P9-DFB-281

Sisters of Holmes County
Three Bestselling Romance Novels in One Volume

WANDA E. BRUNSTETTER

ISBN 978-1-61626-772-8

All scripture quotations, unless otherwise noted, are taken from the King James Version of the Bible.

All German-Dutch words are taken from the *Revised Pennsylvania German Dictionary* used in Lancaster County, Pennsylvania.

This book is a work of fiction. Names, characters, places, and incidents are either products of the author's imagination or used fictitiously. Any similarity to actual people, organizations, and/or events is purely coincidental.

For more information about Wanda E. Brunstetter, please access the author's website at the following Internet address: www.wandabrunstetter.com.

Published by Barbour Publishing, Inc., P.O. Box 719, Uhrichsville, Ohio 44683, www.barbourbooks.com

Our mission is to publish and distribute inspirational products offering exceptional value and biblical encouragement to the masses.

Printed in the United States of America.

A Sister's Secret

Dedication/Acknowledgments

In memory of the precious Amish children
whose lives were taken in the October 2, 2006,
schoolhouse shooting in Lancaster County, Pennsylvania.
And to the victims' families,
who showed the world what God's love
and true forgiveness are all about.
My thoughts and prayers continue to be with you.

For the Lord God will help me;
therefore shall I not be confounded:
therefore have I set my face like a flint,
and I know that I shall not be ashamed.
Isaiah 50:7

Chapter 1

A chill shot through Grace Hostettler. Stepping outside the restaurant where she worked, she had spotted a redheaded English man standing near an Amish buggy in the parking lot. He wore blue jeans and a matching jacket and held a camera in his hands. Something about the way he stood with his head cocked to one side reminded her of Gary Walker, the rowdy Englisher she had dated for a while during her *rumschpringe*, her running around years. But it couldn't be Gary. She hadn't seen him since—

Grace pressed her palms to her forehead. Her imagination was playing tricks on her; it had to be. She forced her gaze away from the man and scanned the parking lot, searching for her sister. She saw no sign of Ruth or of her horse and buggy. *Maybe I should head for the bakeshop and see what's keeping her.*

Grace kept walking, but when she drew closer to the man, her breath caught in her throat. It was Gary! She would have recognized that crooked grin, those blazing blue eyes, and his spicy-smelling cologne anywhere.

He smiled and pointed the camera at her. A look of recognition registered on his face, and his mouth dropped open. "Gracie?"

She gave one quick nod as the aroma of grilled onions coming from the fast-food restaurant down the street threatened to make her sneeze.

"Well, what do you know?" He leaned forward and squinted. "Yep, same pretty blue eyes and ash blond hair, but I barely recognized you in those Amish clothes."

Grace opened her mouth to speak, but he cut her off. "What happened? Couldn't make it in the English world?"

"I–I–"

"Don't tell me you talked Wade into joining the Amish faith." He slowly shook his head. "I can just see the two of you traipsing out to the barn to milk cows together and shovel manure."

Grace swallowed against the bitter taste of bile rising in her throat. "D-don't do this, Gary."

He snickered, but the sound held no humor. "Do what? Dredge up old bones?"

Grace wasn't proud that she'd gone English during her rumschpringe or that she'd never told her folks any of the details about the time she'd spent away from home. All they knew was that she had run off with some of her Amish friends, also going through rumschpringe, so they could try out the modern, English world. Grace had been gone two years and had never contacted her family during that time except for sending one note saying she was okay and for them not to worry. They hadn't even known she was living in Cincinnati, or that–

"So, where is Wade?" Gary asked, halting Grace's runaway thoughts.

She shivered despite the warm fall afternoon and glanced around, hoping no one she knew was within hearing distance. The only people she saw were a group of Englishers heading down the sidewalk toward one of the many tourist shops. "Wade's gone, and. . .and my family doesn't know anything about the time I spent living away from home, so please don't say anything to anyone, okay?"

He gave a noncommittal grunt. "Still keeping secrets, huh, Gracie?"

His question stung. When she'd first met Gary while waiting tables at a restaurant in Cincinnati, she hadn't told him she was Amish. It wasn't that she was ashamed of her heritage; she'd just decided if she was going to try out the English world, she should leave her Amish way of life behind.

But one day when a group of Amish kids came into the restaurant, Grace spoke to them in German-Dutch, and Gary overheard their conversation. He questioned her about it later, and she finally admitted that she was from Holmes County, Ohio, and had been born and raised Amish. Gary had made light of it at first, but later, as his quick temper and impulsive ways began to surface, he started making fun of Grace, calling her a dumb Dutch girl who didn't know what she wanted or where she belonged.

When Wade came along and swept Grace off her feet with his boyish charm and witty humor, she'd finally gotten up the courage to break up with Gary. He didn't take to the idea of her dating one of his friends and had threatened to get even with her. Had he come to Holmes County to make good on that threat?

"Wh–what are you doing here, Gary?" Her voice sounded raspy, almost a whisper, and her hands shook as she held her arms rigidly at her side.

"Came here on business. I'm a freelance photographer and reporter now." He jiggled his eyebrows. "Sure didn't expect to see you, though."

Grace heard the rhythmic *clip-clop* of horse's hooves and spotted her sister's buggy coming down the street. "I–I've got to go." The last thing she needed was for Ruth to see her talking to Gary. Her sister would no doubt ply her with a bunch of questions Grace wasn't prepared to answer.

Gary lifted his camera, and before Grace had a chance to turn her head, he snapped a picture. "See you around, Gracie."

She gave a curt nod and hurried away.

Ruth squinted as she looked out the front window of the buggy. What was Grace doing in the restaurant parking lot, talking to an English man with a camera?

She guided the horse to the curb, and a few minutes later, Grace climbed into the buggy, looking real flustered. "H–how was your interview?" she panted.

"It went fine. I got the job."

"That's good. Glad to hear it."

"Who was that man with the camera?" Ruth asked as she pulled slowly away from the curb and into the flow of traffic.

Grace's face turned red as she shrugged. "Just. . .uh. . .someone taking pictures of Amish buggies."

"It looked like you were talking to him."

"*Jah*, I said a few words."

"Were you upset because he was trying to take your picture?"

Grace nodded.

"Some of the English tourists that come to Berlin and the other towns in Holmes County don't seem to mind snapping pictures without our permission. Either they don't realize we're opposed to having our pictures taken, or they just don't care." Ruth wrinkled her nose. "I feel such *aeryer* when they do that."

Not even Ruth's comment about feeling vexed provoked a response from Grace.

"Guess it's best if we just look the other way and try to ignore their cameras."

"Uh-huh."

As Ruth halted the horse at the second stoplight in town, she reached across the seat and touched Grace's arm. "Are you okay? You look like you're worried about something."

"Just tired from being on my feet at the restaurant all day."

"You sure? That frown you're wearing makes me think you're more than tired."

"I'll be fine once we get home." Grace smiled, although the expression seemed forced. "Tell me about the bakeshop. What will you be doing there?"

Ruth held her breath as the smell of manure from a nearby dairy farm wafted through the buggy. "Mostly waiting on customers while Karen and Jake Clemons bake in the other room," she said, clucking to the horse to get him moving again when the light turned green. "Some days, I'll be working by myself, and others, I'll be with my friend Sadie Esh."

"Are you wishing you could help bake?"

Ruth shook her head and turned the horse and buggy down the back road heading toward their home. "Not really. I'll be happy to keep waiting on customers until I get married some day. Raising a family is my life's dream." Ruth glanced over at Grace. "Of course, I'll have to find a husband first."

"What about Luke Friesen? You think things might get serious between the two of you?"

"I don't know, maybe. For now I'm going to concentrate on my new job." Ruth smacked her lips. "Just thinking about all those delicious pastries and pies at the bakeshop makes me hungry."

"I'm sure Mom will have supper started by the time we get home, so you'll be eating soon enough."

"Speaking of Mom, I heard her mention the other day that she'd like for the two of you to get busy on your wedding dress soon."

Grace nodded and turned toward the window. Was she staring at the vibrant fall colors on the trees lining the road, or was she trying to avoid conversation?

"Do you still want me to help with the flowers for your wedding?" Ruth questioned.

"Jah, sure."

"You'll need several fresh arrangements on the bridal table, and I'm thinking maybe one big bouquet in the center of each of the other tables would look nice."

"Uh-huh."

"Will you want some candles, too?"

Grace nodded.

"Since Cleon's mother and sister make beeswax candles, I'm sure they'll want to provide those."

"Maybe so."

"I hope Cleon knows how lucky he is to be marrying my big sister."

"I–I'm the lucky one." Grace picked at her dark green dress as if she noticed a piece of lint, but Ruth didn't see anything. Of course, she couldn't look too closely as she had to keep her eyes on the road. Just last week, a buggy coming down one of the hills on this stretch of road between Berlin and Charm had run into a deer.

Grace sighed, and Ruth gave her a sidelong glance. If something was bothering Grace, she would talk about it when she was ready. In the meantime, Ruth planned to enjoy the rest of their ride home. Shades of yellow, orange, and brown covered the birch, hickory, and beech trees, and leaves of red and purple adorned the maple, oak, and dogwood.

A dappling of sunlight shining through the trees gave her the feeling that all was right with the world—at least her little world.

Cleon Schrock stepped up to the counter near the front of the restaurant where Grace worked and smiled at Sarah, the owner's daughter. "I came to town on business about my bees, so I decided to stop and see Grace. Would you tell her I'm here?"

Sarah shook her head. "Sorry, but Grace got off work about ten minutes ago. Said something about meeting her sister, who had an interview at the bakeshop."

"Okay, thanks." As Cleon turned toward the door, he felt a keen sense of disappointment. He hadn't seen Grace since the last preaching service, and that had been over a week ago. "Have a good evening, Sarah," he called over his shoulder.

"You, too."

Cleon opened the front door, and just as he stepped out, he bumped shoulders with a tall, red-haired English man. The fellow held a fancy-looking camera in one hand and a notebook with a chunky green pen clipped over the top in the other. "Sorry. Didn't realize anyone was on the other side of the door," Cleon said with a shake of his head.

"Not a problem. As long as you didn't ruin this baby, no harm was done." The man lifted his camera. "She's my bread and butter these days."

Cleon stood, letting the man's words sink in. "Are you a newspaper reporter?"

"Nope. I'm a freelance photographer and reporter, and I've written for several publications." He smiled, revealing a set of straight, pearly white teeth. "The pictures I submit often bring in more money than my articles."

Cleon gave a quick nod; then he started to turn away.

"Say, I was wondering if you'd be willing to give me a quick interview. I'm trying to find out some information about the Amish in this area, and—"

"Sorry, not interested." Cleon hurried down the steps and onto the sidewalk. The last thing he wanted was for the Englisher to start plying him with a lot of questions about the Amish way of life. He'd read a couple of articles about his people in the newspaper recently, and none of them had been accurate. Cleon rushed around back to the parking lot, untied his horse from the hitching rail, and climbed into the buggy. If he hurried, he might catch up with Grace and Ruth on their way home.

Chapter 2

As Cleon headed down the road in his open buggy, all he could think about was Grace and how much he wanted to see her. He was excited to tell her about the latest contacts he'd made with some gift stores in Sugarcreek and Berlin, and if he didn't spot her buggy on the road, he would stop by her folks' place before going home.

The horse arched its neck and trotted proudly as Cleon allowed his thoughts to wander back to the day he'd first seen Grace Hostettler. It was almost four years ago—the day after he and his family had moved here from Lancaster County, Pennsylvania. He'd met Grace during a preaching service that was held at her folks' house. She'd seemed kind of quiet and shy back then, but after a while, they'd become friends and were soon a courting couple.

He'd wanted to ask her to marry him sooner but had waited until his beekeeping business was going strong enough to help support a wife and family. Besides, Grace hadn't seemed ready for marriage until a year ago. She had told him that she'd been gone from the Amish faith for a time before joining the church and that she'd only been back in Holmes County a few months before they'd met. Cleon had tried a couple of times to ask about her rumschpringe years, but Grace didn't seem to want to talk about them, so he'd never pressed the issue. What Grace had done during her running around years was her business, and if she wanted to discuss it, he figured she would.

A horn honked from behind, pulling Cleon's thoughts back to the present, and he slowed his horse, steering the buggy closer to the shoulder of the road to let the motorist pass. He gritted his teeth. At this rate, he would never catch up to Grace's carriage.

Once the car had passed, Cleon pulled back onto the road and snapped the reins to get the horse moving faster. The gelding flicked his ears and stepped into a fast trot, and several minutes later, Cleon caught sight of a black, closed-in buggy. Since no cars were in the oncoming lane, he eased his horse out and pulled up beside the other buggy. He saw Grace through the window on the left side, in the passenger's seat, and Ruth on the right, in the driver's seat.

"Pull over to the side of the road, would ya?"

Ruth did as he asked, and Cleon pulled in behind her rig. He climbed out of his buggy, sprinted around to the side of the Hostettler buggy where Grace sat, and opened the door. "I went by the restaurant hoping to see you, and when Sarah said you'd already left, I headed down the road, hoping to catch up with you."

Grace offered him a smile, but it appeared to be forced. Wasn't she glad to see him?

"I was hoping I could give you a ride home so we could talk."

Her face blanched, and she drew in a shaky breath. "Talk about what?"

"About us and our upcoming wedding."

"Wh–what about it?"

Cleon squinted as he reached up to rub his chin. "What's wrong, Grace? Why are you acting so *naerfich*?"

"I–I'm not nervous, just tired from working all day."

"She's been acting a bit strange ever since I picked her up in the restaurant parking lot," Ruth put in from the driver's seat. She leaned over and peered around Grace so she was looking right at Cleon. "If you want my opinion, I think my big sister's feeling anxious about the wedding."

"I am not." Grace's forehead wrinkled as she nudged Ruth's arm with her elbow. "If you don't mind, I think I will ride home in Cleon's buggy."

Ruth shrugged. "Makes no never mind to me, so I'll see you at home."

As Grace climbed into Cleon's buggy, her stomach twisted as though it were tied in knots. Had Cleon met Gary while he was in town? Could Gary have told him things about her past? Is that why Cleon wanted to speak with her? Maybe he'd decided to call off their wedding.

"Are you okay?" Cleon reached across the seat and touched Grace's arm. "You don't seem like yourself today."

"I'm fine. What did you want to say to me concerning our wedding?"

"I wanted you to know that I lined up a few more honey customers today, and if my business keeps growing, eventually I'll be able to stop farming for my *daed*." Cleon smiled. "Once we're married, you can quit your job."

A feeling of relief swept over Grace. Cleon must not have spoken to Gary or learned anything about her past, or he wouldn't be talking about her quitting her job after they were married.

He picked up the reins and got the horse moving down the road.

Grace pushed her weight against the back of the leather seat and tried to relax. Everything was okay—at least for now.

They rode in silence for a while. Grace listened to the steady *clip-clop* of the horse's hooves as the buggy jostled up and down the hilly road, while she thought about Cleon's attributes. He was strong and quiet, and ever since she'd met him, she'd appreciated his even temper and subtle sense of humor. He was the opposite of Wade, whose witty jesting and boyish charm she'd found appealing. But Wade had never seemed settled, which could have accounted for the fact that he'd worked as a cook for five different restaurants during the time they'd been together.

As they passed an Amish farmer's field, the rustle of corn blowing in the wind brought her thoughts back to the present, and she sighed.

"You sure you're okay?" Worry lines formed above Cleon's brows. "We're almost at your house, and you haven't said more than a few words along the way."

In an effort to keep him from knowing how upset she was over Gary coming to town, Grace forced a smile. "I was thinking how lucky

I am to be betrothed to someone as *wunderbaar* as you."

"I'm the lucky one," he said, reaching over to gently touch her arm. "And it's you who's wonderful, my blessed gift."

If Cleon knew the secret I'm keeping, would he still think I'm wonderful?

Cleon turned the horse to the right and guided it up the graveled driveway past her father's woodworking shop. A few minutes later, her folks' white, two-story house came into view. He pulled back on the reins and halted the horse and buggy in front of the hitching rail near the barn. "Here we are."

"Would you like to stay for supper?" she asked. "I'm sure that, whatever Mom is fixing, we'll have more than enough to go around."

He gave her a dimpled smile, and the flecks of gold in his brown eyes seemed brighter than usual. "I'd be happy to join you for supper. Afterwards, maybe we can sit on the porch awhile and talk about our wedding."

Grace glanced around the kitchen table. Ruth sat to her right, with their younger sister, Martha, on the left. Mom's seat was at the end of the table closest to the stove, Dad sat at the opposite end, and Cleon was seated across the table from Grace and her sisters.

Grace was pleased that she'd invited Cleon to stay for supper. The conversation and joke telling around the table had helped her feel a little more relaxed, and it was nice to see how well Cleon got along with her family. Dad had said several times that he was happy with Grace's choice for a husband, but she wondered what he and Mom would have thought about Wade. She was sure they wouldn't have approved of the way he hopped from job to job, but they might have enjoyed his lighthearted banter and playfulness.

Those qualities of Wade had attracted Grace from the moment he had showed up to interview for a position as cook at the restaurant where she'd worked in Cincinnati. If her parents had known Grace had once been married to an Englisher, she was sure they would have been upset.

"How are things with your woodworking business, Roman?" Cleon asked Grace's father.

Dad reached for the bowl of mashed potatoes and smiled. "Been real busy here lately."

"Guess it's a good thing you hired Luke Friesen as your helper, then."'

"Luke's a good-enough worker," Dad said with a nod. "Unfortunately, the two of us have butted heads a few times."

"About what?" Ruth asked in a tone of concern. She and Luke had only been courting a few months, and Grace was certain her sister didn't want to hear anything negative about him.

Dad shrugged his broad shoulders. "It's nothing for you to worry about, daughter. Luke just needs to learn who the boss is and what I will and won't tolerate."

Ruth opened her mouth as if to say something more, but Martha spoke first.

"Say, Dad, I was thinking that if you're too busy to build a kennel for my dogs, I could see if Luke would have the time."

Dad frowned at Martha and shook his head. "Luke's got plenty of other work he needs to do, but I'll get your kennel built as soon as I can."

"If you need any help with that, I might be able to lend a hand," Cleon spoke up.

"This is a busy time of year, what with the harvest and all," Dad said. "I'm sure between helping your daed and *bruders* on the farm, working with those bees of yours, and trying to get your and Grace's new house done, you've got your hands plenty full right now."

"You've got a point." Cleon glanced over at Grace. "I'm hoping to have our house done by the time we're married, but with everyone being too busy to help me right now, I'm concerned that it won't get done on time."

"Would you rather postpone the wedding?" she asked as a feeling of dread crept into her soul. If she and Cleon didn't get married in December because the house wasn't finished, would they have to wait until next fall? Most Amish couples in their community got married in

October, November, or December when the harvest was done. Grace didn't think she could stand waiting another year to become Cleon's wife.

"Not to worry. You and Cleon can live here after you're married and stay as long as it takes to complete the house." Dad smiled across the table at Mom and gave his full brown beard a couple of pulls. "Isn't that right, Judith?"

"Oh, jah, that won't be a problem at all," she said. "And since their new house is being built on the backside of our property, it will be easy for both you and Cleon to work on it during whatever free time you have."

Grace glanced back at Cleon to gauge his reaction and was relieved when he smiled and said, "That's just fine by me."

Chapter 3

Despite the pleasant evening she'd had with Cleon the night before, Grace awoke the following morning feeling tired and out of sorts. She'd had trouble sleeping, unable to get Gary out of her mind. All during breakfast, she fretted over his sudden appearance, wondering how long he would remain in Holmes County, questioning if he was really a freelance reporter, and worrying that he wouldn't keep quiet about her past. By the time they'd finished eating and Dad had gone out to his shop, Grace had developed a headache. She dreaded going to work for fear of seeing Gary again and hoped no one she knew would have an opportunity to speak with him.

"Are you feeling all right this morning, Grace?" Mom asked as she ambled across the room with a pile of dirty dishes. "You were so quiet during breakfast and hardly ate a thing."

"I didn't sleep well last night, and now I've got a splitting headache, which has my stomach feeling kind of queasy." Grace filled the sink with hot water and took the plates from her mother's hands.

"I'm sorry to hear that," Mom said with a worried expression.

"Why don't you let me wash the dishes?" Ruth suggested, stepping up beside Grace. "Martha can dry while you sit at the table with Mom and have a cup of tea. Maybe by the time we're ready to leave for work, your headache will be gone."

Grace glanced across the room to Martha, who was sweeping the floor. "Would you like me to take over so you can help Ruth with the dishes?"

Martha shook her head. "That's okay. I'm almost done. You'd better do as Ruth suggested and have a cup of tea."

"All right." Grace headed to the stove to get the simmering teakettle, but her mother got there first. As Mom lifted the teakettle, Grace removed two cups from the cupboard, grabbed a box of chamomile tea and a bottle of aspirin, then took a seat at the table.

While Ruth and Martha did the dishes, Martha chattered about her dogs and how she couldn't wait for Heidi, the female sheltie, to give birth to her first batch of puppies. Grace sipped her tea and tried to tune out her sister's prattle but was unsuccessful.

"Can't you think of anything to talk about except those *hund?*" she snapped. "There are more important things in this world than how many *hundlin* Heidi will have and how much money you might make when it's time to sell them."

Martha turned from the cupboard where she'd put the clean plates and blinked. "It may not be important to you, but it is to me. Just because you don't care for dogs so much doesn't mean you have to make my business venture seem like it's of no great concern."

"Sorry for snapping." Grace took another sip of tea. "I'm not feeling like myself this morning."

Martha wrinkled her nose. "You seemed all right last night when Cleon was here. What happened between now and then to make you so edgy?"

"Nothing. I just don't feel so well."

Mom's blue eyes squinted as she reached over and patted Grace's shoulder. "Maybe you should stay home from work today and rest."

"I agree with Mom; you should go back to bed," Ruth put in from her place at the sink.

Grace shook her head. "I don't want to leave the restaurant short-handed." She popped two aspirins into her mouth and washed them down with some tea. "I'm sure I'll be fine once these take effect."

As Ruth and Grace headed toward Berlin in their buggy, Ruth's concern for her sister escalated. Grace hadn't said a word since they'd left home, and when she leaned her head against the back of the seat and closed her eyes, her breathing came out in short little rasps.

"Does your head still hurt?" Ruth asked, reaching over to touch her sister's arm.

"A little."

"Want me to turn the buggy around and take you home?"

"No. I'm sure I'll be fine by the time we reach Berlin."

"Is something bothering you besides the headache?"

"Just feeling tired and a little jittery is all."

"You know what I think you need?"

The buggy jostled as they descended a small hill, and Grace opened her eyes. "What's that?"

"Some fun in the sun before our beautiful fall weather turns cold."

"What kind of fun did you have in mind?"

Ruth smiled. At least she had her sister's full attention. "This Saturday coming, Sadie and I are planning to meet Luke and Toby at the pond for some fishing and a picnic supper. Why don't you and Cleon join us?"

"That sounds like fun, but I have to work this Saturday." Grace yawned and covered her mouth with the palm of her hand. "How are things with you and Luke? Do you think he might be the man you'll marry some day?"

Ruth shrugged as she flicked the reins to get the horse moving up the hill. "We've only been courting a few months, so it's too early to tell."

"But you like him, right?"

"Jah."

"He must like you, too, or he wouldn't ask you to go places with him."

"Maybe he's just being nice because he works for our daed and wants to keep on his good side."

"From what Dad said last night, it doesn't sound like Luke's doing so well keeping on Dad's good side."

Ruth bristled. "I think maybe it's more Dad's fault than Luke's."

"What makes you say that?"

"You know how picky our daed can be. If it's not done his way, then it couldn't possibly be right."

"I guess either Luke will have to learn to keep his opinions to himself or Dad will have to let some of what Luke says roll off his shoulders."

Ruth nodded. "I hope things work out. It's nice to have Luke working nearby, where I can see him more."

Grace lifted her gaze toward the top of the buggy. "Have you forgotten that you're starting your new job this morning? Most days you'll probably be headed for work before Luke arrives at Dad's shop."

Ruth's dark brows drew together. "I hadn't thought of that. I hope he doesn't take an interest in Martha since she's at home all day and he'll see more of her than he does me."

"I don't think you have anything to worry about. Martha doesn't have anything on her mind these days except raising hund."

After donning his overalls, gloves, and veil, Cleon lit some wood chips in the steel smudge pots with leather bellows. He puffed air through the bottom of the smoldering fuel, and it gave off a cool white smoke that quieted the bees so he could take their honey.

As Cleon worked, he thought about supper the night before with Grace and her family. How grateful he was that he'd not only be getting a wonderful wife when he married Grace, but a great family, as well. He seemed to get along well with all of them, especially Roman.

Cleon had just pulled another honeycomb from one of the bee boxes when his younger brother Delbert showed up, announcing that their father was ready to begin harvesting the cornfields and needed Cleon's help.

"Pop's got the help of half the men in our community this morning. He surely doesn't need me," Cleon protested.

Delbert's gray-blue eyes narrowed into tiny slits. "Pop needs all the help he can get, and he pays you to work for him, so you'd better get out to the fields *schnell*."

"Jah. I'll be there as fast as possible. I need to finish up here first."

"Sure don't see why anyone would want to mess around with a bunch of buzzin' bees." Delbert sauntered off before Cleon could respond.

After Cleon took the honeycombs inside to Mom so she could cut them into small pieces, mash them, and heat them on the stove to extract the honey, he headed out to the cornfields. They should finish by suppertime, and then he hoped to pay Grace a call.

Grace glanced at the clock on the wall above the restaurant's front counter. It was almost three—quitting time for her today. They'd been busier than usual at the restaurant during the breakfast and lunch hours, and she was glad her shift was almost over. Her feet ached something awful. Fortunately, Ruth's hours at the bakeshop today were the same as hers, so she figured her sister would be here soon, ready to head for home.

"Can you take that customer who just came in?" asked Grace's coworker Esther. "I've got an order to put in and one that needs to be picked up."

"Sure."

"Thanks. I appreciate it." Esther nodded in the direction of the booth where a red-haired man sat with his head down as though studying something, and then she hurried off toward the kitchen.

Grace grabbed a menu, an order pad, and a pencil before moving over to the booth. When she arrived, she saw what the man was looking at, and her heartbeat picked up. Several pictures of Amish buggies and Plain People lay on the table, and even before he looked up, she knew the man was Gary. Drawing in a quick breath to help steady her nerves, she placed the menu on the table on top of his pictures.

"Hey, watch it! I don't need any of these prints getting ruined." Gary frowned as he looked up, but his frown quickly faded. "Well, well. I didn't expect to see you again—at least not so soon. Have you worked here long, Gracie?"

Ignoring his question, she pointed to the menu. "Today's special is pork chops and sauerkraut."

He wrinkled his nose. "Not one of my favorite dishes, but that's okay because it's too early to be thinking about supper. I just came in to take a load off my feet and go over these prints before I send them off to a publisher."

"So you don't want to order anything?"

"I didn't say that." He picked up the menu, thumbed through it quickly, and handed it back to her. "I'll have a cup of coffee and a hunk of pie."

"What kind of pie?"

"Why don't you surprise me?"

Grace clutched the edge of her apron and gritted her teeth. The man was impossible! "I'm not allowed to choose for the customer. You need to pick something yourself."

He drummed his fingers along the edge of the table in an irritating *tat-a-tat-tat*. "How about a slice of apple? Have you got any of that?"

"I believe so." She turned to go, but he reached out and snagged her wrist, holding it firmly with his cold fingers. "Don't run off. I'd like to talk to you a minute–get caught up on each other's lives, maybe reminisce about our dating days."

She tried to pull away, but he held firm as his thumb brushed her arm in a slow, deliberate movement. "Those were fun days we had together. Don't you miss 'em, Gracie?"

Grace's pulse pounded in her temples. She thought she'd resolved her guilty feelings for leaving the Amish faith for a time and keeping her past a secret from her family, but now, with Gary looking at her with such intensity, guilt rushed back like raging floodwaters. If only she'd felt free to tell her parents the truth about where she'd been living and what had transpired during her rumschpringe years.

But she was certain they wouldn't have understood, especially Dad, who had mentioned several times how angry he was about his only sister leaving the Amish faith and marrying an English man, then never contacting her family again. Just the mention of anyone leaving the faith, whether they'd joined the church or not, caused her father to become irritable for days. If he had known the details of Grace's rumschpringe, he would have been angry with her, even though she hadn't been a church member when she'd left home.

"Gracie, did you hear what I said?" Gary asked, releasing his grip on her arm.

She took a step back and nodded. "I'll turn in your order, and one of the other waitresses will bring it to you in a few minutes."

His forehead creased. "I thought you were my waitress."

"My shift is almost over. I'm just covering for someone who's too busy to wait on you right now."

"If you'll be off duty soon, why don't you have a seat, and we can have a cup of coffee together." He nodded at the bench across from him, apparently not the least bit put off by her cold reception. Of course, he never had known when to take no for an answer.

"I can't. My sister will be here to pick me up soon. Besides, I'm betrothed, and it wouldn't look right for me to be seen having coffee with another man—especially one who isn't part of the Amish faith." Grace winced. She couldn't believe she'd blurted out that she was engaged to be married.

He shook his head. "Gracie, Gracie, Gracie, you sound like such a puritan. Whatever happened to the fun-loving, spunky little gal I used to date?"

"I'm not going through rumschpringe anymore," she said through tight lips. "I've been baptized, have joined the Amish church, and—"

"Yeah, I figured that much. You wouldn't be dressed in those plain clothes if you hadn't gone Amish again." He stared at Grace so hard it made her skin crawl. "The last time I heard from Wade, he said the two of you were happily married. What happened? Did he get bored with his Plain little wife and leave you for some other woman?"

Grace's ears burned, and the heat spread quickly to her face. "Wade is dead."

His face blanched. "Really?"

She nodded.

"How'd it happen?"

"One foggy night, an oncoming truck came into Wade's lane when he was on his way home from work." She paused to swallow around the lump lodged in her throat. "I figured you would've heard about it."

"I moved to Indianapolis soon after you and Wade got married." He shook his head. "I'm sorry for your loss, Grace."

She studied his face, wondering if Gary felt any compassion for her. When she'd been dating him, he'd never said he was sorry for anything.

"So after Wade died, you moved back here and joined the Amish church?"

She nodded. *Does Gary know anything else about my life? Does he know—*

She leaned closer to the table. "Promise you won't say anything to anyone about me being married to Wade?"

He held up his hand. "As I told you the other day, I'm working freelance, and I came to Holmes County to take some pictures and get a few good stories about the Amish here, not tell tales about an old flame."

Grace wanted to believe him, and she hoped he was telling the truth. But Gary had never been trustworthy, and she wasn't sure she could believe anything he said. She didn't even know if he was telling the truth about being a reporter. She was about to question him when she caught sight of Ruth entering the restaurant. "My ride's here. I have to go."

She pivoted away from the table and rushed over to Esther, handing her the order pad. "That customer you asked me to wait on wants some apple pie and a cup of coffee. My sister's here, so I've got to go."

"No problem. I'll take care of it right away." Esther's forehead wrinkled. "Are you okay, Grace? Your face is flushed, and you're sweating like it's a hot summer day."

"I'm fine–just tired and hot from working all day. See you tomorrow, Esther." Grace hurried off before her coworker could comment. She needed to get away from Gary and his probing blue eyes. She needed to go home where she felt safe.

Chapter 4

What's that you're working on?"

Martha looked up from her embroidery work and smiled at her mother, who leaned over the kitchen table with a curious expression. "I'm making a sampler to give Grace as a wedding present. I'll include her and Cleon's names and leave enough room so Grace can add the names of the children they'll have someday."

Mom's blue eyes twinkled like fireflies in the heat of summer. "I'm sure they'll appreciate such a thoughtful gift."

"I considered giving them one of Heidi's puppies because they'll be born soon and should be weaned in plenty of time for the wedding." Martha shrugged. "Since Grace isn't much of an animal lover, I figured she probably wouldn't welcome it."

"I think you're right about that." Mom pulled out a chair beside Martha and sat down. "In all your sister's twenty-four years, she's never had a pet." She frowned. "At least, not to my knowledge. No telling what she did when she was gone those two years during her rumschpringe."

Martha nodded. Her sister's running-around days were not a topic for discussion. Martha had been twelve and Ruth fifteen when Grace left home for a time. Whenever Martha and Ruth were around, Mom and Dad had avoided the subject of their strong-willed daughter and her desire to try out the English way of life. Martha figured her folks probably worried that their other two daughters might follow in their older sister's footsteps, so the less said the better regarding Grace's rumschpringe.

When Grace finally came to her senses and returned home, she was welcomed without question, just like the prodigal son in the Bible had been. Of course, things might have been different if Grace had been a member of the Amish church at the time. But since she hadn't been baptized or joined the faith before she'd gone English, the community didn't shun her, and she didn't need to confess when she returned home.

"Would you like a cup of hot cider or some lemonade?" Mom asked, pushing Martha's thoughts to the back of her mind.

Martha's mouth watered as she thought about the delicious apple cider Dad made every fall. "Jah, sure. Some cider would be real nice."

Mom pushed her chair aside and headed to their propane-operated refrigerator. She withdrew a jug of cider and ambled back across the room, where she poured some of the amber-colored liquid into a kettle and set it on the stove to heat. "Want some crackers and cheese to go with the cider?"

"I'd better not. Don't want to fill up on snacks now and be too full to eat lunch."

"Guess I'll just stick to hot cider, too." A few minutes later, Mom placed a mug of cider in front of Martha. "Here you go. Enjoy," she said before moving over to the counter across the room.

"Aren't you going to join me?"

"I'll drink mine while I make your daed a sandwich. It'll be time for lunch soon, so I'll take it out to his woodworking shop when I'm done."

"Won't Dad be coming up to the house to eat?" Martha asked as she threaded her needle with rose-colored thread.

"He's got a backload of work and doesn't want to take the time for a big meal at noon." Mom opened the breadbox and pulled out a loaf of whole-wheat bread she'd made. "Even with Luke helping him, he's still way behind."

Martha set her embroidery aside and reached for her mug. The tantalizing scent of apple drifted up as a curl of steam rose from the hot cider. She took a sip and smacked her lips. "Umm. . .this is sure good."

"Jah. Your daed makes some of the best apple cider around."

"Say, Mom, I was wondering if you've noticed anything different about Grace lately."

"Different in what way?"

"Ever since she came home from work on Monday, she's been acting kind of odd—like she's off in her own little world or might be worried about something."

Mom shuffled back to the refrigerator, this time removing a package of trail bologna, a head of lettuce, and a jar of mayonnaise. "Maybe she's just tired. Working as a waitress and being on my feet all day would tucker me out."

Martha took another sip of cider. "When we headed for bed last night, I asked Grace if everything was okay."

"What'd she say?"

"Said things were fine and dandy."

Mom was on the other side of the room again, slathering mayonnaise on four slices of bread. "Then they probably are."

Martha shrugged and pushed her chair aside. "Think I'll head out to the barn and check on Heidi. Her time's getting close, and I want to be sure everything goes all right when she gives birth to those pups."

"Jah." Mom reached for the package of bologna. "I'll be in the shop with your daed for a while, in case you need me for anything."

"Would you mind making a delivery for me?" Roman asked Luke. "I promised to have those tables and chairs ready for Steven Bates this week. He's always been a picky customer, and I need to make good on that promise."

Luke pushed some dark hair off his forehead and wiped the sweat away with the back of his hand. "Jah, sure. I can do that right now if ya like."

"That's fine, but don't take too long getting there." Roman grimaced as he rubbed at a kink in his lower back. "And don't dillydally on the way back like you did on the last delivery you made."

Luke shrugged. "Just didn't see any need to run the horse too hard."

"Jah, well, let's get that furniture loaded, and you can be on your way."

Half an hour later with the furniture placed in the back of the wagon, Luke headed down the road, and Roman resumed work on a set of kitchen cabinets he was making for their bishop, Noah King. He'd just started sanding the doors when a gray-haired, middle-aged English man stepped into the shop, holding a notebook.

"Are you the owner of this place?" the man asked.

Roman nodded. "I am."

"Do you own just the woodworking shop or the house and land it sets on, too?"

"Own it all—fifty acres, to be exact."

The man thrust out his hand. "My name's Bill Collins, and I'm scouting out some land in the area, hoping to buy several acres to develop over time."

Ignoring the man's offered handshake, Roman squinted. "Develop?"

"That's right. I want to build a tract of new homes, and I'm also thinking of putting in a golf course, so I—"

"My land's not for sale."

Mr. Collins rubbed his chin as he leaned against Roman's desk. "Come now, Mr. Hostettler—"

"You know my name?"

"The sign on your shop says 'Hostettler's Woodworking.' "

Roman gave a curt nod.

"Anyway, I was hoping you'd be interested in hearing what I have to say. I'm prepared to offer you a decent price for your land."

"Not interested."

"Oh, but if you'll just give me a chance to—"

"One of my neighbors wanted to buy my land once, but I said no, so I'm sure not going to sell it to you."

"Mr. Hostettler, I assure you—"

The door opened again. Judith entered the room carrying a jug of cider and Roman's lunch pail in her hands.

He breathed a sigh of relief, glad for the interruption.

"I know it's not quite noon, but I brought your lunch," she said, offering him a pleasant smile. "Where do you want me to set it?"

"On my desk—if you can find the room, that is." He nodded when Judith pushed some papers aside and set the lunch pail down.

She glanced at the land developer, who hovered near the desk as though he was looking for something. "I hope I'm not interrupting anything," she said.

The man opened his mouth as if to comment, but Roman spoke first. "You're not interrupting a thing. Mr. Collins is on his way out."

"Give some consideration to what I said. I'll drop by again soon and see if you're ready to hear my offer." With that, Bill Collins turned and sauntered out the door.

"What was that all about?" Judith asked when the door clicked shut.

Roman moved away from the cabinets he'd been sanding. "The fellow wanted to buy our land."

Her eyes widened. "Whatever for?"

"Said something about wanting to build a bunch of houses and a golf course, of all things." He flicked some sawdust off his trousers. "I told him I wasn't interested in selling, and if he comes back, I'll tell him the same."

"I would hope so." Judith nodded toward the door. "On my way down from the house, I saw Luke heading out with a wagonload of furniture." She sat in the chair behind Roman's desk. "Is he making a delivery for you?"

"Jah. He's taking a table and some chairs over to Steven Bates's place. He'd better not be late getting back to the shop like he was last time." Roman shook his head. "That young fellow's a fair enough worker, but he's got a mind of his own. Makes me wonder how things are going with him and Ruth since they've begun courting."

"I'm sure they're going fine, or Ruth would have said something. She's not one to keep her feelings bottled up the way Grace has always done."

Roman grunted in reply and moved over to the desk. He had no desire to discuss their oldest daughter and her refusal to talk about things. In many ways, Grace reminded him of his sister, Rosemary, only Grace had finally returned home where she belonged. Rosemary hadn't.

"I'm glad your business is doing so well," Judith said, leaning her elbows on the desk and staring up at him. "When that English fellow John Peterson moved into the area a few months ago and opened a woodworking shop, I was afraid you might lose some of your customers to him."

Roman shook his head. "Nope. Hasn't seemed to bother my business one iota." He lifted the lid of his lunch pail and peered inside. "What kind of sandwich did you make today?"

"Trail bologna and baby Swiss cheese, and I made two in case you're really hungry. I put some of your favorite double crunch cookies in there, as well."

He smacked his lips. "You spoil me, *fraa*."

"That's the part I enjoy the most about being your wife." She grinned and pushed back the chair. "Guess I should head up to the house and let you eat your lunch in peace."

"Why don't you stay awhile and visit? I'd enjoy the company." He grabbed one of his wooden stools and pulled it over to the desk. "What's our youngest daughter up to today? Has she been combing through the ads in the newspaper to see if anymore hund are for sale?"

Judith sighed. "I wish Martha would forget about raising dogs and find herself a real job, like our other two girls have done."

"Let me pray, and then we'll talk about it."

Judith nodded and bowed her head, and Roman did the same. After a few seconds of silent prayer, he opened his eyes and reached into the lunch pail to retrieve one of the sandwiches. "I think we should give Martha the chance to see if she can succeed in her business venture, don't you?"

"I suppose."

He pulled out the second sandwich and handed it to her. "I don't really need two of these, so if you haven't eaten already, you may as well join me."

"*Danki*. I haven't eaten yet."

They sat in companionable silence for a time.

"Martha's concerned that something might be bothering Grace," Judith said, breaking the silence. "Have you noticed anything unusual about the way she's been acting lately?"

Roman squinted as he contemplated her question. "Well, she didn't have a whole lot to say during supper last night, but as you know, Grace is often moody and quiet."

Judith gave a slow nod. "Leastways, she has been since she returned to Holmes County four years ago."

"Maybe she's just feeling naerfich about her upcoming wedding."

"I suppose she could be nervous." She inhaled deeply and released a quick breath, causing the narrow ties of her white *kapp* to flutter. "I'll keep an eye on things, and if I notice her getting cold feet, I'll have a little talk with her."

Roman snapped his lunch pail shut and handed it to her. "Sounds like a good idea. It took Grace some time to settle down and find a good man, so we wouldn't want her to change her mind about marrying Cleon at this late date."

Judith's head moved slowly from side to side. "No, we surely wouldn't."

Chapter 5

The following day as Grace approached the booth where one of her customers sat, she glanced out the window and caught sight of Gary standing on the sidewalk in front of the gift store across the street, talking to Cleon. She flinched. Maybe Gary knew she planned to marry Cleon. He might be trying to turn Cleon against her by spilling her secrets. Maybe she wouldn't marry Cleon in two months, after all.

Grace gripped the water pitcher in her hands so tightly that her fingers turned numb. She ordered her runaway heart to be still. She was doing it again–worrying about things that probably hadn't happened. Knowing Gary, he was most likely making small talk with anyone willing to listen, the way he used to do when they were teenagers. Or maybe Cleon had stopped to ask if Gary knew the time. He often did that whenever he'd forgotten his pocket watch.

Grace felt relief when Cleon finally turned and walked away. The water in the pitcher sloshed as she hurried across the room, knowing she needed to wait on the young English couple who had taken a seat in her section of the restaurant. *I'm sure it was nothing to fret about*, she told herself. *Oh, I pray it was nothing.*

Grace had just finished taking the English couple's order when she spotted Cleon entering the restaurant. He took a seat in a booth near the front door, which was in her section.

When she hurried over to the booth, he looked up at her, his dark eyes crinkling at the corners as he smiled. "It's good to see you, Grace."

"It. . .it's good to see you, too."

"I came to town to deliver some honey, and I've also been seeking some new outlets for the beeswax candles Mom and my sister Carolyn make."

"I see." Grace shifted her weight from one foot to the other, wondering how to ask why Cleon had been talking to Gary without arousing Cleon's suspicion.

"Will you be getting off work anytime soon?" he questioned.

"In another half hour."

"That's good, because I'd like to treat you to a late lunch if you haven't already eaten."

"No, I haven't." She tapped her pencil against the order pad in her hand. "Isn't that why you're here—to eat lunch?"

He chuckled and shook his head so hard some of his dark hair fell across his forehead. "I'm done with business for the day now, so I figured I'd come in here, drink a cup of coffee, and wait for you."

"Since this is Saturday and Ruth has the day off, I rode my bike into town, rather than driving one of our buggies. Guess if I leave it parked out behind the restaurant I can pick it up after we're done eating. Unless of course, you'd like to stay here for lunch."

"You eat here enough, don't you think?"

"Guess that's true," she said with a nod.

"Since I drove my larger market buggy today, I can put your bike in the back and give you a ride home after lunch. How's that sound?"

"That's fine with me." At least Cleon hadn't mentioned his conversation with Gary. If Gary had said anything about knowing Grace, she was sure Cleon would have said so by now.

"Where would you like to eat?" he asked, reaching out to touch her gently on the arm.

She smiled. "Why don't you choose?"

"How about the Farmstead Restaurant? Haven't eaten there in a while, and they serve some real tasty Dutch apple pie."

She nodded at the menu lying before him. "We have that dessert here, too."

"Nothing against the food here," he said in a whisper, "but in my opinion, nobody serves a better Dutch apple pie than the Farmstead."

"All right, the Farmstead it is." Grace glanced out the window and caught sight of a man across the street standing near Java Joe's Coffee Bar. Thinking it might be Gary, she stopped talking to take another look.

"What are you staring at?" Cleon asked, turning toward the window.

"Oh, nothing much." Relieved to see that the man wasn't Gary, she focused her attention on Cleon again. "I. . .uh. . .saw you talking to an English man with red hair a while ago. I'm curious what he said to you."

"Said he's a freelance photographer and reporter and that he sends his work into some magazines and other publications. From what I gathered, he's lookin' to write some stories about the Amish in our area." Cleon grimaced. "He cornered me the other day, wanting me to answer some questions, but I said no. Then he asked again today, and I told him the same thing. Wouldn't let him take my picture, either."

"He didn't say anything else?"

Cleon shook his head. "After I turned down his offer to interview me, he headed on down the street, snapping pictures of some buggies that were passing by."

Grace sighed. If Gary found out she was betrothed to Cleon, he might cause trouble. And if Cleon found out she had once dated Gary, she would face some serious questions.

"Why so concerned about this picture-taking fellow? Has he been bothering you or some of the others who work here?" Cleon asked with squinted eyes.

"Not really. I—I just know how bold some reporters can be with their fancy cameras, tape recorders, and nosey questions. It will be good when he's gone." Grace thought about the day when Gary had taken her picture without her permission. She didn't see the need to mention it to Cleon, though. She would have to admit that she'd spoken with Gary, and more questions would likely follow. She hoped Gary wouldn't use that picture in any of his magazine articles, for she didn't want anyone to think she had willingly posed for it.

"I'll take that cup of coffee now if you're not too busy."

Grace jerked her attention back to Cleon. "Oh, sorry. I'll see to it right away."

He touched her hand in such a gentle way that it caused shivers to spiral up her arm. "No hurry. I've got a whole half hour to wait until you get off work."

She smiled and hurried off, thinking how fortunate she was to be betrothed to someone as kind and good-natured as Cleon. A lot of men weren't so easygoing. Some, like Gary, could be downright mean.

"I'm thankful for the beautiful fall weather we're having, and in my opinion, this is the perfect spot to have our picnic," Ruth commented to her friend Sadie Esh as the two of them stepped down from their buggies.

"Jah. I've enjoyed visiting the ponds in our area ever since I was a girl." Sadie's luminous blue eyes twinkled in the sunlight, making Ruth wish she'd been blessed with blue eyes instead of brown. "Sure hope the fellows show up soon. Since they like to fish so much, I figured they would have been here by now."

"Like as not, they'll be here soon." Ruth reached into her buggy and withdrew the wicker basket she had packed with a variety of picnic foods. "I don't know about Toby, but I'm pretty sure the reason Luke's not here yet is because Dad must have asked him to work later than they'd planned. They've been really busy at the woodworking shop these past few weeks."

Sadie pulled a quilt from under the backseat of the buggy. "It's good that your daed's business is doing so well. That must be why he hired Luke to help him, huh?"

"I suppose." Ruth's sneakers squished through a pile of red and gold leaves as she made her way toward the pond. "How about Toby? Is he working hard at the lumber store?"

"Toby's always been a hard worker, but he doesn't work at his job on Saturdays. I'm thinking he may have had some chores to do at home."

Ruth set the picnic basket on the ground, and as soon as they had the quilt spread out, they both took seats. "It won't be long before winter will be upon us, so we'd better enjoy this sunshine while we can," she said as she closed her eyes and let the sun's warming rays seep into her upturned face. Come next summer, she might not appreciate the heat so much, but right now she felt as if she could spend the rest of the day sitting here, soaking up the sun, listening to the birds chirp, and smelling the aroma of drying wheat shafts from the fields not far from their picnic spot.

"Too bad Grace and Cleon weren't free to join us."

"I did ask, but that was before I realized Grace had to work today." Ruth smiled. "I'm glad I'm not expected to work any Saturdays with my new job."

"Speaking of the new job, are you happy working at the bakeshop?"

Ruth opened her eyes and glanced over at her friend, who sat with her knees bent and her hands clasped around the skirt of her long blue dress. "I like working there, and it's nice that the owners of the bakeshop have a small corral behind the shop where I can keep my horse and buggy." She patted her stomach. "The only drawback is that it's tempting to sample some of the pastries, cookies, and pies. Thanks to you, I'll probably gain weight just from looking at those fattening pastries."

Sadie plucked a blade of grass and twirled it around her fingers. "You've been thin as a reed ever since I've known you, so I don't think you have anything to worry about."

"Jah, well, if I can't control my cravings, I'll have you to blame for getting me the job."

The nicker of a horse followed by the rumble of buggy wheels interrupted their conversation. Ruth turned. Toby King, the bishop's youngest son, hopped down from his buggy and secured his horse to a tree. "At least one of our fellows is finally here."

Sadie jumped up and scurried over to greet Toby, but Ruth stayed seated on the quilt. A few minutes later, the giggling young couple joined her.

"Where's your fishing pole, Toby?" Ruth asked. "I thought you'd have it with you."

Toby motioned to his buggy. "Left it in there, figuring we'd eat before we fished." He looked around. "Say, where's Luke? He passed me on the road a couple miles back, and I figured he would beat me here."

"Luke hasn't shown up yet." Ruth's forehead wrinkled. "Are you sure it was him?"

Toby took a seat on the grass, removed his straw hat, and plunked it over one knee. "I know it was him because he was drivin' an open buggy. I saw his face plain as day, uh-huh." He pulled his fingers through the sides of his reddish-blond hair as his eyebrows furrowed. "This makes no sense to me."

"Don't tell me he suddenly disappeared." Sadie poked Toby's arm. "Maybe an *auslenner* from outer space came down and snatched Luke away."

Toby snickered and reached out to tweak her freckled nose. "What would you know of aliens and outer space?"

"I know what I've read in the newspaper."

He wiggled his fingers in front of Sadie's face. "Maybe Luke's learned how to make himself invisible, like one of those magicians I saw at the county fair last fall."

"You two can make all the jokes you want, but I'm getting concerned." Ruth pushed herself to her feet. Normally, she didn't fret over things, but Luke should have arrived long ago, and she couldn't help but be a little worried.

Sadie stared up at her with a curious expression. "Where are you going?"

"I think we should look for Luke. He could have been in an accident."

Toby shook his head. "Don't ya think I would have seen his rig if it had been smashed up or lying by the side of the road?"

"His buggy could have ended up in the bushes. Maybe you missed seeing it," Sadie said. "I think Ruth's right. We should search for Luke."

The thought of Luke having been involved in an accident sent a pang of trepidation through Ruth. As she hurried to her buggy, she heard Sadie's quick footsteps right behind her.

"Wait up," Toby called. "We can take my rig." He untied his horse, backed him away from the tree, and hitched him to the buggy. He was about to help the girls inside when Luke's horse and open buggy whipped into the clearing, kicking up a cloud of dust.

"Whoa! Hold up there, Gid!" Luke called, pulling back on the reins.

The horse came to an abrupt stop, and Luke hopped down from the buggy. His cheeks were quite red, and his straw hat was slightly askew. Ruth rushed toward him, but before she could get a word out, Toby sprinted over to Luke and hollered, "Where have you been? You had us all worried."

"I had to work a little later than I'd planned." Luke glanced over at Ruth and grimaced. "Sorry if I caused you to worry."

"I'm just glad you're okay," she said, smiling in return. "I was afraid you might have been in an accident or something."

Luke opened his mouth as if to say something, but Toby cut him off. "As I'm sure you must know, you passed me on the way over here, so you should have been ahead of me, not ten minutes behind." He put his hand on Sadie's shoulder. "*Mei aldi* thought you'd been snatched into the outer limits by some evil space invader."

Sadie slapped his hand away. "Your girlfriend was only kidding, and you know it."

Luke shifted from one foot to the other, looking as if he'd been caught in the middle of something he didn't want anyone to know about. "I. . .uh. . .had one stop I needed to make," he mumbled.

"What stop was that? There ain't no places to stop between here and where you passed me on the road." Toby's cheeks flamed, and Ruth was sure it wasn't caused by the warm fall weather.

"Just had to check on something in the woods, that's all."

Toby's dark eyebrows lifted. "Where was your buggy while you were in the woods, huh?"

"I pulled it off the road behind some bushes."

"What were you doing in the woods?" Toby persisted.

"That's none of your nosey beeswax." Luke unhitched his horse and led him over to a tree—the same one Toby's had been tied to earlier. Then he marched back to his buggy, reached inside, and grabbed his fishing pole. "Are we gonna stand around all day yammering about nothing, or did we come here to fish?"

Feeling the need to smooth things over, Ruth stepped up to Luke and touched his arm. "We thought maybe we'd eat first, if that's all right with you."

Toby grunted. "Shouldn't matter what he thinks. He got here late and won't tell us where he was or what he was doin'. As far as I'm concerned, he's got no say in what we do now. I vote we eat first and then fish. Everyone in agreement, raise your right hand."

Sadie's hand popped up, and she looked over at Ruth.

Ruth couldn't believe how bossy Toby was being, and she glanced at Luke to get his reaction. He shrugged, so she lifted her hand, too.

"It's unanimous, uh-huh," Toby said with a nod. "Now let's eat ourselves full!"

Toby and Sadie led the way back to the quilt, and Ruth and Luke followed. Ruth was glad Luke had finally arrived, but she had a niggling feeling that something was amiss. But Luke pushed her doubts aside when he leaned close to her ear and whispered, "Say, what'd ya bring to eat? I'm starving."

"I had a good time with your folks when I ate supper at your place the other night, but it's sure nice having this time alone with you," Cleon said as he leaned forward in his seat across from Grace in a booth at the Farmstead Restaurant.

She nodded and smiled. "I'm enjoying it, too."

"If I can finish building our house in the next couple of months, we can be alone every night once we're married."

"True, but even if you're not able to get it done, I'm sure my family will respect our privacy and give us time alone."

He reached for her hand. "I can't wait to make you my wife, Gracie."

Grace pulled her hand back, feeling like she'd been stung by a bee. In all the time she'd known Cleon, he'd never once called her Gracie.

"What's the matter?" His dark eyebrows furrowed. "Did I say something wrong?"

"What made you call me 'Gracie'?" she squeaked.

He grinned at her. "It just popped into my head, so I said it, that's all. Hasn't anyone ever called you Gracie as a nickname before?"

Only Gary, she thought ruefully. *And because of it, I've never liked the name*. "I'd rather you not use it."

He shrugged. "Okay."

Grace's hands shook as she reached for the glass of water the waitress had placed on the table soon after they were seated. When she lifted the cold glass, she lost her grip, and the glass tipped over, splashing water all over the front of Cleon's shirt.

"I–I'm so sorry." She grabbed her napkin off the table and handed it to Cleon. "Will you forgive me for being such a *dappich dummkopp*?"

"You're not a clumsy dunce," he said with a shake of his head. "It was just an accident, and there's nothing to forgive."

Grace sat in stunned silence, watching as Cleon blotted the water on his shirt, the whole time smiling at her as though she'd done nothing wrong. This little episode had once again reminded her of what a kind, forgiving spirit he had, and it made her wonder if she'd been foolish to withhold the truth from him about her past. Maybe she could tell him her secret without any consequences or judgmental accusations. It might be that their relationship would be strengthened if Cleon knew the truth. Then again, if he didn't respond well to Grace's story, her world would shatter. While Cleon might have a forgiving spirit over a glass of water being splashed on his clothes, it didn't guarantee he would forgive something as big as her secret.

When Cleon excused himself to go to the men's room in order to better dry the front of his shirt, Grace leaned back in her seat and closed her eyes as she gave the matter careful consideration. She wouldn't risk spoiling the afternoon by revealing her secret to Cleon, but perhaps the next time they were together, she would find the courage to tell him the truth.

Chapter 6

I'm going out to the barn to check on Heidi," Martha called to her mother early Monday morning. She pushed an errant strand of chocolate-colored hair away from her face, where it had worked its way loose from her bun, and rushed out the back door.

"Be back in time for lunch." Judith glanced over at Betty Friesen, who sat at her kitchen table sharing a cup of tea, and clicked her tongue against the roof of her mouth. "That girl's in such a hurry to get outside that I doubt she even heard what I said."

"My Luke's the same way. He's always got his mind on something other than what I'm saying." Betty chuckled. "Maybe we should get the two of them together since they seem to have that in common."

Judith reached for her cup and took a drink. "I don't think Martha's interested in finding herself a boyfriend right now. All she talks about is raising puppies. Besides, from what I understand, Luke and Ruth have been seeing each other." She paused, wondering if she'd shared information that Betty didn't yet know.

Betty nodded. "I did hear that Luke had gone fishing on Saturday with Ruth and a couple of their friends, but I wasn't sure if that meant they were actually courting."

"As far as I can tell, they are."

"I don't know why, but Luke's been kind of moody lately. With yesterday being an off-Sunday from preaching, I figured he would want to do some visiting with the rest of his family." Betty frowned. Deep wrinkles etched her forehead. "But all Luke wanted to do was laze around in the hayloft all day. I hope it won't be long before he decides to get baptized and joins the church. Maybe once he does, he'll be ready to settle down to marriage."

Judith grimaced. She hoped Ruth wouldn't think about marrying Luke if he had a moody disposition and seemed lazy at home, but she thought it best not to mention that to Betty. Luke had only been courting Ruth a few months, and as far as she knew, things weren't serious between them.

"Getting back to Martha," Betty said, "someday things will change for her, and she'll want to raise *kinner* instead of hundlin."

"I hope you're right, but at the moment, my youngest daughter doesn't have time to think about children. She has only one thought on her mind: getting her kennel business going."

"Guess you and your oldest daughter must be busy getting things ready for her upcoming marriage to Cleon Schrock, jah?"

Judith nodded. "We'll be shopping for the material for Grace's dress soon."

"She must be excited."

"I believe so, but I think she's also kind of naerfich about things. The last couple of days, she hasn't been acting quite right."

"*Ach*, she'll be fine once they tie the knot."

"I'm sure you're right. She and Cleon are so much in love, things are bound to work well for them once they're married."

Betty reached over and snatched an oatmeal cookie from the plate in the center of the table. "Say, did you hear about the outhouses that got overturned at a couple of schoolhouses up near Kidron?"

"Can't say that I did."

Betty ate the cookie and washed it down with some tea, then leaned forward, resting her elbows on the table. "My Elam told me about it. Said he read it in the newspaper this morning."

"Did your husband give you any details?"

"Said it must have happened sometime during the night because the teachers discovered the damage when they got to their schoolhouses the next morning." Betty shook her head. "It was probably some rowdy English fellows out for a good time."

"Or it could have been Amish boys kicking up their heels during their rumschpringe."

"Maybe so, but they should know better."

Judith took a cookie and dipped it into her cup of tea, then popped it into her mouth, savoring the sweetness. "Seems like there's always something going on, either with English kids playing pranks or Amish fellows sowing their wild oats."

"Sure am glad none of my kinner ever got involved in anything like that."

Judith bit back a reply. If Betty wanted to believe none of her eight boys had ever pulled any pranks, that was her right. Judith was just thankful the good Lord had given her only girls. Grace had been the only one of her daughters to really experience rumschpringe, but thankfully, she'd come back home after living a couple of years in the English world and had settled right down.

Martha stepped into the barn and drew in a deep breath. Dad must have cleaned the horse stalls that morning, because they smelled of clean, sweet hay.

She hurried to the back of the building where she'd made a bed from a wooden crate for her female sheltie and the pups she would give birth to soon. Fritz, the male sheltie she'd bought for breeding purposes, was kept in an empty stall on the other side of the barn during the night and outside on a rope during the day. Eventually, Dad would get around to building a kennel with separate sections for her to house each of her dogs, but in the meantime, the empty barn stalls would have to do.

"Here, Heidi. Where are you, girl?" Martha called when she discovered that the dog wasn't in the crate. Since the sheltie wasn't due to have her pups for a few more days, Martha figured she was probably outside somewhere or had found herself another place to take a nap. If the animal had been nearby, surely she would have answered Martha's call.

Martha headed to the other side of the barn and had just touched the door handle when it swished open. Luke stepped in.

"Whoa! Didn't think anyone would be standing inside the door. We could've bumped heads."

She took a step back. "I—I didn't expect to find you standing there, either."

"Just came to get a couple of cardboard boxes your daed needs. He said I'd find some stacked inside one of the empty horse stalls."

"I can show you the place if you like," Martha offered.

He jiggled his eyebrows playfully. "Might be a good idea. I could get lost in this old barn."

"*Puh!* You're such a tease. I don't know how my sister puts up with you." She turned on her heels and led the way to the horse stalls.

"Ruth tends to be a little more serious than I am," Luke said. "I make her laugh, and she helps me remember that life isn't a dish full of strawberry ice cream. That gives us a healthy balance, wouldn't ya say?"

"I guess it does."

"Last Saturday when Ruth and I met Toby and Sadie for a picnic at the pond, I had them all laughing with my new fishing pole trick."

"What trick was that?" she asked over her shoulder.

"I wasn't paying close enough attention to what I was doing and ended up snagging the top of Ruth's kapp while I was trying to cast my line into the water. Sure got razzed about that little mistake from Toby and Sadie."

Martha chuckled as she stepped into the unused horse stall and lit the gas lamp hanging from the rafters. "All kinds of things are stashed in here, including what you came for." She motioned to the cardboard boxes stacked against one wall.

"Looks like a couple of 'em are just the size I'm needing." Luke reached for the boxes, then halted. "Hey! What's this?"

"What's what?" Martha peered around his outstretched arm and gasped. "Heidi! Why she's gone and had her hundlin inside that old box."

Luke nodded. "That's what it looks like all right."

"I guess she didn't care much for the wooden crate I fixed up for her on the other side of the barn."

"Dogs are like humans in some ways," he said in a tone too serious for someone like Luke. "They're as picky about their birthing boxes as we are about choosin' our mates."

Martha wasn't sure how to respond since she hadn't given much thought to choosing a mate. Truth was, she didn't have a whole lot on her mind these days except getting her kennel business going. "I suppose it would be best to just leave her be since she's picked this place and seems nicely settled in."

He nodded and stared into the box. "How many pups does she have in there, can ya tell?"

Knowing it wouldn't be a good idea to touch any of the puppies yet, Martha squinted and tried to count each little blob. That's what she thought they looked like, too—squirming, squealing blobs with tiny pink noses. "I think there are five," she announced. "Could be more scrunched in there, though."

"Sure are noisy little critters. Are you planning to keep any?"

She nodded. "I might keep one for breeding purposes, but I'll sell the rest because I need the money."

He tipped his head as though studying her. "You're quite the businesswoman, aren't you?"

"I'm trying to be." Martha moved away from the box. "Guess I'll head back inside and see if Mom needs my help getting lunch on the table. Heidi would probably like to be left alone with her brood, anyway."

Luke reached for two of the empty boxes. "I'd better get back to your daed's shop before the impatient fellow comes looking for me."

With no comment on her father's impatience, Martha turned down the gas lantern and followed Luke out the door. She felt good knowing that Heidi had given birth to a litter of pups. At last, she was well on her way to what she hoped would be a successful business venture.

Roman looked up from the paperwork he was doing when Luke stepped into the shop carrying two cardboard boxes. "Took ya long enough," he grumbled. "Couldn't you find the stall I told you about?"

"Found it just fine." Luke set the boxes on the floor. "Martha and I discovered that her sheltie had given birth to five hundlin in a cardboard box inside the stall."

"I'll bet my daughter was happy about that. She didn't think the pups would be born for a couple more days." Roman nodded toward a stack of finished cabinets sitting along one wall. "The set of cabinets Steven Bates ordered for his wife's birthday are ready to go, so I'd like you to deliver them today."

"Sure, I can do that. Want me to go now or wait 'til after lunch?"

"Now would be better. You can eat lunch when you get back."

"Okay."

Roman pushed his chair away from the desk. "I'll help you get them loaded and tied onto the wagon, and then I need to get busy and finish up the paperwork I started this morning."

"I'm sure I can manage to tie 'em in place on my own," Luke said, moving toward the cabinets.

"Okay, but you'd better be certain they're tied on good and tight. Steven's a picky customer, and he won't stand for any scratches or dents."

"I'll make sure everything's firmly in place."

They soon had the cabinets set in the back of the wagon Roman used for hauling, and as Luke began to tie them in place, Roman headed back to the shop. A short time later, he heard the buggy wheels rolling and Luke calling for the horse to "get-a-moving."

"Sure hope he doesn't get that horse moving too fast," Roman mumbled as he reached for his ledger to begin making entries again. "That kid is either running late or moving too fast. No happy medium where Luke's concerned."

For the next hour and a half, Roman worked on the books. Every now and then, he glanced up at the clock on the far wall to check the time. He figured Luke should have been back by now—unless he stopped somewhere to eat his lunch.

The sound of a car door slamming brought Roman to his feet. A few seconds later, Steven Bates entered the shop, looking madder than a bull chasing a dog around the pasture.

"What's wrong? Didn't you like the cabinets Luke delivered? He did deliver them, I hope."

"Oh, yeah. He got 'em a few feet from my driveway, and they slid off the back of your wagon and landed in the street—in several pieces."

Roman's face heated up. "How'd that happen?"

"Guess you didn't get 'em tied on good enough." Steven grunted. "Tomorrow's my wife's birthday, and now I'm in big trouble because our kitchen remodel isn't done."

Roman struggled to keep his temper from flaring. He should have insisted he help Luke tie on those cabinets, and he shouldn't have trusted the kid to do them alone. "It'll take me a few weeks, but I'll make good on the cabinets," he promised.

Steven shook his head. "Don't bother; I'm done."

"Done? What do you mean?"

Steven squinted his beady brown eyes as he rubbed the top of his balding head. "You've been late with work I've contracted you to do before, your work's not the quality I expect, and now this! I'll be taking my business down the road from now on." He turned on his heels and marched out the door, slamming it with such force that the windows rattled.

Roman rushed to the door, but by the time he got there, Steven's car had peeled out of the driveway, sending gravel flying in all directions.

A short time later, Luke showed up, looking more than a little sheepish. "Sorry to be telling you this, but—"

Roman held up his hand. "I already know. Thanks to you, I won't be getting any more of Steven's business."

"I—I thought I had those ropes tied real good, and I can't figure out how it happened."

"Jah, well, what's done is done, but now I'm out the money Steven owed me, so I'll be takin' it out of your pay to make up for what I lost today."

Luke's face turned bright red. "But those cabinets weren't cheap. It'll take me several weeks to pay you back."

Roman gave a curt nod. "And you'll work twice as hard as you've been workin', too."

Luke opened his mouth as if to say something more, but then he closed it with an audible click. "What have you got for me to do now?" he asked, turning toward the workbench.

"You can start by sweeping the floor in the back room, and when you're done with that, I'd like you to clean the front windows."

A muscle on the side of Luke's neck quivered, but he just grabbed the broom from the closet and headed for the other room.

"Always trouble somewhere," Roman muttered under his breath. "I knew I shouldn't have hired that irresponsible fellow."

The door to Roman's shop opened again, and this time Martin Gingerich stepped into the room.

"Can I help you?" Roman asked as he turned to face the young man with light brown hair.

Martin nodded and glanced around the room as if he might be looking for something. "I. . .uh. . .came by to see if you'd have the time to make something for me."

"All depends on what it is."

Martin removed his straw hat and fanned his face with it a couple of times. "My folks' anniversary is coming up soon, and I was hoping to give them something nice."

"Did you have anything particular in mind?" Roman asked as he headed for his desk and took a seat in the chair behind it.

Martin followed and continued to fan his face while he stood on the other side of the desk, facing Roman. "Thought maybe they might like a new rocking chair."

Roman leaned forward, his elbows resting on the desk. "I'm not braggin', mind you, but I think the rocking chairs I make are pretty nice—real comfortable, too."

"Can you have it ready in three weeks?" Martin asked.

Roman nodded. "Jah, sure. Shouldn't be a problem."

"Danki." Martin's gaze dropped to the floor, and he twisted the brim of his hat in his hands.

"Is there anything else I can help you with?"

"Uh. . .no, not really."

Roman pushed his chair aside and stood. "Okay then, I'll put a card in the mail to let you know when the chair's ready."

Martin's head came up. "Oh, no! Better not do that, or my folks will know about my surprise gift." He shuffled his feet a few times. "I'll just plan on dropping by here once a week to check on it."

"Sounds good to me. I'm sure I'll have it done in plenty of time for their anniversary."

Thinking the young man would head out, Roman moved toward the front door. Martin followed, but when he got to the door, he halted and turned to face Roman again. "I. . .uh. . .heard that Ruth got a job in Berlin working at the bakeshop." His voice sounded raspy, almost a whisper.

"Jah, she sure did."

"Does she like it there?"

"I guess so." Roman grinned. "Who wouldn't like working around all those sweet-tasting pastries and pies?"

Martin nodded and glanced around the room again. "Heard you hired Luke Friesen a few months back, but I don't see him anywhere. Does that mean he's not workin' for you anymore?"

Roman nodded toward the back room. "He's doing some cleanup."

"I see. Well, I'd best be on my way, I expect. See you soon."

Roman shook his head as Martin headed out the door. That fellow was sure the nervous type. Nothing like Luke, who never seemed to think twice about what he said or did.

Chapter 7

Cleon pulled into the Hostettlers' place, halted his buggy in front of the hitching rail, and climbed down. As soon as he had his horse put in the corral, he skirted around to the back of the buggy and lifted his bicycle out. Today was another beautiful Saturday with clear blue skies and plenty of sunshine, despite the drop in the temperature that typically came with fall weather. Even though he knew Grace had worked until three this afternoon, Cleon figured they had time to go for a bicycle ride before the sun went down.

He parked his bike near the barn and hurried around the house to the back door, where he found Judith sitting on the porch with a pan of plump, golden apples in her lap and a paring knife in one hand.

"It's good to see you, Cleon," she said, smiling up at him as he stepped onto the porch.

"Good to see you, too." He glanced toward the door. "I'm here to take Grace for a bike ride. Do you know if she's ready to go?"

"She's upstairs changing her clothes, so if you'd like to have a seat and keep me company for a while, that'd be real nice." Judith nodded toward the wicker chair that sat beside her own.

"I believe I will." Cleon liked the way Grace's mother always took time out to visit with him. Not like his mother, who stayed busy from sunup to sunset. But then, Judith didn't have a home-based business where she had to feed several groups of hungry, curious tourists several times a week. Mom also had her candle-making business, and even though she had the help of Cleon's sister with both jobs, she had very little time to sit and visit.

"It's a fine day for a bike ride, jah?"

Cleon nodded. "What are your other two daughters up to this afternoon?"

"Martha's out in the barn hovering over her dogs, like usual, and Ruth went for a walk with her friend Sadie." Judith's lips puckered as she lifted her knife and began to peel one of the apples in the bowl. "Ruth was supposed to go somewhere with Luke this afternoon, but Roman asked him to work today, so she made other plans, which might be a good thing in the long run."

"What makes you say that?"

She shrugged. "If Luke's giving Roman a hard time in the shop, then he might not be the best choice as a suitor for Ruth. She tends to be quite sensitive, and I'm not sure a headstrong man like Luke is what she needs."

The back door swung open, and Grace stepped onto the porch, saving Cleon from having to respond.

"Ready to go?" he asked, feeling a sense of excitement at the prospect of being alone with her again.

Grace nodded and smiled. "Just don't expect me to go speeding down the road. My legs are tired from work, and I'm not sure how far I can go without my strength giving out."

"Would you rather we not ride our bikes? We could go for a buggy ride instead."

She shook her head. "That's okay. I need the fresh air, and the exercise my legs will be getting is different from walking or standing."

"Okay then." Cleon smiled at Judith. "I'll have your daughter home in plenty of time for supper."

Judith's eyes twinkled. "You're welcome to stay and eat with us if you like."

"I might take you up on that offer." Cleon lifted his hand in a wave and hurried down the steps after Grace.

"I can't believe how well this weather is holding out," Ruth commented as she and Sadie turned off the main road and headed onto a wide path into the woods not far from the pond where they'd had a picnic with Luke and Toby the week before.

"Winter will be here soon, which is why we need to do some fun things before it gets too cold."

Ruth poked Sadie gently on the arm. "There are plenty of fun things you can do in the cold, you know."

"Right. Sledding, ice skating, and snowball fights." Sadie swung her arms as they clipped along at a steady pace. "Too bad Toby and Luke weren't free to join us today."

"My daed has a backload of work right now, and he needed Luke's help today."

Sadie nodded. "Since tomorrow's church service will be held at Toby's house, he had to help his brothers get the benches they'll need."

Ruth stopped walking and pointed to a shiny black pickup parked behind a clump of bushes. "I wonder whose truck that is. I don't recall seeing it before, do you?"

Sadie shook her head. "No, but the last time we came to the pond, we never walked back into the woods."

"You're right." Ruth squinted as they moved closer to the truck. "It's empty, and I don't see anyone else around but us."

"Maybe it's abandoned."

"Or maybe someone hid it here."

"Why would anybody do that?"

Ruth's hands went straight to her hips. "Some fellows going through rumschpringe have vehicles they don't want anyone to know about. You ought to know that."

Sadie's blue eyes widened. "You think some Amish fellow owns this truck?"

"Maybe so."

"It's not a new vehicle, but it's clean and polished." Sadie touched the chrome mirror. "I'd say whoever owns it feels a bit of *hochmut* and takes pleasure in keeping it nice."

"If it belongs to an Amish fellow, then he's not supposed to feel pride." Ruth pursed her lips. "I hope he doesn't like having a truck so much that he decides to leave the faith so he can continue to drive it."

Grace's legs were about to give out, and she was on the verge of asking Cleon to stop so she could rest when he pulled his bike to the side of the road and signaled her to do the same. "This hilly road is starting to get to me, and I'm feeling kind of tired," he huffed. "Why don't we push our bicycles awhile? That will make it easier for us to talk, too."

She smiled in appreciation and climbed off her bike.

"I'm glad you were free to spend the afternoon with me, since this is the last chance we'll have to be together for a week or so."

"Oh, why's that?"

"Didn't I tell you that my family and I are leaving for Rexford, Montana, on Monday morning to attend my cousin Sarah's wedding? We'll be gone a week."

She shook her head. "I don't remember you saying that." Of course, lately, she hadn't paid much attention to anything that had been said to her. All she could think about was Gary showing up in town, and whether she should tell Cleon the truth about her past. After another restless night of tossing, turning, and mulling things over, Grace had concluded that it might be best if she revealed her secret now before Gary had a chance to say anything. If Cleon was as understanding as she hoped he would be, then maybe it would give her the courage she needed to tell her folks about it, too.

They walked in silence for a while as Grace tried to decide the best way to broach the subject of her rumschpringe days. Maybe it would be good if she led into it slowly, to see how he felt about things.

"Let's get off the main road and head into the woods," Cleon said, nodding toward a path on the right. "I think this leads to the pond near the Wengerds' place."

Grace pushed her bike off the shoulder of the road and onto the wide dirt path, deciding to wait until she was walking by his side before she spoke again. "Uh. . .Cleon, there's something I want to talk to you about."

His eyebrows drew together. "You look so serious. Is there something wrong? Are you having second thoughts about marrying me?"

Grace moistened her lips with the tip of her tongue and halted her bike. This was going to be harder than she thought. "I'm not having second thoughts, but I think you should know that–"

"Hey, what are you two doing out here?"

Grace whirled around at the sound of her sister's voice. "Ruth, you scared me!"

Sadie chuckled. "I can tell she did. Your eyes are huge as buggy wheels."

"I–I just didn't expect to see either of you here," Grace stammered. It was a good thing she hadn't revealed her secret to Cleon. What if Ruth and Sadie had overheard their conversation? The last thing she needed was Sadie knowing anything about her personal business, because she tended to be a blabbermouth.

"Sadie and I cut through the woods and spent some time at the pond," Ruth said. "It's beautiful there this time of the year." She nodded at Grace. "Is that where you two are headed?"

"Jah," Cleon spoke up. "We were riding on the shoulder of the road but decided to walk our bikes awhile."

Ruth glanced at the diminishing sun filtering through the trees. "It'll be getting dark soon, so I wouldn't stay too long if I were you."

"She's got a point," Cleon said. "Maybe we should head back before we lose our daylight."

"Okay." Grace felt a mixture of relief and disappointment. If they headed for home now, and Ruth and Sadie tagged along, she wouldn't be able to tell Cleon what was on her mind. Still, the girls coming along when they did might have been a good thing, especially if Cleon's response had been negative. Maybe it would be best to wait and tell Cleon sometime after he got back from Montana. That would give her another whole week to think it through and decide the best way to word things to him.

Sure were a lot of folks missing from church today," Mom said as she walked toward the house beside Grace, with Ruth, Martha, and Dad following. "Martin Gingerich, Sadie Esh, and Abe Wengerd were sick, I understand."

"Luke was out with the flu," Ruth put in.

"Leastways that's what his mamm said." Dad grunted. "Truth be told, he was probably lazing in bed because I worked him so hard last week after he wrecked that set of cabinets that was supposed to be for Ella Bates's birthday. Steven was hoppin' mad about that, and he said from now on he won't be giving me any more business."

"I'm sure tired this afternoon," Mom said, making no reference to Dad's problems at work, which he'd already told them about.

He yawned noisily. "Jah, me, too. *Ich bin mied wie en hund*."

"If you're as tired as a dog," Martha put in, "you're very tired indeed. I'm going out to the barn to check on Heidi and her pups as soon as I change out of my church clothes."

Grace couldn't help but smile at her sister's exuberance. It seemed that all Martha talked about anymore were those dogs of hers.

"You can spend the rest of the day in the barn with your hundlin if you want to," Dad said, "but I'm gonna take a nap."

Mom nodded. "I think I'd better take one, too."

As they stepped onto the back porch, Grace noticed that the door hung slightly open. Dad must have noticed it too, for he turned and gave them a curious stare. "Which of you was the last one out the door this morning? And how come you didn't close it?"

"It wasn't me," Grace was quick to say.

Ruth shook her head. "Nor me."

"I may have been the last one out," Martha admitted, "but I'm sure I didn't leave the door open."

"Well, someone did." Dad pushed the door fully open and entered the house, grumbling about all the flies that had probably gotten in.

Grace and her sisters stopped in the hallway, but Mom had already entered the kitchen. "Someone's been in here," she shouted. "Ach! They've made such a mess!"

The others rushed into the kitchen. Mom stood in the midst of chaos—pots and pans littered the floor, chairs were overturned, and several items of food from the refrigerator lay in the middle of the table.

They stood for several seconds in stunned silence. Then Dad groaned and shook his head. "Weren't no critter that sneaked into the house and did all this. Had to be done by human hands—that's for certain sure." He turned on his heels with a huff.

"Where are you going?" Mom called with a panicked expression.

"To check out the rest of the place, what do you think?"

She rushed to his side. "If whoever did this is still in the house, then what?"

"If he is, then we'll have ourselves a little heart-to-heart talk."

Martha bent down and picked up a rolling pin from the floor. "Maybe I'd better go with you."

Mom moved like she was going to stop Martha, but Grace got to her first. "Just what do you think you're doing?" She grabbed the rolling pin and placed it on the counter. "I hope you're not considering using that as a weapon."

"I—I wasn't going to hit anyone, just scare 'em a bit is all."

Dad pointed to the floor. "You'd better stay here and help your mamm clean up while I look through the other rooms." He rushed out of the kitchen before anyone could argue the point.

Grace's hand trembled as she bent to retrieve one of her mother's frying pans. *Who could have done this, and why would they do such a thing?*

"Never in all the years your daed and I have been married has anything like this ever happened to us," Mom said in a shaky voice.

"I–I wonder if anything's been stolen." Ruth's dark eyes were huge, and her face had turned chalky white, making her brunette hair appear even darker.

"I hope not," Mom said, "but we need to remember that nothing we own is really ours. It's all on loan from God."

Grace moved closer to the hallway door and craned her neck. She couldn't see anything, but she could hear her father's footsteps as he moved through the living room. "Dad, are you all right?"

"I'm fine. Just checking things out in here."

"Has that room been vandalized, too?"

He stepped into the hall and shook his head. "Nothing appears to have been disturbed in the living room. Next, I'm going to check upstairs."

Grace gripped the edge of the door and clenched her teeth. *What if someone's been in my room? What if they went through my things? What if. . .*

"I hope everything's okay upstairs," Mom said, breaking into Grace's disturbing thoughts. "I wish your daed had let one of us go with him."

"I'm sure he'll be down soon." Ruth managed a weak smile.

It seemed obvious to Grace that they all felt uneasy about this break-in, and she wouldn't rest easy until she knew if anything had been taken from her room.

"I'll be right back," Martha said, scooting toward the back door.

"Where are you going?" Mom called to her.

"To the barn to check on my dogs." Martha's shoulders lifted, and her breath came out in little spurts. "I want to be sure they're okay."

"Not without your daed, you're not. Whoever broke into the house could be hiding in the barn." Mom shook her head firmly.

Martha raised her chin as if she might argue, but Grace knew her determined little sister would not get her way on this matter.

"We must be patient and wait for Dad," Ruth said, reaching for the jar of dill pickles that had been dumped on the table.

When Grace heard her father's heavy footsteps clomping around upstairs, she glanced into the hallway again.

"Let's try to remain calm and wait and see what he discovers upstairs," Mom said as she wet a dishrag at the kitchen sink and began to wash off the table.

For the next few minutes, Grace and her mother and sisters bustled around the kitchen, picking things up and cleaning off the table. They were nearly finished when Dad showed up again, squinting his dark eyes and scratching the side of his head.

"What's wrong, Roman?" Mom asked, stepping up to him. "Was everything all right upstairs?"

"There's nobody there, and nothing was disturbed in any of the rooms except for Grace's."

"How odd." Mom's forehead wrinkled. "If they messed up one room, you'd think they would have done the same to the others."

"Maybe Heidi or Fritz sensed something was amiss and started barking, scaring anyone off before they could do more damage," Martha suggested.

"That could be," Dad agreed as he reached up to rub the bridge of his nose. "Or maybe it was done randomly, with no rhyme or reason as to which rooms got messed."

Grace stood for several seconds, trying to piece everything together. With a little gasp, she dashed from the room.

"Would you like me to run down to the phone shed and call the sheriff's office?" Martha asked her father.

"I'll go with her," Ruth put in.

Firmly, he shook his head. "We won't involve the sheriff, and I wouldn't press charges even if he was notified and found the person who made this mess."

"I know that, but–"

"I'm sure it was just some pranksters–probably the same ones who turned over those outhouses near Kidron last week."

"So we just allow them to get away with this?" Martha motioned to the remaining items on the table. "I think they need to be stopped, or else they might do the same thing to other folks."

Mom touched Dad's arm. "Our daughter has a point. Maybe we should let the sheriff know about this."

"We'll do what others in our community have done whenever the rowdy English kids have played their pranks. We'll look the other way, turn the other cheek, forgive, and forget." Dad sighed. "Now let's get on with the business of living and forget this ever happened."

Martha made a sweeping gesture with her hand. "How can we forget it happened when our kitchen is such a mess and Grace is upstairs trying to deal with whatever they did to her room?" She moaned. "This isn't right. It's not right at all."

"We can forget it happened by making the choice to put it out of our minds. That's how we'll deal with it." Dad folded his arms in a stubborn pose.

"Do you think Grace is going to forget that a stranger came into her room while we were at church?" Martha nodded toward the door leading to the upstairs.

Before Dad had a chance to answer, Ruth spoke up. "I'm going to see how she's doing. No doubt, she'll need some help cleaning up the mess."

Grace entered her room and skidded to a stop in front of the bed. Articles of clothing were strewn everywhere—white kapps, choring aprons, a pair of black sneakers, and some dresses that had been torn into shreds.

Her heart thudded. Her hands sweat. Her knees nearly buckled. With a sense of dread, she made her way over to the cedar chest at the foot of the bed and flipped open the lid, dipping both hands deep inside and feeling around to see if anything was missing. When Grace's fingers touched the scrapbook she'd kept hidden away, and then she discovered that her faceless doll was still there, she breathed a sigh of relief.

"Are you all right? Has anything been stolen?"

Grace slammed the lid shut and spun around. "Ruth! I didn't hear you come in."

"I came up to see if there was anything I could do to help." Ruth stepped forward and pointed to the mess on Grace's bed. "Oh, sister, I'm so sorry. I can't understand why anyone would do such a thing. It makes no sense why they would mess up the kitchen and your room yet not bother with any of ours."

"I–I don't understand it, either, but to my knowledge, nothing was taken." Grace stood on trembling legs and clenched her teeth, trying to stop the flow of tears.

"Maybe Martha's right about either Heidi or Fritz hearing the intruder and scaring him off before he had time to ransack the other rooms." Ruth glanced around. "It does seem odd that nothing is missing, though."

Before Grace could respond, Martha rushed into the room, her face flushed and her eyes wide with obvious concern. "Did they break anything? Have any of your things been stolen?"

"Not that I can tell." Grace pointed to her bed. "They threw some of my clothes on the bed and tore up a couple of my dresses."

"Look over there!" Martha pointed to the desk on the other side of the room. "They emptied everything out of the drawers onto the floor. Looks like some of your papers have been shredded, too."

Grace pivoted. She'd been so concerned about the things in her cedar chest that she hadn't even noticed the desk. Tears burned her eyes, and she nearly choked on the lump lodged in her throat. Who could have done this? Who could hate her enough to rummage through her room and make such a mess?

She froze as an image of Gary Walker popped into her head. Could he be responsible for this? He'd said he would get even with her someday for breaking up with him. Had he finally made good on his threat?

Chapter 9

It was difficult for Grace to go to work the next day, but she had no legitimate reason for staying home other than feeling traumatized over the break-in at their house. She wished she could tell Cleon about the break-in, but she knew he and his family had left for Rexford, Montana, to attend a cousin's wedding. In all likelihood, they wouldn't be back for a week.

When Grace arrived at the restaurant, she was surprised to learn that Esther was out sick with the flu. That meant Grace was needed more than ever, confirming that she'd done the right thing by coming to work.

She donned her apron, grabbed an order pad and pencil from behind the counter, and headed for the dining room. She'd only taken a few steps when she halted. There sat Gary in a booth in her section, looking as smug as always. Grace had no choice but to wait on him.

Her legs felt like two sticks of rubber as she slowly made her way across the room. When she reached Gary's table, she placed the menu in front of him, avoiding his piercing gaze. "Would you like a cup of coffee?"

"Sure, that'd be great."

"I'll take your order when I bring the coffee." Grace turned and walked away before he could respond.

When she returned a few minutes later, she had calmed down some. She'd decided to come right out and ask if he had anything to do with the break-in at their house when she spotted a notebook lying on the table beside his camera. That's when she remembered that Gary had said he was some kind of reporter. If she mentioned the break-in and he wasn't the one involved, he might want to do a story about it, and seeing a story about their break-in in some publication would make her father furious. Maybe it would be best if she didn't say anything—at least for now. No point in letting Gary know how upset they had all been.

"Are you going to stand there staring at the table all day, or did you plan to give me that cup of coffee you're holding?"

Grace drew in a deep breath and placed the cup on the table; then she reached into her apron pocket and withdrew her order pad and pencil. "What would you like for breakfast?"

He jiggled his eyebrows and gave her a quick wink. "Is a date with you on the menu?"

She moaned. Apparently Gary hadn't changed. He'd always been a big flirt, which she'd been attracted to at first. But when she got to know him better, she'd come to see how moody he could be.

"Aw, come on, Gracie," he drawled. "Don't look so down-in-the-mouth. You and I had something special together once, remember?"

Of course she remembered. Remembering was the easy part. The hard part was forgetting. If Grace had it to do over again, she never would have dated anyone outside her faith during her rumschpringe, and she certainly wouldn't have dated anyone as arrogant as Gary.

He touched her arm, and the contact of his sweaty, hot fingers made her cringe. "You're bound and determined not to warm up to me, aren't you?"

Grace jerked away, feeling like she'd been stung by one of Cleon's honeybees. She could hardly believe she used to enjoy this irritating man's touch or that she'd been sucked in by his smooth talking. Not anymore. She was older, wiser, and more cautious. "Are you going to order or not?" she asked through tight lips.

He grinned up at her and tapped the menu with his pen. "I'll have two eggs over easy, a side of hash browns, and a cinnamon roll to make me sweeter."

If a cinnamon roll would make you sweeter, I would bring you ten.

Grace picked up the menu and turned away, but she'd taken only a few steps when he called out to her.

"Better make that two cinnamon rolls, Gracie. Today, I'll be interviewing several people who work with the Amish, and I might need a little extra energy so I can sweet-talk 'em into telling me what I want to know."

Grace hurried across the room to put in his order. She figured the best thing was to ignore his catty remarks. If he really was a reporter and had only come to Holmes County to get a story on the Amish, then hopefully he would be gone in a few days.

Ruth had just finished waiting on a customer when Luke walked into the bakeshop. "I'm surprised to see you," she said as he stepped up to the counter. "I figured you'd be working for my daed today."

"I am. Just came into Berlin to deliver a table to Paul Hendricks. Last week, he and his wife opened a new bed-and-breakfast across town."

"I heard about that. With all the tourists who come into the area, I guess we need another place for them to stay."

"Jah." Luke leaned against the counter and studied the pastries Ruth had put into the case when she'd arrived at work this morning. "Think I'll buy myself a donut or something. Any suggestions?"

"Normally, I'm kind of partial to cream puffs, but since I have no appetite today, I'd better let you decide."

"What's wrong with your appetite? You're not comin' down with the bug that's been going around, I hope." He lifted his shoulders in a brief shrug. "I felt kind of under the weather yesterday. That's why I wasn't in church."

"Are you doing better now?"

He nodded. "Guess a lot of folks are still sick, though."

"The flu's not my problem," she said with a shake of her head, "but I am a bit *loddrich* after what happened yesterday."

"What happened that's got you feeling shaky?"

"Didn't my daed tell to you about the break-in at our place

yesterday while we were at church?"

"He never said a thing. So why don't you fill me in?"

Ruth glanced around the room to be sure there were no other customers in the store, and then she quickly relayed the details of the break-in. She sniffed and swallowed hard in an effort to hold back the threatening tears. "I know others have been the victims of break-ins and vandalism in the past, but we've never had anything like that happen to us, and it made everyone in the family feel loddrich."

Luke leaned on the counter. "Did your daed phone the sheriff?"

Ruth shook her head. "Dad thinks it was probably a bunch of English kids having some fun. He said we should try and forget it ever happened." She drew in a deep breath and released it quickly. "Of course, that's easier said than done."

"Roman's probably right about it being some English fellows. A group of 'em dumped over some outhouses not long ago. Did you hear about that?"

"It wasn't confirmed that they were English, though, right?"

"Well, no, but—"

"Who's to say that it wasn't some Amish kids going through rumschpringe?"

"Right." Luke shifted from one foot to another, then stepped away from the counter. "Well, guess I'd better be going."

"What about that donut you wanted?"

He turned and lifted his hand in a backwards wave. "Some other time, maybe. I've got things to do and places to go."

As Luke left the store, Ruth's thoughts took her to the day she and Sadie had gone to the pond to meet Luke and Toby. When Luke had shown up late, he'd acted kind of odd, too.

She grabbed a tray of donuts from the shelf behind her and slipped them into the display cabinet, knowing she needed to keep busy so she wouldn't have to think about yesterday's break-in or Luke's strange behavior.

A few minutes later, another customer entered the store. This time it was Donna Larson, their middle-aged English neighbor, who often drove for them when they needed to go places that were too far to travel by horse and buggy.

"I heard you were working here now," Donna said as she stepped up to the counter and pushed a wisp of grayish-brown hair away from her face.

Ruth nodded and pointed to the pastries inside the glass. "We're having a special on donuts today, if you're interested."

"I haven't had time to do much baking lately, so I think I will take a few of those with chocolate glaze." Donna snickered. "Better make that half-a-dozen chocolate and half-a-dozen lemon. Ray has a sweet tooth, and he'll probably eat all the chocolate ones himself."

Ruth smiled, but her heart really wasn't in it. Truth was, she wished she and Grace could have stayed home from work today, since they'd both felt shaky after yesterday's break-in.

"For a young woman with a new job, and a good-smelling one at that, you sure look down in the dumps today," Donna commented.

Ruth wondered if she should tell Donna what had happened at their place. Maybe whoever had broken in had vandalized some of the neighbors' homes, as well. She waited until she had Donna's donuts put in a box and had rung up her purchase, then she leaned across the counter and said, "Did anything unusual happen at your place yesterday?"

"Let's see now, Ray fixed us some omelets for breakfast." Donna grinned and fluttered her eyelashes. "That's pretty unusual for him."

"No, I meant did anything *bad* happen yesterday?"

"Not really. Unless you count Ray falling asleep in the middle of me trying to tell him about the letter I got from my sister the other day."

Ruth grimaced. Beating around the shrubs wasn't getting her anywhere, so she guessed she might as well come right out and say it. "Your house wasn't broken into, was it?"

Donna tipped her head to one side and squinted at Ruth, her gray-blue eyes narrowing into tiny slits. "Of course not. Why do you ask?"

Ruth cleared her throat and lowered her voice to a whisper. "While we were in church, someone broke into our house."

Donna's eyes opened wide. "Was anything taken?"

"No, but they made a mess in a couple of rooms." She leaned closer to Donna. "Did you hear or see anything unusual yesterday?"

"No, I didn't, but then I was inside most of the day watching Ray sleep while I worked on a crossword puzzle." Donna's eyes narrowed again. "Did you notify the sheriff?"

Ruth shook her head. "Dad said no to that idea. Even if he had let the sheriff know, he wouldn't have pressed charges if they'd found the person responsible."

"I understand that's not the Amish way."

"No, it's not. Dad also thinks it was probably a bunch of kids out for a good time and that it isn't likely to happen again."

"He could be right, but I'll tell Ray to keep an eye out just the same. He's always got those binoculars of his trained on the trees in our yard, watching for different birds. I'll ask him to check things out over at your place whenever he gets the chance." Donna plucked the box of donuts from the counter and glanced at her watch. "I'd better run. I've got a hair appointment in ten minutes, and I don't want to be late." With a quick wave, she hurried out the door.

"How are you doing today, Heidi?" Martha asked as she stared into the box where the mother sheltie lay nursing her pups.

The dog responded with a faint whimper but didn't budge from her spot.

She patted the top of Heidi's head. "You're a good *mudder*, and I'm glad you and your little ones weren't bothered by whoever broke into our house yesterday." Just thinking about anyone disturbing her dogs made Martha feel sick to her stomach.

The barn door clicked open, then slammed shut, and she jumped. "Who's there?"

"It's only me," Mom called. "Came out to tell you that I'm taking some lunch to your daed soon. I thought if he's not too busy I would eat with him, and I wondered if you'd like to join us."

Martha waited until her mother was closer before she responded. "Will Luke be there, too?"

"I don't rightly know. Probably so, unless he's planning to go home for lunch today. I guess he does that from time to time." Mom laid a hand on Martha's shoulder. "Why do you ask?"

Martha shrugged. "Just wondered, is all."

"So, did you want to join us?"

"Think I'll spend a little more time with Heidi and her brood, and then I'll take my lunch out back and sit by the creek awhile."

Mom leaned over and looked into the box. "Those puppies are sure cute. I'll bet it's going to be hard for you to part with them after they're weaned."

Martha sighed. "Jah, but I'm raising them for the money, so except for one pup I might keep for breeding, I'll be selling the rest."

"Are you still planning to buy some other breed of dogs to raise?"

"I hope so. If and when I can afford it."

Mom patted Martha's arm. "Be patient, dear one. Only barns are built in a day, and that's because there are so many workers to help with the building."

Martha chuckled. It appeared that her mother had calmed down after yesterday's scare, for her sense of humor had obviously returned.

"Guess I'll head back to the house and gather up the lunch I fixed," Mom said, turning to go. "Come on out to the shop if you change your mind about eating with us."

"Okay."

Mom closed the door behind her, and Martha dished up some dog food for Heidi. When she was done, she dropped to a bale of hay and let her head fall forward in her hands. "Dear Lord," she prayed, "please protect our family, and don't let anything like that awful break-in happen to anyone else we know."

"You're sure late getting back. What took you so long?" Roman grumbled as Luke stepped into the shop with his face all red and sweaty and his straw hat tilted to one side.

"Had a little trouble with the delivery wagon." Luke grimaced. "Guess it was more your horse that gave me problems than the wagon."

Roman set aside the piece of sandpaper he'd been using to sand a table leg and moved over to the window. "What's the problem with Sam?" He peered though the glass and spotted his delivery wagon parked near the stable, but there was no sign of the horse.

"He tried to run away with the wagon when Paul Hendricks and I were unloading his table. I had quite a time gettin' that skittish animal settled down."

"Didn't you have him tied up?"

Luke nodded and hung his straw hat on a wall peg near the door. " 'Course I did, but he broke free, and I didn't realize it 'til the wagon started moving."

Roman thumped the side of his head and groaned. "Don't tell me you lost the table in the street like you did with those cabinets for Steven Bates. If you did, it'll be more than a few days pay you'll be docked for this time."

Luke shook his head, and his face turned even redder. "Me and Paul had just taken the table out of the back when the wagon started moving, and we had to set the table down in order to chase after the horse."

"Where's Sam now?"

"I gave him a good rubdown and turned him loose in the corral. He acted kind of spooky on the way home and was pretty lathered up by the time we got here."

Roman moved back to his sanding job. "I thought he was acting a bit jumpy this morning when I took him out of his stall, but I figured he'd settle down once he was harnessed up."

"Maybe you should have the vet check him over," Luke suggested. "It's not like Sam to carry on like that."

"I'm wondering if it has something to do with what happened yesterday." Roman gave the table leg he'd been working on a couple of swipes. "I didn't mention this earlier, but someone broke into our house while we were at church."

"I heard about that."

"Who told you?"

"Stopped by the bakeshop to say hello to Ruth when I was in

Berlin. She told me about it." Luke grabbed a hunk of sandpaper and started working on one of the other table legs that had been lying on the workbench.

"The womenfolk were pretty shook up when we got home and discovered the kitchen had been ransacked." Roman grunted. "Whoever did it made a mess in Grace's bedroom, too, although nothing appeared to have been stolen."

"Ruth said you had decided not to notify the sheriff."

Roman nodded. "I'm sure this was just a prank—probably done by whoever tipped over those outhouses not long ago."

Luke squinted. "You think that's got something to do with the way your horse acted this morning?"

Roman stopped sanding long enough to reach up and scratch the side of his head. "I'm not sure, but maybe the person who broke into the house went out to the barn and bothered the horses."

"Was anything in the barn disturbed?"

"Not that I could tell."

"Did any of the other horses act jumpy this morning?"

"Nope. Just Sam." Roman gave his earlobe a couple of sharp pulls. "Guess I'll never know what all went on during the break-in, but I'm thankful nothing was stolen and that none of the animals were hurt."

Luke opened his mouth as if to comment, but the door opened, and Judith stepped into the room. "Ready for lunch, Roman?" she asked, lifting the lunch pail she held in her hands.

Roman nodded, grateful for the interruption. He didn't want to give any more thought to yesterday's happenings, much less talk about them.

Chapter 10

As Roman headed to his woodworking shop the following Monday morning, thoughts about the break-in flitted through his mind. During the past week, he'd checked with some Amish families who lived close by to see if they'd had any problems, but apparently no one else had been bothered. If it was some rowdy English boys running amuck, then they probably wouldn't stop with just a prank or two.

Roman slipped his key into the lock and swung the shop door open. He froze. Even without the gas lamps lit, he could see the devastation. Broken tools littered the floor, a couple of tables had been dumped over, and the distinctive odors of lacquer thinner and stain permeated the room.

"*Was in der welt?* What in all the world was someone thinking? Who's responsible for this?" Since the front door had been locked, he knew the only way anyone could have gotten in was through one of the windows or the back door.

Cautiously, he stepped through the mess, making his way to the back room. The door there was slightly ajar, and he saw immediately that the lock had been broken.

He lit the nearest lamp so he could see better. Anger boiled in his chest when he realized how many of his tools and supplies had been ruined. After a thorough search through the cabinets where more tools were kept, he discovered several items were missing—a gas-powered saw, a sander, and his two most expensive hammers.

He bent over to set one of the tables in an upright position. "I don't need this kind of trouble. No one does."

The door swung open just then, and Ruth stepped into the room. "Dad, I came to tell you that breakfast is ready." Her mouth dropped open, and she motioned to the mess on the floor. "Ach, my! What's happened here? It looks like a tornado blew through."

Roman shook his head and grunted. "More like a bunch of *diewe*. Besides making a mess of the place, the thieves stole some of my tools."

She drew in a couple of shaky breaths. "Do you think it could be the same ones who broke into our house a week ago?"

"Don't know. Probably so."

"Are you going to let the sheriff know about this?"

"No need to involve the law. Even though I'm not happy about this, no one was hurt, and I'm turning the other cheek just like the Bible says we should do."

Ruth bent down and picked up a chair that had been overturned. "If it is some rowdy English fellows, it's not likely they'll stop until someone catches them in the act and they're put in jail."

"I know that already, but I'm not going to bother the sheriff."

"Okay." Ruth nodded toward the house. "If we hurry and eat, we can all come back to the shop and help you clean up before it's time for Grace and me to leave for work."

He motioned to the floor. "After seeing this mess, I've lost my appetite. You go on up to the house and eat. I'll get something after I've cleaned things up in here."

Ruth shrugged and headed out the door.

Ruth shivered as she started for the house, and she knew it wasn't from the chilly morning air. Had the same person who'd ransacked their house broken into her father's shop? Why would anyone do such a thing?

Stepping into the kitchen, she told the rest of the family, "Dad's shop has been broken into." She drew in a quick breath. "Broken pieces of furniture are all over the floor."

Mom's face blanched, and she grabbed hold of the cupboard as though needing it for support. "Oh, no, not again."

Martha set the plate she'd been holding onto the table. "Maybe now Dad will notify the sheriff."

Ruth shook her head. "He says no. He'll turn the other cheek as the Bible says we're to do."

"But what harm could there be in letting the sheriff know? It doesn't mean Dad will have to press charges or anything."

Mom walked across the room as if she were moving in slow motion, removed her shawl from a wall peg, and opened the back door.

"Where are you going?" Ruth called.

"Out to speak with your daed."

Martha pulled out a chair and sank into it with a groan. "Mom won't get anywhere with Dad; she never does. Whatever he says, she's always in agreement with, so he won't be phoning the sheriff."

"Is Grace still in her room?" Ruth asked.

Martha nodded. "She hasn't come down yet. Why do you ask?"

"I need to see if she'll ask Cleon to speak to Dad about this."

"Why Cleon?"

"Dad thinks highly of him, and if anyone can convince Dad to notify the sheriff, it will be Cleon."

Later that morning as Grace traveled down the road in her buggy toward the Schrocks' place, she prayed they would be back from their trip and that Cleon would agree to speak to her father. She also prayed that Dad would listen. At Ruth's suggestion, she'd agreed to take a separate buggy so that she could stop by to see Cleon before she headed to work. Passing a phone shed on the way, she felt tempted to pull over and call the sheriff herself but thought better of it. If Dad found out she'd done that, she would never hear the end of it. No, it would be better if Cleon convinced Dad to contact the sheriff.

A short time later, Grace pulled her rig into the Schrocks' driveway. Cleon's twenty-year-old brother, Ivan, was out in the yard. "I'm glad you're home from Montana. When did you get back?" she called as she stepped down from her buggy.

"Got home late last night."

"Is Cleon here?"

"Jah. He's checking on his bee boxes right now." Ivan nodded his blond head in the direction of the meadow out behind the Schrocks' three-story home. "What brings you by so early this morning?"

"I'm on my way to work, but I wanted to speak with Cleon about something."

"Does it pertain to your wedding?"

She shook her head and tied her horse to the hitching rail near the barn.

"Want me to go fetch him?"

"That won't be necessary. I'll head out to the meadow myself. I'd like to see how things are going with his bees."

"Jah, okay. See you later then, Grace."

Grace lifted the edge of her skirt as she stepped carefully over the cow flops in the pasture, then traipsed through the tall grass leading to the open space where Cleon kept his bee boxes. The newly risen sun had cast a beautiful orange haze on the sky, and she could smell the distinctive, crisp odor of fall in the air. If she hadn't been so upset, she might have felt a sense of peace from the scenery.

When she reached the first grouping of bee boxes, she stopped and stared at the bees buzzing around one of the boxes as though looking for a way to get in. She wondered if the bees felt trapped once they were inside the box. That was certainly how she felt—trapped. And there seemed to be no way out. No way to forget the past or make her family feel safe in their own home again.

Grace spotted Cleon across the field, and her frustrations abated some. His easygoing mannerisms and genuine smile made her feel safe and loved. Drawing in a deep breath, she rushed over to him.

"Grace! What a surprise. I was planning to come by your place after you got off work today, but I sure didn't expect to see you here this morning."

"I took my own rig and left the house early. I'll be heading to work soon, but I wanted to speak with you first thing."

He drew her close to his side. "What's wrong? You're trembling. Are you upset about something or just cold?"

She leaned her head against his chest, relishing the warmth of his jacket and finding comfort in the steady beating of his heart. "I'm upset. We're all upset."

"Why's that?"

"There have been two break-ins at our place in the last week—the first one at the house last Sunday, and then this morning, my daed's shop was vandalized."

Cleon held her at arm's length, and a muscle on the side of his face quivered. "Is everyone all right?"

"We're fine, but some of Dad's tools were taken, and lots of other things were ruined."

"What's your daed planning to do about this?"

"Nothing. He thinks it was probably done by whoever turned over outhouses at the schoolhouses near Kidron a few weeks back." Grace swallowed hard in an effort to dislodge the lump in her throat. She wanted so desperately to share her suspicions about Gary with Cleon, but fear of his reaction kept the words in her throat. "Dad thinks it won't happen again and says if we involve the sheriff and he finds whoever did it, we'll be expected to press charges."

"Roman wouldn't do that. It goes against our beliefs."

She nodded. "Even if we can't press charges, don't you think the sheriff should be told so he can keep an eye out for trouble and hopefully catch the person responsible?"

Cleon reached up to rub the bridge of his nose. "I suppose it might be good if the sheriff knew what happened. Maybe there have been some other break-ins in the area, and he might have a better chance of catching whoever did it if he knew what all had been done. Could be some kind of a pattern these kids are using."

She tipped her head and stared up at him. "What do you mean?"

"Maybe they strike once or twice in one area, then move on to some other place and pull a few pranks there."

"What they did to our house and Dad's shop was more than a prank, Cleon."

"You're right, and it could get even more serious if they're not stopped."

"So you'll talk to my daed and offer your opinion?"

He nodded. "Not sure how much influence I have with him, but I will give my two cents' worth."

Grace sighed with relief. If Gary was the one responsible and the sheriff caught him, then even without her father pressing charges, she figured Gary would be hauled off to jail. That would get him out of Holmes County and away from Grace and her family. Then she would never have to worry about revealing her secret.

Ruth had just placed a pan of fresh cinnamon rolls into the bakery case when the bell on the front door jingled. A customer walked in. He was English—the same man she'd seen Grace talking to a few weeks ago in the restaurant parking lot. Ruth recognized his wavy red hair and the haughty way he held himself, like he thought he was something special.

The Englisher stepped up to the counter and stared at Ruth so hard it made her squirm.

"Can I help you?"

"Well, now, that all depends." He raked his fingers through the sides of his hair, and a spicy fragrance permeated the air, causing Ruth to sneeze.

He wrinkled his nose. "Have you got a cold? Because if you do, you shouldn't be working around food."

"I don't have a cold. I think I must be allergic to something." She motioned to the glass case that separated them. "Cinnamon rolls just came from the oven. Would you like to try a sample?"

He shook his head, blinking his eyelids. "I didn't come here for anything to eat."

"What did you come for then?"

"I need some information."

"If you want to know anything about the town of Berlin, the Chamber of Commerce would be your best source."

"I've been there already." He reached into his shirt pocket and pulled out a small notebook. "The people who work there can't give me the kind of firsthand information I'm needing."

She tipped her head in question.

"Personal details about the Amish who live in Holmes County and the outlying areas." He winked at her. "I can see that you're Amish by the way you're dressed, so I thought you'd be a good person to ask."

Ruth glanced over her shoulder, hoping Karen or Jake Clemons, the owners of the bakeshop, might come out of the kitchen and rescue her, but they were still busy baking in the back room.

The man extended his hand across the counter. "My name's Gary Walker. I'm a freelance photographer and reporter. Awhile back I did a pretty big article for a new magazine called *Everyone's World*. Have you heard of it?"

She shook her head. "I don't read many magazines."

"I guess the Amish newspaper is probably more your style, huh?"

"I do read *The Budget*." Ruth glanced toward the front door, hoping another customer would come in and wishing this was Sadie's day to work with her at the bakeshop. "If you already know some things about the Amish, why not write that?"

"I'm not interested in basic facts. I want to know what's going on in the lives of the Amish people in this area compared to what I've learned about Amish settlements in other parts of the country."

"Do people who read your stories want to know that kind of thing?"

"You'd be surprised what curious readers want to know." Gary removed the cap of the pen with his teeth and grinned at her. "So what can you tell me—what'd you say your name was?"

Her cheeks warmed. "Ruth Hostettler."

He started to write it down but lifted his pen and stared at her in a most peculiar way. "Say, you wouldn't be related to Grace Hostettler, would you?"

She nodded. "Do you know my sister?"

"Let's just say we've met a time or two."

"A few weeks ago, I saw you talking to Grace in the parking lot of the restaurant where she works. Were you asking her questions about the Amish, too?"

"As a matter of fact, I was." His forehead wrinkled. "She didn't tell me much, though. Not a very friendly one, that sister of yours."

Ruth bristled. *I'm not about to tell this man anything, either.*

"Have there been any attacks made against the Amish around here?"

Her mouth dropped open. She leaned against the counter, not knowing what to say. Did the man know about the break-ins at their place? Was he hoping she would give him details?

He tapped his foot and glanced around as though growing impatient. "I know of some Amish communities in other parts of the country where the Plain People have been taunted by outsiders trying to make trouble, so I wondered if anything like that has ever happened here."

Ruth wasn't about to give him any information, and she felt relief when another customer came into the bakeshop. "You'll have to excuse me. I need to wait on this lady."

Gary stepped away from the counter and folded his arms. "I can wait."

Ruth shook her head, feeling a little braver now that she wasn't alone with the persistent man. "If you're not here to buy baked goods, then there's nothing more to be said."

"Look, if it's that little remark I made about your sister not being friendly, I'm sorry. I tend to say stupid things when I'm around pretty women."

Ruth's face grew hot, and she turned from Gary and focused on the English woman who had stepped up to the bakery case. "May I help you?"

"I'd like half a dozen cream puffs, two cinnamon rolls, and an angel food cake."

"I'll get those for you right away."

Gary cleared his throat, and when she glanced his way again, he gave her a quick wink and sauntered out the door.

Ruth breathed a sigh of relief. *No wonder Grace didn't want to answer that man's questions. He's pushy and arrogant. I hope he gets done with his stories soon and leaves Holmes County.*

Grace drew in a deep breath and whispered a silent prayer as she carried a tray full of food out to the restaurant's dining room. Her hands shook so badly, she didn't know how she would make it through the day. Ever since she'd heard about her father's shop getting broken into, she'd been a nervous wreck. She hoped Cleon would find time today to talk to her father about notifying the sheriff, and she hoped Dad would listen.

Grace gripped the tray tighter. If only they knew who was responsible for the break-ins. Could the same person who broke into their house have vandalized her father's shop, or were they two separate incidences? Were some rowdy English boys the culprits, or could it have been Gary?

She glanced out the restaurant's front window. No sign of the arrogant man, at least. For the last two weeks, he'd been going from shop to shop, asking people questions about the Amish and snapping pictures whenever he felt like it—even some close-up shots of Amish people. Grace knew this because some of her friends had mentioned that a redheaded Englisher with a fancy camera was nosing around. Grace figured that, after this many days, Gary should have gotten enough information to write ten articles, so it made no sense that he was still hanging around. She'd heard that he'd been seen in Walnut Creek on Saturday, taking more pictures and interviewing anyone willing to talk to him.

As Grace approached an English couple whose order she'd taken earlier, she gritted her teeth with a determination she didn't feel and carefully set their plates of food in front of them. "Will there be anything else?"

The elderly woman smiled. "I'd like another cup of coffee, please."

"One for me, too," the man said with a nod.

"I'll see to it right away."

"Are you okay?" Esther asked as she joined Grace in front of the coffeepot moments later. "Your hands are shaking."

"I'm feeling a little nervous this morning," Grace admitted. "My daed's shop got broken into sometime during the night, and it has us all plenty worried."

Esther's forehead wrinkled, and she patted Grace's arm in a motherly fashion. "That's terrible. I understand now why you're shaking. You have every right to feel nervous."

"I didn't say anything about this before, but someone broke into our house a week ago, too," Grace whispered.

Esther's pale eyebrows lifted high on her forehead. "How come you didn't tell me this sooner?"

"Dad said he thought it was a one-time thing, and since nothing was taken at that time, I saw no point in mentioning it."

"Do you have any idea who might be responsible, and do you think both incidents were done by the same person?"

"We don't know, but Dad suspects it might be some rowdy English fellows." Grace wasn't about to tell Esther whom she suspected.

Esther slowly shook her head. "Let's hope it doesn't happen again—to your family or to anyone else in our community."

Grace nodded and headed back to the dining room with her customers' coffee. Having Gary Walker back in town was hard enough to deal with. Now she had the added worry of whether another break-in would occur.

Chapter 11

"It's good you could meet me and Ruth after work today," Grace said to her mother as the three of them headed down the sidewalk toward the quilt shop, where a variety of fabric was sold.

Mom nodded. "I thought if we looked at some material for your wedding dress, it might take our minds off this morning's break-in."

"Did Dad get everything cleaned up?"

"Jah. He and Martha worked on it while Luke made some deliveries."

Ruth pursed her lips as she slowed her steps. "I don't suppose he changed his mind about calling the sheriff?"

"He says he will turn the other cheek, just like before."

"What if it happens again?"

"Then we'll have to deal with it."

Grace clenched her fingers around the straps of her black handbag. *How do we deal with it?* She wanted to scream out the question but knew it was best to keep silent. When Ruth had met her after work, she'd mentioned that Gary had come into the bakeshop asking questions. It made Grace feel more anxious than ever. What if Gary didn't leave Holmes County? What if he decided to stay and torment her indefinitely? What if more break-ins occurred?

"Oh, there's Cleon's mamm, Irene." Mom pointed to the dark-haired Amish woman who'd just gotten out of her buggy across the street. "If the two of you would like to go inside the quilt store and start looking around, I'll join you in a few minutes. I want to see how the Schrocks' trip to Rexford went and speak to Irene about making some beeswax candles for your wedding."

"Sure, Mom, we can do that," Ruth said as the two of them moved toward the door of the shop.

Ruth nudged Grace's arm as they began looking through some bolts of blue material. "I'm so happy for you and Cleon. I'll bet you can hardly wait for the wedding."

"I am looking forward to it," Grace admitted, "but it's hard to concentrate on wedding plans with what's been going on lately."

"You mean the break-ins?"

"Jah."

"Like Dad said, maybe it won't happen again. Maybe whoever broke into his shop got what they wanted when they stole his tools."

Grace wished she could believe it wouldn't happen again, but she had a terrible feeling that the break-ins were only the beginning of their troubles. If Gary had come here to make good on his threat to get even with her, then there could be more attacks. Should she tell her folks who Gary was—that she'd dated him during her rumschpringe years? Would that be enough to convince Dad that he needed to notify the sheriff?

She cringed. If she told her folks about Gary, wouldn't that lead to more questions? Should she tell them the truth about her marriage to Wade, or would it be better to keep quiet and see what happened with Gary?

"Grace, are you listening to me?" Ruth nudged Grace's arm again.

"Wh-what was that?"

"Do you think there will be more attacks?"

"Oh, I hope not." Grace pulled a bolt of blue material off the rack and held it up. "I think this is the one I want."

"Should we look for some white to make your apron now?"

"Okay." Grace followed Ruth to the other side of the room. Several shelves near the front of the store were stocked with bolts of white material, and she glanced out the window to see if Mom was still talking to Cleon's mother. She didn't see any sign of either woman. "I wonder what could be taking Mom so long," she said, turning to face her sister. "I don't see her anywhere, and I'm getting worried."

"She and Irene probably went into one of the other stores. You know how gabby our mamm can get whenever she's with one of her friends."

Grace nodded. "Jah, she does like to talk."

"What do you think of this?" Ruth asked, as she handed a bolt of white material over to Grace.

"It's nice, but I'd like to keep looking awhile."

"Want me to hold it out in case you decide it's the best one?"

"Sure." Grace looked out the window again, and she nearly dropped the bolt of material she held when she saw her mother standing on the sidewalk talking to Gary.

"What's wrong, Grace? Your face has gone pale as goat's milk," Ruth said in a tone of obvious concern.

"It. . .it's that reporter. He's talking to Mom, and I've got to stop him." Grace thrust the material into her sister's hands and rushed out the door.

Judith heard Grace holler even before she saw her running down the sidewalk, frantically waving her arms.

"What is it, Grace? What's the matter?"

Grace gulped in a quick breath and grabbed hold of Judith's arm. "I–I thought you were with Irene."

"I was, but she was in a hurry to get home, so she left a few minutes ago." Judith turned to the English man she'd been talking to and smiled. "My daughter's choosing the material for her wedding dress today, and she's real excited."

"Is she now?" Gary looked over at Grace and offered her a wide grin. "Who's the lucky man?"

"Mom, are you coming?" Grace gave Judith's arm a little tug, and their elbows collided. "Sorry."

"No harm done. I'll come with you as soon as I've answered this man's questions."

"He's some kind of a reporter, Mom. Dad wouldn't like it if

anything you said was put in some publication for the whole world to read." Grace gripped her mother's arm, and Judith noticed a look of fear in her daughter's eyes.

The man stared at Grace, and his auburn-colored brows drew together. "Say, haven't we met before?"

Grace's eyes darted back and forth, and her face turned crimson. "Mom, let's go."

Judith had never seen Grace act in such a strange manner. She seemed afraid of the man. Did the thought of being asked a few questions make her that nervous, or was she still feeling jumpy about the break-ins?

Judith turned to the reporter and smiled. "I think we'd best be on our way."

He gave her a quick nod. "Sure. I've got some business that needs tending to, anyway."

Judith hurried off toward the quilt shop with her distraught daughter beside her.

"What did you tell that fellow?" Grace asked before they entered the store. "You didn't mention the break-ins, did you?"

"Of course not. If your daed doesn't want the sheriff to know, he sure wouldn't want such news put in some magazine or newspaper for everyone to read."

"What kind of questions did he ask, and what did you tell him?"

Judith shrugged. "He wanted to know my name and how long I've lived in Holmes County. Then he asked me a couple of questions about our family."

Grace halted in front of the shop door. "What kind of questions?"

"Just wondered how many children I have and what type of work my husband does for a living. They were simple questions, and I saw no harm in answering."

"If he tries to talk to you again, I hope you won't answer."

Judith gave her daughter's arm a gentle squeeze. "Why do you fret so much? Why can't you be more like your sister Martha? *Sie druwwelt sich wehe nix.*"

Grace frowned. "What do you mean, 'She doesn't worry about

much of anything'? Martha worries about those dogs of hers more than you realize."

"Maybe so, but she doesn't worry about everything the way you do." Judith nodded toward the store. "Shall we go inside and choose your material now?"

Grace nodded, but her wide eyes revealed fear as she watched the reporter cross the street and begin talking to an Amish man.

"You all right? You seem awfully naerfich this afternoon."

"I'm fine."

"I think you overreacted to that reporter, don't you?"

Grace didn't answer; she just opened the shop door and followed her mother inside.

Roman had just stepped outside his shop to load the rocking chair Martin Gingerich had asked him to make for his folks' anniversary into Martin's market buggy when a truck rumbled up the driveway. It halted a few feet from where he stood, and when the driver got out, he recognized him immediately—Bill Collins, the land developer who'd expressed interest in buying Roman's land.

"Afternoon," Bill said, lifting his hand in a wave.

Roman merely grunted, and Martin, who stood beside his buggy, gave him a strange look.

"I was in the area and thought I'd stop by and see if you've changed your mind about selling your land."

"Nope, sure haven't." Roman glanced over at Martin, thinking the young man didn't need to be in on this conversation. "The chair's secure in your buggy now, so you can be on your way."

Martin hesitated but finally climbed into the driver's seat and took up the reins. As he directed the horse down the driveway, he stuck his head out the window and hollered, "I'll let you know what the folks had to say about the chair, and danki for getting it done early for me."

"You're welcome." Roman turned back to Bill Collins. "As I said before, I'm not interested in selling my land to you or anyone else."

"You sure about that?"

"Very sure." When Roman headed for his shop, Bill followed so close he could feel the man's warm breath blowing on the back of his neck.

"I hope you'll at least take a look at these figures," Bill said, holding a notebook in front of Roman's nose.

Roman scanned the paper quickly, and his spine went rigid. The man was offering a tidy sum. Even so—

"If you'd like to discuss my offer with your family, I'd be happy to leave you a copy of these figures." Bill started to tear off the piece of paper, but Roman stopped him with a shake of his head.

"Don't bother. My place isn't for sale, plain and simple." He pushed past the man. "Now if you'll excuse me, I have work waiting."

"You won't get an offer like this every day," Bill called. "I would suggest that you think on it some more."

Roman gave no reply. Six months ago, the Larsons had asked about buying his property as an investment. He had told them no, too, so he sure wasn't about to sell off his land to some money-greedy land grabber who wanted to turn it into a development of fancy English houses with electricity. And a golf course was the last thing their Amish community needed!

As Martha stood at the kitchen sink peeling potatoes for their supper, she thought about the break-in of her father's shop that morning. Ruth had said that Dad seemed real upset at the time. Yet he'd refused to talk about the incident when Martha had taken some lunch out to him later that afternoon.

Martha knew what the Bible said about forgiveness, turning the other cheek, and loving one's enemies, but she still wondered if the sheriff should be notified.

Forcing herself to concentrate on the matter at hand, she placed the potatoes on the cutting board and cut them into hunks, then dropped them into a kettle, filled it with cold water, and set it aside. She wouldn't start cooking them until her sisters and Mom came home, and the ham she'd put in the oven a short time ago would be okay until then, too. Maybe she would take a book and go sit on the back porch to relax and read awhile.

She hurried up to her room, grabbed the historical novel she'd borrowed from Ruth a few days ago, and headed down the stairs. When she entered the kitchen, she placed the book on the table and opened the oven to check on the ham.

As she closed the oven door, she heard a sound. What was it? A creak? A bump? Hair prickled on the back of her head as she peered out the window. Nothing out of the ordinary, at least not that she could see.

She turned away from the window and had just picked up her book when a deafening crack split through the air. The kitchen window shattered, and a brick flew into the room, landing with a thud on the floor.

Martha let out a bloodcurdling scream, and with no thought for her safety, she dashed out the back door.

Chapter 12

Martha stepped onto the back porch. Cold, damp air sent a shiver rippling through her body. She scanned the yard but saw no one. "Someone had to have thrown that brick; now where did they go?" she muttered.

Taking the steps two at a time and ignoring how cold and wet the ground felt on her bare feet, she sprinted across the yard. Looking around, she listened for any unusual sounds. Nothing was out of the ordinary.

Needing to know if Heidi and her puppies were safe, Martha raced for the barn, her heart pounding like a herd of stampeding horses.

She had almost reached the door when she noticed a straw hat lying on the ground. It didn't look like any of her father's hats, and she bent to pick it up, wondering if he might recently have purchased a new one. *I'd better take this out to Dad's shop when I tell him about the brick, but not until I've checked on Heidi and her brood.*

Martha opened the barn door, lit the lantern hanging from a beam overhead, and peered cautiously around, allowing her breathing and heartbeat to slow. She saw no one and heard nothing but the gentle nicker of the two buggy horses inside their stalls and the cooing of some pigeons in the loft overhead.

She hung the straw hat on a nail near the door and started toward the back of the building, but she'd only taken a few steps, when a mouse darted in front of her. She let out a yelp, screeched to a halt, and drew in a shaky breath as the tiny critter scurried under a bale of straw. *I'm okay.*

It was only a maus. *There's nothing to be nervous about.*

With another quick glance around, she rushed over to the box that had become the temporary home for Heidi and her puppies. A feeling of relief washed over her when she discovered that the pups were nursing and Heidi was sleeping peacefully.

"I'll check on you again after supper," Martha whispered, patting the top of the dog's silky head.

She made her way quickly back to the place where she'd lit the lantern, extinguished the flame, and lifted the straw hat from the nail.

Once outside, Martha scoured the yard one more time; then seeing no one in sight, she dashed for her father's shop.

"You sure have sold a lot of honey lately," Cleon's brother Ivan commented, as the two headed home from town in one of their family's closed-in buggies. After they'd finished helping their father and younger brothers, Willard and Delbert, in the fields earlier that day, the two of them had made some honey deliveries and taken a few orders.

Cleon smiled. "I'm doing real well here of late."

"Think you'll ever quit helping Pop on the farm and go out on your own with the honey business?" Ivan's dark eyes looked full of question as he tipped his head.

"I hope so. Never have liked farming that much. I'll have to find more customers for my honey than just a few stores in the towns around here and a handful of people from our community, though."

"Looks to me like you've got more customers than just a handful." Ivan tapped Cleon's arm. "We delivered twenty quarts of honey this afternoon, and you met with five others who want to become regular customers."

"I'm glad for that, but it's still not enough to make a decent living."

"You'll be gettin' married soon, so I can see why you might need some extra cash."

Cleon nodded. "The wood for the house I'm building on the

acreage behind the Hostettlers' place is costing a lot more than I'd figured, so it's taking longer than I'd planned."

"Building materials aren't cheap anymore, that's for sure."

"Nothing's cheap nowadays."

"So, what'd Grace want when she came by to see you this morning?" Ivan asked. "I got so busy helping Pop with chores all morning, I forgot to ask."

Cleon grimaced. "The Hostettlers had a break-in at their house after church last Sunday, but we didn't hear about it because we left for Montana early the next morning."

"That's too bad. Was anything stolen?"

"Not until this morning."

"They had another break-in this morning?"

"Not at the house, but Roman's shop got broken into. Grace said whoever did it made a mess of things, and some of her daed's tools were stolen, too."

"That's a shame. You think it could have been done by whoever dumped over those outhouses some weeks ago?"

Cleon shrugged. "Could be, but that was several miles from here."

"You've got a point, but there was some cowtipping done at the bishop's place awhile back, too."

"I'm sure that was done by some pranksters."

"Do you have any idea why someone would want to target Grace's family like that?"

"Nope. None at all."

"Well, hopefully, it won't happen again."

"Sure hope not. The Hostettlers don't need this. No one does."

"Changing the subject," Ivan said, "you mentioned before that you thought Grace felt nervous about getting married. I was wondering if you're feeling that way, too."

"Not really. I love Grace a lot, and I'm sure we're going to be happy living together as husband and wife."

"You plannin' to start a family right away?"

Cleon shrugged. "Kinner will come in God's time, not ours."

"Jah, well, I know for a fact that our mamm's lookin' forward to bein' a *grossmudder*, so she'll be real happy when you do have some kinner."

Cleon thumped his brother's arm. "Maybe you ought to find yourself an aldi and get married, too. That way you can take an active part in giving Mamm a bunch of *kinskinner*."

Ivan wrinkled his nose. "I'm in no hurry for that. Besides, women have too many peculiar ideas to suit me."

Cleon grimaced as a vision of Grace came to mind. She'd been acting kind of peculiar herself lately. He hoped she wasn't getting cold feet about marrying him. His whole being ached with the desire to make Grace his wife, and he didn't think he could stand it if she broke things off.

Ivan leaned closer to Cleon. "Say, you'd better watch out for that hilly dip we're coming to. Last week my friend Enos hit a deer standing in the road."

"I'll be careful." Cleon guided the horse up the hill and started down the other side. They had just reached the bottom of the hill when he spotted a black pickup in his side mirror coming up behind them at a pretty good clip. The driver, wearing a pair of sunglasses and a baseball cap, laid on his horn, and Cleon steered the horse toward the shoulder of the road, glad he had one of their more docile mares today. With no traffic coming in the opposite direction, he figured the truck would have plenty of room to pass. Apparently the driver didn't think so, because he nearly sideswiped Cleon's buggy as he whipped around him and raced down the road.

"Whew, that was too close for comfort," Cleon said, sweat beading on his forehead and rolling onto his cheeks. "I wish people wouldn't drive so fast on these back country roads."

"Makes me wonder if that fellow was trying to run us off the road on purpose," Ivan grumbled.

Cleon gripped the reins a bit tighter and directed the horse back onto the road. "What would make you think that?"

"Last week, Willard and I were heading home from a singing, and a truck nearly sideswiped our open buggy. It was dark out, and we couldn't see the color or make of the vehicle, but we knew it was a truck." Ivan's dark brows drew together in a frown. "Willard was driving, and boy, *waar er awwer bees*."

"I can imagine just how angry he was, but it's not likely that it was the same truck. Whoever was driving wasn't trying to hit you on purpose any more than that fellow was trying to hit us just now. Some Englishers get in too big of a hurry and drive too fast, that's all."

"Humph!" Ivan folded his arms and stared straight ahead. "Some English don't think we have a right to be on the road with our buggies, and they don't like the road apples our horses leave, either. It's almost like they're singling us out because we're different."

Cleon thought again about the break-ins that had occurred at the Hostettlers' and wondered if they'd been isolated incidents or if the family might have been singled out. He needed to have a talk with Roman as he'd promised Grace he would do.

"Mind if we stop by the Hostettlers' before we go home?" he asked his brother. "I want to speak with Roman about those break-ins."

Ivan shrugged. "Makes no never mind to me. Maybe the brothers will do our chores if we don't get home on time."

Cleon grunted. "Jah, right. That's about as likely as a heat wave in the middle of January."

"It's past quitting time," Roman said when Luke returned to the shop after loading some cabinets for Ray Larson, their nearest English neighbor. "You're free to go whenever you want."

"You sure about that? We've still got several pieces of furniture that need fixing."

"They can wait until tomorrow. We've both put in a long day, and I'm exhausted."

Luke nodded. "I'm kind of tired myself."

"Sure was nice of John Peterson to come by this afternoon and loan us some tools," Roman said as he put a final coat of stain on a straight-backed chair.

"I hope you don't mind that I mentioned your break-in to John when I went home for lunch and found him visiting my daed." Luke nodded toward the shelf where the hammer and saw lay that John had dropped by shortly after lunch.

"Why would I mind?"

"I know you don't want the incident reported to the sheriff, so I figured you might not want anyone else knowing about it, either."

Roman shrugged. "We live in a small community, and I've told some of my Amish neighbors. I'm sure the news would have gotten out soon enough."

Luke opened his mouth as if to comment, but the shop door opened, and Martha rushed into the room, interrupting their conversation.

"Dad, you'll never believe what happened a few minutes ago!"

A look of fear covered his daughter's face. "What is it, Martha? What's happened?"

"I was in the kitchen getting supper started, and a brick flew right through the window."

"What?" Roman dropped the rag he'd been using to stain the chair and hurried to her side. "Are you all right? Did the brick hit you?"

"I'm okay. It just shook me up a bit."

"Did you see who did it?" Luke asked.

Martha shook her head. "I ran outside right away, but whoever threw the brick must have been a fast runner, because no one was in sight." She lifted the straw hat in her hand. "I went out to the barn to check on Heidi and her pups and found this lying on the ground outside the barn door."

Luke grabbed hold of the hat. "That's mine. I must have dropped it as I was putting my horse in the corral when I got here this morning."

"Are you sure you weren't wearing it when you went outside to load those cabinets for Ray? Maybe you dropped it then."

"I'm sure I didn't have it on." Luke plunked the hat on his head. "Want me to take a look around the place before I head home? Maybe whoever threw the brick is still lurkin' about."

Roman groaned. "I'm guessing the culprit took off like a shot as soon as that brick hit the window."

"I believe you're right, Dad." Martha touched his arm. "I know you won't press charges, but don't you think it's time to notify the sheriff?"

He shook his head. "Psalm 46:1 says, 'God is our refuge and strength, a very present help in trouble.' "

"If someone's out to get us—and it seems like they are—I'm worried that the next attack could be worse." Martha's chin trembled. "If this keeps up, someone's likely to get hurt."

The truth of her words sliced through Roman like a knife. The thought of someone in his family getting hurt gave him the chills, but he had to keep believing and trusting that God would protect his family. He was about to say so when his shop door opened again and in walked Cleon and his brother Ivan.

"I see you made it back from Montana," Roman said. "Did you have a good trip?"

Cleon nodded. "We got back last night." He glanced around the room and grimaced. "Grace stopped by our place on her way to work and told me about the break-ins that happened at your house last week and then here this morning."

"Make that three acts of vandalism," Martha said. "Someone tossed a brick through our kitchen window a short time ago."

Cleon's mouth dropped open. "Was anyone hurt?"

Martha shook her head. "Sure scared me, though."

"Any idea who could have done these things?"

Roman shrugged. "I'm guessing it's some rowdy fellows—maybe the same ones who dumped over those outhouses near Kidron."

"I heard a couple of cows got tipped over awhile back in Bishop King's field," Ivan put in. "One of the bishop's sons saw some English fellows running through their land, so he's pretty sure it was them who pushed the cows over."

"Dumping outhouses and pushing over cows doesn't compare to breaking into someone's home or place of business," Cleon said. "Makes me wonder if someone has a grudge against you. What do you think, Roman?"

Roman contemplated Cleon's question a few seconds. He guessed there might be a few people who weren't too happy with him right now: Luke, because Roman had docked his pay; Steven, because his wife's birthday present had been ruined; and Bill Collins, because Roman refused to sell his land. Even so, he didn't think any of them would resort to vandalism. Of course, he didn't know the land developer personally, so he guessed it might be possible that the determined fellow could resort to scare tactics in order to get Roman to agree to his terms.

"What does the sheriff have to say about all this?" Cleon asked, breaking into Roman's swirling thoughts.

"Haven't told him," Roman muttered, staring at the floor where a blob of stain still lingered.

"How come?" The question came from Ivan this time.

"Saw no need. I wouldn't press charges even if we knew who'd done it. I'm turning the other cheek and relying on God's protection, like the Bible says we should."

Cleon leaned against Roman's desk. "Has anyone else in the community been bothered?"

"Not that I know of."

"If we hear that anyone has, what will you do?" Martha asked.

"I'll get with the others, and we'll have a talk with our church leaders and see how they think it should be handled." Roman put his arm around his daughter's trembling shoulders. "In the meantime, we need to be more watchful while we pray for God's protection over our friends and family."

Chapter 13

Grace awoke the following morning with another pounding headache. Hearing about Martha's scare with the flying brick had about done her in, and she'd gone to bed early.

With great effort, she pulled herself out of bed and padded over to the window. It was a sunny day, yet she felt as if a dark rain cloud hung over her head—the whole house, really. She continued to struggle with the need to tell her folks she suspected Gary might be out for revenge. However, her fear of them finding out about her previous life kept her from saying anything.

Grace moved away from the window, frustration bubbling in her chest. Maybe it would be best either to tell Gary what she suspected or to ask him to leave Holmes County. She clenched her fists and held her arms tightly against her sides. Unless Gary had changed, it wasn't likely that he would be willing to leave the area simply because she asked him to. If he could be cruel enough to break into her home, what else might he be capable of doing?

A knock on the bedroom door brought Grace's thoughts to a halt. "Mom has breakfast ready, and we're going to be late for work if we don't eat soon," Ruth called from the other side of the door.

"I'll be down in a minute." Grace didn't feel up to going to work, but she didn't want to leave her employer shorthanded. Besides, the only chance she had of seeing Gary was in town.

She hurried to get washed and dressed, then took two aspirins for her headache and headed downstairs.

"Are you okay, Grace?" Mom asked, turning from her place at the stove and squinting. "You look awful *mied* this morning. Didn't you sleep well?"

Grace went to the refrigerator and removed a quart of grape juice. "I am a bit tired, and I woke up with a headache, but I'll be okay."

"Are you sure about that?" Ruth, who had been setting the table, clicked her tongue. "Your face is paler than a bedsheet, sister."

"Maybe you're coming down with that achy-bones flu that was going around," Mom said with a look of concern. "Might be good if you stayed home and rested today."

Grace shook her head. "I'll be fine once I've had some breakfast." She glanced around the room. "Where are Dad and Martha?"

"Your daed's still out doing his chores, and Martha went to check on Fritz, Heidi, and the hundlin."

"Those two dogs and the puppies are all our little sister thinks about anymore." Ruth's forehead wrinkled. "What she needs is a boyfriend."

"Martha's only eighteen." Mom broke a couple of eggs into the frying pan and glanced over her shoulder. "She has plenty of time to find the right man."

Ruth placed the last glass on the table and turned to face Grace, who was pouring juice into each of the glasses. "I guess what Mom says is true. Look at how long it took you to find a man and decide to get married."

Grace winced, even though she was sure Ruth wasn't trying to be mean. *What would my family say if they knew my secret? How would Cleon deal with things if he knew? Is it time to tell him the truth?*

The back door flew open, and Martha rushed into the room. Her lips were compressed, and her eyes looked huge. "The pups are all alone in their box crying for their mamm's milk, and I couldn't find Heidi anywhere." She hurried over to their mother. "What am I going to do? Those puppies are too young to make it on their own."

Mom pushed the frying pan to the back of the stove. "Calm down and take a deep breath. I'm sure Heidi is somewhere nearby. Probably just needed a break from her pups, or maybe she went outside to do her business."

"Mom's right," Grace put in. "Heidi will return to her puppies soon; you'll see."

"Are you sure you're up to going to work today?" Ruth asked again when she noticed how Grace was gripping the buggy reins with clenched fingers and a determined set to her jaw. She didn't know which sister to be the most concerned about this morning–Grace, who looked like she should be home in bed, or Martha, who had refused to eat breakfast so she could hunt for her missing dog.

"I need to go to work," Grace said with a nod.

"You could have gone to the phone shed to let your boss know you weren't feeling well."

"My headache's eased some, and I saw no need to stay home. Besides, it would have left them shorthanded at the restaurant, and I know from experience how hard that can be on the other waitresses."

Grace stared straight ahead, gripping the reins so tightly that the veins on the back of her hands stood out.

"You've been acting awful strange for the past couple of weeks. Is it the trouble we've had at our place that has you so *engschderich*?" Ruth questioned.

"I'm not anxious, just concerned."

"We all are."

"First the break-in at the house, followed by Dad's shop being vandalized. Then a brick thrown that could have hit Martha, and now her dog is missing."

"I'm sure Heidi's not really missing. I'll bet by the time we get home from work Martha will be all smiles because Heidi's back in her box with the puppies again."

"Maybe so, but that won't undo what's already been done." Grace's voice cracked as she guided the horse to the side of the road.

"Why are we stopping? Aren't you worried we'll be late for work?"

"I need to tell you something, but you must promise not to repeat to anyone what I'm about to say." Grace's blue eyes flickered, and her chin quivered slightly. "Do I have your word on this?"

Ruth gave a quick nod as she reached over to squeeze her sister's hand. She couldn't imagine what Grace might tell her that she didn't want to have repeated.

Grace leaned forward and massaged her forehead. "You know that reporter in town?"

"The one who says he's doing stories on the Amish here and has been asking all kinds of questions?"

"Jah."

"What about him?"

"His name is Gary Walker, and I went out with him for a while when I first moved away. It was during a time when I lived in Cincinnati."

"You. . .you did?"

"Jah. I thought he was cute and fun at first, but then he started acting like he owned me." Grace lifted her head, and when she looked over at Ruth, tears filled her eyes. "Gary had a temper, and when I refused to go out with him anymore, he said I would be sorry and that he'd make me pay for breaking up with him."

Ruth let her sister's words sink in. If the reporter had been angry because Grace broke up with him, was it possible that he'd come here to make good on his threat? "Oh, Grace, do you think he might be the one responsible for the damage that has been done at our place?"

Grace nodded. "If I see him in town today, I'm going to ask if he's the one."

"Maybe it would be best if I'm with you when you speak to him."

Grace picked up the reins and gave them a snap. "I appreciate your concern, but this is something I must do alone."

Throughout Grace's workday, she kept an eye out for Gary, but he never came into the restaurant, and she didn't notice him outside whenever she looked out the window. Maybe he'd gone to one of the nearby towns to do his research. Or maybe he'd left the area altogether. She hoped that was so, but a niggling feeling told her otherwise. If Gary had come to Holmes County to make her pay for running off with Wade, then he probably wasn't done with her yet.

By the time Grace got off work, her headache had returned. She was glad she'd told Ruth that she would walk over to the bakeshop after work. It would give her time to think. She hoped the fresh fall air would help clear the throbbing in her head, as well.

She'd only made it halfway there when someone called her name. She whirled around and spotted Gary leaning against an Amish buggy parked next to the curb.

Grace's heart pounded so hard she felt it pulsate in her head as she made her way over to where he stood. *I've got to do this. I need to confront him now.*

"Hey, Gracie," he said with a lopsided grin. "Haven't seen you around in a while. Have you changed your mind about going out with me?"

Grace shook her head vigorously. "I'm surprised to see that you're still in Holmes County. I figured you would have enough information to write ten stories about the Amish by now."

He chuckled. "You're right. I do. But I've decided to stick around the area awhile longer and do a couple of stories about some of the events that will be taking place here, as well as in Wayne and Tuscarawas counties, during the next few months."

"The next few months? How can you afford to stay here that long?"

"My granddaddy died six months ago and left me a bundle." He winked at her. "So I've got enough money to stay here as long as I want."

"If he left you so much, then why do you have to work at all?"

"Let's just say I enjoy the work that I've chosen to do. It makes me feel in the know."

She tipped her head. "Are you really a freelance reporter?"

"Of course." He lifted the camera hanging from the strap around his shoulder. "Is it so hard to believe I'm gainfully employed?"

Grace shrugged. When they had been teenagers, Gary had been kind of lazy. While the other kids they'd hung around with all had jobs, he'd been content to take money from his dad, who seemed to have more than he needed. It was hard to imagine Gary holding down any kind of job–much less working on his own as a photographer and reporter. Of course, some people changed when they matured. Grace was living proof of that.

"So, how about the two of us going somewhere for a cup of coffee?" Gary asked.

"I told you before that I'm—"

"I know. I know. You're soon to be married."

"Jah."

"Jah? What's this jah stuff, Gracie? I'm English, remember? So I'd appreciate it if when we're together you would speak English."

"Sorry," Grace mumbled. She was losing her nerve, and if she didn't say what was on her mind soon, she might never say it. "Some. . .uh. . . unusual things have been going on at our place lately. I'm wondering what you know about it."

His forehead creased. "If you're trying to say something, Gracie, then spit it out and quit croaking like a frog."

She glanced around to be sure no one was listening. "The thing is. . .we've had a problem with—"

"With what? What kind of problem are you having?"

She felt his hot breath blowing against her face and took a step back. "Someone broke into our house a week ago, and then yesterday morning my dad discovered that his woodworking shop had been ransacked." She paused to gauge his reaction, but he simply stared at her with a stoic expression. "As if that wasn't enough, someone threw a brick through our kitchen window while my youngest sister was fixing supper last night, and this morning, one of her dogs went missing."

A muscle in the side of Gary's face quivered slightly, but he said nothing.

"Do you know anything about this?"

He shook his head. "What kind of crazy question is that? How would I know anything about some break-ins at your place?"

A sense of frustration welled in Grace's soul. Had she really expected he would admit what he'd done?

"Look, Gracie," he said in his most charming voice. "I don't know anything about any break-ins, but I do appreciate the information."

Her mouth dropped open. "You. . .you appreciate it?"

He nodded.

"Why is that?"

Gary pulled a notebook from his shirt pocket. "Because this will make one great story."

Chapter 14

Are they accepting the little bottle with the formula we made up?" Judith asked as she stepped into the barn and found Martha bent over a box, trying to feed Heidi's puppies.

Martha looked up and offered a weak smile. "They're eating some, but not as well as they would if their mamm was here feeding them."

Judith gave her daughter's shoulder a gentle squeeze. "Even if Heidi doesn't come home, I'm confident that the pups will live; you'll see to it."

"I spent the whole day searching for Heidi. Luke and Dad even helped me look during their lunch hour, but it was a waste of their time." Martha frowned. "If Dad would only let the sheriff know about the things that have been happening to us lately, maybe he could find out who's doing this and why."

"Your daed believes the things that have happened were merely pranks, and he sees no need to notify the sheriff." Judith reached into the box and stroked one of the whimpering pups with the tip of her finger. "Just pray, dear one. That's the best we can do."

When Martha left the barn sometime later, she noticed a gray SUV pulling into their yard. John Peterson opened his door and stepped down, and to her surprise, Toby King climbed out of the passenger's side, holding a cute little sheltie in his arms.

"Heidi!" Martha raced down the driveway and scooped the dog out of Toby's arms. "Where have you been, girl? I was worried about you."

"I found her wandering along the side of the road near my house," Toby said. "I knew you had a couple of shelties, and I decided to bring her over and see if she was yours."

"I was heading to town and saw Toby walking alongside the road, so I gave him a ride," John put in.

"I appreciate that." Martha stroked the top of the dog's head. "Heidi gave birth to a batch of pups not long ago, and she's still nursing. When she went missing this morning, I was afraid she'd been stolen."

John's eyebrows furrowed as he pulled his fingers through the sides of his dark, curly hair. "She probably just went for a run and lost her bearings."

"But she knows where she lives, and she's always come straight home before."

"Maybe she forgot." John tipped his head, making his slightly crooked nose look more bent than usual. Martha figured he'd probably broken it sometime—maybe when he was a boy. She didn't think it would be polite to ask, so she averted her gaze and focused on the trembling dog in her arms.

John pointed down the driveway toward her father's shop. "When I brought some of my tools for your dad to borrow, he said he thought the incidents that had happened to your family were probably done by some rowdy English kids. Does he still think that?"

Martha nodded soberly.

"Luke's been hanging around with some English fellows. I wouldn't be surprised if he wasn't in on some of those pranks." Toby gave one quick nod.

Martha pursed her lips. "I doubt Luke would take part in anything like that, but if I could prevent more pranks from happening to us or anyone else, I surely would."

John shook his head. "You'd best not do anything foolish, girl. I told your dad I would keep my eyes and ears open, and if I hear or see anything suspicious, I'll be sure to let him know."

Martha almost laughed at John referring to her as a girl. He wasn't much more than a boy himself—maybe in his mid-twenties.

"I'll keep a lookout for things, too," Toby said. "And if I find out Luke had anything to do with it, I'll inform my daed."

Martha was on the verge of telling Toby there would be no need for him to tell his bishop father anything, but she figured the less said about Luke, the better.

"I should get Heidi back in the box with her brood." She smiled at the young men. "Thanks for returning her to me."

"Glad we could help," they said in unison.

Grace leaned against the buggy seat and closed her eyes. She was glad Ruth had been willing to drive home, because after the encounter she'd had with Gary awhile ago, she probably couldn't have kept her mind on the road if she'd been the one in the driver's seat.

Ruth reached over and touched Grace's arm. "Does your head still hurt?"

"Jah."

"Sorry about that. Was the restaurant real busy today?"

"No more than usual."

"Things were sure hectic at the bakeshop. Seemed like everyone wanted a dozen donuts, all at the same time. At one point, there must have been twenty customers milling around the store, and even with Sadie's help this afternoon, I could barely keep up."

Grace nodded. She didn't feel like talking right now. All she wanted to do was go home, take a couple of aspirin, and lie down.

"I've been mulling over what you told me on the way to work this morning," Ruth said. "I think you should tell the folks about that reporter fellow."

Grace opened her eyes and blinked a couple of times. "No." The word was nearly a whisper. "I don't want them to know. At least, not yet."

"Why not? It isn't as if you're running around with the Englisher now. You were only a teenager when you dated him, and it was during your rumschpringe, so Mom and Dad should understand."

Grace inwardly cringed. There was a lot more to the story than she'd told Ruth, and if her folks found out everything, she was sure they wouldn't understand. She knew she should have told them that she'd married Wade and that a year later he'd been killed in a car accident. But if she'd told them that much, she might have had to reveal other details she'd rather not talk about.

Grace's thoughts went to Cleon, the way they always did whenever she reflected on her past. If she had only known him when she was a teenager, she might not have run off with her friends to try out the English world. Too bad his folks hadn't moved from Pennsylvania to Holmes County a few years sooner than they did. The love she felt for Cleon was strong–not based solely on physical attraction or having fun, the way it had been with Wade. With Cleon, she felt an assurance that he would always be there for her, through good times and bad. *If that's so, then why haven't I found the courage to tell him the truth?*

"If you won't tell Mom and Dad about the English reporter, then at least let me go with you when you speak to him," Ruth said, breaking into Grace's thoughts.

Grace's eyes snapped open. "Uh. . .I saw Gary this afternoon when I was walking to the bakeshop to meet you after work."

"Why didn't you tell me about this before now?"

"My head hurt, and I–I didn't want to talk about anything unpleasant."

Ruth pulled back on the reins.

"What are you doing?"

"I'm pulling over to the shoulder of the road so we can discuss this some more."

Grace shook her head. "Better keep on driving. There's no point in us being late and worrying Mom. She's had enough to worry about lately."

"That's true." Ruth glanced over at Grace. "What did Gary say when you talked to him? Did you come right out and ask if he's responsible for the awful things that have been done at our place?"

Grace moistened her lips with the tip of her tongue. "I did, but he denied knowing anything about it."

"Do you believe him?"

"No."

"Did he say when he would be leaving Holmes County?"

Grace clenched her fists as she relived the anxiety she'd felt during that conversation. "He says he's got lots of money and plans to stay here longer and write more stories."

"That's not good."

"No, it's not, and there's more. After I told Gary about the break-ins and the brick that was thrown through the kitchen widow, he said it would make a great story. I—I think he's planning to tell the whole world about the troubles we've been having."

Ruth gasped. "Oh, Grace, that would be *baremlich*. Dad will have a conniption fit if this gets written up in some magazine or newspaper."

"I know it would be terrible, and now I'm wishing I had never mentioned it to Gary. Nothing good came from it, since I couldn't get him to admit that he's involved."

"If you're not planning to tell the folks about this, then what are you going to do?"

Grace shrugged. "I don't know."

"Maybe Gary will decide he's got enough information on the Amish, leave the area, and never come back."

Grace pursed her lips. After seeing the determined look on Gary's face today, she felt certain that he would write the story. The only questions remaining were how soon until he found a publisher, and when would the story be released?

Chapter 15

For the next several weeks, life was quiet at the Hostettlers'. Grace felt grateful that her family hadn't been attacked again, and she figured if Gary was behind the earlier incidents, he was lying low so as not to cast suspicion on himself. If he'd written an article about their break-ins, either it hadn't been published or none of the Amish in the area had seen it, because no one had mentioned it.

Since Grace didn't have to work at the restaurant this Saturday, she decided it would be a good opportunity to hem her wedding dress and get the apron and cape made. Ruth and Martha had gone shopping in Berlin; Mom was visiting her friend Alma Wengerd; and Dad would be working in his shop most of the day. The house would be quiet, and Grace would have no interruptions.

As she checked the kitchen table to be sure it had been wiped clean after breakfast, her thoughts went to Cleon. *I've got to find a good time to tell him what's on my mind, and I need to come up with the right words to say,* Grace thought as she spread the white material for her apron on the table.

She hadn't seen much of Cleon lately, between him working on their house, helping his dad and brothers on the farm, caring for his bees, and making honey deliveries.

Her fingers trailed along the edges of the soft white fabric she would wear over her wedding dress. Would it be best to wait and tell Cleon the truth after they were married, or should she keep the secret she'd been carrying for the last four years locked in her heart forever?

Grace picked up the scissors. If she could only cut out her past as she was about to cut out her wedding apron, things might go better for all.

A knock on the back door brought Grace's thoughts to a halt. "I wonder who that could be."

She opened the door. Cleon stood on the porch with a jar of amber honey is his hands. "*Guder mariye*," he said. "This is for you."

"Good morning to you, too, and danki for the honey. It's always so sweet and tasty, and I enjoy putting some in my tea." Grace took the jar and motioned Cleon inside. "I didn't expect to see you today. I figured you'd be helping your daed and bruders on the farm."

"Now that the corn has been harvested, we're pretty well caught up with things, so I decided to use today to make some deliveries to the stores in Berlin that sell my honey." He smiled and leaned so close to Grace that she could smell the minty odor of the mouthwash he must have used that morning. "Thought maybe you'd like to ride along if you're not busy with other things."

Grace nodded toward the table. "I was working on the cape and apron for our wedding, but I can finish up with that later on."

"You sure?"

"Jah." Grace would never pass up an opportunity to spend time with Cleon. "Just give me a minute to clear the table, and we can be on our way."

As Ruth and Martha left the market with their sacks of groceries, Ruth noticed a few more Amish buggy horses had been tied to the hitching rail since she and her sister had arrived. She wrinkled her nose as the sweaty scent of the horses greeted her and wondered as her horse nuzzled the one next to him what these animals would have to say if they could talk.

"Say, isn't that Luke over there with those English fellows?" Martha pointed to the other side of the parking lot, where several cars were parked.

Ruth turned to look. Sure enough, Luke stood beside two young

Englishers dressed in blue jeans and white T-shirts. They leaned against a fancy red sports car and seemed to be engrossed in conversation.

Martha nudged Ruth's arm with her elbow. "I wonder what Luke's doing in town. I figured he would be working for Dad today."

Ruth nodded. "I thought so, too, but maybe he had a delivery to make and stopped by the market to buy something for lunch."

Martha opened the door of the buggy and set her paper sack in the back. "I didn't see anything in his hands, did you?"

"Maybe he hasn't gone into the store yet."

"If you'd like to go over and say hello, I'll wait here with the buggy."

Ruth was tempted to follow her sister's suggestion, but she and Luke hadn't been courting very long, and she didn't want him to think she was throwing herself at him. She placed her own sack of groceries in the back of the buggy and shut the door. "I don't want to interrupt his conversation."

"He'd probably like to introduce you to his friends since you're his aldi and all."

Ruth stared across the parking lot and squinted. "You think those Englishers are Luke's friends?"

"The other day when Toby brought Heidi home, he mentioned that Luke's been hanging around some English fellows, and if they weren't his friends, then why would they be gabbing away like there's no tomorrow?"

Ruth shrugged. "I don't know, but I've never seen either one of them before. If they are Luke's friends, wouldn't you think I would have met them, or at least seen them around Berlin somewhere?"

Martha shrugged. "You'll never know what's up until you go over there."

Ruth hesitated a moment, and when she caught Luke looking her way, she decided it would be rude not to at least say hello. "You're welcome to come with me," she told her sister.

"You wouldn't mind?"

"Not a bit. I'll be less nervous if you're by my side."

Martha chuckled. "Jah, right."

Ruth walked beside her sister, and when they reached the spot where Luke and the Englishers stood, she halted. "Hello, Luke. I'm surprised to see you here. Did you come to town to make a delivery for my daed this afternoon?"

He shook his head. "Uh. . .no. I'm not workin' for him today."

"But I thought Dad was getting behind on things."

"Maybe so, but he said he didn't need me today."

"Oh, I see."

One of the English fellows, whose curly blond hair reminded Ruth of a dust mop, snickered and nudged the other fellow, whose straight, black hair looked like it hadn't been combed in several days. His clothes smelled of smoke, and she turned her head to avoid sneezing.

The other Englisher mumbled something under his breath, but Ruth couldn't make out the words.

When Luke made no move to introduce her, she backed slowly away. "Well, I. . .uh. . .guess we'd best be on our way. It was nice seeing you, Luke."

"Right. See you around, Ruth." He offered her sister a half smile. "You, too, Martha."

"I wonder what's gotten into Luke," Martha said once they had climbed into their buggy. "He sure was acting *kariyos*, don't you think?"

Ruth nodded. "I thought he acted a bit odd, too. Maybe it was because he was with those English fellows and didn't want to let on that I'm his girlfriend." She clutched the folds in her dark blue dress. "But then, if he cares for me, why would he be too embarrassed to let anyone know we're courting?"

"Luke hasn't joined the church yet, and since he's still going through rumschpringe, I'm sure he feels he has the right to run around with those Englishers."

"It's not the Englishers I have a problem with," Ruth murmured. "It's the fact that he didn't bother to introduce me. He barely acknowledged he knew me at all, much less that I'm his aldi."

"Guess you'll have to ask him about it."

"I might the next time we're alone."

"Changing the subject, is there anyplace else you'd like to stop while we're in town, or did you want to head for home now?" Martha asked as she gathered up the reins and backed the horse out of her parking spot.

"Let's stop by the bakeshop," Ruth suggested. "I'll treat you to a lemon-filled donut."

Martha smacked her lips. "Sounds good to me."

Grace and Cleon traveled along the hilly road toward Berlin in his buggy. "The other day when we went bike riding," Grace said, "I was going to discuss something with you, but we got interrupted when Ruth and Sadie came along."

He glanced over at her and smiled. "What was it you wanted to discuss?"

She gulped in a breath of fresh air and blew it out quickly, hoping to steady her nerves. "I have an aunt who moved away from Holmes County and never returned."

"Which aunt is that?"

"Her name is Rosemary, and she's my daed's only sister."

Cleon's forehead wrinkled. "I've never heard your daed mention having a sister. I thought he only had brothers."

"Dad probably wouldn't mention Aunt Rosemary. He rarely speaks of her, and when he does, it's always with a tone of regret."

"How come?"

"From what I've been told, Aunt Rosemary fell in love with an Englisher and left the Amish faith almost thirty years ago."

"I see."

"In all that time, she's never once come home for a visit or contacted any of her family."

Cleon stared straight ahead as he clucked to the horse.

"My daed's whole family was hurt by this—Dad most of all. I don't think he's ever really forgiven her for leaving."

"I can understand why he would be hurt. The fact that his sister went English and left the faith would be hard to take."

Grace's pulse pounded in her temples, and she turned her head away so Cleon wouldn't see her tears.

They rode along quietly for a while, the only sounds being the steady *clip-clop* of the horse's hooves and an occasional *whirr* of an engine as a car whizzed past. Grace hated keeping her secret from Cleon, but if he felt the way Dad did about an Amish woman marrying an Englisher, no good could come from telling him the truth. He would probably call off the wedding, and Grace loved Cleon too much to jeopardize their relationship. The best thing she could see to do was to continue keeping the painful secret to herself. She could only hope it wouldn't be revealed by someone else.

Chapter 16

Grace could hardly believe her wedding day had finally arrived. Sitting at the kitchen table and drinking a cup of tea, she reflected on the day before. Several of their Amish friends and relatives, some of whom would be table waiters during the wedding meal, had showed up early to help out. The bench wagons from both their home church district and from a neighboring district were brought over to the Hostettlers' because they would need more seating at the wedding than during a regular Sunday church service. Much of the furniture had been removed from their house and stored in clean outbuildings, while smaller items were placed in the bench wagons after the men had unloaded the benches, unfolded the legs, and arranged them in the house.

Many hands had prepared the chickens that would be served at the wedding meal as well as mounds of other food items. The four couples assigned as "roast cooks" had divided up the dressed chickens and taken them home to roast in their ovens. Aunt Clara, Mom's oldest sister, was an excellent baker and had made several batches of doughnuts. Some of the other women had made a variety of cookies, and there were three large, decorated cakes, one of which had been purchased at the bakeshop where Ruth worked.

"Guder mariye, bride-to-be," Ruth said as she stepped into the kitchen wearing a smile that stretched ear to ear. "You look like you're a hundred miles away."

"Good morning," Grace said. "I was just thinking about yesterday and all the help we had getting ready for today."

"We sure did." Ruth moved across the room and pulled out a chair at the table. "How are you feeling this morning? Are you naerfich?"

"I am a little nervous," Grace admitted.

"I'm sure I'll be nervous when I get married someday, too." Ruth took a seat beside Grace and reached for the teapot sitting in the middle of the table. "Cleon's a good man, and I'm glad the two of you will be living here until your house is finished."

Grace nodded. "At least our new home is close by so it will be easier for Cleon to work on it when he's not busy with his bees or helping his daed."

"It's obvious that he loves you, and I think you two will have a good marriage."

"I hope we can be as happy as Mom and Dad have been all these years."

"I think one of the reasons they have such a good marriage is because they see eye to eye on so many things." Ruth reached for one of the empty mugs sitting near the teapot and poured herself some tea. "Mom told me once that she believes the most important ingredient in marriage, besides loving the person you're married to, is honesty."

"Honesty?" Grace repeated as a sinking feeling made her stomach feel tied in knots. Years of regret tugged at her heart, and a twinge of guilt whispered to her that she wasn't worthy to marry Cleon—wasn't worthy to bear his children.

"Mom said from the moment she and Dad started courting, she made a promise to herself that she would never intentionally lie or keep secrets from him."

Grace inwardly groaned. She was about to begin her marriage to Cleon with a secret between them—one that could change the way he felt about her and could destroy her relationships with her parents and sisters, as well.

She set her empty mug in the sink and glanced out the kitchen window. It was a cold, crisp day in early December, but at least no snow covered the ground. Her stomach flew up when she noticed several buggies were already lined up in the yard. She knew some of their

English friends and neighbors had also arrived because a couple of vans and several cars were parked outside. It wouldn't be long before the bishop and other ministers arrived, and soon after that, the wedding service would begin. It was too late to tell Cleon her secret. That would have to wait until sometime after they were married, if at all.

Feeling the need to think about something else, Grace focused on the six teenage boys, known as the "hostlers," whose job it was to lead the horses into the barn and tie them up. For the next hour or so, those young fellows would be kept plenty busy, and during the afternoon, they would see to it that all the horses were fed.

"What are you doing in here?" Dad asked, stepping up beside Grace and placing his hand on her shoulder.

"Oh, just watching the goings-on outside."

He chuckled. "There's a lot of activity out there, all right. I imagine the bishop will be here most any time, so it might be good if you headed to the other room and got ready for the service, don't you think?"

Grace nodded and smiled, even though her stomach was still doing little flip-flops. She wanted so much to become Cleon's wife, yet she was full of apprehension and misgivings.

"I'm glad you and Cleon will be living nearby," Dad said. "It would be hard on your mamm if you were to move too far away."

Grace wondered if her father was referring to the time she'd been gone during her rumschpringe. She knew how much it had hurt her parents when she'd moved to Cincinnati and not kept in touch. When she returned home two years later without a word of explanation, they hadn't asked any questions, just welcomed her with open arms. From that day on, Grace had tried to be the perfect daughter, helping out at home without question and adhering to the church rules. Now all she had to do was be a good wife to Cleon, and everything should be fine.

Glancing down at her dark blue dress draped with a white cape and apron, Grace grew more anxious by the moment as she sat rigidly in her seat. Most of their guests had arrived, including two other ministers, but Bishop King was late, and she was getting worried. What if something had happened to him? What if someone had tried to detain the bishop and his family along the way?

Her thoughts went to Gary. Would he stoop so low as to try and stop her from marrying Cleon? Did he even know that this was her wedding day? Since he was a reporter, he might have finagled that information from someone in the community.

"I think I'd better get my horse and buggy and go looking for the bishop," Deacon Byler announced as he headed for the door.

"I'll go with you," Mose Troyer, one of the ministers, said.

Grace glanced across the room to where Cleon sat straight and tall, wearing a white shirt, black trousers, and a matching vest and jacket. Did he feel as nervous as she? Was he having second thoughts? His stoic expression gave no indication of what he might be thinking.

If she'd told him about her previous marriage and everything that had transpired after that, would he have forgiven her for keeping the truth from him? She loved Cleon, but did it really matter if only she knew the details of her rumschpringe days? After all, that was in the past. Shouldn't it stay that way?

Grace clenched her teeth so hard her jaw ached. She wished she could quit thinking about this. She had to get ahold of herself, or the entire day would be ruined.

Since the wedding wouldn't start until the bishop arrived, everyone left their seats. Some of the women went to the kitchen, some sat in groups around the living room, and most of the men went outside to mill around and visit.

Half an hour later, the bishop and his family showed up. He offered his apologies for being late, explaining that one of his carriage wheels had fallen off.

Grace breathed a sigh of relief. At last, the wedding could begin.

The ceremony, which was similar to a regular Sunday preaching service, began with a song from the Amish hymnal, the *Ausbund.* Grace did fine during the first part of the song, but as the time drew closer for her and Cleon to meet with the bishop and other ministers for counseling, she became more apprehensive.

As the people began the third line of the hymn, the ministers stood and made their way up the stairs to a room on the second floor. Grace and Cleon followed, but their attendants—Grace's sisters and two of Cleon's brothers—waited downstairs with the others.

Upstairs in the bedroom that had been set aside for the counseling session, Grace sat in a straight-backed chair, fidgeting with a corner of her apron as she listened to the bishop's admonitions and instructions on marriage.

The counseling session consisted of several scripture references and a long dissertation from Bishop King on the importance of good communication, trust, and respect in all areas of marriage. He reminded the couple that divorce was not an acceptable option among those of their faith, and he emphasized the need to work through any problems that might arise in their marriage.

When Cleon and Grace returned to the main room a short time later, they took their seats again, and the congregation sang another song. The ministers reentered the room during the final verse and also sat down. Next, a message was given by Mose Troyer, followed by a period of silent prayer and the reading of scripture. The bishop rose and began the main sermon.

Grace glanced over at Cleon, and he flashed her a grin, which helped calm her nerves and offered her the assurance she so desperately needed.

The bishop called for the bride and groom to stand before him, and Grace joined Cleon at the front of the room. "Brother," Bishop King said, looking at Cleon, "can you confess that you accept this, our sister, as your wife, and that you will not leave her until death separates you? And do you believe that this is from the Lord and that you have come thus far by your faith and prayers?"

With no hesitation, Cleon smiled at Grace and answered, "Jah."

The bishop then directed his words to Grace. "Can you confess, sister, that you accept this, our brother, as your husband, and that you will not leave him until death separates you? And do you believe that this is from the Lord and that you have come thus far by your faith and prayers?"

"Jah."

The bishop spoke to Cleon again. "Because you have confessed that you want to take this, our sister, for your wife, do you promise to be loyal to her and care for her if she may have adversity, affliction, sickness, or weakness, as is appropriate for a Christian, God-fearing husband?"

"Jah."

The bishop addressed the same question to Grace, and she, too, replied affirmatively. He then took Grace's hand and placed it in Cleon's hand, putting his own hands above and beneath theirs. "The God of Abraham, the God of Isaac, and the God of Jacob be with you together and give His rich blessing upon you and be merciful to you. To this I wish you the blessings of God for a good beginning, and may you hold out until a blessed end. Through Jesus Christ our Lord, Amen."

At the end of the blessing, Grace, Cleon, and Bishop King bowed their knees in prayer. "Go forth in the name of the Lord. You are now man and wife," the bishop said when the prayer was done.

Grace and Cleon returned to their seats, and one of the ministers gave a testimony, followed by two other ministers expressing agreement with the sermon and wishing Cleon and Grace God's blessings. When that was done, the bishop made a few closing comments and asked the congregation to kneel, at which time he read a prayer from the prayer book. Then the congregation rose to their feet, and the meeting was closed with a final hymn.

Grace drew in a deep breath and blinked back tears of joy. In a short time, the wedding feast would begin, and so would her new life as Mrs. Cleon Schrock. Maybe now she could finally leave her past behind.

As several of the men set up tables for the wedding meal, Cleon reflected on the somber expression he'd seen on his bride's face as they'd responded to the bishop's questions during their wedding vows. Grace had taken her vows seriously, which reassured him that everything was as it should be between them.

Once the tables had been put in place and covered with tablecloths, the eating utensils were set out. Foot traffic was heavy and continuous from the temporary kitchen that had been set up in the basement to the eating areas, which included the living room and upstairs kitchen. Food for all courses was soon placed on the table, beginning with the main course, which included roasted chicken, bread filling, and mashed potatoes. They were also served creamed celery—a traditional wedding dish—coleslaw, applesauce, pies, doughnuts, fruit salad, pudding, bread, butter, jelly, and coffee.

As soon as everything was ready for the meal, the bridal party made its entrance, beginning with the bride and groom, followed by Ruth, Martha, Ivan, and Willard, entering single file.

As Cleon and Grace took their seats, she commented about the jars of select celery that had been spaced at regular intervals on each of the tables so the leaves formed a kind of flowerlike arrangement. There were also several bouquets of flowers Ruth had put together.

"Everything looks real nice," Cleon said, leaning close to her as they sat at the corner table known as the *"Eck."* "You and your family did a fine job decorating for our special day."

"Your mamm and sister did well with the candles, too." Grace touched the tablecloth adorning their corner table where the bride and groom traditionally sat. "This is from my hope chest, and two of the three decorated cakes were contributed by friends."

He smiled and licked his lips. "They look real tasty."

"The most elaborate cake, we bought from the bakeshop where Ruth works," she said. "Did you notice what's written in the center of that cake?"

Cleon read the words out loud. "*Bescht winsche*—best wishes, Cleon and Grace." He reached for her hand and gave it a gentle squeeze. "I hope we'll always be this happy."

Tears pricked the backs of her eyes. "Jah, me, too."

Chapter 17

Grace couldn't believe she and Cleon had been married a little over two months already, and as she stood in front of the sink one Saturday afternoon, peeling potatoes for the stew they would have for supper, she reflected on how things had been since their wedding day. She and Cleon were enjoying married life and getting along well at her folks' place, although Grace looked forward to the day when their own house would be done and they could move into it.

During December and January, they'd had several days of snow, and Cleon had taken time out from his honey deliveries and working on the house in order for them to do some fun things together. They had frolicked in the snow, taken a sleigh ride, sat by the fire sipping hot chocolate, and played board games with the rest of her family.

Grace felt happier than she had ever dreamed possible, and she was grateful there had been no more attacks on her family. She was certain this was because Gary Walker had left Holmes County. Esther had told her that Gary had come into the restaurant where Grace used to work and mentioned that he was leaving for Lancaster County, Pennsylvania, to do some stories on the Amish who lived there. Grace hoped Gary never returned to Ohio.

Now, if they could just get their house finished, things would be nearly perfect. It wasn't that she minded living with her folks, but it wasn't the same as having a place of their own. Grace was anxious to set out her wedding gifts, as well as the things she had in her hope chest. Cleon had said the other day that he hoped the house would be finished in a few months, but since he'd gotten so busy with new honey orders, he'd spent less time working on it.

Grace had wanted to do some work on the house herself since she'd quit her job at the restaurant as soon as they were married, but she didn't know a lot about carpentry. Even if Grace had, Cleon made it clear that building the house was his job, and with the help he got from other family members, including Grace's father, Grace knew their home would be finished in due time, so she needed to be patient.

She glanced out the kitchen window and noticed the dismal-looking gray sky. Between that and the drop in temperature, they were sure to have more snow.

Grace had just finished with the potatoes when she heard a knock on the front door. *That's strange. Hardly anyone we know uses the front door.*

She left the kitchen, hurried through the hall, and opened the door. A tall, middle-aged man wearing a dark green jacket and a pair of earmuffs stood on the porch. He held the hand of a petite little girl whose dark brown hair was pulled back in a ponytail. The child wore blue jeans and a puffy pink jacket with a hood, and as she looked up at Grace with a quizzical expression, her clear blue eyes blinked rapidly.

"Can I help you?" Grace asked, thinking the man had probably stopped to ask for directions like other English tourists did when they got lost.

He cleared his throat. Seconds ticked by as they stared at each other. "Grace Davis?"

Her mouth went dry, and she glanced around, relieved that she was alone. She hadn't been called by that name since—

"Is this the Hostettler home?"

She could only nod in reply. Who was this man, and how did he know her previous married name?

"Are you Grace?"

She nodded again as she studied him closer. They might have met before, but she couldn't be sure. Could he have been one of her customers at the restaurant or maybe someone from one of the

English-owned stores in town? But if that were so, how did he know her last name used to be Davis?

Grace glanced at the little girl again. She was certain she'd never met her, yet there was something familiar about the child. "Have. . . have we met before?" she asked, returning her gaze to the man.

He nodded. "Just once–at my son's funeral."

Grace's heart slammed into her chest with such force, she had to lean against the doorjamb for support. The man who stood before her was Wade's father, Carl Davis. She looked down at the little girl standing beside him, and goose bumps erupted on her arms.

"This is your daughter." Carl touched the child's shoulder. "Anna, this is your mother. As I told you before, you'll be living with her from now on."

Anna's eyes were downcast, and her chin quivered slightly.

Grace clung to the door, unsure of what to say or do. She was glad her long skirt hid her knees, for they knocked so badly, she could barely stand. She'd never expected to see Anna again, much less have her show up on her doorstep like this.

"How did you find me? Where have you been all this time? Why are you here?" Grace's head swam with so many unanswered questions she hardly knew where to begin.

"May we come inside?" Carl motioned to Anna. "She's tired from the long plane ride, and it's cold out here."

"Oh, of course." Grace held the door open for them and, on shaky legs, led the way to the living room.

Carl pulled off his earmuffs and took a seat on one end of the sofa, lifting Anna into his lap. Grace seated herself in the rocking chair across from them, fighting the urge to gather the girl into her arms and kiss her sweet face. Anna looked so befuddled, and Grace didn't want to frighten or confuse her anymore than she obviously was.

"Before I answer your questions," Carl said, removing Anna's jacket and then letting her turn and nestle against his chest, "I need to explain a few things."

Grace nodded in reply, never taking her eyes off Anna–the precious little girl she'd been forced to give up four years ago.

"When Wade married you without inviting us to the wedding, my wife was devastated."

"Where is Bonnie?"

"I'm getting to that." Carl leaned over and placed Anna on the other end of the sofa. Her eyes had closed, and her steady, even breathing let Grace know she'd fallen asleep. "When Wade finally called and told us he had moved to Cincinnati and had gotten married, Bonnie insisted that he tell her everything he knew about you—where you were from, what your background was, and why you had convinced him to elope with you and not include us in the wedding."

"But. . .but I didn't convince him," Grace sputtered. "Eloping was Wade's idea, and none of our parents were invited to the wedding." She stared down at her hands, clenched tightly in her lap. "My folks don't know I was ever married to your son or that we had—" She drew in a quick breath. "Go ahead with what you were about to say."

"Wade told us soon after you were married that you'd grown up in the Amish faith and that you had lived here in Holmes County, somewhere between Berlin and Charm. He said your last name had been Hostettler, and that you'd left your faith in order to marry him."

"Actually, I hadn't been baptized or joined the church yet."

"I see. Well, since I knew your family's last name and the general area where they lived, I was able to track you down."

A lump formed in Grace's throat. "I tried to call you and Bonnie soon after you left with Anna, but your phone had been disconnected. I wrote several letters, but they all came back with a stamped message saying you had moved and there was no forwarding address."

"Bonnie thought it would be better if you had no contact with Anna." Carl shifted on the sofa. "So we moved from our home in Michigan to Nevada, where we had some friends, and left no forwarding address."

"Why are you here now after making no contact with me these past four and a half years?"

"Bonnie had a sudden heart attack a few days after Christmas and died."

"I–I'm sorry." Even though Grace had only met Wade's folks when they'd come to his funeral, she'd taken an immediate dislike to his mother. Still, she took no pleasure in knowing the woman was dead.

"I've had my own share of health problems lately, and because of that, I won't be able to continue caring for Anna on my own." Carl swiped his tongue across his lower lip and grimaced. "I want you to know that I never felt good about taking your baby from you. It was Bonnie's idea. She felt we could give Anna a better home."

Too little, too late. Why couldn't you have stood up to your wife back then? Why couldn't you have offered me some financial support instead of taking my child?

Grace lifted her hands to her temples and massaged them with her fingertips. "I was so young, and. . .and I knew I couldn't provide properly for a baby. I was grieving over my husband, and I didn't know what was best for me or Anna at the time." She paused and drew in a quick breath to help steady her nerves. "I wanted to take my little girl and go home to my folks, but I—I was afraid of their rejection."

He opened his mouth as if to comment, but she rushed on. "Ever since the day you took Anna, I've felt guilty for letting someone else raise my daughter and for not having the courage to tell my family about my marriage or that I'd had a baby girl. I was too ashamed to admit I'd given up my rights as her mother, and since I didn't think I would ever see Anna again, I decided it would be best to keep my marriage and my daughter a secret."

He glanced around the room. "Where are they now—your family?"

"My dad's out in his woodworking shop, Mom went to visit a friend, and my two sisters are in town shopping."

Carl leaned slightly forward. "As I said before, I can't take care of Anna myself, so I've brought her to you. You're her mother and should have been the one caring for her these past four years, not me and Bonnie."

Grace closed her eyes as the memory of Wade's funeral and all that had happened afterwards rose before her. It had been enough of a shock to learn that Wade had been killed, but when his parents showed up for the funeral and said they wanted to take Anna, Grace's whole world had fallen apart.

She remembered how Bonnie had insisted that Grace let them raise the child, saying they could offer her more than Grace possibly could. When Grace refused, Bonnie threatened to hire a lawyer and prove that she was an unfit mother, unable to provide for Anna's needs. Bonnie and Carl had promised Grace visiting rights, saying she was welcome to see her little girl anytime she could make the trip to Michigan. But that hadn't happened because they'd moved, and Grace had given up all hope of ever seeing her daughter again.

Grace's eyes snapped open as the reality of the situation set fully in. Wade's father was offering her the chance to raise Anna—something she should have been doing all along. But the child didn't know Grace, and it would be a difficult transition for both of them. Not only that, but agreeing to keep Anna would mean Grace would have to reveal the secret she'd kept from her family and Cleon. She would need to explain why she had hidden the truth.

Grace rose from the chair and knelt on the floor in front of the sofa, reaching out to stroke her daughter's flushed cheeks. "Oh, Anna, I've never forgotten you." She gulped on a sob. "I've never stopped loving you, either."

Carl cleared his throat. "Are you willing to take her? Because if you aren't, I'll need to make other arrangements."

Other arrangements? Grace had already lost Anna once and couldn't bear the thought of losing her again. Regardless of her family's response, she knew what she had to do. "I think God might be offering me a second chance," she murmured.

"Does that mean Anna can stay?"

She nodded. "I will never let her go again."

"I wouldn't expect you to." Carl rose. "I packed some of Anna's winter clothes, and her suitcase is in my rental car. I'll get her things and be on my way before she wakes up." He smiled at his granddaughter as tears welled in his eyes. "It'll be better that way."

Grace started to get up, but he waved her aside. "No need to see me out. I'll just get the suitcase, bring it inside, and head back to the airport."

For the next hour, Grace sat on the floor in front of the sofa, watching her daughter sleep and thanking God for the opportunity He'd given her to be with Anna again.

When the back door slammed shut, Grace jumped, and when she heard the unmistakable sound of her father's boots clomping across the linoleum in the kitchen, she cringed. Her secret was about to be revealed. She could no longer hide the truth.

Chapter 18

Is anybody home?" Dad called.

Grace's heart took a nosedive. She couldn't let him see Anna without explaining things first. Guilt clung to her like a spider's web to a fly. If only she could undo the past. Oh, how she wished she hadn't kept this secret from her family.

"Grace, are you here?"

She jumped up and rushed out of the room, meeting him in the hallway outside the kitchen door.

"I figured you were here, but I wasn't sure about your mamm and sisters. Are they home yet?" Dad asked.

"No, and I—I don't expect them until closer to suppertime." Grace took hold of his arm. "Uh, Dad, we need to talk."

"Sure, I've got time for a little break. Just came in to refill my thermos with something to drink." He nodded toward the living room. "Should we go in there?"

She shook her head. Panic threatened to overtake her. "Let's go to the kitchen. I'll pour you a glass of goat's milk, and we can sit at the table."

"Sounds good to me."

Grace followed her father down the hall. When they entered the kitchen, he pulled out his chair at the head of the table and took a seat, stretching his arms over his head. "Didn't realize how tired I was until I sat down. I've been working too many long hours lately."

Grace took down two glasses from the cupboard and poured some milk.

As she handed a glass to her father, his forehead wrinkled. "Your hands are shaking. Is there something wrong? There hasn't been another break-in, I hope."

She shook her head and sank into the chair across from him. "We had a visitor awhile ago—an English man with a little girl."

He took a drink from his glass and wiped his mouth with the back of his hand. "Oh? Did they come in a car?"

"Jah."

"I'm surprised I didn't hear it pull into the yard. Of course, I've been hammering and sawing much of the day, so most outside sounds would probably have been drowned out." He took another drink. "Who were the English visitors?"

Grace's throat felt so dry and swollen she could barely swallow. She took a sip of milk and nearly choked as the cool liquid trickled down the wrong pipe.

"Are you okay?" Dad jumped up and thumped her on the back. "Take a couple of deep breaths."

She coughed and sputtered, finally gaining enough control so she could speak. "There's. . .uh. . .something I must tell you."

"What is it, daughter? Your face is as pale as this milk we're drinking."

"I think you'd better sit down again. What I have to say is going to be quite a shock."

"You're scaring me, Grace." He lowered himself into the chair with a groan. "Has something happened to your mamm or one of your sisters?"

She shook her head. Tears clouded her vision. "The man who was here is Carl Davis. When I was living among the English, I—I married his son, Wade."

Dad sat, staring at Grace in a strange way. "Is this some kind of a joke? You're married to Cleon, remember?"

"It's not a joke. Wade was killed in a car accident, and I returned to Holmes County soon after his funeral."

His eyebrows furrowed, nearly disappearing into the wrinkles of his forehead. "Does. . .does Cleon know of this?"

She shook her head.

"How come you never mentioned it before now?"

Grace gulped in some air. "I was afraid you wouldn't understand."

He opened his mouth as if to respond, but she held up her hand to stop him. "There's more. I've been keeping another secret these past four and a half years, as well."

"What other secret?"

She glanced toward the door leading to the hallway. "There's a little girl asleep on the sofa in our living room. Her name is Anna, and she. . .she's my daughter."

Dad's mouth dropped open, and his eyes narrowed into tiny slits. "Your what?"

"Anna's my little girl. She was only six months old when her daed was killed. Then Wade's parents took her from me and moved away." She gulped on the sob rising in her throat and steadied herself by grabbing the edge of the table. "I was unable to contact them by phone or mail, so I finally realized I needed to be here with my family and not living in the English world on my own."

The color drained from Dad's face, and he slowly shook his head.

"I know it was wrong to keep this from you and Mom." Grace reached out to touch his arm. "I was so ashamed that I'd given up my baby, and I didn't think I would ever see Anna again, so I—"

"You're just like your aunt Rosemary, you know that?" Dad's fist came down hard, scattering the napkins that had been nestled in a basket in the center of the table. "How could you have done such a thing, Grace? Ach, it's bad enough that you ran off and married an Englisher, but how could you have given up your own flesh and blood?"

"I—I didn't want to, but Wade's mother was so mean and pushy. She insisted that Anna would be better off with them, and she threatened to hire a lawyer and prove I was unfit to raise Anna on my own."

"Were you unfit, Grace?"

Their gazes connected, and Dad's pointed question was almost Grace's undoing. "I was so young, and the only job I'd ever had was working at a restaurant as a waitress. I knew I couldn't make enough money to support myself and Anna, and I thought—"

"You could have come home and asked for help. Surely you knew we wouldn't have let you or your daughter starve. If Rosemary had come home, she would have been welcomed, too."

Silence filled the air in the wake of her father's reproof, and the tears Grace had fought so hard to hold back spilled onto her cheeks and dribbled down her chin. She didn't understand how he could forgive whoever had broken into their home and his shop yet not forgive his sister or his own flesh-and-blood daughter. "You have every right to be angry with me," she said with a sniff. "But no one could be any angrier than I am with myself."

He continued to stare straight ahead, a muscle in his cheek quivering.

"Wade's mother is dead now, and his father's health isn't good, so he brought Anna to me and asked that I raise her."

Dad blinked rapidly, and he tapped his fingers against the tablecloth in quick succession. "Where is this man now?"

"He left soon after Anna fell asleep. Said it would be better that way."

"I see."

"Would. . .would you like to meet your granddaughter?"

He shook his head. "I need time to think about this. I need to understand why you would lie to your mamm and daed—why you would follow in your aunt's footsteps."

"I know it was wrong to keep the truth from you, but I—" Grace bit her lower lip to stop the flow of tears and pushed her chair away from the table. All she wanted to do was hold Anna and promise that she would never let her go again.

Grace left the kitchen, hurried back to the living room, and dropped to the floor in front of the sofa, where her daughter lay sleeping. Her heart thumped with fury and remorse. *I should never have let Wade's folks take Anna from me, no matter what they threatened to do. I should have packed up our things and brought my baby girl home with me, regardless of the consequences. Things would have gone better if I'd told Mom and Dad the truth right away. I should have told Cleon about Wade and Anna, too.*

Grace hiccupped on a sob. Regrets wouldn't change anything, and she knew she had to find a way to deal with her new situation. If only Dad had shown some understanding or offered a bit of support when she'd told him about Anna instead of comparing her to Aunt Rosemary, whom she'd never even met. Would Cleon respond the same way when she told him?

She glanced at the door leading to the hallway. Should she go back to the kitchen and try to talk to her father again? Would it do any good if she tried to explain things better?

Anna stirred, and Grace held her breath, waiting to see if her daughter would wake.

The child sat up, yawned, and looked around. "Poppy? Where's Poppy?" she asked in a small, birdlike voice.

Grace searched for words that wouldn't be a lie. "Your grandpa went home, but he'll come back to visit sometime, I'm sure." She smiled, hoping to reassure the child.

Anna's eyes opened wider. "Poppy left?"

Grace nodded. "He wants you to stay with me now because he can't care for you any longer." She moved closer to Anna and reached out her hand. "I'm your mother. Your grandpa said he told you about me."

Anna scrambled off the couch and raced for the front door. "Come back, Poppy! Come back!"

Grace rushed to her daughter's side, gathering the child into her arms. "It's going to be all right. You're safe here with me."

Roman sat at the kitchen table, trying to let Grace's news sink into his brain. He felt betrayed and didn't understand why she'd kept her first marriage a secret or why she'd hidden the fact that she'd had a baby and had given the child to someone else to raise. The one thing Roman knew was that he was a *grossdaadi*, and that his *grossdochder* was sleeping in the next room.

His shoulders sagged, and he dropped his head into the palms of his hands. This news would affect the entire family. And what of Grace's new husband? How would Cleon deal with things?

His thoughts shifted to a silent prayer. *Dear God, haven't we been through enough these past few months with the break-ins we've had? Must we now endure the shame of our daughter's deception?*

The back door opened and clicked shut, interrupting Roman's prayer. He lifted his head as his wife entered the room.

"*Wie geht's?*" Judith asked with a cheery smile.

He groaned. "I'm not so good, and my day was going along okay until I came into the house awhile ago."

A look of alarm flashed across her face, and she hurried across the room. "Was there another break-in or something else to upset things?"

"Oh, there's an upset all right. Only it's got nothin' to do with any break-ins."

"What is it, husband? You look so *uffriehrisch*."

"I am agitated, and you had better sit down." He motioned to the chair across from him. "What I have to tell you is going to be quite *schauderhaft*."

She sank into the chair, her eyes full of question. "You're scaring me. Please tell me what is so shocking."

"We've got a grossdochder."

Judith blinked as she let her husband's words sink into her brain. "Is Grace in a family way? Is that what you're trying to say?"

He shook his head. "I'm not talking about a granddaughter we might have someday; I'm talking about the one we have now."

Her forehead wrinkled. "What are you saying, Roman? We have no grandchildren yet."

"Jah, we do. She's in the living room, asleep on the sofa."

The muscles in Judith's face relaxed, and she poked her husband on the arm. "You always did like to tease, didn't you?"

His expression turned somber as he leaned forward in his chair. "I'm not teasing. There really is a little girl in our living room, and she's Grace's daughter."

Judith sat rigid in her chair, her mouth hanging slightly open. "What?"

"It's true. Grace was married during the time she lived among the English, and she. . .she had a baby girl."

"But how can that be?"

"I just told you she was married before and–"

She held up her hand. "This makes no sense. If Grace is already married, then how could she marry Cleon?"

"Her husband's dead. Died in a car accident, Grace said." Roman pulled his fingers through the back of his hair and grimaced. "Guess her husband's folks came to the funeral and took Grace's baby to raise."

As Judith tried to digest her husband's astonishing story, her head began to throb. These last four and a half years, Grace had never said a word about having been married–or that she'd given birth to a baby girl. "Why would she do that, Roman? Why would our daughter let someone else raise her child?"

He shrugged. "She said it was because she was young and scared and didn't think she could support the child."

"But she could have come home, let us help raise the baby."

Roman squeezed his fingers around the edge of the table so hard his knuckles turned white. "Grace said she was afraid we wouldn't understand." He slowly shook his head. "She's right–I don't. I think she's got my sister's blood in her; that's what I think."

"What are you saying?"

"Hearing Grace's story brought all the pain back that my family felt when my own sister left the Amish faith. Then Rosemary made things worse by marrying that Englisher who ended up taking her away from her family for good." He squeezed his eyes shut. "Nearly broke our mamm's heart, it did."

Judith stared at a dark spot on the tablecloth and struggled to keep her voice steady. "You can't compare what our daughter did with your sister's act of defiance. Rosemary left home and never returned or made any effort to contact your family or come home for a visit." She swallowed a couple of times. "At least Grace returned home and joined the church, and she's–"

Roman's eyes snapped open, and his fist came down hard on the table, clattering the two glasses sitting there, nearly knocking them over. "She's been lying to us all this time, Judith! Our daughter kept her marriage to an English man and the child she bore a secret, and I doubt Grace would have ever told the truth if her dead husband's father hadn't shown up on our doorstep with her daughter today."

"Is. . .is the man still here?"

He shook his head. "Grace said he left soon after the child fell asleep on the sofa. His wife is dead, and he's not well, so he brought his granddaughter here for Grace to raise."

Judith pushed her chair aside and stood.

"Where are you going?"

"To meet our grossdochder. Wouldn't you like to come along?"

Deep wrinkles formed on his forehead as he released a moan. "I do want to meet her; I'm just not sure I can."

"Of course you can." She held out her hand. "You can't sit here all evening, fretting because Grace kept this secret from us. What's done is done, and we need to put it to rest because we have a granddaughter to help raise."

"But. . .but what will I say to the child—or to Grace?"

Judith shrugged. "I don't know. The words will be on your lips when you need them, same as mine." She moved toward the door. "Are you coming or not?"

He grunted and pushed away from the table.

Anna wiggled free from Grace's embrace and pulled on the door handle. "Leave me be! I wanna go home! I want Poppy!"

Before Grace could react, her mother and father stepped into the room. "What's going on? What's all the shouting about?" Mom asked with a worried expression.

"Oh, Mom, I've made such a mess of things." Grace nodded at Anna, who stood with her little body pressed up to the door, trembling from head to toe. "This is my daughter, Anna, and—"

"I know already. Your daed told me everything." Mom knelt in front of Anna and reached out to wipe the tears from her cheeks. "I'm your grandmother, Anna."

"Grandma's gone away and will never come back. Poppy said so."

"I'm your other grandmother. My name is Grandma Hostettler." She motioned to Grace's father. "That's Grandpa Hostettler."

"Poppy went home! He. . .he's never comin' back."

"That's not true," Grace was quick to say. "I'm sure he'll write you letters and come visit whenever he can."

Anna's lower lip quivered. More tears flooded her eyes. The sorrow Grace saw on the child's face tore at her heartstrings, but she didn't know what she could say or do to make things better–for her or Anna.

Mom stood and reached for Anna's hand. "Why don't we go out to the kitchen for some cookies and milk? Does that sound good to you?"

"Got any chocolate ones?" the child asked with a hopeful expression. It was the first indication that she might calm down, and for that Grace felt some relief.

"I have chocolate chip and peanut butter cookies," Mom said with a smile.

Anna sniffed and quietly nodded.

Mom touched Grace's shoulder, and Grace found a measure of comfort in the gesture. "If we put our trust in God, He will see us through this, just as He helped us through those acts of vandalism awhile back."

As soon as Mom and Anna left the room, Grace turned to face her father, her stomach lurching with nervous anticipation. "I'm sorry for keeping the truth from you. I know how disappointed you must be in me."

"You're right, I am disappointed and feeling more than a little *verhuddelt* right now."

"We're all confused. Anna most of all."

His gave a short nod and then headed for the door. "Luke's gone for the day, but I'm going back to work for a while." He rushed out of the house.

"You've been awful quiet since we left town," Martha commented to

Ruth as their horse and buggy rounded the bend a short distance from home.

"I've just been thinking, is all."

"What about?"

"Luke. He's been acting awful strange for a couple of months, and as time passes, he seems more tense and sometimes unfriendly toward me. It makes me wonder if he wants to break up with me, but I haven't had the nerve to ask."

Martha clicked her tongue and shook the reins to get the horse moving faster. Her stomach had been growling for the last couple of miles, and she was anxious to get home and eat supper. "If Luke were my boyfriend, I'd ask him why he's been acting so peculiar. If he really cares about you, he should be willing to share whatever's on his mind."

Ruth sighed. "I've tried talking to him about his strange behavior a couple of times, but he always changes the subject."

As they pulled into their yard, Martha was glad to see her mother's buggy parked near the barn. She was probably getting the evening meal started. Martha's stomach rumbled again, as she thought about the good food they'd soon be having.

"I'll help you put the horse away," Ruth offered. "That way we can get into the house quicker and help Mom and Grace get supper on the table."

"Danki, I appreciate that."

After the horse had been rubbed down and put into his stall, Martha and Ruth headed for the house. When they opened the back door, Martha was disappointed that no tantalizing aromas greeted them. "Guess Grace and Mom must not be at home after all," she said. "Otherwise we'd smell something."

"Maybe we're having cold sandwiches tonight," Ruth commented.

"Jah, maybe so."

When they stepped into the kitchen a few seconds later, Martha was surprised at the sight. Mom sat at the table with a young English girl. They each had glasses of milk, and the child nibbled on a cookie.

"Wie geht's?" Martha called to their mother. "Who's your little friend?"

Mom looked up and smiled, but the child kept eating, only giving Martha and Ruth a quick glance. "This is Anna, and she's going to be staying with us."

"Just 'til Poppy comes back," the child said around a mouthful of cookie.

Martha looked at Ruth, who merely shrugged. She turned back to Mom. "Who's Poppy, and where's Anna from? Don't think I've ever met her before."

Mom nodded toward the door leading to the hallway. "Grace is in the living room with your daed. It might be best if you let her explain."

Chapter 19

As Cleon headed down the road toward the Hostettlers', he glanced over at the cardboard box sitting on the seat beside him. Inside were six jars of clover honey. He'd had some extra this week and wanted to share it with his in-laws as a thank you for letting him and Grace stay with them while their house was being finished.

A horn blared behind Cleon's buggy. He looked over his shoulder and noticed several cars behind him, so he guided his horse to the shoulder of the road to let them pass. As soon as the cars went by, he pulled onto the highway again and let the horse trot for a bit.

"If only things could stay nice and calm," Cleon murmured, thinking about the Hostettlers again. He was glad they hadn't had any more problems at their place, and he hoped the troublemaker who had destroyed some of their property and stolen Roman's things never struck again.

A short time later, Cleon pulled up to Roman's barn, hopped down, and tied his horse to the hitching rail. Then he reached into the buggy, grabbed the box full of honey, and headed to the back of their house. When he stepped into the kitchen a few minutes later, he spotted Judith sitting at the table with a little English girl.

"I brought you some honey," he said, nodding at the box in his arms.

"That was. . .uh. . .real nice of you." Judith glanced over her shoulder and cleared her throat a couple of times.

He placed the box on the counter nearest the door. "Didn't realize you had company. There was no car in the driveway."

"No. . .uh. . ." Judith's forehead wrinkled. "I think you need to speak with Grace."

Cleon couldn't imagine why he would need to talk to Grace about why there wasn't a car in the driveway, but eager to be with his wife, he nodded. "Where is she?"

"In the living room."

"Okay." Cleon smiled at the young girl sitting at the table, but she never made eye contact with him. He left the room wondering why Judith was acting so strangely.

"I wish you would have told us this sooner," Ruth said, reaching over to take Grace's hand. Grace had just informed her sisters about her marriage to Wade and how she'd allowed her in-laws to take her baby girl.

Martha nodded. "We could have helped you through this, sister."

Tears welled in Grace's eyes. "I know how strongly Mom has always felt about having children, and I was afraid if she knew I had allowed someone else to raise my child, she wouldn't have understood. I was ashamed of what I'd done and thought if no one knew my secret it would be easier to deal with the guilt." She sniffed. "The way Dad reacted to my news only confirms what I suspected. He's still hurting over his sister leaving home when she was a young woman, and he's upset with me now, too."

"I really believe it would have been easier for you to deal with things if you'd had the support of your family," Ruth said.

Grace swallowed hard. "I'm not so sure. You should have seen how upset Dad was with me. I think he and Mom feel that I've cheated them out of knowing the granddaughter they should have met long before now." She drew in a quick breath. "I cheated myself—and Anna, too. Now my little girl sees me as a stranger, and I don't know if anything will ever be right for any of us again."

"You need to give your daughter some time to adjust. We'll help in any way we can. Isn't that right?" Martha asked, turning to Ruth, who sat between them.

Ruth nodded. "Of course we will."

"I'm not sure. . . ." Grace forced herself to complete her thought. "I'm not sure what I've done will be overlooked by the ministers or anyone else in our community."

"But you weren't a member of the church when you went through rumschpringe and married an Englishman, so you won't be shunned," Martha reminded.

"That's right," Ruth agreed. "You were legally married, your husband died, and you returned home and joined the Amish church."

"But I gave away my daughter and kept my previous marriage a secret. If I can't forgive myself, how can I expect others to accept what I've done?" Grace released a deep moan. "And what of Cleon? How's he going to take the news when I tell him the secret I've been keeping?"

"What secret is that, Grace?"

Grace jumped at the sound of her husband's voice, and when he strolled into the room, her heart almost stopped beating. "Cleon. I–I didn't know you were home."

"I came in the back door and stopped in the kitchen to give your mamm some honey. She said you were in here."

Grace's throat felt so swollen she could barely swallow. Had Cleon met Anna? Had Mom told him the whole story? Was that why he looked so befuddled?

Ruth stood and reached for Martha's hand. "I think we should get out to the kitchen and help Mom with supper, don't you?"

"Jah, sure." Martha glanced over her shoulder and offered Grace a reassuring smile. Then both sisters exited the room.

As soon as they were gone, Cleon took a seat on the sofa beside Grace. "There was a little English girl sitting at the kitchen table, but I didn't recognize her as one of your neighbors."

"Didn't Mom introduce you?"

He shook his head.

"Then I guess I need to explain."

"Explain what? Is she a friend of your family?"

"No, uh–"

"Where are her parents?"

Grace squeezed her eyes shut, praying that the right words would come. When she opened them again, Cleon was looking at her in a most disconcerting way.

"What's wrong, Grace? You look so unsettled."

"The little girl's name is Anna," she said in a near whisper. "I–I'm her mother."

Cleon sat with his forehead wrinkled. "What was that?"

"Anna's my daughter."

"Are you joking?"

She shook her head as tears threatened to escape. Her heart thumped furiously.

"I don't understand. How can that English girl be your daughter?"

"When I was going through my rumschpringe, before your family came to Holmes County, I moved to Cincinnati with some other Amish girls who wanted to try out the English world for a while. During the time we were living there, I worked as a waitress in a restaurant, and I. . .well, I dated an English fellow." She gulped in some air. "It was that reporter who was in town for a while, asking questions so he could write stories about our people."

"You. . .you married the reporter?" Cleon's face blanched, and his voice raised a notch.

Grace shook her head vigorously. "I finally broke up with him because he had a temper and acted like he owned me."

"Then who's the *daadi* of the little girl in the kitchen?"

"Wade Davis. He was one of Gary Walker's friends, and the two of us started dating soon after I broke up with Gary."

"So you married this Wade fellow?"

She nodded, unable to speak around the lump in her throat.

"Did your folks know about this?"

Grace shook her head. "I never told any of my family where I was during that time or that I'd gotten married and had a baby." She paused long enough to gauge Cleon's reaction. He sat stony-faced and unmoving. "A year later, Anna was born, and six months after that, my husband was killed in a car accident."

A muscle on the side of Cleon's face quivered. "Where's your daughter been all this time?"

"When Wade died, his parents came to the funeral, and the next day they took Anna away to live with them." Grace's voice trembled. "Bonnie, Wade's mother, said I was an unfit mother, and she threatened to hire a lawyer and take Anna from me if I didn't agree to let them raise her." She drew in another quick breath. "Bonnie insisted that she and Carl could give Anna a better life."

Cleon's eyebrows lifted high on his forehead. "So you gave up your child because your husband's parents said they wanted her?"

She sniffed and swiped at the tears coursing down her cheeks. "I was confused and afraid I wouldn't be able to support Anna. I was afraid my folks wouldn't understand or accept me back if I had a child."

"And your daughter's been living in Cincinnati all this time?"

Grace shook her head. "Wade's folks lived in Michigan at the time, and soon after they took Anna, I changed my mind about letting them have her. I wanted to take my little girl and go home, hoping my folks would accept me back and help raise her."

"Why didn't you?"

"I tried to contact Wade's folks, but their phone had been disconnected. The letters I wrote came back with a stamp that said they'd moved and there was no forwarding address."

"Then what did you do?"

"I moved back home but was too ashamed and too frightened of my family's reaction to admit what I'd done, so I kept the secret from everyone."

He gave a quick nod. "Including me—the man you're supposed to love and trust."

"I was afraid if I told you the truth you wouldn't understand and might not marry me."

"I thought our relationship was built on trust." He stared at the floor, slowly shaking his head. "I was sure wrong about that."

"I'm sorry, Cleon. I never meant to lie to you, but—"

He lifted his gaze and leveled her with an icy stare. "But you didn't love me enough to be honest with me? Isn't that what you're saying?"

"No. I do love you, and after Gary showed up in town, it made me rethink my decision to keep my previous marriage and daughter a secret." She choked on a sob. "I was planning to tell you, but I just couldn't do it."

"Why not?"

"When I told you about my aunt who went English, you said you could understand how my daed felt, so I assumed you would react the same way Dad did when he found out his sister married an Englisher."

Cleon's face turned bright red, and sweat darkened the sides of his hair. "So you were never going to tell me the truth?"

"I don't know."

He stood and headed for the door but then whirled around to face her again. "I can't talk about this anymore. I need time to try to figure out what to do about all this."

Grace was tempted to throw herself into his arms and beg him to stay and talk things out, but she knew Cleon well enough to realize that he needed time alone to deal with his feelings. Maybe a few hours from now they could talk about this again. Maybe by then he'd be willing to forgive her deception.

Chapter 20

As Martha and Ruth helped their mother with supper, Martha kept looking over at little Anna. She'd finished her cookies and milk and sat at the table staring at her folded hands in her lap and looking as forlorn as a lost puppy.

An idea popped into Martha's head. "Would it be all right if I take Anna out to the barn to see Heidi's hundlin?" she asked, leaning close to her mother's ear.

Mom nodded. "Jah, sure, that's a good idea. Ruth and I can finish getting the meal ready. It won't be done for another half hour or so, and that should give you plenty of time to take Anna to the barn. Oh, and if you see your daed out there, tell him supper will be on the table in about thirty minutes."

"Okay." Martha hurried over to the table and bent down so she was eye level with the child. "How would you like to walk out to the barn with me to see some cute little puppies?"

At first Anna shook her head, but then she hopped down from her chair. "Can I hold 'em?"

"Of course you can." Martha extended her hand. "We'll be back in time for supper," she called to Mom as the two of them went out the back door.

Holding tightly to Anna's hand, Martha led the way to the barn. Once inside, she called for her father, but when he didn't respond, she figured he must have gone out to his shop.

Martha directed Anna over to one of the stalls where she had moved Heidi's three remaining puppies. They'd outgrown the box soon after they were born and needed room to run around. Dad had begun working on a dog kennel for her, but it wasn't done.

Anna knelt in the straw with one of the sleepy pups nestled in her arms. Slender and willowy, with a slightly turned-up nose, the little girl reminded Martha of Grace in many ways.

A lump formed in Martha's throat as she thought of how much her sister had missed, knowing she had a daughter, believing she would never see her again, and being afraid to share her secret with them. Everyone in the family had missed out on Anna's babyhood, and it gave Martha a strange sensation to realize that she was an aunt and could have been helping raise this little girl if Grace hadn't been afraid to tell them the truth.

She knelt next to Anna and picked up one of the other puppies. "They're cute little things, aren't they?"

Anna nodded and stroked the pup's furry head. "How come you're wearin' such a long dress?" she asked, tipping her head to one side.

"Because my family and I belong to the Amish church, and we believe women should wear plain, simple dresses, not trousers like men."

Anna squinted and pursed her lips. "Poppy said you dressed different than us."

"That's right, we do, and soon your mother will make you some long dresses to wear; then you'll look like one of us, too."

Anna shook her head. "I don't wanna look like you. I wanna go home and live with Poppy."

Martha patted Anna's shoulder in a motherly fashion, wondering how the child would cope with all the changes she would face in the days to come.

Roman was about to turn down the gas lamps in his shop when the front door opened, and their bishop, Noah King, stepped in. He held a magazine in his hands, and his lips were compressed in a thin line.

"Wie geht's?" Roman asked. "What brings you by so late in the day?"

"I'm here on business, but not the woodworkin' kind," Noah replied with a curt nod.

"What's the problem?"

"This is the problem." Noah held up the magazine and waved it about. "How come you let some reporter write up a story about those break-ins a few months back? Now everyone in the country will know about them, and they'll all get a good look at your daughter, too."

"Huh?" Roman took a step closer to the bishop and squinted. "What's it say in there, and which daughter are you talking about?"

Noah huffed and then handed him the magazine. "See for yourself."

Roman's gaze came to rest on a picture of Grace standing near an Amish buggy that he assumed had been parked in Berlin, because he could see the drugstore and Christian bookstore in the background. His hands shook as he read the article telling about the break-ins that had occurred on their property. "I wonder how the reporter was able to take Grace's picture and get all these facts. And why after all this time is the story coming out?"

"You don't know who gave him the facts?"

"Of course not. What'd you think–that I volunteered all this information?"

The bishop shrugged. "Figured it might have been Grace, since she must have let the man take her picture."

Roman shook his head vigorously. "I'm sure none of my family would give any reporter information such as this, much less pose for a picture."

"Then how'd the article get written up, and how'd the man get this?" Noah's long finger tapped the picture of Grace as he noisily clucked his tongue.

"I have no idea. Someone outside the family must have told that fellow about the break-ins, but I'm sure it wasn't Grace. I'm equally sure she didn't agree to him taking her picture." Roman handed the magazine back to Noah. "How'd you come across this anyway?"

"One of my English neighbors subscribes to the magazine, and he gave it to me." Noah gave his beard a couple of quick pulls. "Sure hope this won't lead to more attacks for you or any of our other people."

Roman's forehead wrinkled. "You think it could?"

"Well, the one who was responsible for your break-ins might read this and decide to do it again because he's getting free publicity. Or someone else might get the idea that if the person who did this got away with it, maybe he can, too." Noah tapped the magazine again. "It says in the article that the sheriff wasn't called, so someone might think they could do whatever they wanted and never get caught."

"You think I should have called the sheriff?"

"*Nee*. I'm only sayin' this article isn't a good thing."

Roman slowly shook his head. "Didn't think this day could get much worse, but it surely has."

"What's wrong? Has there been another break-in?"

"No, but thanks to my oldest daughter and the secret she decided to keep from us these past four and a half years, things are more verhuddelt around here than ever."

Noah's bushy eyebrows drew together. "What kind of secret would Grace be keeping from you?"

Roman pulled out the chair behind his desk and another that sat near one of the workbenches. "Have a seat, and I'll tell you about it."

"Where's Anna?" Grace asked, as she rushed into the kitchen, hoping to find comfort in her daughter's arms.

"She's gone out to the barn with Martha to look at the puppies." Mom turned from the stove, where she had poured some green beans into a kettle. "Where's Cleon? Is he still in the living room?"

Grace winced. "He's gone."

"Gone where?"

"I–I'm not sure. Just said he was leaving and rushed out of the house."

"Did you tell him about Anna?" Ruth, who had been setting the table, questioned.

Grace nodded and steadied herself against the cupboard door. "He. . .he didn't take the news well." With a childlike cry, she hurried across the room, burying her face against her mother's chest. "Oh,

Mom, I'm afraid I've ruined things between me and Cleon. I–I'm sorry I didn't tell everyone the truth right away. How I wish I could change the past, for if I could, I would never have let Wade's folks take Anna away. I would have raised her myself, no matter how hard it might have been."

Mom massaged Grace's shoulders as she rocked her gently back and forth, the way she'd done when she was a child in need of comfort. "It's going to be all right; you'll see. We'll get through this together."

"But you didn't see Cleon's face when I told him the news. He looked so angry and hurt."

"I'm sure in time Cleon will realize that you didn't keep your secret in order to hurt him," Ruth interjected.

Grace stepped back and wiped her nose on the handkerchief Mom handed her. "No, I didn't, but that doesn't mean he'll ever forgive me."

"Cleon loves you, Grace, and I doubt he'll stay mad for long. If he's the kind of man he seems to be, then he'll not only forgive as the Bible says we should do, but he'll be willing to help you raise Anna."

Grace tried to smile but failed miserably. She was so happy to have Anna back, but it seemed like nothing in her life would ever be right again.

"Come, have a seat at the table, and I'll fix you a cup of tea," her mother said.

Grace nodded numbly and pulled out a chair. She'd just taken a seat when the back door opened, and her father stepped into the kitchen followed by Bishop King. Her heart pounded. Had Dad told the bishop about Anna? Had he come here to reprimand Grace for keeping such a secret?

"*Gut-n-owed*, Grace," the bishop said, moving across the room to the table.

"Good evening, Bishop King."

"I came by your daed's shop to tell him about an article that has your picture in it."

Dad stepped forward, waving a magazine in the air. "Did you pose for this, Grace?" he asked accusingly. He plunked the magazine on the table, and Grace gasped.

"I—I didn't pose for that picture. The reporter just snapped it without my permission." She swallowed hard. "I didn't know he was going to use it in a magazine article, either."

"Many people take pictures of us Amish without asking, especially reporters." The bishop pulled out the chair next to Grace and lowered himself into it. "Your daed tells me you have a daughter you've been keeping a secret. I came up to the house thinking you might want to talk about it."

Grace nodded as shame and remorse settled over her like a heavy quilt. "I—I know it was wrong to keep such a secret, but I was afraid my folks wouldn't accept the fact that I'd once been married to an English man, and that they wouldn't understand why I had allowed his parents to raise my child after he died."

Grace's mother moved over to the table, placing her hands on Grace's shoulders as if to offer some comfort. But her father stood with his arms folded, leaning against the cupboard door across the room.

"It would have been much better if you'd been up-front about this from the beginning," the bishop said, "but the past is in the past, and nothing's going to change what's been done." He touched Grace's arm. "Since you weren't a member of the church when this all took place, there's no need for a public confession. However, I do hope you've learned a lesson from your mistake and that you'll never lie or keep secrets from anyone again."

"No. No, I won't." Grace's eyes filled with tears, blurring her vision. "I just want my family's support as I try to help my daughter adjust to a new way of life."

"I'm sure you shall have that, and you can call on me or any of the other ministers for counsel should you feel the need."

Dad said nothing, but Mom gave Grace's shoulders another comforting squeeze. Now, if she could just get through to Cleon, she would feel some hope for the future.

For the past twenty minutes, Cleon had been sitting on the floor in the middle of what would soon be their new living room, thinking about the secret Grace had kept from him and wondering what he should do. He felt betrayed, humiliated, and confused. How could she have kept her previous marriage from him? And what about the daughter she'd allowed someone else to raise? What kind of mother would give up her own child and keep such a secret from her family and the man she was supposed to love?

He scooped up a handful of sawdust from the floor and let it sift through his fingers. "If she'd only told me about this before we were married." He winced as the truth slammed into him with the force of stampeding horses. If Grace had told him the truth, he probably wouldn't have married her. It wasn't his job to raise another man's child—especially a man who didn't share their faith.

He stood and began to pace, going from the front window to the stone fireplace and back again. What he really wanted to do was run away from this problem, but where would he go—back home to live with his folks? What would he tell them? That his wife had a child she'd been keeping from him, and that he felt betrayed and wasn't sure he could forgive her? Cleon knew that divorce wasn't an option and that he needed to figure out a way to deal with Grace's deception, but he also knew it wouldn't be easy.

The back door opened and shut, and he whirled around. Grace entered the room. Her face was red, and the skin around her eyes looked puffy as though she'd been crying. Under different circumstances, he would have reached out to her and offered comfort.

"I was hoping that I would find you here," she said, moving toward him.

He took a step back.

"We need to talk."

"I think we've already said all that needs to be said."

She reached her hand out to him. "I need you to understand why I kept the truth from you about Anna."

"I don't care about your reasons. You obviously don't love me enough to be truthful."

"That's not true. I do love you, Cleon." Grace's voice broke, and she swiped at the tears running down her cheeks. "I–I was afraid of how you would respond, and the way you're acting now tells me what your reaction would have been if I'd told you sooner."

Cleon shook his head. "I'm reacting to you not telling me about your secret."

"So you're not upset about me having been married before or having a daughter you knew nothing about?"

He turned away. "I'm very upset, and I can't talk about this now."

"But we need to talk things through. We need–"

"I want to be left alone." He moved toward the door and pulled it open. "I'll be spending the night here, so you may as well go home to your folks–and your daughter."

"Cleon, please–"

Once more, he shook his head. "I don't want to talk about this right now. Please, just go."

Grace gulped on a sob, turned, and fled from the room.

Chapter 21

It was difficult for Grace to get ready for church the next morning, but she knew she must. When she'd put Anna in bed with her last night, the child had cried herself to sleep. Cleon had apparently followed through on his intention to spend the night in their unfinished house, because he'd never returned to her folks' home.

"Anna, wake up. It's time to get dressed and ready for church." Grace leaned over the bed and gently shook the child's shoulders.

Anna moaned but didn't open her eyes.

"You need to get up and have some breakfast."

Anna finally opened her eyes, which looked red and swollen. "Poppy. I want Poppy," she murmured.

"I know you do, but your poppy had to go home. He's sick and can't take care of you now, so he brought you to me."

Before putting the child to bed, Grace had tried to explain to Anna about her father dying and Grace agreeing to let his parents raise her baby girl because she was young and confused. The look of bewilderment on Anna's face told Grace that the child didn't fully understand, but with time and patience, she hoped to gain her daughter's approval.

Grace opened Anna's suitcase. Carl had packed plenty of winter clothes—several pairs of jeans, some sweaters, blouses, underwear, a pair of tennis shoes, snow boots, white patent leather shoes, slippers, a nightgown, and two pretty dresses—nothing suitable for an Amish child to wear to church. *But she's not really Amish*, Grace reminded herself. *It will take some time for her to feel as if she's one of us*.

"Anna, I believe your grandma is making pancakes for breakfast this morning. So let's hurry downstairs so we can have some."

Anna jerked the covers over her head. "Grandma's gone. Poppy said so."

Grace pulled them gently aside. "I was talking about my mother, Grandma Hostettler."

Anna just lay staring at the ceiling as her eyes filled with tears.

Grace wanted to take the child in her arms and offer comfort, but she'd tried that last night and Anna had become hysterical. So she just stood there feeling as helpless as a newborn calf. When a knock on the bedroom door sounded, Grace hurried across the room, hoping it was Cleon. Martha stood in the hallway.

"I came to see if Anna wants to help me feed Heidi and Fritz," Martha said, peering around Grace and into the room.

Anna shot out of bed before Grace could offer a reply. "Can I hold one of the puppies again?" Her pink flannel nightgown edged with fancy lace hung just below her knees, exposing her bare legs and feet, and her long brown hair was a mass of tangles. But for the first time, Grace saw a hopeful expression on her daughter's face.

Martha leaned down so she was at eye level with the child. "As soon as we're done feeding the dogs, you can hold a puppy."

"Let's go then!" Anna started out the door, but Grace caught her arm. "You can't go outside dressed like that. It's cold, and you need to put some clothes on first."

Anna hurried back across the room, flipped open her suitcase, and removed a pair of jeans and a turtleneck sweater.

While the child dressed, Grace stepped into the hallway to talk to Martha. "I looked through the clothes Anna's grandfather packed for her, and she's got nothing to wear to church except for some fancy dresses and blue jeans. I wish I still had some of the dresses I wore as a child, but they were passed on to Ruth after I outgrew them, and if they were still in good condition, they became yours."

Martha tipped her head. "All my childhood clothes are gone. Once I couldn't wear them anymore, Mom gave them to one of our younger cousins."

"I guess she'll have to go to church wearing one of her fancy dresses," Grace said, "but tomorrow I'll get busy and make her a few plain dresses."

When Cleon stepped into the Hostettlers' kitchen, he realized that they'd already eaten breakfast and that Grace and her mother were doing the dishes.

Grace turned to look at him, her eyes puffy and rimmed with dark circles. Apparently, she hadn't slept any better than he had last night. Cleon had bedded down on the floor of their unfinished living room, using the sleeping bag he'd kept there for times when he'd been working late on the house and had decided to spend the night. Besides the fact that the floor was hard and unyielding, his only source of heat had come from the stone fireplace that had been completed a few weeks ago.

Cleon had lain awake for hours, mulling things over and fretting about the secret Grace had kept from him. When he'd finally succumbed to sleep, he'd slept fitfully and much longer than he should have. Since today was Sunday, and he would be expected to be at the preaching service at the home of Mose and Saloma Esh, he had to go to the Hostettlers' in order to get cleaned up and dressed for church. He'd also intended to get some much-needed breakfast.

"We've already had breakfast, but I'd be happy to fix you something to eat," Judith offered, making no mention of where he'd spent the night. Why hadn't Grace offered to fix his breakfast? She was his wife, after all.

"I'll just have some coffee and toast, but I can get it myself," he mumbled.

Judith shrugged and turned back to the sink, but Grace didn't say a word. Was she angry with him for sleeping at their new house? Well, he was the one who had a right to be angry, not her. If it weren't for Grace's deception, everything would be fine, and they would have slept warm and toasty in their bed together last night.

Cleon glanced around the room. "Where are the others?" What

he really wanted to know was where Grace's English child was. He'd had such a brief encounter with her last evening, he couldn't even remember if he'd been told her name.

"Roman's out in the barn getting a horse hitched to the buggy, Ruth is upstairs changing into her church dress, and Martha's helping Anna get ready."

Cleon pulled his fingers through the beard he'd begun growing since his marriage and ambled to the stove. He didn't know how he could go to church and act as if everything was okay when his world had been turned topsy-turvy, yet he had no legitimate excuse for staying home. So he would do the right thing and drive his wife and her daughter to church, but he didn't have to like it.

The ride to church seemed to take forever, and it wasn't because the Eshes lived far away. Fact was, Mose Esh's place was only a couple miles from the Hostettlers', but the tension Grace felt between Cleon and her made the trip seem twice as long. Her husband kept his gaze straight ahead as he guided their horse and buggy down the road. He didn't say a word. Except for an occasional deep sigh, followed by a couple of sniffs, Anna was quiet, too.

Grace wasn't sure what she should say to others in their community about the daughter they didn't know she had, and she didn't know how well they would accept Anna or how well Anna would accept them. When they pulled up to the Eshes' barn, she climbed down quickly and reached for Anna. Then, forcing a smile, she took the child's hand and led her toward a group of women who stood on the front porch talking with Mose's wife, Saloma.

"Now who's this little girl?" Saloma asked as Grace stepped onto the porch with Anna.

"She. . .she's my daughter."

"Your what?" Saloma's mouth dropped open, and several of the other women gaped at Grace as if she'd taken leave of her senses.

Grace needed to explain Anna's appearance, but she didn't want to do it front of the child. She was relieved when she spotted Ruth and

Martha talking to some of the younger women nearby. "Excuse me a minute," she said, stepping off the porch with Anna in tow. "Would you two look after Anna until church starts?" she whispered in Ruth's ear.

"Don't you think it would be best if she stayed with you?"

Grace shook her head. "Not while I explain to Saloma and the other women who Anna is."

"She can come with me," Martha spoke up. "I'll introduce her to Esta Wengerd and some of the other children who are close to her age."

Grace blew out a sigh of relief. At least one problem was solved.

Chapter 22

As Grace stood in the hallway outside Martha's open door, staring at her sleeping daughter, a lump formed in her throat. Anna had been with them almost two weeks, and she still hadn't accepted Grace as her mother. The child barely looked at her and spoke only when spoken to. Yet Anna seemed to have accepted Martha fairly well, even sleeping in Martha's room and spending all her free time in the barn with Martha and the puppies.

Anna continued to ask for her poppy and often complained because she wanted to watch TV and wear blue jeans instead of the plain dresses Grace had sewn for her, but she'd done better in church yesterday than she had two weeks ago. She hadn't squirmed so much on the hard benches and had even frolicked around the yard after the noon meal with her new friend, Esta, and some of the other children.

Grace had been relieved that the other women at church had been kind and understanding about the situation when she explained it to them. If only her husband and father could be that accepting.

She released a heavy sigh. It didn't seem fair that the two men she loved most seemed so unforgiving, and it wasn't fair that due to Anna's unwillingness to accept her, she was still being deprived of her daughter's love. Grace's only consolation was that Anna was here and didn't cry for her Grandpa Davis as often. Maybe in time, the child would adjust to her new surroundings and learn to love Grace. Maybe with prayer, Cleon and Dad would decide to forgive her, too.

For the last two weeks, Cleon had kept his distance—going to his folks' place to tend his bees early every morning, making honey deliveries the rest of the day, and sleeping on a mattress in the middle of the living room floor in their future home, rather than at the Hostettlers' house with Grace. She wondered if anything would ever be right between them again.

When Grace entered the downstairs hallway a few minutes later, she met Ruth, who had just come in through the back doorway.

"Shouldn't you have left for work by now?" she asked her sister.

"I was getting ready to head out when Cleon stopped me." Ruth handed Grace an envelope. "He wanted me to give you this."

"What is it?"

"I don't know. He said he was on his way to town and asked if I would see that you got it."

Grace's heart raced with hope. Maybe Cleon had forgiven her. Maybe he wanted to make things right between them.

"Well, I'd better go, or I'll be late getting to the bakeshop." Ruth gave Grace a hug and went back out.

Grace stood in the doorway and watched Ruth guide the horse and buggy down the driveway. Then she took a seat on the sofa and opened Cleon's note.

Dear Grace,

I've spent the last two weeks thinking about our relationship and wondering why you didn't love me enough to tell me about your previous marriage and the child you had given up. I can't say how I would have responded if I'd known the truth sooner, but I know how I'm feeling now. I feel betrayed, hurt, and angry. I need more time to deal with this, and I can't do it here where we see each other every day.

I have an opportunity to expand my honey deliveries to some places in Pennsylvania, so I've decided to catch a bus and head there. Ivan will care for my bees while I'm gone, and it will give me a chance to think things through.

As Always,
Cleon

Grace gulped on a sob as she crumpled the letter into a tight ball. What if Cleon never came back? What if—

"Daughter, what's wrong? Why are you crying?"

Grace looked up and saw her mother standing over her, a worried expression knitting her brows.

Releasing more sobs between every couple of words, Grace shared the letter Cleon had written. "I'm afraid I may have driven him away, and now nothing in my life will ever be any good."

Mom took a seat on the sofa and gathered Grace into her arms. "God brought your daughter back to you, and that's a good thing."

Grace nodded.

"After your visit with the bishop the night Anna arrived, he offered you words of comfort and acceptance."

She nodded again.

"The people in our community have been friendly to Anna and tried to make her feel welcome."

"Jah."

"You need to trust God with Cleon. I'm sure that in time your husband will come around, too."

"I—I hope so." Grace sniffed. "Anna may have been returned to me, but she doesn't accept me as her mother. She doesn't seem to want anything to do with me."

"She needs more time to adjust and get to know you better."

Grace reached for the box of tissues sitting on the table next to the sofa. She dabbed her eyes and blew her nose. "That doesn't solve things between Cleon and me. I'm afraid he might decide to leave the Amish faith and begin a new life in the English world without me."

"That's ridiculous. Cleon would never leave the faith or risk a shunning by deciding to do something so unthinkable as to dissolve your marriage." Mom gently patted Grace's back. "He's strong in his beliefs, and I'm sure that deep down, he loves you. Just give him some time to sort things out, and soon he'll be home again."

Grace moaned. "Dad's angry with me, too—not only because of the secret I kept from you, but because he blames me for that magazine article Gary Walker wrote."

Mom shook her head. "Now how can that be your fault?"

"I'm the one who told Gary about our break-ins. I figured he'd forgotten about it because I'd heard he had gone to Pennsylvania to write some stories about the Amish there."

"I see."

"I was as surprised as anyone when that story came out, and when Dad told us about the article and picture the bishop showed him, I believed it would be best to admit that I'd spoken to the reporter." She lifted the tissue to her face and blew her nose again.

"But there were details in the article that you never mentioned to the reporter, right?"

Grace nodded. "That's true, but if Gary is the one responsible for our break-ins, he would have already known everything that happened to us."

"Or someone else might have told him."

"Like who?"

Mom shrugged. "I don't know, but others in our community knew about the break-ins. One of them might have spoken to the reporter and told him the details you left out."

"Maybe so. All I know is when someone makes a decision about something important, the way I did when I allowed Wade's folks to take Anna, it can change their life forever." Grace slowly shook her head. "That's what happens when people don't think about the effect their decisions will have on others. If I'd known that giving up my little girl and keeping it a secret would have affected my family so much, I would have done things differently."

"That's how life goes—we learn and grow from our mistakes."

"And hope we don't make them again," Grace murmured.

"We shouldn't merely hope. We need to ask God to guide us in all our decisions."

Grace nodded. She knew Mom was right, for if she'd sought God's will in the first place, she wouldn't be in the mess she was in right now.

"Martha's gone to Kidron with your daed to look at a pair of beagles, so why don't we hire a driver to take us to the Wal-Mart store in Millersburg and get your daughter some appropriate shoes?"

Grace shook her head. "I don't feel like going anywhere, Mom. Why don't you and Anna go? It'll give you a chance to get better acquainted."

"I don't think staying home feeling sorry for yourself is going to solve anything. I really wish you'd come along."

"I'd rather not."

Mom shrugged. "All right then. Maybe some time alone is what you need."

A short time later, Judith and Anna were on their way to Millersburg in Donna Larson's car. As soon as they entered the Wal-Mart, Anna pointed to the mechanical horse inside the entrance. "I wanna horsey ride!"

Judith gave the child's hand a gentle tug. "Maybe on our way out." She'd hoped, as Grace had suggested, that this would be a chance for her and Anna to get better acquainted.

"I wanna ride the horsey now."

"Not until we finish our shopping." Judith grabbed a shopping cart, scooped Anna into her arms, and placed her inside the cart.

"I don't want new shoes. Let me out. I want out!"

"You might get tired if you walk. It's better that you ride inside the cart."

Anna scrunched up her nose and crossed her arms.

Judith sighed and headed for the shoe department. Anna needed a sturdy pair of dress shoes, and they had to be plain and black. The other day, they'd looked at the boot and harness shop run by their friend Abe Wengerd but found nothing in Anna's size.

A short time later, Judith found a pair of appropriate-looking black shoes for the child and was about to move on to do some other shopping when Anna shouted, "I don't want these shoes! They're ugly, and I won't wear 'em."

Judith drew in a deep breath and prayed for patience. "I know you're upset about the shoes, and I understand that being left with strangers has been hard on you, but I won't tolerate such outbursts, Anna." She bent over so she was at eye level with the child. "Do you understand?"

Anna nodded but said nothing. She sat like a statue with her arms folded, staring straight ahead.

Judith gritted her teeth and maneuvered the cart down the toothpaste aisle. When she finished the rest of her shopping, she went to the nearest checkout stand, paid for her purchases, and pushed the shopping cart toward the door. They'd no sooner left the checkout counter when Anna started hollering, "Horsey! Horsey! I wanna ride the horsey!"

"Shh. I told you before you mustn't yell." Judith wondered what the other shoppers must think seeing a child dressed in plain clothes carrying on in such a manner. Amish children were taught at an early age to behave in public. But of course, none of the people staring at them had any idea Anna hadn't grown up Amish. How different things might have been for all of them if the child had been a part of their family from the time she was a baby.

When an ear-piercing buzzer went off, Anna let out a yelp. Judith halted outside the first set of doors where the scanners were located. She figured the security alarm had been triggered because the clerk who'd rung up her purchases had forgotten to remove the security strip from one of the items. A few seconds later, a clerk rushed over, demanding to see Judith's receipt and then searching her packages. Throughout the entire process, Anna fussed and cried for a horsey ride, which only caused Judith further embarrassment.

When the clerk found nothing in any of the packages, she turned to Judith and said, "You'd better let me see that purse you're holding."

Her forehead wrinkled. "Why would you need to see this? I didn't buy it here. It was a gift from my sister who lives in Indiana, and I was carrying it when I came into the store."

"Our scanners are set up to check for security strips on things going out of the store, not coming in," the clerk said. "Now, are you going to let me see that purse, or do I need to call my supervisor?"

Judith's head began to pound, and as Anna's screams increased in volume, she felt as if she could shriek at someone herself. Gritting her teeth, she handed over the purse.

The clerk snapped it open, and after a few seconds of rummaging around, she said, "I found the problem." She held up a small metallic strip. "This was stuck to the lining of your purse and must not have been removed when your sister purchased it. Since it's full of your personal things, it's obviously yours."

Judith sighed in relief, and miraculously, Anna stopped crying.

"I'm sorry for your trouble, ma'am," the clerk said with a sheepish-looking smile. "This kind of thing doesn't happen often, but we need to check things out to be sure nothing leaves the store that hasn't been paid for."

"I understand." On shaky legs, Judith pushed the cart toward the front door, anxious to get out to the car where Donna waited. Before she could exit the last set of doors, Anna stood up in the cart and hollered, "Horsey ride! Please, Grandma."

Judith halted and reached over to give the little girl a hug. Something good had come from this otherwise stressful shopping trip: Anna had called her "Grandma." Maybe the child would call Grace "Mama" soon. Oh, how she hoped so.

"Anna's asleep," Martha said, as she entered the kitchen later that evening.

Grace looked up from the letter she'd been writing and frowned. "I tried to get her to sleep with me tonight, but she cried and insisted on sleeping in your room again. It doesn't look like she's ever going to accept me as her mother."

Mom, who sat across from Grace drinking a cup of tea, shook her head. "I think you're wrong about that. I didn't say anything before because I didn't want to embarrass Anna in front of everyone during supper, but this afternoon as we were leaving Wal-Mart, she called me 'Grandma.' "

Grace set her pen aside and reached for her own cup of tea, letting the warmth of it seep through her cold fingers. "I'm glad to hear that, but just because Anna seems to have accepted you as her grossmudder and Martha as her *aendi* doesn't mean she will ever accept me."

Martha pulled out the chair next to Grace and sat down. "You need to remember that the only mother Anna's ever known was her grandma Davis. Now that the woman is dead and her grandpa left her with people she'd never met before, the poor little thing doesn't know where she belongs or who she can trust."

"I think your sister's right about that," Mom said with a nod. "I believe you need to work at gaining Anna's trust. If you spend as much time with her as you can, she'll learn that she can trust you, and eventually she'll begin calling you 'Mama.' "

Martha poured herself a cup of tea. "The only reason Anna has taken to me is because of the hundlin. She enjoys playing with them, and it's given us something to do together."

"Speaking of puppies," Grace said, "how'd things go with you and Dad in Kidron? Did you see any dogs you liked?"

Martha nodded, and her blue eyes fairly sparkled. "Found me a pair of beagle hounds for breeding. The male is named Bo, and his mate's name is Flo."

"They sound more like twins than mates."

Martha chuckled. "I think Anna will like the beagles as much as she does Heidi, Fritz, and the pups."

Tears trickled down Grace's cheeks, and she plucked a napkin from the wicker basket on the table and wiped them away. "It hurts so much to know that Anna's accepting you but not me."

Mom reached over and touched Grace's arm. "Maybe if you can find something Anna's interested in, it might do the trick."

"Jah, maybe so. It doesn't look like I'll be spending my free time with Cleon anymore." Grace choked back a sob. "He gave Ruth a note for me this morning, and it wasn't good news."

"What'd it say?" Martha asked.

"He said he was catching a bus and would be going to some places in Pennsylvania where he wants to sell his honey."

"I'm sure he won't be gone long," her sister said.

"I agree," Mom put in. "Cleon will be back before you know it."

"As I'm sure you know, he's been sleeping on the floor in our unfinished house because he's still upset that I didn't tell him the truth about Wade and Anna sooner. I'm afraid he left because of that more than a need to sell honey." A sense of hopelessness welled in Grace's soul.

"I knew he'd been sleeping there," Martha said, "but I thought it was because he wanted to work on the place late at night and early in the morning. I never dreamed it was to get away from you."

"Cleon said he needs time to think about things, and I guess he feels he can't do that here where he would see me and Anna every day."

"Oh, Grace, I'm so sorry. Why didn't you say something about this sooner?"

Grace sniffed, picked up the napkin again, and blew her nose. "I told Mom about Cleon's letter this morning, but I haven't mentioned it to anyone else because I didn't think Anna needed to hear things she wouldn't understand."

Martha placed her hand in the small of Grace's back and gently massaged it. "Maybe it's good that Cleon will be gone awhile. It will give you more time to spend with Anna. I'm sure that after he's had a chance to think things over, he'll realize his place is here with you."

"I hope you're right." Grace stood up and walked toward the hallway.

"Where are you going?" Mom asked.

"Upstairs to check on Anna."

"I told you she's asleep," Martha said.

"I just want to be sure she's okay."

"Will you join us for some popcorn and hot apple cider afterward?" Mom called. "Your daed will be joining us when he's done with his chores in the barn."

Grace gave a quick nod, then rushed out of the room.

Chapter 23

It's been awhile since I've ridden in your buggy," Ruth said as she and Luke headed down the road in his open courting buggy. It was a brisk, windy evening, and she felt grateful for the quilt wrapped around her legs.

Luke looked over at her and smiled. "I'm glad you were free to go with me this evening."

"Me, too."

"Your daed says things are hectic at your house right now, what with Grace's secret daughter showing up and all."

She nodded. "That's why I haven't felt free to go anywhere with you. I wanted to be around home every evening so I could get to know Anna better and help Grace deal with things. It's been quite a shock to have her daughter show up the way she did."

"I imagine."

"Almost every day Anna asks about her other grandpa, wondering when he's coming back for her."

"He's not, though, right?"

"Maybe for a visit." Ruth sighed. "Even though Anna seems to be adjusting in some ways, she doesn't like doing without some of the modern things she's used to. She isn't accepting Grace as her mamm very well, either."

"I'm sure in time she'll be okay."

"I hope so." She lifted her gaze toward the starry sky. It was a clear winter night, and the stars looked so bright and close she felt as if she could reach out and touch them.

"Your daed told me that you've had no more break-ins at your place, but he's worried there might be more because of the magazine article about the troubles you had."

"I think Dad's more concerned about the article bringing attention to the Amish in this area than he is with trying to find out who attacked us."

"Maybe it's best that he doesn't find out."

"What do you mean?"

"If someone in your family started snooping around, trying to play detective, somebody might end up getting hurt."

Ruth blinked as a feeling of dread crept up her spine. She knew Grace had been trying to find out if the English reporter might have been responsible for the break-ins, but the last she'd heard, Gary was gone, so Grace would no longer be asking him questions and putting herself at risk.

"Your daed's a stubborn man; that much I know," Luke said. "We've butted heads about the way I do my work, and he won't listen to reason when I try to show him something new I'd like to try. He's gotten upset with me for being late to work a couple of times or taking longer to get a delivery made. Even docked my pay once because he blamed me for some cabinets that fell off the wagon and got busted." He grunted. "Makes me wonder if I shouldn't try to find another job."

"Has someone offered you a better job?"

"Not yet, but I'm good with my hands, and I'm sure somebody would be willing to hire me as a carpenter."

Ruth hated to think of Luke quitting work for her father, but if he decided to go, she couldn't do much about it. "Let's talk about something else, shall we? This is supposed to be a fun evening, and discussing my daed's business isn't much fun."

Luke reached for her hand. "You're right. Your daed's not my favorite subject, either."

Her face flamed. "I didn't say that—"

He let go of her hand and slipped his arm around her shoulder.

"Getting back to that reporter fellow, do you have any idea who gave him the information he used in that article or how he got Grace's picture?"

She shrugged. "Grace admitted that she'd told him a few things, but she never posed for the picture. He took it without her permission. She believes he might have gotten the rest of his story from someone else in our community."

"Like who?"

"I have no idea."

"Who else knew about the break-ins?"

Ruth pursed her lips. "Let me see. Dad told Bishop King and a couple of our Amish neighbors about them. Grace told Cleon, and then I mentioned it to one of our English neighbors when she came into the bakeshop." She looked over at Luke. "Of course, you knew."

"I never talked to that reporter, so I hope you're not accusing me of anything." Luke's voice raised a notch, and he gave the reins a quick snap, causing the horse to pick up speed. "Giddy-up, there, boy."

"I wasn't accusing you."

"Sure sounded like it to me."

"You asked who else knew about the break-ins, and I answered."

He frowned. "Jah, well, I thought maybe you didn't trust me, that's all."

"Of course I trust you." Ruth flinched as the words rolled off her tongue. For some time she'd felt uneasy whenever she was with Luke. She wasn't sure if it was mistrust or simply confusion because he acted so odd at times. It was almost as if he was hiding something, but she didn't know what it could be.

She thought about the day she and Sadie had met Toby and Luke for a picnic, and how Luke had been late but wouldn't explain why. She thought about that morning when she and Martha had seen Luke outside the market in Berlin talking to a couple of English fellows. He'd acted strange then, too, not even bothering to introduce her.

"I've been wondering about something," she said, gathering up her courage.

"What's that?"

"A few months ago when Martha and I saw you outside the market talking to a couple of English fellows, you seemed kind of edgy and acted like you barely knew me."

His forehead wrinkled. "I don't know what you're talkin' about. Fact is, I barely remember the incident. I'm sure I wasn't acting edgy or said I didn't know you."

"I said you *acted* like you barely knew me."

He removed his arm from around her shoulders and gave the reins another snap. "I was busy, and you probably interrupted my conversation."

Ruth looked away, feeling like a glass of water had been dashed in her face. The passing scenery became a blur as tears stung the back of her eyes. "I wish you would slow down, Luke. The road could be icy, and it makes me naerfich to be going this fast."

"I'm a good driver. There's nothing to be nervous about."

"There have been too many buggy accidents on this road, and the way you're driving could set us up for one."

"You're turning out to be just like your sister Grace, you know that?"

"What's that supposed to mean?"

"You both worry too much."

Ruth folded her arms and compressed her lips. She had a good mind to tell Luke to turn his buggy around and take her home. And if he said one more unkind thing, that's exactly what she would do.

They rode in silence for the next several miles; then Luke reached for her hand and gave her fingers a little squeeze. "I'm sorry for snapping at you. I know most women tend to worry about things—my mamm most of all."

"I never used to worry so much," Ruth admitted. "But when the vandalism went on at our place, I began feeling anxious about many things."

"Guess that's understandable."

Ruth moistened her lips and decided to bring up the previous subject again. "Mind if I ask what you and those English fellows were talking about in the parking lot that day?"

He stared at her in such a strange way it sent chills up her spine. "I can't believe you're bringing something up that happened months ago."

"I wanted to talk to you about it before, but every time I started to, you changed the subject."

He shrugged.

"So I'm asking now, and I'd really like an answer."

"I'd rather not say."

"Why? Is it because you have something to hide?"

Luke's face turned bright red. "I've got nothin' to hide."

"Then why won't you tell me what was being said?"

"Because it's not important."

"What about that day at the pond with Sadie and Toby?"

"What about it?"

"How come you acted so strange and said you were late because you'd stopped in the woods? What did you really stop for, Luke?"

He slowed the horse and released a grunt. "Promise you won't say anything to anyone?"

She nodded, although it made her feel uneasy to make such a promise. What if Luke had been doing something wrong? If she knew about it and kept quiet, wouldn't that mean she was doing something wrong, too?

"If you really must know, I bought myself a truck last summer, and I've been keeping it hidden in the woods so my folks won't know."

Ruth compressed her lips tightly together. So that must have been Luke's truck she and Sadie had seen the day they'd been walking in the woods.

"Now, don't give me that face," he said, wagging his finger. "I'm still in rumschpringe, and I've every right to drive a motorized vehicle if I want to."

"If you think it's fine and dandy, then why hide it from your folks?"

Luke stared straight ahead and shrugged.

"Are you planning to leave the Amish faith?" Ruth dared to ask. She had to know what his plans were, for it could affect their relationship.

He shrugged again.

"Luke, would you please answer my question?"

"Haven't made up my mind yet."

Ruth leaned against the narrow seat and closed her eyes. This whole evening had gone sour, and from the looks of things, it wasn't going to get any better. "I think it would be good if you took me home now," she muttered.

"Whatever you say." Luke directed the horse to make a U-turn.

They rode the rest of the way in silence, and when they pulled into Ruth's yard, she turned to him and said, "I think it would be best if we don't see each other anymore."

His eyebrows lifted high on his forehead. "Now what brought that on?"

"If you don't care enough for me to answer my questions, then I think–"

"I did answer your questions. Well, most of 'em, anyway."

"If you decided to go English, we'd have to break up because I could never leave the Amish faith."

A spot on the right side of his face twitched, and he looked away. "Maybe you're right. Maybe we should go our separate ways before someone gets hurt."

"Jah, I agree. *Gut nacht*, Luke."

"Good night."

Ruth stepped down from the buggy onto the frost-covered grass and shivered. It wasn't until she reached the back porch that she allowed her tears to flow. It had been a mistake to let someone like Luke court her, and she almost felt relief that it was over.

Grace sank into a chair at the kitchen table, where Martha sat with their parents. Dad was reading *The Budget*; Mom had the newest issue of *Country Magazine*; and Martha was doing a crossword puzzle. A bowl of popcorn sat in the center of the table, and they each had cups of hot cider.

"Was Anna asleep when you checked on her?" Martha asked.

Grace nodded with a weary sigh. "I wish she was willing to sleep in my room. Anna, my own flesh-and-blood daughter, wants as little to do with me as possible. She talks more to her new friend, Esta, than she does me."

She blinked, willing her tears not to spill over. She'd shed enough tears since the little girl had come to live with them—tears over Anna not accepting her as mother, tears over Cleon's refusal to forgive her, tears over her own shame and regrets.

"It will get better in time—you'll see," Mom said with a look of understanding.

"I don't think anything will ever be better for me." Grace's head ached, her emotions were spent, and a sense of despair threatened to pull her down. "I–I'm afraid Cleon's never coming back."

Dad's head came up. "Why would you say something like that? Have you heard from him again?"

"I got a letter this morning."

"What'd it say?"

"He's asked his brother Ivan to check on his bees and collect the honey because he's going to be on the road a few more weeks, trying to line up several new customers."

"That makes sense to me," Martha put in. "Someone's got to take care of the bees while he's gone."

"But what if Cleon never comes back? What if—"

"He'll be back. He's just trying to drum up more business so he can provide better for you and Anna," Mom said.

Grace shook her head as tears coursed down her cheeks, despite her effort to keep them at bay.

Mom patted Grace gently on the back. "I'm sorry for your pain."

"Cleon might not have gone if you'd been honest with us in the first place." Dad's chair scraped against the linoleum as he pushed away from the table. "If your husband leaves the Amish faith and never returns, it will be your fault."

Grace trembled as her father's sharp admonition pierced her soul, but as much as his words hurt, she knew they were true.

"Roman, don't be so harsh." Mom set her magazine aside and

joined him at the sink, where he'd gone to put his empty cup.

He groaned. "Nothin's been right around here for months. Not here at home or even with my business. Why, the other day when I was in town, I saw Steven Bates at the drugstore, and the fellow snubbed me. Acted like I didn't even exist. I think he's still put out over those cabinets that broke, and I wouldn't be surprised if he hasn't been badmouthing me to others so I'll lose some business."

"I know I'm not to blame for that," Grace said tearfully, "but I do feel responsible for what's happened between me and Cleon, and now me and Anna."

Martha offered Grace a sympathetic smile. "None of us can do anything about Cleon except pray that he'll come home soon. However, we can all pitch in and do whatever we can to help make Anna feel more at ease."

Mom nodded and turned to Dad. "You always seem to be busy in your shop, but couldn't you make a little time to spend with your granddaughter?"

He shrugged and gave the end of his beard a quick tug. "I suppose I could. I've been wantin' to crack some of those walnuts I've had stashed away, so maybe I'll take Anna out to my shop and show her how to do it."

"That's a fine idea," Mom said with a hopeful-looking smile. "Don't you think so, Grace?"

Grace nodded, as the lump in her throat grew tighter. "I guess I haven't found the right thing to do with her yet."

"You'll think of something. Maybe you could—"

Martha's sentence was halted when Ruth entered the room, her lips turned down at the corners and her eyes swimming with tears.

"What's wrong?" Mom asked, rushing to Ruth's side. "Have you been crying?"

Ruth opened her mouth, but all that came out was a little squeak.

Dad stepped forward and grabbed hold of her arm. "What's the problem? Has there been another attack?"

She shook her head. "It's. . .it's Luke."

"What about Luke? Has he done something to you?" Dad's voice shook with emotion, and a vein on the side of his neck bulged.

"He won't be honest with me about anything, and I'm afraid he may end up going English, so I—I broke up with him." Ruth nearly choked on a sob and bolted from the room.

Grace groaned. Apparently she wasn't the only one in the family with problems.

Chapter 24

"I don't wanna crack walnuts," Anna whined as Roman led her into his shop Saturday morning. "I wanna watch TV."

"We have no TV, Anna, and you know it." He glanced over at her and frowned. It seemed like all the child had done since she'd arrived at their house was pout, complain, and cry for her poppy. The hardest part was seeing what the little girl's sudden appearance had done to Grace and her relationship with Cleon.

Roman grimaced. Truth was, he'd felt just as hurt and betrayed as Cleon when Grace's secret had been revealed. If only she'd told them sooner, when she'd first returned home after living among the English. If they'd known about Anna then, maybe they could have helped Grace get her back. They surely would have offered their support.

Would you have been supportive or judgmental? a little voice niggled at the back of his mind.

He flinched. In all likelihood, he wouldn't have taken the news of her marriage well, and he wouldn't have been happy that Grace had allowed someone else to raise her child. This whole episode continued to remind him of his wayward sister. Had Rosemary been afraid of her family's reaction to her going English, or didn't she care enough to want to see them again? Did Rosemary have any children? Was she still alive? He feared he might never know the answer to those questions.

"How come there's so much wood in here?"

Anna's simple question pulled Roman out of his musings, and he jerked to attention. "This is where I work. I make wooden things."

She shrugged her slim shoulders and wandered around the room as though scrutinizing everything she saw.

"Come, have a seat at my workbench." Roman pulled out a stool for Anna and lifted her onto it. Then he poured some walnuts out of a burlap sack and picked up a hammer. "In my opinion, this is the best way to split open a walnut." *Crack!* The hammer came down, and the walnut shell split in two. "Now, it's your turn." He handed the hammer to Anna, but she stared at the smashed walnut, her eyes filling with tears.

"You killed it!"

"No, Anna, it's—"

"It's dead, just like my grandma."

"Your grandma isn't dead; she's back at the house, probably fixing lunch by now."

"Grandma's dead, and Poppy's gone away." Tears trickled down Anna's cheeks in little rivulets.

Roman looked around helplessly, wishing Judith or Martha were here. They seemed to have better luck at calming the child than he did. "Let's forget about the walnuts for now," he said. "You can sit at my desk while I do some work."

Anna's eyebrows furrowed, and her lower lip jutted out like a bullfrog. "I don't want to. I don't like it here."

"Fine! You can go back to the house, and that will give me the freedom to go somewhere I need to go." Roman set the hammer aside and reached for Anna's hand. So much for them getting to know each other better.

Judith was about to put the last two quarts of applesauce into the pressure canner when she heard a knock on the front door. *That's strange. It's not likely anyone we know would use the front door.*

"Martha, could you see who's at the door?" she called. Then she remembered that Martha had gone to check on her dogs, and Grace was upstairs resting.

Sighing, Judith dried her hands on a towel, stepped into the living room, and opened the front door. An English man stood on the porch. At first she didn't recognize him, but then she remembered him having gone to Roman's shop when he'd asked about purchasing their land.

"Can I help you?" she asked, stepping onto the porch.

"I hope so." He offered her a crooked smile. "In case you don't remember, my name's Bill Collins, and I was here a few months ago, talking to your husband about the possibility of buying your place."

She nodded curtly. "I remember."

"I'd like to talk to you a minute if you're not busy."

"Actually, I was about to put some applesauce into the canner."

"No problem. I can wait until you're done."

Thinking he might take a seat in one of the wicker chairs on the porch, Judith headed back inside, leaving the door slightly open. She'd just entered the kitchen when she heard a man's voice. She whirled around and was surprised to see the land developer standing inside the doorway.

"I'm hoping you and your husband might have reconsidered my offer about selling this place," he said, leaning against the counter and folding his arms.

"Have you spoken to Roman about this again?"

Mr. Collins shook his head. "I thought I'd talk to you first."

She frowned. "My husband would decide if we were to sell, but I'm sure he hasn't changed his mind in that regard."

"I'm prepared to offer you a fair price for the land."

"That may be so, but we have no plans to sell or relocate."

He grunted. "Money talks, and it's not my style to take no for an answer."

She opened her mouth to comment, but a knock sounded on the front door again. "Excuse me. I need to answer that."

"Sure, no problem."

The man stood as though he had no intention of leaving, so Judith headed for the front door, figuring she would ask him to leave as soon as she saw who was at the door.

She was taken aback to see another man standing on the porch, and she grimaced when she realized it was the reporter she'd talked to in town several months ago.

"Mind if I ask you a few questions?" he asked, reaching into his jacket pocket and withdrawing a tablet and pen.

"You've already done a magazine article about the break-ins we had. Shouldn't that be enough?" Judith surprised herself by the boldness of her words and her cool tone of voice. She was usually more pleasant to strangers—even the nosey ones who wanted information about the Amish.

"I was working on some other stories in Pennsylvania, but I've come back to Ohio to do a follow-up story on the break-ins. So I was wondering if there have been any more acts of vandalism here."

"I'd rather not talk about this if you don't mind."

"How about the law? Do they have any leads on who might have been responsible?"

"We didn't involve the sheriff."

"Mind if I ask why?"

Judith opened her mouth to reply when she remembered her jars of applesauce needing to be put into the canner. Besides, that determined land developer was still in her kitchen. All she wanted was for both men to leave so she could get on with the things she'd planned to do. "If you'll excuse me, Mr. Walker, I have something that needs to be taken care of in the kitchen." She left him on the porch and rushed back to the other room. Mr. Collins was still standing in the same place she'd left him.

"As I was saying," he said, following her across the room, "I'd like to discuss the details of my offer with you."

"It's not my place to talk about this with you, so if you have anything more to say, you'll have to meet with my husband." She nodded toward the window. "He's working in his shop this morning, so I'm sure you'll find him there."

He glanced at his watch and moved toward the back door. "I've got an appointment in half an hour, so I won't have time to talk to Mr. Hostettler right now." He handed her a business card he'd taken from his jacket pocket. "If you have any persuasion over your husband, I'd recommend you try and talk some sense into him." He sauntered out through the doorway.

Judith shook her head and dropped the card to the counter as she made her way to the stove. The water in the cooker was already boiling, so she set the jars of applesauce in place, closed the lid, and checked the pressure valve. When she turned from the stove, she was shocked to see Gary standing inside the kitchen door.

"Ach! You scared me. I thought you'd left."

He nodded at the notebook in his hand. "Didn't get any answers yet."

She released an exasperated groan. "I have nothing more to say."

"You never answered my question about the sheriff and why he wasn't involved."

"We're trusting in God for our protection and leaving it up to Him to bring justice to those who did us wrong."

"Are you saying that even if you knew who had done the break-ins, you wouldn't press charges?" His pen flew across the notebook with lightning speed.

"That's right." She nodded toward the stove. "Now if you'll excuse me—"

Just then the back door flew open, and little Anna darted into the room.

"Back already?" Judith couldn't believe they could have finished cracking all those walnuts so quickly.

"Grandpa killed a nut, and then he got mad and sent me back here."

Judith's gaze went to the back door. She saw no sign of Roman. "Where's your grandpa, Anna?"

"He's going somewhere." The child's chin trembled. "He's not nice like Poppy."

Concern welled in Judith's soul. She needed to speak with her husband and find out what had happened between him and Anna and tell him about the pushy land developer and the incessant reporter. With only a slight hesitation, she opened the back door and rushed onto the porch. When she spotted Roman turning his horse and buggy around by the barn, she ran down the walkway, waving and calling his name.

He halted the horse and leaned out the side opening. "What is it, Judith? I'm in a bit of a hurry."

"What happened with Anna, and where are you heading?"

"Didn't she tell you?"

Judith shivered and stepped up to the buggy. "She said you were mad at her, and that you were leaving."

"That's all?"

"Pretty much. Oh, and she said you'd killed a nut."

Roman grimaced. "All she did was whine and complain, and after I cracked the first walnut, she started to bawl. Then she mentioned her other grandpa and said she wanted to go home." His nose twitched and his eyebrows scrunched together. "I figured I'd never get anything done with her howling like a wounded heifer, so I sent her back to the house."

"I see. And where are you off to now?"

"Going into town to get a few things I need in my shop. Is that all right with you?"

"Of course, but I think you should know that Mr. Collins, that land developer, was here a few minutes ago."

"What'd he want?"

"To get me to convince you to sell our land."

"What'd you tell him?"

"That he'd need to talk to you, but I didn't think you were interested in selling."

"You got that right. If and when he does talk to me again, I'll tell him the same thing I told the Larsons when they asked about buying our place: I won't sell for any amount of money." Roman picked up the reins. "I'm off to town now."

Before she could say anything else, he got the horse moving and steered the buggy down the driveway.

Judith blew out her breath and rubbed her hands briskly over her arms. Spring would be here soon, but it was still too cold to be outside without a shawl or a jacket. "I'd best get back inside and see about Anna." She'd only taken a few steps when she realized that she'd left the child alone with a stranger. *What was I thinking? If only I'd thought to call Grace downstairs before I left the house in search of Roman.* She hurried her steps. *Guess I wasn't thinking straight because I felt so flustered over that land developer's pushy ways, the reporter's noisy questions, and then Anna showing up unexpectedly.*

She stepped onto the porch, and was about to open the door when Gary stepped out. She startled and took a step back, nearly losing her balance.

"Sorry if I frightened you, but I've got to go." He hurried down the steps and toward the driveway. She saw no sign of a car. Surely the man hadn't walked here all the way from town.

She reached for the handle of the screen door and was about to pull it open when a thunderous explosion rumbled through the house. Breaking glass crackled.

Judith's heart thudded against her chest as she raced into the kitchen. "Anna!"

Chapter 25

The vibrating floor beneath Grace's bed caused her to waken, and the rumbling roar made her aware that something horrible must have happened. She scrambled off the bed and without even bothering to put on her shoes, rushed from her room. At the bottom of the steps, she nearly collided with Martha as she dashed into the house.

"What happened, Grace? It sounded like something blew up in here. I heard it all the way out in the barn."

Trembling, Grace shook her head. "I—I don't know. I was upstairs in my room and heard a terrible noise. It shook my bed, rattled the windows, and vibrated the walls." Her gaze went to the kitchen. "You don't suppose–"

Martha made a beeline for the kitchen, with Grace right on her heels. Their mother was kneeling on the floor by the table, her arms wrapped around Anna. On the other side of the table lay several broken jars, with blobs of applesauce splattered everywhere.

Grace's heart pounded, and she rushed to her mother's side. "What happened? Is Anna hurt? Are you okay, Mom?"

"The pressure cooker's gauge must be faulty. It exploded when I was out on the porch." Mom's voice trembled with emotion. "Anna's shaken up, but she seems to be okay." She nodded toward the broken glass. "Thankfully, nothing went past that side of the table."

"Dad put a new gauge on the cooker a few weeks ago," Martha said, stepping around the mess and up to the stove. "Makes no sense that it would go like that."

Grace reached for Anna, but the child wouldn't budge. She clung to Mom, weeping for all she was worth.

"That's what I get for leaving the stove unattended and going outside to see where your daed was heading," Mom said tearfully. "That reporter had me so rattled with all his questions, and then when Anna showed up saying her grossdaadi was mad at her and was going somewhere—"

Grace felt immediate concern. "Reporter? What reporter?"

"The fellow who asked me some questions in town the day we went looking for your wedding dress material." Mom clambered to her feet, pulling Anna to her side. "First that land developer showed up, and he followed me into the kitchen. Then the reporter came to the door, and soon after the land developer left, the reporter came into the kitchen. When Anna ran into the house and said your daed was going someplace, I went outside to see what was up."

"I thought Gary had left Holmes County."

"Said he was back now and doing a follow-up story about our break-ins." Mom glanced toward the door. "Without even thinking, I left him in the kitchen with Anna, but he headed out a few minutes before the explosion."

Grace gritted her teeth so hard her jaw ached. Could Gary have had something to do with the pressure cooker exploding? Could he have tampered with the valve while Mom was outside talking to Dad? She glanced down at her daughter, still whimpering and clinging to Mom's skirts; then she moved quickly toward the door.

"Where are you going?" Mom called after her.

"Outside to see if I can find Gary."

"Not without me." Martha caught up to Grace at the door and pushed it open. "If you do catch up to that curious reporter, you shouldn't be alone with him."

Grace offered her sister a grateful smile. "I appreciate your concern."

As Martha followed Grace down the porch steps, her thoughts raced like a runaway horse. What if her sister was right and the reporter was responsible for the break-ins and other attacks? If they couldn't report it to the sheriff or prove that he'd done it, how would they ever make him stop?

"There's no sign of his car." Grace pointed to the driveway. "Guess that means he's already gone."

"Maybe so, but let's look out by the road, in case he parked his car somewhere nearby," Martha suggested.

"Jah, okay."

They hurried down the driveway, and when they approached the mailbox by the road, they saw him standing across the street with a camera pointed at them. Grace turned her head, but Martha marched boldly across the street until she stood face-to-face with Gary. "What do you think you're doing?"

"Just taking a few pictures to go with the article I'm planning to write." He turned the camera toward her, but she put her hand in front of the lens.

"Don't even think about it."

Gary's eyes widened, and his jaw dropped open. Apparently, he wasn't used to hearing an Amish woman speak so boldly.

Grace joined them. "Wh-what are you doing here, Gary?"

"I'm back in the area again, hoping to do another story or two." He nodded at Grace. "I came by to see if there have been any more attacks at your place."

Martha planted both hands on her hips and stared up at him. "Did you mess with the gauge on our mother's pressure cooker?"

"Of course not. Why do you ask?"

"It blew up minutes after you left our house. Since you were alone in the kitchen–"

He held up his hand. "I hope you're not insinuating that I had anything to do with it."

"My daughter was in the kitchen when the cooker blew." Grace took a step closer to him.

His eyebrows furrowed. "Your daughter? That little girl with the whiny mouth is yours?"

Grace nodded. "My secret's out now, so you have nothing to hold over me anymore."

He scratched the back of his head. "What secret are you talking about?"

Martha stepped between them. "Anna. She's talking about Anna."

"Huh?" Gary looked at Grace, over at Martha, then back at Grace again. "You two are talking in circles. I have no idea what secret you're referring to."

"The one about me being married to Wade and giving birth to his daughter."

"I never knew you and Wade had a kid."

"You said you knew he'd married me."

"Yeah, I knew that much."

"After I broke up with you and started dating Wade, you said you would get even with me."

He shrugged. "Guys say and do a lot of things when they're trying to keep a woman."

"It seems odd that we never had any attacks until you showed up in Holmes County," Martha put in. "And since you've been asking all sorts of questions and pestering Grace to have coffee with you and all, you're our prime suspect."

Gary leaned his head back and howled. "Prime suspect? Who do you think you are—the Nancy Drew of the Amish?"

"Who?"

"Never mind." Gary turned to face Grace again. "You and your little sister are acting paranoid. You have no proof that I'm anything other than a reporter trying to do his job." He pointed to his camera. "Do you honestly think I would be stupid enough to jeopardize my chance to sell a dynamic piece to some big publication?"

She opened her mouth to reply, but he cut her off. "As I said, I'm back in the area to do a few more stories on the Amish, and I might do a couple articles about some of the events happening in the area. So whether you like it or not, I'll be sticking around Holmes County for as long as I want."

Grace's face paled, and her whole body trembled. Martha didn't think it was doing either of them any good to continue arguing with the Englisher, so she took hold of her sister's arm and steered her toward the house. "Let's go, Grace."

"Say, Gracie. Did you and that Amish man ever get married?" Gary called after her.

She gave a quick nod.

Martha glanced over her shoulder as Gary headed for his car parked on the shoulder of the road. She felt certain of one thing: If he was responsible for the things that had happened to them, God would deal with him in His time.

Chapter 26

For the next several days, Grace made every effort to spend more time with Anna. They'd baked cookies together and taken them over to the Wengerds' place so Anna could play with Esta while Grace and Alma visited awhile. The next morning, Anna helped Grace feed and water the chickens in the henhouse. At the moment, Grace was sitting in one of the wicker chairs on the back porch, watching her daughter romp around in the yard with Heidi's rambunctious pups.

Anna seemed to be accepting her new life better these days—accepting Grace better, too.

"Thank You, God," Grace murmured as she took a sip of tea from the mug she held. She closed her eyes and drew in a deep breath. *Bless my husband, Lord, and bring him home soon.*

"Are you sleepin'?"

Grace startled at the sound of her father's deep voice, and she turned to face him. "I was watching Anna play with Heidi's pups."

Dad took a seat in the chair beside her and set his cup of coffee on the small table between them. "Watching with your eyes closed, huh?"

Grace smiled. "Actually, I was talking to God."

"Ah, now that's a good thing. I've been doing a lot of that myself here of late."

"Because of the attacks on our family?"

He shrugged. "There've been no more for some time. I'm sure that trouble is over."

"What about the pressure cooker exploding the other day?"

"That was an accident, plain and simple."

"An accident?" Grace could hardly believe her ears.

"The gauge must have been faulty, or maybe the valve was broken."

"You replaced the gauge with a new one, so I don't see how it could have been faulty."

"Maybe it happened because your mamm left the cooker on the stove too long and it overheated."

She touched his arm. "I'm sure that wasn't an accident, and neither were the other things that have happened to us."

"I know you believe the reporter had something to do with it, but I'm equally sure he didn't. The things that were done before were most likely done by some rowdy English fellows who've probably been the cause of a few other destructive things that have been done in our area."

"I still think Gary might be the one responsible, but since I have no proof, I guess there's not much I can do about it." She released a weary sigh. "I'm just glad no one was hurt when the pressure cooker blew up. It would break my heart if something happened to Anna."

"God was watching over your mamm as well as your *dochder*; there's no doubt about that." He smiled, but a muscle in his cheek quivered, letting her know he was more concerned than he was letting on. "It's silly of us to think it could be this person or that. It's just speculation on all our parts."

"That's true, but—"

"Only God knows the truth, and He will handle things in His way, His time. You'll see." He leaned back in his chair and took a drink of his coffee.

Grace mentally scolded herself for being overly suspicious of Gary, but she shuddered to think what could have happened to Anna if she'd been sitting on the other side of the table. The child could have been cut by the broken glass or burned by the hot steam that shot from the pressure cooker when it exploded. *Thank You, God, for watching out for my little girl.*

Dad motioned in the direction of Cleon and Grace's new home.

"Since Cleon's brothers have been coming over to help me work on your place the last couple of weeks, I believe we'll have it ready for you to move in by the time Cleon gets home."

She stared at the silhouette of the two-story structure sitting near the back of her folk's property—the place she had hoped would be her and Cleon's happy home. "I appreciate all the work you've done on the house, and when it's done, Anna and I will move in, but I'm not sure about Cleon."

Dad frowned. "What do you mean? It's Cleon's home, too, and I'm sure when he returns from his business trip, he'll be glad to find the house has been finished."

Grace nibbled on her lower lip as she contemplated the best way to voice her thoughts. "I'm. . .uh. . .not sure Cleon will ever return home. His last letter let me know how hurt he still is, and he said something that made me think he might decide to leave the Amish faith and go English."

"What did he say?"

"That he's still feeling confused and wonders if maybe he's meant to do something else with his life besides what he'd planned."

"He could have been referring to the honey business. Maybe he's having trouble lining up customers and is thinking about doing some other kind of work." Dad pointed in the direction of his shop. "Cleon's carpentry skills are pretty good. Maybe he would consider coming to work for me."

"You already have Luke working for you, Dad, and I don't think you have enough work right now to keep three men busy, do you?"

He shrugged. "Never know what the future holds."

Grace wrapped her arms around her stomach as she was hit by a sudden wave of nausea. She'd been feeling a little dizzy lately and kind of weak but figured it was because she hadn't been eating much since Cleon left. Then again, it might be caused by stress or a touch of the flu.

Dad placed his hand on her shoulder. "Try not to worry so much. Just pray and leave the situation in God's hands."

Grace squeezed her eyes shut and willed her stomach to settle down. It was easy enough for Dad not to worry; it wasn't his mate who'd gone off to Pennsylvania.

"Say, aren't you one of those Amish fellows?"

Cleon turned to the middle-aged English man who shared his seat on the bus and nodded. "Jah, I'm Amish."

"I thought so by the way you're dressed. And from the looks of that beard you've got going, I'd say you might be newly married."

Cleon scrubbed a hand down the side of his face. "Jah, I'm married."

"Me, too. Been with the same woman for close to twenty years. We've got three great kids—two boys and a girl. How about you?"

"I've only been married a couple of months." Cleon chose not to mention Anna. She was Grace's child, not his. Truth was, he and Grace might never have any children.

"Where you from?"

"I live in Ohio, between Berlin and Charm."

"Holmes County, right?"

"Jah."

"I heard that's the largest Amish settlement in the United States."

Cleon nodded.

"So what are you doing in Pennsylvania?"

"I've had business here."

The man studied Cleon intently. "Do you farm for a living?"

Cleon shook his head. "I raise bees for honey, and we also use the wax to make candles."

"Ah, I see. Were you trying to set up some new accounts, then?"

"Jah."

"I'm in sales, too. I sell life insurance." The man stuck out his hand. "My name's Lew Carter, and I work for—"

"I don't mean to be rude, but I've got no use for life insurance."

The man looked stunned. "If you've got a family, then you ought to make some provision for them in case something were to happen to you."

"The Amish don't buy any kind of insurance. We take care of our own." Cleon turned away from the man and stared out the window at the passing scenery. Maybe it was time to finish up his business here and face his responsibilities at home.

Chapter 27

Church was good today, jah?" Mom asked as she glanced over her shoulder and smiled at Grace. They were riding home in their buggy with Dad, Mom, and Martha sitting in front, and Grace, Ruth, and Anna in the backseat.

Grace nodded in response to her mother's question. The truth was she'd barely heard a word that had been said during any of the sermons today. She'd been fighting waves of nausea.

"It was hard for me to see Luke at church today," Ruth whispered to Grace.

"I can imagine. Did he say anything to you after the service?"

"He never looked my way." Ruth sighed. "It's probably for the best since he wants to be so close-mouthed and not share things with me."

"Luke was late to work again on Friday; did I mention that?" Dad asked.

Ruth looked stunned, but it was no surprise to Grace that Dad had overheard their conversation. Mom often teased him about being able to hear a piece of sawdust fall if he was listening for it.

"Did he say why he was late?" The question came from Martha.

"Made some excuse about having an errand to run after he left home and it taking longer than he expected."

"Did you believe him?" Ruth asked.

Dad shrugged. "Not sure what I believe where Luke's concerned. He's got a mind of his own, that's for sure. I think he actually believes he knows more than me about working with wood."

"I'm sure Luke's just trying to share his ideas," Martha put in.

Martha's defense of Luke made Grace wonder if her sister might have more than a passing interest in Ruth's ex-boyfriend.

"When Luke finally showed up for work on Friday, I smelled smoke on his clothes." Dad shook his head. "Sure hope he's not messing with cigarettes during his rumschpringe."

"Did you question him about it?" Mom asked.

"Nope. Didn't think it was my place to be askin'."

Ruth's cheeks turned pink, and she cleared her throat a couple of times. "I. . .uh. . .think it's possible he's doing a lot of things he shouldn't be."

"How do you know that?" Dad asked.

"Well, he's got a—" She fell silent. "Never mind. It's not my place to be saying."

Dad gave the reins a quick snap to get the horse moving faster, as the animal had slowed considerably on the last hill. "Well, whatever Luke's up to during his rumschpringe, my main concern is his work habits. I made up my mind last week that if he was late to work again I would fire him, and I should have done that on Friday morning."

"Why didn't you, Roman?"

Dad reached over and patted Mom's arm. "Figured you would tell me I ought to give the man one more chance."

She chuckled. "You know me well."

Grace leaned against the seat and tried to relax. She and Anna would be moving into their new house tomorrow morning, but it would be without Cleon. She shivered. All this waiting and wondering if he would ever come home was enough to make her a nervous wreck. No wonder her stomach felt upset much of the time. If it weren't for Anna, she would be utterly miserable.

She reached over and took her daughter's hand, and the child smiled at her. *Thank You, God. Thank You for giving my daughter back to me.*

"Do we have to go?" Anna asked as Grace placed a stack of linens into a box she would be taking over to their new home. "I like it here."

Grace smiled and nodded. "I know you do, but at the new house, you'll have your own room. Won't that be nice?"

The child stuck out her lower lip. "But I'll miss Aunt Martha."

"She won't be far away. She'll come over to see us, and we'll go see her and the rest of the family, too."

Anna's forehead wrinkled. "Poppy never comes to see me like he promised."

"That's because he lives far away, and he's still not feeling well, Anna." Grace gently squeezed the child's arm. "He writes you letters, though."

Anna stared at the hardwood floor. "I miss him."

"I know." Grace drew Anna into her arms, but the child just stood, unmoving. One step forward and one back. If there was only something she could do to put a smile on her little girl's face this morning.

Grace's gaze came to rest on her cedar chest. The faceless doll! Why hadn't she thought of it sooner?

She hurried across the room, flipped open the lid, and dug into the contents of the cedar chest until she located the doll. "Look what I've found, Anna."

"What's that?" The child's eyes opened wide, and Grace was pleased that she'd captured her interest.

"It's the doll I made for you when you were a baby."

Anna's forehead wrinkled as she pursed her lips. "It's got no mouth." She touched the side of her nose. "No nose." She pointed to one of her eyes. "No eyes." She shook her head. "She ain't no doll."

Grace resisted the temptation to correct her daughter's English. Instead, she got down on her knees beside Anna and cradled the doll in her arms. "It's hard for me to explain, but Amish people make their dolls without faces."

"How come?"

"It has to do with a verse from the Bible that talks about not making any graven images."

Anna tipped her head and squinted. Obviously, she had no idea what Grace was talking about.

"It's fun to pretend, don't you think, Anna?"

The child nodded. "Last Sunday after church, me, Esta, and some of the other kids took turns pretending to be a horse pulling a buggy along the road."

"Then let's pretend this doll has a face." She looked up at her daughter to get her reaction, but Anna's expression didn't change.

Grace tried again. "Let's start by naming the doll."

Still no response.

"How about if we call her Sarah?"

"I don't like that name."

"How about Phoebe? I had a friend named Phoebe when I was a little girl, but she moved to Wisconsin."

Anna shook her head.

Grace released an exasperated sigh. "What would you like to call the doll?"

"Martha."

Grace nodded. "Martha it is, then." She touched the doll's face again. "Let's pretend that little Martha has eyes. What color should they be?"

"Blue. Like Aunt Martha's."

"Okay. What color hair should the doll have?"

"Aunt Martha has brown hair."

"True." She extended the doll toward Anna. "Would you like to hold her now?"

Anna reached for the doll and snuggled it against her chest. "I like the doll with no face."

Grace smiled. She might not have completely won over Anna, but she was making a bit more headway every day. And now she could see her daughter cuddling the doll Grace had made for her when she was a baby.

Chapter 28

Roman looked up from sanding a chair and frowned when Luke entered the shop. "You're late again, boy. What's the problem this time?"

Luke stayed near the door as if he was afraid to come in. Was he dreading another lecture or worried that Roman might fire him? That's what he'd planned to do if Luke showed up late again without a good excuse.

"Well, how come you're late, and why are you standing by the door?"

Luke made little circles in a pile of sawdust with the toe of his boot as his gaze dropped to the floor. "I. . .um. . .I'm late because I had an errand to run on the way here."

Roman set his sandpaper aside and straightened. "I warned you about this habit of being late. Said if it happened again, I'd have to let you go."

Luke lifted his gaze. "Are you sayin' I'm fired?"

Roman nodded.

Luke shuffled his feet a few times. "I know you and me haven't seen eye to eye on some things, but–"

"That's true, we haven't." Roman took a step toward Luke, and a whiff of smoke permeated his nostrils. Either Luke had taken up smoking, as Roman had suspected, or the boy had been hanging around someone who did.

Luke's eyebrows drew together. "I know you have a fair amount of work right now, and if I leave, you'll be shorthanded."

"That's my problem. I'll do fine on my own until I can get someone else."

Luke shrugged. "I think you're gonna regret having fired me." He pulled a pair of sunglasses from his shirt pocket, turned on his heels, and headed for the door.

Roman grunted and went back to sanding the chair.

"Now how'd that happen?" Judith muttered as she made her way across the yard to check on her drying laundry. The line was down, and clothes were strewn all over the ground. At first, she thought the towels she'd hung must have been too heavy and caused the line to break, but after closer inspection, she realized that the line had been cut. "Who would do something like this?"

She bent to retrieve one of Roman's shirts and noticed a pair of sunglasses lying on the ground a few feet away. No one in her family wore sunglasses like that, and her heart started to race as she realized that whoever had cut the line had probably lost their sunglasses during the act.

Grabbing up the glasses along with one of the dirty shirts, Judith hurried toward Roman's shop. She found him bent over his workbench, sanding on the legs of a straight-backed chair. "There's been another attack," she panted.

He rushed over to her. "What's happened? Has anyone been hurt?"

She shook her head as she held up his shirt. "My clothesline's been cut, and now everything needs to be washed again."

"That's it—just a broken line—and you're all in a dither?"

"It didn't break on its own, Roman. I checked the line, and it was obviously cut." She showed him the sunglasses. "I found these on the ground not far from the clothes."

He reached for the glasses. "These look like the pair Luke had in his pocket. He put them on as he was leaving my shop."

Judith glanced around the room. "Where'd Luke go?"

Roman shrugged. "Don't know. I fired him."

"Why would you do such a thing?"

"He was late to work again, and I'm getting tired of it. That fellow's been a thorn in my side for some time—coming in late to work, arguing with me about how things should be done. I'm even more convinced that he's been smoking."

Judith's eyes widened. "He's always seemed like such a nice young man."

"Looks can be deceiving." He frowned. "Makes me wonder if that *ab im kopp* might be the one who broke into our house and my shop. That crazy fellow's certainly had opportunity."

"Ach, Roman, surely not."

"Luke hasn't joined the church yet, and from what I've heard, he's been seen with a rowdy bunch of English fellows. You never know what kind of pranks he might decide to play."

Judith slowly shook her head. "The things that were done here were more than pranks, and what reason would he have for singling us out?"

He shrugged. "Can't say for sure, but it could have to do with his broken relationship with Ruth, or he might be nursing a grudge against me because we've butted heads so many times. With me firing him just now, he may have decided to retaliate by cutting your clothesline."

She sank into a chair and released a deep moan. "May the Lord help us all."

Chapter 29

I'm glad you were free to go shopping with me and Anna this morning," Grace said to Martha as they drove their buggy toward Berlin. "It's a nice clear day, and I thought it would be good for us to get some fresh air and time together." She glanced over her shoulder at Anna, asleep on the backseat with her faceless doll in her hand. "She's not completely adjusted, but things are getting better between me and my daughter."

"Glad to hear it."

"She likes the doll I made her when she was a *boppli*. Hardly lets it out of her sight."

Martha smiled. "Once Cleon gets back, you'll be a real family."

Grace swallowed back the wave of nausea that hit her unexpectedly. It wasn't good for her to feel this way—not when she had so much to do and was trying hard to be a good mother while she put her faith in God to make things better.

"Are you okay?" Martha reached across the seat and touched Grace's arm. "You look kind of pale, and your hands are shaking."

"I'm all right. Just a bit tired is all."

"Want me take over driving?"

Grace shook her head. "I'll be okay."

"Are you sure?"

Grace opened her mouth to respond, but before she could get a word out, something went *splat* against the front window.

"What was that?" Martha leaned forward and squinted at the red blob.

"Looks like a tomato."

Splat! Splat! Two more hit the buggy.

"*Ich kann sell net geh*—I cannot tolerate that." Martha pointed to the shoulder of the road. "Would you please pull over?"

"What for?"

"We need to see if we can find out who threw those tomatoes."

"It's probably just some kids fooling around."

"They shouldn't be hiding in the woods, throwing things at buggies. It could cause an accident."

Grace pulled back on the reins and guided the horse to the side of the road, knowing if she didn't stop, she would never hear the end of it. She looked around. "I don't see anyone in the woods, do you?"

"Over there!" Martha pointed to a stand of trees on the opposite side of the road. "I thought I saw the back of some fellow's head bobbing in and out between those trees."

Grace craned her neck. "I don't see anyone."

"He ducked behind that tree."

"What'd he look like?"

"I'm not sure. It looked like he was wearing a baseball cap." Martha opened the door on her side of the buggy.

"Where are you going?"

"Across the road to see what's up."

Grace reached across the seat and grabbed her sister's arm. "Are you kidding? There could be more than one person in those woods, and you might get hurt."

"I just want to talk to them."

"Do you really think anyone mean enough to throw tomatoes at an Amish buggy is going to listen to you?"

"They might." Martha compressed her lips as she frowned. "You don't suppose whoever threw that brick through our kitchen window and broke into the house and Dad's shop could be responsible for throwing those tomatoes, do you?"

Grace glanced over her shoulder and was relieved to see that Anna was still asleep. She didn't think it would be good for her daughter to hear this conversation. It might frighten her. "I doubt it could be the same person, but just in case, we're not going to put ourselves in any danger by going into the woods." She gathered up the reins and got the horse moving again. "We need to get our shopping done so we can help Mom do some cleaning."

Martha nodded. "Sure hope Ruth doesn't have any trouble on her way home from work this afternoon."

Grace shook her head. "I'm sure whoever threw those tomatoes will be long gone by then."

For the rest of the morning, Roman had trouble getting any work done. He couldn't stop thinking about how he'd fired Luke or about the clothesline that had been cut in their yard. What if he'd been wrong about rowdy Englishers committing the break-ins? What if Luke had done all those things because he was angry with Roman?

He was also worried about Judith, who had seemed extremely agitated after the clothesline incident. When they'd gotten the laundry picked up and the line put back in place, she'd gone to the cellar to wash everything again. Roman could tell by the droop of her shoulders and her wrinkled forehead that she was deeply troubled.

"Wish there was something I could do to make things better for everyone," he mumbled as he brushed a coat of stain on a chair. It wasn't right that their lives were in such turmoil. He wondered if his prayers were getting through to God, and if they were, why wasn't God answering?

Maybe I should pay a call on our bishop and see what he has to say about this. Jah, that's what I need to do.

As Grace guided the horse and buggy over their graveled driveway, Martha spotted their mother out in the yard. "Look, Mom's hanging out the wash. That makes no sense, because she was hanging it out when we left for town this morning."

"Maybe she found some other things that needed to be washed," Grace suggested as she halted the horse near the barn.

Anna sat up and yawned. "Are we home yet? I'm hungry."

"Jah, we're home," her mother replied. "We'll have lunch as soon as we get the groceries put away."

"The horse needs to be put in the corral, too," Martha added.

A short time later, Grace, Martha, and Anna headed for the house, but they stopped at the clothesline to speak with Mom.

"How come you're still doing wash?" Martha asked. "I figured you'd be bringing in dry clothes by now, not hanging out wet ones."

Mom frowned. "Someone cut the line. I found clothes all over the place."

"That's terrible! Who would do such a thing?"

Mom pointed to the ground. "I found some sunglasses nearby, and your daed thinks they were Luke's."

Grace stepped forward. "What'd they look like?"

"Metal-framed with dark lenses."

"Gary has a pair of metal-framed sunglasses. He was wearing them the day the pressure cooker blew up."

"So it could have been Gary rather than Luke who cut the line." Martha frowned. "Someone threw tomatoes at our buggy on the way to Berlin. I wonder if it could have been—"

Mom motioned to Anna, who stood beside Grace with an anxious expression on her face. "Can we talk about this later?"

Grace nodded and took her daughter's hand. "Let's go into the house, Anna. You can help me make some sandwiches."

"Can we have peanut butter and honey?"

"Jah, sure. We've got plenty of honey."

"I'm going to check on my dogs, and then I'll see about getting our lunch made," Martha said as Grace and Anna headed up the path leading to their new house.

"Jah, okay."

When Martha drew close to the barn, she heard yipping. It sounded like Fritz, only it wasn't coming from the dog kennel Dad had finally finished. It seemed to be coming from the other side of the house.

Yip! Yip! There it was again.

She hurried around the house and halted when she saw Fritz tied to a tree. The rope had been fastened around the dog's neck and left front leg, so that it was pulled up under the animal. The poor dog's water dish had been placed just out of his reach.

Martha let out a shriek and rushed to the animal's side. "Oh, Fritz, you poor little thing. Who could have done this to you?"

The dog whined pathetically, and Martha's fingers trembled as she undid the knot and removed the rope. "Whoever did this has gone too far. Dad has got to notify the sheriff!"

Roman was about to put the Closed sign in his window and head up to the house for lunch when Martha rushed in holding Fritz in her arms. Her face was crimson and glistening with sweat. "What's wrong, daughter?"

"It's Fritz," she panted. "I found him on the side of the house."

"How'd he get there? I thought he was in the kennel with the other dogs."

"All the dogs were in the kennel when Grace, Anna, and I left for town this morning, but when I found Fritz just now, he was tied to a tree, with one leg held up." She paused and gulped in some air. "A watering dish had been placed just out of his reach."

Roman compressed his lips as he shook his head. "Cuttin' your mamm's clothesline is one thing, but cruelty to an animal is going too far."

Hope welled in Martha's soul. "Are you going to notify the sheriff?"

He shook his head. "We have no proof who did it, and even if we did—"

"As I'm sure you know, Grace thinks that English reporter might be trying to get even with her for breaking up with him before she married Anna's daed."

He drew in a quick breath and released it with a huff. "I think she's wrong; I suspect it could be Luke."

"But Luke seems so nice. I can't imagine him doing anything that mean." Martha looked down at the trembling animal in her arms.

"What reason would he have for hurting one of my dogs or for doing any of the other things?"

"You know that Luke and I have butted heads several times. He doesn't like to be told what to do, and when I fired him this morning, he might have been mad enough to get even."

"You. . .you fired him?"

Roman nodded. "I hate to think it could be one of our own, but your mamm did find some sunglasses this morning that looked like Luke's."

"Grace said the reporter had a pair of sunglasses that fit the description of the ones Mom found."

Roman shrugged. "Maybe so, but remember that day when the brick was thrown through the kitchen window and you discovered Luke's hat on the ground near the barn?"

She nodded.

"Doesn't that make him look like he could be guilty?"

"I suppose it does, but if Luke's running with that bunch of rowdy English fellows Ruth and I saw him in town with one day, maybe he thinks playing a few pranks is fun."

Roman's eyebrows drew together. "There's nothing fun about vandalizing someone's property, stealing tools from their shop, or hurting their animals."

Martha rubbed Fritz's silky ear. "He's not really hurt. Just scared a bit—that's all."

He grunted. "Jah, well, the critter could have been hurt if you hadn't found him when you did."

"That's true, and I am upset about what happened. Still, I'm not convinced that Luke's the one who did it."

"We can't solve this problem right now, so why don't you put Fritz back in the kennel with the other dogs, and then we'll go up to the house for some lunch. If Luke shows up to get his sunglasses and I'm able to question him, it might give me a clue as to what's going on. If not, then I may go over to his place and have a little talk with him."

Chapter 30

Martha paced in front of her dog kennels, stopping every couple of minutes to watch Heidi and her remaining three pups frolic on the concrete floor inside the chain-link fence. She had placed another ad in a couple of newspapers, including *The Budget*, hoping to sell the rest of them. So far she'd sold one female pup to Ray and Donna Larson, and a male to an Amish man who lived near Sugarcreek. Flo, the female beagle, hadn't become pregnant yet, but Martha hoped that would happen soon.

Maybe I should go over to the Larsons' after lunch and see how their puppy is doing. It would give me a chance to talk to Donna about the situation here and find out if she or Ray might have heard or seen anything suspicious.

"I invited the folks to lunch at my house," Grace called from the barn doorway. "It's ready now, so are you coming?"

"Jah, okay." Martha took one final look at the dogs and hurried toward the front of the barn. "Did Dad tell you about Fritz?"

Grace nodded with a grim expression. "When he came up to my house a few minutes ago with Mom, he told us the whole story." She touched Martha's arm. "I'm sorry it happened but glad the dog wasn't hurt."

"Dad's trying to blame Luke, but I'm not convinced."

"Me, neither. I've been saying all along that Gary's responsible for the terrible things that have happened to our family." Grace bit her lip and stared at the ground. "Except for the mess I've made with my marriage. That's my fault—no one else's."

Martha slipped her arm around her sister's waist as they started walking up the driveway toward Grace's house. "You made a mistake in keeping the truth from Cleon, but that doesn't give him the right not to forgive."

"Maybe not, but I should have told him sooner, not kept it hidden until Anna showed up."

"No one's perfect, Grace. We all make mistakes."

"I seem to take the prize in that department." Grace stopped walking and drew in a shaky breath. Her face looked pale, and dark circles rimmed her eyes.

"What's wrong? Are you feeling *grank*?"

"I don't think I'm really sick, but I've been having waves of nausea for a couple of weeks."

"Have you missed your monthly?"

Grace nodded soberly.

"Sounds to me like you might be in a family way."

"I–I'm afraid that might be the case."

"It's nothing to look so down in the dumps about. If you're going to have a boppli, that's joyous news."

"It would be if things weren't so verhuddelt around here."

"You're right about things being confused, which is why I'm going over to the Larsons' this afternoon to see if they know anything."

"Why would they know anything? Surely you don't think that nice couple would want to hurt us in any way."

Martha shook her head. "Of course not, but I'm hoping Ray might have seen something with those binoculars he uses for bird watching. Or maybe Donna has heard something from one of the people she drives to appointments."

"I'd feel a lot better if the attacks would stop," Grace said, "but that doesn't solve my problem with Cleon not coming home."

"Have you heard from him lately?"

"Not since he sent that letter saying he was making more contacts for honey sales and didn't know when he might be home."

"Guess you can't write back and tell him you're pregnant, then."

"I haven't seen a doctor yet, so I'm not sure I'm in a family way. Maybe my symptoms are caused from the stress I've been under." Grace halted when they came to the steps leading to her back porch. "Please don't say anything to the folks about this. If I'm still feeling nauseated by the end of the week, I'll make an appointment to see the doctor."

"You promise?"

Grace gave a quick nod.

As Cleon exited the store he'd visited in hopes of soliciting some business, he spotted an English girl skipping down the sidewalk beside her mother. It made him think of Grace's little girl, who was about the same age. After Grace's secret had been revealed, he'd made no effort to get to know Anna, but then, she hadn't seemed that interested in him, either.

A pang of guilt shot through him. Anna might not be his child, but she needed a father. Her own father had died when she was just a baby, and her grandfather—the only father she'd ever known—had left her with strangers to begin a new way of life. Even so, Cleon wasn't sure Anna would ever accept him as her father, and he didn't know if he would ever feel comfortable in that role.

He pulled his gaze away from the English girl and spotted a phone booth down the street. Since his folks had a phone shed outside their home because of Mom's meal-serving business to tourists, he decided to give them a call and let them know he'd be on his way home soon.

Cleon entered the phone booth and dialed his mother's number. Ivan answered. "Cleon, I'm glad you phoned, because I have some bad news."

"Has something happened to Grace? Have there been more attacks at the Hostettlers'?"

"I don't know about that, but there's been one here."

"What's happened?"

Ivan cleared his throat a couple of times. "It's your bee hives—they're gone."

"Gone? What do you mean?"

"They've been destroyed."

Cleon's knees went weak, and he had to brace himself against the phone booth to keep from toppling over. "All of them?"

"Jah. Every last one has been burned. There's nothing left but a pile of ashes."

"Wh–when did this happen?"

"I'm not sure. I hadn't checked on things for a few days, and when I got done helping in the fields earlier today, I decided I'd better see how your hives were doing. That's when I discovered they'd been ruined. Some of the bees were flying around with nowhere to go, but I'm sure a lot of 'em were burned with the hives."

Cleon groaned. With no hives and no bees, he had no more honey to sell. And if he had no honey, he had no job other than farming for his father, which he'd rather not continue to do.

"I can't figure who would do this to you or why."

"Could have been some disruptive kids out for a good time, or maybe it was done by someone who's got something against me."

"Come on, brother. Who would have anything against you?"

Cleon had no answer. "I'll be there as soon as I can."

"Are you going to start up some new hives when you get home?"

"I–I don't know."

"I'm sure Grace will be glad to see you."

Cleon cringed. Despite his anger at Grace, he really did miss her—missed what they used to have together. He knew he'd hurt her by leaving, but she'd hurt him, too, and he wasn't certain he could ever trust her again.

When lunch was over and Grace's folks had left for home, she decided to put Anna down for a nap.

"Are you sure you don't want my help with those?" she asked Martha, who stood near the sink drying the last few dishes.

"No, you go ahead upstairs." Martha waved a soapy hand. "Maybe you should lie down awhile yourself. You're looking even more peaked than before we had lunch."

"I am feeling a bit tired, so maybe I will take a short rest." Grace headed for the door. "See you later, Martha."

A short time later, Grace had Anna situated in her room, so she stretched out on her own bed across the hall. It seemed odd to be living in this house–the home Cleon had started building when they'd first become engaged, the place where they were supposed to be living together.

Tears trickled down her cheeks and splashed onto the dahlia-patterned quilt. *Dear God, I'm so sorry for what I've done to my family and Cleon. Won't You please bring my husband home so I can make it up to him?*

Chapter 31

"You critters are sure messy, you know that?" Martha clicked her tongue, as she hosed out the unpleasant debris that had accumulated on the concrete floor of the dogs' outside run.

Heidi and her pups ran around one side of the kennel, and Fritz occupied the other side with a partition between them. Bo and Flo shared another section of the kennel, which would also be divided once Flo got pregnant. Dad had built the kennel against the back of the barn and connected it to an outside run through a small door Martha could open whenever the dogs needed fresh air or exercise.

Martha thought about Freckles, the pup Donna and Ray had bought from her, and how well the dog seemed to be doing. When she'd gone over to the Larsons' the other day, she'd been pleased to see how much the pup had grown and how well-adjusted it seemed.

Martha had brought Donna and Ray up to date on the attacks at her home. They seemed shocked and promised to keep an eye out for anything strange going on, and Ray had said he would notify the sheriff about the attacks that had already occurred.

Martha felt some measure of relief knowing the sheriff would finally be told, but it wouldn't set well with her father if he thought she'd had anything to do with it. Hopefully, the Larsons wouldn't mention her visit.

As Grace left the doctor's office, her heart swirled with emotions.

What she'd suspected had been confirmed—she was definitely pregnant. She was pleased to learn that she was carrying Cleon's baby, but she was worried about how well she could cope with having another child when everything in her life was so mixed up.

The odor of horseflesh assaulted her senses, and she glanced to the left. Two buggies waited at the stoplight, the horses both pawing at the pavement as though they couldn't wait to go. A car down the street tooted its horn, and an English boy heading up the sidewalk with his mother sneezed. A world where everything seemed normal was going on all around her, while Grace's world had been turned upside down.

When she approached her buggy, parked in the lot next to the doctor's office, she spotted Gary across the street, entering the restaurant where she used to work. How much longer would he be hanging around? Every time she saw him, she was reminded of her past and of her concerns that he might be responsible for the attacks. She wondered if she should confront him again—ask him to stop harassing them, plead with him if necessary.

Grace shook her head. What good would that do? When she'd confronted him before, he'd denied knowing anything about the attacks. Maybe he found pleasure in knowing she and her family were frightened. If she ignored him, he might leave them alone.

Roman had just begun sweeping up a pile of sawdust when John Peterson entered his shop.

"What can I do for you, John?" he asked, setting the broom aside.

John moved closer to Roman and pulled his fingers through the back of his hair. "You've. . .uh. . .probably heard that Luke Freisen has come to work for me."

"Jah, I heard."

"Well, I came by to make sure there were no hard feelings over me hiring him."

Roman leaned against his workbench and folded his arms. " 'Course not. It's not like you lured Luke away or anything. He only went to you because I fired him."

John blinked. "Really? I thought–" He shook his head. "Luke said you'd had a difference of opinion and that he figured he'd do better working for someone who used modern equipment."

"What'd you say to that?"

"What could I say? I wouldn't be happy doing the kind of work I do without the electricity and updated equipment I have in my shop." He glanced around the room. "Not that you do poor work with what you use here."

"I hope things go okay between you and Luke," Roman said with a shrug. He didn't want to make an issue of it, but if he were a betting man, he'd bet Luke Friesen wouldn't last more than a few weeks working for John.

"Luke seems like a pretty smart fellow, and from what I've seen, he's a good-enough worker."

Roman grunted. "He likes to do things his own way, and I'll give you a little warning: He tends to be late to work pretty often. Leastways, he was when he was workin' for me."

"I appreciate the tip, and you can be sure that I'll be keeping an eye on him."

Roman glanced at the fancy pair of sunglasses he'd set on the shelf across the room–the ones Judith had found on the ground near the clothesline. He was tempted to mention that he thought Luke might have something to do with the attacks that had been done at their place but decided against it since he had no proof. He supposed he could mention the sunglasses and ask John to take them and see if they belonged to Luke. On the other hand, if they were Luke's, it might be best to let him come and claim them himself.

John moved away from the desk. "I'd better get back to my shop. I left Luke working on a set of cabinets for Dave Rawlings, and I need to be sure he knows how many coats of stain it will take."

"Jah. Thanks for dropping by." When John closed the door, Roman reached for his broom and gave it a couple of hard sweeps across the floor. Now Dave, one of his steady customers, had taken his business elsewhere. Could Luke be saying bad things about Roman's work in order to lure more customers to John?

Roman grabbed a dustpan and pushed the pile of shavings into it as he thought about the conversation he'd finally had with their bishop the other night. "I've got to quit stewing over things and put my trust in God like Bishop King said I should do."

"I'm glad you're home, 'cause I didn't know what to do about all this."

Cleon grimaced as he and Ivan stood in the middle of the clearing where his beehives had once been. "Not a one left, is there?"

"Nope, and I'm sure sorry about this." Ivan shook his head. "I didn't want to make things worse by tellin' you all the details when I spoke with you on the phone the other day, but the shed where you kept your beekeeping equipment was burned, too."

Cleon huffed. Things seemed to be going from bad to worse for him these days. "It wasn't your fault. This could have happened if I'd been here. It isn't possible to keep an eye on the hives all the time."

Ivan touched Cleon's shoulder. "Have you seen Grace and told her about this?"

Cleon shook his head. "I had my driver bring me here as soon as I got off the bus in Dover."

"I'll bet Grace will be happy to know you're home. She looked awful mied and *bedauerlich* when I saw her in church a few weeks ago."

Cleon shrugged. Grace wasn't the only one who felt tired and sad. Finding out about her secret had made him feel like he'd been butted in the stomach by a charging bull. Now that his beehives were gone, he didn't even have a job he liked to do.

"You going home soon, then?"

Cleon winced. Was his brother trying to make him feel guilty for being gone so long? Didn't he realize the way things were with Grace?

"Guess I'll have to since I have no other place to go."

Ivan opened his mouth as if to say something more, but Cleon cut him off. "Think I'll speak to Grace's daed and see if he'd be willing to hire me in his shop. I'm not the best carpenter in the world, but

I believe I can give him a fair day's work."

"Sounds like a good idea." Ivan made a sweeping gesture of the open field. "You planning to get some more bees soon?"

"I don't know. Maybe." Cleon sighed. "Guess that all depends on how things go when I talk to Roman. I'll need some money in order to buy more bees and boxes, not to mention all the equipment that was burned in the fire."

"I'm sure Pop would loan you–"

Cleon held up his hand to halt his brother's words. "I'd rather do this without Pop's help." He nodded toward their folks' house. "Guess I'll get the horse and buggy I left here and head over to the Hostettlers' place. May as well get this over with."

Ivan's eyebrows lifted high on his forehead, but he said nothing. Truth be told, he probably knew Cleon was in no hurry to see Grace.

Chapter 32

Cleon's boots echoed against the wooden boards as he stepped onto the Hostettlers' porch. He dreaded this encounter with Grace even more than seeing his burned-out beehives. It was hard enough to return home without a job; it would be harder yet to live with a wife he didn't trust.

When he entered the kitchen, Grace's daughter was sitting at the kitchen table with a tablet and a pencil. She looked up and glared at him as though she was irritated with the interruption.

"Hello, Anna," he said. "Is your mother to home?"

The child squinted her blue eyes.

Cleon moved over to the table and pulled out the chair beside Anna. "I need to talk to your mamm—I mean, your mother."

"I know what mamm means, and she's sleepin' in her room right now."

His forehead wrinkled. Why would Grace be asleep in the middle of the day? "Is she sick?"

Anna shrugged.

"Guess I'd better go see." Cleon's chair squeaked against the floor when he pushed away from the table. As he made his way up the stairs, he hoped for the right words to say to Grace.

When he reached her bedroom, he noticed that the door was open. He stepped inside and was surprised to see that Grace wasn't there. For that matter, the house seemed unusually quiet, and he'd seen no one except Anna. Surely the child wouldn't have been left alone in the house.

He hurried down the stairs and was headed for the kitchen when the back door opened and Martha entered the house.

"Cleon! When did you get back? Does Grace know you're here?"

He shook his head. "I haven't seen her yet. I just left my folks' place after seeing what's left of my beehives."

Her forehead wrinkled. "What do you mean?"

"They've all been burned."

"Ach! When did that happen?"

"A few days ago, according to Ivan. All my hives, boxes, and equipment are gone, and that means I'm out of a job."

"I'm so sorry. I'm sure Grace will be, too, but I know she'll be glad to see you."

He nodded toward the kitchen door. "Anna said her mamm had gone to take a nap, but Grace wasn't upstairs in her room."

"She's over at your new house. She and Anna moved in there last week."

Cleon tipped his head. "But it's not finished—at least not enough so Grace could move in."

"Jah, it is. When your brothers weren't helping with things on your farm, they came over here and helped my daed get it done." Martha smiled. "They weren't sure how long you'd be gone, and they thought it would be a nice surprise when you got back."

"It's a surprise—that's for sure."

"Your being here will be a surprise for my sister, too. Why don't you go over to the house and say hello?"

He nodded and moved toward the door. "Guess I'd best do that."

As Grace lay on her bed, tossing, turning, and fighting waves of nausea that had kept her stomach churning for hours, her mind rehashed the past. She was still angry with herself for keeping her secret from her family, but she became more upset whenever she thought about her rumschpringe and how she'd wasted so many days dating Gary Walker. She wished she'd never left home to try out the English way of life. But then, if she hadn't married Wade, she wouldn't have Anna now.

She sniffed and swiped at the wetness under her nose. It did no good to dwell on the past. She needed to concentrate on a future with Anna and on the new life she carried in her womb. Last night, she'd told her folks about the baby, and they'd seemed pleased. If only she could be sure Cleon would feel the same way.

The door creaked open, and thinking it must be Anna, she wiped her eyes and sat up. Shock waves spiraled through her when she saw her husband standing inside the door. She scrambled off the bed and rushed toward him but was disappointed when he took a step back.

Grace held her arms rigidly at her sides. "Did you get a lot of honey orders on your trip?"

He nodded. "Trouble is I can't fill any of 'em now."

"Why not?"

"Hives, bees, and all my equipment are gone—burned out—every last one."

"What? How?" Grace could hardly believe her ears, and she wondered why she hadn't heard anything about this until now.

"Ivan said it looked like someone had deliberately set the fires." Cleon huffed. "I sure didn't need this right now."

"What are you going to do?"

"Don't know. Guess I need to find another job, because it will take some time before I can get any new hives going well enough so I'll have some honey to sell." Cleon's eyes looked weary and spent. "Just when I was beginning to think I might be able to make a decent living as a beekeeper."

Grace took a tentative step toward him. She wanted to offer support and let him know how much she cared but was afraid of his rejection. "I'm sorry, Cleon. Sorry for everything."

His broad shoulders shrugged. "Jah, well, it's all part of life, I guess. You think you've got things figured out and you're on the path to happiness. Then everything gets knocked out of kilter."

Grace was sure Cleon was referring to their messed-up marriage. She moistened her lips with the tip of her tongue and decided a change of subject might help. "Were you surprised to see that the house had been finished in your absence?"

He nodded. "Didn't expect anyone to do the work for me."

"My daed and your bruders wanted to surprise you, and they thought it would be good if Anna and I got moved into our new home."

"It looks nice. They did a fine job." He glanced around the room. " 'Course anything that pertains to building would be done well if your daed had his hand in it."

"You did well with your part of the building, too."

"It was all right, I guess."

A sudden wave of weakness washed over Grace, and she sank to the edge of her bed. "Cleon, I think we should talk about us."

"There's nothing to talk about," he said with a wave of his hand. "You kept the truth hidden from me, and that's that."

"It's not as simple as you make it sound. There's more I'd like to explain."

"It's a little late for explaining, don't you think?"

Grace sat trying to decide how best to respond. Should she list the reasons she had kept Wade and Anna a secret, beg Cleon to forgive her, or suggest that they try to forget the past and move on from here?

Before she had the chance to respond, Cleon spoke. "While I was on the road, I did a lot of thinking."

A ray of hope welled in Grace's soul. Cleon had come home, so that was a good sign. She placed one hand against her stomach, wondering if now was the time to tell him about the child she carried–his child, a product of their love. "Cleon, I–"

"Please, hear me out."

She lowered her gaze to the floor.

"After thinking things through, I realized that I have an obligation to you–and to Anna."

"Does that mean–"

"It means I'm back, and I'll provide for your needs. But I'll be sleeping in some other room."

"So our marriage will be in name only? Is that what you're saying?" Grace almost choked on the words.

He nodded.

"Is there anything I can say or do to make you change your mind?"

"Not unless you can undo the past."

"You know that's not possible." Grace clenched her fists as frustration raged within her like a whirling storm. Cleon had come home, but he hadn't forgiven her. They would be living in the same house but not sharing the same bedroom. He was the father of the baby she carried, yet she didn't feel free to tell him. Not now. This wasn't the right time.

"I'm going out to your daed's shop," Cleon said. "I need to speak with him about the possibility of giving me a job."

Grace nodded. When Cleon left the room, she moved over to the window and pulled the curtain aside. *What am I to do, Lord? Cleon and I used to be so close, and now it's as though we're strangers. I know I can't keep the news of my pregnancy from him indefinitely. Sooner or later, he'll have to know.*

She squeezed her eyes shut as tears threatened to escape. When Cleon had walked into the room moments ago, her hopes had soared. Now she was certain that nothing would ever be right in her world again.

Chapter 33

Ruth had just set an angel food cake in the bakery case when Martin Gingerich entered the shop.

"I heard you started working for Abe Wengerd last week," she said as he stepped up to the counter.

"Sure did, and I think I'm going to enjoy learning how to make and repair harnesses. Always did like the smell of leather." A wide smile spread across his face as he motioned to the counter full of pastries. " 'Course, what you're smelling here every day would be a lot better."

"Jah, it's enough to make me feel hungry the whole time I'm working."

"I imagine it would. Fact is, I'm feeling hungry right now."

"Would you like to sample something?"

He shook his head. "Better not. My mamm's fixing stuffed cabbage rolls for supper tonight, and she'd be sorely disappointed if I didn't eat at least five."

Ruth chuckled. She couldn't imagine anyone eating that many cabbage rolls. If Martin's mother made them as big as Ruth's mother did, she'd be lucky to eat two.

"So what can I help you with?"

"Actually, I didn't come to the bakeshop to buy anything."

"You didn't?"

"No, I. . ." Martin's voice trailed off, and he stared at the floor as his face turned a deep shade of pink. Finally, he looked up, although he kept his focus on the pastries inside the case. "I. . .uh. . .heard that you. . ." He paused and swiped at the sweat rolling down his forehead.

"What did you hear?"

"I heard that you and Luke broke up."

"That's true."

"Mind if I ask why?"

Truthfully, she did mind. The last thing she wanted to talk about was Luke and her mistrust of him.

"If you'd rather not say, I understand. It's just that. . .well, I've heard some things, and—"

"What kind of things?"

"Heard he's been hanging around with a bunch of rowdy English fellows, and my daed mentioned that he thinks Luke might have been in on that cow tipping over at Bishop King's place some time ago." Martin lifted his gaze to meet hers. "I thought maybe you knew about it, too, and that's why you broke up with him."

Ruth swallowed hard. Should she share her suspicions with Martin? She'd known him since they were little, but they'd never been close friends. Besides, she wasn't sure what his reaction would be if she told him what she thought Luke might be up to. She couldn't be sure Martin would keep what she said to himself.

"If you don't want to talk about it, I won't press." Martin's hazel-colored eyes held a note of sympathy.

She nodded. "Danki. I'd rather not."

Martin shrugged. "Anyway, finding out why you and Luke broke up isn't the reason I dropped by." He shifted his weight and pulled his fingers through the back of his thick, Dutch-bobbed hair.

"What is the reason?"

"There's going to be a young people's get-together at our place this Saturday evening. We'll be playing some games, and of course, there'll be plenty of refreshments furnished by my mamm."

"Sounds like fun."

"I came by to see if you might be free to come. Your sister Martha's invited, too, of course."

Ruth's first thought was to decline the invitation because she hadn't felt like doing anything fun since she and Luke broke up, not to mention the stress she'd been under because of all the trouble at home. But as she thought about it more, she decided that she and Martha might need an evening of fun with others their age. "I'll speak to Martha this evening and see if she's wants to go."

"Good. I hope to see you on Saturday then." Martin hesitated but finally turned and headed out the door.

Ruth smiled as the door clicked shut behind him. For the first time in many days, she felt a sense of anticipation.

After Cleon went to his house to speak with Grace, Martha decided to take Anna out to the barn. Mom had gone to visit Alma Wengerd, who'd sprained her ankle a few days ago, and Martha figured Mom might stay awhile, which meant she'd probably have to keep an eye on Anna for most of the day.

"Can I play with the puppies?" Anna asked as they neared the end of the barn where the kennel had been built.

"Jah, sure."

Anna grinned up at her. "I like Rose the best."

"Rose?"

"That one right there." Anna pointed to the runt of the litter—the pup no one wanted.

Martha smiled and patted the top of Anna's head. "How would you like to have Rose as your own?"

"You mean it?" Anna's blue eyes lit up like a firefly.

"If your mamm says it's okay."

"You think Mama will let me keep her at the new house?"

Martha was pleased that Anna had referred to Grace as *Mama*. She finally must have accepted Grace as her mother. "You can ask your mamm after supper tonight. How's that sound?"

Anna's smile quickly faded. "Is that man gonna eat supper with us?"

"What man?"

"The one who came to our house today."

Martha nodded. "I think Cleon will be joining us. He was on

a business trip for a while, but his home is here with you and your mamm."

Anna thrust out her chin. "I don't like him. I wish he'd go away again."

Martha was about to reply when she heard the barn door open and shut. She turned and saw Grace heading their way with shoulders slumped and head down. Martha figured things hadn't gone so well between her sister and Cleon.

"I'll get Rose out of the kennel, and you can sit over there and play with her," Martha said, leading Anna to a nearby bale of straw.

"Okay."

Once the child was seated, Martha stopped by Grace. "I'm going to get one of the pups for Anna to play with, and then the two of us can talk."

Grace nodded.

"As soon as Anna and the puppy are settled, I'll meet you in the tack room."

Grace glanced over at her daughter, who sat on the bale of straw with her chin resting in the palms of her hands. "That's fine."

Grace headed for the tack room, and Martha hurried to the kennels at the back of the barn. A few minutes later, Anna had a sleeping pup nestled in her lap.

"Your mamm and I need to talk, but we'll be back soon." She gave Anna's shoulder a gentle squeeze. "Don't leave the barn, you hear?"

"I won't."

Martha hurried to the tack room and found Grace sitting on a wooden stool, her head down. "Why do you look so sad?"

Grace lifted her head. "Cleon's back."

"I know. He came by looking for you, and when I told him your place had been finished and that you were over there, he headed that way." Martha slipped her arm around Grace's shoulders. "Did he speak with you?"

"Jah. He had some bad news."

"You mean about his beehives being burned?"

Grace nodded. "He's going to Dad's shop to see if he might be able to work there."

"I thought he helped with the farm at his folks' place."

"He's never enjoyed farming that much. I think he'd be happier working in Dad's woodworking shop."

"What did Cleon say when you told him about the baby?"

"I–I didn't tell him."

"You didn't tell him you're pregnant?"

"No."

"Why not?"

"He made it clear that he's only staying with me out of obligation." Grace drew in a quivering breath. "From now on, Cleon and I will be sleeping in separate bedrooms. He'll be my husband in name only."

Martha had known Cleon was upset about Grace's secret, but she didn't think he would still be nursing a grudge. She massaged Grace's shoulders and neck, feeling the tension in her sister's knotted muscles beneath her fingers. "What are you going to do about this?"

"There's not much I can do."

"You could start by telling Cleon that you're carrying his boppli. That might make him see things in a different light."

"Or it might make him feel more resentful–like I trapped him on purpose."

Martha's forehead wrinkled. "That's *lecherich*. It's not like you planned to get pregnant."

"It might seem ridiculous to you," Grace said with a catch in her voice, "but Cleon is full of hurt and bitterness right now, and he might think I'm capable of doing most anything."

Martha moved to face Grace. "You can't hide this from Cleon forever. Before long, you'll be showing."

"I know."

"Besides, you've already told our folks. If you wait to tell Cleon and he finds out on his own, he might accuse you of keeping another secret from him. You don't want that, do you?"

Grace shook her head as more tears pooled in her eyes. "I'll tell him tonight after Anna's in bed."

Chapter 34

Roman was about to close up for the day when a customer entered his shop. At least he thought it was a customer until he looked up from his desk and saw Cleon standing inside the door.

"Cleon! It's good to see you. How long have you been back?"

"Got home this morning."

Roman's forehead wrinkled. "This morning? You've been here that long?"

Cleon nodded. "Went over to see the damage that had been done to my beehives; then I stopped in to see my folks."

"What damage was done to your hives?"

"Somebody set fire to 'em. Every last one is gone."

"I'm real sorry to hear that. Do you have any idea who might have done it?"

Cleon shook his head. "Ivan figures it was probably some rowdy fellows out for a good time. Could even be the same ones who dumped over those outhouses near Kidron and were involved in the cow tipping." He moved closer to Roman's desk. "Since I have no bees, hives, or equipment, I'm out of a job."

"But spring is here, and you'll be farming with your daed again, right?"

Cleon's fingers curled through the ends of his beard. "I've never enjoyed farming, and I'd rather do something else." He took a step forward. "I know I'm not an expert carpenter, but I can handle a hammer and a saw fairly well. So I was wondering if you might be able to use an extra pair of hands here in your woodworking shop."

"As a matter of fact, I could use some help. I had to fire Luke for being late to work so many times, and now he's working for John Peterson." Roman nodded at Cleon. "Judging from the work you did on your new house, I'd say I'd be getting more than an apprentice if I hired you."

Cleon shook his head. "I can't take credit for all the work done on my house. You and my brothers helped in the beginning, and from what Grace told me, you finished it up in my absence. I appreciate all your hard work."

"I figured you and Grace would want to get settled into your own place before the boppli is born."

Cleon's eyebrows drew together. "Boppli? What boppli are you talking about?"

"Surely Grace must have told you."

"Told me what?"

"About her being in a family way."

Cleon's face turned red as a cherry, and a vein on the side of his neck bulged. "I just came from talking to Grace, and she never said a word about any baby."

Roman reached up to swipe the trickle of sweat rolling down his forehead. Apparently Grace hadn't learned her lesson about keeping secrets. "I'm sorry you had to hear it from me. Should have been my daughter doing the telling."

"You're right about that." Cleon grunted. "Of course, she seems to be real good at keeping secrets, so I shouldn't be surprised that she's kept this one from me, as well."

"Maybe she was waiting for the right time."

"The right time? And when would that be?" Cleon crossed his arms.

Roman shrugged. He wanted to defend his daughter, but the truth was, he hadn't quite forgiven Grace for not telling them about her English husband and the little girl she'd allowed her in-laws to take. He couldn't blame Cleon for being angry that Grace hadn't told him about the baby she carried. That should have been the first thing out of her mouth when she'd seen him today.

Cleon's lips parted as if he might have more to say, but the shop door opened. Luke stepped into the room.

"I hope you're not here about getting your job back," Roman said, irritation edging his voice. He motioned to Cleon. "You've been replaced."

Luke's face flushed as he shook his head. "Came to see if I left my sunglasses here. I think I had 'em with me that day you fired me, and—"

"Well, it's about time. What took you so long?"

"Huh?"

"Never mind." Roman pointed to the shelf across the room where the fancy pair of sunglasses lay. "They're right over there. My wife found 'em on the ground, not far from where her clothesline had been cut." He squinted at Luke. "You wouldn't know anything about that, would ya, boy?"

The color in Luke's cheeks deepened. "Are you accusing me of cutting your wife's clothesline?"

Roman shrugged. "Not accusing, just asking, is all."

Luke's eyes narrowed into tiny slits. "Now why would I do something like that?"

"I don't know. Why would somebody burn Cleon's beehives, vandalize our house, or steal tools from my shop?"

Cleon's face blanched. "Surely you don't think one of our own had anything to do with those things?"

"I don't know what I believe anymore, and those aren't the only things that have been done to us, either."

"What do you mean? What else has been done?"

Roman looked at his son-in-law, then over at Luke. "Maybe you should ask him."

Luke's eyes flashed angrily. "Ask me what—whether I know what attacks have been done, or if I had anything to do with them?"

"Both."

"I only knew about the break-ins here at the shop and the house. Oh, and also the brick that was thrown through your kitchen window.

I don't know who's responsible for any of those acts, but—"

Jack Osborn, the middle-aged sheriff in their county, entered the shop.

Roman pushed his chair away from the desk and stood. "Sorry, but that rocking chair you asked me to make for your wife isn't ready yet, Jack."

"I'm not here about the chair." Jack glanced around the room as if he was looking for something. "Got a phone call from one of your English neighbors the other day. They said you folks had been having a few problems. I should have come by sooner, but two of my deputies have been out sick, so I've only had time to respond to urgent calls."

Before Roman could formulate a response, Luke dashed across the room and grabbed his sunglasses off the shelf. "I've got an errand to run, so I'd better go." He rushed out the door like a fox being chased by a pack of hounds.

Jack opened his jacket and pulled a notebook and pen from his shirt pocket. "Now why don't you tell me what's been going on here, Roman?"

"Jah, okay." Roman returned to his seat, and Cleon grabbed one of the wooden stools near the workbench.

For several minutes, Roman related the details of the attacks, and Sheriff Osborn took notes. Roman ended his speech by saying, "My son-in-law here recently had his beehives burned, so I'm thinking that whoever's been bothering us might have ruined the hives, as well."

Jack leaned over and placed both hands on Roman's desk. "You think someone's singled out your family?"

Roman gave his left earlobe a couple of pulls. "Thought at first it might be a bunch of rowdy English fellows, but now I'm not so sure."

Jack's bushy eyebrows rose as he leveled Roman with a questioning look. "I know you Amish don't prosecute, but you could have at least let me know what was going on here so I could have investigated and hopefully brought the criminal to justice."

"God is the only judge we need. He knows who did those things, and if it's His will for them to be brought to justice, then He'll do it in His time, His way."

Jack looked over at Cleon as though he hoped he might say something, but Cleon said nothing. Finally, Jack straightened and slipped the notebook and pen back into his pocket. "Have it your way, but I want you to know that I'll be keeping an eye on things for a while."

"Suit yourself."

"If there are any more attacks made on you or your family, I'd appreciate hearing about it. Some who've committed crimes like this against the Amish have done it simply because you're different, and that doesn't set well with me."

"Nor me, but it will be up to our church leaders and the nature of the crime whether it's reported or not."

Jack shrugged and headed for the door. "Let me know when that rocking chair's done," he called over his shoulder.

"Jah, I surely will."

The door clicked shut, and Roman let his head fall forward into his hands as he released a groan. "I wonder which one of our English neighbors phoned the sheriff, and more importantly, who told 'em about the attacks?"

Cleon shook his head. "Could someone in your family have mentioned it?"

"Maybe so, but I need you to do me a favor."

"What's that?"

"Don't say anything about the sheriff showing up here today, or that he plans to keep an eye on things."

"Why not?"

"I don't want the family to get the idea that they're being watched, and I don't want 'em thinking I called the sheriff."

"I won't say a word unless you speak about it first."

"I appreciate that." Roman slid his chair away from the desk. "Now let's go on up to the house and see if supper's ready. Grace and Anna have been taking most of their meals with us since you left, so I'm sure everyone will eat together at our place tonight."

Cleon nodded.

"If you'd like to meet me here at the shop tomorrow morning, I'll give you some woodworking tools and show you what I need to have done."

"I'll be here, bright and early."

Tension had filled the air between Grace and Cleon all during supper, and Grace had even noticed something going on between Dad and Cleon. It was as if they knew something and had decided not to share it with the rest of the family. She'd been tempted to ask about it but figured it might be best to question Cleon later on—if she got the chance.

By the time Grace took Anna home to their house and was getting her ready for bed, she felt ready to go to bed herself. But she knew she couldn't. Not until she'd told Cleon she was carrying his baby.

She slipped Anna's nightgown over the child's head and pulled back the bed covers. "Hop into bed now."

"Aunt Martha says I can have a puppy of my own," Anna said as she nestled against her pillow.

"Are you sure about that?" Grace knew her sister was trying to build up her business, and giving dogs away wouldn't bring in any money.

Anna nodded, her blue eyes looking ever so serious. "She says I can have Rose if it's all right with you, Mama."

Grace stroked her daughter's arm, relishing the warmth and softness of the child's skin. It felt good to hear Anna call her Mama. They'd been drawing closer every day, and Grace wouldn't do anything to spoil things between them. She nodded and smiled. "You may have the puppy on one condition."

"What's a 'condition'?"

"It means you must agree to help take care of the dog."

Anna's eyes brightened. "I will. I've been helpin' Aunt Martha with the puppies ever since I came to live here."

Grace bent over and kissed Anna's forehead. "All right, then. You can call Rose your own."

Anna snuggled beneath the covers with a satisfied smile, and Grace slipped quietly out of the room. The last she'd seen Cleon, he had been downstairs in the living room reading the latest issue of *The Budget*.

Knowing he needed to speak with Grace before she went to bed, Cleon left the living room and started up the steps. He'd just reached the top when he bumped into Grace.

She covered her mouth with the palm of her hand. "Oh! You startled me. I—I was heading downstairs so we could talk."

He nodded. "You're right. We do need to talk. Let's go to the living room so our voices won't be heard."

Once they reached the living room, Cleon took a seat on the sofa, and Grace sat in the rocking chair across from him. No furniture had been in the house when he'd left Holmes County, so Grace's father must have provided it in his absence.

"I know you're pregnant."

"I'm pregnant."

They spoke at the same time, and Cleon repeated himself to be sure she had heard him.

Grace's mouth dropped open. "You know?"

He nodded.

"Who told you?"

"Does it matter? The point is you didn't tell me, and I'm wondering why."

"I—I was afraid you might think I had gotten pregnant on purpose so I could trap you into staying with me."

Cleon slowly shook his head. "That's lecherich. How could you have gotten pregnant on purpose? It's not like we were using any birth control methods."

She dropped her gaze to the floor. "I know, but I've heard of some women who try to time things around their monthly cycle, and—"

He held up his hand to silence her. "I know you didn't get pregnant on purpose, and under normal circumstances, I'd be looking forward to becoming a daed."

"But not now? Is that what you're saying?" Grace's chin trembled, and her eyes filled with tears. He made no move to comfort her.

"Things are so verhuddelt right now I'm not sure how I feel about much of anything."

"I'm sorry for my part in your confusion."

"You want me to forgive you for keeping Anna a secret, yet you keep another secret from me. That makes no sense."

"I–I was scared you would leave and scared you would stay for the wrong reasons."

He grimaced. "I told you earlier today that I would take care of you and Anna."

"I know, but–"

"Until you can learn to be honest with me, I don't see how we'll ever be able to have a real marriage, Grace."

"Are you saying that you don't love me enough to try to make our marriage work? It takes two, you know."

Cleon flinched. Was that what he was saying? "I'll be starting work for your daed tomorrow morning, so I'd better get to bed." He stood and rushed out of the room, knowing if he didn't get away from Grace, he might say something he would be sorry for come morning.

Chapter 35

When Grace awoke the following morning, she felt as if she hadn't even gone to bed. Besides the morning sickness she'd been dealing with for weeks, her head hurt, and her hands shook so badly that, as she cracked eggs, several pieces of shell fell into the bowl. If only Cleon would forgive her. If he could just show some excitement over the baby she carried in her womb.

Soon after Grace and Cleon had become betrothed, they'd begun talking about the family they would have some day. Cleon had said he wanted a large family, and Grace had looked forward to the day when she could hold another baby in her arms and know it wouldn't be taken from her. Now she would have that baby, as well as her five-year-old daughter, but she feared she would never have her husband again. Not in the real sense of the word, anyway.

A knock at the back door halted Grace's thoughts. Since Cleon hadn't come downstairs for breakfast yet, she dried her hands on a towel and went to see who was at the door. Martha stood on the porch.

"Why didn't you come in rather than knocking?"

"I—I wanted to be sure I could talk to you alone."

Noting how pale her sister's face looked, Grace felt immediate concern. "Are you feeling grank this morning?"

Martha shook her head. "Not physically, but I'm sure sick at heart."

Grace's heart pounded against her chest. "Has there been another attack?"

"I'm not sure." Martha stepped closer, and her voice lowered to a whisper. "Where's Anna? I don't want her to hear what I have to say—at least not yet."

"She's upstairs in bed. I figured I would wait until breakfast was ready to wake her." Grace motioned to a couple of wicker chairs sitting on the other end of the porch. "Let's sit over there."

Once they were seated, Martha leaned over and massaged her forehead. "Rose is dead."

"Rose?"

"The puppy I promised Anna she could have if you said it was okay."

"She asked me about it last night, but I'd forgotten that she'd called it 'Rose.' " Grace touched her sister's arm. "What happened? How did the pup die?"

"I'm not sure. I found both kennel doors open when I went out to feed the dogs this morning, and then I discovered them running around the yard." Martha paused. "Except for Rose; she was dead."

Grace covered her mouth.

"I don't know how I'm going to tell Anna. She really liked that puppy and was looking forward to calling it her own."

"I'm her mamm; it's my place to tell her."

"I feel awful enough about losing one of my dogs, but I hope it won't affect how things are with you and Anna."

"I hope not, either. Do you have any idea why the hundli died or how the dogs got out of their kennel?"

"They got out because the doors were open, and I guess the pup could have climbed onto one of the bales of hay that sat near the barn and then fallen off."

"You don't suppose someone did this on purpose, do you? I mean—let the dogs out of their cage and. . .and killed Anna's puppy?"

"I hope that's not the case."

"How do you think the cage doors got open?"

"I don't know. Maybe I forgot to latch them when I fed them last night."

"But you're always so careful when it comes to things like that."

"That's usually true, but I've had a lot on my mind lately, so I suppose I could have forgotten." Martha released a sigh. "Are you sure you don't want me to tell Anna?"

"No, I'll do it after breakfast."

"Guess I'd better go bury the puppy." Martha released a sigh. "I don't want Anna to see it that way."

"No, that wouldn't be good." As Grace rose from her chair, a wave of nausea hit her, and she clutched her stomach.

"Are you okay?"

"I'll be fine. It's just a touch of morning sickness."

"What did Cleon say when you told him about the boppli?"

Grace rubbed her hands briskly over her arms and shivered even though the early spring weather had turned quite warm. "He already knew."

"He suspected it? Is that what you're saying?"

"I guess Cleon learned about it when he went to Dad's shop to see if he would hire him."

"Dad told Cleon you're in a family way?"

Grace nodded. "I'm sure he thought Cleon knew about the baby. He probably figured I'd already told him. Now Cleon thinks I deliberately kept another secret from him, and—" Grace couldn't finish her sentence.

"Didn't you explain why you hadn't said anything yet, and that you had planned to tell him last night?"

"I tried, but Cleon doesn't trust me anymore, and he—"

"He what, Grace?"

Grace took a few seconds to compose herself as she sniffed and wiped the tears from her cheeks. "Cleon didn't show any enthusiasm about the baby. I—I don't think he wants to be a daed. At least not to any of my children."

Martha wore a look of disbelief and slowly shook her head. "I didn't think things could get much worse around here."

"Me, neither. It makes me wonder if God cares how much we're all hurting."

Unable to control her emotions, Grace leaned her head on Martha's shoulder and sobbed.

When Cleon entered the kitchen, he was surprised to discover that it was empty. When he'd first wakened, he thought he'd smelled coffee brewing, so he figured Grace had to be awake. He had tossed and turned most of the night and needed a cup of coffee to clear the cobwebs from his foggy brain.

He spotted the coffeepot sitting near the back of the stove and was about to take a mug from the cupboard, when he noticed a carton of eggs on the counter, a sure sign that Grace must be nearby. Maybe she was using the necessary room or had gone outside for something.

Cleon poured some coffee and was about to take a drink when he heard footsteps coming down the stairs. A few seconds later, Anna entered the kitchen dressed in a long, cotton nightgown.

"Where's Mama?" she asked, rubbing her eyes and looking around the room.

"I'm not sure. She must have been in the kitchen at one time, because breakfast has been started." Cleon motioned to the coffeepot and then to the eggs. "She wasn't here when I came downstairs, and I don't know where she is now."

Anna padded over to the table and climbed onto a chair. "I'm hungry. I wanna eat now so I can play with Rose."

"Who's Rose?"

"My new puppy. Aunt Martha said I could have her if Mama said it was okay." Anna's head bobbed up and down. "Last night Mama said it was all right with her."

Cleon leaned against the counter and studied the child. Her long brown hair hung down her back in a mass of heavy curls, reminding him of how Grace's pale blond hair had looked on their wedding night after she'd taken it down and he'd begun brushing it for her. His heart clenched as he thought about how soft Grace's skin had felt beneath his touch, and how full of love his heart had been for her that night. He ached with the knowledge of her deception. Didn't honesty come with love? Had she ever truly loved him?

"Are you gonna look for Mama so we can eat?"

Cleon's mind snapped back to the present. "Uh, I'll see if she's outside." He headed for the back door, but it opened. Grace stepped in. Her face looked ashen, and her eyes were red and swollen. Had she been crying because of him, or had something else happened?

He stepped aside. "What's wrong? Have you been crying?"

"I–I can't talk about it right now." She glanced over at Anna and grimaced. "I'll deal with it after breakfast."

Cleon shrugged. If she didn't want to talk about what was bothering her, he couldn't do much about it. He took a seat at the table.

Anna looked up at her mother. "I'm hungry."

Grace nodded and hurried to the stove. "I'll have some breakfast on the table real soon."

"Can we go see Rose after we're done eating?"

Grace shook her head.

"You said I could have the puppy." Anna thrust out her lower lip. "I wanna see her now."

"You need to eat breakfast. We can talk about Rose after you've finished your scrambled eggs."

"I wanna see her now."

"Your mamm said after breakfast," Cleon said before Grace could respond. "Now quit whining and sit there quietly until breakfast is served."

Grace glared at Cleon. "There's no need to be yelling at her."

"I wasn't yelling."

"Yes, you were." Anna pointed at Cleon. "Your face is red, too."

A muscle on the side of Cleon's cheek pulsated. He debated whether he should say anything more and finally decided that if Grace chose to ignore the child's sassy attitude, then she could deal with it, not him.

Anna hopped off her chair and raced for the back door.

"Where are you going?" Grace called to her daughter's retreating form.

"To see Rose."

"No! You can't see her now." By the time Grace started across the room, Anna had already opened the door. "Come back here, Anna!"

She reached out and grabbed the child's arm, pulling her back into the house.

"I wanna see Rose!" Anna screamed as she tried to pry her mother's hands off her arm.

Grace's shoulders trembled, but she kept Anna in her grip. Cleon wondered if he should step in and attempt to calm the child or if it would be best to let Grace handle things.

"Anna, listen to me now." Grace knelt down and wrapped her arms around the child, holding her firmly until she finally calmed down. "Rose is dead. Your Aunt Martha found her that way this morning."

Anna stiffened. She pulled away sharply. "Rose can't be dead!"

"I'm sorry, Anna. Maybe Aunt Martha will give you another puppy when Flo has some." Grace reached out to wipe the tears from Anna's face, but the child jerked open the door and bolted out of the house.

Grace rushed after her. Cleon sat too stunned to move.

Chapter 36

The next few days were difficult. Anna mourned the loss of her puppy, and Grace tried to deal with the emotions swirling around in her heart like a windmill going at full speed. Her relationship with Anna had taken a step back. Her relationship with Cleon was strained and formal. Concern for her family's safety weighed on her heavily.

If they could only learn who was responsible for the attacks and make them stop. If they could just go back to the way the things were before their world had been turned upside down.

As Grace finished the breakfast dishes, she stared out the kitchen window at the tree branches swaying in the wind. Cleon had gone to work in Dad's shop, and Anna was upstairs in her room. Thinking it might help the child get her mind off the loss of her puppy, Grace had suggested that they go to the Wengerds' today so Anna could play with her friend Esta, but Anna hadn't wanted to go.

The quiet and solitude of the house would have been a welcome respite on most days, but this morning, Grace felt as if she were suffocating. She wanted to rush outside and scream out her fears. Instead, she grabbed a scouring pad and scrubbed the frying pan clean. "I need to keep busy. If I keep my hands and mind occupied, I won't have time to think about the troubles I'm facing."

When the back door creaked open, Grace turned to see who had come in. Her mother held a gray and white kitten in her hands. "How are you feeling this morning?"

"My stomach's settled down some, but that's about all."

"Things are no better with Anna's grief over the puppy?"

Grace shook her head. "She's not even interested in visiting her friend Esta today."

"I'm sorry." Mom nodded at the squirming kitten. "Martha offered Anna another puppy, but she refused, so I thought maybe I might interest her in one of Callie's kittens."

"Martha shouldn't be giving her pups away, anyhow. She'll never get her business going if she doesn't start bringing in some money." Grace glanced at the door leading to the hallway. "Anna's upstairs in her room. You can offer her the kitten, but I doubt she'll take it."

"It's worth a try." Mom started toward the door but paused. "Your daed says Cleon's working out well in his shop."

"That's good." Grace went back to washing the dishes, figuring her mother would head upstairs to see Anna, but Mom moved over to stand beside her at the sink.

"Your sullen expression tells me there might be something else bothering you besides Anna grieving for her puppy. Are things any better between you and Cleon?"

The lump in Grace's throat refused to let her say a word. She could only shake her head and shed a few more salty tears.

Mom placed the kitten on the floor and gathered Grace into her arms. "Is there anything I can do?"

Grace swallowed a couple of times, hoping to push the lump down. "I don't think there's much anyone can do. Cleon doesn't trust me anymore. We're still sleeping in separate bedrooms."

"But he knows about the boppli, right?"

"Jah."

"And that makes no difference?"

"I guess not. Dad told him the news before I had a chance to say anything, and now Cleon thinks I was trying to keep my pregnancy a secret from him." She inhaled deeply. "I think, more than anything, Cleon's upset that I was married before. I believe the thought of me having had a child with another man is too much for him to bear."

"*Puh!*" Mom waved a hand. "That's just plain lecherich. We know many widows who have married again, and their new husbands don't sleep in separate rooms or act is if the wife has done something wrong because she used to be married."

Grace dried her hands on a towel that had been lying on the counter. "If I'd been married to an Amish man who had died, Cleon would probably be okay with it. I think what troubles him most is that I was once married to an Englisher."

"Has Cleon said he feels prejudiced toward your deceased English husband?"

"Well, no. . .not in so many words, but from some of the things he's said, I've gotten that impression." Grace dropped her gaze to the floor. "He seems to have trouble with forgiveness."

"Then he needs to read his Bible more and start putting into practice the things he hears in church." Mom nodded toward the back door. "Truth be told, your daed has the same problem concerning his sister. Since it's a touchy subject with him, I try to be understanding and don't question his feelings." She patted Grace's arm. "My advice is to put your relationship with Cleon in God's hands."

"I'll try to be a better wife. Maybe if Cleon sees how much I love him, he'll find it in his heart to forgive me."

"I'll be praying that he does." Mom bent to retrieve the kitten. "Guess I'll head upstairs now and see what Anna thinks about this *siess* little ball of fur."

Grace smiled despite her frustrations. "It is pretty sweet, and I hope she likes it."

"Sure am glad I hired you. You've been a big help to me the last few days."

Cleon looked up from his job of sanding a straight-backed chair and smiled at his father-in-law, who stood nearby hammering nails into a set of cabinets. "I appreciate the job."

"I know it's selfish of me," Roman said, "but I wouldn't mind if you decided to forget about beekeeping and stayed right here working for me. I have no sons, so I'll need to pass on the business to someone, and you're a lot more dependable than my last employee."

"I wonder how things are working out for Luke at his new job. Have you heard any complaints from John?" Cleon asked, making no comment about his interest in taking over the woodworking shop someday. He was taking one day at a time, and even if he didn't rely solely on selling honey, he still wanted to do it on a part-time basis.

Roman pursed his lips. "John came by the other day and said he was pleased with Luke's work, but I'm guessin' he won't be for long—not once that lazy fellow starts showing up late for work." He shrugged. "But then I guess it's not my place to judge."

Cleon recoiled, feeling like he'd been stung by one of his bees. Had that remark been directed at him? Did Grace's dad know Cleon hadn't forgiven Grace? Was this Roman's subtle way of trying to make him feel guilty?

Cleon pushed the sandpaper a little harder against the unyielding arm of the chair and grimaced. *Roman doesn't understand the way I feel. He's not the one who wishes he could leave Holmes County and never look back.*

Ruth smiled when she saw her youngest sister enter the bakeshop. "I didn't know you were coming to town today," she said as Martha stepped up to the counter.

"I got a ride from Donna Larson into Sugarcreek this morning so I could stop by *The Budget* and run another ad for Heidi's remaining pups, since I've decided not to keep any. Then we drove to Berlin."

"I'm sorry you lost that little pup the other day."

Martha frowned. "Sure wish I knew how it happened and whether or not it was an accident."

Ruth leaned on the counter. "Who would want to hurt an innocent puppy?"

"It's hard to say, but if whoever did this is the same person who made the other attacks at our place, then I'd have to say they must be a bit ab im kopp."

"You're right, they must be off in the head, and I hope it's no one we know."

Martha glanced around the room, and her voice lowered to a whisper. "Are you thinking of Luke?"

Ruth nodded. "Dad said those sunglasses Mom found near her clothesline belonged to him."

"How does he know that?"

"Luke came by his shop the other day, looking for his glasses."

Martha shrugged. "So the sunglasses were Luke's. That doesn't prove he had anything to do with cutting the line. He may have dropped his glasses when he was heading for his buggy."

"Jah, maybe so." Ruth didn't want to think the worst of Luke, but he'd acted so strangely the last few months of their courtship. Dad had mentioned that Luke had said and done some things at the shop he didn't care for and that he'd put Luke in his place a couple of times. She supposed Luke could be nursing a grudge, but to try and get even–going so far as to kill one of Heidi's pups? It was too much to fathom.

"Are you still going to that young people's fellowship with Martin on Saturday?" Martha asked.

Ruth's mouth dropped open. "I'm not going with Martin. He just asked if I planned to go and said he hoped to see me there."

"What'd you tell him?"

"That I thought it sounded like fun and I'd try to be there."

"What was his response to that?"

"He said he was glad and would look forward to seeing me on Saturday."

Martha snickered. "Sounds like a date to me."

"It's not a date."

"Whatever you say." Martha winked at Ruth. "Martin's kind of shy, but he's also pretty cute. You'd better make sure you're playing on his side of the volleyball net."

"Go on with you now," Ruth said with a wave of her hand. "And you'd better plan on going with me, because you spend way too much time at home with those dogs of yours. You need to get out more and have some fun."

Martha wrinkled her nose. "Caring for my hund seems like fun to me."

"That might be, but you need to be with people your age." Ruth smiled. "Speaking of which, I was thinking that since this Sunday will be an off-Sunday from preaching, the two of us could go to the pond for a picnic."

"That's a fine idea. Maybe we could take Anna along, too. She's been so sad since her puppy died. She wouldn't even accept the kitten Mom offered her. Maybe a day at the pond will help lighten her mood." Ruth smiled. "It might be good for Grace and Cleon to have some time alone, too."

"Sounds good to me. We can go to the young people's gathering on Saturday evening and spend Sunday afternoon at the pond. By Monday morning, maybe we'll all feel a little better than we have here of late."

Chapter 37

How was the young people's gathering you girls went to last night?" Roman asked, nodding at his two daughters who sat to the left of him at the kitchen table.

"It was all right," Martha said, reaching for a piece of toast.

Ruth just sat there with a dreamy look on her face.

"How about you, Ruth? Did you enjoy the young people's get-together?"

"Jah, it was a lot of fun."

Martha snickered. "Ruth's in love."

Judith's eyebrows lifted in obvious surprise, but Roman looked over at Ruth and frowned. "Did Luke show up there? Are the two of you together again?"

Ruth shook her head. "No, Dad. Luke wasn't there, and we aren't a courting couple."

He breathed out so forcefully that the air lifted a lock of hair from his forehead. "That's a relief. As far as I'm concerned, that fellow can't be trusted."

Martha's forehead wrinkled. "I'm sure Luke's not the one responsible for the attacks against us. He doesn't seem like the type to do something like that."

"Jah, well, you can't always judge a piece of wood by its color."

Judith leaned close to Ruth. "If you're not seeing Luke, then what did Martha mean when she said you were in love?"

Ruth lifted her gaze to the ceiling. "I'm not in love, Mom. I just got to know Martin a little better last night, that's all."

"Martin Gingerich?"

"Jah."

"I talked to Abe Wengerd the other day, and he said he'd recently hired Martin as his apprentice," Roman said.

Ruth nodded. "That's what Martin told me. He said he thinks he's going to like working in the boot and harness shop."

"You should have seen the way Martin looked at Ruth," Martha put in. "If ever there was a man in love, it has to be him."

Ruth elbowed her sister. "Martin's not in love with me any more than I am with him. As I said before, we're just getting to know each other."

"Jah, well, at least Martin's settled down and joined the church. That's more than I can say for Luke, who in my opinion is much too old to still be running around," Roman grumbled.

Martha opened her mouth as if to respond, but he held up his hand. "Enough talk about Luke. Let's get our breakfast finished and decide how we want to spend our day."

"Since this is an off-Sunday from church, I thought it might be nice if we went calling on a few folks," Judith spoke up.

"Martha and I had planned to take Anna on a picnic today," Ruth said.

"We thought it might help take her mind off the puppy she lost," Martha added.

"Besides, it will give Grace and Cleon some time alone together."

"That's a good idea," Judith agreed. "Those two surely need to talk things through. With Anna out of the picture, it might be easier for them."

Roman swallowed some coffee, then said, "If Grace hadn't lied to Cleon, they wouldn't have a problem."

"She didn't actually lie, Roman. She just withheld the facts about her previous marriage and having a daughter."

He grunted. "From what Cleon told me, she didn't tell him about her being in a family way, either."

Judith shrugged, and the girls stared at their plates.

Roman grabbed a piece of toast and slathered it with a glob of apple butter. "I say we forget about Grace and Cleon's problems and finish our breakfast."

Grace paced between the kitchen sink and the table as she waited for Cleon to come downstairs. He'd gotten up long enough to drink a cup of coffee, but then he'd gone back to bed without eating breakfast, saying he had a headache. So Grace had fixed Anna's breakfast and sent her off to spend the day with Ruth and Martha at the pond. She hoped a day of fun might lift her daughter's spirits. Now if something could be done to lift her own.

The sound of footsteps on the stairs drew Grace's attention, and she turned to greet Cleon when he entered the kitchen. "Is your *koppweh* gone?"

He nodded and yawned, stretching his arms overhead. "Can't remember the last time I had a headache like that. A few more hours of sleep finally took it away, though."

"I'm glad." She motioned to the table. "If you'd like to take a seat, I'll fix you something to eat."

He glanced at the battery-operated clock on the far wall as he pulled out a chair and sat down. "It's too late in the day for me to eat a big breakfast. Just a cup of coffee and some of those biscuits we had last night will do."

Grace went to the stove for the coffeepot, then reached into the cupboard to retrieve a mug. After she'd filled it with hot coffee, she set it on the table in front of Cleon and went back to the counter to get the basket of biscuits. "Would you like me to warm them in the oven?"

"They'll be fine the way they are."

She placed the basket on the table, along with a dish of butter and a jar of strawberry jam. "Can I get you anything else?"

He shook his head.

"Ruth and Martha picked Anna up awhile ago, and they're on their way to the pond."

No response.

Grace pulled out the chair beside him and sat down. "I thought the two of us could spend the day together—maybe go for a walk or sit out on the porch swing and talk." She watched his face, hoping to tell what he was thinking. His face was stoic.

He cut a biscuit in two and slathered some butter on both halves. "I'd planned to go over and see my folks today," he mumbled. "Thought maybe I'd talk to Ivan about going in with me on some more beehives."

"I could go along. It's been a while since I visited with your folks."

"I'd rather go alone."

Grace's heart sank. A dozen responses came to mind, but she couldn't gather the presence of mind to verbalize one of them.

"Maybe you can spend the day with your folks," he suggested.

She dared not say anything least she break down and cry, so she stared at a purple stain on the tablecloth until tears blinded her vision. What kind of marriage did they have with him sleeping in another room and the two of them barely speaking? Cleon had made it quite clear that he didn't want to spend any time alone with her. Their marriage was a marriage in name only, just as Cleon had said it would be when he'd come home.

The now familiar churning in Grace's stomach gripped her like a vise, and unable to stand the wall of silence between them, she pushed her chair away from the table and stood. One thing was certain: Only God could mend her broken marriage.

Cleon sat at the kitchen table staring into his empty mug and mulling things over. In his heart, he knew that he still loved Grace, but he felt frozen, unable to respond to her as a husband should respond to his wife. If only he could rid himself of the memory of her lies. How he wished he could erase everything that had happened between them and start over with the day they'd first met. Would Grace have said and done things differently if she'd known how things would turn out between them?

He leaned back in his chair and clasped his hands behind his head, staring at the cracks in the ceiling. The gas lamp hanging overhead hissed softly, and he spotted a fly that had landed in a spider's web in one corner of the room.

That's how I feel, he thought ruefully. *Like a trapped fly*.

Cleon remembered his grandfather saying once that happiness didn't depend on what life dished out to a person but rather on how the person chose to accept whatever came his way.

Guilt lay heavily on Cleon's chest, and tension pulled the muscles in his neck and upper back as he shifted in his chair. It wasn't good for a body to get so worked up, but every time he thought about Grace's deception, it was as though his heart was being ripped in two. As a Christian, he should forgive, but did he have the strength to forget the past and look to a future with Grace and the baby she carried? Could he find enough love in his heart to be Anna's stepfather?

Chapter 38

What a perfect day for a picnic," Ruth said as she and Martha spread a quilt under a leafy maple tree. "The pond looks so clear today. It's almost as blue as the sky above. I'm glad spring is finally here. Makes me anxious for summer."

Martha nodded and glanced down at Anna, who stood off to one side with her arms folded and a scowl on her face. Most children would be excited about going on a picnic, but Anna still grieved for her puppy. Nothing anyone had said or done had helped ease her pain. Maybe today would be different. Maybe something would happen that might make Anna laugh again.

"I thought it might be fun to take a walk in the woods." Martha tapped Anna on the shoulder. "Should we do that now or after we eat our lunch?"

Anna wrinkled her nose. "I'm not hungry."

Ruth placed the picnic basket on the quilt and took hold of Anna's hand. "All right then, the three of us will take a walk now, and we can eat when we get back." She smiled as the thought of the tasty lunch that awaited them made her mouth water. "I'm sure by then you'll have worked up an appetite."

Anna said nothing, but she didn't resist as the three of them walked away.

Martha halted and turned back toward the quilt. "What about our picnic basket? Do you think it's all right to leave it unattended, or should we put it back in the buggy?"

"I'm sure it'll be fine," Ruth called over her shoulder. "No one else is around that I can see, and we won't be gone long. Let's leave it under the tree where it can stay nice and cool."

Martha shrugged and started walking again. If she wasn't careful, she might end up like her older sister—worried about everything.

As Cleon headed to his folks' place on foot, he struggled with feelings of guilt. He'd turned down Grace's offer to accompany him, knowing she wanted them to spend time together. He simply wasn't able to deal with the two of them being alone. He became anxious whenever they were in the same room, and his words often came out clipped or defensive. He knew it was wrong to harbor feelings of mistrust and bitterness, but he couldn't seem to control his emotions where Grace was concerned.

It was an exceptionally warm day for spring, and Cleon reached up to wipe the rivulets of sweat running down his forehead and into his eyes. He wanted to be a father, had wanted it for a long time. This should be a joyful occasion, and he and Grace shouldn't be sleeping in separate bedrooms.

That's your choice, a voice in his head reminded him.

He picked up speed. It was best that he didn't think about this. Maybe he would feel better once he'd talked to Ivan and decided what to do about his beekeeping business.

A short time later, Cleon's folks' house came into view. He found Mom and Pop relaxing on the wide front porch in their rocking chairs, with one of the yellow barn cats sitting at Mom's feet. She kept so busy all the time with her many responsibilities, it was nice to see her doing nothing for a change.

She smiled when Cleon stepped onto the porch. "It's good to see you, son."

"Good to see you, too."

Pop grunted. "You don't come around so much now that your bee boxes are gone and you've begun workin' for Roman."

Cleon took a seat on the top step and swiped at his sweaty

forehead with the back of his hand. "That's one of the reasons I came over–wanted to speak with Ivan about the bees."

"How's Grace and that cute little stepdaughter of yours?" Mom asked. "I'm disappointed you didn't bring them along."

"Anna went on a picnic with Ruth and Martha today."

"And Grace? How come she didn't come with you?"

Cleon winced. Should he tell his folks the truth about his strained relationship with his wife? Should he tell them about her pregnancy? He knew they would find out sooner or later, and he figured the news should probably come from him.

He swallowed hard. "Uh. . .Grace isn't feeling well these days, so I thought it would be best if I came alone."

"What's wrong with her? Is she grank?" Mom's brows furrowed with concern.

Cleon removed his straw hat and fanned his face with it. "Grace isn't sick. She's. . .uh. . .in a family way."

Mom clapped her hands and nearly jumped out of her chair. "Oh, that's wunderbaar!" She nudged Pop's elbow. "Just think, Herman, our first *kinskind* is on the way."

Pop's face broke into a wide smile. "That is good news. Are ya hopin' for a *buwe* or a *maedel*?" he asked, nodding at Cleon.

Cleon shrugged. "Haven't had a chance to think much about whether I'd like a boy or girl. Just found out Grace was pregnant a few days ago." He stood and flopped his hat back on his head. "Is Ivan about? I'd like to talk to him."

"I think Ivan's out in the barn. Said he was goin' to take a nap in the hayloft." Pop chuckled. "Ever since that boy was a kinner, he's liked sleepin' in the hay."

"Okay. I'll see if he's there." Cleon hurried away before his folks could continue discussing the baby.

He entered the barn a few minutes later and tipped his head to stare into the hayloft. "You up there, Ivan?"

No response.

Cleon cupped his hands around his mouth and hollered, "Ivan!"

A muffled grunt, followed by another, came from a mound of

hay. "What's with all the racket?" Ivan peered over the edge of the loft. "Cleon, I didn't know you were comin' over today."

"Since this is an off-Sunday from church, I thought it would be a good chance to drop over and say hello to the folks." Cleon removed his hat and fanned his face with the brim. "Wanted to speak with you about something, too."

"What's that?"

"Why don't you come down here, and we can talk about it. It's kind of hard to carry on a conversation when you have to yell."

"You've got a point." Ivan crawled out of the hay and scrambled down the ladder. When his feet hit the bottom, he shook like a dog, sending pieces of hay flying.

"Hey, watch it!" Cleon jumped back, but not before a couple of stubbles landed on his shirt. He flicked them off and sat on a nearby bale of straw.

"What'd ya want to talk to me about?" Ivan asked as he plunked down on the bale next to Cleon's.

"Bees and honey."

Ivan reached up to pick a chunk of hay out of his hair. "What about bees and honey?"

Cleon pulled out a length of straw and chewed on the end of it as he contemplated the best way to ask his question. "I'm wanting to start up my bee business again, and as you know, I don't have enough cash yet to buy more bees, boxes, and the supplies I'll need."

Ivan nodded. "I still feel bad about you losin' 'em that way."

"I'm making pretty good money working for Roman, but it's gonna be a while before I have enough saved up to start the business again." Cleon reached up to rub his bearded chin. "The thing is, I read an ad in *The Budget* the other day from someone in Pennsylvania who's selling off his beekeeping supplies. So I was wondering if you might be able to loan me enough money to get a start on things. Or maybe you'd like to go halves on the business with me this time around."

Ivan's dark eyebrows drew together. "I do have some money laid aside, but I was plannin' to use it to buy a new buggy horse."

"What's wrong with the one you've got now?"

"Nothing, really. He's just gettin' kind of old and isn't as fast I'd like him to be."

"Ah, I see."

Ivan stroked his clean-shaven chin. "Guess buyin' a new buggy horse can wait awhile, though." He nodded at Cleon. "Don't really want to be your business partner, but I'm willing to loan you whatever you need."

Cleon sighed with relief. If he could get his bee business going again, he'd be earning money from that as well as from working for Roman. Then he not only could pay Ivan back what he'd borrowed, but he'd have enough to pay Roman back for all the lumber and other supplies he'd bought in order to finish Cleon's house. Besides, working with the bees again would give him a good excuse to be away from home when he wasn't at work in Roman's shop. He thumped his brother on the back. "I appreciate the loan, and if Roman doesn't mind me missing a few days' work, I'll head out soon and see about buying what I need."

Martha led the way for Ruth and Anna as they tromped through the woods. Birds warbled from the trees overhead, insects buzzed noisily, and leaves rustled in the breeze. It had turned into such a warm day, but being in the shaded forest made it seem much cooler.

"Should we play hide-and-seek?" Ruth suggested, remembering how the childhood game had always made her laugh whenever she'd felt melancholy.

"That's a good idea." Martha halted and turned around. "I'll close my eyes and count to one hundred while you two hide. Then the first one I find has to hide her eyes next time around."

Anna looked up at Ruth with a hesitant expression. "What happens if I get lost?"

Ruth bent to give Anna a hug. "You won't get lost, because the two of us will be staying close together."

Martha leaned into the nearest tree and closed her eyes. "One. . . two. . .three. . .four. . ."

Ruth grabbed Anna's hand and dashed away in search of a good hiding place. They halted behind a clump of bushes, and Ruth motioned Anna to get down. "Be real quiet. Martha won't find us so easily if she can't hear us."

Anna giggled and covered her mouth with the palm of her hand. Ruth crouched behind her. If Martha found them, she would spot Ruth first. Then Ruth would have to count to one hundred while Martha took Anna off to look for a place to hide. If they kept going like that, Anna would never have to be the one to go looking, and they would know she was safe and couldn't get lost in the woods.

"One hundred!" she heard Martha shout. "You'd better have found a really good hiding place, because here I come!"

Ruth held her breath and squeezed Anna's hand. This reminded her of when she was little, and she and her sisters had run through the woods behind their home playing hide-and-seek. So many times she'd been caught because she'd given herself away by making too much noise. She was determined that wouldn't happen now.

"Anna? Ruth? Where are you?" Martha's voice sounded farther and farther away, and Ruth figured they were safe—at least for the moment. She relaxed a bit and was about to whisper something in Anna's ear, when someone tapped her on the shoulder. She whirled around. Martin Gingerich was staring at her.

"What are you doing down there?" he asked with a crooked grin. "Looking for bugs, are you?"

Anna giggled, and Ruth snickered as she put her finger to her lips. "We're hiding from Martha."

He tipped his head and looked at her as if she'd taken leave of her senses. "Why would you be hiding from your sister?"

"We're playin' hide-and-seek," Anna said before Ruth could respond. "Aunt Martha's it, and if you're not quiet, she's gonna find us."

Martin nodded and dropped to his knees beside them. "I won't say another word."

The three of them crouched there for several more minutes until Martha jumped out from behind a tree and hollered, "Found you!"

When she spotted Martin, she planted her hands on her hips and stared at him. "Now where on earth did you come from?"

"Came from home, same as you." He winked at Anna and offered Ruth a heart-melting smile. In that moment, she realized how easily she could fall in love with this man. Martin was nothing like Luke. He was steady, polite, and attentive, not impetuous, flippant, or brash. She felt certain that Martin was trustworthy, which was more than could be said for Luke.

"I don't know about the rest of you, but I'm hungry as a mule," Martha announced. "I say we head back to the pond and eat our picnic lunch." She nodded at Martin. "We made plenty of food, so you're welcome to join us if you like."

"I appreciate the offer, but I left my brother waiting in the buggy where the road cuts by the pond. The only reason I came into the woods was because I heard you hollering and thought someone might be in trouble." Martin turned and smiled at Ruth again. "Maybe some other time I can join you for a picnic."

Her cheeks heated up. "That'd be nice."

"See you later then," Martin said and dashed away.

Martha nudged Ruth's arm as they started back toward the pond. "I can tell he's smitten with you."

Ruth just kept her gaze straight ahead.

"What's 'smitten'?" Anna asked, looking up at Martha.

Martha chuckled. "It means he can't take his eyes off my sister."

"How come he wants his eyes on her?"

Martha's laughter escalated, and Ruth joined in, too. She hadn't felt this carefree since she was a little girl.

As they stepped out from the darkened trees and into the clearing where they'd left their food, Ruth gasped. "Our picnic basket–it's gone!"

Chapter 39

What in all the world?" Martha planted her hands on her hips and stared at the quilt where they'd left the picnic basket. "Where did our lunch run off to?"

Ruth squinted. "It sure couldn't have walked off by itself."

"Maybe some animal came along and took it," Anna said, looking up at Martha with a frown.

"More than likely it was some human playing a trick on us," Ruth said with a shake of her head.

"You don't suppose Martin did this, do you?"

Ruth looked at Martha as if she'd gone daffy. "Martin?"

"He snuck up on you in the woods, so what's to say he didn't hide the picnic basket, too?"

"I'm sure he wouldn't have done something like that."

"How do you know?"

"I just do, that's all."

"You said you're only beginning to know him, so I doubt you'd be able to tell what he's capable of doing."

Ruth's eyebrows drew together. "It's not like I just met Martin. I've known him since we were kinner."

"We've known Luke that long, too, yet you seem to think he's capable of doing all sorts of terrible things."

Ruth motioned toward Anna, who had taken a seat on the quilt. "Let's not argue about this, okay?"

Martha nodded. "You're right. We should be looking for that

picnic basket, not trying to figure out who took it." She glanced around. "Which direction should we look first?"

Ruth shrugged. "Makes no difference to me. I'm getting hungry and I want to eat."

"Me, too," Anna said in a whiny voice.

"Then let's get busy looking. We can start on this side of the pond, and if we don't find it here, we'll walk around to the other side." Martha reached for the little girl's hand, pulling her gently to her feet.

They broke through a clump of bushes, rounded the bend, and had only gone a short distance when Martha spotted the wicker basket sitting near a pile of men's clothes not far from the water. "There it is!" she and Ruth shouted at the same time.

Martha dropped to her knees and opened the basket lid. Nothing remained except a bunch of empty wrappers and a half-full jug of lemonade. "This makes me so mad," she muttered.

"Look there!" Ruth pointed to the pond. Several young English men floated in inner tubes. "I'll bet they're the ones who took our picnic basket."

Martha shielded her eyes from the glare of the sun and squinted. "I think one of those fellows was with Luke when we saw him talking to some Englishers outside the market several months back. Do you remember?"

Ruth shrugged. "Can't say for sure since they're so far away, but they're obviously the ones who took our food, so I think we should teach them a lesson."

"What kind of lesson?"

"One that's going to leave those fellows with some sore feet on their trip home and probably feeling pretty chilly if the wind picks up." Ruth bent down, grabbed the shirts and shoes, and turned toward the woods.

Martha reached for Anna's hand and followed. They stumbled through a tangle of bushes, past a grove of spindly trees, and went deeper into the forest. As Ruth scurried along, she hung the shoes and shirts on various branches, hiding some under shrubs and inside a hollow log. "That ought to teach them not to take what doesn't belong to them." Her forehead wrinkled as she shook her head. "If they're the ones responsible for the terrible things that have happened at our place lately, then maybe this will make 'em think twice about that, too."

Martha stood, too dumbfounded to say a word. This act of retaliation wasn't like her normally placid sister. It wasn't the Amish way, either, and it wasn't a good example to be setting for Anna. "Do you think you should have done that, sister?"

Ruth folded her arms and gave one quick nod.

"If those English fellows are behind the break-ins and other things that have been done at our place, they may decide to do something worse in order to get even."

Ruth shrugged. "Well, I'm not going to put their clothes back, but if you want to, I won't stop you."

Martha looked overhead at a black and white sneaker flopping in the breeze and shook her head. "I say we take our picnic basket and hightail it out of here before those fellows get out of the water."

"Sure seems quiet around here with everyone gone for the day, doesn't it?" Judith asked Roman, who sat in the wicker chair beside her on their front porch.

He nodded. "Jah. Quiet and peaceful."

"I hope Anna has a good time with the girls."

"I'm sure she will."

"Haven't seen anything of Grace or Cleon, so I'm hoping they're enjoying their day together, too." She reached for his hand. "I'm enjoying my time spent with you, as well, husband."

He smiled. "Same here."

"Things have been so crazy around here for the last couple of months. It's nice to finally have some peace."

"Let's hope it stays peaceful." Roman's eyebrows drew together. "We still don't know who's responsible for the attacks, but I keep praying that whoever's behind it will realize what they did was wrong and that it won't happen again."

Judith nodded. "I wish I knew why we seem to be the only ones under attack. It's as if someone has deliberately singled us out."

"I agree, and I'm fairly sure it's someone who wants to get even with me."

"You? But what could you have done that would make someone angry enough to do such horrible things to our property?"

Roman's forehead wrinkled. "Let's see now. Steven Bates could be trying to make me pay for ruining his wife's birthday present. Or Luke could be getting even because I fired him."

"Grace still thinks that reporter fellow might be trying to get even with her for breaking up with him and marrying his friend."

"I doubt he'd be carrying a grudge that long." He tugged his earlobe. "It could even be that land developer who seemed so determined to get me to sell off our land."

"He did seem determined, but I guess he must have taken no for an answer, because he hasn't been around."

"I heard he's bought some land up near Kidron, so maybe he's given up trying to buy our place."

"Could be that no one has a grudge against us at all. Maybe it was just some wild kids stirring up trouble, like you thought in the beginning. Say, isn't that Cleon walking up our driveway from the main road?"

Roman squinted and stared across the yard. "I believe it is."

"Wonder where he's coming from and why Grace isn't with him."

"Could be she's takin' a nap, and he decided to go for a walk."

Judith wrinkled her forehead. "It's strange we didn't see him leave his house."

"Maybe he left before we came outside."

"But we've been here for some time."

Roman patted her arm. "Is it really so important?"

"I thought one of the reasons the girls took Anna on a picnic was so Grace and Cleon could spend time together. They can't do that if she's in the house sleeping and he's taking a walk by himself."

As Cleon came to the end of the driveway, he turned toward their home. When he reached the porch steps, he stepped up and nodded at Roman. "I. . .uh. . .need to speak with you about something."

"Jah, sure. What's is it?"

Cleon looked over at Judith and shuffled his feet.

"I think I'll go inside and get a jug of iced tea while you menfolk talk," she said, grasping the arms of the chair and rising to her feet. "Would either of you like some?"

"Nothing for me," Cleon was quick to say.

Roman shook his head. "Not right now; maybe later."

She disappeared into the house. *Guess if Cleon had wanted me to hear what he had to say, he would have invited me to stay.*

"Have a seat," Roman said, motioning to the chair Judith had been sitting in.

Cleon sat down and cleared his throat.

"What's on your mind?"

"I've been wanting to get my beekeeping business going again, and my brother Ivan's offered to loan me some money. So I was wondering if it would be okay with you if I took a few days off from work to see about buying some bees, boxes, and other supplies from a fellow who lives near Harrisburg, Pennsylvania, not far from where I grew up."

"I'd thought maybe since you'd come to work for me that you'd decided to quit the bee business."

"I'll keep working for you as long as you want me to, but I enjoyed what I was doing with the bees, and I could use the extra money now that we have a boppli on the way. Since Ivan will probably be helping me part-time, maybe I can tend to the bees when I'm not working for you."

Roman's eyes narrowed. "Workin' two jobs won't give you much time to spend at home with your wife and kinner."

"Taking care of the bees isn't a full-time job, so I'll be around home enough, I expect."

"What's Grace think about this?"

"She. . .uh. . .doesn't know yet."

Roman rubbed the bridge of his nose. "I guess it'll be all right if you're gone a few days, but I hope you'll be back by Friday. It's Grace's birthday, you know, and she'd be mighty disappointed if you weren't there to help celebrate."

Cleon clamped his lips together. He didn't want to appear like a thoughtless husband, but he needed to get those bee boxes and other supplies before someone else got to them. "I can't promise I'll be back by Friday, but I'll try."

After Cleon left for his folks' place, Grace rested awhile. Then she decided to spend some time reading her Bible. She'd been negligent about doing her devotions every day and knew that getting into God's Word might help her depression.

Curling up on the sofa, she opened the Bible to Isaiah chapter 50. When she read verse 7, words of scripture seemed to jump right off the page. "For the Lord God will help me; therefore shall I not be confounded: therefore have I set my face like a flint, and I know that I shall not be ashamed."

Tears coursed down Grace's cheeks, and she sniffed. She needed to rely on God to help her as she set her face like a flint. She had done some wrong things, but she no longer needed to be ashamed of them, because she'd asked God for forgiveness. Even though Cleon hadn't forgiven her, God had, and for that she felt grateful.

When the back door opened and clicked shut, Grace dried her eyes and sat up. "Who's there?"

"It's me," Cleon said as he stepped into the living room.

"Did you have a nice visit with your folks?"

He nodded. "Didn't visit with 'em long, though. Spent most of my time talking with Ivan about the possibility of getting some more bees, boxes, and other supplies."

"I see."

Cleon took a seat in the rocking chair across from her. "When I got back, I spoke with your daed about letting me have a few days off."

She tipped her head. "How come?"

"I read an ad in *The Budget* from some fellow who lives near

Harrisburg, Pennsylvania. He's got a bunch of bee things for sale at a pretty good price, so I want to see about buying them."

"When would you be leaving?"

"Tomorrow morning."

Grace moistened her lips with the tip of her tongue. She didn't want Cleon to think she was trying to tell him what to do, and she wasn't going to mention that she wanted him home to celebrate her birthday. Cleon knew when her birthday was. If he didn't remember this year or didn't want to spend it with her, then she wouldn't bring up the subject. "I–I guess if you feel you need to go, then that's what you should do."

He nodded and stood. "Think I'll walk over to the Larsons' and see if Ray can give me a ride to Dover in the morning so I can catch the bus to Pennsylvania."

Grace stared at him. He finally shrugged and left the room.

She released a sigh that turned into a strangled sob. *Dear Lord, please give me the strength to endure my husband's rejection.*

Chapter 40

Roman was about to close up shop for the day and take Grace and the family to dinner, when John Peterson showed up.

"I was driving by and thought I'd stop in and see how things were going," John said, leaning against the desk where Roman sat.

"I'm keeping busy enough. How 'bout you?"

"Same here. Seems to be a lot more folks in the area who want quality furniture."

Roman nodded. "How are things working out with Luke as your new apprentice? Is he coming to work on time and working steady?"

"So far he's done okay, but I'm keeping an eye on him all the same."

"I gave that young man plenty of chances, but he didn't seem to care enough about his job to do as I asked." Roman gritted his teeth. "I'm glad my daughter broke up with him, because to tell you the truth, I don't trust that fellow."

"Do you make a habit of firing your employees?"

"What's that supposed to mean?"

"I just wondered if Luke was the first employee you've had to fire."

Roman shrugged. "May have had to let a few others go over the years, but it was only because they wouldn't listen to me and wanted to run things their own way."

"Luke thinks you believe he had something to do with the break-ins you folks had awhile back."

"I wouldn't be surprised." Roman shrugged as he ran his fingers through the back of his hair. "Martha found Luke's hat outside in the dirt after that brick went through the kitchen window. Then Judith found his sunglasses not far from the clothesline that somebody cut."

John's dark eyebrows drew together. "That does make him seem guilty. Guess I'd better keep a closer watch on Luke. Sure wouldn't want him tearing things up at my place."

"As long as you don't give him an ultimatum, he probably won't bother your place. It wasn't until I jumped him about being late a couple of times and docked his pay for being careless that things started happening." Roman shook his head. "We've had a couple of incidents since Luke quit working for me, too. Makes me wonder if he might be trying to get even because I fired him."

"I'll be sure and let you know if I hear or see anything suspicious."

Roman glanced at the clock on the wall, and realizing what time it was, he pushed his chair aside and stood. "Sorry to cut this visit short, but I need to head up to the house and get washed and changed. Today's my oldest daughter's birthday, and we're taking her to dinner at Der Dutchman in Walnut Creek."

John smiled and moved toward the door. "Don't let me hold you up. Tell Grace I said happy birthday, and I hope you all have a pleasant evening." Just as he got to the door, he glanced around the room and his forehead wrinkled. "I thought I'd heard that you'd hired your son-in-law to work for you."

"That's right. Cleon started working here a few weeks ago after he got home from a trip and discovered that all his bees, boxes, and supplies had been burned."

"I heard about that, too. The fellow who told me said he thought it was probably done by some kids playing a prank."

Roman nodded. "Could be."

"So if Cleon's working for you now, where is he?"

"Went to Pennsylvania to look at some items for his beekeeping business, which means I'm on my own for a few days."

"He won't be here for his wife's birthday?"

"Nope, afraid not."

The strange look on John's face made Roman wish he hadn't said anything. It was bad enough that Cleon wouldn't be here for Grace's birthday; he didn't need John making something of it.

"Well, guess I'd better get going." John lifted his hand in a wave. "See you around, Roman, and don't hesitate to call if you need anything."

Grace wasn't looking forward to her birthday dinner, but her folks had insisted on hiring a driver and taking the family to Der Dutchman. She didn't want to disappoint them. Besides, a meal out with her family was better than sitting home alone with Anna. Grace would have spent the evening wishing Cleon could be with her and that their relationship was on track. If only there was something she could do to earn back his trust and his love.

As Grace sat in the backseat of Ray Larson's van, she realized that at times she actually felt relieved that her husband wasn't around, looking at her as if she were a terrible person and making her feel guilty for the secret she'd kept.

When Ray pulled into the restaurant's parking lot, he turned to look at Grace's father. "I've got some errands to run, so I'll be back to get you folks in a couple of hours. Is that okay?"

Dad nodded. "You're welcome to join us for supper if you like."

"No, thanks. I'd better get my errands run, or I'll have to answer to Donna."

"Okay then," Dad said as he and the rest of the family climbed out of the van.

Grace took Anna's hand and followed her family inside the building. A long line of people waited for service. Anna and Martha busied themselves at the revolving rack near the checkout counter. It featured lots of postcards and books about the Amish, as well as some novels and a few children's books. Several English people, who were obviously tourists, commented on how cute Anna was as she squatted down to look at the books.

Any other time, it probably wouldn't have bothered Grace, but this evening her nerves were taut. She resisted the urge to tell everyone to quit staring at her daughter. Instead, she sat on a bench with her hands clenched in her lap, hoping they would soon have a table.

After thirty minutes of waiting, they were ushered into the dining room. Soon after they'd placed their orders and the waitress had brought beverages and rolls, Anna announced that she needed to use the restroom.

"Want me to take her?" Martha asked, looking over at Grace.

"I'll do it." Grace pushed her chair aside and reached for Anna's hand.

When they stepped out of the ladies' restroom a short time later, Grace collided with a man. Her heart thumped erratically when she realized it was Gary.

"Well, now, isn't this a pleasant surprise?" he drawled. "It's been a while since I've seen you, Gracie. Where have you been keeping yourself?"

Grace opened her mouth to respond, but before she could get a word out, Anna looked up at Gary and announced that today was her mama's birthday. "We're having supper to celebrate," she added.

A look of recognition registered on his face as he stared at Anna. "Oh, that's right—I remember you. Aren't you the little girl I saw at the Hostettlers' house a while back?"

Anna nodded. "I'm Anna, and this is my mamm."

Grace squeezed her daughter's hand. "Haven't I told you not to talk to strangers?"

"Come now, Gracie. I'm hardly a stranger—at least not to you." Gary offered Grace a lopsided smile, and it fueled her anger.

"I want you to go back to the table now," she said, giving Anna a nudge in that direction.

"What about you? Aren't you comin', too?"

"I. . .uh. . .need to use the ladies' room, but I'll be there as soon as I'm done."

"You didn't have to go before."

Grace gave Anna another nudge. "Go on now. Tell Grandpa and Grandma I'll be there soon."

Gary winked at Anna, and she gave him a quick smile, then darted off toward the dining room.

Grace turned back to face Gary. "How much longer will you be staying in Holmes County?"

He rubbed his chin and looked at her in a most disconcerting way. "Well, now, that all depends."

"On what?"

"On how many more interesting stories I find here."

"Are you sure you're not hanging around just to make trouble?"

He chuckled. "You're really direct and to the point these days, aren't you, Gracie? Not like the timid young woman I used to date, that's for sure. Must be those years you spent living among the English that made you so bold."

She grimaced. This man certainly had a way of getting under her skin.

He folded his arms and leaned against the wall. "I remember spending one of your birthdays with you, Gracie. Let's see now—which one was that?"

She glanced back at the table to be sure Anna had joined her family again.

"Say, here's an idea. Why don't I join your little birthday party? While I'm there, maybe I can get someone in your family to open up and tell me more about the vandalism at your place. I really need to get that story wrapped up, you know."

"You wouldn't dare follow me back to the table."

"Wanna bet?"

He started in that direction, but she reached out and touched his arm. "What information do you want that you don't already have?"

His eyebrows jiggled up and down. "I'd like to know why you left me for that simpleton, Wade Davis."

"Why would you talk about Wade like that? I thought he was your friend."

"He was until he snatched you away." Gary frowned. "What I'd really like to know is how come you gave up the English way of life for this." He motioned to her plain dress and eyed her up and down.

"I chose to return to my Amish roots after Wade died because I knew that's where I really belonged. I should never have left home in the first place."

He motioned toward the dining room. "I only see one man sitting at your table. Where's that new husband of yours?"

Grace could hardly swallow around the lump in her throat. She would never admit to Gary that her husband cared more about starting up his beekeeping business than celebrating her birthday. "Not that it's any of your concern, but my husband is away on business right now. Now, if you'll excuse me, I need to get back to my family."

"Sure, Gracie. Don't let me stop you." He snickered. "Oh, and happy birthday."

"What's wrong?" Ruth asked, taking Grace's hand when she returned to the table. "Are you having a wave of nausea? Is that why you went back to the restroom?"

Grace shook her head. "I'm fine."

"Are you sure?"

Grace gave a quick nod.

"Anna said you were talking to a man in the hallway outside the restroom," Mom put in. "Was it someone we know?"

Grace's face paled as she shook her head. "Can't we talk about this later?"

Their father nodded. "Grace is right. Let's pray so we can eat."

All heads bowed for silent prayer, and then everyone dug in. Everyone but Grace. She toyed with the piece of chicken on her plate.

"For one who was supposed to be hungry, you're sure not eating much," Dad said, reaching for another biscuit from the basket in the center of the table. "Are you feeling bad because Cleon couldn't be here to help celebrate your birthday?"

Grace shrugged. "It would have been nice, but he's got important business to tend to."

"It'll be good when he gets his bee boxes set up again," Mom put in from across the table. "Nice for us to have some fresh honey again, too."

"That's for sure." Dad lifted a drumstick off his plate and had just taken a bite, when he scrunched up his nose and released a moan.

"What's wrong, Roman?" Mom's eyebrows furrowed, and she reached over to touch his arm.

He opened his mouth, stuck two fingers inside, and withdrew a porcelain crown.

"Oh, no." Mom clicked her tongue noisily. "Looks like you'll be making a trip to the dentist tomorrow morning."

"No, I won't," he said with a shake of his head. "You know how much I hate going to the dentist."

"But, Dad, you can't go around with the nub of your tooth exposed." Ruth grimaced. "You'll need to get that crown cemented on right away."

"I've got some epoxy cement in my shop. Maybe I'll use that."

Martha's mouth dropped open, and she looked at their father as if he'd taken leave of his senses. "You wouldn't."

He nodded. "Sure would. It'll save me a chunk of money."

Ruth couldn't believe how stubborn her father could be at times. She glanced over at Grace, who had been unusually quiet all evening. Grace stared at her half-eaten food as if she didn't care that Dad had lost a crown. Something was going on with Grace, and Ruth hoped it wasn't anything serious.

Chapter 41

I don't see why you felt the need to follow me out here," Roman said to his wife as they stepped into his shop after they'd returned home from dinner.

"Because I know what you plan to do, and I'm hoping to talk you out of it. It's just plain *eefeldich* to try and glue your crown back in place." She frowned. "It won't hold, you know."

"It may seem silly to you, but I know what I'm doing, and this will save us some money." Roman ignited one of the gas lamps.

Judith pulled out the chair at his desk and took a seat. "If you insist on doing this, then at least let me help so you don't get it glued on crooked or put glue where it doesn't belong."

He shrugged and started toward his supplies. Most women worried too much, especially his wife.

"Grace seemed sad tonight, didn't she?" Judith said.

"Guess she was missing Cleon," he called over his shoulder.

"I still don't see why he couldn't have waited to make that trip until after her birthday."

"I'm heading into the back room now, so can we talk about this later?"

"Jah, sure."

Roman stepped into the room and turned on another gas lamp. When he opened his toolbox to retrieve the epoxy cement, several things were missing. "Now that's sure strange."

"What's strange?"

Roman whirled around. Judith had followed him into the room. "Some things in this case are missing, including the epoxy cement."

Her forehead wrinkled. "What all is missing?"

"A hammer, a couple of screwdrivers, a pair of pliers, and two tubes of cement."

"Maybe you put them somewhere and forgot."

"Don't remember puttin' them anywhere but here."

She covered her mouth with one hand. "I hope someone hasn't broken into your shop again. I'm getting so tired of these attacks."

"If it is another attack, we just need to hold steady and keep trusting the Lord." He looked around the room. "We don't know if the missing tools really are part of an attack, and I don't see anything else missing. The front door was locked when we came in, so it doesn't seem as though anyone broke into the place while we were gone."

"You think maybe Cleon borrowed the tools and forgot to tell you?"

Roman leaned against the workbench. "I suppose that's possible. I'll ask when he gets back." He closed the lid on the toolbox and turned down the gas lamp. "Guess I'll have to see the dentist whether I like it or not, because without that cement, I can't glue my crown back on."

Judith smiled. "At least one good thing came out of your supplies being gone."

He grunted and touched his mouth. "Jah, right."

As Cleon entered a café on the outskirts of Harrisburg, he noticed a small calendar sitting on the counter near the cash register. *Oh, no, today was Grace's birthday, and I didn't even send her a card.*

He seated himself at a booth near the window and reflected on his wife's last birthday, when he'd been invited to her folks' house for supper. They'd made homemade ice cream after the meal, and he and Grace had spent the rest of the evening sitting on the porch swing, talking about their future and holding hands. Cleon had hung around until almost midnight, wishing he could be with Grace forever. Things had sure turned out differently than he'd imagined they would.

He wondered what Grace had done to celebrate her birthday, and as he reached for the menu the waitress had placed on the table, a feeling of guilt swept over him like a raging waterfall. Even if he was Grace's husband in name only, the least he could do was to acknowledge her birthday.

Cleon thought about a verse from Matthew 6 he had read in his hotel room: *"For if ye forgive men their trespasses, your heavenly Father will also forgive you."* He still loved Grace, and he needed to forgive her. But if he couldn't trust her, then how could he fully forgive and open his heart to her again?

Maybe I'll buy her a gift before I head for home. At least that way she can't say I didn't care enough to do something for her birthday. And when she finds out that I've bought enough bees, boxes, and supplies to start my business again, maybe she'll realize that I'm not going to shirk my duties, and that I plan to take care of her and the baby.

A lump formed in Cleon's throat, and he swallowed a couple of times, trying to dislodge it. God had put Grace in his life for a reason. It wouldn't be enough to give her a gift and let her know he didn't plan to wriggle out of his duties to her and their unborn child. Grace's secret wasn't the problem. His unforgiving actions and refusal to trust her were keeping them apart.

Truth be told, he hadn't given Grace a chance to tell him about the boppli and then had blamed her for not telling him the news. He had to give his hurts over to the Lord, for only God could break down the barriers Cleon had erected between him and his wife. He'd been running from what he wanted the most. He and Grace belonged together. He needed not only to forgive Grace, but to seek Anna's forgiveness, as well. Cleon resolved to do that as soon as he returned home.

As Grace and Anna headed for their house, Anna chattered about how Ruth had hid somebody's clothes in the woods when they'd gone on a picnic the other day. Grace barely let the words sink in. She was still feeling flustered over her encounter with Gary, and she wasn't looking forward to spending the rest of the night in an empty house, knowing Cleon wouldn't be coming home. A lump formed in her throat. He hadn't even bothered to give her a card, much less a gift.

"Look, Mama, somebody must have left you a birthday gift," Anna said as they stepped onto the back porch.

Grace bent down and picked up a small package wrapped in plain brown paper. She wondered if it could be from Cleon. Maybe he'd bought it before he left for Pennsylvania and asked someone from his family to deliver it to Grace on her birthday.

"Open it! Open it!" Anna shouted, hopping up and down.

"Calm down. I'll open it when we get inside."

Grace pushed the door open and stepped into the kitchen. She placed the package on the table, turned on a gas lamp, and pulled out chairs for Anna and herself.

"Can I open it?" Anna asked.

"Jah, sure, go ahead."

Anna ripped off the paper, pulled open the lid, and screeched with horror. "Dead mouse! Dead mouse!"

Thinking the child must be joking, Grace reached for the box and peered inside. "Ach! It is a dead maus!" She shuddered and tossed the package to the floor.

Anna started to sob, and Grace gathered the child into her arms. "It's okay. I'm sure someone's just playing a trick on Mama."

As Grace sat rocking Anna back and forth, the bitter taste of bile rose in her throat, and she swallowed to push it down. Who could have done something so horrible? Who could hate her so much that they would want to ruin her birthday?

Her thoughts turned immediately to Gary. When she'd seen him at the restaurant tonight, she'd mentioned that it was her birthday. Could he have driven over here and put the dead mouse on her doorstep?

Chapter 42

When Grace awoke the following morning, she looked out the window. Large droplets of water splattered against the glass, and a streak of lightning zigzagged through the dreary sky. Her stomach twisted as she thought about the night before–missing Cleon, encountering Gary, finding the package with the dead mouse on her porch.

She moved back across the room and sank to the edge of her bed as a wave of nausea hit. Her head pounded, and her hands shook. Maybe yesterday's doings had taken more of a toll on her than she'd realized. If only she could be free of the pain. If she could just let go of the past and release her fears to God. If she could keep her focus on the good times she and Cleon used to have, maybe she could find the strength to go on.

"For the Lord God will help me; therefore shall I not be confounded: therefore have I set my face like a flint; and I know that I shall not be ashamed."

"Thank You, Lord," Grace whispered. "I needed the reminder that You're here to help me." She rose from the bed and, with a sense of renewed determination, left the room and headed downstairs to fix breakfast.

Anna sat at the kitchen table with a piece of paper and a pencil. Her faceless doll lay in her lap. It was good to see her taking an interest in things again.

"Good morning, daughter." Grace bent to kiss Anna's forehead. "What are you doing?"

"Me and Martha with no face are drawin' a picture for Poppy. We want him to come see us soon."

Grace took a seat beside Anna. "You still miss your Grandpa Davis, don't you?"

Anna nodded, and tears welled in her eyes.

"The last letter we had from your poppy said he's feeling some better but isn't up to traveling just yet."

"Can we go see him?"

"I don't think so, Anna."

"How come?"

"We're busy with things here." Grace pressed her hand against her stomach. "And I'm not feeling well myself these days, so a long trip isn't a good idea."

Anna's eyes opened wide. "Are you gonna die like Grandma Davis and my puppy?"

"No, dear one, I'm not sick; I'm pregnant." Grace reached for Anna's hand and gave it a gentle squeeze. "That means in a few months you'll have a little sister or brother to play with."

The child's mouth fell open. "You're gonna have a boppli?"

Grace nodded and smiled. It pleased her to hear Anna speaking German-Dutch.

"A baby sister would be better'n havin' a puppy," Anna said with a grin. "Can I name her?"

"Don't you think we'd better wait and see whether it's a boy or a girl?"

Anna giggled. "Guess it would be kinda silly if a boy had a girl's name, huh?"

"Jah. We'll also have to wait and see what the baby's daadi has to say about choosing a name."

Anna's eyebrows drew together. "Who's the baby's daddy gonna be?"

"Why, Cleon, of course. He's my husband."

Anna shook her head forcibly. "My daddy's name was Wade. Poppy said so."

"I used to be married to Wade, and he was your daadi. But now I'm married to Cleon. He's the daadi of the boppli I'm carrying."

Grace placed Anna's hand against her slightly protruding stomach.

"I don't like Cleon. He don't like me, neither."

Grace sat dumbfounded, not knowing how to respond. She'd seen the way Cleon reacted to Anna—seeming to barely tolerate her. He wasn't Anna's father, but he was her stepfather, whether he liked it or not. Just because he was angry at Grace gave him no right to ignore Anna the way he did.

"I'm sure Cleon doesn't dislike you, Anna," she said, wrapping her arms around the child. "It's going to take some time for the two of you to get better acquainted."

Anna sat staring at the table.

Grace finally pushed her chair aside and stood. "What would you like for breakfast?"

No comment.

"How about pancakes and maple syrup?"

A little grunt escaped the child's lips as she shrugged her slim shoulders.

"All right, then. Pancakes, it is."

As Judith prepared breakfast for her family, she thought about the missing items in her husband's toolbox. Could Roman have misplaced them, or was it possible that Cleon had borrowed some things and forgotten to mention it? She grimaced as she stared out the window. Rain rattled against the roof. Maybe someone had been in Roman's shop and stolen the tools. But if that were so, how did they get in without breaking a window or tampering with the lock on the door?

Thunder clapped. Judith gasped. "Oh, how I dislike *dunner* and *wedderleech*. Haven't liked it since I was a girl."

Roman stepped up behind Judith and put his arms around her waist. "No need for you to fear. I'm here to protect you."

She leaned against his chest and sighed. "I wish we were safe from all outside forces."

"We need to trust God with every area of our lives—the weather included."

"I wasn't thinking about the weather. I was thinking about the attacks and wishing they would stop."

"We can't be sure those missing things from my toolbox were stolen, if that's what you're thinking."

Judith turned to face him. "Have you remembered where you put them?"

"No, but I'm pretty sure Cleon must have borrowed them." Roman shrugged. "We'll know soon enough, because I'm certain he'll be home soon."

"It isn't good for him and Grace and to be apart like this. They're newlyweds, and they shouldn't be sleeping in separate bedrooms."

"Give them time to work things out, and whatever you do, don't meddle."

"Jah, I know." She nodded toward the window. "Sure hope this rain lets up. I've got some washing to do today, and I was counting on hanging the clothes outside on the line. I also need to go down to the phone shed to make that dental appointment for you."

He shook his head. "You stay put in the house. I'll make the call myself."

She nodded as another clap of thunder rumbled, shaking the house. "Sure hope no one's barn or house gets struck by lightning today."

Grace spent the rest of her day cleaning, mending, and trying to keep Anna occupied. The rain hadn't let up, and the child was anxious to go outside and play. At the moment, she was taking a nap, which gave Grace enough time to get some baking done. She'd just put two rhubarb pies in the oven when she heard footsteps on the porch, and the back door creaked open.

"You busy?" Martha asked as she stepped into the room, holding a black umbrella in her hands.

"Just put a couple of pies in the oven. Come on in. We can have a cup of tea."

Martha placed the umbrella in the old metal milk can sitting near the back door, removed her lightweight shawl, and took a seat at the table.

"Sure is nasty weather we're having," Grace commented.

Martha nodded and glanced around the room. "Where's Anna?"

"Upstairs taking a much-needed nap."

"I'm glad she's not about, because I don't think it would be good for her to hear what I have to say."

Chills ran up Grace's spine as she took a seat across from her sister. "What's wrong? Has something happened to another one of Heidi's pups?"

Martha shook her head. "The dogs are fine, but I can't say the same for poor Alma Wengerd."

"Ach! What's wrong with Alma?"

"She's dead. Dad got the news when Bishop King dropped by his shop this morning."

"What happened to Alma?"

"She'd gone out to feed the chickens, and when she didn't come back to the house, Abe went looking. He found her on the ground a few feet from the chicken coop. She'd been struck by a bolt of lightning."

Grace gasped. "Oh, that's baremlich!"

Martha nodded soberly. "I know it's terrible. Alma was a friend of Mom's, and she's terribly broken up over this."

Grace stared at the table as tears gathered in her eyes. "After last night, I didn't think things could get much worse around here, but I guess I was wrong."

"What happened last night?"

"First, I ran into Gary Walker in the hallway outside the women's restroom at the restaurant."

"Did he say something to upset you?"

"Gary always says things to upset me." Grace swallowed hard. "I wish he'd leave Holmes County and never come back."

"I've been praying for that–not just because you think he's the one responsible for the attacks, but because I know that seeing him makes you think about the past."

Grace sniffed and turned to reach for a tissue from the box sitting on the counter behind her. "Something else happened last night that upset me, too."

"What was it?"

"When Anna and I got home, we found a package on the porch."

"A birthday present?"

"I thought so at first." Grace blew her nose and dabbed at the corners of her eyes. "I made the mistake of letting Anna open it, and–"

"And what, Grace? What was inside the package?"

"A dead maus."

"That's *ekelhaft*! Who in their right mind would do such a disgusting thing?"

"Gary Walker, that's who."

"You really think he's responsible?"

Grace nodded. "As I've told you before, he said he would get even with me someday."

"That was several years ago. Surely the man's not still angry because you married his friend."

The back door opened, and Ruth stepped into the room. "Whew, this is some weather we've been having. You should have seen all the water on the road. I had a hard time seeing out the front buggy window on my way home." She set her umbrella in the milk can next to Martha's, hung her shawl on a wall peg, and hurried over to the table. "Have you got any tea made? I could sure use some about now."

Grace reached for the pot sitting on the table and poured her sister a cup of tea.

"Have you heard about Abe's Alma? Is that why you're here?" Martha asked as Ruth took the offered cup.

"Haven't heard a thing about Alma. What about her?"

"She's dead. Struck down by a lightning bolt right there in her yard."

Ruth's eyes widened. "Ach, what a shame!"

"That leaves Abe with six kinner to raise. He's surely going to need some help in the days ahead," Grace put in.

Ruth nodded with a somber expression. "I'm sure their relatives will pitch in."

Grace moaned. "So much sadness going on around us these days. Sometimes I wonder how much more we can take."

Ruth set her cup down and reached over to touch Grace's hand. "Despite the sad news about Alma, I've got another piece of news that might bring a smile to your face."

"What news is that?"

Martha leaned forward. "I'd be interested in hearing some good news for a change, too."

"That reporter you used to date came into the bakeshop today, and he mentioned that his work was done here and that he'd be heading to Wisconsin soon to do some stories about the Amish there." Ruth squeezed Grace's fingers. "Now you can quit worrying about running into him every time you go to town. And if the attacks on us should quit, we'll know he was responsible."

Grace sighed as a feeling of relief flooded over her. Maybe now they could stop worrying about being attacked and concentrate on helping Abe and his family plan Alma's funeral and make it through the days ahead.

Chapter 43

The sky was a dismal gray, and the air felt much too chilly for a spring morning, but at least there was no rain on the day of Alma Wengerd's funeral. As family and friends gathered at the cemetery to say their final good-byes to Alma, Ruth's heart ached for the six children Alma had left behind. Molly, age two; Owen, who was four; six-year-old Willis; Esta, age eight; ten-year-old Josh; and the oldest, Gideon, who was twelve, huddled close to their father as they stood near Alma's coffin.

Alma had been only thirty-two years old when she'd been snatched from the world so unexpectedly. The sweet-tempered woman, still in the prime of her life, would never see her children raised or enjoy becoming a grandmother someday. It tore at Ruth's heartstrings to think of these little ones without a mother, and she wondered how Abe would manage to take care of the house, do all his chores, watch out for the children, and run his harness shop.

She glanced over at Martin, who stood near his parents. He hadn't attended the main funeral that was held at Abe's house, but he'd shown up in time for the graveside service. Ruth wondered if he would be expected to do more work at the harness shop now, since Abe would have additional family responsibilities. Martin seemed like such a kind young man, and she felt sure he would do all he could to help lighten Abe's load.

If Ruth didn't already have a job at the bakeshop in town, she might offer to work for Abe as his maid, but she'd heard that his unmarried sister who lived in Illinois would be coming to care for his children.

As Alma's four pallbearers lifted the long, felt straps that had been placed around each end of the coffin and lowered it slowly into the ground, Ruth drew her attention back to the gravesite. Death was a horrible thing, and she couldn't imagine how Abe must feel after losing his wife of thirteen years. The closest people Ruth had ever lost were her grandparents, and she couldn't conceive of how it would be to lose a mate.

As short boards were placed over the casket by one of the men, Abe bent down and scooped his youngest child into his arms. Maybe Molly had become fussy, or perhaps Abe had picked her up in order to offer himself some measure of comfort. The tall man with reddish-brown hair and a full beard to match showed no outward signs of grief other than the somber expression on his face.

Gideon leaned over and whispered something in Josh's ear, and little Esta moaned as she clasped her two younger brothers' hands.

Ruth wanted to dash across the space between them and gather the children into her arms. Instead, she reached one hand out to Martha, who stood to her left, and the other hand out to Anna, who stood on her right, looking as though she might break into tears. Was Grace's daughter thinking about the passing of her English grandmother? Had Alma's death been a reminder of what Anna had lost? Grace looked on the verge of tears, too. Perhaps her greatest sorrow came from the fact that her husband wasn't at her side, for Cleon hadn't returned home yet and probably didn't even know about Alma's death.

As the pallbearers filled in the grave, the bishop read a hymn from the Ausbund, a few lines at a time, and a singing group followed. Then the grave was filled in and the soil mounded. Everyone turned away, wearing solemn expressions, and moved slowly toward their buggies.

Everyone but Esta, that is. The young girl dashed across the grass and, sobbing as though her heart would break, threw herself on the ground next to her mother's grave.

Abe stood as if he was torn between getting his other children into the buggy and going back to offer comfort to his grieving daughter.

No one else was close enough to notice the child. Even Ruth's family had left the gravesite, but she'd stayed put, waiting to see what Abe would do. Finally, when she saw him move toward his buggy again, she rushed over to Esta and knelt on the ground beside her. Gathering the little girl into her arms, she rocked back and forth, gently patting her back.

"Mamma. . .Mamma. . .why'd you have to leave us?" the child sobbed. "Don't you know how much we all need you?"

Tears coursed down Esta's face, wetting the front of Ruth's dress and mingling with her own tears. At that moment, Ruth promised herself that she would not only pray for the Wengerd family, but she would also drop by their place as often as possible and offer to help in any way she could.

As Grace directed her horse and buggy down the road after she and Anna had left Alma's funeral, she was filled with concern—not only for Abe and his children, but also for Anna, who hadn't spoken a word since they'd left the burial site. The child was shaken by the death of Esta's mother, but she'd refused to talk about it. Due to Anna's melancholy behavior, Grace had decided to get Anna home as quickly as possible, rather than stay for the dinner at Abe's house.

She glanced over at the child, who sat in the seat beside her with her arms folded and her eyes downcast. If only she knew what was going on in her daughter's head.

Grace was glad her parents and sisters had stayed for the funeral dinner, for the women's help was needed serving the meal. Dad and Abe had done a lot of business with each other, as well as sending customers one another's way, so she knew Dad would want to hang around and offer encouragement to Abe. Grace had noticed that Ruth had taken Esta Wengerd under her wing, and that she'd even been the one to walk the crying child to Abe's buggy after the graveside service.

Ruth would make a good mother someday, and Grace hoped her sister would find a nice Amish man to marry when the time was right.

Maybe it would be Martin Gingerich. He'd certainly shown an interest in Ruth. Martin was rather quiet and shy–nothing like Luke Freisen–but he seemed like a kind man, and from what Abe had told Dad a few weeks ago, Martin was a hard worker.

Grace's thoughts went to Cleon as she placed one hand against her stomach. *He'll be sorry when he hears of Alma's passing. Sorry for Abe and sorry he wasn't here for the funeral.* She swallowed against the burning lump clogging her throat. *Would Cleon mourn if something were to happen to me, or would he be relieved to have me out of his life?*

She shook her head. She shouldn't allow herself to think this way. It wasn't good for her to focus on the negative. It wasn't good for the baby she carried to have its mother feeling so distraught.

As they came down a slight incline, the buggy horse whinnied, halted, and pawed at the ground.

"What's the matter with you, Ben?" Grace snapped the reins, but the horse refused to move, shaking his head from side to side. His behavior made no sense. Cars weren't whizzing past, and from what she could see, nothing in the road signaled danger.

She snapped the reins again and reached for the buggy whip. "Giddy-up there, Ben. Move along now, schnell!"

The horse finally moved forward, but he acted skittish, and Grace had to keep prompting him with the buggy whip. Finally, they reached the driveway leading to her folks' home, and when she turned Ben to the right, he tried to rear up. She pulled back on the reins. "Whoa, now. Steady, boy."

The horse finally calmed enough so she could get him moving again, but they'd only made it halfway up the driveway when she smelled smoke. Grace forced the horse to keep moving until her Dad's shop came into view. Nothing wrong there; it looked the same as it had this morning. Past Mom and Dad's house they went; it looked fine, and so did the barn. She'd just started up the incline to the second driveway when she saw it–smoke and flames coming from her and Cleon's house!

At first, Grace wasn't sure what to do. Should she run for the hose and try to put out the fire on her own, or turn the buggy around and head to the closest English neighbors' to call the fire department? Trying to put out the fire by herself was ridiculous. However, it would take some time for the fire trucks to get there, and the house could be gone by then. If only Dad or Cleon were here, she could go for help while they fought the fire.

Anna squealed and crawled over the seat just as Grace halted the buggy. She turned to reach for the child, but Anna scooted away, climbed out the back opening, and ran toward the burning building.

Grace opened her door and jumped down, too. "Anna, stop! Don't go near the house!"

The child kept running, and by the time Grace reached the front porch, Anna had already opened the door and slipped inside.

"Oh, dear Lord, no," Grace panted as she raced in after the child. "Please don't let anything happen to my little girl!"

When Cleon's bus arrived in Dover, Henry Rawlings, one of the English drivers he sometimes used, picked him up. But Henry needed to make a stop in Berlin, and since Cleon was anxious to get home and make things right with Grace, he headed there on foot.

As he trudged along the shoulder of the road, he thought about his trip to Pennsylvania and how well things had gone. Not only were some bees and hives being shipped home, but also he'd purchased a honey extractor, some goat-hide gloves, a bee veil, a smoker, and a hive tool that would be used to pry frames out of the beehives. He'd also found a couple of outlets that wanted to buy his honey. If things went well, by this time next year, he could have a thriving business again.

He'd also bought Grace a package of stationery with bluebirds scattered along the top of each page. It wasn't much, but at least it would let her know that he hadn't forgotten her birthday.

About halfway home, Cleon heard a horn honk. He turned and saw John Peterson's SUV pull onto the shoulder of the road behind him. "Need a lift?" John called through his open window.

"I'd appreciate that." Cleon pulled the door open on the passenger's side and climbed in.

"Heard you'd been on a trip to buy some bees," John said as he pulled onto the road again.

Cleon nodded. "Bees and boxes, both."

"Did you have any luck?"

"Sure did. Had the bees, boxes, and beekeeping supplies shipped to my folks' place. They should be there by now, I'm guessing."

"Is that where you're headed then—to see your folks'?"

Cleon shook his head. "Figured I should stop by my own house first and let Grace know I'm home."

John gave the steering wheel a couple of taps. "There's been some excitement in the area since you've been gone."

"What kind of excitement—good or bad?"

"Afraid it's not good. We had a pretty rough storm a few days ago, and Alma Wengerd was hit by a bolt of lightning."

"I'm real sorry to hear that. Was she hurt bad?"

"She's dead. Her funeral was today, although I didn't attend. Since I'm not Amish and haven't been in the community very long, I wasn't sure I'd be welcomed." John shook his head. "Your neighbor Ray Larson wasn't there, either. I saw him at the pharmacy in Berlin not long ago."

A chill ran up Cleon's spine, and he shivered. Abe's wife was dead—struck down in the prime of her life. He couldn't imagine how he would feel if something like that happened to Grace.

"You okay?" John asked, nudging Cleon's arm. "You look kind of pale."

Cleon popped a couple of knuckles and reached both hands around to rub the kinks in his neck. "I was thinking about Abe losing his wife like that. Must have been some shock for him."

John nodded. "I heard he was the one to find her not far from the chicken coop where she'd gone to gather eggs."

"How terrible. Abe's got six kids, you know, and it won't be easy for him to raise them on his own."

"He'll probably be looking for another wife soon. That's what most Amish men do when they lose a mate, isn't it?"

Cleon shrugged. "Some do; some don't. All depends on the

circumstances." *Would I be looking for another wife if Grace died? Could anyone make me as happy as she does? How would I feel if Grace was taken from me before I had a chance to ask for her forgiveness?*

When they turned onto the Hostettlers' driveway, Cleon noticed a thick cloud of smoke hanging in the air. The acrid smell stung his nostrils, and when they began the climb to his driveway, he realized that his house was on fire. His spine went rigid, and his heart pounded. *Dear God, don't let them be in there. Don't let it be too late for us, please.*

He turned to John. "Can you call the fire department for me?"

"Of course." John fumbled in his shirt pocket and frowned. "Rats! Must have left my cell phone at home. I'll go there now and make the call."

Cleon opened the door, jumped out of the vehicle, and raced up the driveway. He spotted Grace's horse and buggy parked nearby. *She must be home. She could even be in the house.*

"Grace, where are you?"

Silence except for the crackle of flames shooting into the air.

"Anna! Anna, come back here! No, don't go upstairs!"

Cleon halted. That was Grace's voice coming from inside their house. Apparently Anna was there, too. His heart nearly stopped beating. If he lost Grace now, without making things right between them, he didn't think he could go on living.

Noting that the fire seemed to be coming from the second story, where it shot out the bedroom windows and through the roof, Cleon pulled a quilt from the buggy, wet it in the horses' watering trough, and threw it over his head. He jumped onto the porch, flung open the door, and raced inside.

Chapter 44

Rather than helping the other women serve the funeral dinner, Ruth decided it would be best to stay with Abe's children, especially Esta, who had refused to eat anything.

"If you promise to eat a little something," Ruth coaxed as she sat on a bench beside Esta, "then I'll ask your daed if you can come over to our place tomorrow so you can see how my sister's puppies are growing." She smiled. "I'm sure Anna would enjoy having someone to play with, too."

Esta stared up at Ruth, her dark eyes looking ever so serious and her long lashes sweeping across her cheeks with each steady blink. "You think Martha might let me have one of them hundlin?"

Ruth knew Martha had given Anna one of Heidi's puppies, but that pup had died, and Martha was counting on getting paid for the other two she still hoped to sell. She took hold of Esta's hand. "If they were my hundlin to give, I'd say, jah, but I'm pretty sure Martha's planning to sell the others."

Esta's lower lip protruded. "I've got no money, and I'm sure Papa won't give me none, neither. He always says we can buy only what we need."

Ruth had some money saved up from her job, and she couldn't think of a thing she needed it for right now. "I'll tell you what, Esta," she said, gently squeezing the little girl's fingers, "If your daed says it's okay, then I'll buy you one of Heidi's hundlin."

Esta's eyes opened wide. "Really?"

"Jah."

"Okay." Esta grabbed a sandwich off her plate and took a bite.

Ruth smiled and turned her attention to her own plate of food. *I hope I have a child as sweet as Esta some day.*

After the meal, the men and women gathered in groups to visit, while the children and young people visited with friends. Since Esta seemed content to play with one of the other children who'd brought along her faceless doll, Ruth decided it was a good time to go off by herself for a while to think and pray.

As she wandered through the yard, heading for the stream near the back of Abe's property, her thoughts went to Grace, who had taken Anna home some time ago. The sad expression on her sister's face concerned Ruth, and she was sure it wasn't only due to Alma's death. Grace anguished over her strained marriage and worried about the assaults against their family over the last several months.

If there's something I can do to help my sister deal with this, please show me how, Lord, Ruth prayed as she dropped to a seat on the grass not far from the stream. She lifted her face to savor the warmth of the sun and closed her eyes. *And help me know what to do to help Esta and her brothers and sisters in the days ahead.*

"Are you sleepin'?" a male voice asked.

Ruth's eyes snapped open. Toby King and Sadie Esh stared down at her.

"I didn't realize anyone else was here."

"We weren't. I mean, we just got here," Toby mumbled.

"Too many people were milling about the Wengerds' yard, so we decided to take a walk by ourselves," Sadie said, her cheeks turning rosy.

Ruth nodded.

"Seems like nearly everyone in our community came out for Alma's funeral. Everyone but Luke." Toby shook his head. "I wouldn't be surprised if he isn't spending the day with his English buddies. Seems to have more time for them than he does his Amish friends these days, uh-huh."

Ruth made no comment, preferring not to discuss her ex-boyfriend.

She had other, more important things on her mind. Things like how she could help little Esta and her siblings cope with the loss of their mother.

Toby gave Sadie's arm a tug. "Are we goin' for a walk or not?"

"Jah, sure," she said with a nod. "See you at work tomorrow, Ruth."

Ruth lifted her hand in a wave and closed her eyes again as she leaned back in the grass. A few minutes later, she heard a man clear his throat, and her eyes snapped open.

Her insides quivered when she saw Martin standing over her.

"Saw you heading this way awhile ago and thought I'd come talk to you," he said, his face turning a light shade of red.

She patted the ground beside her. "Would you like to have a seat?"

"Jah, sure." Once Martin was seated, he removed his hat and flopped it over his bent knees. "Sure was a sad funeral, wasn't it?"

She nodded, afraid if she voiced her thoughts, she might dissolve into a puddle of tears.

"Just goes to show that no one knows what the future holds. You can be going along fine one minute, and the next minute some unexpected tragedy occurs." He shook his head. "I'll bet Abe never dreamed when Alma went out to feed the chickens that he'd never see her again—leastways not in this life."

She nodded again.

"I couldn't help but notice the way you were comforting Abe's kinner—especially Esta when she was so upset."

Ruth swallowed around the lump in her throat. "They're all going to miss their mamm, that's for sure."

"Seemed like you got her calmed down, though."

"I did my best."

Martin pulled up one blade of grass after another. Finally, he turned to Ruth, cleared his throat a couple of times, and said, "I enjoyed the time we spent with each other at the young people's gathering the other night."

"Me, too."

"I was wondering. . .that is. . .would it be all right if I came calling on you at your home sometime next week?"

Ruth didn't want to appear too anxious, but the thought of being courted by this kind, gentle man made her feel so giddy she could barely breathe. "Jah, Martin. I'd be happy to have you come calling," she said with a nod.

"I'm sure sorry about Alma," Roman said as he clasped Abe's shoulder. "If there's anything I can do, please let me know."

Abe nodded. "I appreciate that."

"Will someone from your family help with the kinner?"

"My youngest sister, Sue, who isn't yet married, said she'd move in and take over their care." Abe ran his fingers through the back of his reddish-brown hair as he leaned against the barn door. Tears welled in his eyes. "Alma was only thirty-two when she died. Don't seem right for one so young to be snatched away from her family, does it?"

Roman shook his head. Judith was forty-four, and he couldn't imagine losing her.

Abe groaned. "We celebrated thirteen years of marriage a few weeks ago. Alma was nineteen, and I'd just turned twenty when we tied the knot."

Roman clasped his friend's shoulder again. "From what I knew of Alma, she was a fine Christian woman."

"You're right about that, and she was a good mudder to our six kinner." Abe stared across the yard where his two oldest boys played a game of tug-of-war with some of the other children. "Losing Alma is gonna be hard on us all, but I'm especially worried about Esta. At the end there, I was torn between helping her and getting my other five back to the buggy. I finally decided to tend to them first and then see about Esta, but when I caught sight of your daughter Ruth comforting Esta, I figured I'd let her handle things."

He turned to face Roman. "Esta's the oldest of my girls, you know, and the truth is she got along with her mamm better than she did me. I'm thinking now that Alma's gone, Esta will need the hand of a woman to guide her along."

"I'm sure my wife and daughters will be willing to do whatever they can to help, along with your sister, of course."

"We'll appreciate any help we get." Abe turned away from the barn. "Guess I'd better go visit some of the others for a bit. Although, if I had my druthers, I'd go in the house, climb into bed, and pull the covers over my head."

Roman nodded in understanding. Ever since the attacks on his family had begun, he'd felt the same way.

As Grace dashed through the house screaming for Anna, her eyes stung with tears, and her lungs filled with smoke. "Anna! Anna, where are you?"

All she heard was the crackle of flames lapping against the wooden structure of her home. Unless help came soon, they would lose everything. But Grace couldn't worry about that right now. She had to find Anna and get her out of this inferno.

Coughing and choking, Grace looked everywhere, hoping for some sign of her daughter. She could barely see for all the smoke and worried that Anna might have gone upstairs. "Anna! Anna, where are you?"

The front door *swooshed* open, and Cleon burst into the room. Grace gulped on a sob and threw herself into his arms.

"Thank the Lord, you're all right," he panted, squeezing her so tightly she could hardly breathe. "When I got home and saw the place was on fire, I was afraid you were inside and had been—"

Grace pulled away and hiccupped on a sob. "Anna's missing, Cleon. I'm afraid she may have gone upstairs."

Cleon motioned to the door. "It's not safe for you to be in here with all this smoke. Go outside, and I'll search for Anna."

Grace hesitated, but the intense heat from the flames made her realize that she needed to get out of the house. They all did—especially Anna, her precious little girl. "Oh, Cleon, I—I don't think I could stand it if something happened to Anna. I need to find her—to be sure she's all right."

"I promise I'll find her," he said, practically pushing Grace out the door. "I love you, Grace, and right now you need to take care of yourself so that boppli you're carrying has a chance at life, too."

Grace blinked a couple of times as she let Cleon's words sink in. He'd said he loved her and was concerned about the child she carried. Did that mean he'd forgiven her, too? There was no time for questions, and Grace didn't argue further, for she knew Cleon was right. He had helped on the volunteer department and would have a better chance of saving Anna than she ever could.

Moments later as Grace knelt on the grass in their front yard, she whispered a prayer. "Help us, Lord. Help Cleon find Anna, and keep them both safe."

With each passing second, she struggled against the desire to run back into the house and help search for her little girl. What if Cleon couldn't find the child? What if he and Anna both perished in the flames?

She stood on trembling legs and was about to head back to the house when Cleon emerged from the building, Anna in his arms.

"Oh, thank the Lord!" Grace rushed forward and reached for her daughter, who clutched her faceless doll in her hands. "Where was she?"

"Found her upstairs in her room, trying to rescue her dolly."

"Is she hurt?"

"I think she breathed in quite a bit of smoke, but I didn't see any burns, and I think she's gonna be—"

Before Cleon could finish his sentence, Anna buried her face against Grace's neck and cried, "Poppy saved me from the fire!"

"Oh, no, daughter," Grace said, as she patted the child's back. "It was Cleon who went into the burning house to rescue you."

Anna turned her head toward Cleon as tears rolled down her flushed cheeks. "Can I call you Papa?"

"I'd like that." Tears welled in Cleon's eyes. "I owe you an apology, Anna. I've been selfish, thinking of my own needs, and never considering what it must be like for you coming here to live with people you didn't know and trying to adjust to a new way of life."

Anna reached out and touched Cleon's damp face. Then she leaned forward and kissed his cheek.

His gaze turned to Grace. The look of tenderness she saw on his face caused her to choke on a sob.

"One day while I was off buying some beekeeping supplies, I thought about a verse of scripture, and it made me realize—" He gulped in a deep breath. "I love you, Grace. That's never changed. And I'm sorry for my unforgiving spirit. Will you forgive me for being such a stubborn *narr*?"

"You're not a fool," Grace said with a shake of her head. "You were just deeply hurt by my deception."

"That doesn't make it right," he said, leaning down to kiss her lips. "I promise to be a better husband from now on."

Tears pooled in Grace's eyes, clouding her vision. "And I'll try to be the best wife I can be." She sank to the ground, placing Anna in her lap; then pointed to the house as angry flames lapped at the sides and shot through the roof. "Oh, Cleon, if help doesn't come soon, we're going to lose the whole house."

He knelt beside Grace and reached for her hand. "John Peterson gave me a lift home, and when we realized the house was on fire, he said he'd call for help. The fire trucks should be here soon, but even if we should lose the house, it doesn't matter."

She blinked several times. "What do you mean, 'it doesn't matter'? We've worked hard to build our home, and if we lose it—"

"The house doesn't matter; it can be rebuilt. What counts is you and Anna—that you're both unharmed."

"You're right," she murmured. "God has given us a second chance, and all that matters is that we obey Him and try to do what's right."

Sirens blared in the distance, and Cleon took Anna from Grace as they clambered to their feet. Two fire trucks roared up the driveway, followed by John's rig. Several firemen hopped out of the vehicles and set right to work, but the house was nearly gone. It looked hopeless.

"Do you have any idea how the fire got started?" the fire chief asked Cleon.

He shook his head as he put his arm around Grace's shoulders.

"There's been no more lightning since the day one of our Amish women was struck down, so it couldn't have been that," she replied. "Were any of your gas lamps left burning inside the house?"

"I thought I had turned them off before my daughter and I left for Alma Wengerd's funeral this morning, but then I've been so upset about Alma's death, I guess I might have left one on without realizing it."

"Once the fire is out, we'll conduct an investigation," the fire chief said. "In the meantime, you all need to let the paramedics check you over."

Cleon nodded, and his arm tightened around Grace's shoulders as they headed for the rescue vehicles. "When I think how close I came to losing you, I feel sick all over." He grimaced. "And I feel even sicker when I think how terrible I treated you after Anna arrived and I learned the truth about the secret you'd been keeping."

"As Bishop King said to me the night Anna showed up on our doorstep, 'The past is in the past, and nothing's going to change what's been done.' "

Cleon stopped walking and turned to stare at their home. The fire was out now, but the house was burned beyond recognition.

Grace leaned her head on his shoulder and sighed. "It's going to be all right. We have a boppli to look forward to, and with the love and support of each other and with God as the head of our home, I know we can face whatever might come in the days ahead."

"You're right, my blessed gift." He kissed her tenderly on the mouth, then leaned down to kiss the top of Anna's head. The little girl smiled up at him.

Grace's heart filled with joy. "And from now on," she promised, "we won't have any more secrets."

A Sister's Jest

Dedication

To my sister, Joy, who is also my friend.

But he knoweth the way that I take:
when he hath tried me, I shall come forth as gold.
Job 23:10

Chapter 1

Ruth, watch out! Get out of the way!"

Ruth Hostettler halted. A hammer slid down the roof of her sister's new house. *"Ach!"* She jumped back as it bounced off the sheets of plywood, just missing her head.

Martin Gingerich scrambled down the ladder and rushed to her side. "Are you okay, Ruth?"

Ruth nodded as she looked up at his strong, handsome face. She saw tenderness there, and something more. Did she dare believe he might be falling in love with her?

Her heart pounded like a blacksmith's anvil as Martin pulled her to his side.

"You need to stay away from the work site. It's too dangerous." His hazel-colored eyes were wide with obvious concern.

"I—I was coming to see if the workers wanted something to drink."

Martin wiped the rivulets of sweat running down his forehead; then he bent to pick up the hammer lying in the dirt near Ruth's feet. "I think we could all use a break." He leaned his head back and stared at the roof. "Luke most of all, since he's the one who lost his grip on that hammer."

Ruth's gaze followed Martin's. Luke Friesen sat near the edge of the roof, shaking his head. "Are you all right, Ruth?"

"I'm okay. Just a bit shook up."

"I thought I had a good grip, but that hammer slipped right out of my hand."

"You need to be more careful!" Martin's harsh tone took Ruth by surprise. Usually he was very soft-spoken.

"*Jah*, well, she shouldn't have been standing where she was. The work site's no place for a woman." Luke grunted. "Hand me that hammer, would ya, Martin?"

"Why don't you come down and take a break? Then you can get the hammer yourself."

"Guess I will."

As Luke descended the ladder, Martin smiled at Ruth, lifted his straw hat, and brushed back his coffee-colored hair. "Would you like me to go with you to get something to drink for the workers?"

"That would be nice." Ruth appreciated Martin's kindness. In all the time she and Luke had courted, Luke had never offered to help with anything. For that matter, he'd never shown much concern for her welfare, not even when her family's home had been broken into and other acts of vandalism had taken place. Instead, Luke had admitted to Ruth that he owned a truck he kept hidden in the woods and made her promise not to tell anyone. On several occasions, he'd acted as if he might be hiding something. Ruth was sure she'd done the right thing by breaking up with him. Having Martin as a suitor made her happier than she'd ever been during her courtship with Luke.

"I'm glad you weren't hit by Luke's hammer," Martin said as they started for the house. "It's bad enough that your sister and her husband lost their home in that horrible fire a few weeks ago. The last thing we need is for anyone to get hurt today."

Ruth nodded. "We were all relieved that nobody was hurt in the fire. I know Grace and Cleon appreciate all this help building their new home. This is the second Saturday in a row that they've had a large crew working on it."

"That's what friends and family are for."

Martin's dimpled smile made Ruth feel tongue-tied and tingly. She hadn't felt like that when she and Luke were together. More than anything, she'd felt irritated the last few months they'd been courting.

"Sure is a good turnout today," Martin said.

"Jah. The house is almost done, and it will be good for Grace and Cleon to have their own place again."

"I heard your *daed* say that the fire chief found a cigarette lighter on the ground outside their old house. He thinks the fire might have been intentional."

Ruth nodded, wondering if she should tell Martin that Grace thought the English reporter she used to date might have started the fire before he left the area. She decided it would be best not to say anything since they had no proof it was Gary Walker. Besides, Dad had his own suspicions about who might have set the fire.

When they reached the home of Ruth's parents, she turned to Martin. "If you'd like to have a seat on the porch, I'll run inside and see if Mom's fixed anything to drink yet."

"Okay."

Martin took a seat on the porch swing, and Ruth hurried into the house.

She found her mother and two sisters in the kitchen, along with a few other Amish women and their nearest English neighbor.

Mom smiled at Ruth and pushed a wisp of dark brown hair back into her bun. "Are the men ready to take a break?"

"Jah. I came in to get them something to drink."

"There's iced tea and lemonade in the refrigerator." Grace motioned toward the stove. "We've got some coffee heating, too." Her blue eyes twinkled like sparkling water.

"You'll need help carrying the beverages out," Ruth's younger sister, Martha, put in.

"Martin's waiting on the porch to help me with that."

"Martin Gingerich?" Sadie Esh asked.

Ruth nodded, and her cheeks turned warm.

"That fellow's really sweet on my sister, and I think she's equally sweet on him." Martha grinned at Ruth, and the skin around her blue eyes crinkled. "Look how red in the face she's getting."

Ruth shrugged. She couldn't deny her interest in Martin, but she wasn't about to admit it, either.

"Leave your sister alone," Mom said, shaking her finger at Martha. "When you find a fellow you like more than your dogs, you'll turn red in the face whenever his name's mentioned, too."

"How are things going with the new house?" Grace asked.

"Everything was fine until I nearly got hit in the head," Ruth said as she removed a jug of iced tea from the refrigerator.

Mom gasped. "Oh, Ruth, are you all right?"

"I'm fine. It just shook me up a bit."

"How'd it happen?" their English neighbor Donna Larson questioned.

"A hammer tumbled off the roof. It could have hit me if Martin hadn't shouted a warning."

"Was it Martin's hammer?" Cleon's mother, Irene, asked.

"No, it belonged to Luke."

Mom pursed her lips. "Luke Friesen's here today?"

Ruth set the jug of iced tea on the counter and turned to face her mother. "He and his boss both came to help."

"Your daed's not going to like that. He doesn't trust Luke, and if he thought for one minute—"

"Ach, Mom, surely you don't think Luke would intentionally let his hammer fall." Martha's face had turned red as a pickled beet. "I think Dad's still angry because Luke's not working for him anymore."

"Luke was fired, and you know it."

"That was only because he didn't see eye to eye with Dad on everything."

Mom squinted at Martha. "Luke came to work late on several occasions, and he thought he knew more than your daed about things. And don't forget about those sunglasses of Luke's that were found near my clothesline after it had been cut."

Martha stared down at the table. "That doesn't prove he cut the line."

"Toby says Luke's been acting strange for several months," Sadie put in. "He thinks Luke hasn't been right in the head since he started running with some rowdy English fellows."

Ruth was glad Luke's mother hadn't come today. It wouldn't be good for her to hear such talk about her son. In fact, she didn't think they should be having this conversation, especially not in front of Donna Larson.

Martha shot Sadie an exasperated look. "You can tell your boyfriend that *he's* done some strange things, too. Does that make *him* a suspect?"

Sadie opened her mouth as if to comment, but Cleon's mother spoke first. "It's not our place to judge Luke or anyone else. It might be good if we change the subject."

"I agree." Ruth headed back to the refrigerator for a pitcher of lemonade. "I'm taking this outside. If some of you would like to bring out the coffee and cookies, I'm sure the men would appreciate it."

As Martin waited on the porch swing for Ruth, he thought about her near mishap with the hammer and thanked God that she hadn't been hurt. He'd had an interest in Ruth for a long time—ever since they were children. Even back then, he thought she was beautiful, with her dark brown hair and matching eyes, not to mention her gentle, sweet spirit. During their teen years, when they'd first started attending singings and other young people's functions, he'd been too shy to ask if he could give her a ride home in his buggy. Then Luke Friesen began courting Ruth, and Martin figured his chances were nil. Now that Luke was out of the picture, Martin hoped he might be able to win Ruth's heart.

"What's the matter, Martin? Did you get tired of crawling around on the roof?" Abe Wengerd asked as he clomped up the steps to the back porch.

Martin motioned to the house. "I came here to help Ruth get something to drink for the workers."

Abe glanced around, then tipped his head in Martin's direction. "Don't see any sign of Ruth. Looks to me like you're taking a break."

Martin chuckled. "Guess I am at that. But just until Ruth returns from the kitchen."

"How come you didn't go in with her?"

"Figured I'd only be in the way." Martin's cheeks warmed. "Besides, she asked me to wait out here."

"Reminds me of the way my Alma used to be." Abe reached under his straw hat and pulled his fingers through the ends of his unruly reddish-brown hair. "That woman could get me to do most anything." A shadow crossed his face as he stared down at his boots. "Sure do miss her."

Martin couldn't imagine what it must be like for Abe, losing his wife after she was struck by a lightning bolt. Now the poor fellow had six children to raise on his own. Martin wondered whether Abe would marry again—and if so, whether it would be for love or so his children could have a mother.

"Did you come up to the house for a particular reason or just to see if I was loafing off?" Martin asked.

Abe leaned against the porch railing. "From what I've seen of your work habits at the harness shop, I'm convinced you're not the kind to loaf around." He nodded toward the back door. "In answer to your question, I was heading in to use the facilities."

"What's wrong with the portable outhouses that were put up for the workers to use?" Roman Hostettler asked as he stepped onto the porch. "Are they too smelly for your sensitive nose?" He snickered and bumped Abe's arm with his elbow.

Abe nudged him right back. "They were both in use. I figured you wouldn't mind if I used the one inside."

"Don't mind at all." Roman pushed the screen door open. "Go right on in."

When Abe disappeared into the house, Roman flopped into one of the wicker chairs that sat near the swing and fanned his damp face with the brim of his hat. "Sure has turned into a warm day, jah?"

Martin nodded. "That's why Ruth went into the house to get something cold to drink. As soon as she comes back, we'll take it to the workers."

"It's nice of you to want to help," Roman said with a sly-looking smile. His brown eyes twinkled, as though he knew Martin's secret.

Martin's ears burned with embarrassment. Did Ruth's dad know how much he cared for his daughter? Would Roman approve of his courting Ruth? He was tempted to ask but decided to bring up another subject instead. "Did you see that hammer fly off the roof a while ago?"

"Sure didn't. Did anyone get hurt?"

"No, but the hammer almost hit Ruth."

Roman's dark bushy eyebrows drew together. "How'd it happen?"

"It was Luke's hammer. He said it slipped out of his hand."

"Humph! As much training as that fellow's had using a hammer, he shouldn't be losing his grip. That was just plain careless." Roman's eyes narrowed as he glanced at the place behind his house where the section of property he'd given Cleon lay. "I never invited Luke to this work frolic. If I'd had my way, he wouldn't have come."

"Who invited him?"

"Cleon. He invited Luke and his English boss, John Peterson. Guess he wanted all able-bodied carpenters to help so we could get the job done quicker."

"Even so, if he knew you didn't want Luke invited—"

"Since it's Cleon and Grace's house, I didn't think I had the right to say who could help and who couldn't." The scowl on Roman's face was enough to curdle fresh goat's milk. "Now that I know one of my daughters could have been injured because of Luke's carelessness, I have a right to say what's on my mind." He stood and pivoted toward the porch steps.

"Where are you going?"

"To send Luke Friesen home!"

Chapter 2

As Ruth neared the back door with a jug of iced tea and a pitcher of lemonade in each hand, she almost collided with Abe Wengerd, who had just entered the house.

"Ach, sorry. I didn't know anyone was there." His face had turned nearly as red as his hair.

"No harm was done." Ruth took a step back, being careful not to spill the beverages. "How are your *kinner* doing? I assume they're home with your sister today?"

Abe nodded. "They're getting along okay with Sue, but they still miss their *mamm*. That's especially true with Esta. She seems to be taking Alma's death harder than the others." He smiled, but it appeared to be forced. "I appreciate the kindness you showed Esta on the day of Alma's funeral."

As Ruth thought about that sorrowful day, she remembered her promise to buy Esta one of Martha's puppies. "Esta seemed interested in having one of my sister's *hundlin*. Would that be all right with you?"

Abe's forehead wrinkled. "I can't afford to buy any pedigree dogs right now."

"Oh no. I was planning to buy the dog for Esta."

The lines in his forehead deepened. "Why would you do that?"

"I thought having a puppy to care for would be good for Esta. It might help her deal with losing her mamm better if she had a dog to take her mind off her grief."

Abe compressed his lips, mulling the offer over. Finally, he nodded. "Jah, okay, but she'll have to be responsible for the *hundli*. My older kinner already have critters to care for, so they won't have time to babysit hers."

"I'll make that clear to Esta when I bring the puppy over." Ruth smiled. "Would tomorrow be a good time, since it's an off-Sunday from church?"

Abe nodded. "That'll be fine."

"I'll be over sometime before noon." Ruth moved toward the door again. "I'd better get these cold drinks out to the men."

Abe held the door, and Ruth stepped outside. Martin was sitting on the porch swing, and her heart skipped a beat when he smiled at her.

"What took you so long?" he asked.

"I was on my way out when Abe Wengerd came into the house. I asked if it would be okay with him if I brought one of my sister's puppies over to his house tomorrow. I'm buying it for Esta."

"That's real nice of you." Martin stood and reached for the jug of iced tea. "Let me carry that for you."

"Danki."

As they walked up the driveway leading to Cleon and Grace's new house, Martin commented on the unseasonably warm spring weather they were having.

Ruth nodded. "I hope it's not a sign that summer will be hot and dry."

"Never know what the weather will bring."

As they neared the house, he stopped and turned to face her. "Say, I was wondering. . ."

She tipped her head. "What were you wondering?"

"Would you mind me going with you when you take the puppy to Esta? It would give us a chance to spend some time together."

"That sounds like fun."

"Maybe afterward, we can drive over to the pond near Abe's place and see if the fish are jumping."

"I'd like that," she said as they began walking again.

When they reached the work site, the crisp scent of wood being sawed mingled with the acidic aroma of sweaty bodies, and Ruth knew the men were in need of a break. She set the jug of lemonade on a piece of plywood that had been placed over some sawhorses, and Martin did the same with the iced tea.

"Guess I'll have a glass of lemonade and then get back to work," he said.

"Aren't you going to take a break with the other men?"

"I took my break while I was waiting for you on the porch." Martin gave her a heart-melting smile and headed toward the house.

Martha and Sadie showed up with a tray of cookies and a pot of coffee. Ruth motioned Martha to one side. "Can I speak to you a minute?"

"Jah, sure. What's up?"

"I'd like to buy one of Heidi's hundlin."

Martha's eyebrows lifted. "I never thought you'd want to buy one of my puppies."

"The puppy's not for me; it's for Esta Wengerd. I thought it might help her deal with her mamm's death a little better."

"Then I should just give her a pup."

Ruth shook her head. "You're trying to build up your business so you can buy more dogs for breeding. I insist on paying for the puppy."

"You're a good sister and a good friend to little Esta." Martha gave Ruth a hug. "When did you plan to take the puppy to her?"

"Since tomorrow's an off-Sunday, I thought I'd head over to the Wengerds' sometime after breakfast."

Martha smiled. "Sounds good to me. I'll have the puppy ready for you then."

"Guess I'll go back to our place now and see what Mom has for me to do."

"Sadie and I will serve the men their snacks, then we'll come back to the house to help get lunch ready to serve."

When Ruth returned to the house, she found Grace and Mom sitting at the table, drinking lemonade. "I figured you'd be making sandwiches by now," she said.

Mom smiled. "They're already made, and since the rest of the women have gone outside to either check on their kinner or see how things are going with the house, Grace and I decided to take a break."

"Guess I will, too, then." Ruth pulled out a chair and sat down. "I'll be taking one of Martha's puppies over to Esta Wengerd tomorrow, so I hope you haven't made any plans that will include me."

Mom shook her head. "Your daed and I thought we would visit my sister, Clara, but there's no need for you to go along."

"If you're goin' to see Esta, can I go, too?"

Ruth turned at the sound of Anna's voice. She hadn't realized her six-year-old niece had come into the room. The child's vivid blue eyes were wide with expectation, while a wisp of dark-colored hair peeked out of her *kapp* and curled around her ear. Not since before the fire had Ruth seen Grace's daughter looking so enthused. There was no way she could say no to Anna's request. "If it's all right with your mamm, you can ride along," she told the child.

Anna hurried to her mother's side. "Can I go with Aunt Ruth to see Esta?"

Grace nodded and gave her daughter a hug. "It's fine with me."

Ruth thought about Martin's offer to drive her over to Abe's place and wondered how he would feel about Anna tagging along. It meant they wouldn't get to spend time alone, but she hoped he would understand.

Martin had just started up the ladder on the back side of the house when he heard angry-sounding voices nearby. He glanced to the left and spotted Ruth's dad talking to Luke.

"Your carelessness could have caused serious injury to my daughter." Roman squeezed his fingers around his straw hat so tightly that his knuckles turned white.

"It was an accident; the hammer slipped out of my hand." Luke looked over at Martin. "You were there when it happened. Tell Roman I didn't drop the hammer on purpose."

Martin swallowed hard, not sure how to respond. Even though it had appeared to be an accident, he wasn't sure it was. Fact was, he didn't trust Luke Friesen and had been relieved when Ruth broke up with him.

"Speak up," Luke said, moving closer to Martin. "Tell the man how the hammer slipped out of my hand and slid down the roof."

"It did that, all right," Martin said with a nod. "And if you'll recall, I told you that you needed to be more careful."

"What he needs to do is stay away from my daughter." Roman planted his hands on his hips and stared hard at Luke. "I don't trust you. Haven't since we found your sunglasses on the ground under my wife's clothesline that *somebody* cut."

"Well, it wasn't me." Luke's eyes darkened to the color of the night sky.

Roman continued to glare at Luke. The tension between them blazed like a hot fire. "Why'd you come here today?"

"To help rebuild Cleon and Grace's house, same as all the others who came."

"Everywhere you go, trouble seems to follow. I'd appreciate it if you'd go home." Roman's eyebrows furrowed. "Better yet, go on back to John Peterson's woodworking shop and do some work there. He's still your employer, isn't he?"

Luke kicked at a dirt clod with the toe of his boot. "John and I both took the day off so we could help here."

"I appreciate John showing up, but you can spend your day off doing something else, because you're not welcome in this place!"

Luke grabbed his work pouch from the patch of grass where he'd laid it and stalked off.

Roman looked over at Martin and slowly shook his head. "I don't trust that fellow."

Martin glanced across the yard. When he saw Luke heading toward his buggy, he made a promise to himself. *Whenever Luke's around Ruth, I'm going to keep a close watch on things.*

Chapter 3

As Martin headed down the road toward the Hostettlers' place the following day, a wave of excitement coursed through his body. He could hardly wait to see Ruth again, and he looked forward to the time he would spend with her on the drive to Abe's place. If he had his way, he would ask Ruth to marry him today. He figured he'd better not rush things, though. He had to be sure she cared as much for him as he did for her. He needed to know that her folks approved of him, as well.

When Martin pulled into the Hostettlers' yard a short time later, he was surprised to see Grace's daughter, Anna, sitting on the porch steps beside Ruth.

After securing his horse to the hitching rail near the barn, Martin sprinted across the yard and stepped onto the porch. "*Guder mariye,*" he said, smiling at Ruth.

"Good morning."

"Are you ready to go?"

"I am, and I hope you don't mind, but I said it was okay if Anna went with us today." Ruth slipped her arm around Anna's shoulders. "Esta's a good friend of Anna's, so she'd like to be there when we deliver the puppy."

Even though Martin was disappointed that he wouldn't have Ruth to himself, he understood why Anna would like to go along. "We can make the drive to the pond some other time," he said.

"I'm sure we can." Ruth reached for Anna's hand. "Shall we go out to the kennels and see if Martha's got that hundli ready for us?"

Anna nodded and clambered to her feet. "I hope Esta lets me help her name it."

Martin seemed awfully quiet on the way over to Abe's, and Ruth wondered if he was unhappy about her bringing Anna along. Of course, the reason he hadn't said much could be because Anna had been talking nonstop ever since they'd left home. The little girl had turned into a regular chatterbox.

"I hope Esta likes the hundli," Anna said from her seat behind Ruth. "She's lost her mamm and needs this little fellow to comfort her."

"I'm sure she'll like it fine," Ruth replied.

Martin smiled at Ruth. "Anna's caught on to the *Deitsch* pretty well, hasn't she?"

"She had a little trouble fitting in and learning our Pennsylvania Dutch language when she first came to live with my sister," Ruth whispered, "but she's finally adjusted and is looking forward to her mamm having a *boppli* soon."

Anna tapped Ruth on the shoulder. "What do you think of the name Winkie for Esta's puppy?"

"Why would you want to call him that?" Ruth asked the child.

" 'Cause he likes to wink. If you watch him real close, you'll see his one eye wink when I pet him behind the ear." She stroked the pup behind its ear, and one eye closed, then opened again.

Ruth laughed. "That's some *schmaert* dog we're giving Esta."

"*Schmaert* means smart, right?"

"Jah."

"Sounds like you're pretty schmaert, too," Martin called over his shoulder.

"Danki."

Ruth turned to look at Anna. With the little reddish-brown and white sheltie nestled in her arms, the little girl looked quite content. "Are you sure you wouldn't like another dog, Anna?" she asked. "I could have given you one for your birthday two weeks ago."

Anna shook her head. "I don't need one of my own, 'cause I'll have a baby sister to play with soon. Besides, I can play with Esta's puppy whenever I visit her."

"Okay." Ruth hoped Anna wouldn't be too disappointed if she ended up with a baby brother. The child had already faced so many disappointments. Even on her sixth birthday, she had suffered the disappointment of not having much of a celebration. Cleon had spent most of the day cleaning up the mess that had been left after their home had been burned. Mom had invited Grace's family for supper that evening, but Cleon and Dad had returned to work on the cleanup right after they'd eaten their meal. Of course, Anna had received some gifts, but Ruth had seen the dejected look on her niece's face and knew she felt let down because there hadn't been a real party to celebrate her special day.

Ruth glanced back at Anna again and was pleased to see the dreamy look on the little girl's face. Apparently her disappointing birthday had been forgotten, for her concentration seemed to be on the puppy she held.

When they arrived at Abe's place, Ruth spotted three of his children—Owen, age four; Willis, age six; and Josh, age ten—playing in the yard. None of them wore jackets, despite the chilly wind and dark clouds hovering overhead. Ruth was sure if their mother were still alive, they wouldn't have been playing outside on a day like this without jackets. She was tempted to mention the chilly weather to the children but decided it wasn't her place to do so. Abe's sister, Sue, had left her parents' home in Illinois and moved into Abe's house to care for his children soon after Alma died. It was Sue's responsibility to look after Abe's kinner now.

Eight-year-old Esta darted out of the barn as soon as Martin pulled the horse up to the hitching rail. Her older brother, Gideon, who was twelve, stepped out from the door behind her.

"Where's your daed?" Martin asked as he hopped down from the buggy and went around to help Ruth and Anna out.

"He's in the house takin' a nap." Gideon's forehead wrinkled. "He's been sleepin' a lot since Mama died."

Esta nodded. "That's right. As soon as Papa's done eating supper every night, he goes right to bed."

"Your daed works hard in his harness shop," Martin said in his boss's defense.

"It ain't the harness shop that's got him feelin' so tired," Gideon mumbled. "He misses Mama, same as we do."

"Only we don't sleep so much," Esta said as she sidled up to the buggy and stood on her tiptoes. "Papa said you were bringin' me a hundli. You got him in there?"

"Of course we do," Anna replied. "Winkie's right here." She handed the puppy to Esta.

Esta stared at the pup. "Winkie? Where'd you get that funny name?"

"I chose it 'cause he likes to wink."

Gideon snorted. "Jah, right. Like any dog knows how to wink."

"This one does," Anna said with a nod.

"It's true," Ruth put in. "I saw the puppy wink."

Gideon shook his head. "People wink; dogs don't."

"Uh-huh." Anna stepped closer to Esta and reached out to stroke the puppy behind its right ear. Winkie closed one eye, opened it, and closed it again.

"I told you he could wink. That's why his name should be Winkie," Anna said.

"I like that name." Esta looked up at Ruth with a dubious expression. "Are you sure he's mine?"

"Absolutely. But you must promise to take good care of him."

Esta's head bobbed up and down. "I'll feed him and make sure he gets plenty of exercise, too."

Ruth bent down and gave Esta a hug. "I'm sure you will."

"Winkie's a dumb name," Gideon mumbled as he shuffled back to the barn.

Esta's lower lip protruded. "I don't know why my *bruder* has to be so mean."

Martin patted Esta on the head. "Maybe he's jealous because you've got a new puppy and he doesn't."

"That's just plain silly," Esta said with a shake of her head. "Gideon's got a goat and a whole lot of other barn animals to care for. He's a mean old *schtinker*."

"Does Gideon smell bad?" Anna asked.

Esta grunted. "Sometimes, after he's been workin' in the barn."

Ruth chuckled. "I think Esta was calling her brother a stinker because he wasn't acting nice about the name you chose for the puppy."

Anna nudged Esta. "Are you gonna keep the name *Winkie* for him?"

"Don't see why not. He can wink real good, so I think it's a fittin' name." Esta motioned to her brothers playing in the yard. "Let's show the others my new puppy."

The girls scampered across the lawn.

"She seems real happy to have the hundli, doesn't she?" Martin asked as he and Ruth followed the girls.

"Jah. It's good to see her smiling again."

"It was nice of you to buy the dog from your sister."

"I could almost feel that little girl's pain the day her mother was buried." Ruth stopped and turned to face him. "I wanted to do something to give her a sense of joy again."

"You did that, all right." Martin nodded toward Josh, Willis, and Owen, who had gathered around Esta, begging to hold the puppy. "I think you'll make a fine mamm someday, Ruth."

"I hope so."

"What's going on here?" Abe called as he stepped out of the house and headed for the group on the lawn. "All that hollering woke me from my nap."

"We're lookin' at the hundli Ruth brought over for Esta," Josh announced. "Come see how cute he is, Papa."

Abe left the porch and joined them. "It's a nice one, all right," he said with a yawn.

"Where's Aunt Sue and baby Molly?" Esta questioned. "I want them to see my new puppy, too."

Abe grimaced. "Molly woke up fussy from her nap, so Sue's trying to get her calmed down."

Ruth was tempted to ask if she could be of assistance but figured Abe might not appreciate her butting into his family's business.

"It's not fair that Esta gets a puppy and we don't," Willis complained to his dad.

Abe patted the boy's head. "There are plenty of animals around our place for you to play with."

"I'll share Winkie with everyone." Esta held the pup out to her brother. "You can play with him whenever you want."

Abe quirked an eyebrow. "Winkie, is it?"

"I gave him the name," Anna explained. "It's because he winks whenever I do this." She stroked the pup behind its ear, and just like before, the puppy winked.

Everyone laughed. Ruth was glad she'd given the dog to Esta. Despite all of the horrible things that happened in people's lives, it was good to still have some things to laugh about.

Chapter 4

Would you be interested in seeing the harness shop while you're here?" Martin asked Ruth as they sat with Abe on his back porch, watching the children frolic in the yard with the puppy.

"Oh jah," she said with an eager nod. "I think that would be quite interesting."

Abe grunted. "Don't see what's so interesting about a bunch of leather harnesses, straps, and buckles, but if you'd like to see my shop, I'd be happy to show you around."

"Will the kinner be all right?" Ruth questioned.

"Sure," Abe said with a nod. "Sue's in the house if they need anything, and we'll be within hollering distance."

"Let's head out to the shop, then, and give Ruth the grand tour." Martin reached for Ruth's hand as she rose to her feet, and their gazes met. He looked pleased at her interest in his work.

When they stepped into Abe's harness shop, Ruth's nose twitched at the distinctive odor of raw leather and pungent dye. It seemed strange that she'd never visited here before. But whenever Dad had come to see Abe during Ruth's childhood, she'd either been in school or been doing chores at home. Now she kept busy with her job at the bakeshop and never had a need to visit the harness shop on her own.

"This is quite impressive," Ruth said as she gazed around the room, awed by all of the equipment and supplies. She pointed to a tall machine on one side of the room. "What's that over there?"

"It's a riveter. We use it to punch silver rivets into leather straps." Martin glanced over at Abe and shrugged. "Guess I should let you do the telling since this is your shop."

"No problem," Abe said. "You go ahead and show Ruth around. I'll take a seat at my desk and relax awhile."

After the comment from Gideon about Abe sleeping so much since Alma died, Ruth wondered if Abe had lost his zest for working. Could he be putting the workload on Martin's shoulders while he sat around feeling sorry for himself?

Ruth mentally scolded herself. She had no right to judge the man. She hadn't walked in his shoes, and it wasn't fair to speculate on how Abe ran his business or how he was coping with Alma's death. Besides, he had come to the work frolic the other day and worked hard to rebuild Grace and Cleon's house.

"Here are all the buckles, snaps, rings, and rivets we use." Martin pointed to a group of open-faced boxes lining one wall.

"I don't know how you keep track of everything," Ruth said, letting her gaze travel from the boxes, to the harnesses and bridles looped from ceiling hooks overhead, to the scraps lying on the cement floor, looking like thin spaghetti noodles.

"We know where everything is." Martin moved to stand between two oversized sewing machines. "This is what we use to stitch leather straps together. They're run by an air compressor."

"It's all so impressive. I like what I see."

A wide grin spread over Martin's face. "So do I."

Ruth felt the heat of a blush cover her cheeks. Did Martin mean he liked looking at her, or was he referring to the harness shop? She didn't dare ask.

"How did you learn the trade of harness making?" Ruth asked, turning to face Abe.

He leaned back in his chair with his fingers locked together behind his head. "Learned it from my daed, and he used to say he learned it from making mistakes."

"Your daed must have taught you well," Martin said, "because you've got a lot of customers who are always telling me what a good job you've done for them." He grinned. "You're teaching me real well, too."

"That's because you're a good learner, and you've always been cooperative." Abe looked back at Ruth. "Not like Luke Friesen, who gave your daed nothing but trouble when he was working as his apprentice."

Ruth wasn't in the mood to talk about Luke, and she wished Abe hadn't brought him up.

"Come over here and take a look at all the tools we work with," Martin said, steering Ruth across the room. She figured he knew talking about her ex-boyfriend made her feel uncomfortable.

Ruth followed Martin around the room as he explained how they cleaned and repaired old harnesses and made new ones. She reached out to touch a strap that lay on one of the workbenches. "This feels so soft and oily."

"It's recently been dipped in neat's-foot oil," Martin explained.

Ruth glanced over at Abe and noticed that his eyes were closed. She figured the poor man must be either very tired or bored with playing chaperone for them. Or maybe he was trying to shut out the world as he suffered the loss of his wife in silence.

Martin stepped closer to Ruth and whispered, "Would you be interested in going to the pond with me next Saturday for some fishing and a picnic?"

"Just the two of us?"

He nodded. "Since we couldn't go there today, on account of bringing Anna along, I thought maybe next Saturday would work better. You don't have to work at the bakeshop, do you?"

"I have that day off. What about you? Won't you be working here at the harness shop?"

"Nope. Abe's only got the shop open one Saturday a month now, and that won't be this Saturday."

Ruth hesitated before giving Martin her answer. The last time she'd gone to the pond with a man, it had been Luke. He'd acted odd and secretive that day, despite his kidding around. Of course, now she knew that was because Luke had a truck hidden in the woods not far from the pond and didn't want anyone to know about it.

"Maybe you'd rather we make it a double date," Martin said. "We could ask your friend Sadie and her boyfriend, Toby, to join us."

"That's a good idea," Ruth was quick to say. "Sadie's been after me to go someplace with her, and that would be a nice way for us to spend the day."

Martin tipped his head. "For who—you and Sadie, or you and me?"

"Both."

His face relaxed into a smile. "Do you want to speak to Sadie about it, or should I talk to Toby?"

"Sadie and I are both scheduled to work at the bakeshop on Monday, so I'll ask her then. But if you happen to see Toby between now and then, feel free to mention it to him, as well."

Abe released a sigh as he sat at his desk, resting his eyes and listening to Martin and Ruth's conversation. The joy of being young and in love. He could still remember how excited he felt when he and Alma first started courting. He couldn't wait to be with her. Whenever they went somewhere together, he didn't want to take her home. Even after they'd been married a few years and had started their family, he'd continued to enjoy her company and looked forward to their time alone after the kinner were in bed.

Abe thought about his sister, whose boyfriend, Melvin Zook, lived in Illinois. He knew it had been hard for Sue to leave Melvin and her family to come care for his kinner. He also knew that should Sue and Melvin decide to marry, he would lose his housekeeper.

"Then what'll I do?" he mumbled.

"Were you speaking to me, Abe?"

Abe's eyes snapped open, and he squinted. Martin stood a few feet from his desk, and Ruth was right beside him. "Uh. . .no. I was just thinkin' out loud, is all."

Martin nodded. "I do that sometimes, too."

Abe grunted. "Been doin' it a lot more since Alma died."

"I'm sorry for your loss." Ruth's pained expression revealed the depth of her compassion.

Abe swallowed hard. "You know what happened the first time I brought Alma out here to show her around?"

"What happened?" Martin asked.

"She ran around the room touching everything in sight, saying how much she liked the place. Alma was full of love and life, and I sure do miss her. Even though my kinner and Sue are around, I feel lonely without Alma."

"Of course you do. It's only natural that you and your children would miss her," Ruth said, touching Abe's shoulder. "My grandma Hostettler used to say that when we're lonely, we should reach out to family and friends and allow them to reach out to us in return."

Abe sniffed. "Esta's got her puppy now, but I wish there was something that could help my oldest boy cope with his mother's passing. Gideon hasn't shed a tear since Alma died. Yet I know he's grieving. He's been acting moody and kind of sassy lately."

"Would you like me to speak with him?" Ruth asked. "Maybe I can help in some way."

"I appreciate the offer," Abe replied, "but I believe in time the boy will come around."

"I think we'd better go," Martin said before Ruth could respond. "We don't want to get Anna back to her folks too late, or they might start to worry."

"Oh, okay." Ruth glanced over her shoulder as Martin led her toward the door. "Danki for letting me see your shop, Abe. It's very interesting in here."

"Jah, sure. I'm glad you like it."

Grace entered her new living room and seated herself in the rocking chair near the fireplace. She leaned her head against the cushion and placed both hands on her stomach.

"You feeling all right?" Cleon asked as he took a seat on the sofa across from her.

"I'm fine," she said with a nod. "I just felt the boppli kick."

"He's an active one, isn't he?"

"Jah, but it could be a girl, you know."

He shrugged. "I guess Anna would like a baby sister."

"What about you? Will you be disappointed if the babe is a girl?"

"I'll be fine with whatever God chooses to give us," he said.

"Me, too." Grace smiled. "I was pleased to see how Anna perked up when she found out Ruth was taking the puppy over to Esta. I'm glad Ruth didn't mind taking Anna with her."

"I'm not sure Martin was so pleased about Anna tagging along, though."

"What makes you say that?"

"I've got a hunch Martin wanted to be alone with your sister today."

"Then he should have said so."

"Probably didn't want to hurt Ruth's or Anna's feelings."

"Anna would have been disappointed, but I'm sure she'd have gotten over it." Grace stopped rocking and stood.

"Where are you going?"

"I've got a cramp in my leg, so I need to walk around a bit."

Cleon was immediately at her side. "Want me to rub it for you?"

Grace appreciated her husband's concern, but sometimes he could be a bit overprotective. "If it doesn't relax soon, I might take you up on that offer," she said with a smile.

Despite the uncomfortable knot in her calf, Grace felt peace and joy in her heart. It was hard to believe that just a few weeks ago things had been strained between her and Cleon. Then the day their house had burned, Cleon had apologized for his part in their marital problems, and she'd done the same. Grace had never felt closer to him, and with each passing day, their relationship seemed to grow stronger. *Let it always be so,* she silently prayed. *Let peace and joy reign in this house.*

Chapter 5

When Martin pulled his buggy into a grassy area near the pond, Sadie and Toby were already there. He and Ruth hadn't planned to meet them until noon. According to his pocket watch, it was just a little past eleven thirty. So much for spending time alone with his girlfriend.

Ruth looked over at Martin and smiled. "Looks like they beat us here."

"Jah." Martin halted the horse, climbed down, and secured the animal to the nearest tree. He hurried back to the buggy to help Ruth down, but by the time he got there, she had climbed out on her own.

"Hey, you two," Sadie hollered with a wave. "Looks like we've got the perfect day for a picnic."

Ruth lifted her face toward the sun. "Jah, it's a beautiful spring day. Much better than the low-hanging clouds and gusty winds we had earlier in the week."

"Let's hope the fish are biting today." Toby thumped Martin's shoulder. "I'd like to catch a couple of big ones. How about you?"

"That'd be fine with me." Martin scooted around to the back of his buggy and withdrew his fishing pole.

"No fishing until we've had our lunch," Sadie said with a shake of her head. "If you fellows put your lines in the water now, we'll never get to eat, and I'm hungry."

"Aren't you the bossy one today?" Toby tweaked Sadie's freckled nose. "Sadie Esh, my bossy little *aldi*."

She pushed his hand away, and her blue eyes flashed indignantly.

"I may be your girlfriend, but I'm not bossy."

"Are so." Toby whipped off his straw hat, revealing a thick crop of reddish-blond hair, and plunked the hat on Sadie's head.

"Hey, you're crushing my kapp!" Sadie lifted Toby's hat and sent it sailing through the air.

Ruth looked over at Martin and rolled her eyes skyward. "Shall I get the picnic food?"

"Might as well," he replied with a nod.

Ruth and Martin spread a quilt on the ground and retrieved their ice chest from the buggy while Sadie and Toby did the same.

Once everyone was seated on the quilt, all heads bowed for silent prayer. Afterward, Ruth and Sadie passed out golden brown chicken, macaroni salad, coleslaw, carrot sticks, dill pickles, and lemonade.

"Everything looks good," Toby said, smacking his lips. He reached for a drumstick and took a bite. "Jah, it's *appeditlich*."

"If you think the chicken's delicious, wait until you taste some of Ruth's strawberry-rhubarb pie," Martin said. "I had some at her house last Sunday when I brought her home from Abe Wengerd's place."

"What were you doing at Abe's?" Toby asked, looking at Ruth.

"We took one of Martha's little shelties over to Esta, hoping it might help her deal with the grief of losing her mother," she replied.

"It was nice of Martha to give away one of her pups," Toby said as he reached for another piece of chicken.

Sadie swatted his hand. "You haven't finished the first piece you took, and already you're taking another?"

"Actually, giving Esta a puppy was Ruth's idea," Martin said. "Ruth even paid for the hundli."

Toby set the chicken leg down and licked his fingers. "Is that a fact?"

"Sure is." Martin smiled at Ruth. "My aldi's real kindhearted and generous."

Ruth blushed a crimson red, and he figured he'd probably embarrassed her. At least she hadn't denied being his girlfriend.

"You're right about Ruth being kindhearted," Sadie said, touching Ruth's arm. "My good friend is the nicest person I know."

The color in Ruth's cheeks deepened. "I'm not perfect, you know."

Sadie shook her head. "Never said you were. Just meant you're a good friend, and a nice one at that."

Ruth finished her lunch in quiet as she mulled over what Martin and Sadie had said about her. She did care about others who were hurting, which was why she'd been concerned for Esta Wengerd. She'd always tried to be an obedient daughter, a helpful sister, and a trustworthy friend. But at times, Ruth felt as if she were being tested—always trying to do what was right, yet struggling with feelings of discontent. Her feelings of frustration over the break-ins at their home and Dad's shop were examples of how imperfect she was. Then there was the anger she'd felt toward Luke when he had refused to be honest with her.

"You're awfully quiet," Martin said, nudging Ruth. "Are you bored with being here?"

"Not at all. I was just thinking."

"I've been thinking, too." Toby grabbed Sadie's hand and pulled her to her feet. "I've been thinking it might be a good idea to take a walk in the woods and work off some of the food I ate so I don't fall asleep while I fish." He glanced down at Ruth and Martin. "You two want to join us?"

Ruth looked over at Martin to get his opinion and was pleased when he said, "I'd rather stay here and enjoy the sunshine."

Ruth nodded. "Me, too."

"Suit yourself," Toby said as he and Sadie hurried away.

Martin leaned close to Ruth, and she could feel his warm breath caress her cheek. "I enjoy being with you," he murmured.

She swallowed a couple of times, hoping she could speak without stammering. "I enjoy being with you, too."

He reached for her hand, and they remained on the quilt, visiting and watching the ducks float on the pond until Toby and Sadie finally returned.

"You'll never guess what we found in the woods," Toby said as they plunked down on the quilt.

"A big black bear?" Martin asked in a teasing tone.

Toby snorted. "Jah, right. We found a big black pickup truck covered with a layer of dust. But no one was in sight." He squinted at Ruth. "Sadie says she's seen it before, and so have you."

Ruth nodded slowly. "Jah, that's true. We spotted it there one day when we were taking a walk."

"Do you know who it belongs to?" Toby questioned.

Ruth merely shrugged in reply. "It's not important. Let's talk about something else, okay?"

"No way!" Toby got right in her face. "If you know who owns that truck, then tell us. *Raus mit*–out with it!"

Ruth curled her fingers into the palms of her hands, remembering the day Luke had told her about the truck he'd hidden in the woods so his folks wouldn't know. She had promised she wouldn't tell anyone, and until now, she'd never been tempted.

"I'll bet it belongs to one of those rowdy English fellows who have been seen pulling some pranks in our area." Toby grunted. "I heard that a couple of 'em were caught throwing dirt clods at some buggies going down the road near Sugarcreek the other day."

Ruth gave a nonchalant shrug.

"I say we drop this subject," Sadie said, squeezing Toby's arm.

Toby turned his hands palms up and grunted. "Whatever."

"Why don't you and I do some fishing while the women visit?" Martin poked Toby's arm. "That's what we'd planned to do in the first place, right?"

Toby nodded and rose to his feet.

Martin glanced over at Ruth and smiled, then headed for the buggy to get his fishing pole.

Sadie nudged Ruth with her elbow. "I've been thinking about that truck in the woods."

"What about it?"

"You sure acted funny when Toby mentioned it. Do you know who owns the truck?"

"Do we have to talk about this? Can't we just enjoy our day?"

"Does that mean you know who owns the truck and just won't say?"

Ruth clenched her teeth. "I do know, but it's not for me to say."

"How come?"

"Because the person who owns the truck asked me not to say anything."

"You can tell me. I won't tell anyone else, I promise."

"Sure is a beautiful day. Just listen to the birds twittering in the trees overhead."

Sadie sighed. "All right, then, don't tell me who owns the truck."

Ruth leaned back on the quilt and closed her eyes. "Ah, that warm sun feels so good on my face."

"Remember last spring, when the two of us were here with our boyfriends?"

Apparently Sadie had given up on learning who owned the truck, and Ruth was glad. Sadie was her friend, but she was also being courted by Toby, who tended to be a blabbermouth. If Ruth told Sadie that the truck belonged to Luke, and Sadie repeated it to Toby, the word would soon get out to everyone in their community, including Luke's parents. If Dad was right about Luke, and he *was* trying to get even with Ruth for breaking up with him, he might think up even more malicious things to do in retaliation.

"Did you hear what I said about last spring?"

"Jah, I heard, and I do remember coming here."

"Only you were being courted by Luke instead of Martin." Sadie nudged Ruth's arm, and Ruth's eyes popped open. "I think Martin's a better match for you than Luke."

"Martin and I have been getting along pretty well," Ruth admitted. "The only thing is. . .*sis mer bang.*"

"You're afraid?"

"Jah."

"Why are you afraid?"

Ruth swallowed hard, refusing to give in to her swirling emotions. "Whenever things are going well, it seems as if they suddenly turn bad."

"Are you talking about the way things went with you and Luke?"

"That and all the things that have happened at our place over the last year."

"The break-ins and vandalism, you mean?"

"Jah, and also the fire at Cleon and Grace's house. Just when we thought things had settled down, something else happened to test our faith. It makes me afraid of being happy for fear something will go wrong and spoil it."

"Guess there will always be things in life that test our faith," Sadie said. "But we can't let it keep us from falling in love or finding joy in things."

Ruth smiled. "When did you get so schmaert, anyway?"

"I've always been smart; you've just been too busy to notice." Sadie motioned to the fellows. "Sure is nice to see how well they get along, isn't it?"

Ruth nodded. "Toby seems to have a better relationship with Martin than he does with Luke."

"You're right. For some time now, I've noticed tension between Toby and Luke, but I've never figured out the reason for it."

"Guess there doesn't have to be a reason," Ruth said. "Some folks just get along better with certain people than they do others."

"Maybe so, but it's like there's some kind of competition going on between Toby and Luke. Almost seems as if Toby wants to make Luke look bad."

"Why would he do that?"

Sadie shrugged. "Beats me, but the other day I heard Toby speaking with his daed about Luke. He said he knows that Luke's been running around with some rowdy English fellows."

"What'd the bishop say about that?"

"Said he was aware that Luke had been keeping company with some Englishers, but there wasn't much he could do about it since Luke's still going through his *rumschpringe*."

Ruth sighed. "I had hoped he would get that out of his system, settle down, and join the church while we were courting, but he seems bent on kicking up his heels."

Sadie patted Ruth's arm. "You're better off without him."

Ruth nodded. "I know."

"That lunch Ruth and Sadie fixed sure was tasty," Toby said as he baited his hook with a plump worm. "Made me almost wish I was married."

Martin cast his line into the water and took a seat near the edge of the pond. "Why aren't you, then?"

"I'm not quite ready to settle down."

"But you've joined the church."

"That's true."

"And you've got an aldi you seem to like."

"Uh-huh. Sadie and me have been courting a little over a year."

"Then what's the problem? Why don't you ask her to marry you?"

Toby shrugged.

"Are you in *lieb*?"

"In love with Sadie?"

Martin's gaze went to the sky. Sometimes Toby seemed so dense about things. "Of course I meant Sadie. She's the only one you're courting, right?"

"Jah, but I'm not sure what I feel for her is love." Toby dropped his line into the water and sat back on his heels. "I like her a lot, and we get along pretty well, but–"

"Are you afraid of marriage?"

"Why would I be afraid?"

"Don't know. Just asking, is all."

"I ain't afraid of nothin'."

Martin chuckled. "Jah, right."

As Martin fished, he found himself thinking of Ruth and wondering about her response to the pickup Toby and Sadie had found in the woods. Whose secret was Ruth keeping, and why? He was tempted to press her about it but didn't want to do anything that might drive a wedge between them. Maybe after they'd been courting longer, he would feel free to ask about the truck. If she was honest about it, she could be trusted and might be the right woman for him. If not, he didn't know what he would do.

Chapter 6

"Are you sure you want to move these?" asked Cleon's brother Ivan as he and Cleon lifted one of the bee boxes onto the back of an open wagon early Monday morning.

Cleon nodded. "I think it will be better if I have the boxes closer to home. That way I won't have to leave so often in order to check on the bees and extract the honey."

"Guess that makes sense." Ivan wiped the sweat from his brow and squinted his dark eyes. "Sure hope no one will try to burn out your bees again."

"Me, too. At least with these new boxes out behind our house, I can keep a closer watch on things." Cleon grimaced. "First my bee boxes were burned and then my house. Makes no sense why someone would want to do such hateful things."

"I heard that the firemen found a cigarette lighter outside your home the day of the fire," Ivan said as they headed over to get the next bee box.

"Jah, that's right."

"You know anyone who smokes?"

Cleon shrugged. "None of my Amish friends."

Ivan's forehead wrinkled. "I've heard rumors that Luke Friesen smokes."

"Where'd you hear that?"

"Toby King mentioned that Luke's been hanging around a bunch of English fellows who smoke and that he's smelled smoke on Luke's clothes a time or two."

"That doesn't prove he's a smoker. Could be that Luke just smells like smoke because he's been with others who do."

"Maybe so."

"As far as who's responsible for the fires that were started. . .it could be the same person who broke into the Hostettlers' place, took some of Roman's tools from his woodworking shop, and did several other acts of vandalism."

Ivan's eyes narrowed. "You think Luke could have done all those things?"

"I hope not. Grace thinks it was Gary Walker, that reporter who hung around the area for a time taking pictures and asking a bunch of nosy questions." The brothers set the bee box on the wagon.

"Why would the reporter want to do anything to hurt the Hostettlers, or you?" Ivan asked.

Cleon pulled his fingers through the back of his hair and frowned. "You know the story. Gary Walker used to date Grace when she left home to try out the English world. After she broke up with him, he said he would get even with her someday."

"But the reporter left Holmes County to do some other stories. So if he's the one who did the attacks, then they're not likely to happen again."

Cleon nodded, but his mind raced on. What if the reporter wasn't responsible for any of the crimes? He hated to think it could be Luke or anyone else they knew. The one thing he did know was that he planned to keep a close eye on Grace and the rest of her family. That was the real reason he'd decided to move the bee boxes from his folks' property.

"Say, Ivan, I was wondering. . ."

"What's that?"

"Would you be willing to make some of my honey deliveries when you're not helping Pop in the fields?"

"You don't plan to make your own deliveries anymore?"

"I will when I can, but with me working for Grace's daed and tending my bees, I don't have as much time for making deliveries."

Ivan nodded. "I'll help whenever I can."

"I appreciate that, and I'll pay you something for your time." Cleon clasped his brother's shoulder. "Could you start this afternoon?"

"Making deliveries, you mean?"

"Jah. There are a couple of shops in Charm that sell my honey. The last time I was there, they were getting down on their supply."

"I can't do it today," Ivan said with a shake of his blond head. "I promised Pop I'd help him clear that back field."

"What about Willard and Delbert?"

"They'll be helping, too. The ground's really rocky there, and it's gonna take all four of us to get the job done."

Cleon grunted. "Guess I'll have to deliver the honey myself. Maybe I'll take Grace and Anna along. It's been a while since they've been to Charm."

Grace stood at her bedroom window, watching Cleon and his brother unload the bee boxes they'd brought to the field behind their new home. She was glad he'd decided to move the boxes so he wouldn't be gone so much.

She pressed her hand against her lower back to ease out some of the kinks and moved away from the window, knowing it was time to wake Anna and get breakfast on the table before Cleon came inside.

A short time later, Grace, Cleon, and Anna gathered around the kitchen table. "Too bad Ivan couldn't join us for breakfast," Grace said after their silent prayer. "He would have been more than welcome."

"I'm sure he would have stayed if he hadn't had to get home and help our daed and *brieder* clear a new field. We'll invite him some other time." Cleon gave his dark brown beard a quick tug, then looked over at Anna and smiled. "How would you and your mamm like to go with me to Charm this morning to deliver some honey to Grandma's Homestead Restaurant and a couple of other places?"

Anna's eyes brightened. "Could we eat at the restaurant?"

Grace chuckled and pointed to the child's plate, still full of fluffy french toast and sticky syrup. "You're eating right now, silly girl."

Anna shrugged her slim shoulders. "Figured we could eat lunch at the restaurant."

"Sorry," Cleon said, "but I've got to get the deliveries made right after breakfast. Then I'll need to hurry back home and go to work in your grandpa's woodworking shop."

Anna's lower lip protruded. "Seems like you're always workin', Papa."

"That's what daeds do when they've got a family to support." Cleon reached for the bottle of syrup. "The good news is I won't be gone so much now that my bee boxes have been moved closer to our home. Ivan's agreed to make some of my honey deliveries, which means I can spend more time with you and your mamm."

Anna grinned and forked a hunk of french toast into her mouth.

Grace looked over at Cleon, and he winked at her. Despite the fact that Anna was the daughter of Wade Davis, an Englisher who had died when Anna was a baby, Cleon had accepted her as his own child, and Grace felt grateful. During the time when her family had been under attack, she'd looked toward the future with dread. Now she anticipated the new baby who would be coming soon and hoped they would have many happy days ahead.

"I was talking with Irene Schrock the other day, and she mentioned that her daughter slipped on the stairs and broke her arm a few days ago," Ruth's mother said as Ruth helped her and Martha clear the breakfast dishes from the table.

"Does that mean Carolyn won't be able to help Irene with the dinners they do for tourists?" Ruth asked.

Mom nodded. "Not for several weeks. Carolyn won't be able to do much with only one hand."

"I could go there and help," Ruth offered.

"What about your job at the bakeshop?" Mom asked.

"I'm usually off by early afternoon, so that shouldn't get in the way of my helping Irene. I could help on my days off, too."

Mom shook her head. "I don't know. . .seems like a lot of work to me, especially since you already have a job."

"Guess I could help," Martha said. "Of course, Ruth's better at cooking than I am."

"I'm sure you would do fine." Mom patted Martha's back.

Martha shrugged. "I'd better let Ruth do it."

"I think I'll drop by the Schrocks' on my way to work and speak with Irene about helping." Ruth smiled. "Since Abe Wengerd's place is on the way, I might stop and see how Esta's doing with her puppy."

Mom nodded. "That's a good idea. We need to check on Abe and his kinner often."

Martin reached for a piece of leather that hung on a hook above him and spotted Ruth outside the window, talking with Esta. When Ruth bent down and gave the little girl a hug, he thought about how well she got along with Abe's children. No doubt she would make a good mother someday, and he hoped the children she had would be his.

"What's so interesting?"

Martin whirled around at the sound of Abe's resonant voice. "Huh?"

"Out the window. You've been holding that piece of leather and staring out the window for several minutes."

Martin's face heated up, and he dropped the hunk of leather to the workbench. "I. . .uh. . .just noticed Ruth Hostettler's here. She's in the yard, talking to Esta."

Abe moved over to the window and nudged Martin's arm. "You're in love with her, jah?"

Martin couldn't deny it, yet he didn't want to admit it, either. "Would you mind answering a personal question?" he asked.

"What do you want to know?"

"I was wondering when you first knew you were in love with Alma and how long you waited until you asked her to marry you."

Abe chuckled. "I can't imagine why you'd want to know that."

Martin glanced out the window again. He hoped Ruth would drop by the harness shop and say hello.

Abe tapped Martin on the back. "Are you gonna stand there all day staring out the window, or did you want to hear the answer to your question about when I fell in love with Alma?"

Martin pulled his gaze back to Abe. "I do want to hear it."

Abe motioned to a couple of wooden stools. "Have a seat, and I'll tell you about it."

Martin listened as Abe told the story of how he'd taken an interest in Alma soon after she and her folks had moved to Ohio from Pennsylvania. "When Alma turned sixteen and started attending some of the young people's functions, I asked if I could court her. Soon after our first date, I knew I was in love. Two years later, I asked if I could marry her," Abe said, dropping his gaze to the floor.

Martin figured talking about Alma must have conjured up some nostalgic feelings. He wished he hadn't brought up the subject of Abe and Alma's courtship. "Sorry if I've upset you."

"I miss my wife, but it's good for me to talk about her." Abe touched his chest. "Keeps her memory alive in here."

Martin nodded solemnly. If he were married to Ruth and lost her the way Abe had lost Alma, he didn't know how he could go on living. No wonder Abe slept so much when he wasn't working. It was probably the only way he could deal with his grief.

"Want my advice, Martin?" Abe asked as he stood.

"Jah, sure."

"If you're in love with Ruth, don't let her get away. Don't waste a single moment you have together."

Martin's forehead wrinkled. "Are you saying I shouldn't wait to ask her to marry me?"

"That's got to be your decision. But if it were me, I wouldn't wait too long." Abe lifted his shoulders in a brief shrug. "One never knows what the future holds. One never knows how much time they have left on this earth."

"You're right, Abe. Danki for the good advice. I'll be thinking on what you said."

A few seconds later, the shop door opened, and Ruth stuck her head inside. "I'm on my way to work, so I can't stay," she said, smiling at Martin. "But I wanted to say hello."

"Glad you did. It's always nice to see you." Martin moved toward the door. "I had a good time with you at the pond last Saturday," he whispered.

She nodded. "I enjoyed myself, too."

"Maybe we can do it again sometime soon."

"That'd be nice." She glanced toward her horse and buggy, parked outside the harness shop. "Guess I'd better go."

Martin fought the urge to hug her; he knew it wouldn't be appropriate. Especially with Abe right behind him, no doubt watching and listening to their conversation. "See you soon, Ruth," he said. "Have a good day."

As Martin returned to his workbench, Abe shot him a knowing look.

Martin grabbed a hunk of leather and set right to work. Every time he saw Ruth, he fell deeper in love with her. How long would he have to wait until he felt free to ask her to marry him?

As Ruth headed down the road toward the Schrocks' place, the pleasant scent of wildflowers growing in the woods wafted through the open buggy flap, and she drew in a deep, satisfying breath. She was glad she had been able to stop by the harness shop to see Martin.

Ruth's thoughts turned to Esta. She'd been pleased to see how well the child was doing. From what she could tell, the puppy had adjusted to its new home. As time allowed, she hoped to continue her visits to the Wengerds' to check on Abe's children.

Ruth was about to turn into the Schrocks' place when a black truck whizzed past, causing the horse to whinny and veer to the right. She hadn't been able to get a good look at the driver, but she thought he was wearing a baseball cap and sunglasses.

"Sure wish folks wouldn't drive so fast," she muttered.

A few minutes later, she spotted a horse and buggy up ahead. It didn't take her long to realize it was Martha's rig. Ruth followed as the horse and buggy turned to the right and headed up the Schrocks' driveway past the sign reading Schrocks' Home Cooking.

"How'd your visit with Esta go?" Martha asked as she stepped up to Ruth moments later.

"It went fine." Ruth squinted. "What are you doing here? I thought you weren't coming to speak with Irene."

"Changed my mind. Since my dog business isn't doing too well yet, I figured I could use some extra money."

"I doubt Irene will need us both."

"Then I guess she'll have to choose between us."

Ruth frowned. She didn't think it would be fair to put Irene in that position, and Martha should have realized it, too. "Never mind. You can have the job."

Martha shook her head. "I won't work for Irene if you want to. I just figured since you already have a job—"

"You're right. I don't need two jobs. I'd much rather spend my free time with Martin—and of course little Esta, who still needs extra encouragement."

"Speaking of which, is the pup doing okay?"

"Seems to be."

"I'm glad." Martha motioned to the Schrocks' house. "Guess I'd better go see what Irene has to say about me helping her."

Ruth gave Martha a hug. "See you this evening."

"Jah. Have a good day." Ruth climbed back in her buggy, feeling good about things. Martha would be earning some extra money, Esta was getting along well with Winkie, and Martin was definitely showing interest. This was the beginning of a very good day.

Chapter 7

One early summer morning, Grace entered the barn to look for Martha. She drew in a deep breath, enjoying the pleasant, prickly aroma of fresh hay as she leaned against one of the wooden beams. She felt the baby kick and placed one hand against her bulging stomach. "I wonder if you're a *buwe* or a *maedel*."

"Are you talking to yourself or me?"

Grace turned and saw Martha heading toward her. "I was talking to my boppli, wondering if it's a boy or a girl."

Martha grinned. "I think Anna's hoping for a maedel."

"Jah, and speaking of Anna, I was wondering if you could watch her so Mom and I can go to town to get some material for baby things."

"What time will you be back?"

"Soon after lunch, I expect."

Martha nodded. "That should be okay, since I don't have to be at Irene's until three o'clock."

"I'd forgotten about your new job. Would you prefer that we take Anna with us?"

"I'm sure you'll be back in plenty of time. Besides, I enjoy spending time with Anna. It'll be better than being out here alone, fretting over my failing business."

"Things aren't going so well with your plans to raise dogs, are they?"

Martha shook her head and handed Grace a breeders magazine. "I was reading this and spotted an ad about trading dogs to strengthen the breeding lines. I might consider doing such a thing if I had some extra dogs to trade."

"I'm sorry Flo still isn't pregnant."

"I may allow Heidi to get pregnant again soon," Martha confided, "since she did so well with her first batch of puppies."

"She did okay giving birth, but things went a bit sour after that."

"You mean with the one puppy dying?"

"Jah."

"That was too bad, especially since you had just said Anna could have the pup."

"Hopefully nothing like that will happen again," Grace said firmly. "I'm sure everything will work out."

Grace touched Martha's arm. "I'd better head back to the house. As soon as Mom's ready to leave for town, I'll send Anna to the barn."

Martha held up the magazine in her hand. "Thought I'd sit on a bale of straw and thumb through the rest of this. Then I need to get busy and clean out the kennels. Maybe Anna can help."

Grace started for the door but turned back. "We'll probably stop by the bakeshop and see Ruth while we're in town. Is there anything special you'd like me to bring home as a thank-you for watching Anna?"

Martha shook her head. "No payment's needed. But if you're stopping at the bakeshop, I wouldn't turn down a couple of lemon-filled doughnuts."

Grace chuckled. "Consider it done."

Martha had just started cleaning Heidi's cage when Anna darted into the barn. "Mama said I get to spend the morning helping you!"

Martha smiled. "It's a good thing, too, because there's lots of work to be done. I'm in need of a big helper like you."

"What do you want me to do?"

"All the cages need to be hosed out."

Anna's forehead wrinkled. "That's a dirty, smelly job, and Mama wouldn't like it if I got wet."

"How about if I do the hosing? When I'm done, you can put clean straw in the dogs' beds."

"Okay."

Martha motioned to a bale of straw. "If you'd like to have a seat over there, we can visit while I work."

"I hope Heidi has some more puppies soon. I liked playing with 'em," Anna said as she flopped onto the straw.

"You can play with Esta's puppy whenever you go over to the Wengerds'."

Crack! The window shattered, and a small canister crashed to the floor. Anna screamed, and a terrible odor permeated the barn.

Martha's eyes began to water. She grabbed Anna's hand and ushered her quickly out the door.

"How come the window broke? And what was that awful smell?" Anna asked, rubbing her eyes.

Martha glanced around the yard. No one was in sight. "I think it was a homemade stink bomb. We'd better let Cleon and your grandpa know about this right away."

Cleon had just begun to sand a new chair when the door to Roman's shop flew open. Martha and Anna rushed into the room.

"I think the attacks are beginning again! Someone just threw a stink bomb through one of the barn windows!" Martha panted.

Roman looked up from the hunk of wood he'd been sanding. "Are you sure about that?"

"Of course I'm sure. I heard the window break and saw the cylinder hit the floor, and Anna and I definitely smelled the putrid stench."

Anna nodded vigorously. "It smelled like rotten eggs, and it made my eyes water."

Cleon dropped the sandpaper he'd been using and rushed across the room. "Are you all right?"

"She's fine. It just took us by surprise," Martha replied before Anna could respond.

"Did you see anyone?" Roman asked, moving over to Martha.

Martha shook her head.

"It was probably some prankster. I heard some English kids have been fooling around the area again, doing all sorts of goofy things."

"I don't know. I think maybe. . ." Martha's voice trailed off when she noticed Anna's wide-eyed expression. "I'd better go back to the barn and get things aired out."

"I'll take care of that," Roman said before he rushed out the door.

Cleon picked Anna up and seated her in the chair behind Roman's desk. "Why don't you draw awhile?" He handed Anna a tablet and pencil, then moved toward the door and motioned Martha to follow.

"I think it would be best if we didn't say anything to Grace about this," he whispered. "With her expecting our first boppli this fall, I don't want her getting upset or worrying that this could be another attack on her family."

"I won't mention it, but Anna might blab."

"I'll have a talk with her," Cleon said with a nod.

Martha's fingers curled around the doorknob. "Guess I'd better go talk to my daed and make sure he doesn't say anything, either."

Ruth had just finished waiting on an English woman when Mom and Grace showed up at the bakeshop, chattering about the baby things they had bought that morning.

"Anna's excited about being the baby's big sister," Grace said as she stepped up to the bakery counter, wearing a smile that stretched ear to ear. "I think she's hoping for a maedel."

"Not Cleon, though," Mom put in. "He told your daed that he'd like it to be a buwe."

Grace stroked her stomach. "It doesn't matter to me whether it's a boy or a girl. I just want it to be born healthy."

"We're all praying for that," Mom agreed.

Ruth smiled despite the pang of jealousy she fought. She wished she was starting a family. If Luke hadn't been so undependable and secretive, she might be planning a fall wedding right now. Instead, she was in the early stages of courtship with Martin, and it could be another year or two before he proposed, if at all.

"Do you have any lemon-filled doughnuts?" Grace asked, breaking into Ruth's thoughts. "I promised to bring some home for Martha."

Ruth pointed to the section in the bakery case where the doughnuts were kept. "Still have half a dozen lemon ones left."

"I'll take them all," Grace said with a wink in Mom's direction.

"That way there'll be enough for our menfolk to have some."

Mom chuckled. "Better give the doughnuts to the men before Martha gets her hands on the tasty treats, or there might not be any left."

Ruth reached into the case and removed the last of the lemon-filled doughnuts, placed them inside a small cardboard box, and handed it to Mom. She'd just put the money into the cash register when the bell above the door jangled and a red-haired English man stepped into the room.

"Hello, ladies," Gary Walker said, stepping between Grace and Mom. "Have you come for some sweets to make you sweeter?"

Mom blinked a couple of times, and Grace grabbed the side of the counter, as if needing it for support. "Wh–what are you doing here?" she rasped. "I thought you had left Holmes County for good."

He wiggled his eyebrows. "I did go to Pennsylvania for a while, Gracie, but I decided with all the interesting people here, I needed to come back and do a few more stories."

Grace's face turned paler than goat's milk as she swayed unsteadily. Ruth feared her sister might pass out, so she skirted around the counter and slipped one arm around Grace's waist. "There's a stool in the back room. Would you like to sit awhile?"

Grace shook her head and moved toward the door. "I'll be fine. I just need some fresh air."

Mom scurried to the door and was about to open it, but Gary beat her to it. "May I help you outside to your buggy?" he asked, looking at Grace.

"I can make it on my own," she mumbled.

Gary looked her up and down. His gaze came to rest on her stomach. "Well, well," he said with a smirk. "When's the blessed event?"

Grace hurried out the door behind Mom.

Gary lifted his shoulders in an exaggerated shrug as he turned to look at Ruth. "That sister of yours sure is testy."

Ruth clenched her fingers into tight balls and moved back to the bakery counter. "May I help you with something?"

He sauntered over to the counter and glanced at the baked goods, then looked back at her. "Nothing looks quite as good as the one selling these sweet treats. How'd you like to have supper with me after you get off work?"

Gary's piercing gaze sent shivers up Ruth's back, and she shook her head.

"Ah, come on, Ruthie. I just want to get to know you a little better." Gary leaned across the counter, and the spicy scent of his aftershave caused Ruth to pull back, feeling like a turtle being poked with a sharp stick.

"You're sure jumpy," he said with a smirk. "I don't bite, you know."

Ruth's face heated up. "If you don't want anything, then—"

"Oh, I want something, all right, but it's not one of these," he said, motioning to the pastries.

Ruth swallowed against the bitter taste of bile rising in her throat. This man frightened her. No wonder Grace got so upset whenever Gary came around. She clasped her hands tightly behind her back to keep them from shaking.

Just then, Jake Clemons stepped out of the back room, where he and his wife did the baking. "Is there a problem here, Ruth?"

Before Ruth could reply, Gary looked at Jake and shook his head. "Nope. No problem at all. I just came in to get something for my sweet tooth." He pointed to a layer of maple bars. "I'll take two of those."

Ruth released a sigh and quickly filled the man's order. When Gary left the store, she turned to Jake with a grateful smile. "Thanks for coming to my rescue. That man makes me nervous."

Jake skimmed his fingers along his temples and into his receding blond hair. "If he ever bothers you again, please let me know."

"I will."

When Jake returned to the other room, Ruth leaned on the counter and closed her eyes. *Dear Lord, please don't let Gary Walker stay in town.*

Chapter 8

How's it going in here?" Martha asked her father when she stepped into the barn and found him holding a spray can in one hand.

"I sprayed some of your mamm's room deodorizer around and opened all the windows. I think the smell will be gone before she and Grace get back from town." Dad's eyebrows pulled together in a frown. "I think it's best if they don't know about this. No point in causing them to worry for nothing."

"I'm in agreement with that, but I don't think this is nothing." Martha motioned to the shattered window across the room. "Someone deliberately threw that stink bomb into the barn. If it's the same person who did the other things to us, then we have every reason to be worried."

Dad set the can of deodorizer on a shelf. "Regardless of who's responsible for this, I don't want the rest of the family getting all upset. Especially not your mamm. She's been through enough these past several months."

"I don't think the attacks affected Mom nearly as much as they did Grace," Martha said. "With her being in a family way, it wouldn't be good for her to have more stress added."

Dad nodded solemnly. "Unfortunately, most of Grace's upsets have been of her own doing."

Martha didn't argue. She had a hunch Dad hadn't completely forgiven Grace for leaving home when she was a teenager or for keeping her previous marriage and the birth of her daughter a secret for so long.

"How's that new job you've got with Irene Schrock working out?"

Dad asked, redirecting their conversation.

"It's okay." Martha nodded toward the back of the barn, where the inside section of her dog kennels had been built. "With summer being here, more tour buses are scheduling dinners at the Schrocks'. Even though Carolyn's able to help again, Irene asked if I would continue to work for her. So once I get enough money saved up, I'm going to buy a few more dogs. Maybe a couple of poodles this time."

Dad grunted. "Poodles are too prissy to suit me. Besides, they yap too much."

"Maybe I should get a pair of hunting dogs. From what I've read in the breeders magazine, they seem to have more puppies than some of the smaller breeds."

"Now that makes good sense." Dad removed his straw hat and slapped the brim of it against his knee, sending sawdust blowing off his pants in every direction. "Why don't you get some German shorthaired pointers? Then Cleon and I can do some pheasant hunting this fall."

"Since when have you ever gone hunting?"

"Went all the time when I was a boy. Might be nice to try it again."

"I'd like to go hunting sometime," Martha said.

"Hunting's for men, not girls."

"I'm not a girl, Dad. I turned nineteen a few months ago, remember?"

He grunted. "That may be so, but you've never shot a gun. It wouldn't be safe for you to hunt."

Martha's defenses rose. Even though she'd never shot a gun, she didn't think it would be too hard to learn. She couldn't help but wonder if Dad was disappointed because he'd never had a son. Maybe that was why Dad and Cleon got along so well.

"If Cleon doesn't want to hunt, I could see if Abe would like to go," Dad continued. "Might do Abe some good to get out in the fields and away from his harness shop awhile."

"Ruth mentioned that Abe's been sleeping a lot. Do you think it's to avoid thinking about his loss?"

Dad nodded. "Everyone deals with grief in their own way, but it's my job as Abe's friend to help him." He took a seat on a bale of straw, and Martha did the same.

"That's what friends are for," she agreed. "To encourage each other and help during times of need."

Dad pulled a piece of straw from the bale he was sitting on and slipped it between his teeth. "Between your job at Irene's and raising your dogs, I guess you'll be plenty busy all summer."

"Jah."

"Doesn't leave much time for socializing."

Martha merely shrugged in reply.

"A woman your age ought to be courting by now." He eyed her curiously. "Have you got your sights set on any particular fellow?"

Martha cringed. She did have an interest in someone, but she didn't dare say so. Dad would have a conniption if he knew she'd come to care for Luke Friesen. Especially since he thought Luke might be the one responsible for the attacks against them.

Dad nudged Martha's arm. "Is there someone you're interested in?"

"I'm too busy with other things to be worried about having a boyfriend," she said, carefully choosing her words.

"Guess there's still time for you to find the right man."

"Jah."

When Martha heard the rumble of buggy wheels outside, she stood. "Do you suppose that's Mom and Grace back from town? If so, they didn't stay very long. I figured they wouldn't be back until this afternoon."

"Only one way to find out," Dad said, rising to his feet. "Let's go have a look-see."

As Grace climbed out of the buggy, her legs shook so hard she could barely stand. All the way home, she couldn't stop thinking about Gary showing up in town. When he'd left a few months ago, she had hoped they'd seen the last of him. Her plans to treat Mom to lunch at the Farmstead Restaurant had been forgotten when Gary came into the bakeshop. All she'd wanted to do was go home.

"I didn't think you'd be back so early," Martha said as she and Dad stepped out of the barn. "Figured you'd have lunch after you finished shopping."

"We ran into that reporter fellow at the bakeshop." Mom took hold of Grace's arm. "After that, Grace didn't feel like eating."

Dad's lips compressed into a thin line. "What's that guy doing back in town? I thought he'd left Holmes County for good."

"He said he's decided to do a few more stories on the Amish in our area." Grace's voice trembled as she spoke. It was all she could do to keep from crying. She'd been especially emotional lately and figured it had to do with her changing hormones. The distress she was dealing with right now, however, had nothing to do with her pregnancy. She was worried that Gary had come back to the area to fulfill his promise to get even with her for breaking up with him after they'd dated awhile during her rumschpringe years. Grace's life was just getting back to normal, and she didn't think she could deal with more attacks on her family.

Dad looked at Martha, and they exchanged worried glances. "Maybe you should get Anna so Grace can go home and rest," he said.

Martha nodded. "That's a good idea."

"Where is Anna?" Grace asked. "Is she in the barn?"

"She's at the woodworking shop with Cleon," Dad said.

"What's she doing there? I've told her not to bother Cleon when he's working."

Dad rocked back and forth on his heels. "She. . .uh. . .came out there with Martha to talk to us."

Grace frowned as she turned to face her sister. "I thought you were going to keep Anna entertained in the barn, not haul her out to the shop to bother the men."

"I didn't *haul* her out there. We went there because—" Martha stopped speaking and glanced over at Dad.

"What's going on, Roman?" Mom asked. "You and Martha are acting so *missdrauisch*. Is there something you're not telling us?"

"We're not acting suspicious," he was quick to say. "It's just that—well, we had a little incident in the barn a while ago, and I didn't want to worry you."

"What kind of incident?"

"Someone threw a stink bomb through one of the barn windows, and Martha brought Anna out to the shop to tell us about it."

Mom hurried into the barn, and the rest of them followed.

Mom's nose twitched. "I do smell something funny in here."

"I thought I had the barn aired out pretty good, but I guess the putrid odor will linger awhile." Dad motioned across the room. "I'll have the window fixed before the day's out."

Grace's stomach clenched as she gripped her mother's hand. "This was Gary's work. I'm sure of it."

Dad shook his head. "*Sell kann ich mir gaar net eibilde.*"

"What do you mean you can't conceive of that? Gary's back in Holmes County. He promised to get even with me someday, and I'm sure he's the one who did all those horrible things to us before he left for Pennsylvania." Grace's knees nearly buckled, and she leaned against a wooden beam for support. "I think Gary may have come here and thrown the stink bomb into the barn before he went to town. I–I'm afraid if he's not stopped, he'll continue to do more things."

"You're worried for nothing, Grace. I'm guessing that stink bomb was thrown by some prankster," Dad said.

"You said that before, when the attacks first began. But things only got worse." Grace drew in a deep breath to settle her nerves. "Anna or I could have been killed when our house was set on fire. I don't think that was done by any prankster."

"She's right, Roman," Mom put in. "Whoever did most of those things to our property was out for more than a good time."

Dad stared at the ground, and a muscle in the side of his cheek quivered. "Cleon and I will keep an eye on things; I can promise you that."

Grace shrugged and headed out of the barn. "I need to get Anna and put her down for a nap."

"I'll do that," Martha said. "Mom, if you'd like to walk Grace up to her house, I'll be there with Anna real soon."

Mom nodded, and they started up the driveway toward Grace and Cleon's new home, Mom leading Grace by the arm.

Martin hurried down the sidewalk toward the bakeshop. He'd come to Berlin to pick up some supplies for the harness shop, and since Abe

had told him to take all the time he needed, he figured he may as well stop at the bakeshop and say hello to Ruth. He might even pick up a few doughnuts and take them to Abe.

When he stepped into the bakeshop, the pleasant aroma of freshly baked pastries flooded his senses and made his stomach rumble. He was pleased to see that no customers were there at the moment, but then he spotted Ruth sitting behind the counter with her head resting in the palms of her hands.

"Ruth, what's wrong?" he asked, rushing over to the counter. "Do you have a *koppweh*?"

Ruth lifted her head, and his heart clenched when he saw the weary look on her face.

"I don't have a headache, but I have had a rough morning," Ruth said, rising to her feet.

"What happened?"

"That reporter, Gary Walker, is back in town. He came into the bakeshop a while ago, while Grace and Mom were here."

Martin pursed his lips. "Grace used to date that fellow, right?"

Ruth nodded. "She thinks he's the one responsible for all those acts of vandalism that were done at our place."

"What do you think?"

"I–I'm not sure, but I do know that Gary is a troublesome fellow."

"Did he do or say anything to bother you?"

Her gaze dropped to the floor. "Well–"

"What did he say?"

"He just gave me a hard time, but Jake put a stop to it."

"What exactly did the reporter say to you?"

Ruth's face flushed the color of ripe cherries. "He wanted me to have supper with him after I got off work today."

Martin's spine went rigid, and he clenched and unclenched his fingers. He had enough to be concerned about, worrying whether Luke was still interested in Ruth. He didn't need some fancy-talking Englisher chasing after her.

"I wouldn't have gone with Gary, even if Jake hadn't come into the room," Ruth was quick to say. "So you needn't look so concerned."

"How long ago did the reporter leave the bakeshop?"

"Twenty minutes or so."

"Maybe he's still in town." Martin turned toward the door.

"Where are you going?"

"To see if I can find him."

"What for?"

Martin stopped walking and turned to face her. "I think it might be good if I had a talk with him–asked him to stop bothering you."

Ruth dashed around the counter. "Oh no! Please don't do that."

"Why not?"

"I don't trust the man. If Gary is the one who did those attacks, then he could be dangerous."

"I'm not afraid."

"Well, I am." Ruth clutched his arm, and tears glistened in her eyes. "Please don't go looking for him."

"All right, I won't. But if he ever bothers you again, I want to know about it."

Chapter 9

Cleon couldn't believe his eyes. Sometime during the night, Roman's shop, house, and barn had been covered with long strips of toilet paper.

He spotted Roman standing outside his shop, shaking his head and muttering, "I don't have time for this. Don't have time at all."

"I wonder if the same person who threw the stink bomb through the barn window did all this," Cleon said, motioning to the tangle of toilet paper draped over the shop.

Roman grunted. "I don't know, but I think whoever did it must be a smoker."

"How do you know?"

Roman reached into his shirt pocket and withdrew a pack of cigarettes. "Found these on the ground near our back porch. I'm thinking that whoever hung toilet paper all over our buildings must have dropped his cigarettes." Roman frowned deeply. "I told the women yesterday that I thought the stink bomb was the result of a prankster. But Grace thinks it might have been done by Gary Walker, that reporter who likes to write articles about our people." He grunted. "Want to know what I really think?"

Cleon nodded.

"I believe Luke may have done this, as well as thrown the stink bomb yesterday."

"What makes you think that?"

"I've smelled smoke on his clothes a time or two, and since he doesn't care for me—"

"But he could have smoke on his clothes just from hanging around other folks who smoke," Cleon interrupted.

Roman made a sweeping gesture toward the mess above them. "Either way, he still could have been involved in this."

"If you're convinced Luke's the one who did this, then maybe you should talk to him or his folks about it."

"I've thought about that, but I'm not sure if I should."

"Why not?"

"If I speak with Luke, it might give him some sort of satisfaction to know he's got me riled. And if I talk to his folks, it might upset them too much." Roman reached up and snatched a strand of toilet paper from the roof. "Guess I'd better get this disaster cleaned up before we begin work for the day. Judith was pretty distressed when she woke up and saw the mess. I don't want it hanging around all day to remind her of what happened."

"If you have something you need to get done in the shop, I can take care of getting the toilet paper down," Cleon offered.

Roman shook his head. "Nothing pressing. If we clean this up together, we'll get to work that much quicker."

"Sounds good to me." Cleon shielded his eyes from the glare of the sun and stared in the direction of his home. "Grace was quite disturbed last night about the stink bomb episode, not to mention seeing that reporter again. I think it would be good if we get this cleaned up before she has a chance to see it."

Grace held Anna's hand as they headed down the driveway toward her folks' house. She hadn't slept well. Had Gary really come back to Holmes County to write more stories, or did he have evil on his mind? Were the attacks some sort of test to see how much her family could endure? *Maybe a good talk with Mom over a cup of tea might make me feel better.*

She gritted her teeth and tried to focus on something positive—the cloudless sky overhead, the emerald grass beneath her feet, the bounty of multihued flowers in bloom, a warbling bluebird calling to its mate. The babe in her womb kicked just then, and she smiled. She had good things to think about, and as the Bible reminded in Philippians 4:8, she would try to think on those things.

"Can we go see Esta today?" Anna asked, giving Grace's hand a tug. "I wanna see how Winkie's doing."

"Maybe after lunch."

As they neared her folks' place, Grace noticed a strip of toilet paper hanging from a branch in the maple tree. Her gaze traveled around the yard. Had Mom and Dad been the victims of a TP party? If so, it seemed odd that there was just one strip of toilet paper hanging from the tree. "That's sure *fremm*," she murmured.

"What's strange, Mama?" Anna asked as she tromped up the back steps.

"It's nothing for you to worry about."

When they entered the house, Grace found her mother sitting at the kitchen table with her Bible open and a cup of tea in her hand.

"Wie geht's?" Mom asked as Grace took a seat at the table and Anna dropped to the floor beside a milky white kitten.

"I'm feeling a little better than yesterday." Grace reached for the teapot sitting in the center of the table and poured herself some tea.

"You looked so pale and shaken when we returned from Berlin yesterday. I was worried about you."

Grace glanced over at her daughter, who sat cross-legged on the floor with the kitten in her lap. "Anna, why don't you take the kitten out to the porch and play with her there?"

"Why can't I stay here?"

"Outside's a better place for the kitten."

Anna clambered to her feet and headed out the door.

Mom pushed a jar of honey in Grace's direction. "With the boppli coming soon, you need to get plenty of rest and remain calm."

Grace added a spoonful of honey to her tea. "It's hard to relax knowing Gary is back and might have been the one who threw the stink bomb into Dad's barn."

Mom nodded. "Did you see the mess we woke up to?"

"What mess was that?"

"Someone strung toilet paper all over the house, barn, and your daed's woodworking shop."

"I saw a piece of toilet paper hanging from a branch in the maple tree, but that was all."

"The men cleaned it up before they went to work this morning."

Grace shivered and leaned back in the chair, her thoughts racing.

"Are you cold? Would you like one of my shawls to drape around your shoulders?" Mom asked with a look of concern.

Grace shook her head. "I'm not shivering because I'm cold. I'm afraid Gary might have come back to continue harassing our family. The stink bomb and TP mess could be just the beginning."

"I hope not." Mom lowered her voice, even though Anna was no longer in the room. "Your daed mentioned that Luke dropped a hammer during the work frolic on your new house and that it almost hit Ruth. Did you hear about that?"

Grace shook her head, then pushed her chair aside and stood.

"Where are you going?"

"I think I should make another trip to Berlin to see if I can find Gary. If he's hanging around town, I'm going to have a talk with him."

"Ach, Grace, I don't think that's a good idea. And I don't think Cleon would like you going into town alone—especially if he knew what you had in mind."

"I won't go alone. If you're able to watch Anna, I'll see if Martha's willing to ride along."

"I guess I could watch Anna, but—"

"Where is that little sister of mine?"

"Out in the barn as usual."

"I'll go see if she's free." Grace rushed out the door before Mom had a chance to respond.

Since there was a lull between customers, Ruth decided it was a good time to clean the outside glass of the bakery case, where fingerprints from customers were always a problem. She enjoyed her job at the bakeshop but looked forward to the day when she became a wife and mother. Cooking, cleaning, and wiping children's runny noses would be more rewarding than waiting on impatient customers all day.

Ruth squirted liquid cleaner on the front of the glass and began wiping it with a clean rag, but her thoughts were on Martin and his gentle, caring ways. She was quickly falling in love with him and hoped the feeling was mutual. *Will Martin ask me to marry him someday? I'd say yes if he did.*

She smiled, picturing Martin's deep dimples and the genuine smile he so often gave her. *If we were to marry, I wonder if our kinner would have his cute little dimples.*

The telephone rang, and Ruth's musings were halted. Someone probably wanted to place a bakery order.

A few minutes later, she hung up the phone and had just slid a tray of maple bars into the bakery case when she heard a man clear his throat. She looked up and saw Gary Walker standing on the other side of the counter, staring at her with a look so intense it made her toes curl inside her shoes. "Y-you're back," she stammered.

"Sure am," he said with a twisted grin.

She gestured to the baked goods inside the case. "Do you want more maple bars?"

"No, but I wouldn't mind a strong cup of coffee."

"We don't serve coffee here, just baked goods."

He raked his fingers through the back of his thick auburn hair. "How about you and me having a cup of coffee somewhere? Maybe we could go to that restaurant on the other side of town where your sister used to work."

She shook her head. "I can't leave the bakeshop. My boss wouldn't like it if I left the front counter unattended."

Gary placed both hands against the display case and leaned toward her.

So much for cleaning the glass.

"You do get breaks, don't you?" he asked.

She nodded and leaned away from the disgusting odor of cigarette smoke that made her want to sneeze. She hadn't noticed a smoky smell on him before. Maybe his spicy aftershave had covered it up.

"Tell me when your break is, and we'll meet wherever you like."

Ruth's mouth felt so dry she had to swallow several times in order to speak. "Wh-why would you want to meet me for coffee?"

"I'd like to talk to you about some things, and it would be easier to do it away from here."

She looked over her shoulder, hoping Jake would come into the room, but she figured he probably couldn't hear the conversation over the noisy mixer running in the back room.

"I don't believe we have anything to talk about," she said through tight lips.

He leaned so close she could feel his sultry breath blowing against her face. "You'd be surprised how much we might have to talk about."

Ruth closed the sliding door on her side of the bakery case. "If you'll excuse me, I have work to do."

Gary chuckled. "From what I can tell, I'm your only customer right now. Don't you think I deserve your undivided attention?"

Ruth gripped the edge of the counter so hard her fingers turned numb. "If you didn't come here to buy anything, then I'd appreciate it if you'd leave."

"I'll take a maple bar."

"Just one?"

"Yep." He thumped his stomach. "Don't want to get fat, or pretty women like you may not find me attractive."

Ruth clenched her teeth, placed a maple bar on a square of waxed paper, and handed it to him. "That will be fifty cents."

He paid her, then bit into the maple bar and smacked his lips. "This tastes almost as sweet as your big sister's lips." He gave her a flirty wink. "How about you? Have you ever been kissed by an English man?"

Ruth heard the echo of her heartbeat in her head.

An English couple entered the bakeshop. Gary grunted and stepped aside as they approached the counter.

"May I help you?" Ruth asked.

The man nodded. "We'd like a dozen chocolate doughnuts and an angel food cake."

As Ruth reached into the bakery case to remove the items, she looked up and saw Gary heading for the door. "I'll come back when you're not so busy," he called over his shoulder.

Ruth cringed. The last thing she wanted was to see that man again!

Chapter 10

When Martha pulled her buggy up to the hitching rail near the back of the bakeshop, she pointed to Gary Walker as he came around the corner of the building. "There he is. Are you sure you want to speak with him, sister?"

Grace nodded despite her sweaty hands and rapidly beating heart.

"I'll park the buggy and go with you."

"I think it would be better if I speak with Gary alone. Why don't you wait for me inside the bakeshop?"

Martha's forehead wrinkled. "I don't think–"

"I'll be fine."

Martha shrugged and stepped down from the buggy.

As her sister headed for the bakeshop, Grace hurried toward Gary, who was almost to his car.

He whirled around to face her. "You following me, Gracie?"

When she opened her mouth to reply, the only thing that came out was a little squeak.

"I wouldn't think a married woman who's expecting a baby would be running down the street chasing after other men."

"I'm not. I mean, I just wanted to ask you a question."

He leaned on the hood of his car and folded his arms. "About what?"

"I was wondering how long you plan to stay in Holmes County."

"As long as it takes."

"For what?"

"For me to write the stories I'm after." He leveled her a penetrating look that sent shivers up her spine. "Are you feeling the need to check up on me, Gracie?"

She swallowed hard, unsure of how to respond.

"I didn't come back to Holmes County to make your life miserable, if that's what you're worried about."

The urge to ask if he had toilet-papered their buildings and thrown the stink bomb into the barn was strong, but Grace figured he might take satisfaction in knowing she was afraid. "I would think you could find other things to write about than the Holmes County Amish," she said as a horse and buggy rumbled by and turned into the cheese store parking lot across the street.

Gary leaned away from his car and moved closer to her. "None quite as interesting as you."

Before she could comment, he snickered and said, "I think your sister who works at the bakeshop is pretty interesting, too."

Grace's fingers pressed into her palms until the nails dug into her flesh. "Stay away from Ruth."

"If I don't?"

"I'll tell the sheriff what I think you're up to."

Gary snorted and slapped his knee. "It's a free country, Gracie. I have every right to visit the bakeshop whenever I get the urge for something sweet. Besides, it's not like the sheriff's going to arrest me for buying a few doughnuts."

"The sheriff's aware of the break-ins and vandalism that went on at our place several months ago. He told my dad that he plans to keep an eye on things."

"I told you before that I had nothing to do with any of those occurrences." Gary flung open the car door. "Now if you'll excuse me, I've got work to do."

"That man makes me so angry," Grace fumed as Gary pulled away from the curb. "I'm sure he's the one responsible for those attacks, and he's probably trying to make it look like it's someone else."

"I can't believe you let Grace speak to that reporter by herself," Ruth said after Martha came into the shop and told her what Grace had decided to do.

"I tried to talk her out of it, but she wouldn't listen." Martha groaned. "You know how stubborn our big sister can be when she makes up her mind about something."

"Jah, I know." Ruth skirted around the front counter and hurried over to the window near the door. She craned her neck to see up the street but saw no sign of Grace or Gary.

"Do you want me to go after her?" Martha asked.

"She probably wouldn't like it. Besides, I'm sure Gary wouldn't do anything foolish right here in town." Ruth moved back to the bakery case, and Martha followed.

When Grace stepped into the bakeshop a few minutes later, her face looked pale, and she shuffled across the room as if she had no strength in her legs.

Ruth rushed into the back room and grabbed a stool. "You'd better sit down."

Grace nodded and did as she was told. "I held up pretty well while I was talking to Gary, but after he left, my knees felt so shaky I thought I might not make it here."

"What did the man have to say?" Martha asked.

"I asked how long he plans to stay in Holmes County, and he said as long as it takes to get the stories he wants. Then he mentioned Ruth, and I threatened to notify the sheriff if he doesn't stay away from her."

Ruth's heart slammed into her chest. "I hope Gary doesn't think I'm interested in him, because I'm surely not."

Martha looked over at Grace. "Did you ask if he knew about the stink bomb or the toilet-papering?"

Grace shook her head. "I didn't want him to know what I suspect. I think it gives him pleasure to know I'm scared."

"You shouldn't have spoken to him alone." Martha pursed her lips. "You should have let me go with you."

Grace stared at her hands clasped tightly in her lap.

"The stink bomb and the toilet paper mess could have been pranks like Dad mentioned," Ruth said. "I'll bet if we asked some of our neighbors, we'd find out that their places were toilet-papered, too."

Martha touched Grace's shoulder. "I think we should go. You look all done in and need to get home, where you can rest."

Grace nodded and slipped off the stool.

As Ruth's sisters headed out the door, she offered up a prayer. *Lord, please be with my family–especially Grace.*

Cleon had just finished staining the legs of a table when Judith and Anna entered the woodworking shop.

"We brought you some lunch," Judith said, holding out two metal lunch boxes.

Roman moved away from the desk where he'd been doing paperwork and greeted her with a smile. "We appreciate that."

Cleon straightened and set his staining rag aside. "Where's Grace? She usually brings my meal if I don't go home for lunch."

"Mama went to town," Anna said.

Cleon's brows knit together as he looked over at Judith.

"She was upset when she found out about the toilet-papering. So she decided to go to Berlin, hoping she might see Gary Walker there."

"What?" Cleon's voice echoed in his ears. "She went to town alone–to speak with that man?"

Judith shook her head. "She's not alone. Martha went with her."

"As if that's supposed to make me feel better. Doesn't my wife ever think things through? Must she always make decisions without asking my opinion or getting my approval?"

Judith glanced down at Anna, whose eyes were huge as saucers; then she looked back at Cleon and shook her head. "I think this discussion can wait, don't you?"

After seeing the frightened look on Anna's face, Cleon realized he had let his emotions get the better of him. He knelt on the floor in front of the child. "I'm sorry for yelling. I'm just worried about your mamm."

"Did Mama do somethin' wrong?" Anna's chin quivered as she stared up at Cleon.

"She didn't do anything wrong. I just wish she'd told me where she was going."

"Maybe you should go after her," Roman suggested as he tapped

Cleon on the shoulder. "Just to be sure everything's okay."

Cleon stood. "You wouldn't mind? I know you have a lot of work going."

"Nothing I have to do here is as important as the safety of my girls. I know you won't get much work done if you stay here stewing over things."

"Danki. I'll have Grace and Martha back soon," Cleon called over his shoulder as he hurried out of the shop.

"I guess we'd better go, too," Judith said. She steered Anna toward the door.

Judith and Anna had no more than left the shop when Bishop King showed up. "Wie geht's?" Roman asked.

"I'm doing all right. How about you?"

Roman blew out his breath in a huff that lifted the hair off his forehead. "There have been a couple of attacks here lately. At first I thought they were just pranks, but now I'm not so sure."

"What kind of attacks?" the bishop asked as he moved closer to Roman's desk.

"Someone tossed a stink bomb through one of the barn windows the other day. Then this morning we found toilet paper all over the house, barn, and my shop."

Bishop King compressed his lips. "Any idea who's to blame?"

"I can't be sure, but I found a half-empty pack of cigarettes lying next to the barn, and I've got a hunch whose it is."

"Who would that be?"

"Luke. I told you once before that I thought Luke might be upset with me for firing him. I wouldn't be a bit surprised if he's trying to get even."

"What makes you think the cigarettes are Luke's?"

Roman's eyes narrowed. "I smelled smoke on Luke a time or two when he was working for me."

The bishop raked his fingers through the ends of his beard. "Now that I think of it, not long ago, my son Toby made mention of smelling smoke on Luke."

"Remember the time Judith's clothesline was cut?"

"Jah."

"She found a pair of sunglasses on the ground not far from the line, and they turned out to be Luke's."

"Did he admit to cutting the line?"

"No, but–"

"Would you like me to speak with Luke?"

"Can you do it without letting him know I told you what I suspect?"

Bishop King nodded. "I'll feel him out–maybe tell him what's been going on here and see what kind of reaction I get."

"Sounds good. You'll let me know what he has to say?"

"Jah, sure." The bishop shifted from one foot to the other. "I'm a bit concerned about your attitude, though, Roman."

"What do you mean?"

"Seems to me as if you're jumping to conclusions–judging Luke with no real evidence. Don't you think you should give him the benefit of the doubt?"

"I just think he's the one with the most likely reason to want to get even with me. If that's the case, it could be why he won't get baptized and join the church."

"The fact that Luke hasn't left the faith and gone English gives me hope that eventually he'll settle down and do what's expected of him. More than likely that will happen when he finds the right woman and decides to get married."

"Maybe so. I'd still appreciate you talking to him, though."

"No problem." The bishop glanced around the room. "So do you have that set of dressers I ordered last month ready for me yet?"

"Sure do. We can load them into your buggy right now."

Cleon had just begun hitching a horse to his rig when another horse trotted up the driveway, pulling a buggy. He realized right away that it was one of Roman's mares, so he hurried over to the barn and waited by the hitching rail until the horse came to a stop. "Are you okay?" he called to Grace through the open buggy flap.

She nodded, although he noticed that she looked exhausted.

Martha climbed down from the driver's side, and Cleon helped Grace out of the buggy. "Why'd you run off like that without telling me where you were going?"

"Because I was afraid you would say no." Grace spoke so softly he could barely hear the words.

"You're right, I would have. You're in no condition to go traipsing around after someone you *think* might be responsible for the things that have been done here these past two days."

"I needed to speak with Gary and see how long he plans to stay in Holmes County." She drew in a ragged breath. "It's not just what's been done here recently, either. There were other attacks that took place when he was here before."

"So what did you find out?"

"Gary said he's come back to the area to write more stories and that he'll be here until they're done."

Cleon took hold of Grace's arm and looked over at Martha, who stood near the buggy with a concerned look on her face. "Would you let your folks know that you and Grace are home?"

Martha nodded. "Jah, sure."

"Oh, and would you see if Judith can keep Anna for the rest of the day? My *fraa* looks exhausted and needs to go to bed."

"Your wife will be just fine once she's had something to eat and has rested awhile, so there's no need for Mom to keep Anna," Grace argued.

Cleon slipped his arm around her waist. "I can't go back to work in your daed's shop unless I know you're resting."

Grace finally nodded, and Cleon felt relief. He might not be able to do anything about the vandalism that had been done at his in-laws' place, but he could take care of his wife.

Chapter 11

When Martha directed her buggy up Abe Wengerd's driveway, she spotted Martin walking toward the harness shop. She needed to be at Irene's by three o'clock but had decided to stop on her way and see how Esta was getting along with Winkie.

Martha halted the horse near Abe's barn and climbed out of the buggy. She was greeted by Esta, who had been in the yard playing with the puppy.

"Wie geht's?" Martha asked.

"I'm doin' good," Esta replied. "Just givin' Winkie some exercise."

Martha smiled. "Winkie's a cute name."

Esta nodded. "Anna chose it 'cause the pup likes to wink one eye."

"Jah, she told me."

"How come Anna didn't come with you? I like it when she comes over to play."

"I didn't invite her because I can't stay very long."

"Why not?"

"I'm on my way to work, and I'll need to leave soon." Martha bent down and stroked the puppy's ears. "I'm glad Winkie has a good home."

Esta nodded and scooped the little sheltie into her arms. "I'm takin' good care of him."

"I'm sure you are." Martha squeezed Esta's shoulder. "I'll try to bring Anna along the next time I come over."

"Okay."

As Martha started for her buggy, she spotted Luke coming out of

Abe's harness shop, and her heart missed a beat. She wished she didn't feel so giddy every time she saw Luke. She was sure he had no interest in her. If Dad knew she had a crush on Luke, he wouldn't approve.

"Hello, Luke," she said as he approached. "How are you?"

"Fair to middlin'," he replied with a shrug. "And you?"

"Doing okay." She was tempted to mention the acts of vandalism earlier in the week but thought better of it, in case Luke was the one responsible. She hoped he wasn't. Even if Luke was angry because Dad had fired him, Martha couldn't imagine Luke being behind any of the things that had been done to her family. Dad had asked around the day after they'd discovered all of the toilet paper on their buildings, but none of their neighbors had been bothered. That made Martha wonder if more attacks would be forthcoming.

"How's the dog business going?" Luke asked, pulling her thoughts aside.

"Not so well. The female beagle I bought still isn't pregnant, but I'll be breeding Heidi and Fritz again when the time is right."

"Maybe you should sell off the beagles and buy some other breed of dog."

"I've thought of that, and I might put an ad in *The Budget* soon."

"Or you could try the *Bargain Hunter*," he suggested. "Might have better luck there."

"That's a good idea. Maybe I'll run an ad in both papers."

Luke moved away from the building. "Guess I'd better go. Just came by to check on a bridle Abe's making for my daed. Now I've got a delivery to make for John."

"How are things going with you working for him?" she asked.

"Compared to your daed, John's real easy to work for." He averted his gaze. "Guess I shouldn't be saying this, but working for your daed every day was like going to the dentist to get a root canal."

Martha bristled. As much as she liked Luke, she didn't care for him saying things against her dad. "From what I hear, you weren't so easy to work with, either."

Luke shook his head. "Your daed didn't like that I had my own ideas about how things should be done. He blamed me for Steven Bates's cabinets falling off the wagon, and it wasn't even my fault."

"It doesn't matter who did what or who said what. My daed let you go and you should accept that."

His eyes narrowed. "Who says I'm not?"

"You wouldn't try to get even with Dad, would you?"

"No way. I'd never do that, no matter how much he might irritate me."

A sense of relief flooded Martha's soul. "I didn't think you would try to get even, but we've had a few more incidents at our place this week, so—"

"What's been done?"

"A stink bomb was thrown into our barn, and then our house, barn, and Dad's shop got toilet-papered."

Luke frowned. "Sounds like some pranksters to me. I heard there was some toilet-papering done at one of the schoolhouses near Berlin the other day."

"Dad thought it might be pranksters at first, but then he mentioned that he thought it could have been—"

"Me?"

She nodded.

"Puh! I've got better things to do than make stink bombs and spread TP all over the place." Luke started walking toward his buggy.

Martha was more certain than ever that Luke wasn't the one responsible for any of the attacks. The only question unanswered—who *was* responsible?

As Martin headed down the road in his buggy, his stomach twisted as though it were tied in knots. He'd come to a decision about his relationship with Ruth, and this evening he planned to talk to her about it.

When he arrived at the Hostettlers', he spotted Ruth sitting in the glider under the maple tree in the backyard, reading a book. He halted the buggy, secured his horse to the hitching rail, and sprinted across the lawn.

"I'm surprised to see you," Ruth said as he approached her. "I didn't know you'd be coming by this evening."

He licked his lips, and the knot in his stomach tightened. "I thought

I would surprise you."

"You did that, all right." She set the book aside and patted the cushion beside her. "Would you like to join me?"

Martin took a seat. "I. . .uh. . .need to talk to you about something." He removed his straw hat and twisted the edge of the brim.

"Are you all right? You seem kind of *naerfich*."

"I am feeling a bit nervous."

"How come?"

"Well. . .I. . ." He scooted a bit closer. "I know we haven't been courting very long, but I've come to care about you."

"I care about you, too."

"Enough to be honest with me?"

"Of course."

He drummed his fingers along the armrest of the glider. "Remember that day at the pond when you said you knew about the truck Toby and Sadie found in the woods?"

She nodded.

"You acted like you knew who owned the truck, but you didn't seem to want to talk about it."

She stared at her lap, and her chin trembled slightly. "I. . .uh. . .do know who owns the truck, but I promised I wouldn't tell anyone."

"Does it belong to someone I know?"

"Jah."

He reached for her hand. "If we're going to have a close relationship, then I don't think we should keep secrets from each other, do you?"

She slowly shook her head.

"I'd like to know who owns that truck."

Ruth's forehead creased. "If I tell, will you promise not to repeat it to anyone?"

"Jah, if you don't want me to."

"The truck belongs to Luke."

"Luke Friesen?"

"Jah. He keeps it hidden there so his folks won't know."

Martin groaned. "I knew Luke was still going through rumschpringe, but I had no idea he owned a truck. Doesn't it seem strange that he would keep it hidden—especially since many Amish young people openly own cars?"

Ruth nodded. "The fact that he kept secrets from me and wouldn't settle down and join the church was the reason I broke up with him."

Martin brushed his thumb back and forth across the top of her hand. "I can't say that I'm glad Luke's not settled down, but I am glad you broke up with him." He swallowed a couple of times. "I. . .uh. . . have another question I'd like to ask you."

"What's that?"

"Will you be my wife?"

Her mouth hung slightly open. "You—you want to marry me?"

He nodded. "I love you, Ruth. I know it's sudden, but I feel a strong need to make you my wife as soon as possible."

A blush of pink cascaded over her cheeks.

"It's not just a physical need," he was quick to say. "It's a sense of urgency I can't explain."

"I—I don't understand."

"I have a feeling that if we don't get married soon, we might never marry."

"Is it because you're worried about the attacks against my family? Are you afraid something will happen to me?"

He nodded. "Could we be married this fall—maybe early October?"

She lifted her gaze to meet his. "Most couples have a longer courtship than that."

"I know." He squeezed her fingers. "Will you at least give some consideration to my proposal?"

"I don't need to consider the proposal, Martin." A smile spread across Ruth's face as a flicker of light danced in her dark eyes. "I'd be honored to marry you."

"Really?"

She nodded. "Shall we go inside and discuss this with my folks? I want to be sure we have their approval."

"Maybe it would be better if you talked to them alone. In case they don't approve of you marrying me."

"I don't see why they wouldn't approve."

"Jah, okay."

When Ruth and Martin stepped into the kitchen, Ruth spotted her parents sitting at the table, each reading a section of the newspaper. Her throat felt so swollen she wasn't sure she could speak. What if they didn't approve of her marrying Martin? What if Mom and Dad wanted them to wait until they'd been courting longer?

Martin squeezed Ruth's hand, and the warmth of his fingers gave her the confidence she needed. "Mom, Dad. Martin and I have something we'd like to tell you."

"What's that?" Mom asked, glancing up from her paper. She smiled at Martin. "It's good to see you."

"Good to see you, too," he replied.

Dad merely grunted as he kept reading the paper.

Ruth shifted uneasily. "Martin has asked me to marry him."

"What?" Mom and Dad said in unison.

Dad dropped his paper to the table, and Mom reached to steady the glass of iced tea sitting before her.

"I've asked Ruth to be my wife." Martin gave Ruth's fingers another squeeze. "She said she's willing–that is, if you approve."

Dad squinted as he leveled Martin with a most serious look. "I have no objections to you courting my daughter, but I think it's too soon for you to be thinking about marriage."

Ruth opened her mouth to comment, but Martin spoke first. "I love Ruth, and I'd like us to be married as soon as possible."

Dad held up his hand. "What's the rush?"

Martin moved closer to the table. "I–I feel a sense of urgency to marry her."

"He's worried something will happen to me," Ruth quickly explained.

Mom's eyebrows furrowed as she looked at Martin. "Why would you think that?"

"All the things that have happened in our community lately have made me realize life is fragile, and one never knows when they'll lose someone they love."

"Are you thinking about Abe losing Alma?" Dad asked.

Martin nodded. "That's part of it. I'm also concerned about all the attacks on your family. If Ruth and I were married, she would be in my care."

A muscle in Dad's cheek twitched rhythmically. "Are you saying I haven't cared well for my fraa and *dechder*?"

Martin's face flamed. "I'm not saying that at all. I'm sure you're doing a fine job caring for your wife and daughters."

"I do my best," Dad mumbled.

Mom reached over and patted his arm. "Of course you do, Roman."

Ruth cleared her throat. "Do you have any objections to Martin and I being married in October?"

"I think it would be better if you waited until November," Mom said. "That will give us time to get some celery planted, make your wedding dress, and get everything done before the wedding."

"It will give you more time for courting, too," Dad put in.

Ruth looked at Martin and was relieved when he nodded and said, "November it'll have to be, then."

She smiled and bent to hug her mother. "Where's Martha? I want to share our good news with her."

"Out in the barn with those dogs of hers," Dad said with a scowl. "Where else would she be?"

Ruth kissed her father's forehead. "Danki, Dad." Then she grabbed Martin's hand, and they rushed out the door.

Chapter 12

On a Friday morning two weeks later, Ruth stepped out of the house to hitch a horse to her buggy and discovered a message in bold black letters written on the side of their barn. It read You'll Pay!

"Oh no," she gasped as a shiver zipped up her spine. "Who could have done this? Why would they do such a thing?"

Ruth rushed around the corner of the house, knowing her father was probably heading to his shop by now. That's when she saw her mother's garden. All of the plants had been destroyed.

"Ach! My celery!" she screamed.

Dad rushed toward her then, his eyes wild. "What's all the yelling about?"

"Look over there!" Ruth's hand shook as she pointed to her mother's garden. "Someone's ruined all our plants, and—and they wrote a threatening message on the side of the barn."

Dad's eyebrows furrowed. "What message?"

"You mean you haven't seen it yet?"

He shook his head.

"Come see for yourself." Ruth led the way to the barn and halted in front of the message. "Who could have written such a thing, and what would someone think we need to pay for?"

"Not *we*," he said with a shake of his head. "It's me that's being targeted; I'm sure of it."

"But why? What have you done that would make someone want to ruin our garden and paint a hateful message on the barn?"

Dad moaned as he bent to pick up an empty can of spray paint.

"Several people might be carrying a grudge against me–Steven Bates, Luke, and that land developer who wanted to buy our property."

"But the land developer left our area some time ago, Dad."

He nodded. "That's true."

"You don't think it could be the English reporter who used to date Grace, do you? Maybe it's her he's trying to get even with, not you."

Dad shook his head. "If the attacker wanted to make Grace pay, then the attacks would have been against just her, not the rest of the family."

"But if it's someone wanting to get even with you, then wouldn't he have done things to hurt just you?"

"Anything that hurts my family hurts me," Dad said as he hurled the empty can into a box full of trash near the barn door.

"The more things that happen, the more scared I become." Ruth gulped in some air. "I just wonder how much longer this will go on."

"I don't know. Our bishop came by the shop yesterday morning and said he'd spoken to Luke."

"What did Luke have to say?"

Dad shrugged. "Guess he told the bishop that he thinks I've got it in for him and that he's not responsible for any of the attacks against us."

"Do you believe him?"

"No, and I've been thinking about talking to Luke myself, but I don't want to rile him. He might be capable of doing even worse things if he gets mad enough."

"I can understand that he might have been upset with you for firing him, but that was some time ago. Why would he be doing spiteful things to us now?"

"Maybe he heard about your betrothal to Martin and feels jealous because you're marrying him."

"Oh, Dad, I don't think so. If Luke had wanted to marry me, he wouldn't have kept secrets during our courtship. I think he was relieved when I broke up with him."

"Maybe so, but he wasn't relieved when I fired him."

"Are you talking about Luke?" Martha asked, stepping up to them.

Dad nodded and pointed to the garden. "Look what was done to your mamm's vegetable plants."

Martha's eyebrows lifted high on her forehead. "What in all the world would cause someone to do such a thing, and who could have done it?"

"The same one who did that." Ruth pointed to the writing on the side of the barn. "*Somebody's* trying to make *someone* in this family pay for *something*."

Martha clasped her father's arm. "You've got to phone the sheriff. We can't allow this kind of thing to continue. Sooner or later someone's going to get hurt."

Mom stepped into the yard just then. "What's going on? I figured Ruth would be on her way to work by now. And you, too, Roman. What are you all doing out here on the lawn?"

"Look," the three of them said in unison as they pointed to the garden.

Mom let out a yelp and lifted her hands. *"Ich kann sell net geh!"*

"There isn't much you can do except tolerate it." Dad slipped his arm around Mom's waist. "What's done is done. We just need to hold steady and keep trusting God to protect us and our property."

"How can we trust God when things keep happening and we never know when or why?" Ruth questioned.

Before Dad could reply, Cleon showed up. "What's going on? Why are you all standing out here in the yard?"

"Someone left a message on our barn, and they—they killed my garden," Mom said in a shaky voice. "Somebody's out to get us, and I'm very much afraid."

"That's what they want—to make us afraid." Dad's lips compressed into a thin line. "We can't give in. We must hold steady."

Cleon frowned. "When Grace hears of this, she's going to be awfully upset. Probably more convinced than ever that the reporter is behind it."

"Grace might be right," Ruth agreed. "That reporter seems real sneaky to me."

"I think it's safe to say that whoever's been doing this must be someone close by, as they seem to know our family's comings and goings," Cleon said. "I wouldn't be surprised if they're not keeping a watch on the place."

"As I've said before, I'm not convinced the reporter's doing it," Dad said with a grunt. "I still think it could be Luke."

"I don't believe Luke's the one responsible," Martha protested.

"We won't solve anything by standing around playing guessing games." Dad nodded at Cleon. "We've got work in the shop that needs to be done."

"What about the garden?" Ruth wailed.

"I'll see about getting another spot plowed and spaded as soon as I'm done for the day," Dad said. "Then you and your mamm can begin planting tomorrow morning."

Cleon leaned close to Mom. "Would you go to my house and speak with Grace? I don't want her coming out here and seeing what's happened without some warning."

She nodded. "Jah, sure. I'll do that now." Mom headed up the driveway toward Cleon and Grace's house, and the men turned toward the woodworking shop.

Martha paced in front of her mother's garden, anger bubbling in her soul. "Something needs to be done about this."

Ruth knelt on the grass and let her head fall forward into her outstretched hands. "I have a terrible feeling that I'll never marry Martin—that something will prevent our wedding from taking place."

Martha dropped down beside Ruth and gave her a hug. "Maybe I should go out to the shop and talk to Dad again—try to convince him to phone the sheriff."

"Sheriff Osborn knows about some of the other things that have happened here, and what good has that done?"

"He said he'd keep an eye on things."

"True. But he can't be watching our place all the time."

"Even so, I think Dad should let the sheriff know about these recent happenings." Martha rose to her feet and was about to walk away, when Sheriff Osborn's car pulled into the driveway. It stopped beside her father's shop, and the sheriff got out of the car and went inside.

"Now that's a surprise," Ruth said. "I wonder what he's doing here."

"I'm going to see what the sheriff has to say." Martha sprinted toward the shop, leaving Ruth sitting on the grass by herself.

"Got a call from one of your neighbors," Martha heard the sheriff say when she stepped into the shop a few minutes later. "They said someone had written something threatening on the side of your barn."

"Don't tell me. Ray Larson called. He was probably checking things over with those binoculars of his. After that first round of attacks against us several months ago, Ray's wife said she would ask him to keep an eye on things." Dad folded his arms and grunted. "I never thought that was necessary, though."

Sheriff Osborn shrugged. "The caller didn't identify himself. Just mentioned seeing the writing on your barn."

"There was more done than that," Martha announced as she closed the door behind her. "Somebody put weed killer on my mother's vegetable garden, and now everything's ruined."

Dad shot Martha a look of irritation. "What are you doing out here, girl?"

"I saw the sheriff's car pull in, and I wanted to see if he knew anything about what's been going on here lately."

Sheriff Osborn tipped his head in Dad's direction. "Has something happened besides the message on the barn and the garden being ruined?"

Dad waved a hand. "It wasn't much. Just a stink bomb thrown into the barn, and some toilet paper draped all over our buildings."

"Sounds like whoever bothered you before might be at it again." The sheriff pulled a notebook and pen out of his shirt pocket and began writing. "When did you say these other things happened?"

"A couple weeks ago," Dad answered.

"Did you see anyone lurking around the place before or after the incidents?"

"Nope."

"Just Ray Larson." Cleon spoke up from across the room, where he'd been quietly working on a set of cabinets. "I spotted him walking up and down our fence line the day before the stink bomb happened. His binoculars were hanging around his neck." He shrugged. "I figured he was out looking for some unusual birds."

"How come you never mentioned this before?" A muscle in Dad's cheek twitched.

Cleon shrugged again. "Didn't seem important at the time. It just came to mind now, when the sheriff asked if we'd seen anyone hanging around the place."

Martha stepped between the sheriff and her father. "There's no way Ray Larson could be responsible for any of the things that have been done to us."

"How do you know?" the sheriff asked, turning to face her.

"I just do. Ray and Donna are good neighbors. They often drive us places we can't go with the horse and buggy, and they bought one of Heidi's pups."

The sheriff arched one eyebrow and stared at Martha as if she'd taken leave of her senses. "I hardly thinking buying a puppy is reason enough to remove the Larsons' name from our list of suspects."

Martha's eyes widened. "You have a list?"

The sheriff nodded. "The last time your father and I spoke, he mentioned a few people he thought might have a grudge against him."

"You never told us you'd given the sheriff a list of names," Martha said, turning to face her father.

"I talked to him about it once when he stopped by my shop to see if there had been any more attacks." Dad gave his earlobe a quick pull. "Saw no need to mention it."

Martha turned back to the sheriff. "Did Dad tell you about Gary Walker?"

"Who?"

"He's that reporter who's been hanging around Holmes County doing stories about the Amish," Cleon explained. "He used to date my wife when she was going through her running-around years."

Sheriff Osborn nodded. "Ah, I remember now. He's the one who wrote that article some time ago that included a picture of Grace and told about some of the acts of vandalism that had been done at your place."

"That's right," Dad said. "We were afraid the article might make things worse by giving someone the idea that they could get away with doing such a thing." He grunted. "And maybe it has, because things sure have gotten worse since that article came out."

"Might be good for me to speak to this reporter." The sheriff scribbled something else on his tablet. "Find out what he knows and feel him out."

"I doubt he's going to admit anything," Martha said. "I was with Grace one day when she confronted him, and he was real arrogant and denied knowing anything about our problems."

"He might be willing to talk to me." Sheriff Osborn looked over at Dad. "Were any clues left after these recent attacks? Something that might point to the one responsible?"

"Just a pack of cigarettes I found on the ground after the toilet-papering was done," Dad said. "I suspect the culprit's a smoker."

"Do you still have the cigarettes?"

Dad shook his head. "Threw them out that same day, just like I did with the empty spray can I found on the ground near our barn this morning. Martha could get that for you."

"If there are any more attacks and you find any clues, I don't want you to touch them–and certainly don't throw them away." The sheriff frowned. "I might be able to check for fingerprints." He started for the door but whirled back around. "Let me know if you see or hear anything suspicious."

Dad nodded, and Martha hurried out the door after the sheriff. After she showed him where the can of spray paint was, she said, "You will let us know what Gary Walker has to say after you speak to him, I hope."

The sheriff nodded. "If there's anything worth repeating, your dad will be the first to know."

Chapter 13

Do I have to go to school, Mama?" Anna whined as she sat at the table, poking her scrambled eggs with the tip of her fork.

Grace nodded and took a sip of her tea. "This is your first day of school, and you should be happy about attending the first grade."

Anna's lower lip protruded. "What if I don't like my teacher? What if the work's too hard?"

"Clara Bontrager is a good teacher, and I'm sure you'll do fine. Your friend Esta will be there, and you know most of the other children, so you won't be alone."

Anna's forehead wrinkled. "I wonder if Esta will miss her puppy while she's in school. Winkie makes Esta laugh, you know. He helps her forget she lost her mamm."

"I'm glad about that. I'm also pleased that you and Esta have become such good friends." Grace gave Anna's shoulder a gentle squeeze. "Now hurry and finish your breakfast so I can take you to school."

"Can't I walk? The schoolhouse isn't far down the road."

Grace shook her head. "If you had older brothers or sisters to walk with you, I might allow it, but it's just you, and I want to be sure you get to school safely."

Anna shrugged her slim shoulders. "Jah, okay."

A short time later as Grace directed their horse and buggy down the driveway past her folks' place, she was shocked to see the writing on her father's barn. She halted the horse and climbed out of the buggy so she could get a better look at the words that had been painted in bold black letters.

Her heart pounded. "Gary's at it again," she fumed. "That man won't rest until he's made me pay for breaking up with him and marrying Wade."

Mom rushed up to her. "I hated for you to see this, and I was coming up to tell you about it," she said, motioning to the barn. "Your daed and Cleon won't have time to paint over it until they're done working for the day. They promised to dig a new garden plot for me, too."

Grace's forehead wrinkled. "You already have a garden plot. Why would you need a new one?"

"Whoever painted those threatening words on the side of our barn also put weed killer on my garden." Mom slowly shook her head. "Everything's dead—including the new shoots of celery we planted for the creamed celery dish we were going to serve at Ruth's wedding."

Grace glanced at the buggy. She was grateful Anna hadn't gotten out. She didn't want her daughter to know what had happened. Anna was already nervous about her first day of school; she didn't need something else to worry about.

"I'm so sorry, Mom," Grace said, clasping her mother's hand. "If there was something I could do to make these horrible attacks stop, I surely would."

"There's nothing we can do but pray. Things will ease up. We just need to hold steady and trust God, like your daed has said many times."

Grace stared at the ugly words written on the barn until they blurred before her eyes. "I don't think things will ever ease up unless Gary Walker leaves town for good." Without waiting for Mom to comment, Grace climbed into the buggy, grabbed up the reins, and headed down the driveway.

As they traveled to the schoolhouse, all she could think about was the latest act of vandalism. By the time she pulled into the schoolhouse parking lot, she'd developed a headache.

"Oh, there's Esta," Anna said, clambering across the seat and hopping out of the buggy.

"Don't you want me to walk you inside?" Grace called after her.

Anna shook her head. "I'll walk with Esta."

The child scampered off, and Grace took up the reins. She didn't feel like going home and looking at the words on Dad's barn, so she decided to drive over to Abe Wengerd's place to see how he was getting along and maybe visit with Sue. Focusing on someone else's problems might help take her mind off her own.

As Martin hauled a piece of leather over to a tub of black dye, his thoughts went to Ruth and how interested she had seemed the day he'd shown her the harness shop. She'd said she liked it here, and that was a good thing since they would be getting married in a few months. He would probably come home from work every night smelling like leather, neat's-foot oil, or pungent dye.

Martin remembered how nervous he had felt when he'd proposed to Ruth, and how relieved he'd felt when she said yes. He could hardly wait to make her his wife.

Martin's thoughts were halted when Abe's youngest boy, Owen, burst into the room, shouting, "Molly won't let me play with her wooden blocks!"

Abe stepped away from the oversized sewing machine where he'd been working and lifted the boy into his arms. "Molly's only two, son. She doesn't understand yet about sharing."

Owen's lower lip quivered. "I always have to share with her."

"I know." He patted the child's back. "Did you speak with Aunt Sue about it? Maybe she can convince Molly to share the blocks with you."

Owen shook his head. "Aunt Sue's busy bakin' bread."

"I'm sure Molly will take a nap after lunch." Abe placed Owen on the floor. "So while she's asleep, you can play with the blocks. How's that sound?"

"Okay." Owen hugged his father around the legs.

Abe opened the door and ushered the boy out. "You be good now."

Martin was impressed with Abe's patience. He could only hope he would be that patient when he and Ruth had children someday.

"Sorry about the interruption," Abe said, smiling at Martin. "Sometimes family business comes before work."

"No problem. It was nice to see the way you handled things with Owen. Sure hope I'll be as good a daed as you when Ruth and I have kinner."

Abe thumped Martin on the back. "I'm sure you'll do just fine."

"Guess I'd better get this hunk of leather dyed. Then I've got some straps that need cutting," Martin said, turning back to the tub of dye.

"I'd better get busy on those straps I was stitching, too."

Except for the steady hum of the air compressor, the men worked in silence.

When the door to Abe's shop opened again, Martin was surprised to see Grace Schrock step into the room.

"Wie geht's?" Abe called, turning off his machine. "What can I do for you this morning?"

"I just came by to see how things are going here and to tell you about some vandalism done at our place during the night."

Martin's ears perked up. "Is Ruth okay?" He'd been consumed with worry ever since Ruth's family had come under attack.

Grace nodded. "No one was hurt, but someone wrote the words 'You'll pay' on the side of my daed's barn. They also put weed killer on Mom's garden—which means the celery that had been planted to be served at your wedding meal was ruined."

Martin sucked in his breath, and Abe released a groan.

"I was hoping there would be no more attacks at your folks' place," Abe said.

"So were we."

Martin could see by the expression on Grace's face that she was frightened. Well, he was scared, too. Scared for everyone in the Hostettler family. Ruth most of all.

He turned to Abe. "Would it be okay if I take my lunch break a little early so I can go to town and speak with Ruth? I know she'll be upset about the celery."

"Jah, sure," Abe said with a nod. "You can head to Berlin right now if you like."

"You wouldn't mind?"

"Nope. We don't have much work today, so take all the time you need."

"Danki." Martin grabbed his straw hat off the wall peg and dashed out the door.

After Martin left the shop, Abe turned to Grace. "I'm sorry about the things that have been done to you folks. Nobody should have to live in fear."

"You and your family have been through a lot lately, too," she said.

"It helps to know we have the prayers and assistance of others in our community."

She nodded.

"Maybe you'd like to go up to the house and say hello to Sue and my two little ones," Abe suggested. "Sue would probably enjoy a chat with someone closer to her age. She looked kind of frazzled this morning, and I think she's having a hard time keeping the house running smoothly and taking care of my six *raubels* kinner."

"Your children aren't so rowdy from what I can tell," Grace said. "In fact, they seem pretty well behaved compared to some I know."

"They did real well when Alma was alive, but since she's been gone, they've been kind of unruly and moody." He grimaced. "Never know what Gideon will say or do next. I'm a little concerned about how he'll do in school this year."

"We'll continue to pray for all of you." Grace smiled. "Guess I'll go see Sue now."

After Grace left the shop, Abe turned the air compressor on again and resumed work at the sewing machine. It was good to keep busy. It kept his mind off missing Alma. If he didn't keep busy, he might want to sleep, and that wasn't a good thing during working hours.

Abe had sewn only a couple of straps together when Ivan Schrock entered his shop.

"What can I do for you, Ivan?" he asked the young man.

Ivan shuffled his feet a few times. "Just dropped by to see if you might need any help."

"Help with what?"

"Here, in the harness shop."

"Have you had any experience with harness making?"

Ivan's face flooded with color. "No, but I'm sure I could learn."

"Don't you have a job working for your daed on his farm?"

"Did have until last night."

Abe tipped his head in question.

"Pop announced during supper that he was getting out of the farming business. Said there wasn't enough money in it anymore and that he's planning to sell off some of our land. Guess he got an offer to work at the lumber store in Charm. My brothers, Delbert and Willard, may work there, too."

"I see." Abe drew in a quick breath. "The thing is, I've barely got enough work to keep me and Martin going right now, so I can't afford to hire another man."

Ivan's gaze dropped to the floor, and he made little circles in the dust with the toe of his boot. "Guess I'll have to look elsewhere for a job. I can't expect to live at home and not pull my share of the load. The only money I'm making is what Cleon gives me whenever I make a few honey deliveries for him. So unless something else turns up, I may end up applying at the lumber store, too."

"Sorry I can't help," Abe said. "If things change and I get real busy, I'll let you know."

"I appreciate that." Ivan pulled the door open and stepped outside.

"Everyone has their troubles these days," Abe muttered as he returned to his work. "Some more than others, but each has his own."

"It's nice we're both working today," Sadie said to Ruth as they stood behind the bakery counter, slipping fresh pastries inside. "Don't get to see you much when we have different hours."

"We see each other every other Sunday during church," Ruth reminded her friend.

"That's true, but there's always so much going on before and after preaching that it's hard to visit."

Sadie placed a tray of banana muffins in the case. "Anything new at your place these days?"

"As a matter of fact, there is," Ruth replied. "This morning we woke up to find a threatening message painted on our barn."

Sadie squinted. "What kind of message?"

"It said 'You'll pay.' "

"That's *baremlich*!"

"I know it's terrible, and that's not all. Mom's garden is dead; someone sprayed weed killer all over the plants."

Sadie's eyes grew wide as she slowly shook her head. "What about the celery you planted for your wedding? Did that get ruined, as well?"

Ruth nodded. "Every last plant is gone, and now we'll have to start over."

"Any idea who did it?"

Just then the door to the bakeshop opened, and Martin stepped in.

"I heard about what happened at your house this morning, and I wanted to see if you were okay," he said, rushing over to the counter.

"I'm fine. Just upset over losing our garden and all the celery we'd planted for the wedding."

"Grace dropped by the harness shop a while ago and told Abe and me what happened." Martin's eyebrows drew together. "She said someone had painted 'You'll pay' on the side of your daed's barn."

"Whoever did that has to be sick in the head," Sadie put in. "I hope the sheriff catches the crazy fellow and puts him in jail."

Martin turned to Sadie. "How do you know it's a man? Could be a woman who's been bothering Ruth's family."

Sadie snorted in an unladylike manner and wagged her finger. "No woman I know could think up all the horrible things that have been done to the Hostettlers."

"Whether it's a man or a woman doesn't really matter. What counts is keeping Ruth safe." Martin leaned across the counter. "Now do you see why I wanted us to get married right away? I want to be there to watch out for you every day."

"I'm okay," Ruth assured him. "No harm came to any of us—just our garden."

"Maybe not today, but what about next time?"

"Let's hope there is no next time," Sadie said.

Deep wrinkles formed in Martin's forehead. "I couldn't stand it if anything happened to you."

Ruth smiled. It was nice to know Martin was concerned about her. Luke never seemed to care so much. "God will watch over us," she said with a nod. "We just need to trust Him and try to not worry."

Chapter 14

It's nice to have things back to normal again," Mom said to Ruth as the two of them hung out the wash one Monday morning in early fall.

Ruth nodded. "I'm glad they are, and I'm hoping it's because the sheriff's been keeping an eye on our place."

"Now we can keep our focus on getting ready for your wedding."

"I'm glad I have today off," Ruth said. "It gives me a chance to wash and dry the material I bought for my wedding dress."

Mom reached into the basket of clean clothes and withdrew a towel. "Have you and Martin decided where you'll live once you're married?" she asked, clipping the towel to the line.

"We'd talked about staying with his folks for a time, but Martin found a little house to rent near Abe's place. It's owned by the Larsons, and Martin plans to talk to them about renting it soon."

"It makes sense that he'd want to live near his job."

Ruth nodded. "And since we'll be living close to Abe's, I can stop in more often to see how Esta and the other kinner are doing."

"Speaking of kinner," Mom said, reaching into the basket for another towel, "Grace says Anna's adjusting well in school, and she seems to like her teacher."

"I figured she would. She's smart and gets along well with others." Ruth smiled. "Even though she's a couple years younger than Esta, they've become best friends. You should see how much fun the girls have playing with Winkie."

"That was a thoughtful thing you did when you gave Esta the

puppy." Mom squeezed Ruth's shoulder. "You'll make a fine *mudder* someday."

"I hope so. I'm also hoping Martin and I will be blessed with kinner right away." Ruth clipped the piece of blue material that would soon be her wedding dress to the clothesline. "I love Martin, and I'm sure he'll make a good daed."

"I think you're probably right about that." Mom reached for the empty basket. "Now that our wash has been hung, I guess I'll head back inside and see about baking some bread." She smiled. "Oh, and speaking of bread, I just want to say that I think Martha's gotten pretty good at baking since she started working for Irene."

"She'll need baking skills if she's ever to marry."

"She's got to find herself a boyfriend first."

"I'm sure she will when the time is right. I hope it's someone as *wunderbaar* as Martin."

"Are you getting nervous about your wedding day?" Abe asked as he cut a piece of leather and handed it to Martin to trim the edges.

"A bit."

"I thought so. You've been acting kind of jittery lately, and you haven't said more than two words since you came to work this morning."

"I've been trying to stay focused on the job at hand."

"More than likely you're thinking about that little woman we'll soon be calling Martin's Ruth."

Martin smiled. "I suppose I have been thinking about her some."

Abe bumped Martin's arm with his elbow. "Some?"

"Okay, more than some. I've been thinking about Ruth a lot these days." Martin sucked in his breath. "I hope I can always keep her safe."

"There are no guarantees of that."

Martin's heart went out to Abe. It had to be hard for him to come to work each morning and stay focused when his heart was full of sorrow and regrets. It couldn't be easy for him to go home every night and father his kids when all he wanted to do was retreat to his room and sleep away the pain.

Abe grabbed a hunk of leather that had been dyed cinnamon

brown and snipped a curved shape with his scissors. "Guess we'd better quit gabbing and get back to work."

Martin nodded. "Harnesses sure don't get made themselves."

"I'll go out and check the clothes drying on the line if you like," Martha said to Mom as they finished washing the dishes after lunch.

"That would be much appreciated. As soon as Ruth comes up from the cellar, she can help you."

Martha grabbed the wicker basket from the utility room and scurried out the back door. As she came around the side of the house, she screeched to a halt. "Someone's shredded the clothes!"

Mom rushed outside, with Ruth right behind her.

"Ach!" Ruth cried. "My material is ruined!"

Mom stood there shaking her head. "I don't understand why anyone would do something like this."

Martha headed for her father's woodworking shop.

"Where are you going?" Mom called after her.

"To tell Dad what's happened."

"He's not there. He had a dental appointment, remember?"

Martha started running. Dad might not be there, but Cleon would be.

Ruth sat on the grass holding what was left of her wedding dress material and rocking back and forth. "Why, Mom? Why did this have to happen now when everything was going so well?"

Mom knelt beside Ruth and gently patted her back. "I don't know, dear one. I just don't know."

A few minutes later, Martha showed up with Cleon at her side.

"Martha said someone ruined the clothes you hung on the line this morning," he said, a look of concern etched on his face.

Ruth choked back a sob. "Every last one has been shredded."

"Look there." Cleon pointed to a set of footprints in the dirt that seemed to be headed in the direction of the Larsons' place. "Whoever did this must have gone that way."

"Surely the Larsons wouldn't be involved in something so terrible," Mom was quick to say. "They're our good friends and neighbors."

"Maybe it was Drew, that rowdy fourteen-year-old grandson of theirs who's been visiting them this week," Martha put in. "Think I'll go over and ask a few questions." She took off running before anyone could stop her.

"Want me to go after her?" Cleon asked, looking at Mom.

She shook her head. "She'll be all right. I'm sure neither the Larsons nor their grandson had anything to do with this."

"Let me help you clean up this mess." Cleon bent down to grab a couple of shredded towels.

"That's okay; you have work to do in the shop. Ruth and I can manage. Right, Ruth?"

Ruth nodded as she stood, but she couldn't seem to find her voice.

"It will be all right," Mom said, stroking Ruth's back. "We'll get more material tomorrow, and then we can start making your wedding dress as planned."

Tears welled in Ruth's eyes. "And then what, Mom? Do we make the dress, wash it, then hang it on the line again so someone can shred it in two?" She let her gaze travel around the yard. "Where was the sheriff when this was done to our clothes? Why wasn't he watching out for us the way he said he would?"

"Sheriff Osborn can't be everywhere," Mom reminded. "He's got other obligations and isn't able to keep an eye on our place all the time. Besides, this is the first attack we've had in many weeks. The sheriff probably figured things were fine and dandy around here since he hasn't heard anything to the contrary."

Ruth stared at her mother as she gulped in deep breaths; then she dashed across the yard and sprinted up the driveway to Grace's house.

Grace had just taken a loaf of bread from the oven when the back door swooshed open and Ruth rushed into the room, wide-eyed and waving a piece of blue material in her hands.

"He's at it again, Grace! Whoever attacked us before has shredded all the clothes on our line, including the material for my wedding dress!"

Grace hurried across the room. "Ach, I'm so sorry," she said, wrapping her arms around Ruth. "This had to be Gary's doing."

"But why?" Ruth sobbed. "Why would he want to ruin the material for my wedding dress?"

Grace shook her head. "It's me he wants to hurt, not you." She swallowed around the lump in her throat. "I'm sorry to say this, but he's hurting my family in the process."

Ruth leaned her head on Grace's shoulder. "How are we going to make it stop?"

"I don't know. I suppose we could talk to the sheriff."

Ruth's mouth dropped open. "Without Dad's permission?"

"If that's what it takes."

"But I thought Sheriff Osborn was supposed to be keeping an eye on our place. If so, it hasn't done much good."

"Maybe he's been too busy or decided to give up patrolling the area because things have quieted down. Since Anna's in school, I'm free to go with you to town. We can see Sheriff Osborn first, and then we'll head over to the fabric outlet and get more material for your wedding dress."

"Are you sure you feel up to it?" Ruth asked with a look of concern. "Maybe it would be better if you stayed home and rested. I can go by myself to see the sheriff."

Grace shook her head. "I'm fine, and I insist on going to town with you."

Ruth offered Grace a weak smile. "Danki. You're a good sister."

By the time Martha arrived at the Larsons' place, she was panting for air. She gave a couple of sharp raps on the front door and leaned against the porch railing, trying to catch her breath.

A few seconds later, Donna Larson opened the door. "What a nice surprise," she said, motioning Martha to come inside.

Martha stepped into the living room. "I hope I'm not interrupting anything, but I—"

"Not at all. Did you come to see how the little sheltie we bought from you is doing?"

"I. . .uh. . .yes, it would be nice to know how the dog's getting along."

"Real well. In fact, my grandson, Drew, is out in the barn feeding it right now."

"Speaking of Drew. . ." Martha cleared her throat a couple of times.

"What about him?"

"I was wondering where he's been all morning."

"Right here. He went to the barn to feed the dog and do a few chores." Donna motioned to the sofa. "Would you like to have a seat?"

Martha shook her head. "I can't stay long. I need to get back home and see how Mom is doing."

"Is something wrong with Judith? She's not sick, I hope."

"Not physically, but she was quite upset when she discovered that all the clean clothes she'd hung on the line had been shredded."

Donna's face blanched. "When did that happen?"

"Sometime this morning after Mom and Ruth hung some clothes out to dry. The material for Ruth's wedding dress was ruined."

"I'm sorry to hear that."

"We found footprints in the dirt that appeared to be heading in the direction of your place."

Donna's forehead creased as she pressed her lips tightly together. "I hope you don't think Drew had anything to do with the clothes being cut."

"Well, I–"

"Drew does tend to be a bit rowdy, but I know he would never do anything like that."

"Like what?" Ray asked as he stepped into the room from the kitchen.

Donna turned to face her husband. "Someone shredded the clothes on the Hostettlers' line this morning. Martha says there are footprints leading from their place to ours. She thinks Drew may have done it."

"I didn't say that–"

Ray's bushy brows puckered as he frowned. "Drew's been in the barn with me all morning, except for the short time he came into the house to pack his suitcase. He'll be going home in the morning," he added, looking at Martha.

"I see."

"I'm sorry about the clothes and all the other things that have been done at your place over the last several months." Ray tapped his foot and stared right at Martha. "I'm watching your place whenever I can, so my advice to you is to quit trying to play detective."

Martha recoiled, feeling like a glass of cold water had been dashed in her face. "Sorry to have troubled you." She turned and rushed out the door.

"I think we should stop at the bakeshop before we go home," Ruth said to Grace as the two of them left the sheriff's office. "Sheriff Osborn didn't offer much help other than to say he's spoken with Gary Walker and that Gary claims he's innocent." She wrinkled her nose. "They don't allow smoking in the offices, but it sure smells like a lot of smokers work there. After a few minutes, I could barely breathe, much less think clearly enough to ask the right questions. Maybe a couple of doughnuts will make us feel better."

"The sheriff does seem to smoke a lot," Grace agreed. "Or at least, someone who works in his office does."

"So should we head to the bakeshop?"

"Don't you want to get the material for your wedding dress first?"

Ruth shook her head. "We can do that after we've had our doughnuts."

"Okay."

They hitched their horse to the rail behind the bakeshop and headed for the building.

Sadie greeted them with a smile. "I'm surprised to see you today, Ruth. I figured with this being your day off you'd be home sewing your wedding dress."

Ruth grunted. "I would be if the material I bought hadn't been torn to shreds."

Sadie frowned. "How'd that happen?"

"Someone shredded all the clothes Mom and I hung on the line this morning."

"Not *someone*," Grace put in. "It was Gary Walker; I'm sure of it."

"Gary Walker, the reporter?"

Ruth and Grace nodded at the same time.

"He was here earlier," Sadie said. "Came in to get a maple bar."

"How long ago was that?" Grace questioned.

"A few minutes after we opened."

Ruth was about to comment, but Sadie cut her off.

"He said he had one thing he needed to do, and then he'd be heading out of town and wasn't sure if or when he might be back again."

"That *one* thing was to destroy the clothes on Mom's line," Grace said with a groan.

Ruth touched Grace's arm. "I hope Gary is gone for good this time and never returns to Holmes County."

Grace released a gusty sigh. "I pray that's true."

Chapter 15

"What's got you looking so happy today?" Abe asked as Martin walked across the room carrying a large sheet of leather. "You've been wearing a silly grin on your face all morning."

Martin's smile widened. "Guess I'm excited about getting married. It won't be long now; just a few more weeks."

Abe's heart clenched when he thought of how happy he'd been as he'd looked forward to his own wedding day. He had never expected to lose Alma at such a young age, and the thought that he might be left to raise six kinner by himself had never even entered his mind.

"Have you found a place to live yet?" Abe asked, knowing he needed to think about something else.

Martin dropped the leather onto one of the workbenches and turned to face Abe. "Found a little house to rent that's not far from here. It's owned by Ray and Donna Larson, the English neighbors who often drive for Ruth's family."

"Didn't realize the Larsons owned any land except their own."

"Oh, jah. They own a couple of places. From what I've heard, they tried to buy Roman's place some time ago, too."

"I do recall Roman mentioning that, but I didn't realize they'd bought other pieces of property." Abe leaned against his desk. "The Larsons seem like pleasant enough folks, and I'm sure they'll make good landlords. Even so, it'll be nice when you and Ruth can have a place of your own."

Martin nodded. "I'd like to build a house like Cleon and Grace's place—one with plenty of space and lots of bedrooms for all the kinner we hope to have someday."

Abe grunted. "After what went on at my house last night, I'd gladly have given you a couple of my *beschwerlich* kinner."

Martin looked stunned. "I've never heard you refer to your kids as troublesome before. What happened last night?"

Abe gave his beard a quick yank. "Right before supper, Esta's puppy piddled all over the kitchen floor." He grimaced. "If I've told her once, I've told her a dozen times not to leave that critter in the house unattended."

"Doesn't your sister monitor things like that?"

"She's supposed to, but with six kinner to look after, not to mention cooking and cleaning, a lot goes on that Sue doesn't seem to know about or catch in time."

"I suppose it would."

"To give you another example of how things went last night, Molly spilled her milk on her plate of stew. Then she started howling and dumped the whole thing onto the floor." Abe shook his head. "Sue was so upset about having to clean the floor again, she broke into tears." Abe moved away from his desk and turned on the air compressor for one of the sewing machines. "I love my kinner, but they sure try my patience at times."

"I guess that's how it is with most parents, although I'm still looking forward to Ruth and me having children."

"And you should be." Abe nodded to the sewing machine. "Guess it's time we quit jawin' and get back to work."

As Ruth and her family sat around the supper table that night, she noticed deep grooves lining her father's forehead. Had Mom told him about the shredded clothes, or was something else troubling him?

"How'd your dental appointment go, Dad?" Ruth asked. "Did you have much pain with that root canal you were supposed to have done?"

Dad groaned. "Seems like all I do these days is go to the dentist. Dr. Wilson had me so numbed up, I couldn't feel a thing." He grimaced. "After the appointment, when I ran into Steven Bates, I felt pain."

"Pain from your tooth?" Martha asked.

Dad shook his head. "Pain because one of my used-to-be loyal customers won't speak to me anymore."

Mom reached over and patted Dad's arm. "Did you say hello to him?"

"I was going to, but he walked by like he didn't even see me." Dad wiped his mouth with a napkin and frowned. "Looked right at me when I came out of the dentist's office, and then he stuck his nose in the air and hurried into the building without so much as a word."

"Do you think he's still angry about those cabinets that fell off your delivery wagon a while ago?" Ruth asked.

Dad gave a quick nod.

"If you two don't mind cleaning up the kitchen without me this evening," Mom said as she pushed away from the table and picked up her dishes, "I think I'll go to bed."

"We don't mind," Ruth was quick to say. It was obvious by the dark circles under Mom's eyes that she was all done in. She probably didn't want to listen to Dad's complaints tonight, either.

Dad's forehead furrowed as he stared at Mom. "Are you feeling *grank?*"

She shook her head. "I'm not sick–just tired. I've been fighting a headache most of the day, too."

"Probably came about because of the clothesline incident," Martha said with a scowl.

Dad's eyebrows shot up. "What clothesline incident?"

Ruth looked up at her mother. "You didn't say anything to Dad about what happened?"

She shook her head.

Dad's face filled with concern. "What happened with the clothesline?"

"Someone shredded all the clothes we hung on the line."

Dad strode across the room to where Mom stood at the sink. "Someone shredded the clothes, and I'm just hearing of it now?"

"I didn't want to worry you, Roman." Mom placed her dishes in the sink. "Besides, I knew what your response would be."

"What's that supposed to mean?"

"I figured you'd probably say it was done by some pranksters. And I was sure you wouldn't bother the sheriff."

Ruth and Martha exchanged glances. When she and Grace had returned home from town, they'd told Martha they'd gone to see the sheriff. Then Martha had told them about her visit with the Larsons. If Dad found out about either incident, he wouldn't approve.

"No point in bothering Sheriff Osborn," Dad said with a look of disdain. "He knows about the other attacks, and what good has that done?" He made an arc with his arm. "Came around asking a bunch of nosy questions and saying he'd keep an eye on the place, yet here we go again with another attack."

Mom shuffled across the room. "I'm going to bed. Are you coming, Roman?"

He shook his head. "I'm not tired. Guess I'll go out to the barn awhile and think things through." He turned toward the table, where Ruth and Martha still sat. "If anything else happens, I want to be the first to know. Do you understand?"

They both nodded.

"Good." He tromped across the room and went out the back door.

Martin felt a sense of excitement as he pulled into the Hostettlers' and tied his horse to the hitching rail. He was anxious to see Ruth and tell her that he'd put a deposit on the house they would be living in after they were married.

Taking the steps two at a time, he knocked on the door. A few seconds later, Martha answered. "*Gut-n-owed*," she said. "Won't you come in?"

"Good evening," Martin replied as he entered the house. "I came to see Ruth."

"I figured as much. She's in the kitchen." Martha stepped onto the porch. "Tell my sister I've gone out to the kennels to check on my dogs," she called over her shoulder.

Martin found Ruth sitting at the kitchen table with a cup in her hands. "Are you busy?" he asked.

She looked up and smiled. "Just having some tea. Would you like to join me?"

"Sounds good, if you've got some cookies to go with it."

"I think that can be arranged." Ruth set the cup down and scurried across the room. A few seconds later she was back with a plate of cookies and a cup for him. "These are ginger cookies from the bakeshop, and they're really good, so help yourself."

"Danki."

"So what brings you by this evening?" she asked after taking a seat.

"Came to see you, of course." He grabbed a cookie and bit into it. "Mmm. . .this is good."

She nodded. "Most everything from the bakeshop is pretty tasty."

"I'll bet the Clemonses are going to miss your help when you quit work after we're married. Speaking of which, I stopped over at the Larsons' this morning and gave them our first month's rent."

"So we're definitely taking the place?"

"Jah, if you're still okay with the idea of living there until I'm able to build our own house."

"I'd be willing to live anywhere with you." Ruth's tone was sincere, and the tender look she gave Martin made him wish he could marry her right then.

He took her hand. "Just a few more weeks, and we'll be husband and wife for the rest of our lives."

"If I can get my wedding dress done in time," she said, dropping her gaze to the table.

"I thought you were going to make it today."

"I was until the material got shredded."

"Huh?"

"Someone shredded all the clothes Mom and I hung on the line this morning—including the material for my wedding dress."

The rhythm of his heartbeat picked up. "Someone deliberately shredded your clothes?"

She nodded. "We found footprints leading from the clothesline into the field that separates our place from the Larsons'. We think whoever did it ran over there."

Martin's jaw clenched as he mulled things over. "If I'd known about this sooner, I would have mentioned it to the Larsons when I went by their place."

Ruth leaned forward with her elbows on the table. "Martha thought it might be Drew, the Larsons' grandson who's been visiting for the past couple of weeks. After we discovered the footprints, she headed over there to ask about it."

"What'd they say?"

"They assured her that Drew hadn't left their property all morning."

"Did Martha believe them?"

Ruth shrugged. "I guess so. She had no reason not to."

"Was Sheriff Osborn notified?"

"Grace and I went to town while Martha was at the Larsons', and we stopped to see the sheriff."

"What'd he say?"

"Just that he'd be keeping a closer eye on things and that we should let him know if anything else happens. Oh, and also that he's questioned Gary Walker and doesn't think he's had anything to do with the attacks."

"That's it? He didn't come out to look at the footprints or check around the place for evidence?"

She shook her head. "If you want my opinion, he hasn't taken anything that's been done to us seriously enough. But don't tell Dad I said so, because as you know, he doesn't want the sheriff involved any more than he already is."

Martin nodded. "So if it wasn't the Larsons' grandson who shredded the clothes, do you have any idea who might have done it?"

"Grace thinks Gary Walker, that reporter, did it. According to Sadie, Gary has left town now, so hopefully things will settle down again."

"Let's hope so," he said, giving her fingers a gentle squeeze. "I can't have my bride wearing shredded wedding clothes."

She offered him a feeble smile. Martin had a hunch that Ruth was a lot more upset than she was letting on. He leaned close to her ear and whispered, "Everything will be all right once we're married; you'll see."

"I'm worried about your mamm," Roman said as he entered the section of the barn where Martha kenneled her dogs and found her kneeling on the floor, brushing the female sheltie.

"You mean because she went to bed early this evening?" she asked, looking up from her job.

He nodded and took a seat on the wooden stool sitting in the corner of the room.

"It's been a trying day, and Mom said she had a headache. I'm sure she'll feel better by morning."

"Sure hope so." He drew in a deep breath and released it with a groan. "I'd really hoped these attacks would end, but it doesn't look like they will until someone is caught."

Martha put Heidi back in her cage and set the brush on the table where she kept her grooming supplies. "How's that ever going to happen, Dad?"

"I don't know." He gave his left earlobe a tug. "Were there any clues near the clothesline?"

She shook her head. "Nothing except for some footprints leading to the Larsons' property."

"The Larsons'?"

"Jah. I'd thought at first it could have been done by their grandson, Drew, but when I went over there to talk to them, I learned that Drew had been there all morning."

"Hmm. . . Sure wish I knew for sure who's been doing all these things."

"I hope you don't still suspect Luke."

"Well, his sunglasses were found on the ground after your mamm's clothesline was cut. And then his straw hat was found near the barn right after that brick was thrown through the kitchen window."

"Those incidents happened last year," she reminded him. "Besides, Luke admitted the items were his and said he had dropped them."

Roman folded his arms. "I didn't believe him then, and I've got my suspicions that the pack of cigarettes I found the day our place got toilet-papered might have belonged to Luke, too."

"Maybe someone's trying to make it look like Luke's the one responsible. Have you thought of that possibility?"

He shrugged. "Guess anything's possible, but Luke more than any of the other suspects on our list has reason to get even with me."

"How do you know the one doing the attacks is trying to get even with you? Maybe it's as Grace says, and the reporter's trying to get even with her."

"I suppose it's possible, but—"

"I don't believe Luke would boldly commit acts of vandalism against his own people, even if he is angry with you."

"Bishop King thinks I'm being too harsh and judgmental where Luke's concerned."

Martha stared at the floor.

"Well," Roman said as he stepped down from the stool, "we won't solve anything by gabbing. I've got some horses that need to be fed."

"And I still need to brush Fritz," Martha said, reaching for the dog brush.

"Don't stay out here working with those dogs too late, you hear?"

"I won't, Dad."

As Roman headed for the horse stalls, he offered up a silent prayer. *Father in heaven, please keep my family safe.*

Chapter 16

You don't look so well. Are you feeling all right?" Cleon asked Grace as they sat at the breakfast table the next morning.

She pushed her spoon around in her bowl. "I'm tired and not so hungry."

"Can I have your piece of toast?" Anna asked. "I'm very hungry this morning."

Grace handed her toast over to Anna. "Do you want more oatmeal, too?"

Anna shook her head. "I think I'll be full after I eat the toast."

Grace offered Anna a feeble smile as she reached for her cup of tea.

"Are you still upset about what happened yesterday?" Cleon asked.

"A little," she replied with a shrug. "But I think everything's going to be okay now that Gary has left town."

"We don't know if he's the one who. . . ." Cleon's voice trailed off when he noticed Anna staring at him. "Let's talk about this later, okay?"

Grace nodded and pushed away from the table. "Right now I need to get lunches fixed for you and Anna so you can be off to work and I can take her to school."

"Would you like me to take her this morning?" he asked.

"I'd better to do it since you have to open the woodworking shop."

"I'm sure your daed's done that already."

Grace shook her head. "While you were out checking on your bee boxes earlier, Dad stopped by the house and said he was taking Mom to see the chiropractor this morning. She complained of a headache yesterday, so he thinks her neck might be out of adjustment."

"Sorry to hear she's hurting." Cleon stood and moved over to the counter where Grace had begun making their lunches. "I could still drive Anna to school and then open the shop after I get back."

"There's no need for you to do that."

Cleon reached for his lunch box. "Guess I'll head to work, then. If you're feeling up to it, stop down during my lunch hour and we can talk some more."

She nodded. "I will."

Cleon gave Grace a kiss on the cheek and started for the door. His fingers had just touched the doorknob when Anna called out to him.

"Have a good day, Papa."

He turned and smiled at her. "You have a good day, too, Anna."

By the time Grace returned from taking Anna to school, she'd noticed some pain in her lower back, so she decided to rest on the couch awhile.

She punched the pillow under her head a few times, trying to find a comfortable position, then finally dozed off.

Sometime later she awoke. Finding the sofa damp, she realized her water had broken. Her stomach cramped, and she groaned. "I think I'd better get to the birthing center as soon as I can."

Figuring her folks were probably back from town by now, Grace headed over to their place to see if Mom would walk down to the phone shed and call someone to give her a ride to the Doughty View Midwifery Center, where many Amish women from their community went to have their babies.

By the time Grace reached her folks' house, the pains had increased. They were still far enough apart that she figured they had plenty of time to get to the birthing center before the baby came.

She opened the back door and stuck her head inside. "Mom? Are you to home?"

No answer.

"Martha, are you here?"

No response.

Grace stepped into the kitchen and leaned against the counter as another contraction gripped her stomach. When it eased, she moved over to the table to take a seat and spotted a note lying there. It was from Martha, letting Mom know that she'd gone to work at Irene's.

"I'd better go down to the woodworking shop and let Cleon know what's happening," Grace murmured. "I don't think this boppli will wait until Mom gets home."

Cleon had just begun sanding a set of cabinets when Grace entered the shop, looking pale and shaken.

"What's wrong?" he asked, moving quickly to her side. "Has there been another attack?"

She shook her head. "I'm in labor."

Cleon's mouth fell open. "Are you sure?"

"My water broke, and I'm having some pretty hard contractions." Grace grasped the edge of his workbench. "Mom and Dad still aren't home, and Martha left a note on Mom's table saying she was going to your mamm's place to work. So I came here to see if you'd call someone to drive me to the birthing center."

Cleon nodded. He led Grace over to a chair behind her dad's desk. "Sit right here. I won't be long."

He made a dash for the door and ran all the way to the phone shed. His fingers trembled as he dialed the Larsons' number, and he felt relief when Donna answered on the second ring.

"Grace is in labor. We need a ride to the Doughty View Midwifery Center," he panted.

"Ray's gone for the day, but I'll be right over," Donna said.

"We'll be waiting for you at Roman's shop."

When Cleon returned to the shop, he found Grace slumped over the desk. "What's happened? Are you okay?"

She lifted her head. "Yes."

"I spoke with Donna, and she's on her way. We should be at the birthing center soon."

"I hope so, because the pains are coming quicker."

"Do you think I should call 9-1-1 and get an ambulance here?"

Grace shook her head. "I'm sure we have enough time to get there before the boppli's born."

"That had better be the case, because I've never delivered a baby before—just a couple of calves."

Grace gritted her teeth, and Cleon figured she was having another contraction. "I don't think you'll have to deliver this baby, so you needn't look so worried," she said.

A horn honked. "That must be Donna." Cleon helped Grace out the door and into Donna's car. "I'd better ride in the back with my wife," he told Donna.

She nodded. "No problem."

They'd only gone a short distance when Donna's car overheated and she had to pull onto the shoulder of the road. "I told Ray to check under the hood the last time he filled my car with gas," Donna mumbled. "I suspected there was a leak in the radiator, but he said he would check things out and take care of it if there was a problem."

Grace moaned and clutched the front of Cleon's shirt. "The pains are coming faster."

Cleon's mouth went dry. Was he going to have to deliver this baby?

As Ruth headed down the road toward home, her thoughts went to Martin. In just a few weeks they would become husband and wife, and she could hardly wait. She planned to work on her wedding dress this evening, and things were coming together. Cleon's sister, Carolyn, would provide candles for the tables, and Martha and Sadie had agreed to be her attendants. Martin's brother, Dan, and the bishop's son, Toby, would be his attendants.

Ruth's thoughts were halted when she spotted Donna Larson's car stopped along the side of the road with the hood up and a curl of steam pouring out. Donna stood beside the car shaking her head.

Ruth guided her horse and buggy to the shoulder of the road, climbed down, and hurried over to Donna's car. "What's the problem? Did your car overheat?"

"Yes, and your sister's in the backseat, about to have her baby." Donna grimaced. "I left my cell phone at home, so I can't even call for help. I was hoping another car would come by, but you're the first person I've seen since the car overheated."

Ruth hurried around to the back of the car and jerked the door open. She was surprised to see Cleon there, red-faced, wide-eyed, and hunched over Grace. "Don't push, Grace. Not yet," he instructed.

Grace's face twisted in obvious pain. "It's coming, Cleon. The boppli is coming."

Ruth's knees nearly buckled as she struggled against a wave of dizziness. She couldn't just stand here like a ninny; she had to do something to help her sister. The only experience she'd had with birthing was watching one of their barn cats deliver her kittens, so she wasn't sure what to do.

Cleon didn't seem to notice Ruth as he continued to coach Grace. "Easy now. We're almost there. That's it. . . . I can see the head. . . . Okay now, push!"

Unable to watch, yet reluctant to look away, Ruth felt her eyes mist as she witnessed the miracle of birth. A few seconds later, she heard a lusty cry, and a newborn babe lay across her sister's stomach.

"It's a buwe!" Cleon cried. "We have ourselves a boy!"

Grace lay exhausted against the seat as she stroked her son's downy dark head. "*Gott is gut*," she murmured. "Jah, God is good."

Chapter 17

As Grace settled herself against the cleaned sofa cushions, snuggling a tiny bundle of joy in her arms, she reflected on all that had transpired during the last twenty-four hours. She'd fully intended to have her baby at the Doughty View Midwifery Center. Instead, she'd ended up giving birth in the backseat of Donna Larson's car, with Cleon acting as midwife. After Ruth went to the nearest phone shed to call for help, Grace and the baby had been taken by ambulance to the hospital in Millersburg to be checked over. Then Ruth had gone home to tell her folks and Martin's family the news and to see that Anna was picked up from school. This morning, Cleon had called Ray Larson to pick them up at the hospital, and now Grace and the baby were home where they belonged.

"Come say hello to your little bruder," Grace said, motioning for Anna to take a seat beside her.

The child hovered near the sofa, wearing an expectant look on her face, but she finally sat down. "He's sure tiny and red in the face. What's his name?" she asked, leaning close to the baby.

"Don't put your face so near to his," Cleon said as he took a seat on the other side of Grace. "You've had a cold, and I don't want you giving it to the boppli."

Anna scrunched up her nose. "That was last week, Papa. I'm feelin' fine now."

"Even so, I'd prefer you not breathe any germs on the baby."

Grace pursed her lips. "Cleon, I don't think—"

He held up his hand. "She can look at the boppli without putting her face right up to his."

Grace figured Cleon was just being overprotective and would soon relax, so she decided it was best not to make an issue of it.

"What's his name?" Anna asked again, looking up at Grace.

"Daniel," Cleon said before Grace could respond. He reached over and touched the baby's dark head. "Daniel Jacob Schrock."

Anna's forehead wrinkled. "Is he gonna cry all the time? Esta said her little sister, Molly, cried so much when she was a boppli that Esta had to stuff cotton in her ears so she could sleep."

"Some babies do cry a lot, but hopefully Daniel won't cry much at night," Grace said.

"Can I hold him?"

"Yes."

"No!"

Cleon and Grace had spoken at the same time, and Anna appeared confused.

"He's too little for you to hold yet," Cleon said.

Again, Grace fought the urge to dispute what he'd said. She didn't want Anna to think she was usurping Cleon's authority. Except for Carl Davis, Anna's English grandfather, Cleon was the only father the child had ever known. They had developed a good relationship over the last several months, and Grace didn't want anything to spoil it.

Grace patted Anna's arm. "You can hold him when he's a little bigger, okay?"

Anna nodded, but her eyes were downcast. She sat a few seconds, then hopped off the couch.

"Where are you going?" Grace called.

"To my room to play with my faceless doll. At least she's not too little for me to hold."

Grace turned to Cleon and was about to comment on his behavior toward Anna when Ruth stepped into the room, followed by Martha, Mom, and Dad.

Anxious to see her nephew, Ruth rushed into the room ahead of her family. "What a sweet little bundle of joy," she exclaimed as she approached the sofa.

Grace smiled. "Danki. We think we'll keep him."

In a confused babble of voices, everyone asked Grace how she was doing, how much the baby weighed, and what name had been chosen for him.

"His name is Daniel Jacob," Cleon said. "He weighs eight pounds, four ounces, and Grace is doing fine."

"A nice, healthy size." Mom extended her hands. "May I hold my first grandson?"

Grace looked over at Cleon as if waiting for his approval. When he nodded, she handed the baby to Mom.

"It feels so good to hold him," Mom said as she took a seat in the rocking chair. "Makes me think of the days when you girls were *bopplin*." She smiled at Ruth. "Isn't he a fine-looking baby?"

"He certainly is," Ruth replied. "And when you get tired of holding him, it'll be my turn."

"I'll hold him after that." Martha turned to Dad. "Guess you'll have to go last."

He hunkered down next to the rocking chair. "Makes no never mind to me. Whenever I hold a boppli, they usually start crying."

Mom's gaze went to the ceiling. "You know that's not true, Roman. As I recall, our girls used to fall asleep as soon as you picked them up."

"Humph! That's not much better–saying I was so boring I put our girls to sleep."

"That's not what I meant, Roman."

"Where's Anna?" Ruth asked, changing the subject. "I figured she would be the first in line to hold her little bruder."

"Anna's upstairs in her room. She said she wanted to play with her faceless doll," Grace was quick to say.

"She's probably pretending she has her own boppli." Mom placed the baby over her shoulder and patted his back. "I remember when Martha was born, Grace and Ruth played with their dolls and pretended they were little *midder*."

Cleon reached for Grace's hand. "Are you getting tired? Would you like to go to our room and rest awhile?" he asked.

She shook her head. "I'm fine."

Ruth could see the weariness on her sister's face, and she felt concern. "Maybe it would be best if we went home and let Grace and the baby get settled in," she suggested. "The rest of us can hold the boppli tomorrow."

"You're right," Mom said as she handed the baby to Ruth. "You can put this little guy back in his mamm's arms, and we'll be on our way." She smiled. "I've got a big batch of stew simmering on the stove, so I'll have Martha bring some over for your supper."

"Danki, that'd be nice," Grace replied with a yawn. "It'll be a few days before I feel up to doing much cooking."

"We'll chip in to help wherever we're needed." Ruth stared down at baby Daniel, and a lump formed in her throat. Oh, how she longed to be a mother.

"Did you hear that Grace had her baby yesterday afternoon?" Martin asked Abe as he stepped into the harness shop and hung his hat on a wall peg near the door.

"Nope, I hadn't heard that. What'd she have?"

"A boy, and he was born in the backseat of Donna Larson's car." Martin moved over to the desk, where Abe sat making a list of supplies he needed. "Ruth came over to my folks' place last night and told us about it."

Abe's eyebrows lifted. "How'd that happen?"

"Donna was giving them a ride to the Doughty View Midwifery Center, and her car overheated. I guess Cleon was in the backseat with Grace when the boppli decided it couldn't wait to be born."

"Whew!" Abe let out a whistle. "I can't imagine what it must have been like for Cleon to deliver his own son. I'd have been a nervous wreck."

"Ruth was on her way home from work and spotted Donna's car. When she stopped to see if there was a problem, she discovered Grace in the backseat about to give birth." Martin leaned on Abe's desk and smiled. "I can't wait until Ruth and I are married and can start our own family."

"You might change your mind about that when you have to change dirty *windle* and are kept up all night with a colicky baby." Abe grunted. "Never liked either of those things, but then I—"

Abe's oldest son, Gideon, entered the shop. "Aw, Papa, do you have to work today?" he grumbled. "It's Saturday, and I was hopin' we could go fishing."

"Not today, son." Abe motioned to the stack of papers on his desk. "I've got supplies to order and bills that need to be paid."

Gideon kicked a scrap of leather lying on the floor and grunted. "If you're not workin', you're sleepin'. If you're not sleepin', you're workin'."

"I've got to make a living," Abe said. "Otherwise there'll be no food on our table."

Gideon shuffled out the door with his head down and shoulders slumped.

Abe looked up at Martin. "See what I mean? Being a daed isn't all sugar and cream. Fact is, there are times when it's more like vinegar and sauerkraut. 'Course, I wouldn't trade my kinner for anything. On their good days, they can be a real blessing."

Martin moved over to the cupboard where the dye was kept. One thing he knew: When he became a father, he would never be too busy to spend time with his kinner.

Chapter 18

I can't believe Ruth is getting married today," Grace said as she placed a dish of oatmeal in front of Cleon. "It seems like only yesterday that you and I were preparing for our wedding."

He smiled. "Are you sure you're feeling up to going? It's only been a few weeks since the boppli was born, and I know you're still pretty wrung out."

"I'll be fine," she said, taking a seat across from him. "There's no way I'm going to miss my sister's wedding."

Cleon nodded. "If you get tired or Daniel gets fussy, you can always come home and rest, since the wedding will be at your folks' place."

"That's true." Grace looked over at Anna, who sat in the chair beside her. "Are you excited about attending your aunt Ruth's wedding?"

Anna merely shrugged in reply.

"There'll be lots of good food served during the wedding meal."

"Will Esta be there?"

"I'm sure she will, and the rest of Abe's family, too."

"Will Daniel be going?"

"Of course. We sure wouldn't leave him home by himself." Cleon frowned at Anna.

Anna reached for a piece of toast. "Can I take my doll along? Then I'll have a boppli to bring to the wedding, too."

"That's fine with me." Grace pushed her chair away from the table. "Speaking of babies, I hear your little brother fussing in the other room, so I'd best tend to his needs."

"Want me to get him?" Cleon asked.

"I'd better do it. He's probably ready to eat by now." Grace smiled. "And then we'd better hurry or we'll be late to the wedding."

As Ruth listened to Bishop King deliver the main wedding sermon, her hands turned sweaty, and her mouth felt so dry she could barely swallow. It seemed as if she'd waited her whole life for this moment. Becoming a wife and mother was what she had dreamed about ever since she was a girl. She glanced over at Martin, who sat across from her, and the rhythm of her heartbeat picked up when he smiled. Today was their day—a perfect day with clear blue skies and plenty of sunshine. Their families and friends were here to see them become husband and wife. There had been no more attacks on Ruth's family for the past several weeks, and despite the swirling sensation of excitement she felt in her stomach, her soul was filled with peace.

" 'Wives, submit yourselves unto your own husbands, as unto the Lord. For the husband is the head of the wife, even as Christ is the head of the church: and he is the saviour of the body,' " the bishop quoted from Ephesians 5:22–23.

He paused and said, "We have two people who have agreed to enter the state of matrimony—Martin Gingerich and Ruth Hostettler. If anyone here has objection, he has this opportunity to make it known."

Ruth breathed a sigh of relief when everyone in the room remained quiet. Not that she thought anyone would really protest.

"Since there are obviously no objections, you may come forth in the name of the Lord," the bishop said.

Martin and Ruth left their seats and stood before him.

As Ruth stared into Martin's eyes and answered each of the bishop's questions, her heart swelled with joy and hope for the future—a future as Mrs. Martin Gingerich.

After the wedding service, Martha took a seat at the table with the others from the wedding party and glanced across the room. Her breath caught in her throat when she spotted Luke sitting with a group of young men.

He smiled and seemed to be joking around, so she was fairly certain he wasn't upset about Ruth marrying Martin. Funny thing, though, she hadn't seen him hanging around any other Amish women since he and Ruth broke up. She figured either Luke had decided he wasn't interested in courting right now, or he was seeing some English girl on the sly.

I don't suppose he'd be interested in anyone like me, she thought ruefully.

"You're awfully quiet." Sadie poked Martha's arm. "Are you upset because Ruth will be moving out of your house and settling into a new home with Martin?"

Martha frowned. "Of course not. I'm happy that both of my sisters have found good husbands."

"Martin and Ruth didn't have a very long courtship, did they?" Before Martha could comment, Sadie added, "Then there's me and Toby. He's been courting me over a year now, and still no proposal of marriage. I'm beginning to wonder if he'll ever ask me to marry him."

"Maybe he's having too much fun courting and doesn't feel ready to be tied down to marriage yet."

Sadie grunted. "Jah, well, if he doesn't make up his mind soon, I might just look for another fellow."

Martha blinked. "Do you have someone else in mind?"

Sadie shook her head. "There's no one I'd rather be with than Toby."

Martha glanced at Luke again. He wore his Dutch-bobbed hair a little longer than it should be, but she thought he looked appealing. The jaunty way he held his head whenever he spoke caused Martha's heart to race and made her wish she could be his girlfriend.

"How are things going with your business these days?" Sadie asked, changing the subject.

"Not so well." Martha sighed. "Flo still isn't pregnant, and neither is Heidi. As soon as I have enough money saved up from my job working for Cleon's mother, I hope to buy a couple more dogs."

"Have you considered offering boarding services?"

Martha nodded. "I have. In fact, I mentioned that idea to my daed not long ago, and he said he would think about it."

Sadie smiled. "Now that Ruth's married and won't be returning to the bakeshop, you might consider applying there if you need more money."

"Between my part-time job working for Irene and taking care of my dogs, I'm pretty busy these days. But I'll keep the bakeshop in mind."

"Don't wait too long to decide, because I'm sure the Clemonses will find a replacement for Ruth as soon as they can."

Martha shrugged. She caught sight of Luke and two other young men leaving their places at the table and heading out the door. She figured they were probably in need of some fresh air or wanted to visit without having to talk over the loud voices in the room. She was tempted to follow but knew that wouldn't be proper. Besides, she was one of Ruth's attendants, and her place was right here.

"Mama, is it all right if I spend the night at Esta's?" Anna asked as she tugged on Grace's dress sleeve.

"Jah, sure, that'll be fine," Cleon said before his wife could respond.

Grace turned in her chair and gave him an icy stare. "Don't I have anything to say about this?"

"I figured you'd be okay with the idea," Cleon said. "It'll be nice for us to have a quiet evening alone with Daniel."

Grace's eyes narrowed into tiny slits. Cleon knew she wasn't happy about what he'd said—but didn't she realize how important it was for them to have quality time with the baby without Anna being there asking questions and begging to hold her little brother?

"Is it all right if I go home with Esta?" Anna asked, giving Grace's sleeve another tug.

"Does Esta's daed know about this?" Grace questioned.

Anna nodded. "He said it's fine with him, and so did Esta's aunt Sue."

"All right, you may go." Grace squeezed her daughter's shoulder. "Grandma Schrock's holding baby Daniel right now, so I'm free to walk you home to get your nightgown and a change of clothes for tomorrow."

Cleon shook his head. "You look tired, Grace. I think we should go home now. You can pack Anna's things, and I'll bring her back over here so she's ready whenever Abe says it's time for his brood to go."

Grace didn't argue, and he felt relief. She did look done in.

Cleon pushed his chair aside and stood. "I'll get the boppli from my mamm, and we'll be on our way."

"Everything's going well today, wouldn't you say?" Martin asked Ruth as they sat at their special corner table eating a piece of wedding cake.

She smiled. "All our guests seem to be having a good time."

He thumped his stomach and grinned. "Can't remember the last time I ate this much food."

Ruth nodded. "There's so much chicken, mashed potatoes, dressing, gravy, salads, and vegetables, not to mention all the desserts and cakes. This morning I felt so nervous I could barely eat breakfast. But I've more than made up for it this afternoon."

Martin glanced across the room and spotted Abe sitting at a table with his boys. His shoulders were slumped, and he wore a forlorn expression, making Martin wonder if the man wasn't having a good time. Poor Abe still missed Alma and was probably thinking about their wedding day. It had to have been hard for him to come here today. Abe was not only Martin's boss, but a good friend. Martin was sure Abe had come to the wedding to let him know that he approved of his marriage.

Martin was about to excuse himself to speak with Abe when—*kaboom!*—an explosion sounded from outside, causing the windows to vibrate.

"Wh-what was that?" Ruth's eyes widened, and her mouth hung slightly open.

"I don't know, but I'm going to find out."

Martin, along with several other men, rushed outside. A quick glance around the yard revealed that one of the portable outhouses set up to accommodate the guests had been blown up.

"Talk about starting your marriage off with a bang." Toby slapped Martin's back. "Looks like some of our *yuchend* thought it would be fun to shake things up a bit."

Everyone laughed, and someone pointed to what was left of the outhouse. Martin was fairly certain it had been blown up by one of his youthful buddies as a prank. Well, he wasn't going to let it rile him. With a chuckle and a shrug, he headed back inside to carry on with the wedding meal. Someone else could clean up the mess.

Chapter 19

Ruth's heart hammered so hard she feared it might burst open. "What was it?" she asked when Martin returned to the house. "What caused that horrible noise?"

"It's nothing to worry about," he said, taking a seat beside her. "Someone blew up one of the outhouses."

"What?" Ruth touched his arm. "Oh, Martin, have the attacks on my family begun again?"

"I don't think so. Some of the fellows were outside snickering, so I'm pretty sure they had something to do with the outhouse blowing up."

"How can you be so sure? I mean, with all the other things that have gone on—"

He smiled and took her hand. "It wasn't an attack—just some tomfoolery going on with some of the single fellows who wanted to be sure we remembered our special day."

"I'll always remember our wedding day." Ruth's voice was thick with emotion. "We sure didn't need some *verhuddelt* friends of yours blowing up an outhouse in order to make this day special."

"Someday when we're old and gray, we'll look back on our wedding day and laugh about what those mixed-up friends of mine did." Martin chuckled. "Just think what a fun time we'll have telling our kinner and *kinskinner* about it."

She nudged him in the ribs. "You might have fun telling that story, but I sure won't. I don't think it's one bit funny."

"I agree with Ruth," Martha said as she took her seat again. "What if someone had been using that outhouse when it blew up? They could have been seriously hurt."

"I wonder what Dad has to say about all this." Ruth glanced around the room, trying to locate her parents. "I don't see him or Mom anywhere."

"Mom's in the kitchen making sure everything's going okay," Martha said. "Dad's out on the porch, talking to Bishop King."

"I think they're discussing the outhouse incident," Toby put in as he joined the group at the table. "I told my daed that I'd seen Luke hanging around the outhouses when I went outside for some fresh air. Makes me wonder if he wasn't the one responsible for the explosion."

Martin's forehead wrinkled. "Why would Luke do something like that?"

"You don't know?" Toby asked.

He shook his head.

Toby motioned to Ruth. "You stole his girl. Maybe he's trying to get even."

Ruth shook her head. "Martin didn't *steal* me. I broke up with Luke before Martin asked if he could court me."

"Well, there you go. Luke's probably mad because you dumped him." Toby grunted. "That fellow's been acting strange for some time now. I wouldn't put anything past him."

Martha glared at Toby. "You have no proof that Luke blew up the outhouse or that he wants to get even with Ruth for breaking up with him." She breathed in deeply. "Besides, it's not your place to judge."

Toby squinted at her and dropped into a chair. "That may be true, but my daed's the bishop, and if he thinks Luke needs to be questioned, then he'll do it."

"So what do you think about that outhouse being blown apart? Do you think it's another attack on our family?" Roman asked the bishop as they took seats in wicker chairs on the porch.

Bishop King folded his arms and stared out at the yard. "From what Toby said, it appeared to be a prank. Probably done by some of Martin's friends, hoping to make him remember this day."

"Humph!" Roman said with a huff. "I can think of better ways to help a friend remember his wedding than to scare all the guests half out of their wits."

The bishop pulled his fingers through the ends of his lengthy beard. "I remember on my wedding day, some of my friends took the wheels off my buggy and then set the rig on wooden blocks. I soon discovered that they'd also stuffed a bunch of straw inside." He chuckled. "Peggy and I were plucking straw out of our clothes for weeks after that."

Roman smiled despite his concerns over the outhouse incident. Maybe it had just been a prank. He certainly hoped that was all it was.

As Abe headed down the road with his children and Anna in tow, he felt a sense of relief. He had decided to leave the Hostettlers' right after he'd finished eating the meal. It had been hard enough to sit through the wedding and watch Martin and Ruth say their vows, and he had no desire to stay all afternoon and into the evening as many other folks probably would do.

"Danki for letting Anna come home with us," Esta said as she snuggled against Abe's side. "We're gonna play with Winkie as soon as we get home. Right, Anna?"

Anna, who sat beside Esta, lifted the faceless doll in her lap. "I'd like to play with our dolls, too."

"Okay," Esta said with an agreeable nod.

Abe smiled. It was good to see his daughter smiling again. Abe hoped Martin realized how fortunate he was to be getting such a fine woman for his wife. Ruth had a heart full of love; she'd shown that the day of Alma's funeral, when she'd comforted Esta, and then later when she'd given Esta the puppy.

Abe heard a grunt and glanced over his shoulder. Gideon sat in the backseat with his shoulders slumped and his head down. He hadn't said a word since they'd left the Hostettlers' place. Josh sat next to Gideon, leaning against the seat with his eyes closed. It was obvious that he'd fallen asleep. Abe's other three children had ridden in another buggy with Abe's sister, since there wasn't room for them all in one rig.

"Say, Gideon," Abe called over his shoulder, "how would you like to go fishing with me and Martin soon?"

No response.

"We've been talking about taking next Saturday off, since work's slowed up a bit. We'll do some fishing at the pond. What do you say?"

Gideon grunted.

"Would you like to go or not?"

"Maybe."

Abe smiled and shook the reins as the horse took them up a small hill. A day of fishing might do him and Gideon both some good.

Cleon took a seat on the sofa next to Grace and studied his son's precious face. The baby had just finished nursing and looked relaxed and sleepy.

"He's a good baby, jah?" Cleon looked over at Grace and smiled.

She nodded. "Anna was a good boppli, too."

"I wouldn't know about that since I wasn't around to see her as a baby."

She flinched as if she'd been slapped. "As you know, I missed most of my daughter's babyhood."

"Then how do you know she was a good baby?"

"I was with Anna for her first six months. During that time, she hardly ever cried unless she was hungry or needed her windle changed."

Cleon stroked the baby's soft cheek with his thumb. "The Lord was good to give us this boppli to raise. Maybe it'll help make up for the years you lost when Anna's English grandparents took her away."

Grace shook her head. "I'm glad we have Daniel, but it doesn't bring back the years I missed with Anna."

"No, I don't suppose, but–" Cleon halted his words, realizing it would do no good to rehash the past. It couldn't be changed. They had a future to look forward to now. Reaching his arms toward the baby, he said, "How about I hold the little fellow for a while?"

She lifted the baby over her shoulder and patted him on the back. "He needs to burp first."

"Jah, okay."

The minutes ticked away on the battery-operated clock across the room.

"What's wrong with him? Why hasn't he let loose with a burp?" Cleon asked, feeling a sense of impatience.

"He will when he's ready."

Several more minutes went by, and finally Daniel released a loud burp.

Cleon held out his arms again, but then Daniel started hiccupping.

Grace continued to pat the little fellow's back, and Cleon's impatience grew stronger.

"Can't you do something to make him stop?"

She compressed her lips and glared at him. "I'm doing the best I can. Can't you learn to have more patience?"

"You don't have to be so snappish. I just want to hold my son."

"He's my son, too, and right now he needs his mother." She continued to pat the baby's back, rubbing her fingers up and down his spine between each little thump.

"Want me to try?"

She shook her head.

"Maybe you're not firm enough with your touch."

With an exasperated sigh, Grace handed the baby to Cleon and stood.

"Where are you going?"

"Out to the kitchen to fix him a bottle of warm water. That always stopped Anna's hiccups."

Grace left the room, and Cleon continued with the pat-rub-pat-rub method she had begun, but Daniel's hiccups seemed to increase. By the time Grace returned to the living room, Cleon was ready to turn the baby over to her again.

She took a seat in the rocking chair, and Cleon placed the baby in her lap. After a few ounces of water, the hiccupping subsided.

Cleon was about to ask if he could hold Daniel again, but Grace spoke first.

"There's something I've been wanting to speak with you about, Cleon."

"What's that?"

"It's about Anna and the way things are between you."

His forehead wrinkled. "What's that supposed to mean?"

"Strained, like they were before when you were upset with me for not telling you about my past."

"I forgave you for that," Cleon said, feeling his defenses rise. "And I asked you and Anna to forgive me for the way I'd treated you both."

She nodded. "I know you did, and you were an attentive father to Anna until Daniel was born. Now you've started giving him all your attention and treating her like she doesn't matter."

"I haven't done that."

"Jah, you have. It's obvious to me that Anna's feeling your rejection, which might cause her to resent her little brother."

Cleon grunted. "I think you're making more out of this than there is."

"No, I'm not. I really believe that—"

He jumped up and started for the door.

"Where are you going?"

"I don't feel like arguing with you, Grace. I think I'll go over to your folks' and see if they need help with anything."

Cleon heard the rocking chair squeak and figured she had started rocking the baby, but he didn't turn around. So much for a quiet, pleasant evening with just the three of them.

Chapter 20

I'm so *uffgschafft*," Ruth said a couple of days later as she followed Martin into their little rental house.

Martin set the box he'd been carrying onto the kitchen counter and grinned. "I'm real excited, too."

"I like it here." Her nose twitched. "Even if it does smell like *schtinkich* paint."

"Jah," he agreed, "but it won't take long for the smelly odor to settle down."

"I'm looking forward to setting out my hope chest items, as well as all the wedding gifts we received."

He pulled her into his arms and kissed her tenderly. "You make me feel so happy. I'm thankful God brought us together."

Ruth nestled against his chest and sighed. "I hope He gives us many good years together."

He nuzzled her cheek with the tip of his nose. "Many good years and lots of kinner to love."

"Jah."

He pulled away slowly. "As nice as this feels, we have some work to do if we're going to make it over to my folks' for supper by six o'clock."

"Your mamm said she was planning to fix your favorite meal—stuffed cabbage rolls." She poked him playfully in the ribs. "And I wouldn't want to make you late for that."

He chuckled and gave her another hug.

"We won't get any work done that way."

He surveyed the small kitchen, and his face sobered. "Both of our families were a big help in getting our things moved over here yesterday, and then your daed brought us that load of wood for our stove last night. I think we ought to have them all over for a meal sometime after the first of the year."

"Since I'm no longer working at the bakeshop, I'll be home all day and will have time to cook up a storm." Ruth smiled. "I think it would be good if we had Abe and his family over soon, too. It would be a nice break for Sue."

Martin drew her into his arms again. "You're such a thoughtful fraa. Have I told you how much I love you?"

"Only about a hundred times since our wedding."

He snickered. "But that was two days ago. I'm going to need to say it at least a hundred more times before this day is out."

"And I'll never tire of hearing it," she murmured.

"Are you busy, Dad?" Martha asked as she stepped into her father's woodworking shop. "I'd like to ask you a question."

He looked up from the cabinet he was sanding and smiled. "I've got work to do, but I'm never too busy for you."

She moved quickly across the room, stopping briefly to say hello to Cleon, who was staining a rocking chair.

"What would you like to ask me?" Dad gave the cabinet door a few good swipes with the sandpaper he held.

"It's about my dog business."

He chuckled. "Why am I not surprised?"

"Guess I do talk about my dogs quite a lot."

"That's okay. I know how important they are to you."

She showed him the newspaper in her hand. "I spotted an ad for a pair of cocker spaniels in the paper this morning. Now that I've made some money working for Cleon's mamm, I thought I might buy them. Just wondered what you thought of the idea."

Dad shrugged. "Guess it would be all right, but remember, your other dogs haven't made you any money."

She nodded. "I know, and I'm thinking of selling Flo or trading her at one of the dog auctions."

"Suit yourself. She's your dog."

Martha stared at the newspaper as she contemplated how to bring up her other idea.

"You got something else on your mind?"

"Jah."

"Then raus mit–out with it."

"I was wondering if you've thought about the idea of me boarding some dogs. That might give me a steady income."

His eyebrows drew together. "Boarding dogs would mean building more kennels, and that would be a lot of work."

"I know, but I'll help in whatever way I can."

"I'd be willing to build the extra kennels she'll need," Cleon put in.

Dad shook his head. "I can't ask you to do that. You've already got too much going, what with working for me, your beekeeping business, and helping Grace with those two young ones of yours."

"I could ask Martin about helping," Martha said.

"He's newly married and has a job working for Abe," Dad said.

"How about Luke? He's good with wood, and–"

"Absolutely not!" Dad's face turned red, and a muscle on the side of his cheek began to pulsate. "I don't want that troublesome fellow anywhere near you."

"But, Dad–"

He waved the piece of sandpaper in front of her face. "Do not ask Luke Friesen for anything; you hear?"

She nodded as a lump formed in her throat. There'd been no proof that Luke was responsible for any of the things that had happened to them. In fact, everything had been quiet around their place for some time.

"I don't think you need to board any dogs right now," Dad said. "Maybe in a few months, I'll reconsider. By then, I might have the time to build some extra kennels."

Martha opened her mouth to say something more but decided against it. Instead, she whirled around and rushed out the door.

"That was a great meal, Mom." Martin leaned back in his chair and thumped his stomach. "Danki for fixing my favorite dish."

Mom nodded and looked over at Ruth, who sat in the chair beside her. "If you want to keep my son happy, you'll need to fix stuffed cabbage rolls at least once a week."

"Or more," Martin said with a chuckle.

"I'll be happy to fix cabbage rolls anytime Martin wants, but I doubt I can make them as tasty as yours," Ruth said. "Do you have a special recipe, and if so, would you be willing to share it with me?"

"Jah, sure, only I don't have the recipe written down. It's right here." Mom tapped the side of her head and smiled.

Martin's dad nodded. "My wife's a good cook. Most everything she makes comes from memory."

"Maybe someday I'll have all of Martin's favorite recipes memorized." Ruth looked over at Martin and gave him one of her prettiest smiles.

Martin grinned, thumped his stomach again, and looked over at his mother. "So, Mom, what's for dessert?"

As Martin and Ruth drove home in their buggy, her head lolled against the seat, and her eyes drifted shut.

"You sleepy?" he asked, reaching over to take her hand.

She yawned. "A little."

"It was a good supper we had, jah?"

"Uh-huh."

"Did you get that recipe for stuffed cabbage rolls written down?"

"It's right in here." Ruth tapped the black handbag lying in her lap.

"When do you plan to make them?"

Her eyes snapped open. "Martin Gingerich, your belly's still full of cabbage rolls and dutch apple pie, and you're already asking when there will be more?"

He snickered. "It's a good thing I've never had a problem with gaining too much weight."

She poked him gently in the ribs. "You might have a problem if you keep eating the way you did tonight."

"I doubt it. Ever since I was a boy, I've been able to eat whatever

I want without gaining a bunch of weight."

"Well, there's a first time for everything."

He shrugged. "Would you still love me if I were chubby?"

"Jah."

"If my hair started falling out and I went completely bald, then would you love me?"

"Of course."

"How about if I jabbed myself with a knife while cutting a hunk of leather and got a nasty scar that made me look ugly. Would you love me then?"

Ruth pursed her lips. "You shouldn't even tease about such things. Just thinking about you getting hurt makes me feel grank."

He leaned closer and nuzzled her neck. "Sorry."

She pointed to the hill up ahead, and the buggy jostled. "You'd better keep your mind on your driving, or you might run off the road."

"All right, I'll be good." He gave her a quick wink. "For now, at least."

Ruth smiled as she relaxed against the seat and snuggled under the warm quilt tucked around her legs. This stretch of road was beautiful during the day—with plenty of trees on both sides, well-kept farms, and fields of fresh-cut hay along the way. During the night, however, she couldn't see much. But that was okay. She and Martin were together, and that was all that mattered.

Ruth's head drooped against Martin's shoulder. She was nearly asleep when he nudged her and said, "We're home."

She shivered and rubbed her hands briskly over her arms. "Guess I should have worn a coat instead of my shawl tonight. The quilt kept my legs warm, but not the upper half of my body. I can almost taste the cold."

"Never heard it put quite that way before." He smiled. "If the weather keeps getting colder, we'll soon have snow."

"Maybe you should forget about your plans to go fishing with Abe tomorrow," Ruth said. "I sure wouldn't want to fish in weather this chilly."

"Abe promised Gideon he could go, and I'm looking forward to it, as well."

She shrugged. Truth was, she'd hoped she and Martin could spend his day off together—maybe get the house organized.

Martin hopped down from the buggy, then came around to Ruth's side and helped her down. "I'll get an armload of wood and bring it up to the house as soon as I put the horse away. It'll be good to have a nice warm fire this evening."

"Okay. See you inside." Ruth sprinted to the house, where she lit the gas lamps to dispel the darkness. It was almost as chilly inside as it was outside, so she grabbed a dahlia-patterned quilt from the sofa and wrapped it around her shoulders, then took a seat.

The gas lamps sputtered and hissed but brought her no warmth. "What we need is a fire," she murmured.

Martin entered the house a short time later, but his hands were empty.

"Where's the wood you said you would bring in?" she asked.

He shrugged, then shook his head. "It's gone."

"How can it be gone?"

"I don't know, but it is—every last piece."

Her forehead wrinkled. "Did you look all around?"

He nodded. "There was no wood in sight, but I did see some large tire marks near where the pile used to be. I think whoever took it might have been driving a truck."

Ruth's heart pounded. "Oh, Martin, you don't suppose whoever took it is the same person who did all the horrible things at my folks' place, do you?"

Martin took a seat on the sofa beside her. "More than likely it's one of my friends—maybe the same ones who blew up the outhouse at our wedding." He touched her hand. "It'll probably be back by morning."

"Maybe we should go see Dad and tell him what's happened."

"What good would that do?"

"He's the one who gave us the wood. It's only right that he knows it was stolen."

Martin shook his head. "I don't think that's necessary."

"Why not?"

He squeezed her fingers. "I'm your husband now. It's my job to look out for you. Besides, your daed didn't seem to care much about the attacks that were done at his place. What makes you think he'll care that our wood was taken?"

Ruth's mouth dropped open. She'd never expected to hear her husband speak out against her father, and she told him so.

"I'm not speaking against him. I'm just stating facts."

Ruth folded her arms and stared straight ahead. "I think he does care about the attacks. He's just chosen to turn the other cheek and trust God to protect our family." She pursed her lips. "I think he has the right to know that the wood he gave us is gone."

"Maybe so, but it can wait until morning."

She shivered. "But I'm cold."

"Then let's go to bed and get warm under the quilts."

"You can go to bed if you want to," she said, rising to her feet.

"Where are you going?"

"I've got work to do in the kitchen."

"What kind of work?"

"We've still got boxes that need to be unloaded and put away."

"They'll be there in the morning, Ruth."

"I want to do them now."

"It's too cold in here to be milling about the kitchen. Let's turn off the gas lamps and head upstairs to bed."

Ruth was tempted to argue, but she didn't want the two of them to spend the night mad at each other. Besides, Martin was right—they could empty boxes in the morning. Maybe by then the wood would be back.

Chapter 21

When Ruth awoke the following morning, she was surprised to feel warm air drifting through their bedroom floor vent. She rolled over and discovered that Martin was gone. Apparently he'd gotten up and built a fire. Maybe the wood had been returned.

Ruth scrambled out of bed and hurried to get dressed.

When she stepped into the kitchen a short time later, she was pleased to find a cozy fire crackling in the woodstove. Martin wasn't in the kitchen. She hurried to put the teakettle on, and a few minutes later, steam began to rise out of the spout. The whistling kettle had a rich, comfortable sound to it, not a shrill sound as it did during the hotter summer months.

When the water was hot enough, she poured some into a cup, plopped a tea bag in, and stepped toward the table. There, she discovered a note.

Dear Ruth,

I've gone fishing with Abe and Gideon. I didn't want to wake you, so I had a piece of leftover apple pie Mom sent home with us last night. Now I'm about to head for Abe's place. The woodpile wasn't back when I got up, so I went over to my folks' and got enough wood to get you by for the day. I shouldn't be gone too late. Oh, and you might want to have the frying pan ready, because I aim to bring home a mess of fish.

Love,
Martin

Ruth sighed and sank into a chair at the table. She had hoped Martin might decide to stay home today on account of the cold weather. It upset her to know that whoever had taken their wood hadn't brought it back, but it frustrated her more that Martin thought fishing was more important than helping her unload boxes.

Ruth took a sip of tea and held the warm liquid in her mouth awhile before swallowing. *Maybe I won't unload those boxes, either. I think I'll go visit Grace and the baby this morning. After that, I'll stop over at Abe's place and see how his kinner are doing.*

"Can I come, too?" Anna asked when Cleon announced during breakfast that he was going to check on his bee boxes.

Cleon shook his head and reached for his cup of coffee. "I'll be extracting honey from the hives today, and it's not safe for you to be around the bees."

"But I'd like to see where all that honey comes from," the child persisted.

"You would need to wear protective gear, and I don't have any your size."

Anna's lip jutted out, but Cleon seemed to ignore her. The child looked over at Grace. "Can we do something fun after breakfast, Mama—maybe bake some cookies?"

Grace released a weary sigh. "Not today, Anna. I have to bathe the boppli, and after that I've got some sewing to do."

"I could give the baby a bath while you sew."

"Absolutely not!" Cleon shouted before Grace could respond.

"How come?"

"You're not old enough to bathe Daniel. You might drop him or let him slip into the water, and then he could drown."

Anna's chin trembled, and tears gathered in her eyes.

Grace frowned. "You don't have to scare her like that."

"Well, it's true," he said with a grunt. "Anna's barely old enough to bathe herself, and she's sure not capable of caring for her baby brother."

"Many Amish kinner care for their younger siblings," Grace argued.

"That's part of a child's training."

"She can learn on one of her dolls, not my child." Cleon pushed his chair away from the table and stood. "I've got work to do."

When the door clicked shut behind him, Grace patted Anna's hand. "We'll find something for you to do today."

Anna poked at the last bit of eggs on her plate. "Since you're so busy with the boppli, and Papa won't let me help with the bees, can I visit Aunt Martha? Maybe I can help feed the dogs."

Grace nodded. "As soon as you've finished your breakfast." She figured having Anna out of the house might be better for her, too. Ever since Daniel had been born, Grace had felt irritable and depressed. Maybe it had to do with the fact that Cleon seemed so overprotective of the baby and hadn't spent much time with Anna. Grace had tried talking to him on several occasions, but he always said there wasn't a problem, despite the fact that his relationship with Anna seemed to be going downhill.

After Grace had bundled Anna into a warm jacket, she herded her to the door. "I'll watch you from the porch to be sure you make it to Grandma and Grandpa's."

"I'll be fine, Mama."

"Just the same, I'll feel better when I see that you've made it there safely."

Anna shrugged and took off at a run.

Grace couldn't see the back side of her folks' place from the first house Cleon had built for them, but from their new house, Grace was able to see all the way down the driveway.

Leaning on the porch rail, she watched until Anna entered her folks' house, then she stepped back into the warmth of her kitchen. She shouldn't have to worry about her daughter's safety right here on their own property. It wasn't right that everything they did, everywhere they went, she had to be anxious about whether another attack would occur.

Grace tiptoed into the baby's room and was relieved when she found him asleep. His baby breath smelled sweet, and he looked ever so peaceful, sleeping on his side with his little thumb stuck in his mouth. She leaned over the crib and kissed Daniel's downy head. *Bless my baby, Lord. Bless Anna and Cleon, too.*

She left Daniel's room and curled up on the sofa in the living room, deciding that she needed a nap. She'd only been resting a few minutes when someone called out, "Grace, are you to home?"

Grace sat up just as Ruth stepped into the room. "I didn't expect to see you today."

"Martin went fishing with Abe and Gideon, so I decided to drop by and see how you and the boppli are doing." Ruth draped her coat over the back of the rocking chair and took a seat.

"Daniel's doing well; he's sleeping right now."

"And you?"

"I'm kind of tired and feeling a bit weepy as of late."

"Do you think it's postpartum depression?"

Grace shrugged. "I suppose it could be, but what's got me feeling down more than anything is the way Cleon's been acting since the boppli was born."

Ruth's forehead wrinkled. "How's he been acting?"

"Possessive of Daniel. He hardly pays Anna any attention unless it's to scold her for something."

"Have you tried talking to him about it?"

"Jah, but he doesn't think he's doing anything wrong."

Ruth grunted. "Men sure can be stubborn."

"Surely you can't mean Martin. You two haven't been married long enough for you to see his stubborn side."

Ruth leaned slightly forward. "Last night after we got home from Martin's folks', we discovered that the pile of wood Dad had given us was gone."

"It was?"

Ruth nodded. "Martin said he thought some of his friends might have taken it as a prank and figured it would be back in our yard by morning."

"Was it?"

"No. By the time I got up, Martin had already gone fishing, but he left me a note saying he'd gotten up early and gone over to his folks' to get some wood before he left for Abe's."

Grace shifted on the sofa. "You don't suppose whoever took it was the same one who blew up the outhouse at your wedding, do you?"

Ruth shrugged. "That's what Martin thinks, but I'm not so sure. There were large tire tracks in the dirt near where the woodpile was, and that makes me think whoever took the wood was driving a truck."

"Do you think it might be another attack–done by whoever has been trying to scare us?"

"Maybe so."

"Have you spoken to Dad about this?"

"Not yet. I wanted to tell him last night, but Martin said it could wait and that we needed to see if the wood was returned."

"Are you going to tell him now?"

"I suppose I could, but it would probably be best if I waited until Martin gets home and we can discuss it more."

"I suppose you're right."

"Where are Anna and Cleon today?" Ruth asked.

"Cleon's checking his bee boxes, and Anna went down to the folks' to see Martha."

"I'm planning to go over to Abe's place to see how his kinner are doing," Ruth said. "Do you think Anna would like to join me?"

"Probably so. Anna looks for any excuse to be with Esta."

"I'd better go now and let you rest awhile before the boppli wakes up." Ruth left her seat and gave Grace a hug. "If you don't get over your depression soon, maybe you should speak with the doctor about it."

Grace nodded. "I will."

"I'll have Anna home in plenty of time for lunch," Ruth called as she retrieved her coat and headed for the door.

"Sure hope we catch some big old trout so Sue can fix 'em for supper," Abe said as he rowed his boat to the middle of the pond. "Wouldn't that be good, son?"

Gideon, who sat near the back of the boat, shrugged.

"I'm hoping to catch enough fish so Ruth can fix some for our supper, too," Martin put in from his seat at the front of the boat.

"This looks like a good place to fish." Abe slipped the oars inside the boat and cast out his line. Martin did the same. Gideon just sat with his arms folded.

Abe's patience was beginning to wane. "Come on, Gideon, you've been after me for weeks to take you fishing. Now we're here–so fish."

Gideon grunted. "It's too cold."

"Then you should have stayed home and sat around the stove all day." Abe took no pleasure in snapping at his son, but he was irked that he'd taken the day off to spend time with Gideon, only to have the boy gripe about the cold and refuse to fish.

"Maybe he'll get more enthused when he sees some trout," Martin said.

"Let's hope so."

For the next several minutes, Abe and Martin visited quietly as they kept an eye on their lines. Gideon continued to sit with a scowl on his face.

Suddenly Martin shouted, "I saw a big one jump clean out of the water!"

Abe turned and saw two more fish jump. "I'd better move the boat over that way. Looks like they're just waiting to be caught."

Gideon perked up a bit and leaned over the edge of the boat. "I don't see anything. Where were they jumpin'?"

"Over there." Martin pointed to the left.

Gideon stood up and shouted, "There's one! That old fish must have jumped three feet out of the water!"

Abe grunted. "Sit down, boy; you're rocking the boat."

Gideon had only taken a few steps when suddenly the boat flipped over, dumping them all into the frigid water.

"I can't swim!" Abe shouted before taking in a mouthful of murky water. *And neither can Gideon.*

Chapter 22

Are you really going to get rid of Flo?" Anna asked Martha as the two of them sat on a bale of straw while Martha brushed the female beagle.

"I've got to, Anna. She can't have puppies, which means she won't make me any money that way. I plan to use the money I make selling her to buy another dog." Martha grimaced. By the time she had responded to that ad about the pair of cocker spaniels, they'd been sold. That meant she had to keep looking, and it wasn't likely that she'd find another pair as reasonably priced as the ones in the paper had been.

"I wish Mama couldn't have any more babies." Anna stroked Flo's floppy ears, and the dog let loose a pathetic whimper as though in tune with the child's feelings.

Martha frowned. "What makes you say a thing like that?"

"If she hadn't had Daniel, Papa would still love me."

Martha set the brush aside, and Flo crawled on her belly to the corner of the room. "I'm sure he still loves you," she said, wrapping her arms around Anna.

"He won't let me hold the boppli. Whenever I ask if I can help with somethin', he always says no."

"What kinds of things have you asked to help with?"

"I wanted to bathe Daniel so Mama could get some sewing done. Papa said I'm too little for that." Deep creases formed on Anna's forehead. "Then I asked if I could help with his bees. He said no to that, too."

"Working around bees can be dangerous, Anna. You might get stung."

"That's what he said."

"Hey! What are you up to in here?" Ruth asked as she stepped into the barn.

"Aunt Martha was brushin' Flo so she looks nice when someone sees the sign out by the road and comes to look at her," Anna answered before Martha could respond.

"I saw that sign when I drove in with my horse and buggy." Ruth took a seat on another bale of straw. "Has anyone stopped to ask about the dog yet?"

Martha shook her head. "Of course, I just put the sign up last night, so I haven't lost hope." She clapped her hands and called for Flo. The dog returned to her with its tail between its legs and released a high-pitched howl.

"Maybe I should have bought Flo to give Esta instead of one of Heidi's pups," Ruth said. "That way you could have kept Winkie for breeding purposes."

"I don't think Esta would have wanted a full-grown dog that likes to howl at everything she sees." Martha picked up the brush and began brushing Flo again.

"You're probably right." Ruth reached over and squeezed Anna's arm. "Speaking of Esta, I'm heading over to see her now. Would you like to go along?"

Anna nodded eagerly. "Guess I'd better ask Mama first."

"I was already at your house and saw your mamm. She said it was fine if you ride over to see Esta with me."

Anna jumped up and raced for the door.

Ruth turned to Martha. "Would you like to come along?"

"I'd better stick around here in case someone comes to see Flo." Martha smiled. "Maybe when you bring Anna home, you can join us for lunch."

"That would be nice. Martin went fishing with Abe and Gideon, and I doubt he'll be home until late this afternoon."

"See you later, then. And be sure to say hello to Abe's kinner for me."

"I will." Ruth headed out the door.

A short time later, Martha heard a vehicle rumble up the driveway, followed by the tooting of a horn. She put Flo inside one of the empty horse stalls and went outside to see who it was. When she stepped out of the barn, she saw John Peterson getting out of his SUV.

"I was driving by and saw the sign out front advertising a female beagle. Is it one of your dogs?" he asked.

She nodded. "I bought a pair of beagles for breeding purposes several months ago, but Flo can't have any pups, so I've decided to sell her as a hunting dog."

He grinned. "Which is exactly what I'm needing. How much do you want for her?"

"I paid a thousand dollars for the pair, so if I could get—"

"I'll give you six hundred. How's that sound?"

Martha's mouth fell open. "Don't you want to look at her first?"

"Guess I probably should." John reached up to rub the bridge of his slightly crooked nose and squinted. "Unless she's sick, crippled, or just plain dumb, I'm sure she'll work out fine for me."

"She's none of those things." Martha motioned to the barn. "Follow me, and you can see for yourself."

Inside the barn, Martha took Flo out of the horse stall and led her over to John. He knelt on the concrete floor beside the dog and gave her the once-over. "She looks good to me. I'll take her."

Martha could hardly believe she had found a home for Flo so quickly. She was pleased to know the dog would be put to good use.

"Help! Help!"

Martin came up out of the water, gulped in some air, and spotted Gideon, kicking and splashing for all he was worth. "Can you swim?" he called to the boy.

"He can't, and neither can I!" Abe, who was several feet away, also struggled.

The frigid water stung Martin's skin and took his breath away. Even though he considered himself to be a good swimmer, he knew he needed to get out of the icy water as quickly as possible. Needed to get Abe and his son out, too.

Since Gideon was the closest and seemed to be having the most trouble staying afloat, Martin swam over to the boy, grabbed hold of his shirt, and pulled him toward shore. He kept pulling until they were in shallow water and he knew Gideon could stand. "Climb out and wait on the shore," he instructed.

Coughing and gasping for air, Gideon did as he was told.

Martin dove back into the water and swam toward where he'd last seen Abe. Only Abe wasn't there!

Treading water, Martin looked around frantically. "Abe!" he hollered. "Where are you?"

"Don't let Papa die!" Gideon shouted from the shore.

Martin whirled around. "Don't come back in the water! Stay right there while I look for your daed."

He dove down and spotted Abe under the water near where the boat had capsized. His hand snaked out and grabbed Abe's arm, then he kicked hard, pulling them both to the surface. Abe wasn't moving, and Martin feared the man might have drowned. *Dear God,* he prayed, *don't let him be dead.*

Several grueling moments later, Martin pulled Abe onto the shore.

Gideon rushed over and dropped down beside his father. "Don't die, Papa," he sobbed. "Don't leave me like Mama did!"

Martin had learned CPR when he'd done volunteer work with the local fire department, so he quickly set to work on Abe. The cold air stung his eyes, and he struggled with each breath. His lungs burned, and he feared his strength would give out, but he wouldn't give up. Abe was his friend, and if their roles were reversed, he knew Abe would do the same for him.

Finally, Abe coughed and spit water out of his mouth.

Martin breathed a prayer of thanks. "He's going to be all right," he said to Gideon, whose eyes were wide with fear. "We need to get back to your house so we can get out of these wet clothes."

"I'm glad you came over to see me today," Esta said as she and Anna took a seat on the porch with Winkie perched between them.

Ruth smiled as she seated herself in one of the wicker chairs beside Abe's sister. "Nothing makes a little girl happier than to be with her best friend."

Sue nodded. Her blue eyes seemed to have lost the sparkle they'd had when she'd first come to help her brother and his family.

"Is everything all right?" Ruth asked, concerned. "Are you working too hard?"

Tears welled in Sue's eyes, and she blinked a couple of times. "I'm feeling kind of homesick."

"That's understandable. You've been away from your folks for several months now. I'm sure you miss them."

"I also miss Melvin."

"He's your boyfriend, right?"

"Jah. Melvin and I started courting six months before I left home. We've been writing letters, but it's not the same as seeing each other and being able to go places together."

"No, of course not." Ruth couldn't imagine being separated from Martin even for a few weeks, much less several months. "Maybe Melvin can come for a visit."

"I'd like that, but he's been busy helping his daed in their masonry business and hasn't been able to get away." Sue released a sigh. "I'd like to go home for Christmas, but I wouldn't feel right about leaving Abe in the lurch."

"Maybe some of the women in our community could take turns coming in to clean house, cook, and watch the kinner."

Sue shook her head. "I think it would be hard on everyone, especially Abe, if I went home for the holidays. It's going to be difficult for him to get through Christmas without Alma. I think he needs my support."

"I understand. I would make that sacrifice for either of my sisters."

The puppy growled as it leaped off the porch and romped in the yard with Josh, Willis, and Owen. "It was nice of you to give Winkie to Esta," Sue said. "The dog's filled a big hole in that little girl's life, and having a pet to care for is teaching her responsibility."

"I was glad to do it." Ruth turned to the girls, who sat on the steps watching the boys and Winkie play a game of tug-of-war with an old sock. "It won't be long until Christmas. Have either of you thought about what you'd like to receive for a present?"

Esta nodded eagerly. "I'm hopin' for some ice skates. Of course, we've gotta have cold, icy weather first."

"It was awfully cold last night," Ruth said. "I imagine it won't be long before your daed's pond will be frozen over."

Esta nodded. "Me and Josh found a ladybug nest on the trunk of a pine tree the other day. Mama used to say that was a sure sign of winter comin'."

Ruth smiled. She remembered how excited she used to get when she was a girl looking forward to winter games, hot chocolate with marshmallows, and gifts at Christmas.

Esta nudged Anna. "How 'bout you? What are you hopin' to get for Christmas?"

Anna shrugged. "If we get snow, a new sled would be nice."

Esta looked up at Ruth. "What are you hoping for?"

Ruth touched her stomach. The best gift she could receive would be to find out she was going to have a baby. "I'll be happy with whatever I get," she murmured.

A buggy rolled into the yard, and Sue stood, lifting Molly into her arms. "Looks like the men are back. They must have either caught lots of fish or got tired of trying, because they're here sooner than I thought they would be."

Ruth's heart gave a lurch when she noticed how wet the men's clothes were when they climbed out of the buggy. When she saw Martin put his arm around Abe's shoulders and walk him to the house, her heart nearly stopped beating.

"What happened?" she and Sue cried at the same time.

"Had a little accident with the boat," Martin replied.

"Did you fall into the water, Papa?" Esta grabbed Abe's hand as he stepped onto the porch.

"Sure did."

"But you can't swim," Sue said in a quavering voice.

"No, but Martin can. He saved us both from drowning," Gideon spoke up.

"You're all shaking." Ruth jerked open the front door. "You need to come inside and get warm."

Martin slipped his arm around Ruth's waist. "That's the last time I go fishing against my wife's better judgment. *Wasser schwimme macht mich gensheidich.*"

"Swimming in cold water gave me goose pimples, too," Abe agreed.

Ruth swallowed against the lump in her throat. *Thank You, God. Thank You for saving each of these men.*

Chapter 23

"I can't believe it's Christmas Eve and that we're having a white Christmas," Ruth said as she and Martin traveled down the road in his buggy toward her parents' house. She wished they were riding in an open sleigh so she could lift her face toward the sky and catch snowflakes on her tongue, the way she'd done as a child.

Martin reached for her hand. "Life's pretty good, jah?"

She smiled. "It is now. Last month when our wood was taken, and you, Abe, and Gideon got dumped into the pond, I wasn't so sure about things being good."

"But we're all okay, and your daed gave us another load of wood."

"That's true, but we never did find out who stole it."

He shrugged. "It makes no never mind to me. I'm keeping my focus on the future with you, my *schee* fraa."

She squeezed his warm fingers. "Will you still think I'm your pretty wife when I'm pregnant and *gross* around the middle?"

"I'll always think you're pretty, even when you become big around the middle."

Ruth sighed. "I hate to admit it, but I'm having a little trouble not feeling jealous whenever I see Grace with her baby. I want so much to be pregnant."

"I know, and I'm looking forward to being a daed," Martin said. "We just need to be patient. After all, we haven't been married quite two months yet. There's still plenty of time for you to conceive."

"But what if I'm barren like Martha's female beagle? You can't just sell me off, the way Martha did with Flo." She groaned. "If I'm unable to conceive, then you'll be stuck with a wife who can't give you any kinner."

He leaned over and nuzzled her neck with his cold nose. "The only reason I'll be stuck with you is because I love you. If we can't have any kinner, then we'll either live without 'em or take in foster children, the way some in our community have done."

Ruth nodded, but internally she struggled with the idea of never being a mother. Ever since she'd been a young girl playing with her dolls, she had wanted to hold a baby of her own. Surely God would answer that prayer and let her conceive.

"Are you looking forward to spending the evening with your family?" Martin asked, taking their conversation in another direction.

"Jah, of course. And tomorrow, it will be nice to spend Christmas Day with your family."

"Mom and Pop really like you, Ruth. They think you're just what I need."

"And you're what I need," she replied, snuggling closer to him.

Blinding headlights from behind flashed against the buggy's front window, and Ruth whirled around. A truck bore down on them, going much too fast. But the shadowy night sky and blowing snow kept her from seeing the color of the vehicle.

"Looks like someone's in a hurry to get wherever they're going on Christmas Eve," she said. "No doubt they'll whip around us and be gone into the night."

Martin opened his mouth as if to comment, but before he could get a word out, they were bumped from behind.

Ruth grabbed the edge of her seat and hung on, while Martin gripped the reins. "What's going on? Do you suppose that vehicle hit a patch of ice?"

"I—I don't know. We haven't hit any in our buggy."

Ruth's heart hammered. "Maybe you should pull over and let him pass."

Martin pulled on the reins, and the horse slowed, but before he could guide it to the shoulder of the road, they were bumped again, harder this time. "There's no ice here. I'm guessing whoever is driving that truck must have been drinking," he mumbled. "What does that *ab im kopp* driver think he's doing? He's either got to be crazy or a real *siffer* to keep ramming our buggy like that."

"You think he could be a drunkard?" Ruth started to turn around, but the vehicle rammed them once more. Her head jerked forward, sending a spasm of pain up the back of her neck.

Twice more the truck hit the back of their buggy. The horse whinnied and reared up as Martin struggled to keep hold of the reins. The vehicle pulled out as though it was going to pass, but then it slammed into the side of the buggy, flipping it over and sending it rolling into the ditch.

"Ach!" Ruth screamed; then everything went black.

"Danki for the new ice skates," Esta said as she took a seat on the sofa beside Abe.

He smiled and patted her knee. "You'll be careful to skate only when others are around, won't you?"

She nodded. "I promise, 'cause I wouldn't want to end up in the pond like you and Gideon did when you went fishing."

"I should say not," Sue put in from the recliner, where she sat with Molly in her lap. "Besides the fact that you can't swim, that water under the ice would be freezing cold."

"The first day Martin and I were back to work after that dunking we took, he said he'd be happy to teach my kinner to swim as soon as the spring thaw comes and it's warm enough to go in the water," Abe said.

"It might be a good idea if he teaches *you* how to swim first, brother." Sue leveled Abe with one of her more serious looks. "Either that, or you'd better give up fishing, because we all need you around."

Abe thought about Alma. There was nothing she could have done to prevent the lightning strike that took her life, but there was something he could do to protect himself from drowning. "Jah," he said with a nod. "I'll see if Martin will teach me how to swim, too."

"Can I go *gschwumme?*" Owen questioned. He'd been sitting on the floor near Willis, playing with the little wooden horses Abe had asked Roman to make.

"When you're old enough to learn how to swim, then you can go swimming," Abe said with a nod.

Owen's lower lip jutted out. "I ain't no boppli." He pointed to his rosy-cheeked little sister, who was almost asleep in Sue's lap. "Molly's the boppli."

"You act like a boppli whenever you're asked to do some chore," Josh countered. He and Gideon sat at a table across the room playing a game of checkers.

"Do not!" Owen shook his head forcefully. "Just 'cause you're bigger 'n me don't mean you're my boss. Only Papa can tell me what to do." He looked over at Sue. "Aunt Sue, too, now that Mama's gone to heaven."

The room turned deathly silent. The children had been hiding it well as of late, but Abe knew they still missed their mother.

Sue rose from her chair. "Molly's fallen asleep, so I'm going to put her to bed. When I come downstairs, I'll make a batch of popcorn and some hot apple cider. Would anyone like to help?"

The children nodded with eager expressions, and Abe offered Sue an appreciative smile. He knew she'd wanted to go home for Christmas, but she had stayed to care for them and was doing all she could to make the holiday pleasant.

Abe leaned back in his chair as a sense of appreciation washed over him. He suddenly realized he wasn't sleeping so much during the day and was sleeping better at night. God was good, and he prayed things would go better for them in the coming year.

"Why don't you let me hold that little fellow awhile?" Mom said when Grace sank to the sofa with a weary sigh. She and Cleon had walked over to her folks' house with Anna and Daniel.

Grace held out her arms gratefully. "He's been fussy all day, and nothing I've done has helped."

"Maybe he's got a touch of the colic," Mom said as she took the squalling baby and seated herself in the rocking chair across from Grace. "Have you tried giving him a bit of catnip tea?"

Anna, who had taken a seat on the floor by the fireplace next to

Martha, looked up and frowned. "Catnip's for *katze*, not bopplin."

"That's true, cats do like catnip, but one of my herb books says it can also be used by itself or in combination with fennel and peppermint to help ease a baby's colic," Mom said.

"You've got to be careful when you're fooling around with herbs." Dad left his recliner and shuffled across the room to stand beside Mom. "Maybe we should try the 'colic carry.' That always worked when our girls were bopplin."

Cleon took a seat beside Grace on the sofa. "What's the 'colic carry'?"

"First, you extend your arm with your palm up." Dad bent down and took Daniel from Mom. "Then you position the boppli like this." He placed the baby chest-down and forehead resting in the palm of his big hand. "You've got to make sure the little fellow's legs are on either side of your elbow." Dad positioned the baby's legs in the manner he'd described. "Now you support the boppli with your other hand and walk around the room, keeping him in this position." He looked over at Mom and gave her a nod. "I'm sure this will help."

Cleon jumped up and rushed over to Dad. "I think I'd better take Daniel."

Dad's eyebrows pulled inward. "What's the matter, son? Are you afraid I might drop him?"

"Roman's had plenty of experience with bopplin," Mom said before Cleon could respond. "He used to carry our three around like that when they were fussy babies."

Deep grooves appeared on Cleon's forehead. "Even so—"

"Dad, maybe you should give the baby to Mom," Grace said, hoping to smooth things over between her father and Cleon. "I think if she rocks him awhile, he'll settle down."

Dad grunted and handed the baby back to Mom; then he moved over to stand in front of the fireplace. "I wonder where Ruth and Martin could be," he said, glancing at the clock on the wall above the mantel. "They should have been here by now."

Martha nodded. "I spoke with Ruth on Monday afternoon, and she said they would be here by six o'clock."

"Maybe the roads are icy because of the snow," Mom said.

"I'm hungry," Anna complained. "When are we gonna eat supper?"

"We're waiting for Aunt Ruth and Uncle Martin to get here." Mom placed the baby over her shoulder and patted his back.

"But I'm hungry now."

"You can wait." Cleon took a seat beside Grace again. "I'm sure they'll be here soon."

"Is there anything in the oven that needs tending to?" Grace asked, looking at her mother.

Mom shook her head. "The soup's staying warm on the stove, and the open-faced sandwiches Martha and I made earlier are in the refrigerator."

"Let's sing Christmas carols while we wait," Martha suggested.

Mom smiled. "Good idea. That'll make the time go quicker, and it'll help us stay focused on the meaning of Christmas."

"Can we sing 'Jingle Bells'?" Anna asked. "I like that song."

" 'Jingle Bells' is not a Christmas carol." Cleon frowned at Anna.

"Why don't we start with 'Silent Night'?" Mom said. "That was Grace's favorite Christmas song when she was a girl."

Martha was the first to lead off, and the rest of the family joined in as they sang, "Silent night! Holy night! All is calm, all is bright, round yon virgin mother and Child. Holy Infant, so tender and mild, sleep in heavenly peace; sleep in heavenly peace."

When the song ended, Grace looked over at her baby, sleeping peacefully in Mom's arms. Maybe tonight they would all sleep in heavenly peace.

They sang several more songs until Dad held up his hand and said, "It's almost seven. Ruth and Martin should have been here by now."

"Maybe we should go look for them," Cleon suggested. "If they did hit ice, their buggy might have skidded off the road."

"You're right," Dad said. "We need to head out and see if we can spot them along the way."

The men donned their coats and stocking caps, then hurried out the door.

As they headed down the road in Cleon's buggy, it didn't take Roman long to realize there were some patches of ice. It had begun to snow quite heavily, too, and he became even more apprehensive.

"You don't suppose they saw how hard it was snowing and decided to stay home, do you?" Cleon asked, turning in his seat to look at Roman.

"I guess they might have. Knowing Ruth, though, she would have moved heaven and earth to be with her family on Christmas Eve."

"You're probably right."

"Sure is cold out tonight," Roman said. "I can see my breath, even here in the buggy." He squinted as he studied the road ahead.

Suddenly Cleon pointed to the left. "Look, there's a buggy flipped over on its side, and it doesn't look good." He guided his horse to the shoulder of the road and jumped down. Roman did the same.

As they raced around to the front of the mangled buggy, a shiver shot up Roman's back. The mare that had been pulling the buggy lay on its side, and two people lay crumpled in the snow. "Ach! It's Ruth and Martin!"

Chapter 24

"Ruth, can you hear me? Please—look at me."

Ruth tried to open her eyes, but they wouldn't cooperate. Where was she? Who was calling her name?

"Ruth. . .Ruth. . ."

Her eyelids fluttered.

"I think she's trying to wake up."

"Are you sure my daughter's going to be all right?"

"She came through the surgery well. Given some time, she should heal from all her injuries."

"Thank the Lord."

Mom, is that you? The words formed on Ruth's tongue, but she couldn't open her mouth.

"She should be fully awake soon, and then the sheriff will want to question her."

Question me about what? Why can't I open my eyes or speak to Mom?

"My son-in-law and I have already spoken to the sheriff, so I don't see what good it will do for—"

Dad, is that you? Tell me where I am and why I can't see you and Mom. Reaching from deep within, Ruth cracked one eye open, then the other. Blurry faces came into view—faces she recognized.

"Wh-where am I?" she rasped.

"You're in the hospital," Dad said.

"What happened? Why does my stomach hurt so much?"

"You were in a horrible accident." Mom's face looked pale, and her chin quivered slightly.

"Do you know how it happened, Ruth?" Dad questioned. "Did your buggy hit a patch of ice on the road?"

Ruth closed her eyes and tried to remember. She and Martin had been driving down the road, heading to Mom and Dad's on Christmas Eve. It had been snowing, and they'd been talking about wanting to have a baby. Then a truck had come barreling up behind them, and then–

"Martin! Where's Martin?"

Dad opened his mouth as if to respond, but Mom shook her head. "You need to rest, Ruth. We can talk about this when you're feeling better."

The look of sadness on Mom's face sent a jolt of panic through Ruth's body. She tried to sit up, but a woman wearing a white uniform placed a restraining hand on her shoulder.

"Lie still, dear," she said. "You've just come from surgery and you've lost a lot of blood. You don't want to rip open your stitches."

"Stitches? Where do I have stitches?"

The nurse looked over at Mom. "Perhaps it would be best if we let her sleep. She needs to remain calm."

A warm, tingling sensation shot up Ruth's arm, and she moaned. *I must be dreaming. Jah, that's all it is; just a strange dream.*

As Grace sat in the hospital waiting room with Cleon beside her, her brain felt as if it were in a fog. What had started out to be a pleasant Christmas Eve had turned into a terrible nightmare.

She glanced across the room, where her folks stood talking to Martin's parents. Mom had her arm around Flossie's shoulder, no doubt offering words of comfort. Dad was doing the same with Martin's father, Elmer.

"I just can't believe what's happened tonight," Grace said, clinging to Cleon's hand. "When the doctor came out and told us that Martin was dead and that they'd done surgery on Ruth because her intestines and uterus had been damaged, my brain wouldn't let me believe it."

"I know–it's a terrible thing. At least we can take comfort in knowing that Martin's in heaven." Cleon let go of Grace's hand and slipped his arm around her shoulders. "Ruth doesn't know the extent of her injuries, does she?"

"Not yet." Grace gulped down a sob. "When she finds out she'll never be able to have kinner, I'm sure she'll fall apart. All Ruth's ever wanted is to be a wife and mother. She loved Martin so much."

Cleon squeezed her shoulder. "Someday, when the pain of losing Martin has subsided, Ruth might find love again, and then—"

"How you can say such a thing?" Tears stung Grace's eyes, and when she blinked, they spilled onto her cheeks.

"I'm not suggesting she find another man and get married as soon as she comes home from the hospital. I just wanted you to realize—"

Grace shook her head. "I can't believe Ruth has been put to the test like this. It's not fair! She's always had such a sweet, tender spirit. She doesn't deserve to have something so terrible happen to her."

"No one deserves it, Grace. Rain falls on the just, same as it does the unjust. We need to ask God to give Ruth strength and help her deal with this loss."

A *thump-thump-thump* woke Abe from his slumber. He rolled over and groaned. It sounded as though someone was knocking on the back door.

He shoved the covers aside, swung his legs over the side of the bed, and stepped into his trousers. Stumbling down the hallway, he bumped into Sue at the bottom of the stairs.

"I heard knocking and came to see who it was," she said.

"Me, too." Abe pulled the back door open and was stunned to see Ivan Schrock standing on the porch. "Ivan, what are you doing here on Christmas morning?"

Ivan's solemn expression caused Abe immediate concern. "I got word from Cleon this morning. There was a horrible accident last night."

"A buggy accident?"

"Jah. It was Martin's buggy."

"Martin Gingerich?" Sue and Abe asked at the same time.

Ivan nodded. "Sorry to be tellin' you this, but Martin's dead, and Ruth's in the hospital with serious injuries."

Abe's knees nearly buckled, and he heard Sue's sharp intake of breath. Instinctively, he reached for her hand. "How did it happen? Was it caused by ice on the road?"

"We're not sure. All I know is that Cleon and Roman got worried when Ruth and Martin didn't show up at their place on Christmas Eve, so they went looking for them." Ivan drew in a quick breath. "Guess they found Martin's mangled buggy overturned on the shoulder of the road. The horse was dead, and Martin and Ruth were unconscious and bleeding pretty bad. Martin died soon after they got to the hospital, and the doctors did surgery on Ruth."

"What kind of surgery?" Sue asked.

Ivan's gaze dropped to the porch as his face flamed. "A hysterectomy. She had some damage to her intestines, and her uterus was messed up when she fell on a broken buggy wheel."

"That's baremlich!" Sue cried.

"Terrible isn't the word for it!" Abe steadied himself against the doorjamb. "Is Ruth going to be okay?"

Ivan shrugged. "I think so—in time."

Abe slowly shook his head. "I can't believe that my good friend, who saved me from drowning, is dead." Hot tears stung his eyes. "First my Alma, and now Ruth's Martin. Dear Lord, how much more can we take?"

Ruth opened her eyes and blinked against the invading light. She'd been dreaming—a horrible, frightening dream about her and Martin riding in their buggy and a truck ramming them from behind. But it couldn't have happened. She was safe and warm in her bed at home. Everything was as it should be.

She turned toward Martin's side of the bed. He wasn't there. All she saw was a strange-looking machine with a long piece of plastic tubing that was connected to—

Ruth screamed as a sharp pain shot through her abdomen. "Where am I? What's happened to me?"

"It's all right, Ruth. You're in the hospital. We're taking good care of you."

A young woman wearing a white uniform stepped up to the side of the bed and placed a cool hand on Ruth's forehead. "The sheriff's outside. He wants to ask you a few questions."

"The sheriff?"

"That's right. He needs to talk to you about the accident."

"Accident?"

"The one you were involved in last night."

So it wasn't a dream. There really had been an accident. As the reality set in, Ruth trembled. "Wh-where's my husband?"

The woman glanced over her shoulder, then Ruth's mother stepped forward.

"Mom! I'm so glad you're here. Martin and I were in an accident. Somebody rammed the back of our buggy, and–"

"I know." Mom clasped Ruth's hand. "You were hurt badly, Ruth. When the buggy tipped over, one of the wheels broke, and you landed on it when you were thrown from the buggy. The broken wheel punctured your belly, causing some intestinal damage, as well as damage to your uterus." She paused and sniffed a couple of times. "The doctors–they had to do an emergency hysterectomy. You'll have to take antibiotics for some time to fight any possible infection."

"Wh-what are you saying?" Ruth's throat felt so dry and swollen she could barely swallow.

Mom sank into the chair beside Ruth's bed as tears dribbled down her cheeks. "The surgery to fix your bowels was a success, but I'm sorry, daughter. . . . You'll never have any babies."

"What? Oh no, that just can't be. Martin and I want a big family. We–"

Mom slowly shook her head. "Martin's gone, Ruth. He died soon after you were brought to the hospital."

Ruth stared at the ceiling. Surely Mom was wrong. Martin couldn't be dead. They'd been on their way to Mom and Dad's to celebrate Christmas Eve. It was going to be a happy time–her and Martin's first Christmas together.

"No! No! No!"

Chapter 25

As Ruth lay in her bed, staring at the cracks in the ceiling, her fingers curled into the palms of her hands and dug into her flesh. Last night, she'd been released from the hospital in order to attend Martin's funeral today. Mom and Dad had brought her home to stay with them, and the doctor had given Ruth a prescription for antibiotics and instructions to get plenty of rest. He'd said she could attend her husband's funeral, but only if she used the wheelchair Dad had rented.

I don't want to go to Martin's funeral, Ruth silently wailed. *I just want to close my eyes and never wake up.*

Ruth's mind took her back to the day Sheriff Osborn had showed up at the hospital, asking her to tell him what she remembered about the accident. Her brain had been foggy, but she'd been able to remember a few things—looking over her shoulder, seeing a truck bearing down on them, being rammed over and over. She'd told the sheriff that it had been dark outside and snowing. She hadn't seen the license plate and couldn't be sure about the color of the vehicle. What she hadn't told the sheriff was that Luke had a truck he kept hidden in the woods, and she feared it may have been him who had rammed their buggy.

Tears stung the back of Ruth's eyes. *Could Luke have followed us on Christmas Eve? If so, why would he do such a horrible thing?*

"I brought you a bowl of oatmeal and some toast with your favorite strawberry jam," Mom said as she stepped into the room carrying a wooden tray in her hands.

"I'm not hungry."

"You've got to eat something. You won't get your strength back if you don't."

Ruth shook her head. "I don't care if I ever get my strength back. My husband's dead, and I can never have any children. There's nothing left for me to live for."

"Ach, don't say such a thing." Mom placed the tray on the nightstand and seated herself on the edge of Ruth's bed. "You have me, your daed, and the rest of the family to live for. We all love you, and we're grateful to God for sparing your life."

"Jah, well," Ruth said as the bitter taste of anger rose in her throat, "I wish He'd taken me instead of Martin."

Mom clutched Ruth's hand. "It wasn't your time to go, and you shouldn't be wishing it were so."

"What are you saying—that it was meant for Martin to die?"

"I can't say that God meant for it to happen, but He did allow it, and we need to accept it as His will."

Ruth swallowed hard and nearly choked on a sob. "I—I don't think I can do that. Someone rammed our buggy on purpose, and they need to pay."

" 'For we know him that hath said, Vengeance belongeth unto me, I will recompense, saith the Lord,' " Mom quoted from Hebrews.

"I know, but. . ." Ruth looked away, unable to finish her sentence.

Mom patted her hand. "Eat your breakfast. Folks will be arriving for the funeral soon, and Cleon will be up to carry you down so you can attend the services."

Ruth gave no reply. She didn't want to attend Martin's services. Hearing the bishop's words and seeing Martin's body lying in that cold wooden coffin would only confirm that her husband was dead.

Abe directed his horse and buggy behind the long procession of black buggies heading down the narrow, hilly road leading to the Amish cemetery where Martin Gingerich's body would be laid to rest. It was a raw, dreary day. The steel gray sky looked as though it might open up and pound the earth with pelting rain, but it was too cold for that. If the clouds dropped anything, it would be more snow.

Abe observed the frozen fields on each side of the road as a bone-chilling wind lapped the sides of his buggy. He felt as if he were reliving Alma's funeral. It hadn't been quite a year since her death, but it seemed as if it were yesterday. The death of a Christian was a celebration, because he or she had left an earth full of struggles and made it to heaven. Yet for the ones left behind, there remained heartache and a silent sense of loneliness that went beyond anything Abe had ever known.

"God will see you through," Bishop King had told Abe the day they'd placed Alma's body in the grave. *"The Bible tells us in Psalm 147:3 that God 'healeth the broken in heart, and bindeth up their wounds.' "*

As Abe reflected on those words, he knew they were true. He still missed Alma, but with every new day, the pain became less. He was now able to find a sense of joy in the little things that occurred in his everyday life. His children, whom he'd previously taken for granted, had become more important to him, as well. His desire to help others during their time of need seemed stronger than ever before. Most of all, Abe's personal relationship with God had taken on new meaning, for he spent more time praying and reading his Bible, which had strengthened his faith and given him purpose in life.

Abe glanced over his shoulder at his children in the backseat. Despite his sorrow over losing a good friend, he knew life must go on.

When Abe stepped down from his buggy a short time later, a blast of frigid air hit him full in the face, and he shivered. *Lord, help Ruth's body to heal, ease her sorrow over losing her mate, and as she regains her strength, please give her the same sense of peace You have given me.*

Martha stood behind her sister's wheelchair, listening to the bishop's final words and watching Ruth's shoulders tremble as she fought to control her emotions. This horrible tragedy that had befallen Ruth wasn't fair. She and Martin had only been married a short time. They'd had their whole lives to look forward to until Martin's life was cut short.

Martha blinked against stinging tears and the biting December wind as she thought about her sister's injuries. Ruth had always wanted children. Martha was sure that having the hope of giving birth to babies of her own and then having it dashed away had only added to Ruth's agony over losing her mate.

How would I feel if I were in Ruth's place? Martha asked as she listened to Bishop King read a hymn. *If the man I loved had been taken from me, would I accept it as God's will or become bitter and full of self-pity?*

When Martha had gone to the hospital to see her injured sister, Ruth had said she hoped whoever was responsible for Martin's death would pay for his transgressions. She'd said she couldn't find it in her heart to forgive that person.

Martha shuddered as a group of Amish men sang a song while the pallbearers shoveled dirt into the grave. What if Ruth never got over her bitterness and self-pity? How could she find inner peace if she didn't forgive?

Grace clung to Cleon's arm as they stood behind her parents, who had positioned themselves behind Ruth's wheelchair, one on the left, one on the right. Mom's hand rested protectively on Ruth's shoulder, and Dad had his arm around Mom's waist. Knowing one of their daughters had suffered such a great loss and seeing Ruth having to witness the burial of her husband had to be hard on Mom and Dad.

I can still remember how lonely and sick with grief I felt when Wade died, Grace thought ruefully. At least she had been left with a child. Ruth would never know the joy of having children of her own.

Tears trickled down Grace's cheeks. *I had a child and gave her up because I was afraid I couldn't make it on my own.* She sniffed and reached up to swipe at the tears. All of the regrets in the world wouldn't change the past. Now she and Cleon had Anna and baby Daniel to raise.

She glanced down at her daughter, who stood like a statue between her and Cleon. They'd left the baby with Abe's sister today, which meant they would have to get Daniel as soon as the graveside service was over so Grace could feed him.

Grace's thoughts were pulled aside as the bishop asked the congregation to silently pray the Lord's Prayer, which meant the service was almost over. Martin's mother stood a few feet away with her husband and their five eldest children, all of whom were married and lived in other parts of Ohio. Flossie wept openly, and Elmer patted her back. Martin's funeral had to be hard on them, too.

When the service was over and the people had started for their buggies, Ruth let out a piercing cry and slumped over in her wheelchair.

Dad and Cleon grabbed the handles of the chair and pushed it quickly toward Dad's buggy. This day had obviously been too much for Ruth.

Chapter 26

Look who's come to visit!"

Ruth turned her head toward the door and saw Grace enter her room carrying Daniel. She knew she should say something, but she couldn't seem to find the words. She could only stare in silence at the opposite wall.

"I'm surprised to see you still in bed. It's almost ten o'clock," Grace said as she took a seat in the chair beside Ruth's bed. "It's been three weeks since you came home from the hospital. You should be getting some fresh air and a bit of exercise, don't you think?"

"I don't care about fresh air or exercise. I want to be left alone."

"Why don't you sit on the edge of your bed? You can hold Daniel while I brush your hair."

Ruth's temples throbbed, and her spine went rigid. She couldn't hold Daniel without being reminded that she could never have children of her own.

"Ruth, did you hear what I said?"

Ruth jerked her head and turned her face into the pillow. "I don't want to have my hair brushed."

Grace didn't say anything, but Ruth could hear her sister's heavy breathing. Several minutes went by, then the chair squeaked and the door clicked shut.

A few weeks ago, Ruth would have welcomed a visit from her sister. Holding baby Daniel would have been a delight. Not now. Ruth knew that whenever she looked at a baby, she would think about her loss. She remembered how desperate Martin had been to marry her, saying he was worried that something bad might happen and he wanted to protect her. It was Martin who needed protection—only there was nothing Ruth could have done to save him.

Ruth squeezed the edge of the pillow. Last night as she lay in her rumpled, damp sheets, she had stared into the darkness, imagining that she could see Martin's face. He was gone. She had to accept it as fact.

She thought about his funeral and how empty she had felt when she'd looked at his face for the very last time. She couldn't accept his death as God's will. All these months since Alma's death, Ruth had tried to reach out to Abe and his family, wanting to help heal their pain but never really understanding it until now.

Ruth had said nothing about her suspicions concerning Luke. She'd allowed her anger and resentment to fester like a bad splinter left unattended. Maybe she should have told the sheriff. Maybe she still could. She wasn't well enough to drive to town in order to speak with him, but she could use the phone shed near her father's shop.

Abe had just begun to look at some paperwork on his desk when Ivan Schrock entered the harness shop. "Are you busy?" he asked, moving toward Abe's desk.

Abe nodded. "Been even busier now that Martin's not here to help."

Ivan leaned on the corner of Abe's desk. "That's why I came by."

"To see if I'm busy?"

"To see if you could use some help."

"I suppose I could." Abe had almost forgotten that Ivan had asked about working in the harness shop awhile back. Abe hadn't needed him then. Besides, Ivan knew nothing about harness making.

"If you're willing to train me, I'd like to come work for you," Ivan said with an enthusiastic nod.

Abe chewed on the end of his pencil as he mulled things over. With all of the jobs he had to finish, he knew he couldn't keep working by himself. It would be better if he could find someone who knew the trade. But there were advantages to training someone, he supposed.

"I'll give you an honest day's work," Ivan said. "Always did for my daed; you can ask him if you like."

Abe shook his head. "No need for that."

"Then you'll consider hiring me?"

"I guess we can give it a try."

Ivan smiled. "You won't be sorry."

"When can you begin work?"

"Right now if you like."

"Jah, sure, you can begin today." Abe nodded toward the back room. "Put on a leather apron, and I'll show you what needs to be done."

Ivan rubbed his hands together. "Okay!"

The first job Abe put Ivan on was cleaning and oiling a bunch of dirty harnesses.

"How often do most folks bring in their harnesses for cleaning?" Ivan asked as Abe filled a tub with warm water and saddle soap.

"About once a year, though some folks wait much longer." Abe pointed to another metal tub, filled with pale yellow neat's-foot oil. "That's for oiling the straps so they'll be nice and soft after they dry."

"You want me to get some harnesses washed first, or should I work on oiling those up there?" Ivan asked, pointing to some straps and buckles from an old harness that hung on a giant hook.

"Those have been done already," Abe said. "Take a feel of how smooth and oily the straps feel."

Ivan reached up and ran his fingers over the leather straps. "I see what you mean. They feel soft as a cow's ear."

"You can work on cleaning those straps now, and I'll go back to my desk to get my paperwork done." Abe wandered back to his desk, and as he took a seat, his gaze came to rest on an old saddle lying on the floor across the room. It had been one of the last things Martin had worked on before his death, and there it lay, still needing to be cleaned and repaired.

Thinking about Martin made Abe wonder how Ruth was getting along. When she'd collapsed in her wheelchair at the close of Martin's graveside service, Abe had been concerned. Later when he'd attended the meal held at the Hostettlers' home, he'd been told that Ruth was resting in bed.

Might be good if I take Esta over to visit Ruth this Saturday, he decided. *Good for Ruth and good for Esta.*

"I'm deeply concerned about Ruth," Mom said as she and Martha rolled out some pie dough. "Whenever I try to coax her out of bed, she seems agitated and says she wants to be left alone."

"I know," Martha agreed. "Ruth's physical injuries are beginning to heal, but she stays in bed most of the time and doesn't want to be around anyone."

Mom nodded. "I've tried everything I can think of to get her to talk about her feelings, but she refuses to discuss Martin or the accident."

"You think we can talk her into helping us with these apple pies?"

Mom opened her mouth as if to respond, but Ruth walked into the kitchen just then.

"It's good to see you up." Mom pulled out a chair at the table. "Would you like to peel some apples for the pies Martha and I are making?"

"I'm not interested in making pies." Ruth plucked her coat off the wall peg and slipped her arms into the sleeves.

She was about to head out the door when Martha called, "Where are you headed?"

"I'm going for a walk. I need some fresh air."

"Would you like me to go along?"

"No thanks." Ruth stepped outside and closed the door behind her.

Mom looked over at Martha and frowned. "It's good to see her up and dressed, but I don't like the way she's acting. I don't think it's a good idea for her to be out walking in the cold by herself."

"I'll go with her, even if she doesn't want the company." Martha wiped her floury hands on a clean dish towel, grabbed her coat, and rushed out the door. She hurried down the stairs and spotted Ruth tromping through the snowy yard. "Ruth, wait up," she called.

Ruth kept walking.

"Where are you going?"

No reply; just the *crunch, crunch, crunch* of Ruth's footfalls in the snow.

Martha picked up speed. "It's cold out here," she said, taking hold of Ruth's arm. "You should come back inside where it's warm."

Ruth halted. "I am not cold. I don't want company."

"What if you become weak and faint, like you did the day of the funeral?"

Ruth's chin trembled, and her eyes glistened with tears.

"I know you're hurting," Martha said, carefully choosing her words, "but you can't keep your feelings bottled up forever."

"Thanks to the one who rammed our buggy, I'll never have any children." Ruth placed her hand against her belly, and Martha could see the anguish in her sister's eyes.

"When I first realized that Flo couldn't have any puppies, I was upset. But then I figured there were other things Flo could do, so—"

"Oh, please. I can't believe you're comparing me to a dog! Flo being unable to have puppies is nothing like my situation."

"I just wanted you to see that your sense of self-worth shouldn't be centered around whether or not you can have bopplin. God spared your life, and someday, when your pain has subsided, you'll realize that God has a purpose for you."

Ruth shrugged and started walking toward the phone shed near the end of their driveway.

"Are you planning to make a phone call?"

Ruth halted and whirled around. "If you must know, I'm going to phone Sheriff Osborn."

"What for?"

"I'm going to tell him who I think rammed our buggy on Christmas Eve."

"You saw who did it?"

"No, but I've figured it out." Ruth clenched and unclenched her fingers, and she began to shiver.

"Who do you think rammed your buggy?"

"Luke. He has a truck he keeps hidden in the woods. I'm sure the vehicle that hit our buggy was a truck."

Martha's heart pounded. "Luke has a truck?"

Ruth nodded. "He confessed it to me shortly before we broke up, and I promised not to tell anyone." She grunted. "I was stupid. I should have told Dad or the bishop right away. Dad thinks Luke's the one responsible for the other things that have been done to us. I'm sure he'll want to do something about it when I tell him I believe it was Luke who rammed our buggy."

"Don't you think you should talk to Luke first–find out what he has to say about it?"

"No. I want to tell the sheriff. I'm sure he. . ." Ruth's voice faltered, and she swayed unsteadily on her feet.

"Are you okay?"

"I'm fine."

Martha grabbed Ruth's arm. "Please don't tell Dad or the sheriff that you think it was Luke who rammed your buggy."

"Why not?"

"Even if it was a truck that hit the buggy, you have no proof it belonged to Luke. Please don't say anything to anyone about your suspicions until I've had a chance to speak with Luke."

"I. . .I don't know. . . ." Ruth's face had turned as pale as the snow. "Oh, I feel so light-headed." She wobbled and sank to her knees.

"I'll get Dad!" Martha raced to the woodworking shop and jerked open the door. "Ruth's fallen in the snow!"

Dad dropped the hunk of wood he'd been holding, and Cleon left the cabinets he'd been sanding. They rushed out the door. A few seconds later, Cleon lifted Ruth into his arms and carried her toward the house.

"What were you two doing out here in the cold?" Dad asked, giving Martha a stern look. "Haven't you got better sense than to go traipsing through the snow with a sister who's only been out of the hospital a few weeks?"

Martha blew out her breath. "We weren't traipsing, Dad. Ruth came down from her bedroom a while ago, and when she said she needed some fresh air, I went after her." Martha thought it best not to mention the reason for her sister's trek through the snow. If Dad had any idea Ruth thought Luke was responsible for their accident, he'd be all over the poor fellow, trying to get him to fess up.

Martha pursed her lips as she made a decision. The first chance she had, she would talk to Luke.

Chapter 27

Is Ruth feeling better now, Papa?" Esta asked as she turned in her seat at the front of the buggy.

"I hope so, daughter. It's been three weeks since the accident, and I'm hoping she'll feel up to some company."

"I'm glad you waited until Saturday when I wasn't in school to visit Ruth," Esta said, grinning at him. "But I wish you woulda let me bring Winkie along."

Abe shook his head. "I'm not sure Ruth will be up to having that much excitement today. You know how crazy Winkie can get when he's excited to see someone."

Esta giggled. "When Bishop King came by to pick up that harness you made for him last week, Winkie got so excited, he piddled on his boot."

"That wasn't a good thing," he said, giving Esta a sidelong glance. Truth was, Bishop King had asked for the accident since he'd gotten the dog riled up when he first arrived.

"Josh was mad 'cause he couldn't come with us today."

"I explained to him and the other kinner that I thought it might be too much if we all barged in on Ruth. Maybe later, after she's had more time to recuperate from her injuries, we can all pay her a visit."

Esta's forehead wrinkled. "I heard Aunt Sue talkin' to Ruth's sister Martha the other day. They were sayin' that Ruth can't have no bopplin. Is that true, Papa?"

Abe nodded. "Ruth had some serious injuries that required surgery and left her unable to have children."

"That's a shame. I know for a fact that Ruth likes kinner and wants to be a mudder; she told me so."

"Some things aren't meant to be."

Esta sat with her lips pursed. Finally, she looked over at Abe and said, "You think you'll ever get married again, Papa?"

"What makes you ask such a question?"

She shrugged her slim shoulders. "I was just thinkin' that since you don't have no fraa anymore, and Ruth don't have no *mann*, maybe the two of you could get married. Then she could be our mamm and wouldn't feel sad 'cause she can't have no bopplin."

Abe's jaw clenched. Just the idea of his replacing Alma with another wife made him feel unfaithful to her memory. And married to Ruth Gingerich of all people! Why, the woman was a good ten years younger than him! Besides, she'd been married to his good friend and loyal worker. That just didn't seem right to Abe.

"Papa, did ya hear what I said?" Esta asked, nudging Abe's arm.

"I'm not looking for a wife right now, and it's way too soon for Ruth to even be thinking about marriage again."

"Maybe someday?"

"Esta, girl, if the good Lord desires for me to find another wife, then He'll have to drop her right in my lap."

Ruth was lying on the sofa, reading a book, when Mom entered the living room with Abe and Esta Wengerd. "You've got company, daughter."

Ruth set the book aside and pulled herself to a sitting position, tucking in the quilt draped over her legs.

"It's good to see you," Abe said as he and Esta took seats in the chairs across from Ruth.

"How are you feelin', Ruth?" Esta asked in a near whisper.

Ruth shrugged.

"Abe, would you care for something to eat?" Mom asked. "I baked some gingerbread this morning, and it should be plenty cool by now."

"Danki, that'd be nice," he replied.

"How about you?" Mom smiled at Esta. "Would you like a glass of milk and a hunk of gingerbread?"

Esta nodded with an eager expression. "Sounds real good."

Mom turned to Ruth. "Would you care for some gingerbread?"

"No thanks; I'm not hungry."

"How about a cup of tea?"

"That would be fine."

"Would you like some tea, Abe?" Mom asked.

"I've never had much appreciation for tea, but a glass of milk would suit me just fine."

Mom reached out her hand toward Esta. "Would you like to help me whip up some cream in the kitchen?"

"Can I lick the bowl?"

"Jah, sure. Martha usually licks the bowls around here, but since she's gone on an errand this morning, you can take over her job."

"Can I go up to Anna's house and see if she wants some gingerbread, too?"

"If it's all right with your daed, it's fine by me."

Abe gave a quick nod. "Be sure you put your coat on."

"I will." Esta skipped out the door behind Mom, leaving Ruth alone in the room with Abe.

He leaned slightly forward in his chair. "I. . .uh, know what it's like to lose a mate, so I think I have a pretty good understanding of what you must be feeling right now."

Ruth gave no response.

"Losing Alma hurt more than words can tell." Abe stared at his clasped hands. "But God's been with me every day since Alma died, and He's given me the strength to get through it."

"Does it help to know that she died from a freak act of nature and not because someone killed her in a senseless attack?"

He lifted his gaze to meet hers. "What?"

"Whoever rammed our buggy did it on purpose," Ruth mumbled, barely able to speak around the lump lodged in her throat. "It was no accident."

"Maybe the driver of the vehicle hit a patch of ice. Could be he just lost control."

Ruth gulped down a sob that threatened to erupt. "The person who killed Martin and left me unable to have children rammed our buggy six times!"

"Does the sheriff have any idea who might be responsible? I mean, is he conducting an investigation?"

Ruth thought about her attempt to phone the sheriff. She would have tried again if Martha hadn't begged her to wait until she'd spoken with Luke herself. Well, if Martha didn't find out something soon, Ruth was going to let the sheriff know her suspicions whether Martha liked it or not!

"I don't know what the sheriff thinks," she said in answer to Abe's question. "He asked me all kinds of questions about the accident and said he would be checking things out." She sighed. "I've not heard anything since."

"I guess investigations take time."

She grunted. "If the sheriff had kept a closer eye on things like he said he was going to do, maybe the culprit would have been caught by now."

Abe drummed his fingers along the arms of his chair. "With no husband to support you, I know it's going to be hard for you financially."

"I can't stay in the house Martin and I rented," Ruth said, feeling the agony of her bitterness weighing her down. "My folks don't mind me staying here, and since Dad's willing to support me for as long as I need his help, I guess I'll manage."

"What about your hospital bills? I know you'll need help with those."

She nodded. "Some of it has already been taken care of through the community fund. Dad says there's been talk of a benefit auction to raise the rest of the money."

Abe drew in a deep breath as he pulled his fingers through the ends of his reddish-brown beard. "Martin was a good friend. I miss seeing his smiling face when I come to work each day."

Not nearly as much as I miss him every night, Ruth thought regrettably. "Have you hired anyone to take his place?" she asked.

"Jah. Ivan Schrock."

"I see."

Mom stepped into the room just then carrying a tray, which she placed on the narrow table near the sofa.

"Where's my daughter?" Abe asked.

"She and Anna are out in the kitchen having their snack at the table." Mom handed Abe a plate of gingerbread. "Those girls have been chattering ever since they got back from Grace and Cleon's."

Abe nodded and forked a piece of gingerbread into his mouth. "This is sure good."

"Danki."

Ruth swung her legs over the side of the sofa. "I'm feeling kind of tired. If you'll excuse me, I think I'll go up to bed."

Before either Mom or Abe could comment, she skirted out of the room.

Martha's heart pounded as she tied her horse to the hitching rail and headed for John Peterson's woodworking shop. She had stopped by the Friesens' to speak with Luke and had been told by Luke's folks that John had asked Luke to work today. Deciding this would be a good chance to see how Flo was getting along, as well as to speak with Luke, she'd headed over to John's.

She found John sitting at his desk, talking to a customer. Luke sat on a stool in front of one of the workbenches, sanding the arm of a chair.

He looked up and smiled when she approached. "Wie geht's, Martha? What brings you over here today?"

"I'm doing okay, and one of the reasons I came by is to ask John how Flo's getting along."

"See for yourself." Luke pointed across the room to where the female beagle lay near the potbellied woodstove. "She's happy as a pig with a bucket of slop."

Martha smiled. "Glad to hear she's adjusted so well."

"From what I could tell, she took to John right away."

"That's good to hear." Martha shuffled her feet a few times, trying to think of the best way to broach the sensitive topic on her mind.

"You're lookin' kind of thoughtful. Is there something else you wanted to say?"

"Well, I was wondering. . ." She leaned closer to Luke. "Do you still have that truck you keep parked in the woods?"

His eyebrows lifted high on his forehead. "How do you know about that?"

"Ruth told me."

He grunted. "So she couldn't keep a secret, huh?"

"That doesn't matter. What matters is whether you still have a truck hidden in the woods."

His only reply was a quick nod.

"And your folks don't know about it?"

He shrugged. "Can't really say, but they've never mentioned it, so I don't think they know."

Martha shifted her weight again.

"Anything else you want to know?"

"Actually, there is. I was wondering what you did on Christmas Eve."

"Had supper with my folks."

"Were you there the whole evening?"

"All except for the short time I drove over to the Kings' place to borrow something my mamm needed."

"Did you drive there in your truck?"

"Now how would I do that when it's parked in the woods? I took one of our buggies over to the Kings'. Jah, that's what I did, all right."

"What time was that?"

"Around four, I think."

Martha felt a sense of relief. If Luke had been home all evening except to make a quick trip to the Kings' at four o'clock, there was no way he could have been driving the vehicle that rammed Martin's buggy sometime after six. She was sure Ruth was just being paranoid about this situation and would change her mind when she heard what Luke had said.

"I'd best be going," she said, turning away from him.

He tapped her on the shoulder. "What about John? I thought you came to ask him how Flo's doing?"

She nodded at the sleeping dog. "I can see for myself the answer to that."

"Oh, right."

"See you later, Luke," Martha said as she rushed out the door.

Chapter 28

Won't you have a couple of cookies to go with your tea?" Mom asked as she took a seat on the sofa beside Ruth one morning in late February.

Ruth shook her head. "I'm still full from breakfast."

"But breakfast was a few hours ago, and you hardly ate a thing."

Ruth set her teacup on the table so hard that some splashed onto her hand. "Ouch!"

"Did you burn yourself?" Mom leaned over and took hold of Ruth's hand. "Maybe I'd better get some aloe to put on that."

"Don't bother. It'll be fine."

"It might leave a scar if you don't tend to it right away."

Ruth pulled her hand away.

"At least let me get a cold washcloth."

Ruth studied the red blotch on her hand. "It's nothing serious. I don't need a washcloth."

Mom shrugged.

They drank their tea in silence, then Mom looked over at Ruth and smiled. "It might be fun if we went to Berlin later this week. We could do some shopping and have lunch at—"

"I don't feel like shopping or going to lunch."

"But you've been cooped up in the house for so long. Some fresh air might do you good."

"I went out to the chicken coop to gather eggs yesterday. The air was cold, and I didn't like it."

Mom laid her hand on Ruth's arm. "It will get better. Give it time."

Ruth fingered the edge of her empty cup. "The weather always improves when spring comes."

"I wasn't talking about the weather. I was referring to the distress you're feeling over Martin's death. It's going to take a while, but eventually you'll work through the pain and move on with your life. I think it would be good if you talked about the way you're feeling."

Irritation welled in Ruth's chest. She didn't want to talk about her feelings. She just wanted to be left alone. "Why must you hover over me and try to make me say things I don't want to say?" she snapped.

Mom pulled back as if she'd been stung by a bee. "I'm just concerned."

Ruth gave no reply.

"Maybe I'll go over to Grace's house for a bit," Mom said, rising to her feet. "I'd like to see how the boppli's doing and find out whether Grace has been able to get his colic under control. Would you like to come along?"

Ruth shook her head.

Mom held out her hand. "I'm sure Grace would like to see you. And the boppli is growing so much these days. Why, in no time at all, he'll be crawling."

Ruth gritted her teeth. "I can hardly look at Grace's baby."

Mom's mouth hung open like a broken window hinge. "Oh, Ruth, how can you say such a thing?"

"You want me to be honest, don't you? Isn't that what you said a few minutes ago—that I should talk about my feelings?"

Mom nodded slowly.

"Seeing how happy Grace is with her boppli only reminds me that I'll never have any bopplin of my own."

Mom seated herself on the sofa again. "I think I understand a little of how you feel."

"Oh?"

"I miscarried a son before Grace was born, and every time I saw my sister, Clara, holding her baby, I wept."

"But you had other children later on."

"That's true, but—"

"So your situation isn't the same as mine."

"Not exactly. When that miscarriage occurred, I didn't know whether I could ever get pregnant again. I grieved until I came to realize that I couldn't change the past any more than I could control the future. I had to go on living and look to God for my strength." Mom touched Ruth's arm. "My advice is for you to take small steps toward doing some of the things you used to enjoy."

"There's nothing I want to do."

"What about little Esta?"

"What about her?"

"Don't you want to continue your friendship with her?"

Ruth shook her head. "Esta doesn't need me now. She's got her dog, and Anna's her friend. She seems to be happy and well adjusted." She released a deep moan. "Truth is, no one needs me, and I have nothing to live for."

"Please don't say that. We all need you–me, your daed, Martha, Grace, and Grace's two precious kinner."

Ruth shook her head. "You and Dad have each other; Grace has Cleon and their little ones; Martha has her dogs. I have no one."

"You have us."

Ruth gave no response.

With a shake of her head, Mom stood. "I'm heading over to Grace's now. If you change your mind, that's where I'll be until it's time to start lunch."

Ruth leaned her head against the sofa cushions and closed her eyes. When she heard footfalls on the hardwood floor, she knew her mother had left the room.

She was tired and wanted to sleep, yet sleep wouldn't come. Some folks in their community had referred to Martin's death as an accident, but it was no accident. Ruth knew whoever had hit their buggy had done it on purpose. The bitterness she felt over this reality mounted with each passing day. She and Martin had been married less than two months, and he'd been snatched away from her in the blink of an eye. It wasn't fair. They'd made so many plans–plans to have their families over for supper, plans to build a house of their own, plans to have a baby. Someone needed to pay for Martin's death. No one should be allowed to get away with murder.

Ruth thought about how Martha had gone to see Luke a while back and how he'd told her that he hadn't been driving his truck on Christmas Eve.

"I don't believe him," she mumbled.

"Who don't you believe?"

Ruth's eyes snapped open. Sadie Esh stood just inside the living room door.

"Ach, Sadie, you scared me! I didn't hear you come in."

"Let myself in through the back door. When I didn't see anyone in the kitchen, I came out here." Sadie glanced around the room. "You seem to be alone, Ruth. Who were you talking to, anyway?"

"Myself."

Sadie lowered herself into the rocking chair. "I do that sometimes, too."

Ruth sat staring at her tightly clasped hands.

"The reason I came by was to see how you're feeling and ask if you might consider coming back to work at the bakeshop. The woman who was hired to take your place when you got married had to quit, and the Clemonses haven't found anyone to replace her yet."

Ruth shook her head. "I'm not up to that."

"Maybe in a few weeks?" Sadie asked with a hopeful expression.

"I don't think so."

"Are you still feeling tired and sore from your surgery?"

Ruth shrugged. "Tired, but not sore anymore."

"What are your plans for the future?"

"I have no plans."

"Oh, but–"

"Nobody around here understands how I feel. No one seems to care that Martin was murdered."

Sadie's eyes widened. "Murdered? But I thought you were involved in an accident."

"Someone rammed our buggy from behind, and they kept doing it until the buggy flipped over." Ruth nearly choked on the sob rising in her throat. "I think whoever did the other attacks against my family is the same one who rammed our buggy. I think if Dad had let the sheriff know about things sooner, Martin would still be alive."

"Have there been any more attacks since your buggy was rammed?" Sadie asked.

Ruth shook her head. "I think whoever's at fault is lying low because the sheriff's been patrolling our area more since Christmas Eve." Tears slipped out of her eyes and dribbled down her cheeks. "Every time I see a buggy going down the road, I'm reminded of the night Martin was killed." She placed both hands against her stomach and gritted her teeth. "I don't think I'll ever forgive the one who did it, either."

"I'm at my wit's end trying to help Ruth deal with her grief," Mom said when she and Grace took a seat at Grace's kitchen table. Grace had just put the baby down for a nap, and she hoped that she and Mom could visit without interruption.

"Ruth's grief is understandable." Grace handed her mother a cup of coffee. "I grieved for a time after Wade died, and even more after his folks took Anna from me."

Mom nodded, her eyes revealing obvious compassion. "That must have been hard."

"It was, but at least I knew Anna was alive and the potential of having more kinner hadn't been taken from me."

Mom leaned forward, her elbows resting on the table. "What concerns me more than Ruth's grief is her growing bitterness and refusal to talk about things."

"I don't know what we can do to help other than pray and keep suggesting things she might like to do."

"I wanted her to go shopping and out to lunch with me later this week, but she said no to that idea." Mom slowly shook her head. "Ruth doesn't want to do anything but sit around the house and pine for what she's lost."

Grace reached over and clasped her mother's hand. "It's hard being a parent, jah?"

Mom nodded as tears welled in her eyes. "But there are many rewards."

How well Grace knew that. She wouldn't trade a single moment of motherhood—not even those days when the baby was fussy and Anna whined about everything. Her heart went out to her sister.

Dear Lord, Grace prayed silently, *please give Ruth's life joy and meaning again, and help me be more appreciative of all I have.*

Chapter 29

Why don't you go to the dog auction with Martha today?" Mom suggested when Ruth entered the kitchen one Friday morning in early March. "It should be fun."

"I'm not interested in watching a bunch of yapping dogs get auctioned off," Ruth said with a shake of her head.

"It would be good if you could find something you're interested in."

Ruth clenched her teeth as she struggled not to say something unkind. She knew Mom meant well, but she didn't understand. No one did.

"Ruth, did you hear what I said?"

Placing the jug of milk she'd taken from the refrigerator onto the table, Ruth turned to face her mother. "I heard, but I'm not going to the auction with Martha. I woke up with a koppweh."

Mom's eyebrows furrowed. "If you've got a headache, why don't you go back to bed? I'll bring you a breakfast tray."

"I don't need a breakfast tray, and I wish you'd quit treating me like a child." Ruth's hands shook as she picked up a stack of napkins and began setting the table.

"I'm sorry." Mom started across the room toward Ruth, but Martha entered the kitchen and stepped between them.

"What's going on?" she asked, looking at Ruth. "I could hear your shrill voice all the way upstairs."

Tears burned the back of Ruth's throat, and she swallowed hard, unable to answer her sister's question.

Martha turned and gave Mom a questioning look.

"I suggested that Ruth go to the dog auction with you today, but she says she's got a headache."

"I'm sorry to hear that." Martha shrugged. "You'd probably be bored watching a bunch of hyper dogs get auctioned off anyhow."

Ruth nodded and hurried over to the cupboard to get out the dishes. At least Martha hadn't suggested she go back to her room and be served breakfast in bed.

"What time will you be leaving for Walnut Creek?" Mom asked, smiling at Martha.

"In an hour or so."

"Your daed will be in from doing his chores soon, and then we can eat."

"What would you like me to do?" Martha asked.

"Why don't you make some toast while Ruth sets the table? I've got a pot of oatmeal cooking, and it should be done soon."

"Okay."

"Would you like some aspirin?" Mom asked, stepping up to Ruth.

"I'll get it."

"I bought a new bottle when I went shopping yesterday. It's in the cupboard above the sink," Mom said.

"You've had a lot of headaches lately," Martha put in. "Maybe you should see the chiropractor for a neck adjustment."

"It's not my neck causing the headaches."

"Maybe some valerian root would help," Mom said as she lifted the lid on the oatmeal and peeked inside.

Ruth dropped the silverware to the table with a clatter. "I don't need any herbs or chiropractic adjustments. I need to be left alone!" She whirled around and dashed out of the room.

As Cleon sat at the breakfast table with Grace and Anna, he made up his mind that he would try to show his stepdaughter a little more attention this morning.

"How are things going with you at school these days?" he asked, looking over at Anna.

"Okay."

"Have you learned anything new?"

Anna reached for her glass of milk and gulped some down. "I guess so."

"What have you learned?"

"Hmm. . ."

"Well?"

The child shrugged.

Cleon's patience was beginning to wane, and he gritted his teeth to keep from snapping at Anna.

Grace gently poked his arm. "Would you please pass the syrup?"

"Jah, sure." He handed Grace the bottle of syrup and turned to Anna again. "Are you looking forward to summer coming so you can spend time with your baby brother?"

Anna's forehead wrinkled. "He cries too much. I'm gonna spend all my time with Esta this summer."

"Not all your time," Grace corrected. "You'll have chores to do, remember?"

"Jah, I know."

Cleon reached for his cup of coffee. "When you're not doing chores, you should get to know Daniel better. Maybe you and your mamm can put the boppli in the stroller and wheel him down to the woodworking shop to see me and your grandpa."

Anna looked over at Grace. "I wonder why my other grandpa hasn't sent me no more letters."

"It's *any more*, not *no more*," Grace said, touching the child's arm. "And you did get a letter and some money from your grandpa Davis for Christmas."

Anna's lower lip protruded. "That was a long time ago. I wish we could see where Poppy lives since he's still not feelin' so good."

"Maybe after Daniel gets a little bigger."

"Really, Mama?" Anna's expression turned hopeful.

Grace opened her mouth as if to say something, but Cleon cut her off.

"I don't think that's a good idea."

"Why not?"

"Jah, Papa, why not?" Anna looked at Cleon with questioning eyes.

"For one thing, it's going to be a while before Daniel's big enough to take a long trip." He glanced at Grace, hoping she would help him out, but she just stared at her plate of half-eaten pancakes.

"Linda Mast said she and her family went to Florida last summer, and they took their boppli along," Anna argued.

Cleon grunted. "That may be true, but the Mast baby is older than Daniel."

"So we can't go?"

"Things are really hectic around here right now," he said. "Your aunt Ruth is still hurting from the loss of Martin, and your mamm needs to be here for her."

"But she's got Grandma and Grandpa Hostettler and Aunt Martha, too."

"We can talk about this later," Cleon mumbled.

"When?"

"I don't know."

"But I need to know when," Anna persisted. "I'm gonna write Poppy a letter when I get home from school. I want to tell him when I can come—"

Cleon held up his hand. "Don't tell him anything; do you understand?"

With a strangled sob, Anna pushed back her chair and dashed from the room.

"Did you have to make her cry?" Grace slowly shook her head. "I hate to send her off to school with her eyes all red and swollen."

Cleon frowned. "Why is it that every time I say something to Anna, she ends up crying and then you take her side?"

"I was not taking her side. If I'd been taking her side, I would have tried to make you realize that Daniel will be old enough to travel by summer."

"No, he won't, because I don't want him going halfway across the country. I don't think it would be good for Anna to see her grandpa right now."

"Why not?"

"You know how strained things have been between me and Anna since Daniel was born. If she saw her grandpa Davis again, she might not want to come home."

"I don't relish the idea of her seeing him again, either, but that's not the point."

"What is the point?"

"I think if you would start paying Anna more attention, things might not be so strained between you two, and she wouldn't be thinking about her grandpa Davis so much."

"Oh, so it's all my fault, is it?" Cleon's face heated up. "I was trying to make conversation with her, and you saw the kind of response I got. She barely answered any of my questions."

Grace opened her mouth to respond, but the baby's cry halted her words. "I'd better tend to Daniel." She pushed her chair away from the table and rushed out of the room.

Cleon grabbed his cup to drink the last of his coffee but discovered it had turned cold. "That figures," he mumbled. This was not the beginning of a good day.

Chapter 30

Ruth had been lying on the sofa for quite a while when she heard a knock on the front door. Her mother had gone to the woodworking shop to take Dad his lunch, and Martha was still at the dog auction. No one but her could answer the door.

Reluctantly, she sat up and plodded over to the door. When she opened it, she discovered a middle-aged English woman with short, chestnut-colored hair and dark brown eyes standing on the porch.

"May I help you?"

The woman nodded. "My name's Rosemary Cole, and I'm looking for my brother."

Ruth squinted against the invading light streaming through the open door. "I don't know anyone with the last name of Cole living nearby," she said.

"My brother's last name is Hostettler."

"Hostettler?"

"That's right. Roman Hostettler."

Ruth's mouth fell open, and she leaned against the doorjamb for support. "Are—are you my dad's sister?"

"Yes."

Ruth stared at the woman, trying to piece things together. Finally, she opened the door wider and said, "I'm Ruth—Roman's daughter. Please, come inside."

Rosemary followed Ruth into the living room and took a seat on the sofa. "Is—is my brother here?"

"He's out in his woodworking shop right now," Ruth said as she seated herself in the rocking chair across from Rosemary. "Would you like me to take you there?"

"Yes. No." Rosemary gave her left earlobe a tug, a habit she and Roman had begun when they were children. "Sorry, I'm feeling kind of nervous right now. I'd like a few minutes to compose myself before I see my brother."

Ruth nodded.

"I. . .uh. . .I'm not sure what his reaction will be when he sees me. It's been a long time, and. . ." Rosemary's voice trailed off, and she stared at her trembling hands.

"Would you like something to drink? Maybe a glass of tea or cold water?"

"Yes, yes. That would be nice."

"I'll be right back."

After Ruth left the room, Rosemary leaned her head against the back of the sofa and closed her eyes. *So my brother has his own woodworking shop. He always did like fooling around with wood. He's obviously married, or he wouldn't have a daughter named Ruth. I wonder how many other children he has.*

She opened her eyes and glanced around the room. The furnishings were simple, and the place had a homey feel. Several potted plants sat in one corner of the room, a scenic calendar adorned the wall, a pair of wooden sconces with white candles bordered an antique-looking clock, and several quilted throw pillows lay on the sofa. Roman's wife obviously had good taste, even though her home wasn't fancy like most English homes.

Rosemary thought about her visit to the home where she and her brothers had grown up. She'd driven to it before coming here and found someone else living there—a young Amish couple, Michael and Karen Mast. The Masts had told Rosemary that the elderly couple who used to live there were dead. When she'd asked about her brothers, Michael had said the only one still living in the area was Roman. He'd given Rosemary the address and said it was just a few miles down the road.

Rosemary's thoughts were halted when Ruth returned with a tray of cookies and a glass of iced tea. She placed the tray on the low table in front of the sofa and returned to her seat. "Please, help yourself."

Rosemary reached for the glass and took a sip. The cool liquid felt good on her parched throat. "Are you the only one at home?" she asked.

Ruth nodded. "My mother went to the shop to take Dad his lunch, my sister Grace is at her house, and my sister Martha has gone to Walnut Creek to a dog auction."

Rosemary's interest was piqued. She loved dogs—had ever since she was a girl. But Bob wouldn't let her have a dog. He'd said they were too much trouble.

Ruth shifted in her chair. "Did my dad know you were coming?"

"No, I—" A burning lump formed in Rosemary's throat. "I stopped by the home where we grew up, but the young couple who live there said my folks had died."

Ruth's chair squeaked as she pumped her legs up and down. "Grandpa Hostettler passed away five years ago, and Grandma died a year later."

Rosemary flinched. "I should have been here. I—I didn't know."

Ruth continued to rock, wearing a troubled look on her face. Did she think Rosemary was a terrible daughter because she hadn't returned home in all these years? Rosemary had thought about it—even mentioned it to Bob a couple of times. But he'd always said no—that her family didn't care about her, which was obvious because they'd never responded to any of her letters.

I was a fool to believe him, Rosemary thought with regret. *I should have made an effort to see my family despite the things he said.*

She finished her iced tea and set her glass back on the table. "I'm ready to see my brother now."

Martha smiled at the female beagle she'd bid on to replace Flo as a mate for Bo. The dog's name was Polly, and she'd already had one litter of pups, so Martha was sure things would work out for her to raise some beagles. If Polly gave her a good-sized litter and Martha made enough money when she sold them, she hoped to buy a pair of cocker spaniels.

"Up you go," Martha said as she lifted Polly into the dog carrier she'd brought from home. "I'm taking you to meet Bo."

"Who's Bo?"

Martha whirled around at the sound of a male voice. "Luke! I didn't know you'd be here today."

He motioned to the ginger-colored cocker spaniel he held on a leash. "Came to buy my mamm a birthday present."

A pang of envy shot through Martha. She wished she'd been able to buy a pair of cocker spaniels, but she needed to be practical. Since she already had a male beagle, it made sense to buy him a mate.

"She's beautiful," Martha said, bending down to pet the spaniel. *"Was is dei name?"*

"Her name's Cindy, and she's a purebred with papers. I think my mamm's gonna like her, don't you?"

"Oh jah." Martha's heart skipped a beat when Luke smiled at her. How could anyone think he could be responsible for the terrible things that had been done to her family? Besides, no one had proven that Luke had been behind the break-ins or horrible attacks. He'd told her that he hadn't taken his truck out on Christmas Eve, so she was sure he wasn't the one who had rammed Ruth and Martin's buggy.

"I see you bought yourself another beagle," Luke said, motioning to the dog carrier in the back of Martha's buggy.

"I got her to replace Flo."

Luke nodded. "John's happy with her, too. Said she does a real good job running down rabbits for him."

"Glad to hear it." Martha shook her head. "She sure wasn't able to give me the puppies I needed to get my business going good."

"Maybe this beagle will work out better for you."

"I hope so. The paper that came with her said she's already had one litter of pups. At least I know she's not barren."

Luke scuffed the ground with the toe of his boot. "I've been wondering—how's your sister getting along these days?"

"Which sister?"

"Ruth."

"She's still struggling with her grief over losing Martin, but we're trying to help her through it, and she's taking it one day at a time."

"That's the best way to deal with anything. Jah, just one day at a time," he said with a nod.

Martha smiled. If Luke had been the one responsible for Martin's death, he surely wouldn't be asking about Ruth or looking so sad-eyed right now. She was sure he was innocent. If only he would get baptized and join the church, maybe her dad, the bishop, and others in their community would realize Luke was one of them.

Martha glanced at the cocker spaniel again. "I would have liked to bid on a pair of spaniels to breed, but I figured it would be best to get a mate for Bo."

"Say, I've got an idea." Luke's dark eyes seemed to dance with enthusiasm. "Why don't you get yourself a male cocker and breed it with my mamm's female?"

"That's a nice thought, but it won't work."

"Why not?"

"The pups your mamm's dog might have would be hers, not mine. If she sold them, the money would be hers, too."

Luke reached up to scratch the side of his head and knocked his straw hat to the ground. "Maybe Mom would be willing to split the profits with you. After all, she'd have to pay for stud service if she wanted to breed the dog on her own," he said, bending over to retrieve the hat.

"I might have to talk to your mamm about this. After I'm able to buy a male cocker, that is."

"I'm making pretty good money working for John. Maybe I could loan you what you need to buy the dog."

"I couldn't let you do that."

"Why not?"

Martha didn't feel she could tell Luke that her dad would have a fit if he got wind that Luke had loaned her money, but she couldn't accept his gracious offer, either. "If I'm going to build up my business, then I want to do it on my own."

"Guess I can understand that. I pretty much feel the same way about what I'm doing."

"But you work for someone; I'm trying to build my own business."

Luke shrugged. "I've got plans for the future, though. Plans I haven't told anyone about."

Martha didn't feel it would be right to press him about whatever plans he might have, so she gave the cocker spaniel another pat and said, "Guess I'd better get home. I told my mamm I'd be there around noon."

"I should go, too. Gotta give this critter to my mamm before it starts thinkin' I'm its master."

Martha laughed and climbed into her buggy. "I hope to see you at the next preaching service, Luke."

"Jah, sure." He lifted a hand in a wave as he led the cocker spaniel away.

As Martha pulled out of the parking lot a few minutes later, a sense of hope welled in her soul. She was glad she had met up with Luke today.

Rosemary's palms turned sweaty, and her legs felt like two sticks of rubber as she followed Ruth down a dirt path toward a white building. Would Roman recognize her after all these years? Would she know him? Would he welcome her home or turn her away?

"Dad, there's someone here to see you," Ruth said as they stepped into the woodworking shop a few minutes later.

Rosemary fought the urge to sneeze as the sharp odor of stain came in contact with her nose.

A young man with dark brown hair and a square jaw looked up from the chair he was staining and smiled. Rosemary knew he wasn't her brother. The man was too young to be Roman.

"Who's with you, Ruth?" a deep voice called out. "I'm about to have lunch with your mamm."

When Rosemary peered around Ruth, she caught sight of a middle-aged Amish woman standing in front of a workbench, and when the woman moved aside, Rosemary's heart felt as if it had stopped beating. The man sitting at the workbench had to be her brother. Hair that had once been full and dark was now thinning and streaked with gray, but the slight hump in the center of his nose was still there, and so were his piercing dark eyes.

"Roman, it's me," she said, moving closer to him. "I-I've come home."

He tipped his head and stared at her. "Do I know you?"

She nodded, unable to answer his question.

"Dad, it's your sister, Rosemary," Ruth said, touching Rosemary's elbow with her hand.

Roman jerked his head. The woman beside him gasped. But neither said a word. After several awkward moments, he spoke. "Where have you been all these years?"

"I've been living in Boise, Idaho, with my husband, Bob, but he died a few months ago. So I decided to come home and see my family."

"You think you can just sashay in the door and pick up where you left off thirty-some years ago like nothing's ever happened? Is that what you think?" Roman's voice sounded harsh, and the scowl on his face spoke volumes.

"I—I would like to explain. There are things you don't know—things you need to understand."

Roman's fist came down hard on the workbench, jiggling his lunch box and sending a napkin sailing to the floor. "It's been over thirty years, Rosemary! Do you know how much can happen in that time?"

She opened her mouth to respond, but he cut her off.

"Mom and Dad are dead. I'll bet you didn't know that, did you?"

"Not until I went by their house before I came here."

"Do you have any idea how hard Mom cried after you left home? When you didn't write and let her know where you were so she could write back, she was brokenhearted."

"I did write. I—"

"Pig's foot! If you'd written, we at least would have known where you were and that you were okay." He waved his hand as if he were swatting at a fly. "Now everyone but me is gone."

"My other brothers are dead?" Rosemary's head began to pound, and she placed her fingers against her throbbing temples.

"They're not dead; they moved to Wisconsin with their wives twenty years ago. Everyone except for Walt."

"Where is he?"

"Walt and his family are living up in Geauga County now. Have been for the last couple of years. I'm the only one from our family still living in Holmes County." He compressed his lips tightly together, grabbed the mug on his workbench, and took a drink.

The woman who stood at Roman's side reached out her hand. "I'm Roman's wife, Judith, and this is Ruth, one of our three daughters," she said, nodding at Ruth.

"It's nice to meet you, Judith. I met Ruth up at your house."

Judith motioned to the young man Rosemary had seen when she'd entered the shop. "That's our son-in-law, Cleon. He's married to our oldest daughter, Grace."

Rosemary glanced over at Cleon and smiled, then she turned to face Roman. "Can we sit awhile and talk? I'd like to explain a few things."

He shook his head. "I've got nothing to say, and there isn't anything you could say that I want to hear."

"Dad, don't you think you should listen to Aunt Rosemary?" Ruth spoke up.

Roman set his cup down with such force, a splash of coffee spilled on the sandwich that lay before him. "If she'd wanted to say something to me, then she would have written or come for a visit." He picked up the sandwich, tossed it in the lunch box, and slammed the lid. "Appetite's gone now."

Cleon stepped over to the workbench and laid his hand on Roman's shoulder. "I think you'd better take a deep breath and count to twenty. You're getting all worked up, and it's not good for your health."

"Maybe we should go up to the house," Judith suggested. "I'll fix some iced tea and we can sit in the living room and talk things through."

"No way!" Roman folded his arms in an unyielding pose. "I've got work to do." He glared at Rosemary. "Besides, I've got nothing to say to the likes of you, and neither does anyone in my family."

Tears stung the back of Rosemary's eyes, blurring her vision. Coming here had been a mistake. She should have stayed in Idaho, just as her son and daughter-in-law wanted her to do.

"I'm sorry I bothered you. I should have known you would still be stubborn like you were as a child." With a strangled sob, Rosemary rushed out the door.

Chapter 31

Unable to stand the dejected look on her aunt's face, Ruth hurried out of the woodworking shop after Rosemary. She thought her father was being cruel in his unwillingness to listen to what his sister wanted to say, and it wouldn't be right to let the poor woman leave without someone saying something to her.

Aunt Rosemary was almost to her car when Ruth caught up to her. "Don't go," she panted. "You need to talk things through with my dad."

Rosemary turned toward Ruth and sniffed deeply. "You heard what he said; he has nothing to say to me."

"Dad's upset right now. Give him some time to calm down and think things through."

"Are you suggesting I try again?"

Ruth nodded. "Not right now, but maybe in a day or two."

Rosemary shook her head. "I'm not so sure—"

"Mom will talk to him, and so will I. Please, won't you come back in a few days?"

Tears glistened in Rosemary's eyes. "There's not much left for me here anymore. But I came all this way, so I suppose I should stay awhile longer."

"Life is so short, and one never knows when their loved ones will be snatched away." Ruth drew in a quick breath. "If you were to leave without making things right between you and Dad, you might regret it for the rest of your life."

"I already do. I never should have left home in the first place."

Rosemary opened her car door and stepped into the driver's seat. "I've taken a room at Hannah's House, a bed-and-breakfast in Berlin, so I'll be back in a couple of days."

As Ruth watched her aunt drive out of the yard, a lump lodged in her throat. Nothing was right anymore. Misunderstanding, misery, and confusion abounded at every turn. There seemed to be no answers for any of it.

With a heavy heart, she made her way back to her father's shop. Maybe Mom had been able to talk some sense into Dad by now. Maybe when his sister returned, he would be willing to listen to what she had to say.

As Martha guided her horse and buggy up the driveway leading to her house, a gray compact car passed her on the left. A middle-aged woman with short brown hair sat in the driver's seat. Martha didn't recognize her. Maybe she was a tourist who had gotten lost and needed directions. Or maybe she'd had business at Dad's woodworking shop.

Martha directed the horse to the hitching rail near the barn and climbed down from the buggy. After she unhitched the horse and led him to the corral, she went around to the back of the buggy to remove the dog carrier.

"Did you have any success at the auction?"

Martha turned and smiled at Grace, who held baby Daniel in her arms. "Jah, I got another female beagle to take Flo's place."

"That's good. Let's hope this one isn't barren."

"She's already had one litter of pups, so I'm sure she'll be able to have more." Martha reached over and stroked the top of Daniel's head. "Are you two out for a walk?"

"Not really. Cleon was supposed to come home for lunch, but it's after one and he hasn't shown up. I thought I'd better go down to the shop and see if he's still planning to eat lunch at the house or if he wants me to bring him something there."

Martha glanced toward the woodworking shop. "If you'll wait a minute, I'll walk with you. I'd like to show Dad my new dog."

"Sure, we can wait."

Martha took the dog out of the carrier and clipped a leash to its collar. "We're ready."

Grace smiled. "She's a nice-looking dog. What'd you name her?"

"Polly. She already had the name when I got her."

"I like it," Grace said as they started walking down the path toward the shop.

"I saw Luke Friesen at the dog auction. He bought a female cocker spaniel to give his mamm for her birthday. We discussed the idea of me getting a male cocker later on and breeding the two."

"Better not mention that idea to Dad." Grace frowned. "I don't think he'd be pleased about you making plans that involve Luke."

"Dad's been irritated ever since he fired Luke." Martha grunted. "I used to think Dad liked Luke, and I can't believe he and Ruth suspect Luke might have done all those terrible things to us. Luke seems like a nice fellow. I'm sure he would never do anything criminal."

"I don't think he could, either." Grace stopped walking and turned to face Martha. "It's been several months since there was an attack–not since Ruth and Martin's buggy was rammed."

"And we don't know for sure that the person responsible for the accident was the same one who broke into our house and did all of the other acts of vandalism to our property."

"That's true. Whoever hit the buggy could have been drinking. Maybe they got scared and fled the scene when they realized they had caused an accident."

Martha shook her head. "Try telling that to Ruth. She thinks the person who hit them did it on purpose, and she's convinced that Luke is the one responsible for that, too."

"How could it have been Luke when he drives a horse and buggy?"

"He owns a truck and keeps it hidden in the woods."

Grace's mouth dropped open. "Really? This is the first I've heard that."

Martha clamped her hand over her mouth. She couldn't believe she'd blurted that out. Especially after Ruth had asked her not to say anything.

"Does Dad know what Ruth suspects?"

"No, but I talked to Luke soon after the accident. In fact, I came right out and asked what he was doing on Christmas Eve."

"What'd he say?"

"Said he was home all evening, except for a quick trip to the Kings' place to borrow something his mamm needed."

Deep lines etched Grace's forehead. "Then he could have done it."

Martha shook her head vigorously. "I asked Luke if he'd been driving his truck on Christmas Eve, and he said he hadn't."

"And you believe him?"

"Jah. He said he went to the Kings' around four o'clock. Since Martin and Ruth's accident happened sometime after six, he couldn't have done it."

"Well," Grace said, releasing a sigh, "we can't solve anything standing here speculating. Let's get into the shop before my arms give out." She smiled at Daniel, fast asleep in her arms. "This young man feels like he weighs a ton."

Martha chuckled. It was good to see Grace feeling better these days. For a while after Daniel was born, Grace had been sullen and mildly depressed.

They stepped onto the porch of Dad's shop, and Martha had no more than opened the door, when she heard Mom's pleading voice.

"Roman, won't you please listen to reason? This may have been your only chance to—"

"My only chance?" Dad bellowed. "It's that woman who had a chance. But she threw it out the window the day she left home."

"What's going on?" Grace asked, looking at Cleon, who stood off to one side with an anxious expression. "I thought you were coming up to the house for lunch."

"I was, until things got sticky in here. Figured I'd better hang around and see if I could help get your daed calmed down."

Martha felt immediate concern. "What's wrong with Dad?"

Cleon nodded toward the workbench where Dad stood beside Mom. "Better let him explain."

Martha hurried across the room. "What's going on? Why were you shouting at Mom?"

"My sister came home," he said with a groan.

Martha gasped. "The sister who's been gone more than thirty years?"

Dad gave one quick nod.

"That's wunderbaar," Grace said.

"Your daed doesn't think so." Mom shook her head. "He sent Rosemary away."

Martha glanced out the window. "That must have been her in the car I passed when I came up the driveway. Oh, Dad, how could you have sent her away? Didn't you think we'd all like to meet her?"

"Ruth met her," Mom said. "Apparently Rosemary went up to the house, and then Ruth brought her down here."

"Did she say where she's been all these years?" Grace asked.

"Boise, Idaho. She said her husband died recently, so she came here to see her family."

"It's too late for that," Dad mumbled. "She never cared a whit about her family before, so why now?"

Mom frowned. "If you'd given her the chance to explain, you might have the answer to your question."

Polly whined and pulled on her leash, and Martha looked down. She'd almost forgotten her reason for coming to the shop. "I came here to tell you that I bought a female beagle today," she mumbled. "But I guess that's not so important right now."

"It is important, dear one." Mom patted Martha's arm. "But at the moment it's hard to get enthused about anything."

"Will Aunt Rosemary be back?" Grace asked. "I'd like to meet her."

Dad shook his head. "If I have my way, I'll never have to see that woman again."

"I'm sorry about lunch being late," Sue said as Abe pulled out a chair and took a seat at the table. "Molly got into a jar of petroleum jelly and made a mess of not only herself but the sofa cushions in the living room."

Abe grimaced. Instead of things getting better for his sister, they seemed to be getting worse. Even with the four older ones in school,

Sue had her hands full caring for Molly and Owen during the day.

"I'm sorry to hear about your troubles." He glanced over at Molly's high chair and saw that it was empty. "Where's my little girl now?"

"I gave her a bath after she made the mess. As I was drying her off, she fell asleep. I put her to bed and figured she could eat when she wakes up."

"That makes sense." Abe looked over at Owen and then back at Sue. "Should we bow for prayer?"

They nodded and lowered their heads. When the prayer was over, Abe helped himself to a piece of bread and slathered it with butter.

"I got a letter from home this morning," Sue said.

"Was it from the folks?"

She nodded. "It was from Dad, letting me know that Mom fell and broke her hip last week. He asked if I could come home."

Abe nearly choked on the bread he'd put in his mouth. "Ach! I'm sorry to hear about Mom."

"I hate to leave you in the lurch, but she really needs me right now, so—"

Abe held up his hand. "No problem. You're needed there more than here. I'm sure I can find someone to take your place." He grabbed his glass of water and gulped some down. "I'll start looking for a helper right away."

Chapter 32

How did the dog auction go the other day?" Irene asked Martha as the two of them peeled apples for the pies Irene would serve to a group of tourists later in the day.

"It went well." Martha smiled. "I got another female beagle, and I'm hoping she'll give me lots of pups."

"What'd you name her?" Irene's teenage daughter, Carolyn, asked from where she stood making a fruit salad.

"She already had a name–Polly."

"I like it. Sounds real *lebhaft*," Irene put in.

"Polly seems to be pretty sprightly, all right. When I introduced Polly to Bo, she got so excited she knocked the poor critter to the ground." Martha reached for another apple. As she sliced into it, the tangy aroma wafted up to her nose and made her mouth water. Apple pie was her favorite, and she hoped there would be some left over so she could have a piece.

"Guess we know who'll be the boss in that family," Carolyn said with a chuckle.

A knock sounded at the back door.

"I wonder who that could be." Irene wiped her hands on a dish towel and went to answer the door. When Irene returned, Martha was shocked to see Gary Walker standing beside her.

"Wh-what are you doing here?" she squeaked.

"I heard about the Amish meals that are served here, so I came by to see if I could get an interview to put in one of the local papers." Gary offered Martha a slanted grin and lifted his notebook and pen.

She ground her teeth together. "I thought you had moved on."

"I did, but I missed the place so much, I decided to come back." Gary smiled at Irene, a more genuine smile than he'd given Martha. "In fact, I've decided to relocate to Holmes County, and I've been looking for a place to live. You wouldn't know of anything that's available, would you?"

Irene opened her mouth as if to respond, but Martha spoke first. "Why would you want to move to Holmes County?"

"I like it here. Besides, I've been offered a job at the newspaper in Millersburg. I'll be doing a regular column for them from now on, as well as some freelance stuff."

Martha's heart gave a lurch, and her palms grew sweaty. If Gary moved to Holmes County and he *was* the one responsible for the things that had been done to them, they could probably expect more.

Gary turned to face Irene. "Would you mind answering a few of my questions about the home-cooked meals you serve?"

"I suppose it would be all right," she replied sweetly. "In fact, some free advertising might be good for my business."

Gary pulled out a chair at the table and took a seat. "Is there anything in particular you'd like my readers to know?"

Ruth lay curled in a fetal position on her bedroom floor. The circle of sun shining through her window did nothing to diminish the loneliness encompassing her soul. When Ruth was a child, she used to lie in the sun, enjoying its warmth, finding it to be healing and comforting whenever she felt sad or lonely. Not anymore. Even the heat of the sun brought no healing or comfort. There seemed to be no reason for her to go on living.

She stared at the dust particles floating past her face. One. . .two. . . three. . . How many specks of dust were there, and where did they all come from?

Caw! Caw! Caw! The persistent chatter of a crow outside her window sounded foreboding, and she shivered. Her nose twitched as she drew in a shallow breath. When was the last time the braided throw rug on which she lay had been cleaned?

She rolled onto her back. Gazing at the cracks in the ceiling, she tried to pray, but no words would come. What was the point of praying? God never answered her prayers.

A groan escaped Ruth's lips. She needed someplace to think—somewhere to clear her head.

The floorboards squeaked as she rose to her feet, feeling as though she were in a dream. She shuffled across the room. . .one. . .two. . . three. . .four steps to the door. Her hand clasped the knob. A few more steps and she slowly descended the stairs. The house seemed so quiet. Somewhere in the distance she heard a steady *tick-tock, tick-tock.*

Dad's taken Mom to see the chiropractor. Martha's at Irene's. No one needs me. I'm all alone.

She meandered into the kitchen and leaned against the wall, stricken with grief and a longing so strong she felt as if her heart might burst. *Martin, I miss you so.*

Ruth jumped as the clang of the dinner bell beating against the side of the house rattled the kitchen window. She needed fresh air. Needed to clear her head.

She jerked open the back door and stepped onto the porch. The sun still shone, but a gust of wind whipped around her face and took her breath away.

As if her legs had a mind of their own, they led her toward the barn. She halted in front of the silo and looked up. She had climbed up there several times when she was a girl, whenever one of her sisters had dared her to do it. Ruth wasn't afraid of heights, and the silo had seemed like a good place to sit and think. She remembered how she had enjoyed the view—gazing at the lush green pasture where the horses nibbled grass, watching the clouds drift lazily overhead, counting the cars zipping past their house.

Ruth reached up and grabbed hold of the ladder, bringing one foot up behind her and then the other. Slowly, she made her way up until she reached the opening near the peak of the silo. Turning, she took a seat on the ledge, her legs resting on the top rung of the ladder. As she stared at the vastness below, her head started to spin. What was going on? She wasn't afraid of heights. Why the woozy feeling?

She closed her eyes, and an image of Martin flashed into her mind. Oh, how she missed him. It had been three months since he'd been killed, but the ache in her heart hadn't diminished. With each passing day, the bitterness toward the one who had caused the accident escalated. Forgiveness seemed an impossible feat.

Ruth's eyelids fluttered, and hot tears dribbled down her flushed cheeks. She drew in a ragged breath and struggled against the temptation to jump. *Oh, God, I know it would be wrong to take my life, but I don't want to live anymore. I want the pain to end. I want to be with Martin.* She gulped, and a pang of fear twisted her insides. *Help me, Lord. Show me what to do.*

As Rosemary left her rental car and started walking toward her brother's woodworking shop, doubts filled her mind. Was she foolish for coming here again and trying to make things right between her and Roman? Would he listen to her this time? Could she make him understand the way things were? Or would he order her out of his shop again?

She sent up a silent prayer, opened the shop door, and stepped inside. Roman's son-in-law sat at a metal desk in the center of the room, but she saw no sign of Roman.

"Is my brother here?" she asked, stepping up to the desk.

Cleon shook his head. "He took Judith to see the chiropractor this morning. As far as I know, Ruth's the only one at home right now."

Rosemary stared at the floor, wondering if she should leave a message for Roman, go up to the house to visit Ruth, or head back to town.

"Ruth would probably like some company," Cleon said. "She lost her husband in a buggy accident a few months ago. She's been sad and lonely ever since."

Rosemary could relate to that. She'd been sad and lonely since Bob died, despite his deathbed confession that he'd intercepted all of the letters she'd written to her family over the years.

"Do you know when Roman will be back?" she asked. "I really would like to speak with him."

Cleon shrugged. "I'm not sure. He said something about taking

Judith out to lunch and then doing some shopping before coming home. He might not be here for several hours."

Rosemary fiddled with the strap on her purse, then turned toward the door. "I guess I will stop and see Ruth. Maybe by the time we're done visiting, Roman and Judith will be home."

Cleon smiled. "In case you miss Roman, I'll be sure to tell him you were here."

"Thanks."

As Rosemary walked up the path toward her brother's house, she thought about what Cleon had said concerning Ruth. No wonder the poor girl had seemed so sad and disconnected when she'd visited with her the other day. *I should have recognized the look of pain on her face. I've seen it often enough when I've looked in the mirror. Maybe I can say something to help Ruth deal with the loss she's sustained.*

Rosemary stepped onto the porch and knocked on the door. Several seconds went by, but no one answered.

Maybe Ruth is in her room and didn't hear my knock.

Rosemary turned the knob and opened the door. "Hello! Is anyone home?"

No answer.

She stood below the stairs and cupped her hands around her mouth. "Ruth, are you up there?"

No response.

Maybe she's sleeping or went out back to check on the clothes I saw hanging on the line when I arrived.

Rosemary stepped outside and started around the house. "Hello! Is anyone here?"

No reply and no sign of Ruth. *I may as well head back to town. Maybe I'll come back tomorrow.*

She started toward her car but stopped to watch a twittering blue jay as it pecked at seeds in a nearby feeder. A downy woodpecker swooped in just then, and the blue jay took flight. She watched it soar over the treetops, past the barn, and up toward the silo.

Rosemary blinked and shielded her eyes against the glare of the sun. It looked as though someone was sitting on the ledge near the top of the ladder. It couldn't be. No one in their right mind would be foolish enough to climb up there and sit on the ledge.

She tipped her head back and stared. It was a woman dressed in Amish clothes. Could it be Ruth? Had she climbed up there to— *Oh, dear God, no!*

Rosemary hurried toward the silo, a sense of urgency pressing her forward. Despite her fear of heights, she dropped her purse to the ground, grabbed the side of the ladder, and started to climb.

She'd only made it halfway up when Ruth called out, "Don't come any farther!"

Rosemary halted and looked up. "It's me, Ruth—Aunt Rosemary."

"Go away."

"I'd like to speak with you."

No response.

"Please, Ruth, come down."

"No."

"If you don't come down, I'm coming up."

When Ruth didn't move, Rosemary began climbing again. The metallic taste of fear sprang to her mouth. *Please, God, don't let her jump.*

By the time Rosemary reached the top rung, her hands shook so badly, she could barely hang on. "I'm afraid of heights," she confessed. "You need to come down so we can talk."

Ruth shook her head.

"I understand your pain. As I told you the other day, I lost my husband, too."

"Was he murdered?"

"No. Bob died of a heart attack."

"Did you lose your ability to have children when he died?"

"No, but—"

"I know it would be wrong to take my own life, but I—I have nothing to live for." Ruth emitted a pathetic-sounding sob. "I want the person who rammed our buggy to pay for what he did."

"I'm aware of what it's like to feel anger and resentment," Rosemary said. "I was angry with my husband when I found out he had betrayed me."

Ruth stared straight ahead, her chin quivering and tears streaming down her cheeks. "H-how did he betray you?"

"I'd rather not discuss the details of that right now. But I do want you to know that one day while I was reading my Bible, I came across Matthew 6:14. It says, 'For if ye forgive men their trespasses, your heavenly Father will also forgive you.' " She paused and drew in a quick breath. "Ruth, the only way you'll ever have peace is to let go of your anger and forgive the one responsible for your husband's death."

Tears coursed down Ruth's cheeks. "I–I'm not sure I can, but I know taking my life isn't the answer."

Rosemary breathed a sigh of relief. "Then you'll come down the ladder with me?"

Ruth nodded.

"Thank You, God," Rosemary murmured. She knew without a shadow of doubt that she couldn't leave Holmes County. Even if she never got through to Roman, she would stay because Ruth needed her. Truth was, Rosemary needed someone, too.

Chapter 33

Wie geht's?" Abe asked as he entered Roman's woodworking shop on Friday morning and found Roman kneeling on the floor beside an old rocking chair.

"I'm doin' okay. And you?"

"I was fine until Sue told me during lunch yesterday that our mamm broke her hip. Now Sue will have to return home to help out."

Roman's forehead wrinkled. "You've got a problem with your sister helping your mamm?"

"It's not her caring for Mom that bothers me; it's the fact that she'll be moving back to Illinois, and I'll be left without anyone to watch my kinner and keep up with the house."

"Sounds like you're going to need a *maad*."

Abe nodded. "I need a maid, all right, and I came by to see if you think Ruth might be interested in the job."

Roman's eyebrows shot up. "I don't think so. Ruth's been struggling with depression since Martin died."

"I think her going to work is a great idea," Cleon said from where he was sanding cabinets.

Roman looked at him with a dubious expression. "You do?"

Cleon nodded. "It's been three months since Martin died, and Ruth will barely go anywhere or take part in anything the family does. I think it would be good for her to get involved in someone else's life and do something useful. Might help take her mind off her own problems."

"Cleon's right," Abe said as a feeling of hope welled in his chest.

"I speak from experience when I say that it's not good for a body to sit around and dwell on her pain. If Ruth came to work for me, she'd not only be helping us out, but it would give her something meaningful to do." He smiled. "Besides, I know for a fact that my kinner think a lot of Ruth."

Roman stood, yawned, and stretched his arms overhead. "You might be right about that." He reached around to rub a spot on his lower back. "Ruth's not only good with kinner, but she's a fine cook and knows how to keep house real well. I'm sure she would do a good job for you."

"Will you speak to her about the job?" Abe asked.

"Why don't you ask her yourself?"

Abe poked a finger under the side of his hat and scratched his head. "I figured she might respond better if you do the asking."

"I doubt that." Roman grunted. "I don't have a lot of influence on any of my daughters these days."

"I could ask her, but that might seem kind of odd," Cleon said. "I agree with Roman; you should speak to Ruth yourself, Abe."

"She's up at the house with Judith. I think they were planning to bake some cookies." Roman wiggled his eyebrows. "If you ask real nice, you might get a few."

Abe nodded. "Jah, okay. I'll head up there and see what Ruth has to say."

"Could you please check on those cookies in the oven?" Mom asked, glancing over her shoulder at Ruth. "I need to use the necessary room." She hurried from the kitchen before Ruth could respond.

With a weary sigh, Ruth opened the oven door and peered inside. The soft molasses cookies were rising nicely, but they weren't quite brown enough. She figured they needed a few more minutes.

She reached for the teakettle at the back of stove, poured herself a cup of hot water, and added a tea bag. She was about to take a seat at the table when a knock sounded at the back door. Since Mom was still in the bathroom and Martha had gone to the barn some time ago, Ruth went to answer the door. She was pleased to find her aunt on the porch.

"I hope you're not busy," Aunt Rosemary said, "because I'd like to take you to lunch in Millersburg. Afterward, I thought it might be fun to go shopping at Wal-Mart."

Ruth sucked in her breath. She hadn't been anywhere other than church since Martin died. The thought of going out to lunch or shopping in a big store made her feel queasy. "I—I don't know—"

"It'll be good for you to get out of the house and do something fun." Aunt Rosemary gave Ruth's arm a gentle squeeze. "I need to buy a few things, and it would be nice to have someone along to keep me company."

Ruth opened her mouth to respond, but Mom came out of the bathroom just then. "Who was at the door, Ruth?"

"It's Aunt Rosemary." Ruth stepped aside and motioned her aunt into the house.

"Oh, good. I'm glad you came back. Have you been to the woodworking shop to speak with Roman?"

Rosemary shook her head. "Not today. I came by to see if Ruth would like to go shopping and out to lunch with me." She smiled at Ruth's mother. "You're welcome to join us if you like."

"That's nice of you," Mom said, "but Grace is coming over soon, and we'd planned to do some sewing." She slipped her arm around Ruth's waist. "I think you should go. It would do you a world of good to get out of the house for a while."

Ruth was on the verge of saying that she didn't feel up to going when she caught a whiff of something burning. "Ach, the cookies!" She rushed into the kitchen, flipped the oven door open, and withdrew the cookie sheet. Every one of the cookies was overly dark and crispy around the edges.

"Are they ruined?" Mom asked as she and Aunt Rosemary stepped into the room.

Ruth nodded. "I'm afraid so. It's a good thing the two batches we made earlier turned out okay." She glanced over at her aunt. "Would you like to try one of the good ones?"

Aunt Rosemary shook her head. "The offer's tempting, but I don't want to spoil my appetite for lunch. Speaking of which, have you decided whether you'll go to Millersburg with me?"

"She'll go," Mom said before Ruth could open her mouth. "And when you get back, maybe you'll have a chance to talk to that *glotzkeppich* husband of mine."

"Roman always was a stubborn one, even when he was a boy." Aunt Rosemary shook her head. "I will try to speak with him again, but I'm not holding my breath that he'll listen to anything I have to say."

"I'll be praying that he does. There's been enough misunderstanding in this family."

Ruth grimaced. She knew her mother was probably referring to the secret Grace had kept when she'd returned home after going English for a time. Ruth wasn't sure whether Dad had ever come to grips with the knowledge that Grace had kept her previous marriage to an Englisher from him for some time.

"Well, now," Aunt Rosemary said, touching Ruth's arm, "should the two of us head for town?"

Ruth glanced at the charred cookies sitting on the counter. "I've still got a couple more batches to bake."

"Never mind that," Mom said with a shake of her head. "You run along with Rosemary, and I'll finish the cookies."

Ruth figured she wasn't going to argue her way out of going, so she plucked her sweater and purse off the wall peg near the door and had just touched the doorknob when a knock sounded.

"Must be our day for company," Mom said. "Open it, Ruth, and see who's come calling."

When Ruth opened the door, she was surprised to see Abe Wengerd standing on the porch holding his straw hat. "Guder mariye," he said, shifting his weight from one foot to the other. "Mind if I come in a minute?"

"No, of course not." Ruth opened the door wider. "If you came to see Dad, he's working in his shop right now."

"Been there already. It's you I'm here to see."

"Me?" Ruth couldn't imagine what Abe would need to see her about.

"I was wondering if you'd be interested in coming to work for me."

"In the harness shop?"

"No, no," he said, looking a bit flustered. "I meant as a maad."

"But you have Sue helping you with the household chores. Isn't she able to handle things on her own?"

"She'll be leaving on Monday—going back home to help our mamm, who recently fell and broke her hip."

"I'm sorry to hear that," Mom said, stepping out of the kitchen. She nudged Ruth gently on the arm. "I think it would be a good idea for you to work as Abe's maid."

"No. I couldn't do that," Ruth said with a shake of her head.

"Why not?" The question came from Aunt Rosemary, who had stepped up behind Mom.

"Well, I. . ." Ruth's face flushed with heat, and her hands began to shake. "I'm needed here, helping you."

"Nonsense." Mom draped her arm across Ruth's shoulder. "I can get by with Martha's help, just like I did when you first got married."

Ruth flinched at the reminder. Ever since Aunt Rosemary had talked her down from the silo, she'd been trying not to think about Martin or the anger she felt toward the one who had killed him.

"I really think it would be good for you." Aunt Rosemary moved to stand beside Ruth and leaned close to her ear. "Remember the things we talked about the other day?"

Ruth knew what Rosemary was referring to—things they'd discussed after they'd climbed down from the silo, things about Ruth making an effort to start living life again.

"I've seen how well you get along with my kinner," Abe put in as if he thought Ruth needed a bit more persuasion. "And I'll pay you a decent wage."

Ruth didn't care about the money. But it would be nice to be around Abe's children. Besides, if she was gone all day, Mom wouldn't be able to hover over her.

She nodded slowly. "All right. I can begin work on Monday morning."

As Grace headed down the path toward her folks' house, she spotted Ruth and an English woman, whom she guessed might be their aunt Rosemary, coming out the back door. She would have waved, but since she had a squirming baby in her arms, she didn't think that was a good idea. By the time she got close enough to call out to them, they'd gotten into the car she'd seen parked in the driveway and pulled away.

"Was that Dad's sister with Ruth?" Grace asked her mother when she entered the house a few minutes later.

Mom nodded as she opened the oven door and removed a sheet of plump, golden brown cookies. "Rosemary came by to see if Ruth wanted to go shopping and out to lunch."

"And Ruth agreed to go?"

"She did."

"I'm surprised. She hasn't wanted to do much of anything since Martin died, not even visit with her family."

"I know." Mom set the cookie sheet on a cooling rack and nodded toward the table. "Have a seat, and I'll fix you a glass of milk to go with a couple of these soft molasses cookies."

"Sounds good to me." Grace took a seat and placed Daniel in her lap.

"There's an even bigger surprise," Mom said, handing Grace a glass. "Ruth's going to work for Abe as his maad."

"I thought Abe's sister was taking care of his house and kinner."

"She was, but she's going back to Illinois to help her mamm, who recently broke her hip."

"That's too bad." Daniel hiccupped several times, and Grace rubbed the small of his back until the hiccups subsided. "How'd you talk Ruth into working for Abe?"

"I didn't. Rosemary took care of that." Mom poured milk into Grace's glass, brought a plate of cookies to the table, and took a seat. "She seems to have some persuasion over Ruth that none of the rest of us has."

"Maybe it's a good thing she's come back to Holmes County."

"I was thinking that, too." Mom held out her hands. "How about I hold the boppli while you eat those cookies?"

"Are you sure? Daniel's cutting a tooth, and he's been fussy all week."

Mom clicked her tongue. "Have you forgotten that I raised three girls of my own? I do know a thing or two about fussy bopplin."

"Guess you've got a point." Grace handed the baby to her mother. "Has Aunt Rosemary tried to speak with Dad again?"

"Not yet, but she said she might try after she and Ruth get home from Millersburg."

"I hope he'll listen. Maybe there's a good reason Aunt Rosemary never contacted any of her family."

Mom nodded. "There are always two sides to every story. Your daed ought to be smart enough to listen to his sister."

A knock sounded at the door, interrupting their conversation.

"Want me to get it?" Grace asked.

"That would be good since I've got my hands full of baby right now."

Grace pushed her chair away from the table and hurried to the back door. She found Donna Larson on the porch holding an angel food cake.

"I was at the bakeshop in town early this morning," Donna explained. "They had angel food cake on sale, so I bought two—one for me and one for your mother." She peered around Grace. "Is she at home?"

"She's in the kitchen. Would you like to come in and have some freshly baked molasses cookies and milk?"

"The cookies sound good, but I'd prefer coffee if you have any."

"Mom probably has a pot on the stove. She usually keeps some warming for my dad."

Donna followed Grace into the kitchen. "I brought you an angel food cake from the bakeshop in Berlin," she said, smiling at Mom.

"That was nice of you," Mom replied. "Why don't you join us at the table?"

"Don't mind if I do." Donna set the cake on the counter and took a seat. "That baby of yours is sure growing," she said, smiling at Grace when she handed her a cup of coffee.

Grace nodded. "He seems to grow an inch every day."

"How's Ruth getting along? Is she dealing any better with the loss of her husband?"

"I think so," Mom replied. "Abe Wengerd came by a while ago and asked if Ruth would come to work for him as his maid."

"I thought his sister was helping."

"She was, but she'll be going home to care for her mother, who was injured recently." Mom smiled. "Miracle of miracles, Ruth agreed to take Sue's place as Abe's maid."

"Where is Ruth today?" Donna asked.

Mom explained about Aunt Rosemary and how she'd been gone for thirty-some years but had come back to Holmes County. She ended the story by saying, "Rosemary's the one who convinced Ruth to agree to work for Abe. The two of them left a while ago to go shopping and out to lunch in Millersburg."

"It's good to hear Ruth's getting out. I hope working for Abe will help with the pain of her loss."

"That's what I'm hoping for, too," Mom said with a nod.

Donna blew on her coffee then took a sip. "How's everything else around here? Have there been any more acts of vandalism?"

"Not since Ruth and Martin's buggy was run off the road. We're hoping things stay that way." Mom bent her head and kissed Daniel's cheek. "It's not easy to spend your days and nights worrying that something bad might be just around the corner."

Donna tapped her fingernails on the edge of the table. "If the attacks should start again and you and Roman decide you need to move someplace else, I hope you'll let Ray and me know before you put the place on the market." She smiled at Mom then at Grace. "We'd like to be given the first opportunity to buy your land."

"Roman thinks moving would be the coward's way out," Mom replied. "He said it would be like giving in to the attacker. If the attacks should start up again, we're hoping the sheriff will catch the criminal. In the meantime, we'll keep trusting the Lord to keep us safe."

Donna looked as though she was going to say something, but Martha burst into the room, interrupting their conversation. "You should see how well Bo and Polly are getting along. I think things will work out better with this dog." She skipped across the floor but halted when she spotted Donna. "Sorry. I didn't realize we had company."

"I'm not really company," Donna said with a wave of her hand. "I'm just your friendly neighbor who decided to drop by with an angel food cake because I know it's one of your mother's favorite desserts."

Martha eyed the cake sitting across the room. "Looks real tasty."

"There's soft molasses cookies, freshly baked," Mom said, motioning to the plate in the center of the table. "Pull up a chair and have a few. It'll tide you over until lunch."

Martha took a seat and plucked two cookies off the plate.

"Don't you think you should wash your hands first?" Grace asked.

"I washed them at the pump outside before I came in."

"Oh."

Martha looked over at Grace, and her eyebrows pulled together. "There's something I've been meaning to tell you, and the reason I didn't say anything sooner is because I know how shaken up everyone's been over Aunt Rosemary's sudden appearance. I didn't want to give you one more thing to worry about."

"What is it, Martha?" Mom asked. "What's happened that might make us worry?"

"When I was working at Irene's the other day, she had an unexpected visitor."

"Who was that?" Grace asked.

"Gary Walker."

Grace's mouth dropped open. "But I thought he had left Holmes County and wasn't coming back."

"He said he's been hired at the newspaper office in Millersburg and that he's decided to move here permanently."

Grace clutched the edge of the table as a sense of panic gripped her like a vise. If Gary was moving to Holmes County, then the attacks would surely begin again.

Chapter 34

As Ruth stood in front of Abe's kitchen window, watching Anna and Esta play a game of hide-and-seek, she reflected on the past. She could still remember how it used to be when she and her sisters played hide-and-seek as children. Playing childhood games used to make her happy whenever she felt sad. Now, thanks to her depression, very little made her laugh. Even her trip to Millersburg with Aunt Rosemary hadn't helped much, although she did feel comfortable in the woman's company.

Aunt Rosemary had seemed disappointed that Dad wasn't in his shop when they'd returned home that day. She'd told Ruth she would return in a few days and try again. The woman obviously wasn't one to give up easily. The fact that she'd been able to talk Ruth into taking the job as Abe's maid was a good indication of her ability to make people do things they didn't want to do. Maybe in time, she would get through to Dad.

Ruth moved away from the window and over to the door. Stepping outside, she took a seat on the porch swing to better watch the children. Anna had come home with Esta after school so the girls could play, and soon after their arrival, they'd initiated the game of hide-and-seek with Esta's siblings. All but Gideon. He kept to himself most of the time and had gone to the barn as soon as he'd arrived home from school.

Ruth's eyes drifted shut as she thought about how well things had gone on her first day working for Abe. She had arrived early this morning in time to feed the children breakfast and make the older ones' lunches for school. After breakfast, Abe had gone to his harness shop. Soon after that, Gideon, Josh, Esta, and Willis had headed for school. Ruth spent the rest of the morning washing clothes, baking bread, and keeping an eye on Owen and Molly.

She reflected on how warm and cuddly Molly had felt as she'd held the little golden-haired girl in her arms and rocked her to sleep after lunch. Molly had called her *Mammi* before she'd fallen asleep, and it had touched Ruth's heart to the very core. *If only I was her mammi,* she thought. *I'd give most anything to have a child of my own.*

"Here I come, ready or not!"

Ruth's eyes snapped open, and she saw Willis zip past the porch, obviously on his way to seek out the hiding places of the other children. A few minutes later, she heard giggling and figured one of the girls had probably hidden under the porch.

She yawned and was on the verge of drifting off again when a shrill scream jolted her fully awake.

With her heart pounding like a herd of stampeding horses, Ruth jumped off the swing and dashed into the yard. There lay Willis, holding his nose and whimpering. She dropped to the ground beside the boy. "What happened?"

"I was chasin' after Josh and run into the tree." Willis removed his hands, and Ruth gasped when she saw blood oozing from his nose.

She pulled out the handkerchief tucked inside the band of her choring apron and covered the boy's nose with it. "Come inside so I can get that bleeding stopped," she said, helping him to his feet.

The other children came out of their hiding places and followed Ruth and Willis into the kitchen.

"Is he gonna be all right?" Esta asked as Ruth seated Willis on a chair and placed a small bag of ice against the side of his nose.

"His *naas* doesn't appear to be broken," Ruth said. "Once we get the bleeding stopped, he should be fine."

"My nose bled like that once," Anna said, leaning over to stare at Willis's nose. "It was when I was livin' with Poppy and Grammy Davis. It happened 'cause I had a bad cold and blew too hard. Poppy soaked a piece of cotton in vinegar and put it inside my nose."

"Eww." Esta puckered her lips. "That must have stung."

"It did. But it made the bleeding stop real quick." Anna looked up at Ruth. "Are you gonna put vinegar in Willis's nose?"

"I hope the ice will do the trick." Ruth motioned to the plate of peanut butter cookies sitting on the counter. "Why don't you all help yourselves to a couple of cookies and go back outside to play?"

"What about Willis?" Owen wanted to know.

"He'll stay with me until his nose stops bleeding. Then he can have some cookies."

The children each grabbed a handful of cookies and tromped out the door.

Several minutes later, Abe stepped into the room. "What's going on?" he asked. "Josh told me Willis had a run-in with a tree."

"Jah, he did." Ruth placed her hand on Willis's shoulder. "He was looking for one of the others in a game of hide-and-seek when it happened."

Abe knelt on the floor in front of Willis and touched the boy's knee. "You gonna be all right, boy?"

Willis nodded, although a few tears trickled down his cheeks.

"The bleeding's probably stopped by now," Ruth said, removing the ice bag to take a look. "Jah, it seems to be fine." She extended the plate of cookies to Willis. "Why don't you take a couple of these and go sit on the porch? No playing or running around, though."

Willis snatched up three cookies and grinned at her. "I'll sit real still; I promise."

"Good thing he's got youth on his side," Abe said when Willis had left the kitchen. "If that had happened to me, I'd probably be bleeding like a stuck pig."

Ruth smiled. It was the first genuine smile she'd been able to offer since Martin's death. "Would you like a cookie?" she asked.

He took a seat at the table. "Danki. They look good."

"I brought them from home," she said, sitting in the chair across from him. "My mamm made them on Saturday."

Abe chomped one down and smacked his lips. "They taste as good as they look. Only thing that might make 'em better would be a glass of cold milk for dunking."

"You sound like my daed. He's always got to have milk to go with his cookies." Ruth started to rise. "I'll get you a glass."

"Don't trouble yourself. I can fetch it." Abe hopped up. "Would you like one, too?"

"I believe I would."

Abe was back soon with two glasses and a jug of milk.

"Danki," she said when he handed her a glass.

"How'd everything go here at the house today?" Abe asked, wiping his mouth with a napkin. "Did you have any problems?"

"Except for Willis's little accident with the tree, everything went well."

"Glad to hear it." Abe leaned his elbows on the table. "If you ever remarry, I think you'll make a fine mudder."

Ruth dropped her gaze to the table. "I thought you knew that I can't have any children." She drew in a quick breath, hoping to keep her emotions in check. She would not allow herself to break down in front of Abe, no matter how much her heart might be breaking.

Abe slapped the side of his head. "Ach, what a *dummkopp* I am. I did know about your injuries and the surgery you had; I just wasn't thinking."

Ruth lifted her gaze to meet his. "I'm sure you've had a lot on your mind, especially with Sue moving back home."

"It's still no excuse. I'm sorry I brought it up."

"Even if I could have children, I doubt I would ever remarry," Ruth said as a feeling of bitterness threatened to choke her.

"Why not?"

"I don't think I could ever love anyone the way I loved Martin."

"I know what you mean. I doubt there's anyone who could fill the place in my heart left by Alma." Abe grunted and pushed his chair aside. "Think I'll go out to the barn and see if Gideon's done all his chores."

Ruth nodded. "I'd better check on Willis. Then I'll get supper started."

"What are we having?" Abe asked as he reached the door.

"Chicken and dumplings."

"Sounds good. That's one of my favorites."

When the door closed behind Abe, Ruth put their glasses and the cookie plate in the sink. She glanced out the window and saw Abe in the yard, tossing a ball for Esta's dog to fetch.

A sense of despair came over her, and she nearly doubled over with the pain. *I'll never know the joy of watching my husband laugh and play with our kinner. I'll never know love again.*

Chapter 35

Guder mariye," Grace said when Martha stepped into her kitchen. "What brings you over here on this warm spring morning?"

"Came to deliver this." Martha held out a loaf of bread. "It's cinnamon-raisin. Aunt Rosemary brought a couple of loaves by our house right after breakfast."

"Dad's sister was here again?"

Martha nodded.

"Did she talk to Dad?"

"She tried to, but he mumbled something about being late to work and hurried out the door." Martha frowned. "I don't know why he's being so stubborn. He ought to at least hear what she has to say. Don't you agree?"

"I do—but then, what I think has never mattered much where Dad's concerned. I'm not sure he's ever gotten over my keeping the secret about Anna and Wade from him and the rest of the family."

"He never mentions it," Martha said.

"Maybe not, but I'm sure it comes to mind." Grace sighed. "With Aunt Rosemary showing up, Dad has been touchier than ever." She motioned to the kitchen table. "Would you like to join me for a cup of coffee and some of that delicious-looking bread you're holding?"

"Jah, sure. That'd be nice." Martha placed the bread on the table and pulled out a chair. "It's awfully quiet in here. Anna must have left for school already."

Grace nodded as she took plates from the cupboard and set them on the table. "Cleon's at work in Dad's shop, and Daniel fell asleep right after I nursed him, so it's been quiet for nearly an hour."

"Do you ever miss working at the restaurant in Berlin?" Martha asked as she cut a slice of bread and placed it on Grace's plate.

"Not really. I enjoy being at home with my kinner more than waiting tables and trying to keep all those hungry customers happy."

"I like my job working part-time for Irene," Martha said, "but I enjoy being at home where I can work with my dogs a lot more."

"Maybe in time you'll make enough money so your business can turn into a full-time operation."

"I hope that's the case."

They finished their snack, then Martha pushed back her chair and stood. "Guess I should head home so you can get busy with whatever you had planned for the day."

"Before you go, I was wondering if you could do me a favor."

"What is it?"

"Could you stay here with Daniel while I walk down to the mailbox? Cleon's expecting a beekeeping catalog he ordered a few weeks ago."

"I don't mind staying with Daniel," Martha said, "but I'd be happy to go to the mailbox for you."

Grace shook her head. "I appreciate the offer, but if the catalog is there, I'll want to stop at the woodworking shop and give it to Cleon."

"I could do that, too."

"I know you could, but I had something I wanted to say to Cleon at breakfast, and he rushed out the door before I got it said. This will give me a chance to do that, as well."

Martha sat down again. "Sure, no problem. Take your time."

"If Daniel wakes before I get back, he'll probably need his windle changed. Can you handle that for me?"

"Jah, sure." Martha wrinkled her nose. "I'll just sit here and enjoy another piece of bread and pray he wakes up clean and dry."

Grace chuckled and headed out the back door. A blast of warm air greeted her, but it felt good on her face. Summer was almost here, and she preferred the hot days to the bitter cold of winter.

As Grace approached the two mailboxes at the end of her folks' driveway, her throat constricted, and her heart pounded so hard she heard it thundering in her ears. Both metal boxes had been smashed in, and a note was attached to the side of her and Cleon's mailbox. It read I'm Not Done with You Yet.

With a strangled sob, Grace tore the note off the box and rushed to the woodworking shop.

"I'm going to be busy cleaning house the rest of the morning," Judith said as Roman took a seat at his desk to do some paperwork. "That's why I brought your lunch out a bit early."

"No problem." Roman took the lunch box and placed it on one end of the desk. "Have a nice day."

Her forehead wrinkled as her eyebrows drew together. "Are you trying to get rid of me?"

" 'Course not. Since you've got housecleaning to do, I figured you'd want to be on your way."

Her face relaxed, and she gave his shoulder a squeeze. "From the looks of this stack of papers on your desk, I'd say you do, too."

Judith was almost to the door when Cleon called out, "If you see Grace, would you tell her I'll be home for lunch around twelve thirty?"

"Jah, sure."

At that moment, Grace rushed into the shop waving a piece of paper. "He's done it again!" Her eyes were wide, her face pale.

"Who's done what?" Judith asked, taking hold of Grace's arm.

"I–I went to get our mail, and–and this is what I found tacked to the side of our smashed-in mailbox." She thrust the piece of paper into her mother's hands.

Judith pushed her glasses to the bridge of her nose. "It says 'I'm not done with you yet.' "

Roman jumped to his feet and hurried across the room. "Let me have a look at that." He snatched the paper from Judith, and his eyelids twitched as he studied the note.

"Was it our mailbox or your folks' that got bashed in?" Cleon asked, coming to stand beside Grace.

"Both mailboxes." Her chin quivered, and her eyes filled with tears. "He's come back, Cleon. Martha told me the other day that Gary Walker is back in Holmes County. He's taken a job at the newspaper in Millersburg and plans to move here permanently." She gulped in a quick breath. "I'm sure he's the one who wrote the note and smashed our mailboxes."

"How can you be certain? There's no way you could recognize his handwriting, because whoever put this note together didn't write it by hand. It was typed in bold letters." Judith clutched Roman's arm. "Will these attacks ever stop? Will we spend the rest of our days living in fear and wondering what's coming next?"

He groaned. "I hope not—we can't stop living."

"So much for Sheriff Osborn keeping an eye on our place," Judith said bitterly. "Makes me wonder if he even cares what's happening to us."

"I'm sure he cares," Cleon put in. "But he and his deputies can't be everywhere at once."

"Donna Larson came by the other day." Judith looked at Roman. "She said if we decided to move, she and Ray would still be interested in buying our place."

Roman shook his head. "I am not selling out because someone smashed in our mailboxes."

"It's not like this is the first attack." Grace's voice sounded unsteady, and her eyes were wide with fear. "They stop and start. Just when we begin to think the attacks are over, another one happens again."

"She's right, Roman." Judith sniffed. "There must be something we can do about this."

Roman patted Judith's back, hoping to offer her comfort. " 'God is our refuge and strength, a very present help in trouble,' " he said, quoting Psalm 46:1. "We must continue to trust Him."

"It's fine to trust God and believe He will help us, but we need to do something to put an end to these attacks." Grace's voice sounded stronger, and the look of determination Roman saw on her face let him know that she meant what she said.

"What do you think we need to do?" Judith asked.

"It's me Gary is trying to punish. I'm going to find him and demand that he stop harassing us."

"No, you're not." Cleon shook his head vigorously. "I'm your husband. It's my job to look out for you. If anyone's going to talk to Gary, it will be me."

As Ruth moved over to the sink, she spotted Abe's empty lunch box sitting on the counter. She couldn't remember whether Abe had said he would be coming up to the house for lunch today or if he'd asked her to make his lunch and bring it out to the harness shop. Things had been so hectic during breakfast this morning, she'd barely had time to make lunches for the children and send them off to school, much less remember anything Abe might have said. Molly had poured her glass of apple juice on the floor and followed that by splattering oatmeal down the front of her clean dress. Owen had whined throughout much of breakfast because he couldn't go to school with his older brothers. Gideon and Josh had gotten into an argument about whose turn it was to muck out the horses' stalls. And Willis had accidentally poked Esta in the eye with his elbow when he reached for a piece of toast.

Ruth took a sip of water and let the cool liquid trickle down her parched throat. *Maybe I'm not up to this job. Abe might be better off if he found someone else to care for his kinner and take charge of his house.* She sighed deeply. *But I enjoy spending time with the children. It gives me something meaningful to do–a reason to get up every morning.*

She set the glass in the sink and reached for the metal lunch box, deciding to make Abe's lunch and take it out to him. It was a balmy, bright day, and the walk to the shop would be good for Molly and Owen–and for Ruth, as well.

A short time later, with Abe's lunch box in her hand, she and the children headed to the harness shop.

When they stepped inside, Molly squealed when she saw her father, and Owen zipped across the room and grabbed Abe's leg. Ruth glanced to the left, and the sight of Cleon's brother standing in front of the riveting machine, wearing the same leather apron Martin used to wear, caused her to flinch.

The knowledge that Ivan was working in her husband's place and that Martin would never work in Abe's shop again was almost unbearable. Even the pungent odor of leather and neat's-foot oil reminded Ruth of Martin.

"Are you all right?" Abe asked, nudging Owen aside and stepping up to Ruth. "You look pale and kind of shaky."

"I'm fine; just a bit tired, is all." She lifted the lunch box. "I wasn't sure if you wanted to eat at the house or planned to have your lunch here, so I fixed you something and brought it out to you."

"Danki." Abe bent to pick up Molly, and then he looked back at Ruth. "Are you working too hard? Do you need a day off?"

She shook her head. "I like to keep busy. Besides, Sunday's coming, and since there won't be church this week, I can rest all day."

"I've got an idea," Abe said, nuzzling his daughter's rosy cheek.

"What's that?"

"I've been promising to take my brood on a picnic, so maybe it would be good to take this Saturday off and make good on that promise. Why don't you join me and the kinner at the pond?"

"Oh, I don't know—"

"It would help if you came along. Handling my six alone can be quite a job."

Ruth's gaze came to rest on Owen, who stared up at his father with an expectant expression. Then she looked at little Molly resting her head against Abe's broad shoulders, and her resolve weakened. It would be nice to spend the day soaking up the sun, playing with Abe's children, and watching the ducks floating on his pond. "All right," she said with a nod. "I'll pack a picnic lunch and go with you and the kinner on Saturday."

"You don't have to make the lunch," Abe was quick to say. "I'll fix some sandwiches and bring along some of those good-tasting cookies you made earlier in the week. That ought to be plenty."

"How about if I fix a jug of iced tea for us and bring some cream soda for the kinner?"

Abe nodded. "That'd be nice." He kissed Molly's cheek and handed her over to Ruth, then bent down and ruffled Owen's hair.

"You be good for Ruth, ya hear?"

The boy nodded soberly and followed Ruth out the door. As she led the way to the house, a feeling she hadn't felt in many months settled over her like a welcoming breeze on a hot summer day: the feeling of anticipation.

Chapter 36

As Ruth reclined on the quilt Abe had spread on the ground near the pond, she lifted her head and stared at the cloudless sky. It was a beautiful summer day, and the sun felt good as it bathed her face with its warm, soothing rays.

Squeals of laughter from Abe's children blended with the call of a dove. It was the first time in a long while that Ruth had felt relaxed.

"Do you like being here at the pond?" Abe asked, taking a seat on the quilt beside her.

"Very much. It's peaceful here, and I feel calmer than I have in many weeks."

"Can you see the quiet?"

She smiled. "Jah. Almost."

Abe shifted on the quilt. "Are you hungry? I could get the ice chest and bring out the sandwiches I made this morning."

"I'm not quite ready to eat, but if you're hungry or you think the kinner need to eat, then please go ahead."

He shook his head. "I think they'd like to play awhile longer."

Ruth shielded her eyes from the glare of the sun and watched as Gideon, Josh, and Willis splashed around in their inner tubes. She smiled at Esta, who held Molly and Owen's hands, walking barefoot in part of the pond that was shallow.

"It's good to see you smile," Abe said. "You have nice dimples in your cheeks."

A flush of heat climbed up the back of Ruth's neck and covered her face. "Danki."

As though sensing her embarrassment, Abe quickly changed the subject. "My kinner can't swim," he said, "so I aim to keep a close watch on them. Sure don't want to take the chance of anyone drowning."

Ruth thought about the day Martin had saved Abe's and Gideon's lives after their boat had capsized. Little had she realized that Martin would be dead less than two months later. How quickly things could change in one's life. If only there was a way to be more prepared for unexpected tragedies.

"Ach, now you're frowning." Abe nudged Ruth's arm with his elbow. "You've put those dimples into hiding again."

She released a sigh. "I was thinking about Martin and the day he saved you and Gideon from drowning."

Now it was Abe's turn to frown. "I'll always be grateful he was such a strong swimmer and cared enough to risk his life for a friend."

Ruth nodded. "Martin was a kind, caring man, and. . ." Her voice faltered, and she swallowed a couple of times.

"I know you miss him, Ruth," Abe said in a near whisper. "I miss Alma, too. Fact is, hardly a day goes by when I don't think about something she said or did. Especially with Esta looking so much like her mamm and often saying something the way Alma would have said it." His sigh lifted the hair off his forehead. "But life goes on, and I take comfort in knowing Alma's resting peacefully in the arms of our heavenly Father. Martin's there, too; I'm sure of it."

"I have that assurance, but it doesn't take away the pain of knowing he was killed by that *narrisch* man who kept ramming our buggy."

Abe's forehead wrinkled as he frowned. "I agree that the person had to be crazy if they did it on purpose, but seeing the look of anger on your face lets me know you haven't forgiven the one responsible."

Ruth swallowed against the burning in her throat. Abe was right; despite Aunt Rosemary's encouragement, she hadn't been able to forgive Martin's killer. Would it help if she knew who the man was, or would that only intensify her anger?

"Let's not talk about this anymore," she said. "I'd like to spend my time here listening to the birds singing, soaking up the sun's warming rays, and watching your kinner frolic in the water."

"You're right. We shouldn't talk about anything negative today."

"Have you heard from your sister lately?" Ruth asked.

"As a matter of fact, I got a letter from her this morning."

"How's your mamm doing?"

"Much better. Sue says she's healing nicely."

"Will Sue return to Holmes County?"

Abe shook his head. "She's become betrothed to Melvin, so she wants to stay and prepare for their wedding, which will take place this fall."

"That makes sense." Ruth moistened her lips with the tip of her tongue. "Will you want me to continue caring for the kinner, then?"

He nodded. "As long as you're willing."

"I'm more than willing." Ruth wouldn't have admitted it to Abe, but she was glad Sue wouldn't be returning to care for his children. She had come to care a great deal for them. The thought of staying home every day with nothing to look forward to wasn't a pleasant prospect. Now that Ruth worked for Abe, she felt needed and appreciated—something she hadn't felt since Martin died.

Abe rose to his feet. "Think I'll move closer to the pond so I can keep a better eye on things. Would you like to join me?"

"No thanks. I'm comfortable right here."

After Abe walked away, Ruth stretched out on the quilt, placing her hands behind her head and gazing at the lazy clouds overhead. *I wonder what it would be like to be the mother of Abe's kinner. Of course, it would mean I'd have to be married to Abe, and that idea is too ridiculous to even think about.*

Abe glanced over his shoulder. Ruth lay on the quilt looking up at the sky as though she didn't have a care in the world. Today was the first time he'd seen her looking so relaxed since Martin's death. Truth was, Abe found himself being drawn to Ruth more every day, and that fact scared him. He couldn't allow himself the luxury of falling in love with her. Ruth was too young for him. Besides, she was newly widowed, and he was sure she wasn't ready for another man in her life. He was equally sure Ruth would never be romantically inclined toward him.

"Well, would ya look at this?"

Abe jerked his attention back to the pond. Esta held a plump little frog in her hands, and Molly and Owen stood on tiptoes trying to get a look at the critter.

"Can we take him home, Papa?" Owen asked, tipping his head in Abe's direction.

"Where would you keep him?" Abe asked the boy.

Owen shrugged. "Don't know."

"Could we put him in a jar?" Esta questioned. "I'll bet there's one in our picnic basket."

"I brought along some pickled beets. I suppose we could dump them onto a paper plate, and then you can wash the jar out in the pond and take the frog home that way." Abe squatted down on his haunches beside the children. "The frog can't live that way for long. You'll have to let it go soon or it'll die."

"Like Mama did?" Owen stared up at Abe with wide eyes.

Abe nodded as a lump formed in his throat. Why was it that they could be having a good time one minute, and the next minute something was said or done that reminded him of Alma?

Owen tugged on Abe's shirtsleeve. "Papa, can me and Molly go swimmin' in tubes, like the brieder are doin'?"

Abe shook his head. "You're not big enough for that, son."

"Guess I'm not, either," Esta said.

"Not yet. When you learn to swim."

"But the brothers can't swim," she said, jutting her chin out.

"That's true, but they're staying near the shore, so if they have a problem I can wade out and grab 'em." Abe thought about the day Martin had saved him and Gideon from drowning. Martin had said he'd be happy to teach Abe and his kinner to swim, but that hadn't happened because Martin had been killed in a senseless buggy accident. No wonder Ruth hadn't come to grips with her husband's death. At least Alma hadn't been taken from Abe in such a violent way. Though her death had been hard to accept, the fact that it had been caused by an act of nature made it a bit easier to deal with.

"Papa, I'm hungry," Owen said, tugging on Abe's shirt again.

"Jah, okay. We can empty that jar of pickled beets, put your frog in the jar, and then we'll eat lunch." Abe cupped his hands around his mouth. "Come out of the water now," he called to his three older sons.

The boys paddled their way to shore, slipped the inner tubes over their heads, and trudged onto the grassy bank. Abe bent down, grabbed some towels, and handed them to the boys. Maybe by now Ruth would be hungry, too.

What am I doing here? Rosemary asked herself as she left her car and headed for Roman's woodworking shop. She'd been here to see him several times already, and each time he'd given her the cold shoulder. Would it be any different today?

The last time she'd tried talking to him, he'd said he was too busy to listen to her lies and had asked her to leave.

"They aren't lies," she muttered under her breath.

Rosemary had been tempted to tell Judith or one of Roman's daughters what had happened to the letters she'd written home all those years ago, but she'd decided against it. She needed to tell Roman before she told anyone else, and she didn't want him to think his wife and daughters were playing go-between.

The front door swung open, and Rosemary bumped into Roman.

"I was on my way out," he said in a brusque tone. "Got some deliveries to make."

"Can't you spare a minute? I'd like to speak to you."

"Don't have the time." Roman brushed past her and headed for the buggy shed.

Rosemary hurried after him. "I was wondering if you could give me our brothers' addresses. I'd like to write them. And since Geauga County is only a couple hours away, I might drive up there and see Walt."

Roman halted and turned to face her. "If you didn't care enough about them to write before, you don't need their addresses now."

Rosemary clenched her fingers around the handles of her purse. "If you'd let me explain why you never got my letters—"

"I'm not interested!" Roman stalked off with a huff.

"Maybe I should forget about reconciling with my family," Rosemary muttered as she turned toward her car.

Don't give up, a voice in her head seemed to say. *This is just a testing of your faith.*

Chapter 37

As Ruth headed for Abe's harness shop with his lunch box, she mentally lectured herself. *Martin's not here; Ivan's taken his place. Life goes on; I must accept the way things are. With God's help, I'll make every day count, for I know how short life can be.*

When she stepped into the harness shop a few minutes later, the pungent odor of neat's-foot oil tickled her nose, and she sneezed.

"*Gott segen eich.*"

She caught sight of Abe down on his haunches, oiling an old saddle. "Danki for giving me God's blessing. Now here's a blessing for you," she said, setting Abe's lunch box on his desk. "My mamm baked some cinnamon-raisin bread on Saturday, so that's what your sandwich is made with today."

Abe smacked his lips. "That does sound like a blessing."

Ruth smiled. Abe was such a kind, appreciative man.

"Where are my little ones today?" he asked. "They usually tag along when you come out to my shop."

"Martha came over and got them a while ago. She took all but Gideon home with her so they could play with Anna and see Martha's new dog."

"How come Gideon didn't go along?"

"He said he had work to do in the barn."

"If he'd gotten it done first thing this morning, he would have been free to go." Abe grimaced and rose to his feet. "Seems I've got to stay after that boy all the time. I'd have him working for me here a few hours every day, but he's not dependable."

Ruth wondered if there was something she might do to make Gideon see the error of his ways, but she figured he was Abe's boy and Abe should take care of the problem.

"I'll be up at the house washing clothes if you need me for anything." She was about to walk away, but Abe tapped her on the shoulder.

"I was wondering if you'd like to go out for a meal one night next week with me and the kinner."

"But I've got all your meals planned already," she was quick to say.

"That might be so, but I figured the kinner would like an evening out at a restaurant. Since next Friday is Esta's birthday, I thought having supper out would be a nice way to celebrate."

"I hadn't realized her birthday was coming up. She never said a word about it, and neither did anyone else."

Abe smiled. "So what do you say—shall we take my brood to supper at the Farmstead Restaurant on Friday night?"

She nodded. "That sounds like fun."

Cleon had no sooner entered the newspaper office than he began to have second thoughts. He'd promised Grace that he would seek out Gary Walker and speak to him about the mailbox incident and the other attacks against the Hostettlers, but he wasn't sure what he should say or how it would be received. If Gary was the one responsible, he might become angry at the accusations and further harass Grace's family. On the other hand, Gary needed to know that the sheriff had been informed and had promised to keep an eye on the place. That might deter him from trying anything else.

"I understand you have a reporter working here by the name of Gary Walker," Cleon said, stepping up to the receptionist's desk.

The young woman sitting behind the desk looked up at Cleon and smiled. "That's right. He started working here last week."

Cleon shifted uncomfortably from one foot to the other. "I was wondering if I might speak with him."

"I'm sorry, but Mr. Walker isn't in right now. He left early this morning to cover a story in Sugarcreek, and I'm not sure what time he'll be back."

"Oh, I see." Cleon turned to go, feeling a sense of disappointment. He didn't know when he'd have the chance to come to Millersburg again, and he wouldn't feel right asking Roman for more time off this week.

He headed for the door and had just stepped outside when he spotted Gary Walker coming down the street. He stopped walking and waited until the man approached. "You're Gary Walker, the reporter, right?"

"That's correct."

"I'm Cleon Schrock–Grace's husband."

Gary studied Cleon a few seconds, then gave a slow nod. "You must be her second husband. She told me about you, but we haven't had the privilege of meeting until now."

"Actually, we have met. You tried to interview me in Berlin a couple of times."

Gary shrugged. "I've interviewed a lot of Amish folks."

Cleon cleared his throat and wiped his sweaty palms on the sides of his trousers. "I was wondering. . . The thing is. . ."

"If you've got something to say, Mr. Schrock, then just say it. I'm a busy man and don't have any time to spare this morning."

"As I'm sure you know, my wife's family has been attacked several times in the last several months."

Gary gave a quick nod.

"On Saturday morning, we discovered that our mailboxes had been smashed in, and there was a note attached to one of the boxes."

"What'd the note say?"

" 'I'm not done with you yet.' "

"Sounds like someone has an ax to grind with one of the Hostettlers, doesn't it?"

Cleon clenched his teeth. "Grace thinks–"

"I already know what she thinks. She believes I'm the one responsible because I told her once that she'd be sorry for breaking up with me." Gary grunted. "That woman is so paranoid. Doesn't she realize that guys say a lot of things they don't mean when they've been jilted?"

Cleon wasn't sure how to respond. Maybe Grace had read more

into Gary's warning than there was. Maybe it hadn't been a threat but rather the wounded pride of a hotheaded teenager trying to scare his girlfriend into coming back to him.

"So you're not responsible for the vandalism to our mailboxes or any of the other things that have gone on at the Hostettlers'?"

"Nope. I'm an innocent man." Gary brushed past Cleon. "Now if you'll excuse me, I've got work to do."

Cleon watched as Gary entered the newspaper office. Maybe the man was telling the truth. But if Gary wasn't responsible for the attacks, who was?

Chapter 38

I'm glad you came out to supper with us," Esta said, smiling at Ruth as she sat at a table with Abe's family at the Farmstead Restaurant on Friday evening.

"I'm glad I did, too. Happy birthday, Esta." Ruth patted the child's arm.

Esta grinned at Ruth. "Danki for the birthday present you gave me." The child looked down at the small black handbag in her lap. "Mama had one like this, only it was bigger."

Ruth smiled. "I'm glad you like it."

Esta looked at her father. "Since we've already said our silent prayer, can we go to the salad bar now? I can't wait for some pickled eggs."

Abe tweaked the girl's nose. "Sure, go ahead." He nodded at Ruth. "If you'd like to go with the older kinner, I'll wait here with Molly. Then I'll go for my salad when you get back."

"Mammi. . ."

Ruth smiled at Molly, who was sitting in the high chair the restaurant had provided, eating a cracker. She patted the little girl's chubby arm and turned to face Abe. "I don't mind waiting with Molly if you'd like to go to the salad bar first."

He shook his head. "I'll wait."

"Okay. I'll see what's there that Molly can eat and bring her something back." Ruth slid her chair away from the table and followed Abe's children to the salad bar. She was ready to take a plate when she spotted her friend Sadie coming into the restaurant with her boyfriend, Toby. Sadie didn't appear to notice Ruth as she hurried to the ladies' room. Toby didn't see her, either, for he was busy talking to the hostess.

Ruth bent down and whispered in Esta's ear, "I'll be right back. Can you help Owen and Willis get their food?"

"Where are you going?" Esta looked up at Ruth with questioning eyes.

"Just need to use the restroom."

"Jah, sure. I'll help the boys get whatever they need."

Ruth smiled. Esta might be only nine years old, but she seemed so grown up at times.

When Ruth entered the ladies' room, she discovered Sadie at the sink, washing her hands. Sadie must have spotted Ruth in the mirror, for she turned and smiled. "I'm surprised to see you here. Did you come with your folks?"

"I came with Abe and his kinner. We're celebrating Esta's birthday."

"How nice." Sadie smiled. "How's your job going at Abe's?"

"I'm doing my best to keep up with things at the house, and it's nice to spend time with Abe's kinner." Ruth sighed. "It makes me feel useful and gives my life purpose."

"Everyone needs a purpose." Sadie nudged Ruth's arm. "Maybe you'll end up marrying Abe. Then your life will have purpose for years to come."

"What?"

"I was thinking you might marry Abe."

"That's ridiculous, Sadie. Abe's ten years older than me, and—"

"So what? My mamm's eight years younger than my daed."

"Even if there was no age difference, there's no love between me and Abe."

"Who says there has to be love? A mutual respect might be all that's needed." Sadie turned her palms up. "Look at my relationship with Toby. I love him, and he says he loves me, yet he still hasn't asked me to marry him. What good has love done me?"

Ruth mulled things over a bit. Maybe Sadie was right about love not being a necessary ingredient in marriage—especially if it meant she could be a mother.

She glanced at her reflection in the mirror and noticed that the dark circles she'd been plagued with for the last several months had diminished. *Would Abe even consider asking me to marry him?* She looked away. *Surely not. He's still in love with his wife. And I love Martin.*

"Martin would want you to find happiness again," Sadie said, seeming to read Ruth's thoughts.

Ruth shrugged. "Maybe so, but I'm sure Abe would never ask me to marry him."

"How do you know?"

"I just do."

A slow smile spread across Sadie's face. "Then why don't you ask him?"

Ruth's spine went rigid. "Ach, I could never do that!"

"Why not?"

"It would be too bold." She squinted at Sadie. "I don't see you asking Toby to marry you."

Sadie's face flooded with color. "No, but I've thought about it."

Ruth folded her arms across her chest. "When you become bold enough to propose to Toby, then I'll think about asking Abe to marry me."

Martha was bent over a small table in the section of her father's barn that had been turned into a kennel when she heard the barn door open and click shut.

"Is anyone here?"

Martha recognized her aunt's voice immediately; Rosemary had been coming over once or twice a week ever since she'd returned to Holmes County.

"I'm back here by the kennels."

"What are you up to?" Aunt Rosemary asked when she joined Martha.

Martha lifted Heidi's left front paw. "I've been clipping my dog's toenails."

Aunt Rosemary reached over and stroked Heidi behind her ear. "How's your business doing these days?"

"The female beagle I bought several weeks ago still isn't pregnant, but I haven't lost hope."

Aunt Rosemary released a sigh and leaned against the table. "Wish I could say the same regarding your dad and me."

"He still won't talk to you?"

"No."

"Dad can be real stubborn sometimes," Martha said with a shake of her head. "Have you tried talking to Mom about this? Maybe she can make him listen to reason."

"I just came from seeing her at the house—after I'd been to your dad's shop and gotten nowhere."

"Dad's still working in the shop at this hour?"

Aunt Rosemary nodded. "I saw the lights on when I drove in, so I stopped there first and found him restoring an old chair. Then I went up to the house and saw your mother. I was tempted to tell her my story but decided it would be best if your dad heard it from me, not secondhand." She sighed. "If I ever get him to listen, that is. He makes me feel so frustrated."

"I know what you mean about frustration." Martha placed Heidi back in her kennel and turned to face her aunt. "Nothing's been the same around here since someone started attacking my family, and things are getting steadily worse."

Aunt Rosemary's eyebrows shot up. "What kind of attacks? No one's mentioned anything about that to me."

"Dad thinks it's better if we don't talk about it, and Mom pretty much agrees."

"And what do you think, Martha?"

"I'd like to find out who's behind the attacks and make them stop." Martha grunted. "Of course, unless the sheriff does more than promise to keep an eye on our place, that's not likely to happen."

"You've spoken with the sheriff?"

"A couple of us have. He's been out to our place a few times to ask questions and look around, too."

"And he's been patrolling the area?"

"That's what he says. But the attacks have continued, and we have no idea why we're being singled out." She shrugged. "Of course, each of us has our own idea about who could be responsible."

"You mean you have a list of suspects?"

"I guess you could say that."

"Does the sheriff know this?"

"Yes. Dad has talked to him a few times."

"Well, the man should be making every effort to do something about it."

"I agree."

"Maybe I'll pay a call to the sheriff tomorrow morning. Would you like to accompany me?"

Martha nodded. Since Aunt Rosemary wasn't Amish, maybe Sheriff Osborn would take her more seriously than he had the others.

Aunt Rosemary gave Martha a hug. "Until tomorrow, then."

"What are you doing in *my* barn, talking to *my* daughter?" Dad shouted as he stepped out of the shadows.

Martha jumped. "We were just visiting," she said before her aunt could respond.

"I wasn't talking to you, daughter. I was talking to *her*." Dad whirled toward Aunt Rosemary and scowled.

"Martha's right; we were visiting."

"Jah, well, you're not welcome here. And I'll thank you to stay away from my family."

Martha's mouth opened wide. "Dad, you can't mean that."

His forehead wrinkled as he gave one quick nod. "This woman is nothing but trouble. I don't want her influencing you."

"She's not."

"It's okay. You don't have to defend me." Aunt Rosemary gave Martha's shoulder a squeeze. "I'll be going now."

As Martha watched her aunt walk out of the barn, a sense of despair washed over her. Would Aunt Rosemary be back tomorrow so they could see the sheriff together? Or would she be on the next plane headed for home?

Chapter 39

That man was no help at all," Rosemary mumbled as she and Martha left the sheriff's office the following day. "All we got for our troubles was the scent of smoke from his clothes." She flapped her hand in front of her face. "Sheriff Osborn must be a chain smoker."

Martha shrugged. "He did say he's been patrolling our area whenever he can. I guess that's something to feel good about."

"Didn't you get the feeling that he's not very interested in finding out who's behind the attacks on your family?"

Martha halted on the sidewalk and turned to face Rosemary. "What makes you think that?"

"He hasn't found any suspects—not even for the accident that killed your brother-in-law." Rosemary gritted her teeth. "Wouldn't you think the sheriff would have investigated that incident thoroughly?"

"He said he did the best he could with the little bit of information he was given."

"Puh!" Rosemary shook her head. "Did he try to gather evidence?"

"I don't know. He questioned Ruth about what she saw that night, and she told him she'd seen a truck but couldn't see the license plate and wasn't sure of the color of the vehicle because it was dark and snowing."

"Did he question the neighbors—someone who might have seen the vehicle?"

"No houses are in the area where they were hit. And no other cars on the road, I guess."

"Hmm. . ."

"The other problem the sheriff mentioned is the fact that except for the buggy accident, he usually hasn't heard about the attacks until several days later." Martha frowned. "Dad didn't like it when Sheriff Osborn showed up at his woodworking shop after one of the attacks and told him that he'd heard what had happened."

"I wish there was something I could do about this," Rosemary muttered. "If I could find out who's responsible for attacking your family, maybe Roman would forgive me for being gone all those years and never contacting my family."

"I'm sorry Dad's not willing to accept your apology."

"I've been here over three months already, and still he won't listen to me. It's a good thing my husband left me with adequate funds, or I wouldn't have been able to make this extended trip."

"I wish you could stay with us."

"Your dad would never allow that." Rosemary touched Martha's arm. "I don't know about you, but I'm hungry. Why don't the two of us go somewhere for lunch?"

Martha smiled. "Sounds good to me."

"Afterward, I think I'll drop by Abe Wengerd's house and see Ruth. Would you like to come along?"

"I'd better not. I'm working at Irene's tonight, and I need to be home by three."

"Maybe some other time we can go there together," Rosemary said as they approached her car. "Today I'll go alone."

Ruth tiptoed out of Molly's room, relieved that she'd finally gotten the little girl down for a nap. Molly had been fussy all morning, and Ruth had rocked her almost an hour before the child had fallen asleep. Since the other children were outside playing, Ruth thought this would be a good time for her to get some sewing done. The children were growing, and the older ones would be back in school soon. That meant several hemlines needed to be adjusted.

Ruth removed a needle and thread from her sewing basket and had just taken a seat on the sofa when Sadie stepped into the living room.

"Looks like you're keeping busy."

"I am. I'm surprised to see you here, though. Aren't you working at the bakeshop?"

"Today's my day off," Sadie said as she dropped into the chair opposite Ruth. "I wanted to tell you my good news."

"What news?"

"Toby and I are getting married in November."

"What?" Ruth grimaced as she jabbed her finger with the needle.

"It's true. We set the date last night, when Toby brought me home from supper at the Farmstead Restaurant."

"I can't believe he finally asked you to marry him," Ruth said, dabbing the end of her finger with a tissue.

Sadie's face flooded with color. "Actually, it was me who did the asking."

Ruth's mouth dropped open.

"Well, don't look so surprised. I told you I might."

Ruth shook her head. "No, you suggested that I ask Abe to marry me."

Sadie chuckled. "And you said you would whenever I asked Toby."

Ruth sucked in her breath. She had said something like that. But she'd never dreamed that her friend would put her to the test, or that Sadie would be bold enough to ask Toby to marry her.

Sadie left her chair and took a seat on the sofa beside Ruth. "I'd like you to be one of my *newehockers*. That is, if you're not already married by November."

Ruth's forehead wrinkled. "Why would I be married? I'm not even betrothed."

"But you might be if you ask Abe like you said you would."

"I was only kidding, Sadie. I really didn't think you would propose to Toby, or that–"

"Or what? That he would agree to marry me?" Sadie's downcast eyes let Ruth know she'd hurt her feelings.

"That's not what I meant." Ruth touched Sadie's hand. "I was going to say that I didn't think you would really expect me to propose to Abe." Her face grew warm. "I could never do that, Sadie. It wouldn't be right."

"Why not? Ruth in the Bible let Boaz know she wanted to be his wife by lying at his feet."

Ruth covered her mouth with the palm of her hand. "Ach, I could never lie at Abe's feet! What would he think of me if I did something like that?"

Sadie shook her head. "You wouldn't have to lie at his feet, silly. I'm sure if you thought about it awhile, you could come up with something else to do that would let Abe know you're interested in him and would like to be his wife." She patted Ruth's knee. "Think about it, okay?"

Ruth gave no reply.

"In the meantime, I'd like your answer about whether you'll be one of the newehockers at my wedding."

Ruth nodded slowly. "I'd be pleased to be your attendant."

"Glad to hear it." Sadie stood. "Be sure and let me know when you and Abe become betrothed." She rushed out of the room before Ruth could say a word.

Ruth reached for her Bible, which she had tucked inside the sewing basket she'd brought from home. Turning to the book of Ruth, she found chapter 3, where Ruth's mother-in-law, Naomi, told Ruth that she should mark the place where Boaz would lie and then go there and lie at his feet.

Ruth couldn't deny her attachment to Abe's family. Truth was, she often found herself wishing his children were hers. But could she ask Abe to marry her as Sadie had suggested? *Oh, that would be so bold!*

She closed her eyes. *Dear Lord, You know how much I long to be a mother. But I still love Martin, and I'm not sure I could be a good wife to Abe–if he would have me, that is.*

Ruth's prayer was interrupted when a knock sounded at the door. She went to answer it and was surprised to see her aunt standing on the front porch.

"What a nice surprise."

Aunt Rosemary smiled. "I've been meaning to come by for some time, but I've been busy getting settled into my new home."

"What new home?"

"It was too inconvenient to keep staying at the bed-and-breakfast in Berlin, so I've rented a small house owned by your neighbors, Ray and Donna Larson. They said I could rent it on a month-to-month basis, since I don't know how long I'll be staying in Holmes County."

Ruth's mouth dropped open. "Is the house near here?"

"Just a mile or so down the road."

"Why, that was the house Martin and I rented when we first got married." Ruth stared at the toes of her sneakers. "After Martin died, my dad and Cleon went over to the rental and cleared out all of our things. I wasn't up to going, and I haven't been back to the house since the night Martin died."

"I'm sure it would be a painful reminder," Aunt Rosemary said.

Ruth nodded. Then, remembering her manners, she stepped aside. "Won't you come in?"

Aunt Rosemary followed Ruth into the living room and took a seat on the sofa when Ruth motioned for her to do so. "It looks like you've been doing some sewing," she said, gesturing to the pile of clothes lying on one end of the sofa.

"Yes, I have," Ruth said as she seated herself beside the clothes. "Abe's children are growing like cornstalks. I need to get their clothes ready for school since it will be starting up again in just another month."

"I've been away from the Plain life so long I'd almost forgotten that Amish children start school several weeks before most English kids do." Rosemary touched Ruth's arm. "You're looking well. Are you feeling better these days?"

"Some. Being here with Abe's kinner has made me feel needed."

"I'm glad to hear it." Rosemary motioned to the Bible Ruth had left on the sofa. "Have you found forgiveness in your heart for the one who caused the death of your husband?"

Ruth opened her mouth to respond, but her words were halted when Gideon rushed into the room.

"Ruth, come quickly! Papa's been kicked by a horse!"

Chapter 40

Ivan, get the horse!" Abe shouted from where he lay on the ground near his buggy. He had been trying to hitch the new horse he'd bought last week to his rig, and the animal had spooked and kicked him in the leg. It was broken; Abe was sure of it. Not only did the leg hurt like crazy, but it was bent at a very odd angle. Abe knew he couldn't stand up on his own. All he could do was lie there helplessly as Ivan dashed across the yard after the gelding. If the crazy animal got out on the road, they might never see him again.

"I got him, Abe!" Ivan shouted several minutes later. "Want me to put him in the corral or the barn?"

"The corral."

"You doin' okay?"

"I'll be all right. Just get the horse put away." Abe grimaced as a stab of pain shot up his leg. Where was Ruth? It seemed as though Gideon had been gone an awfully long time.

A few seconds later, he heard footsteps running across the gravel. His five oldest children were soon at his side, and so were Ruth and her aunt Rosemary.

"Papa!" Esta cried as she dropped down beside him. "Please don't die and leave us like Mama did."

"I'm not going to die," he assured the girl.

"What happened?" Ruth asked breathlessly. "Gideon said you were kicked by a horse."

Abe nodded and ground his teeth together as another ripple of pain exploded in his leg. "It was that new horse I bought last week.

I was trying to get him hitched to the buggy when he got all riled and kicked me in the leg." He grimaced. "I'm sure it's broken."

Rosemary knelt beside him and studied his leg. "I'm no doctor, but it looks like a serious break to me. I think you should get to the hospital right away."

"Can you drive me there?" Abe asked.

"I don't think we should risk moving you—not with that leg looking the way it does." She pulled a cell phone from her purse. "I'm calling 9-1-1."

"Someone should ride to the hospital with Abe," Ruth said. She looked over at her aunt. "Would you mind staying with the children while I go?"

Esta grabbed Ruth's arm and hung on for all she was worth. "I don't want you to go!" Tears streamed down her ashen face.

"Aw, don't be such a boppli," Gideon grumbled. "We can stay here alone."

"No, you can't." Abe gritted his teeth. The pain in his leg was almost unbearable.

"I'll go with Abe," Ivan said as he joined the group. "Ruth can stay with the kinner."

"Are you sure you're gonna be all right?" Josh asked, bending close to Abe's ear.

"I'll be fine."

Ruth knelt on the ground beside Abe. "Would you like me to get word to my daed? He's one of your closest friends, and I'm sure he would like to know what's happened."

Abe nodded. "I'd appreciate that."

"I'll drive over to your folks' and tell him," Rosemary volunteered.

Ruth looked dubious. "Are you sure you don't mind?"

"Not at all. If your daed wants to go to the hospital, I'll drive him there."

When Abe heard sirens in the distance a while later, he breathed a sigh of relief.

"You want me to start sanding that set of cabinets for the bishop now?"

Cleon asked as he stepped up to Roman's desk.

Roman glanced up from the invoices he'd been working on. "Jah, sure. Those need to get done by the end of the week."

"I'll get right on it."

"Say, I've been meaning to ask how things are going with your bees. Are they producing lots of honey?"

Cleon shrugged. "A fair amount."

"Are you wishing you could be doing that full-time instead of working for me?"

"I had hoped to generate enough honey sales to support my family, but after losing all of my bee supplies in that fire last year, it's going to take a while to build up the business again."

Roman leaned his elbows on the desk and stared at Cleon. "When you do build it back up, will you want to quit working for me?"

"I don't know. I wouldn't want to leave you in the lurch. Maybe I could continue to do both."

Roman opened his mouth to reply, but just then the shop door banged open. Rosemary rushed into the room.

"I came to tell you that your friend Abe's been taken to the hospital," she said breathlessly.

Roman's mouth went dry. "What's wrong with Abe? Is he sick?"

"One of his horses kicked him in the leg. It looked like a nasty break."

Abe leaned back in his chair and groaned. "Abe doesn't need this right now. How's he going to work and support his kinner if he's laid up with a broken leg?"

"Ivan's working for him," Cleon said. "I'm sure he can handle things in the harness shop until Abe's able to work again."

Roman looked at Rosemary. "Do you know which hospital Abe was taken to?"

"The one in Millersburg."

He pushed his chair away from the desk and stood. "I'll need to call for a ride so I can go to the hospital and see how Abe's doing."

"I can take you," Rosemary said. "Then I'll be able to check on Abe's progress and give Ruth and the children a report on my way home."

Roman contemplated her offer a few seconds. He didn't relish the idea of being alone with Rosemary, but it would be quicker than calling someone else for a ride and having to wait around until they showed up. He finally nodded and said, "Jah, okay." Then he turned to Cleon. "Can you manage okay while I'm gone?"

"No problem."

"Let's be off." Roman followed Rosemary out the door.

Rosemary couldn't believe she'd been given the opportunity to be alone with her brother, but here they were, heading down the highway toward Millersburg.

She glanced over at Roman and wondered what he was thinking. His head was turned toward the window, and his shoulders were slumped. He hadn't said a word since they'd gotten in the car.

"Are you worried about your friend?" she asked.

He nodded. "Abe's been through enough this past year. He doesn't need anything more."

"From what I understand, you've been through a few things yourself over the last year."

"What do you mean?"

"The break-ins and vandalism that have occurred at your place."

"Who blabbed that information?"

"It doesn't matter who told me. What I'd like to know is why nothing's been done about it." Rosemary glanced at Roman out of the corner of her eye.

"Not much we can do except hope and pray it comes to an end." He grunted. "I figure whoever's behind the attacks is out for some kind of revenge. Once he realizes we won't be intimidated, he'll get tired of the game and leave us alone."

"I hardly think ramming Ruth and her husband's buggy is a game. I think you should have reported each attack to the sheriff right away."

"Jah, well, what would you know about it? You ran off and left your people a long time ago, so it's obvious that you don't understand our ways." His voice was laced with bitterness and a deep sense of pain. "You, who didn't even care enough about her family to let 'em know where you were or how you were doing. Don't you realize how much that hurt our mamm and daed? How does it make you feel to know they went to their graves thinking their only daughter cared nothing about them?"

Rosemary swallowed against the lump in her throat. Hearing the anger in Roman's voice and being reminded of her parents' deaths made her feel extremely guilty. She gripped the steering wheel, praying for the right words. "It's not the way you think, Roman. I didn't deliberately stay away or avoid contact with my family."

No response.

"I did write to Mama several times, but she never responded."

"Puh! If our mamm had gotten a letter from you, she would have written back."

"I thought so, too, until I got no letters in return."

"You got no letters because you sent no letters."

"That's not true. I wrote home several times."

"Then what happened to your letters?"

"They were intercepted by my husband." Rosemary grimaced. "I didn't know about it until he told me the truth shortly before he died."

"Why would he want to keep you from writing home?"

"Bob was a very controlling man. He admitted to me that he'd been afraid if I kept in touch with my family, I might want to return to the Amish way of life."

Roman sat silently, as though deep in thought.

"When I wrote those letters and put them in our mailbox, I had no idea my husband followed behind me to remove and destroy them. I assumed the letters had gone out and that the reason I didn't get a response was because my family didn't want any contact with their wayward daughter."

More silence.

"I'm not making this up, Roman. I've tried to tell you on several occasions, but you've never been willing to listen."

Nothing. Not even a grunt.

"I can't undo the past. All I can do is look to the future. I want that future to include you and your family. That's why I came back—to spend time with my Amish family and try to make up some of the years I've lost."

Roman said nothing as they continued their drive, and Rosemary was certain she hadn't gotten through to him. He probably thought she'd made up the story about Bob intercepting the letters in order to worm her way into the lives of his family.

When they pulled into the hospital parking lot a short time later, Rosemary left the engine running and turned to face Roman. "Would you like me to wait and give you a ride home?"

He reached over and clasped her arm. Tears welled in his eyes, and he released a guttural groan. "I'm sorry, sister. Will you forgive me for being such a dummkopp?"

Tears filled Rosemary's eyes as she placed her hand on his. "I'll forgive you if you forgive me. If I hadn't left home in the first place, I would have been here when Mama and Papa died. I wouldn't have missed out on seeing you get married and start a family of your own. If I'd stayed in Holmes County—"

He shook his head. "Enough with the regrets. It's time to look to the future."

Chapter 41

In the weeks that followed, Ruth settled into a routine of going over to Abe's place every day to care for his children, cook his meals, and clean the house, while Ivan spent the nights there. It had been Ivan's idea to do so, saying Abe would need help during the night and that it wouldn't be proper for Ruth to stay. Ivan had taken over the harness shop, and Gideon had been helping some. But Monday would be the first day of school, so Gideon, along with Josh, Esta, and Willis, would be gone all day, leaving Ivan to run the harness shop and Ruth to care for Abe, Owen, and Molly.

Since today was Saturday and Ivan had given Gideon the day off, the boy had taken Josh and Willis fishing at the pond behind their house. Ruth had sent the boys off with a picnic lunch an hour ago. Esta was out on the porch keeping Owen entertained with a jar of bubbles. Molly was taking a nap. That left Ruth alone in the house with Abe, who was reading his Bible on the sofa in the living room.

Deciding that Abe might like some refreshments, Ruth carried a tray into the living room and placed it on the small table near the sofa. "I brought you some milk and cookies," she said, smiling down at him.

He set the Bible aside and sat up. "Danki. That was nice of you."

Ruth handed him the glass. "How's the leg feeling this afternoon?"

"Not so bad. I should be able to start working in the shop a few hours a day beginning next week." He motioned to his leg, encased in a heavy cast. "Why don't you sit here on the sofa so we can visit awhile?"

Ruth gulped. *If I take a seat on the sofa, I'll be sitting at Abe's feet. . . almost like Ruth from the Bible.*

"If you have something to do in the other room, I'll understand," Abe said. "But it would be nice to have the company. I get tired of sitting around when I should be out in the shop working."

"I have the time." Ruth lowered herself to the sofa and shifted uncomfortably when her elbow brushed the bottom of Abe's cast. "Sorry. I hope that didn't hurt."

"Nope. Didn't feel a thing." Abe took a drink of milk. "This is refreshing. Danki."

"You're welcome."

A few moments of awkward silence passed between them. Then he smiled and said, "Your help's been appreciated. You're not only good with the kinner, but you can cook and keep the house well—better than my sister did."

"She was young and inexperienced."

"You're not so old yourself," Abe said with a crooked grin.

Ruth's face heated with embarrassment.

Abe took another swallow of milk. "I'm sure you still miss Martin, but a young woman like yourself ought to think about getting married again. You'd make a good helpmate."

Ruth stared at the floor. *If Abe were to marry me, I could be his kinner's mamm. I could be his helpmate.*

She lifted her gaze to meet his. "What about you, Abe? Would you think of me as an acceptable wife for you?"

"Ach, Ruth, we're a good ten years apart. You could find a much younger man than me."

"But I wouldn't have anything to give a younger man."

"What makes you say that?"

"I couldn't give him children." She dropped her gaze again.

"Ruth, look at me."

She forced herself to face him, hoping he wouldn't see the tears threatening to escape her lashes.

"I know you would make a good mudder for my kinner, and a fine fraa for me, as well, but without love, a good marriage would be impossible."

"Are—are you saying you won't marry me?"

He nodded. "It wouldn't be fair to—"

"Papa! Papa, come quick!" Josh hollered as he burst into the room.

Abe's face blanched. "What is it, boy?"

"It's Willis! He fell in the pond when Gideon was in the woods lookin' for me, and—" Josh gulped down a sob. "And—and Gideon drug Willis out of the water, but he won't wake up."

Abe grabbed his crutches and pushed himself to his feet.

Ruth stood, too, as her heart gave a lurch. "What are you planning to do?"

"I'm going to the pond."

"But it's too far to go there on crutches. You're not up to walking that far. I think it would be better if you wait here and let me go."

He shook his head and hobbled toward the door. "Josh, hitch up the pony cart. We'll use that to get us to the pond." His eyes were wide as he looked at Ruth. "Run down to the phone shed and call 9-1-1."

Ruth's heart pounded as she hurried out the door and sprinted toward the phone shed near the end of Abe's driveway. *Dear Lord,* she prayed, *please let Willis be okay.*

"Where are you going, Papa? Why's Ruth running down the driveway?" Esta asked as Abe hobbled toward the barn behind Josh.

"There's been an accident at the pond. Take Owen in the house and wait there with him and Molly until we get back."

Esta's eyes widened, and her chin trembled like a leaf caught in a breeze. "Has—has someone been hurt? Is it one of my brieder?"

"Willis fell in the pond. I've got to get to him quick. Now get up to the house, *schnell!*"

Abe didn't look back to see if Esta had done what he'd asked; he just kept moving toward the barn, praying with each step he took. *Don't take my boy, Lord. Don't take my boy.*

By the time Abe got to the barn door, Josh had one of their smaller horses hitched to the pony cart. "Here, take my crutches!"

Josh took the crutches and held them with one hand while keeping a tight hold on the horse's bridle. Abe gritted his teeth and climbed into the cart; then Josh handed him the crutches and climbed in beside him.

"Papa, I'm scared," the boy whimpered. "What if—"

"You hush now; don't even say it. Just get us to the pond as quick as you can!"

As the horse trotted across the fields, Abe continued to plead with God for the life of his son. He'd already lost one family member; he couldn't bear the thought of losing another.

The pond came into view a few minutes later, and Abe caught sight of Gideon bent over his little brother. "Get the horse next to them," he told Josh. "We'll need to put Willis in the cart."

Josh did as he was told, and Abe climbed out of the pony cart. Ignoring his crutches, he hobbled on one foot over to Gideon. "Is your bruder breathing?"

Gideon slowly shook his head. "I don't think so, Papa."

Abe dropped to the ground beside Willis. The boy lay deathly still, and Abe quickly began CPR, praying with each breath he took and each breath he released into his son's mouth.

"Papa, I'm sorry." Gideon leaned close to Abe. "I was only away from Willis a short time." He sniffed a couple of times. "He was playin' in shallow water, so I don't know what happened. I–I waded in and pulled him right out, but–"

"Stand back and give me some room!" Abe didn't look up to see Gideon's reaction. He just kept pushing on Willis's chest and sharing his breath with the boy. He was tempted to put Willis into the pony cart and take him up to the house to wait for the ambulance, but with him not responding to CPR, he figured the best thing he could do was keep trying to breathe life back into his son.

After what seemed like hours, Abe heard sirens in the distance. When the ambulance arrived, Abe's hopes were renewed. The paramedics had more training than he did, and their vehicle was full of lifesaving equipment. He hoped they could accomplish what he hadn't been able to do.

Abe moved aside as the paramedics took over.

"How long was his head under the water?" one of the men asked.

"I don't know." Abe looked at Gideon, but the boy shrugged.

As the paramedics worked on Willis, Abe continued to pray. Finally, one of the men stepped up to Abe and said, "I'm sorry, Mr. Wengerd, but your son is dead."

Chapter 42

As Abe stood near his six-year-old son's coffin, a feeling of despair settled over him like a heavy fog. It seemed like only yesterday that he'd been right here, watching his wife's casket being lowered into the grave.

Abe's nose and eyes burned with unshed tears, and he shifted uncomfortably as his crutches dug into his armpits. *Dear God, why did You allow this to happen? Wasn't it enough that You took my wife? Did You have to take one of my precious kinner, too?*

Abe glanced at Gideon, who stood to his left. The boy's head was down and his shoulders shook, but he made no sound. Abe knew Gideon felt responsible for Willis's death, and well he should. The boy was supposed to watch both of his brothers, not run off in the woods to look for Josh, leaving Willis alone.

I should have seen that my kinner learned how to swim. Martin warned me that something could happen if they didn't. Since Martin wasn't here to teach us how, I should have asked someone else. Abe clenched his fingers around the crutches until they ached. *It's my fault as much as Gideon's that Willis is dead. I may as well have drowned the boy myself.*

Josh, Esta, and Owen clustered around Abe, while Ruth stood to his right, holding Molly in her arms. The little girl would grow up never knowing she'd had a brother named Willis or that she'd had a mother. Truth be told, Molly was fast becoming attached to Ruth. She'd even begun calling Ruth Mammi.

Abe noticed the sorrowful look on Ruth's face, and his heart clenched. She was no doubt reliving the pain of losing her husband.

She'd grown attached to Abe's children, and he was sure that at least part of her grief was over losing Willis.

He pulled his gaze back to the coffin as the bishop read a hymn. A group of Amish men sang as the pallbearers filled in Willis's grave. With each shovelful of dirt, a stab of pain pierced Abe's soul. It wasn't fair. It wasn't right. Death was a fact of life, and he knew it must be dealt with, but he felt as if God had let him down.

All during the funeral dinner, Ruth kept a close watch on Abe's children—all except Gideon, who had gone to his room saying he wasn't hungry and wanted to be alone.

Ruth's heart went out to the boy, as well as to Abe. She could feel the pain of his loss, as she'd come to care for young Willis, and now she felt as if she'd lost another loved one.

"Would you like me to take Molly for a while?" Ruth's mother asked as she stepped into the living room where Ruth sat rocking the child.

Ruth shook her head. "If I put her down, she'll cry. I don't want to move her until she's asleep and I'm able to put her to bed."

Mom shrugged and took a seat on the sofa. "You look exhausted. You really should rest."

"Mom's right," Grace said as she entered the room carrying Daniel. "You've been working hard ever since you came here to help Abe and his family. And since Willis's death, you've hardly slept a wink.

"The kinner need me." The chair squeaked as Ruth continued to rock Molly. How sweet she smelled. How soft and warm she felt. This dear little girl was so innocent and unaware of life's trials.

"You'll be no good to anyone if you wear yourself out," Grace argued.

Ruth patted Molly's back. "I'm resting now."

Mom and Grace exchanged glances, but neither said a word. Grace took a seat on the sofa beside Mom and handed her the baby.

"Danki," said Mom. "I was itching to hold that boppli." She nuzzled Daniel's chest with her nose. "You're sure growing; you know that, little one?"

"Do you think Abe's going to be all right?" Grace asked, turning to face Ruth. "I saw him talking with Dad during the meal, and he'd hardly eaten a thing."

Ruth sighed. "Abe's been through a lot. First losing Alma, having his sister move back home, breaking his leg, and then Willis dying. I feel sometimes like I've been put through a series of dreadful tests, but it seems I'm not alone in that regard."

Mom nodded. "You're right. Troubles come to all, but that's when we need to grab hold of God's hand and hang on tight. It's the only way we can get through the trials life brings our way." She smiled as she released a sigh. "One thing I've learned over the years is that trials can lead us to greater blessings and help us look forward to heaven."

"If Alma were still alive, she would be able to help Abe through this difficult time. It has to be so hard for him to raise his kinner alone and then be faced with something as horrible as losing one of them," Grace put in.

Ruth thought about her impromptu suggestion that Abe marry her, and she cringed. *What must he think of me for being so brazen? Should I say something–apologize for making such a bold implication?* She drew in a deep breath. Now wasn't the time. It would be better to wait until Abe wasn't grieving so much. For now, the best thing she could do was take good care of his children.

"That was one of the saddest funerals I've ever been to," Martha commented from her seat at the back of her father's buggy. "Sure don't know how Gideon's going to deal with the loss of his brother."

"Gideon?" Dad said sharply. "What about Abe? Didn't you see how much he was hurting? He barely said two words today, and I couldn't get him to eat a thing."

"Abe and his family will miss little Willis, but Ruth will be there for the kinner. And you'll be there for Abe, same as you were when Alma died." Mom reached across the seat and patted Dad's arm.

He nodded. "I'll do my best, but I can't help him if he won't talk to me."

"Give him time. He's still in shock over losing Willis."

"It was good to see so many of our English neighbors at the funeral, wasn't it?" Martha asked.

"Jah, and your aunt Rosemary, too," Dad said.

Martha smiled. She was glad Dad and his sister had patched things up.

"I had thought the Larsons might be there today," Mom said. "But I guess Donna had a headache, and Ray had some kind of appointment in town."

Dad shrugged. "Not all from our Amish community were there, either. That's just the way of it sometimes."

Martha thought about Luke, since he'd been one who hadn't attended the funeral. For that matter, he hadn't been at Martin's funeral or Alma's, either. Was it possible that he had an aversion to funerals? Or did he think it was best to stay away since he was still going through rumschpringe and hadn't joined the church? Luke had told Martha once that his parents and the church leaders were after him to settle down and make a decision about getting baptized and joining the Amish church. Martha didn't understand why he kept putting it off. She'd joined the church soon after her sixteenth birthday and had no regrets. She couldn't help but wonder if Luke planned to leave the Amish faith. But if that were true, why hadn't he already? What was he waiting for?

"Ach! Someone's horses are out," Mom shouted as they rounded the bend near their home and found several horses trotting down the road.

"Those animals are mine!" Dad halted the horse and handed the reins to Mom.

"What are you going to do?" she asked in a shaky voice.

"I'm getting out so I can round up the horses."

"Without a rope?"

"There's one here in the back," Martha said. "Want me to help you, Dad?"

"Jah, that'd be good," he said as he climbed down from the driver's seat.

Martha grabbed the rope and stepped out, too, while Mom headed their buggy up the driveway.

The next several minutes were chaotic as Martha and her father raced up and down the road, chasing the horses. Dad finally caught one and started up the driveway. "Maybe the others will follow," he called to Martha.

She waved her hands and blocked one of the mares from going the opposite way. She finally got the animal to follow the gelding Dad was leading. After that, the other four horses trotted in behind, and Martha took up the rear in case one of them tried to head back toward the road.

By the time they got to the barn, Martha was out of breath. When she heard Mom holler, her knees almost buckled.

"What's wrong, Judith?" Dad called.

Mom stood trembling on the grass. She pointed across the yard where more than a dozen chickens lay dead. "Someone's been here while we were gone, Roman. Look what they've done!"

"Go inside and wait there," Dad called to Mom. He looked over at Martha with a panicked expression. "We've got to get the horses put away first thing."

Martha glanced back at her mother. The poor woman was screaming and waving her hands. "Wh–what about Mom? Can't you see how upset she is over the chickens?"

"She'll be all right. Your mother's a strong woman." Dad cupped one hand around his mouth while hanging on to the rope with the other hand. "Judith, go into the house and wait for us there!"

Martha wasn't so sure about her mother's strength. Each attack they'd suffered seemed to make Mom more jittery than the one before.

"Martha, schnell!" Dad shouted. "We need to get the horses into the corral!"

Martha sent up a prayer on her mother's behalf and herded two horses through the corral gate while Dad got the other four.

When they were safely inside and the gate had been locked, Dad released a deep moan. "The horses didn't open that gate themselves. Someone did it on purpose."

Chapter 43

In the weeks that followed, Ruth tried to reach out to Abe, but he didn't respond. He seemed to have pulled into a shell, and the friendship they'd previously established seemed all but gone. Was it because Abe was grieving the loss of his son, or had Ruth's bold suggestion of marriage caused the distance he'd put between them? She still hadn't felt led to ask.

Then there was the situation at home. Mom had been a ball of nerves ever since they'd returned home from Willis's funeral and found their horses running free and dead chickens lying on the lawn. This time Dad had phoned Sheriff Osborn, but when one of the sheriff's deputies came out to look things over, Dad was told that there was no evidence linking anyone to the attack and that nothing could be done. Dad kept saying that they needed to keep trusting the Lord and that in time God would punish the offender.

I know it's wrong to seek revenge, but I hope whoever's responsible for killing Martin and doing such terrible things to my family is caught and brought to justice, Ruth thought as she stood at the gas stove, stirring a pot of soup for Abe's lunch.

She moved from the stove over to the window. Abe's older children had gone to school this morning, and Molly and Owen were playing in the living room, so the yard was empty and quiet. Abe, though still hobbling on crutches, had gone back to work in the harness shop. Ruth had tried to talk him out of it, knowing he couldn't do much with his leg still in a cast and him barely able to function because of his grief. But Abe said there was too much work for Ivan to do alone and that he needed to support his family.

Ruth knew from a few things she'd overheard Abe say to her father that Abe was not only missing Willis but also battling a sense of bitterness toward Gideon for not watching his brother. To Ruth, Abe had said none of those things. He seemed to be avoiding her. Whenever they were in the same room, he only spoke if she asked him a question.

Ruth sighed and glanced at the clock on the far wall. *If only I could turn the hands on that clock back to a more joyful time–when my family wasn't under attack; when Alma, Martin, and Willis were still alive; when the future looked bright and hopeful. Would I do things differently if I were given a second chance?*

Tears welled in her eyes, blurring her vision. *If only people would learn to make the most of each precious moment. No one knows when a tragedy might occur or a loved one will be snatched away.*

A loud crash, followed by a child's wail, jolted Ruth's thoughts back to the present. She dashed into the living room and discovered that the potted plant that had been sitting on a table near the window had fallen to the floor. Broken pieces of the clay pot, dirt, and chunks of green foliage lay on the floor. Molly sat in the middle of it all, sobbing her heart out. Owen stood off to one side, pointing at the plant and shaking his head.

Knowing the first order of business was to get the children out of the room so she could clean up the mess, Ruth bent over to pick up Molly. Just as she reached for the child, a painful spasm gripped her back. Her knees buckled, and she dropped to the floor.

"Ach! Owen, run out to the harness shop and get Ivan," she panted. "I don't think I can get up."

Rosemary stepped into Roman's shop and spotted him sitting at his desk with his lunch pail before him. "Looks like I got here at the right time," she said with a smile. "At least I'm not disturbing your work today."

"Nope, you're sure not. Cleon went home to have lunch with Grace, and I'm eating in peace and quiet," Roman said around a mouthful of sandwich. He nodded to the wooden stool near his desk. "I've still got plenty in my lunch box if you'd like to join me."

"Thanks for the offer, but I've already had lunch. I will sit a few minutes, though." Rosemary scooted the wooden stool over to his desk and took a seat.

"Is there something on your mind," he asked, "or is this just a friendly visit?"

"A little of both."

He tipped his head and gave her a questioning look.

She moistened her lips with the tip of her tongue. "Actually, I came to say good-bye."

His eyebrows shot up. "You're going back to Idaho?"

She nodded. "Ken's found a buyer for my house, so I need to go home and finalize the sale. Then I'll have boxes to pack for my return trip here."

He looked relieved. "You'll be moving here permanently, then?"

"Yes. The little house I've been renting from the Larsons has an option to buy, and I think it will fit my needs. Once I've filled the place with my own things, it will seem more like a real home to me."

"What about your son? Is he in agreement with you moving here?"

"I have Ken's stamp of approval." Rosemary smiled. "In fact, he and his wife plan to use some of their vacation time to help me move. It will give them a chance to meet all of you."

"That would be nice. I'd like to get to know my nephew and his wife."

Roman took a drink from his thermos. "How long do you think it will be before you get moved?"

She shrugged. "I'm not sure. A couple of months, maybe."

"That's not so long."

She reached across the desk and touched his arm. "I'm sorry for all the pain I put my family through when I was gone all those years."

He shook his head. "Apologies have already been said. No need to say 'em again. What counts is the now, not the past."

"You're right, and I plan to make the most of whatever time I have left on this earth."

"Me, too."

Rosemary stepped down from the stool and gave him a hug. She was pleased when he patted her back and said, "I love you, sister."

"I love you, too." She blinked back tears. "Guess I'll say good-bye to Judith and the rest of the family now."

"That'd be good. I'm sure Judith will be glad to hear that you're planning to move to Holmes County permanently. She's been terribly upset since that last attack. Maybe this will give her something to smile about."

"Still no clue as to who let the horses out and killed your chickens?"

"No, and I'm beginning to think we'll never know who was behind any of the attacks."

"Would you like me to speak with the sheriff and see if he has any leads or suggestions as to what you might do to prevent further attacks?"

He grunted. "I think he's pretty much given up on finding the one responsible."

Rosemary's heart went out to her brother. She could see the look of despair on his face and wished there was something she could do to make things better. "I'll be praying," she said. "Praying that God will uphold you through this difficult time and that the culprit will be found and brought to justice."

As Abe sat at one of his workbenches, cutting strips of leather, his thoughts went to Ruth and how she had looked holding Molly this morning after breakfast. There was a look of love on Ruth's face whenever she did anything with his children. He knew without reservation that she would make a good mother. He thought about the day she'd been sitting on the sofa near his feet and had asked if he would like to marry her. Even now, he could see the desire in her eyes, but he knew it wasn't a desire to be his wife; it was a longing to be his children's mother.

He gripped the piece of leather tightly. *Ruth's a good woman, and I've allowed myself to feel something for her that I have no right to feel.*

"You're lookin' kind of thoughtful there," Ivan said, stepping up to the workbench. "Is there something you'd like to talk about?"

Abe shook his head. "No point talking about what can't be changed."

"Are you thinking of Willis?"

"Jah, that and a few other things."

Ivan opened his mouth as if to respond, but the shop door flew open just then, and Owen dashed into the room. "*Daadi, kumme*—schnell!"

Abe's heartbeat picked up speed. "Where do you want me to go quickly, son?"

Owen pointed to the door. "Ruth! *Sie is yuscht umgfalle.*"

"Ruth fell over?"

Owen nodded, and his dark eyes widened with obvious fear. "Kumme, kumme."

Abe grabbed his crutches and hobbled across the room behind Owen.

"I'd better come with you," Ivan said from behind.

Cleon hurried into the barn with the intent of getting some boxes in which to load several jars of honey he planned to deliver to some stores in Walnut Creek. He'd only taken a few steps when he heard Anna's voice.

"It's not my fault baby Daniel got borned." *Sniff.* "It's not fair that Papa don't love me no more." *Sniff. Sniff.* "If I got a new doll, I'd still love you, little faceless friend. I'd love you both, not one more than the other."

Cleon leaned against the wall, too stunned to move. Did Anna really think he didn't love her anymore? Maybe he had shown Daniel a lot of attention since he'd been born, but he was just a baby, and babies needed attention. Even so, he knew he'd been remiss in spending time with Anna, and maybe he'd been a bit short-tempered with her, too. And if he were completely honest about it, he'd have to admit he'd chosen to discount Grace's warnings about Anna's feelings.

Deciding that the boxes could wait awhile, Cleon hurried toward the empty horse stall where he'd heard Anna's voice. "Anna, what are you doing?" he called.

She darted out of the stall, eyes wide and body trembling. "I didn't do nothin' wrong, Papa. I was just–"

"Anna, we need to–"

The child pushed past Cleon and dashed across the room to the ladder leading to the hayloft. She was halfway up before Cleon reached the bottom of the ladder.

"Anna, don't go any farther," he called.

She halted, turned to look at him, then whirled back around. Her foot had just touched the next rung when–*snap!*–the rung broke. Anna screamed as she fell backward.

Cleon leaped forward and caught the child in his arms. "It's okay, Anna," he said, hugging her tightly. "Papa's got you now."

Anna's tears wet the front of his shirt as she buried her face against his chest and sobbed. "I could've fallen. You saved me, Papa."

He stroked her back. "I love you, Anna."

She pulled back and looked up at him with tears clinging to her lashes. "Really, Papa?"

"Jah. You're my special little girl."

"As special as Daniel?"

He nodded. "Just as special."

"But you talk about the boppli all the time and won't let me hold him."

"I'm sorry about that, Anna," he said, his throat thick with emotion. "I've been a bit overprotective of Daniel, and I haven't been fair to you. Will you forgive me, daughter?"

She nodded and hugged him around the neck.

"Why don't you get your doll now and go into the house? I've got some boxes to get, and then I'll join you and your mamm for lunch."

"Okay."

He set Anna on the floor, and she scurried into the empty horse stall. She returned a few seconds later with her faceless doll. "See you in the house, Papa," she said as she skipped out the door.

As soon as Anna disappeared, Cleon made a beeline for the broken ladder. "This makes no sense," he mumbled. "I've had that ladder only a few months, and it shouldn't have broken like that."

A chill shot through him. What if someone had come into the

barn and cut the rung on purpose? Could this have been another attack?

He grabbed the ladder and laid it on its side near the back of the barn. He would replace the rung as soon as he could, and he would keep the barn door locked from now on!

Chapter 44

Are you comfortable enough? Is there anything else I can do for you?" Mom's wrinkled forehead and the concern in her voice let Ruth know how worried she was about her.

"I'll be fine," Ruth said as she tried to find a comfortable position on her bed. Even after several visits to the chiropractor, she was still experiencing back spasms. The doctor said she needed rest and couldn't return to work until her back was better. Much to Ruth's chagrin, Abe's neighbor, Marlene Yoder, was helping in her absence. Marlene was an older woman whose children were grown and married, so she had the time. Ruth's only concern was whether Marlene could keep up with Abe's active children, especially the two youngest ones.

I miss Abe's kinner so much. Ruth grimaced. *I find myself missing Abe, too.*

"You are in pain. I can see by the look on your face that you're hurting." Mom moved closer to the bed and stared down at Ruth.

"As long as I don't move, I don't hurt." Ruth compressed her lips. "What hurts the most is not being able to care for Abe's kinner."

"You'll return to your job once your back has healed."

Ruth groaned. "I still can't believe the way it went into a spasm just because I bent over wrong."

"Dr. Bradley said it's a fairly common occurrence—especially when someone's had to deal with the kind of stress you've had." Mom's hand shook as she reached up to swipe at a wisp of hair that had worked its way loose from her bun. "I understand that, because all the attacks that have occurred around here have made me feel jittery as a June bug. They've affected my ability to sleep well, too."

"I know, and now here you are taking care of me." Ruth hated to be laid up like this. Seeing how tired her mother looked today made her feel guilty for being such a bother.

"I don't mind." Mom patted Ruth's hand. "Martha's been helping when she isn't working for Irene or spending time caring for her dogs. Heidi's going to have another batch of pups now, you know."

"Jah, Martha told me."

"I still wish she'd give up the notion of raising hundlin."

"It's what she enjoys, and we can't fault her for that." Ruth sighed. "I enjoy my job working for Abe, which makes it all the harder to be stuck here in bed."

"You really miss his kinner, don't you?"

"Jah." Ruth almost said that she missed Abe, too, but she caught herself in time. No point giving Mom any hope that she and Abe might marry. He'd made it clear enough the day she'd mentioned marriage that he had no interest in her.

"Well," Mom said as she moved away from the bed, "I'm going downstairs to start lunch. I'll bring up a tray for you when it's ready."

"Danki. In the meantime, would you give me my *Biwel*? I'd like to read a few chapters."

Mom picked up the Bible from the table by Ruth's bed and handed it to her. "I'll be back soon."

"Okay." Ruth turned to the book of Ruth and read the account of how the biblical Ruth had made herself known to Boaz. "It may have worked for Ruth from the Bible, but it sure didn't work for me," she mumbled when she'd finished reading it. "Whatever possessed me to do something so bold? Is the strained relationship I now have with Abe just one more test I'm being faced with?"

Knowing that Job went through numerous tests, Ruth flipped to the book of Job. " 'But he knoweth the way that I take: when he hath tried me, I shall come forth as gold,' " she read from the twenty-third chapter.

She closed her eyes. *Are the tests Abe and I have been faced with refining us, Lord? Will we someday come forth as gold?*

Her eyes popped open. *As soon as my back is better, I'm going to share that verse with Abe.*

Abe entered the kitchen to join his two youngest children for lunch and was shocked to discover a mess. Several boxes of cereal were strewn on the floor, along with some smaller boxes of candy-coated gum. Molly and Owen sat in the middle of it, wearing blue smiles on their faces.

"Bloh," Molly said, holding up both hands, which were also colored blue.

"Jah, blue hands, blue teeth, and blue lips." Abe bit back a chuckle. It was comical to see how the children looked, but he had to wonder how they'd managed to make such a mess.

"Where's Marlene?" he asked Owen.

The boy pointed to the door leading to the living room. *"Schlofkopp."*

"Sleepyhead?" Abe repeated in English.

Owen nodded.

Abe stepped into the living room and discovered Marlene stretched out on the sofa, fast asleep.

He cleared his throat.

No response.

He moved closer to the sofa and bent close to her ear. "Marlene, wake up!"

"Was is letz do?" The poor woman jumped up as though she'd been stung by a bee.

"What's wrong here is that my two youngest kinner have been in the kitchen making a mess while you've been asleep." Abe frowned. "And I'm hungry as a mule and there's no lunch ready."

Marlene clambered off the sofa. "Ach! I had no idea it was lunchtime already. I came in here to rest my eyes a minute. Guess I must have dozed off."

"Aren't you getting enough sleep?"

"I sleep well at night, but I'm not used to running after little ones all day. To tell you the truth, I'm feeling plumb tuckered out." She sighed and pushed an errant strand of grayish-brown hair away from her face. "How soon do you think it'll be before Ruth comes back to work?"

Abe grimaced. He wasn't sure he wanted Ruth to continue working for him. He'd come to realize that not only did his offspring miss having Ruth around, but he did, as well. It wasn't just the good job Ruth had done with the house and children that Abe missed, either. It was her smiling face, caring attitude, and gentle ways. Even so, he wondered if it might be better if Ruth didn't come back once her back was healed. He had feelings for her, which she obviously didn't return. He figured having her around so much would only complicate things. On the other hand, if she didn't come back–

"Abe, did you hear what I asked about Ruth?"

Abe blinked. "Jah. Just don't have an answer for that right now."

Marlene shrugged and turned toward the kitchen. "I'd better tend to Molly and Owen. Then I'll get something put together for your lunch."

"Just worry about lunch," Abe said, following her into the other room. "I'll clean up the kinner."

"I'm not sure who I'm most worried about–Mom or Ruth," Grace said as she placed a sandwich on a plate and set it in front of Cleon. Since Anna was in school and the baby was asleep, Grace hoped she and Cleon would have a chance to visit without interruption.

He looked up at Grace, and his eyebrows drew together. "It won't do any good to worry. I'm sure they'll both be fine."

Grace pulled out a chair and sat down. "I'm not so certain about that."

"What do you mean?"

"First off, Ruth's back seems slow in healing, and she's getting depressed lying around all day."

"The doctor took X-rays and determined it was nothing more than a pulled muscle, right?"

She nodded.

"Then in time, she'll heal."

"I suppose, but Ruth's been through enough already. I hate to see her go through more." Grace grunted. "Now Mom's busy caring for Ruth when she can barely take care of herself." She grimaced. "Even though there haven't been any more attacks since the horse and chicken incident, Mom's been so naerfich. It's hard not to worry or blame myself because—"

"Here you go again, feeling guilty because you think Gary Walker's the one behind the attacks and you're convinced he's trying to get even with you for something that happened over six years ago." Cleon shook his head. "It could be anyone, Grace. No one but the attacker is to blame." He touched her hand. "Let's pray," he suggested, "and then we can talk while we eat if you have more to say on the subject."

She nodded. "Okay."

They bowed their heads, and Grace thanked God that things were better between Cleon and Anna. Then she petitioned the Lord to calm her mother's fears, heal Ruth's back, and protect her family from further attacks.

Chapter 45

Ruth, where are you going?" Mom asked as Ruth plucked her black outer bonnet off the wall peg and slipped it over her white kapp. "Since Martha's gone to town to do some shopping, I thought the two of us could get a little sewing done on this rainy Saturday morning."

"Some other time, Mom. Right now, I'm going over to Abe's," Ruth replied.

Mom's eyebrows shot up. "To work?"

"Not today, but I'm hoping I'll be able to start on Monday morning."

Mom scurried across the room. "Oh, Ruth, it's only been a few weeks since you hurt your back. Do you think you're ready to return to work so soon?"

Ruth opened her mouth to reply, but Mom rushed on. "Fixing meals for Abe's family is one thing, but doing housework is quite another. If you bend over wrong or pick up something too heavy, you could reinjure your back."

"I'll be careful, Mom. If there's something heavy that needs to be picked up, I'll leave it until Abe or Ivan can take care of it."

"Speaking of Ivan," Mom said, "I was talking to Irene the other day, and she mentioned that Ivan's been seeing Amanda Miller as of late."

"Is that so?"

Mom nodded. "Irene said she'd been hoping you and Ivan might hit it off and then she'd have two of my girls for daughters-in-law."

Ruth shook her head. "I would never consider marrying Ivan, even if he was interested in me in a romantic sort of way."

"You don't care for Ivan?"

"He's a nice man, but I'm not attracted to him. Besides, I couldn't allow myself to become romantically involved with any young man."

"Why not? Is it because you're still pining for Martin?"

"I do miss him, and I guess I always will, but if I were to find love again, it couldn't be with a younger man."

Mom raised her eyebrows. "I'm verhuddelt."

"It's not confusing, Mom. As I'm sure you must know, most young men want to raise a family when they get married. I can't have any children, so I wouldn't make a good wife for a young man."

Mom released a sigh. "Oh, Ruth, I wish you wouldn't say things like that."

"Why not? It's true."

"If a man really loves a woman, it shouldn't matter whether or not she can give him kinner."

Ruth slipped into her sweater. "It doesn't make any difference, because I have no interest in marrying Ivan." *It's Abe I want to marry,* she added mentally. *But he doesn't want me.*

Mom pulled Ruth into her arms and gave her a hug. "Tell Abe I said hello and that we'll have him and the kinner over for supper sometime soon."

"I will. See you later, Mom."

Martha had just left the market in Berlin and was about to load her purchases into the back of her buggy when someone touched her shoulder.

She whirled around and was surprised to see Luke behind her. "Ach, you scared me!"

"Sorry." He brushed back his hair from his forehead and offered her an impish grin.

"W-were you shopping in the store?" Martha stammered. She didn't know why she always felt so flustered whenever Luke was around.

"I was, but we must have missed seeing each other." Luke reached into Martha's shopping cart and lifted the bag of dog food as if it were a feather. "Better let me help you with that."

"Danki. It was kind of heavy when I pulled it off the grocery shelf."

Luke placed the dog food into the back of her wagon, and she put the paper sacks inside.

"Have you had lunch?" he asked after she'd secured the buggy flap.

"Not yet."

"How'd you like to share a pizza with me at Outback Pizzeria?"

Martha contemplated Luke's offer. She was a little worried that someone might see her with him and tell her father, but her desire to spend time with Luke finally won out. "Jah, I would enjoy some pizza."

"Should we take separate buggies, or would you like to ride with me and then pick up your buggy after we're done?"

"Guess I'd better take my own buggy since it's got stuff in it that I don't want stolen." Truth be told, Martha was more concerned about someone seeing her riding in Luke's buggy than she was about someone stealing her purchases. If anyone she knew spotted her having lunch with Luke, they might think the two of them had arrived at the pizzeria at the same time and decided to share a table. But if she and Luke were seen riding in the same buggy, folks could get the impression that they were a courting couple.

"Okay. I'll see you at the pizzeria in a few minutes." Luke offered Martha another heart-melting smile and sprinted across the parking lot to his rig.

With a feeling of anticipation, Martha unhitched her horse and climbed into her own buggy.

When she arrived at the pizzeria, Luke was already there, sitting at a table near the back of the room. He waved, and she hurried over to join him.

"I ordered a plain cheese pizza and a couple of root beers," he said. "I didn't know what kind of meat you liked, so figured I couldn't go wrong with cheese."

She smiled as she took a seat opposite him. "Cheese is fine with me."

"So how are things going at your place?" he asked, leaning his elbows on the table and resting his chin in the palm of his hand.

"Okay. Ruth's back is doing better now. I think she'll probably return to work for Abe soon."

"I knew she was missing from church on the last Sunday we had preaching, but I didn't know there was anything wrong with her back." Luke frowned. "Is it serious?"

Martha shook her head. "I don't think so. The chiropractor said it was just a pulled muscle. After several treatments and bed rest, she's finally doing better."

"That's good to hear. My daed's back has gone out on him a time or two, and he was always in a lot of pain."

Martha took a sip of root beer. "This is good but not nearly as tasty as the homemade kind my daed makes."

Luke stared at Martha with a peculiar expression, making her squirm.

"What's wrong? Have I got root beer foam on my naas?"

He grinned. "Your nose looks just fine."

She smiled in response.

"What else is new at your place? Have there been more attacks?"

"Not for several weeks. Did you hear about that last one?"

He shook his head. "What happened?"

"It was the day of Willis Wengerd's funeral. When we arrived home, we discovered that someone had let our horses out of the corral."

"Maybe the gate wasn't latched, and the horses got out themselves."

"We thought that at first, but there were dead chickens all over our front yard." She grunted. "It was obvious that someone had come onto our property while we were at the funeral."

Luke squinted his dark eyes. "Got any idea who might have done it?"

She shrugged. "Probably the same person who's done all the other horrible things at our place."

"Did you find any clues or evidence?"

"No." Martha sighed. "Bishop King came by the other day to talk to Dad about the problem. They both think that whoever's doing these things is either trying to get even with someone in the family or wants to take our property and is hoping to scare us off."

"Why would anyone want your property?"

"I don't know."

"So what's gonna be done about the situation?"

"As far as I know, nothing. Dad thinks if we just keep trusting the Lord, eventually the attacks will stop." Martha grimaced. "I have to wonder if God doesn't expect us to do something about our problems, not just sit around and wait for Him to do everything for us."

Luke studied her intently. "What do you mean?"

"I've been thinking about this for quite a spell. I've come to the conclusion that if there's another attack, it'll be time for me to take action."

"Take action?"

She nodded. "I plan to start investigating things and see if I can figure out who's behind the attacks."

Luke's eyebrows shot up. "You're kidding, right?"

"No, I'm not."

"That's not a good idea, Martha. It's not a good idea at all."

"Why not?"

Luke leveled her with a piercing look that went straight to her heart. "Playing detective could be dangerous. You shouldn't even be considering such a thing."

"Oh, but I—"

"Not only could it be dangerous, but if your daed found out what you were up to, I'm sure you'd be in trouble with him. He's not the easiest man to deal with, you know." Luke grunted. "When that man sets his mind one way, there's no convincing him otherwise. I know that better than anyone."

She took another sip of root beer. "I'll worry about my daed's reactions to me playing detective when the time comes."

Abe headed to the barn to get some cardboard boxes he'd stored in an empty horse stall and spotted Willis's little red wagon. He remembered how Josh had broken it the day before Willis drowned. Abe had promised Willis that he would fix the wagon as soon as his leg healed and he found the time. There was no point fixing it now. Willis was gone, and it was Gideon's fault.

Abe grunted as he bent over and grabbed the boxes. For the past several weeks, he'd only been going through the motions of living. His leg had finally healed and he could get around on it fairly well, but the pain that pricked his heart daily was worse than any physical hurt he'd ever endured. Not only did he miss Willis, but he missed Ruth. A few days ago, he'd talked to Roman and heard that Ruth's back was doing better. But she hadn't returned to work, and he wondered if she might be staying away on purpose. Since Abe had turned down Ruth's suggestion that they marry, he wondered if she'd decided that he and his brood didn't need her anymore.

I was stupid for saying no, he berated himself. *I love her, and even if she doesn't love me, at least I could have given her my name and the opportunity to be a mudder to my kinner.*

Abe started out of the stall but halted when he heard whimpering. He tipped his head and listened. It sounded as though someone was crying, and it seemed to be coming from the other side of the barn.

He placed the boxes on the floor and started in that direction. As he neared a stack of baled hay, he saw Gideon sitting on the floor, head bent and shoulders shaking.

Abe rushed forward. "Son, what's wrong? Have you been hurt?"

Gideon looked up, his eyes swimming with tears. "It's not me who's been hurt, Papa. It's you. I hurt you real bad when I let Willis die. I–I'm awful sorry. I miss my bruder, too." He hiccupped on a sob. "I don't deserve to be called your son anymore. I—*hic*—should've been the one to die, not Willis."

Abe let Gideon's words sink into his brain. Losing Alma had hurt tremendously, but he'd come to grips with her death because it was an accident. But Willis's death could have been prevented if Gideon had been watching the boy as he'd been told to do. For the last several weeks, Abe had been carrying around unresolved anger and resentment toward Gideon, toward himself, and toward God for allowing Willis's death to happen. But at what cost? Was it fair to allow Gideon, who was still just a boy, to go on blaming himself for his brother's death?

Abe thought about Willis's wagon again and how the child had forgiven Josh for breaking it. "It's okay," Willis had said to his brother. "If Jesus could forgive those who put Him on the cross, I oughta be able to forgive my own bruder."

Abe reflected on Matthew 6:14: "For if ye forgive men their trespasses, your heavenly Father will also forgive you." Gideon was Abe's son, not some man who had trespassed against him. How could he have shut the boy out and made him feel responsible for his brother's death?

Abe swallowed and nearly choked on the sob that tore from his throat. He had lost one son; he couldn't risk losing another. Falling to his knees beside Gideon, he pulled the boy into his arms. "I forgive you, son, but I need you to forgive me, as well. I shouldn't have blamed you for Willis's death. It was an accident and might have happened even if you had been right there with him. Will you accept my apology?"

"Jah," Gideon said through his tears. "And I promise to be the best boy I can be—and never let you down again."

"I don't expect you to be perfect." Abe wiped the tears from Gideon's face. "Only God is perfect. We just need to do the best we can. I know when you ran into the woods after Josh that you didn't expect Willis to fall in the pond while you were gone."

"No, I surely didn't." Gideon sniffed deeply. "If there was any way I could bring him back, I would."

"I know." Abe rocked Gideon back and forth in his arms the way he had when the boy was a baby. "Dear God," he prayed aloud, "forgive me for the sin of unforgiveness."

When Ruth stepped into the barn and heard Abe's voice, she halted. She had stopped at the harness shop to see him, but Ivan had told her that Abe had come to the barn to get some boxes. She'd never expected to see him kneeling on the floor, holding Gideon in his arms and praying out loud. Abe was asking God to forgive his sin of unforgiveness.

I've never really done that, Ruth thought regretfully. *Ever since Martin died, I've been struggling to forgive the one who rammed our buggy off the road. Despite my busyness and determination to do something useful with my life, my broken heart has never completely healed.*

Ruth trembled as a sense of shame welled in her soul. She knew it was a sin to harbor anger and resentment toward the person who had caused Martin's death, even though she wasn't sure who that person was and couldn't forgive him to his face.

She leaned against one of the wooden beams and closed her eyes. "Dear Lord, forgive my sin of unforgiveness and heal the hurt in my heart."

"Ruth, is that you?"

Ruth's eyes snapped open as the heat of embarrassment flooded her cheeks. She moved over to the bales of hay where Abe knelt beside his son. "Jah, it's me. I–I came over to let you know my back's doing better and that I can start working for you again on Monday." She shifted from one foot to the other, feeling suddenly shy and unsure of herself. "That is–if you still want me to come back."

Abe stood, pulling Gideon to his feet. "Son, why don't you run into the house and see if Marlene has lunch ready? I'm going to stay out here and talk to Ruth awhile."

Gideon looked at Ruth, then back at his father. "Jah, okay." He gave Abe a hug and darted out of the barn wearing a smile on his tear-stained face.

"Things are better between me and my boy," Abe said.

"I'm pleased to hear it."

He motioned to a bale of hay. "Would you like to sit down?"

She nodded and started to take a seat, but tripped on her shoelace and fell into Abe's lap.

He looked stunned.

"Ach, I'm so sorry." She scooted away and lowered herself to the bale of hay, feeling another blush warm her cheeks.

"No harm done," he mumbled.

"I. . .uh. . .heard part of your conversation–the one you were having with God."

"Did you now?" Abe asked, taking a seat beside her. He wore a silly grin on his face, and she couldn't figure out why.

"The words you said made me realize that I needed to find forgiveness in my heart toward the one who killed Martin."

"I'm glad." His expression turned serious. "One can't find joy and a sense of purpose if their heart is full of anger and bitterness."

"I know. Now that I've confessed my sin to God, I feel clean inside."

"Same here."

"Abe, there's something else I wanted to share with you."

"What's that?"

"I was reading my Bible the other day, and I came upon Job 23:10. It says, 'But he knoweth the way that I take: when he hath tried me, I shall come forth as gold.' "

Abe sat several seconds, staring at his hands. Finally, he lifted his head and looked at Ruth. "I believe that verse applies to both of us."

"I think so, too. That's why I felt the need to share it with you. After reading it, I was filled with a sense of hope that despite the trials and testing I've been through, God will use it for His good." She smiled. "Someday, I hope to come forth as gold."

He nodded. "It's good when we let God's Word speak to us, jah?"

"Jah."

Abe moistened his lips with the tip of his tongue. "Uh. . .Ruth. . .I have something I need to say to you."

"What's that?"

"I don't want you to come back to work for me as my maad."

"You–you don't?"

He shook his head.

"Is it because Marlene's a better maid than me?"

"She's done the best job she can, but she's not a better maid." He fingered the end of his curly red beard. "Nor would she make me a good wife."

"What?" Ruth's forehead wrinkled as she tried to digest what he had said.

The skin around Abe's dark eyes crinkled, and he reached over and took Ruth's hand. "I love you, Ruth. I'm not afraid to say it anymore. If you don't think I'm too old and will have me as your husband when you feel the time is right, I'll do my best to make you happy, even though I know you don't love me in return."

"Oh, but I do! During the time I was home resting my back, I came to the realization that I not only love your kinner, but I love you, as well." Ruth gasped and covered her mouth. "I'm being too bold again."

Abe slipped his arm around her waist and drew her close to his side. "I think maybe your boldness is one of the things I've come to love about you."

Ruth's cheeks grew even warmer.

"You know," he said, leaning close to her ear, "Esta asked me once if I would ever marry again, and I told her that if the good Lord desired for me to find another wife, He'd have to drop her right in my lap." He chuckled. "Looks to me like He did just that a few minutes ago. I think maybe now is the time for me to listen."

Ruth stared down at the floor, unable to meet his gaze.

"You haven't said if you're willing to marry me."

She lifted her gaze as tears dribbled onto her cheeks. "Jah, Abe. I'd be honored."

He stood and reached out his hand. "Shall we go inside and tell the kinner our good news?"

"I think we should." Ruth slipped her hand into the crook of Abe's arm as they walked out of the barn. For the first time in many months, she felt a sense of peace, knowing that with God's help, and Abe at her side, she could deal with any test she might be faced with in the days ahead.

A Sister's Hope

Dedication/Acknowledgments

To my dear friends, Jake and Sara Smucker,
whose hope is fixed on Jesus.

With great appreciation, I wish to thank
the following Ohio friends who shared information
with me related to Holmes County, Ohio:
Esta and Melvin Miller, Monk and Marijane Troyer,
Tom and Connie Troyer, Lori Schlabach,
Marlene Miller, and Sig and Evie Kobus.
I also want to thank Rebecca Germany
and Becky Durost Fish, my helpful editors.
Most of all, I thank my heavenly Father,
who continues to give me the inspiration
and desire to write for Him.

Be of good courage,
and he shall strengthen your heart,
all ye that hope in the Lord.
Psalm 31:24

Chapter 1

Ar-ou-ou! Ar-ou-ou!

Piercing howls roused Martha Hostettler from her sleep, and she rolled over in bed.

Ar-ou-ou! Ar-ou-ou!

There it was again. That couldn't be Polly. The beagle had a high-pitched howl, not deep and penetrating. Polly's mate, Bo, must be making that awful noise.

Martha turned on the flashlight she kept on the nightstand and pointed the light at her battery-operated clock. It was three o'clock. None of Martha's dogs ever barked or howled during the night unless something was amiss. Could Heidi have had her pups? The sheltie wasn't due for another week or so. Maybe Bo had sensed what was going on and wanted to let Martha know.

She shook her head, trying to clear away the cobwebs of sleep. *That's ridiculous. Bo might be able to sense that Heidi's having a problem, but I doubt he's smart enough to let me know. Something else must have disturbed the dog.*

Martha thought of the day she'd found her sheltie Fritz tied to a tree. One of his legs had also been tied up, and a bowl of water had been placed just out of his reach. Another time, Martha had found one of her puppies in the yard with its neck broken. She had wondered if whoever had been vandalizing her family's property and attacking them in other ways could have been responsible for the puppy's death.

A tremor shot through her body. What if someone was in the

barn right now? What if they planned to hurt one of her dogs?

She pushed the covers aside and jumped out of bed. Dashing across the room, she slipped into her bathrobe, stepped into her sneakers, grabbed the flashlight, and rushed out of her room.

When Martha stepped outside, she shivered as a chilly breeze rustled the leaves. Martha hurried across the yard. As she approached the barn, she tipped her head and listened. Bo had stopped howling. The dog could have been spooked by one of the horses on the other side of the barn. She was probably worried for nothing.

Holding the flashlight with one hand and grasping the handle of the door with the other, Martha stepped into the barn. *Clunk! Splat!* Something cool and wet hit the top of her head. The sticky liquid dripped down her face and oozed onto her neck.

Martha aimed the flashlight at the front of her robe and groaned. She was covered in white paint! She flashed a beam of light upward and gasped. A bucket connected to a piece of rope had been suspended above the barn door. Someone had deliberately set this up! Was it a prank by some unruly kids? *Or could this be another attack?*

She reached for a cardboard box on a nearby shelf and fumbled around until she located a clean rag. She blotted the paint from her face the best she could. The ammonia smell identified the paint as latex. At least it would clean up with soap and warm water.

Martha hurried to her dog kennels in the back of the barn. Relief swept over her when she saw that all of the dogs—Polly, Bo, Fritz, and Heidi—were okay. And Heidi still hadn't delivered her pups.

When Martha reached through the wire fencing and patted Bo on the head, he looked up at her and whined.

"Go back to sleep, boy. Everything's fine."

But it wasn't fine. Someone had sneaked into their barn and rigged up the bucket. How long ago had it been done? Could they still be in the barn?

Martha swept the barn with her flashlight but saw no one. Satisfied that nothing else seemed to have been disturbed, she hurried outside. Glancing down, she noticed an empty pack of cigarettes on the ground.

Rustling sounded in the distance. She aimed her flashlight toward the field of dried corn behind their house. A man was running through the fields. She sucked in her breath. It was hard to tell much from this distance in the dark, but it looked like he wore a straw hat, the kind Amish men used.

Martha shuddered. *If I tell Dad about seeing the man, he'll think it was Luke.* For some time, her father had suspected Luke of attacking their family, but she was convinced Luke was innocent. At least, she hoped he was.

Martha hurried to the house and headed straight for the shower. She needed to get the paint washed off. She needed time to think.

When she stepped out of the bathroom a short time later and saw a man standing in the hallway, her breath caught. "Dad! What are you doing here? I. . .I didn't think anyone else was up."

"The sound of the shower running woke me." He frowned and pointed to her clothes lying on the floor outside the bathroom. "I've heard of folks sleepwalking during the night, but I never knew anyone who liked to paint in their sleep."

"I wasn't. I–"

"What's going on?" Mom asked as she joined them in front of the bathroom door.

Martha quickly explained what had happened in the barn.

"*Ach!*" Mom gasped. "Was this another attack?"

"I. . .I don't know," Martha stammered. "It's hard to say."

Dad looked over at Martha, his brows furrowing. "Did you see anyone?"

"I. . .uh. . .thought I saw someone running across the field, but I didn't get a good enough look to tell who it was."

Ruth showed up on the scene, rubbing her eyes and yawning. "It's the middle of the night. What's everyone doing out of bed?"

Martha recounted her story again and ended by saying, "I'm sorry I woke everyone."

"We needed to know what happened." Mom slipped her arm around Martha's waist. "It's not safe for you to go to the barn during the night."

"I just wanted to check on my *hund*. Besides, it's not right that we can't feel safe on our own property." Martha looked at Dad. "Will you let the sheriff know about this?"

"What's the point? Sheriff Osborn hasn't done a thing to prevent any of the attacks from happening. It's not likely he'll start now." Dad shrugged. "What's done is done. Notifying the sheriff won't change a thing."

As Luke Friesen headed down the road in his open buggy, the pungent smell of horseflesh filled his senses. Despite the fact that he owned a pickup truck he kept hidden in the woods because his folks wouldn't approve of it, Luke preferred horse and buggy transportation. He'd only bought the pickup because some of his Amish friends, who were also going through their running-around years, owned a vehicle. Luke figured it was expected of him. Besides, having the truck gave him the freedom to travel wherever he wanted. And it gave him an in with Rod and Tim, the English fellows he'd been hanging around for a time. Luke's folks didn't approve of his rowdy English friends, and they'd been after him to settle down and join the Amish church for some time. But he wasn't ready. Some things he wanted to do, he couldn't do as a member of the church. Besides, there was no point in joining the church when he wasn't ready to get married. He would consider it if and when he found the right woman.

A vision of Martha Hostettler flashed across Luke's mind. She was spunky and daring—the complete opposite of her sister, Ruth, who never liked to take chances and had seemed so subdued during the time they'd been courting. Under the right circumstances, Luke might consider courting Martha.

Luke gritted his teeth as he thought about the way Martha's father, Roman, had fired him for being late to work a few years ago, and how, after the Hostettlers had come under attack, Roman had pointed a finger at Luke. Even though Luke had denied having anything to do with the attacks, Roman had given him the cold shoulder ever since. If the man had any idea Luke was interested in his youngest daughter,

Luke was sure he and Martha would both be in trouble.

At least I have a job working for John Peterson. Guess that's something to be grateful for. Luke snapped the reins to get the horse moving faster. *If I'm not careful, I'll end up being late for work because I'm allowing my horse to plod along while I think about someone I can't have.*

The buggy jolted and leaned to the right. "Whoa! Steady, boy." He pulled back on the reins and grimaced when he saw his left buggy wheel roll onto the opposite side of the road. Good thing there were no cars going by at the moment.

Luke guided the horse and buggy to the shoulder of the road, jumped down, and sprinted over to the buggy wheel. "Great," he muttered. "Now I will be late for work."

Luke lugged the wheel over to his buggy and spent the next several minutes looking for the nut that had come off. When he couldn't find it, he reached into his toolbox in the back of the buggy and took out another nut. He'd just squatted down in front of the buggy to set the wheel in place, when Sheriff Osborn's car pulled up behind him.

"Looks like you lost a wheel," the sheriff said as he sauntered over to Luke.

"That's what happened, all right." Luke grimaced. "It's gonna make me late for work."

"Need any help?"

"Sure, I'd appreciate that." Luke's nose twitched as Sheriff Osborn knelt on the ground next to the buggy wheel. The sheriff's clothes reeked of cigarette smoke, which made Luke think the man was either a heavy smoker or had recently been around someone who smoked.

"Are you still working for John Peterson?" the sheriff asked as he helped Luke lift the wheel and set it in place.

Luke nodded. "Sure am."

"Do you like working for John better than you did Roman?"

"John's a good boss—always patient and fair with me," Luke said without really answering the sheriff's question. "Of course I don't know how he'll react to me being late today."

"I'm sure he'll understand when you tell him what happened with your buggy wheel."

"I appreciate your help," Luke said once the wheel had been securely fastened.

Sheriff Osborn reached into his pocket, pulled out a pack of gum, and popped a piece into his mouth. "No problem. Glad I came along when I did. If you'd had to fix the wheel yourself, you'd be even later for work." He turned toward his car. "Guess I'd better get back to the business at hand. I got a report that there have been too many cars going over the speed limit on this stretch of road, so I figured I'd better nip it in the bud."

Luke shuffled his feet a few times, trying to think of the best way to say what was on his mind.

"You're looking kind of thoughtful there," Sheriff Osborn said as he chomped on his wad of gum. "Have you got something on your mind?"

"I. . .uh. . .was wondering if you've had any leads on who's behind the attacks against the Hostettlers."

"Nope, sure don't. As far as I know, there haven't been any more attacks at their place in some time." The sheriff stuck another piece of gum in his mouth. "I might have caught the culprit responsible for the attacks if Roman had let me know about them sooner." He kicked a pebble with the toe of his boot. "From what I understand, it's not against the Amish religion to notify the police, so I can't figure out why Roman kept quiet about most of those attacks."

Luke shrugged. "I guess he figured it was best to turn the other cheek and not involve the law unless it became absolutely necessary."

"You're probably right." The sheriff turned toward his car again. "I'd better be on my way and let you get to work. Wouldn't want to see you lose your job on my account." He waved as he climbed into his car.

Luke checked the wheel over once more for good measure, gave his horse a quick pat, and stepped into his buggy.

When he arrived at John's shop, he found John sitting behind his desk, talking on the phone. Figuring it best not to disturb him, Luke hurried to the back room to put away his lunch box. When he returned, John was off the phone.

"Sorry for being late," Luke apologized. "One of my buggy wheels fell off, and I had to stop and fix it."

"Of course you did." John smiled. "Your being late's not a problem. Some things happen that we can't control."

Luke wiped the sweat from his forehead as he drew in a quick breath. "I appreciate your understanding. I was afraid you might fire me the way Roman did when I worked for him."

A deep wrinkle formed above John's slightly crooked nose. "No one should be punished for something that isn't his fault."

Luke nodded. Working for John was sure easier than working for Roman had been. Nothing had ever seemed to be good enough for that man. Every time Luke had an idea about how something should be done, Roman had vetoed it.

"What would you like me to do this morning?" Luke asked as he moved toward John's desk.

John motioned to several cabinet doors stacked against the wall. "You can begin sanding those while I go over to Keim Lumber to pick up some supplies." He stood. "I shouldn't be gone long. If any customers show up, go ahead and write up the orders."

Luke nodded. It felt good to have John's trust. Roman never trusted him. He grimaced. *Why do I keep comparing John to Roman, and why can't I stop thinking about how things used to be when I worked for Roman?*

When John left the shop, Luke began working on the doors. John's beagle, Flo, who'd been lying on an old rug near John's desk, ambled over to Luke with a pathetic whine.

He bent down, and the dog licked his hand. "You don't miss John already, do you, girl? Are you craving some attention?"

The dog responded with a low whimper then flopped on the floor a few feet from where Luke stood.

As Luke plucked a piece of sandpaper, he thought about Martha and wondered how her dog business was doing. She'd sold Flo to John because the dog was barren, and she'd used the money to buy another dog she hoped to use for breeding purposes.

Luke wished he felt free to stop by the Hostettlers' to see Martha, but he knew if Roman saw him talking to her, he wouldn't like it.

Luke and Roman would probably end up having words. He thought too highly of Martha to cause trouble between her and her dad. Luke figured it was best if he stayed away from the Hostettler place. Besides, there were other things he needed to do today.

Chapter 2

Martha stood in front of the counter in Irene Schrock's kitchen, rolling out dough for the pies they would serve when a busload of tourists came for supper the following evening. Her thoughts wandered as she pushed the rolling pin back and forth. She couldn't forget about the incident in the barn. Even though Martha had been the one who'd gotten doused with paint, Mom had been so distraught that her hands shook all during breakfast, and poor Ruth had seemed equally shaken. Dad hadn't said more than a few words. He'd gulped down his oatmeal and rushed out the door, saying he needed to get out to his woodworking shop because he had a backlog of work.

A trickle of sweat rolled down Martha's forehead, and she lifted the corner of her work apron to wipe it away. Who had put that bucket of paint above the door, and why had they done it?

She drew in a deep breath and closed her eyes. *Dear Lord, please make this insanity stop.*

Someone touched her shoulder. Martha dropped the rolling pin and whirled around.

"Are you okay?" Irene asked. "You're not feeling *grank*, I hope."

"I'm. . .uh. . .no, I'm not feeling sick. At least not physically."

Irene's dark eyebrows furrowed. "What do you mean, not physically?"

"Something happened at our place early this morning that left us all feeling troubled."

"What happened?" Irene's eighteen-year-old daughter, Carolyn, asked.

"Someone rigged up a bucket of white paint and hung it above our barn door. When I went out to check on my dogs, the paint spilled on me."

Irene gasped. "Ach! Who would do such a thing?"

"We have no idea." Martha wasn't about to mention the Amish man she thought she'd seen running through the field. No point in giving Irene something to talk about with others in their community. There had been enough talk already as to who might be responsible for these attacks.

"Did your *daed* notify Sheriff Osborn?" Carolyn asked.

Martha shrugged. "I doubt it. Just like most of the other times when we've been attacked, Dad thinks he should turn the other cheek and say nothing to the sheriff."

"Do you agree with that, Martha?"

Martha wasn't sure how to answer Carolyn's question. Even though she had her own opinion, she didn't want to say anything that would make Dad look bad. "I think whoever has been doing the attacks will keep on doing them until they are caught," she replied.

"But how will they ever be caught if your daed refuses to notify the sheriff?"

"The best thing for all of us to do is to pray about the matter," Irene intervened. She patted Martha's arm. "In the meantime, we have some pies that need to be baked."

"You're right. I should get busy." Martha grabbed the rolling pin. She would keep her hands busy when she was working for Irene or caring for her dogs, but during her free time, she hoped to find out who was behind the attacks. She only wished she could talk to someone about this. But who could she trust not to say anything to Dad?

I'll begin by making a list of every attack, she decided. *After that, I'll make a list of suspects, which will include a motive and any opportunities they might have had to attack.*

"I guess it won't be long now until your sister gets married," Irene said.

Martha nodded. "Ruth and Abe's wedding will be two months after Sadie and Toby's. I'll have a part in both."

"What will you be doing?" Carolyn asked as she reached into the cupboard for a bag of flour.

"I'll be an attendant at Ruth's wedding and a table server at Sadie's."

Irene slipped two apple-crumb pies into the oven and shut the door. "It's nice that Ruth and Abe have found love again. I think they'll have a good marriage and Ruth will make a fine *mudder* to Abe's *kinner*."

Martha couldn't argue with that. Ruth had talked about becoming a mother ever since she was a little girl playing with her dolls. Sadly, Ruth's hopes had been dashed on Christmas Eve, nearly a year ago. Her husband's buggy had been rammed off the road, and Martin had been killed. Ruth's injuries had left her unable to have children.

Irene touched Martha's shoulder. "Will your aunt Rosemary be able to attend Ruth's wedding?"

"I hope so. She found a buyer for her house in Boise, Idaho, so if she gets everything wrapped up soon, she should be moved here to Ohio in plenty of time for the wedding."

Irene smiled. "It's nice that Rosemary's part of your family again. I'm sure your daed missed her very much when she was gone those thirty-some years."

Martha nodded. Dad had missed his sister, but until a few months ago, he'd never admitted it.

"Since Rosemary will be moving back to Holmes County, maybe she'll consider joining the Amish church."

Martha made another pass with the rolling pin over the dough and turned to face Irene. "I think if Aunt Rosemary had it to do over again, she wouldn't have left the Amish faith and married an Englisher. But she's been English most of her life, so I doubt she'd be willing to give up all the modern conveniences she's become used to." She lifted the dough and placed it in an empty pie pan. "Besides, her son and his wife are English. It might make it hard on their relationship if she went Amish again."

Irene smiled. "I see what you mean."

"Will Rosemary's family be coming to Ruth's wedding?" Carolyn asked.

"As far as I know. I'm anxious to meet them, too." Martha smiled. "Until Aunt Rosemary's surprise visit to Holmes County several months ago, I didn't even know I had an English cousin." Martha smiled.

A knock at the back door interrupted their conversation, and Carolyn scooted to the other side of the kitchen to answer it. A few seconds later, Martha's brother-in-law, Cleon, entered the room, carrying a cardboard box.

"These are for you," he said, smiling at his mother. "I figured with all the dinners you've been hosting lately, you might be running low on honey."

"*Danki*, son." Irene motioned to the counter. "Why don't you set the box over there? Carolyn can put the jars of honey in the pantry after we finish with the pies."

"Sure thing." Cleon set the box down then turned to face his mother. "If my bees keep producing the way they are now, eventually I might be able to build a small store on my property. I'd like to have a place close to home where I can sell some of my honey, as well as those nice beeswax candles you and Carolyn make."

Irene smiled. "I think that's a good idea."

Cleon moved closer to Martha. "I heard about the dousing you got in the wee hours of the morning."

She nodded. "Dad wasn't too happy about having to clean up the mess in his barn, and I wasn't happy about the mess all over me."

"I suggested that Roman keep the barn locked. That's what I've been doing with my own barn since I discovered one of my new ladders had a broken rung." Cleon grimaced. "I'm sure someone cut it."

"What did Dad say?" Martha asked.

"He said he'd think about locking the barn at night."

"Why only at night?" Carolyn asked.

"I guess he figures no one's likely to come around during the day—especially since someone in the family is usually around."

"That's true," Irene said. "Most of the attacks against your family have occurred at night."

"Or when we've been away from home," Martha quickly added. "Truthfully, I doubt that Dad will take Cleon's suggestion about locking the barn, but I hope he will. After what happened last night, I'm worried about my dogs."

As Luke left John's woodworking shop and headed toward home, he spotted another buggy ahead of him and realized it was Martha Hostettler's. He flicked the reins to get his horse trotting and pulled into the oncoming lane to pass her. As his buggy came alongside Martha's, he slowed the horse and motioned her to pull onto the shoulder of the road. Once her rig was stopped, he pulled in behind her, hopped down, and skirted around to her side of the buggy. "*Wie geht's,* Martha?"

"I'm fine now, but I wasn't doing so well in the wee hours of the morning," she replied.

He tipped his head in question.

"I got doused with a bucket of paint when I went out to the barn to check on my dogs."

Luke's mouth dropped open. "How did that happen?"

"Someone rigged the bucket so it would spill when the barn door opened."

"You weren't hurt, were you?"

Martha shook her head. "Just looked a mess, with white paint all over me and my clothes." She grunted. "It's a good thing the paint was water based, or I'd probably still be wearing a white face."

Luke grimaced. "I suppose your daed will blame me for what happened."

"Why would you think that?"

"Because he's accused me of doing other things to your family." Luke shook his head. "I'd never do anything like that. You believe me, don't you, Martha?"

She stared at her hands, folded in her lap. "*Jah,* I do."

A feeling of relief washed over Luke like a fresh spring rain. If Martha believed Luke was innocent, maybe she could convince her dad that he had nothing to do with the attacks. If Luke could get Roman to see the truth, he might have a chance at courting Martha. Truth was, ever since he and Martha had shared a pizza together a few months ago, she'd been on his mind.

"I had a little calamity myself this morning," Luke said.

"What happened?"

"I was heading to work, and my left front buggy wheel came off."

Her forehead wrinkled. "Did you have the tools you needed to fix it?"

Luke nodded. "Sheriff Osborn happened along, and he helped me put the wheel back on. Even so, I was late for work."

"Did you get in trouble with John?"

"Nope. Not even a harsh word." He grunted. "Not like when your daed jumped all over me for being late a couple of times. He was after me for just about everything I did when I worked for him."

Martha's mouth turned down. "I'm sorry about that, Luke. I truly am."

He shook his head. "It's not your fault your daed's so hard to please."

She gave no reply.

"I hope I didn't offend you," Luke was quick to say. "I probably sound like I'm griping. It's not right for me to be bad-mouthing your daed—especially not to you."

"It's okay; I'm not offended. I know how difficult my daed can be at times."

Luke figured it was time for another topic. "How are things going with your dogs these days?" he asked.

"Fairly well. My sheltie Heidi is due to have her *hundlin* any day, and Polly, the beagle I bought at the dog auction some time ago, is also expecting."

"That's good to hear. If you're going to raise dogs, you need some puppies you can sell."

Martha smiled. "I enjoy working for Irene, but I hope someday I'll make enough money with my kennel business to support myself."

"Speaking of kennels, did you read the article in the newspaper this morning, accusing some Amish folks of running puppy mills?"

Martha shook her head. "I didn't have time to read the paper. What did the article say?"

"It said that some Amish are raising puppies without a kennel license and that a few of them have been investigated and accused of neglecting and even abusing their dogs."

Martha shook her head. "I would never neglect or abuse any dog. No one I know who raises dogs would, either." She sucked in her lower lip. "Did Gary Walker write the story? It would be just like him to write something like that."

Luke shrugged. "I can't remember who wrote the article. Fact is, I was so disturbed while reading it that I didn't pay any attention to the reporter's name."

Martha sniffed as though some foul odor had permeated the air. "Gary Walker is so arrogant and pushy." She leaned toward Luke. "Between you and me, I think my sister might be right about him being to blame for the attacks against my family."

A sense of relief shot through Luke. *If Martha thinks Gary is responsible for the attacks, then she must believe I had nothing to do with any of them. Maybe there's some hope for us. Should I ask her out? Would she think I was being too bold?*

He stared down at his boots, unable to make eye contact with her. "Uh. . .remember the day we had pizza together?"

"Jah."

"I enjoyed being with you."

"I enjoyed our time together, too," she said in a near whisper.

He lifted his gaze to meet hers. "I was wondering if you'd like to go out for pizza again."

She hesitated and stared at her hands. "I'd like that, Luke, but—"

"Are you worried about someone seeing us together and telling your daed?"

She nodded.

"How about we meet at the pizza place in Berlin this Saturday at noon? If anyone sees us there, we can just say we happened to meet and are sharing a table."

"I. . .I guess that would be all right."

"Great. I'll look forward to seeing you then." Luke turned and sprinted for his buggy. He liked Martha's spunky attitude and thought she was fun to be with. Now if he could only gain her daed's approval.

Chapter 3

As Martha sat across from Luke at a table in the pizza place on Saturday, her heartbeat picked up speed. She could hardly believe Luke had suggested they meet for lunch. Did his invitation mean he had more than a casual interest in her? She hoped it did. There was only one problem: Dad. Martha was certain he would never give his blessing for her to be courted by the man he thought might be responsible for the attacks against their family.

"After we met the other day, I went home and read that newspaper article you'd mentioned about the puppy mills," Martha said, pushing her thoughts aside.

"What'd you think?"

"I was right—the reporter was Gary Walker. It made me wonder if he's trying to make all Amish look bad."

"Why would he want to do that?"

She shrugged. "It could stem from his anger when Grace broke up with him during her *rumschpringe* years."

"Do you really think that he's still carrying a grudge about something that happened during your sister's running-around years?"

"Grace thinks he is. She's sure Gary's responsible for every attack, even though she has no proof." Martha fingered the edge of her water glass. "I keep hoping the attacks will end, but it's beginning to look like they never will—at least not until we know who's been doing them and they're made to stop."

"I agree," Luke said with a nod. "But since there's nothing we can do about that at the moment, how about we order some pizza?"

"Sounds good to me."

"What kind would you like?"

Martha studied the menu their young English waitress had brought to the table. "With the exception of anchovies, there isn't any pizza topping I don't like." She smiled at Luke. "Why don't you decide?"

"How about sausage and black olives? Does that sound *gut* to you?"

"It sounds real good."

"Should we get a pitcher of root beer to go with it?"

"That's fine with me."

When the waitress returned to the table, Luke placed their order. After the waitress walked away, he leaned across the table to say something but was interrupted when Toby King and Sadie Esh entered the restaurant and sauntered up.

"I didn't expect to see you two here today—especially sittin' at the same table." Toby thumped Luke on the shoulder. "Are you and Martha courting?"

Luke's face turned bright red. Martha figured hers had, too, for her cheeks felt as hot as fire. "Luke and I are just sharing a pizza together," she was quick to say. No point in giving Toby something to gossip about.

Toby gave Luke's shoulder another good whack; then he pulled out the chair next to him and sat down. "Mind if Sadie and I join you?"

"Looks like you already have," Luke mumbled.

Toby looked at Sadie, who stood beside Martha's chair with a bewildered expression. "Aren't you gonna sit and join us?"

Sadie shuffled her feet and glanced at an empty table across the room. "I. . .uh. . .sort of figured—"

"Aw, I'm sure Luke and Martha don't mind if we join 'em. Besides, we'll be alone plenty after we're married." Toby gave Sadie a quick wink. "Have a seat."

Sadie hesitated but finally sat down.

Martha reached over and touched Sadie's arm. "November will be here in a few more weeks. It won't be long until you and Toby are married. How are your wedding plans coming along?"

Sadie's face relaxed. "Pretty well. My *mamm* and I have begun cleaning the house for the wedding meal, and—"

"If everyone who got an invitation shows up, we might have over three hundred guests," Toby interrupted. "Since my daed's the bishop in our church district, I figure we'll have a real good turnout."

Luke cast Toby a disapproving look, and Martha grimaced. She didn't think Toby should be bragging about how many guests might be at his wedding. Truthfully, she'd never understood what Sadie saw in Toby, but then she guessed love was blind when it came to certain things. *Look at me,* she thought ruefully. *I've allowed myself to foolishly fall for Luke.* Martha refused to let herself believe Dad might be right about Luke. If only she could prove Luke's innocence. *Maybe I can. If I keep notes and study that list of suspects I made the other night, I might discover who the attacker is and clear Luke's name.*

Toby nudged Luke. "Do you still have that truck you keep hidden in the woods? I think everyone but your folks knows about it."

Luke's mouth dropped open. "Well, I—"

"You oughta sell that truck, find yourself a nice young woman to marry, and join the church." Toby grinned over at Sadie. "It took me awhile to realize I wanted to get married, but once I made up my mind, there was no stopping me from proposing."

Sadie's eyebrows furrowed. "Excuse me? If you'll recall, I was the one who asked if you'd be willing to marry me."

Toby gave her a sheepish grin; then he elbowed Luke again. "So what do you say? Are you gonna sell that truck and settle down to marriage soon?"

"I'll sell it when I'm good and ready." Luke's dark eyes flashed angrily. "It's not your place to be telling me what to do!"

Martha swallowed hard and reached for her glass of water. She took a quick drink and stood.

"Where are you going?" Toby asked.

"To the ladies' room."

"I'll go with you." Sadie rose from her chair and glanced down at Toby. "When the waitress comes, would you please order a medium-sized pizza with Canadian bacon and mushrooms?"

He squinted. "I thought you only liked pepperoni and cheese."

She shook her head. "It's *you* who likes pepperoni. I prefer Canadian bacon with mushrooms."

He lifted his shoulders in an exaggerated shrug. "Jah, okay."

Martha scurried off toward the restroom with Sadie beside her. Once they were inside, she turned to Sadie and said, "I just can't figure out what the problem is between Toby and Luke."

"I don't know. Toby and Luke used to be such good friends. I first noticed some problems between them when Luke was dating Ruth." Sadie groaned. "It made me wonder if Toby might be jealous."

Martha squinted. "Why would Toby have been jealous of Luke dating my sister?"

"For a while, I thought maybe Toby might be interested in Ruth, but when I asked him about it, he said he had no designs on Ruth. When she broke up with Luke and started dating Martin Gingerich, Toby said he was glad—that he thought Martin was a better choice for Ruth and he hoped they'd be real happy." Sadie frowned. "Ruth was happy, but for such a short time—until Martin's life was taken by whoever rammed their buggy last winter."

Martha nodded as the memory of that fateful night invaded her mind. She and her family had been waiting for Ruth and Martin to show up for Christmas Eve supper, but they never came. Dad and Cleon had gone out looking for Martin's buggy and discovered they'd been in a horrible accident. At the hospital, they'd been told that Martin was dead and Ruth needed a hysterectomy. Ruth had been devastated when she'd learned that she'd not only lost her husband of two months but would never be able to have any children of her own, either.

"I'm glad Ruth's found love again," Sadie said. "She deserves to be happy. I know she'll make a fine *fraa* for Abe and be a good mudder to his kinner."

Martha nodded. "All of Abe's children, especially Esta, have taken a liking to Ruth."

"So, are you and Luke courting?" Sadie whispered.

"Of course not. I told you at the table that Luke and I are just sharing a pizza." Martha slid over in front of the mirror to be sure her *kapp* was on straight.

"I can tell you like him. It's written all over your face." Sadie stood beside Martha. "I think Luke likes you, too."

"What makes you think that?"

"I never saw Luke look at Ruth the way he looked at you out there."

Martha felt the heat of a blush sweep across her face, and she covered her cheeks with her hands. "Even if I do feel something for Luke, and even if he returns those feelings, there's no hope of us ever being together."

"Why not?"

"Unless someone can prove that Luke's not responsible for the attacks against our family, Dad would never give his blessing for Luke to court me."

Sadie's eyes widened. "You don't really think Luke had anything to do with those horrible things, do you?"

"Not me. But my daed suspects Luke."

"He has no proof, right?"

Martha shook her head. "There's no proof of Luke's innocence, either."

"What are you going to do?"

Martha shrugged. She wasn't about to tell Sadie that she planned to do some investigating on her own. Sadie might tell Toby. Knowing Toby, he'd probably blab it to his dad or someone else. For now, Martha would tell no one what she planned to do.

Luke leaned his elbows on the table and stared at Toby. "Are you trying to make me look bad in front of Martha?"

Toby's eyes narrowed. "What do you mean?"

"I think you know what I mean. You brought up my truck, made it sound like I wasn't a good person because I hadn't joined the church, and suggested I marry Martha."

"Huh?" Toby's eyebrows shot up. "I never said that."

"Jah, well, you said I should find a good woman to marry, and you looked right at Martha when you said it." Luke grunted. "What were you trying to do, give her some hope of something that's never going to happen?"

"Does that mean you don't like her?"

"Jah, I like her; Martha's very nice. But that doesn't mean I'm going to marry her."

Toby ran his index finger around the middle of his glass. "If you started courtin' Martha, you might fall in love and decide to get married, jah?"

Luke shrugged.

"Is there something holding you back?"

"Of course there's something. Martha's daed, that's what's holding me back!"

Toby gave him a knowing look. "That's right. You're not one of Roman Hostettler's favorite people these days, are you?"

Luke shook his head. "Unless I can prove I'm not responsible for the attacks that have been made on Roman's family, I'll probably never be accepted by him."

"How you gonna prove that?"

"I don't know."

"If you ask me, the best thing you can do is sell that truck and—"

Luke held up his hand. "Enough about my truck. Like I said before, I'll sell it when I'm ready."

Toby wrinkled his nose. "You always did like to have the last word, didn't you?"

Luke opened his mouth to defend himself but closed it again. What was the point of discussing something with someone who obviously wanted to goad him into an argument? For some time, Toby seemed to need to make Luke look bad. Ever since they were twelve years old and Luke had been declared the winner of a game of horseshoes Toby thought he should have won, there'd been a competitive spirit between them. Could Toby still be holding a grudge because Luke had always been able to do things better than him?

Luke balled his napkin into the palm of his hand. *Can I help it if*

I'm better at playing ball, buggy racing, and fishing than Toby? He ought to grow up.

Martha and Sadie returned to the table just then, and Luke pushed his thoughts aside. He didn't want his lunch with Martha to be ruined, so he would do whatever was needed in order to keep the peace with Toby.

Luke was glad when their pizzas finally came. Now he could concentrate on eating.

By the time they'd finished their pizza and Sadie and Toby had left the restaurant, Martha's nerves were taut. Not only had she and Luke not been able to visit during their meal, but there'd been such tension between Luke and Toby that it had been hard to think of anything to talk about. She hadn't enjoyed her pizza that much, either.

"What was the problem between you and Toby?" Martha asked Luke as they walked out the door and approached her buggy.

Luke leaned against the driver's side of the buggy and folded his arms. "I think Toby is *falsch*."

"Resentful? Why do you think that?"

"Ever since we were kinner, I've been able to do things better than him."

She pursed her lips. "Lots of people can do things better than me, and I don't feel falsch toward them."

"Jah, well, Toby's the bishop's son. I think he feels he has to live up to his daed's expectations to be perfect."

"That's *narrisch*. I doubt anyone expects Toby to be perfect just because his daed's the head minister in our church."

"It might seem crazy, but if Toby thinks he's expected to be perfect and knows he's not. . ." Luke reached under his straw hat and scratched his head. "And if he's struggling with issues concerning me. . ."

"Then he needs to get over it," Martha interrupted. "He needs to be the best person he can, not compare himself to you or anyone else."

"That's what I think, too." Luke moved away from the buggy and reached out to stroke Martha's horse behind its ear. "I've been thinking about the attacks at your place. I wonder if someone might be trying to make me look guilty in order to get even with me for something."

"Like who?"

He turned his hands palm up. "I don't know, but I'm aiming to find out."

"How?"

Luke shrugged. "Haven't figured it out yet."

Martha drew in a deep breath and decided to say what was on her mind. "Would it be all right if I asked you a personal question, Luke?"

"Ask away."

"Would you mind telling me where you were around three o'clock on Thursday morning?"

"In bed, of course. Where else would I be in the middle of the night?"

She swiped her tongue over her lower lip as she struggled for the right words. Should she tell Luke that she'd seen a man dressed in Amish clothes running across the field?

Luke took a step closer to Martha. "Why did you ask where I was early Thursday morning? You don't think I had anything to do with you getting doused with that bucket of paint, I hope."

She swallowed hard. "When I left the barn, I shined my flashlight on the field behind our house, and I saw a man who looked like he was wearing Amish clothes running through the field."

Luke slapped his hands together, causing Martha to jump and her horse to whinny. "I told you someone's trying to make it look like it's me!" He shook his head vigorously. "It wasn't me, Martha. You've got to believe me."

"I want to believe you, and I'm hoping to do some investigating so I can find out who's responsible."

Luke's face blanched. "You're kidding, right?"

She shook her head.

"Snooping around could get you in trouble with your daed, not to mention that it could be dangerous if the culprit finds out you're onto him."

"Or her. It could be a woman, you know."

Luke grasped Martha's arm. "Promise you won't do anything on your own?"

"I can't make that promise. I–"

"How about we work together on solving these crimes?" he suggested. "After all, 'two heads are better than one.' "

She nodded as a sense of relief flooded her soul. If Luke wanted to help her find out who was responsible for the attacks, then he couldn't be responsible.

Chapter 4

Where are you going?" Mom asked as Martha headed for the back door. "If we don't get this kitchen cleaned up right away, we'll be late for Sadie and Toby's wedding."

Martha grabbed a shawl from the wall peg near the door. "I know, but I want to check on Heidi's puppies."

Mom sighed as she lifted her gaze toward the ceiling. "You and those hundlin. I wouldn't be surprised if you weren't late for your own wedding because you were checking on some dog."

"Heidi's puppies are only a couple of days old, Mom. I need to be sure all five are getting plenty of milk. One of them's a runt, you know."

"I'm sure everything will be fine. Heidi did well with her last batch of pups, didn't she?"

Martha nodded. "Except for that one pup I found dead in the yard."

"Accidents happen," Mom said.

"I know."

"My point is," Mom said in a patient tone, "that you spend too much time with your hundlin and not enough time socializing. You'll never find a husband if you don't take an interest in courting."

"I'd need to find someone interested in courting me first."

Mom reached for the dishwashing liquid. "I'm sure the right man's out there. You've just got to look for him."

I've already found him; I just can't tell you who he is, Martha thought as she draped her woolen shawl across her shoulders. *Besides, Luke may never come to like me the way I do him.* "I'll dry the dishes as soon as I get back from the barn," she said.

Ruth entered the room just then. "I'll dry the dishes so Martha can check on her hundlin." She grabbed a sponge from the counter and began wiping off the tablecloth. "I know she wants to be sure they're all right before we leave for the wedding."

"Danki, Ruth."

"You're welcome." Ruth made a clicking noise with her tongue as she wagged a finger in Martha's direction. "Just make sure you're not checking on puppies the day of *my* wedding. I can't have my main attendant being late to the service."

"I promise I won't be late." Martha slipped out the door and hurried for the barn. She found it unlocked, but that was no surprise since Dad had done his chores earlier that morning. Ever since the paint episode, he'd been locking the barn door at night. It remained unlocked during the day, but Martha wasn't too concerned because someone was usually at home.

When Martha entered the dog run where she kept Heidi and her pups, she gasped. One of the puppies was dead! Her thoughts went to the day she'd found one of Heidi's first batch of pups with a broken neck. It was the puppy she'd promised to give Grace's daughter, Anna. The child had been devastated, refusing the offer of another pup. Martha had never figured out the reason the puppy had broken its neck, but she had a hunch someone might have done it on purpose.

"I'm sorry, Heidi," Martha said, patting the sheltie's head. "I hope this puppy wasn't the victim of another attack."

Heidi whimpered and lifted her head as Martha reached into the box and picked up the dead pup. It was the runt of the litter. Maybe it hadn't been foul play, after all. The barn door had been locked last night. Perhaps the puppy hadn't been getting enough milk or had gotten stuck under its mother and smothered. Now she was down to only four puppies, which meant one less pup to sell. Would she ever get her kennel business going well enough to make a decent living?

Hopefully, Polly, her female beagle who was due to have a litter soon, would deliver a healthy bunch of pups. Most shelties sold for anywhere from $300 to $350, but beagles only brought in $200 to $250 if they were trained to run rabbits. Martha would be grateful for whatever she made from either of her female dogs.

She glanced down at the limp pup in her hand. *Maybe I'm not supposed to raise hundlin. Maybe I should look for a full-time job.* She shook her head. *No, I'm happiest when I'm caring for my dogs.*

"What do you mean you've got to work today?" Luke's mother asked when Luke announced that he wouldn't be going to Sadie and Toby's wedding.

"It's Thursday, Mom," Luke said around a mouthful of oatmeal. "John wasn't invited to the wedding, and he's open for business as usual."

"Couldn't you have asked for the day off to attend your friend's wedding?" she persisted.

"I didn't feel like I could. We've got a lot of orders. John needs me in the shop while he makes some deliveries. Besides, Toby and I aren't getting along so well these days. I doubt he'll even miss me."

"Of course he will." Mom reached over and touched Luke's arm. "You and Toby have been friends since you were kinner."

"We used to be friends. Here lately, though, all we do is argue."

"Can't you bury your differences for one day? You know what the Bible says about—"

"If the boy says he has to work today, then he has to work," Luke's dad said as he stepped into the room. "We should be grateful our son has a good-paying job, Betty."

Mom's dark eyebrows furrowed as she took a sip of her tea. "I am grateful. I just think Luke should be at Toby's wedding."

Luke opened his mouth to comment, but his dad cut him off. "It's not as if he's one of Toby's witnesses, you know."

"That's true. Even so—"

"We'd better drop this discussion and eat our breakfast, or the two of us will be late for Toby's wedding," Pop said as he sat at the head of the table.

Mom nodded. "Jah, okay,"

The spicy aroma of cinnamon wafted up to Luke's nose as he poked his piece of toast into the oatmeal and dipped it up and down. Mom always seemed to be fussing about something these days. She wanted him to join the church, find a good woman, and get married. Luke had other things on his mind right now, and marriage wasn't one of them. At least it hadn't been until he'd taken an interest in Martha.

I need to do something to fix things between me and Roman, he thought. *I need to find a way to get back into his good graces and remove my name from the list of suspects Martha's working on.*

Martha had a hard time concentrating on Sadie and Toby's wedding as she sat on one of the backless wooden benches with some other women her age. All she could think about were Heidi's pups and whether the four surviving ones would be all right. She'd been relieved that Dad had agreed to lock the barn before they left home that morning. At least she didn't have to worry about anyone breaking in while they were gone.

She glanced over at the men's side of the room, searching for Luke. He wasn't in sight. Had he stayed home from the wedding because of the disagreement he'd had with Toby the other day, or had he been expected to work for John? Probably the latter, she decided. Luke might not appreciate the way Toby got under his skin, but Martha didn't think he would deliberately skip out on the wedding because he had a grudge against Toby.

Martha clutched the folds in her dress. *I hope he's able to be at Ruth and Abe's wedding in January. It's going to be a joyous occasion, but it won't be nearly as joyous for me if he's not there.*

When Toby's father called for the bridal couple to step forward, Martha's attention was drawn to the front of the room. Her eyes misted when she saw Sadie look lovingly at her groom. Toby looked happy, too, wearing a smile as wide as the Ohio River.

If Luke would only look at me like that. If he would just ask to court me.

Anxious to get out of the stuffy house where a third group of guests had been served their wedding meal, Roman stepped onto the Eshes' back porch for a breath of fresh air. The sun shone brightly on this crisp November afternoon. A group of children frolicked on the lawn, while several young people milled about.

"You're looking kind of wistful," Bishop King said as he stepped up beside Roman and motioned to the children in the yard. "Are you wishing you were young again?"

Roman shook his head. "Although I'd be happy to have half their energy."

"Me, too."

"How's it feel to have your youngest *buwe* married off?"

"It feels rather good. I'm happy my boy's found a nice fraa and will soon be starting a family of his own." The bishop grunted. "Not like Toby's so-called friend, Luke, who didn't care enough to come to the wedding."

"Maybe he had to work today."

"Humph! You'd think he could have taken the day off to see his friend get married."

"Could be his boss had lots of work and wouldn't give Luke the day off." Roman didn't know why he was defending Luke. Truth was, he didn't trust the fellow any further than he could throw one of his buggy horses. The whole time Luke had been working for him, he'd acted cocky, like he thought he knew more than Roman did about woodworking. Luke had been late to work on more than one occasion, too, which made Roman think he was lazy and undependable. If Luke were his son, he would lay down the law and tell him he either had to settle down and join the Amish church or move out. But no, Luke's folks simply looked the other way while Luke pretty much did as he pleased.

Roman grimaced. *Who am I to talk? My oldest daughter took off for a time during her rumschpringe, and we didn't even know where she was. Then there was my sister, Rosemary, who left the Amish faith when she was eighteen years old. For the next thirty years, we never heard a word from her.*

The bishop nudged Roman's arm. "What's wrong? You look like you've just been given a hefty dose of cod liver oil."

"I'm fine. Just thinking about the past, is all."

"How far back were you thinking?"

"Back to when Rosemary left home."

"But she came back last year, and the two of you have made your peace. I don't see why you'd be brooding about that now."

Roman stretched his arms over his head then lowered them and reached around to rub the small of his back. His muscles always tightened up whenever he felt overly stressed. "Sometimes, even when I think I've let go of the past and given everything over to God, something happens or someone says something that brings it all to light again."

Bishop King's bushy eyebrows drew together. "I hope it wasn't anything I said that got you mulling over the past."

Roman shook his head. "I guess the mention of Luke Friesen is what set me off."

"You don't still think he's responsible for the attacks against you, I hope."

"I don't know." Roman shrugged. "I guess several people might have a grudge against me, but Luke seems the most likely."

The bishop leaned against the porch railing and stared into the yard. "I've never really believed Luke was capable of doing any of those things to your family, but after a couple of discussions I've had with him and his folks, I'll have to admit that I am a bit concerned."

"You think Luke's the guilty one?"

"It's not that. What's got me concerned is that Luke is twenty-two years old and still hasn't decided to join the church." The bishop grimaced. "From what Toby's told me, Luke's still running around with a couple of wild English fellows."

Roman nodded. "So I've heard."

The bishop's voice lowered as he leaned closer to Roman. "Toby also told me that Luke's got a truck he keeps hidden in the woods because he doesn't want his folks to know."

"Puh!" Roman waved his hand. "A lot of young Amish fellows who haven't yet joined the church own a car. Many keep 'em right on their folks' property."

"That's true, but Luke's parents have always been very strict about that kind of thing. They've never let any of their kinner keep a car on their property, so I'm sure they won't abide by Luke doing it, either."

"You're probably right."

"Toby's told me a lot about Luke over the years, and one of the things he's said is that Luke tends to be strong willed and moody and always wants his way on things." The bishop slowly shook his head. "Unless Luke has a change of heart, I fear he might never settle down and join the church."

"You think he'll decide to jump the fence and go English?"

"Could be."

Roman grunted. "Maybe it would be for the best if he did. I wouldn't want someone like Luke courting or marrying any of my daughters!"

"Grace is already married, and Ruth will be soon, so that only leaves you one daughter to worry about."

"Jah, well, I'm sure Martha would never be interested in the likes of Luke Friesen. She's got better sense than that."

"That was sure a nice wedding, wasn't it?" Mom asked as she turned and smiled at Martha and Ruth, who sat in the back of their family's buggy.

Ruth nodded. "Sadie seemed real happy to be marrying Toby."

"They'd been courting quite awhile before they were published," Mom said. "Sadie might have been worried that Toby would never ask her to marry him."

"Oh, Toby didn't ask her; it was the other way around." Martha winced when Ruth's elbow connected with her ribs.

"You weren't supposed to say anything," Ruth protested. "I told you that in confidence."

"Sorry. It just slipped out."

"Did Sadie really propose marriage to Toby?" Mom asked.

Ruth nodded, and her face flamed. "She wanted me to do the same with Abe, and I sort of did."

"You did what?" Dad craned his neck to look back at Ruth.

Martha, fearful that their buggy might run off the road, pointed up ahead.

"Don't worry," Dad said with a shake of his head. "Jeb won't leave the road unless I tell him to."

Mom touched Dad's shoulder. "Just the same, Roman, I'd feel more comfortable if you kept your focus straight ahead."

"Jah, okay," he mumbled, turning back around.

"Now, Ruth," Mom said, "tell us about how you sort of proposed to Abe."

The color in Ruth's cheeks deepened. "Well, Sadie had mentioned reading the story of Ruth in the Bible, and she got the bright idea that I should do something that would let Abe know I was interested in him and wanted to be his wife."

"Don't tell me you lay at Abe's feet?" Mom said with a gasp.

Ruth shook her head. "Of course not. I did, however, take a seat at the end of the sofa, and his legs were stretched out–one still in a cast."

"What happened?" Martha prompted. "Did you ask him to marry you?"

"I asked if he could think of me as an acceptable wife."

"How did Abe respond?" Mom asked.

"He reminded me that we're ten years apart and said he thought I could find a younger man." Ruth paused and sucked in her bottom lip. "I can't imagine what Abe must have thought about my boldness."

"He must have agreed to marry you, or else you wouldn't be making plans to be married in January," Martha pointed out.

"Our conversation was interrupted when Abe got the news that Willis had fallen in the pond." Ruth sighed deeply. "Some time after Willis's funeral, I found Abe in the barn, offering Gideon comfort because he blamed himself for his brother's death. It was then that Abe finally asked me to marry him."

"I'm sure it was the Lord's timing," Mom said as she turned back to the front of the buggy. "Just as all things are."

"Wasn't that Steven Bates's car I saw going in the opposite direction?" Ruth asked.

Dad grunted. "Jah, and I gave him a friendly wave, but he didn't bother to wave back."

"Maybe he didn't know it was you," Mom said.

"I'm sure he knew who I was, Judith. The man looked right at me as he went past. He never cracked a smile."

Mom said nothing more. Martha figured it was because she knew Dad would only rehash the past if the subject of Steven Bates continued.

Martha's thoughts went to Luke. A couple of years back when Luke was still working for Dad, some cabinets Steven had ordered for his wife fell off the back of the wagon Luke had used to deliver them. Steven had blamed Dad for it, and Dad put the blame on Luke. Steven had also told Dad that he was done doing business with him. Ever since then, Steven hadn't spoken to Dad. Talking about Steven, the broken cabinets, or Luke always set Dad on edge.

Martha leaned her head against the back of the padded wooden seat. Would God see fit to bring her and Luke together, the way He had Ruth and Martin and then Ruth and Abe? It seemed doubtful, since Dad didn't care for Luke.

The buggy jostled this way and that, and Martha's eyes grew heavy.

Sometime later, the buggy lurched as Dad gave a sharp pull on the reins and guided the horse up their driveway. They drove past Dad's woodworking shop, and then their house came into view.

"Look, Roman," Mom cried. "Someone's thrown eggs all over the side of our house!"

Ruth gasped. "There's a headless scarecrow on our front porch, too!"

Dad halted the horse and jumped down from the buggy. Martha watched as he leaped onto the porch, bent over to study the scarecrow, and plucked something off the scarecrow's shirt. With a grim expression, he marched back to the buggy and waved a piece of paper in the air. "I can't believe it!"

"What is it?" Mom asked, leaning out the opening on her side of the buggy.

He handed her the paper. "This!"

Mom's voice quavered as she read the words: "It's not over yet. Be prepared for more."

Chapter 5

Martha sank to the edge of her bed with a moan. For the last few days, Mom had been acting jumpier than usual. Dad hadn't notified the sheriff about the latest vandalism, and he kept saying that Mom was overreacting—that pranksters could have egged the house.

The recent attack had made Martha even more determined to learn who was responsible. Last night, she'd updated the list she'd made of the previous attacks, adding the egging and headless scarecrow.

Since it was Monday and Martha didn't have to work for Irene, she'd decided to go over her list of suspects and try to figure out who might have egged the house. It had to be someone who wasn't at Toby and Sadie's wedding.

During the wedding meal, Martha had spoken to Luke's mother. Betty had mentioned that Luke hadn't come because he'd had to work for John. *Did Luke really work for John on Thursday, or could he have. . . ?*

Martha thumped the side of her head. *It couldn't have been Luke. I don't want it to be him, but I need to know for sure he didn't egg our house or leave the scarecrow on our porch with the threatening note.*

She stared at the notebook in her hand and read the list of suspects:

Luke—upset with Dad for firing him.
Gary Walker—said he would get even with Grace for breaking up with him.

Steven Bates–stopped doing business with Dad and said Dad would be sorry for ruining the cabinets that fell off the wagon and broke.

Bill Collins, the land developer who wanted to buy our land–left the area some time ago but could have hired someone to cause trouble.

Ray Larson–has been using his binoculars to watch our place from his neighboring property and once asked about buying our land.

Martha drew in a deep breath and released it quickly. As much as she didn't want to admit it, Luke *was* a suspect.

She rose from the bed. *The first thing I need to do after breakfast is pay a visit to John's woodworking shop and find out from Luke where he was during Toby and Sadie's wedding.*

"Do you want me to stain that set of cabinets in the back room?" Luke asked John when he'd finished sanding the legs of a table.

"You'd better wait and do the cabinets after lunch. I've got some deliveries to make, and I'd like you to be near the front of the shop so you can wait on customers and answer any phone calls while I'm gone."

Luke nodded. "I can do that, but wouldn't you like me to get some work done while you're gone?"

John pushed an unruly strand of dark, curly hair off his forehead. "I guess you could finish up sanding that table you've been working on and then do the chairs that go with it. You can do that by the front of the store."

"Sure, no problem."

John clasped Luke's shoulder and gave it a squeeze. "Just want you to know that I'm glad you came to work for me. You're a hard worker, and I appreciate all that you do."

Luke smiled. "Thanks." It made him feel good to know John appreciated him.

"I plan to stop by the bakeshop while I'm in Berlin," John said.

"Would you like me to bring you back something?"

"Maybe a lemon-filled doughnut."

John quirked an eyebrow. "Just one?"

Luke chuckled. "Better make that two or three."

John grinned and headed out the door.

As Luke continued sanding, he thought about John and how easy he was to work for compared to Roman. He did wonder, though, why John made most of the deliveries himself. After all, Luke had a driver's license.

Maybe John doesn't trust me as much as I thought. He does know about those cabinets that fell off Roman's wagon a few years back when I was making a delivery to Steven Bates. Maybe he's afraid something like that will happen while I'm working for him. Luke grimaced. He wondered if anyone trusted him these days.

The bell above the shop door jingled, and Luke looked up. His heart skipped a beat as Martha stepped into the room.

"Wie geht's?" he asked with a smile.

"I'm doing okay." She glanced around the room. "Where's Flo? I didn't see her outside anywhere."

"John had some deliveries to make, and he took the dog along." Luke shook his head. "When you first sold Flo to John, I thought the poor critter would never quit howling, but it didn't take the dog long to warm up to John. Now she's his constant companion."

"As nice as John is, I'm surprised he doesn't have a wife and houseful of kids by now."

"Maybe he hasn't met the right woman yet."

"That could be." Martha moved closer to Luke. "We missed you at Sadie and Toby's wedding last Thursday."

"I had to work that day," he said with a shrug. "How'd the wedding go?"

"It went fine, but I'm sure Toby was disappointed that you weren't there."

"John has a lot of work going right now, and I didn't think I could ask him for the day off." Luke gave the table a few solid swipes. "Besides, I don't think Toby really missed me."

"Why do you say that? You and Toby have been friends since you were little."

"Lately, I've begun to think Toby has it in for me."

Martha's forehead wrinkled. "You really think that?"

Luke nodded. "You heard the way he was goading me at the pizza place a few weeks ago. It's like he's got an axe to grind or something. Toby's always been very competitive, and whenever I've done anything better than him, he's gotten jealous."

Martha leaned against a workbench. "So you think Toby's trying to make you look bad?"

"I wouldn't put it past him. Toby's gone tattling to his daed more than once in the last few years about something I said or did that he didn't like. If nothing else, I think he's hoping I'll get in trouble with my folks." Luke dropped the sandpaper to the floor and stood. "I wouldn't be a bit surprised if Toby's connected to the attacks in some way and is trying to make it look like I'm the one responsible."

"Do you think Toby's capable of doing something so terrible?"

"I'm not sure, but I do know Toby likes to rattle me, and we can't rule anyone out until we know for sure that they're not involved."

"I agree." Martha moved away from the workbench and took a step closer to Luke. "Which is why I've made a list of suspects."

Luke's interest was piqued. "You've made a list already?"

"Jah. I started working on the list after we had pizza together." She shifted her weight from one foot to the other and stared at the floor. "I added to it after what happened on Thursday."

"What happened on Thursday?"

"You haven't heard?"

He shook his head. "Since yesterday was an off-Sunday from church, I haven't seen anyone who would have told me what's been going on."

Martha frowned. "When we got home from Sadie and Toby's wedding Thursday evening, we discovered someone had egged our house and put a headless scarecrow on the front porch with a note pinned to it."

Luke's eyebrows pulled together. "What'd the note say?"

"It said, 'It's not over yet. Be prepared for more.' " Martha's frown deepened as she slowly shook her head. "Mom's been on edge ever since. These attacks have gone on way too long. I don't know how much more any of us can take."

"I'll do whatever I can to help you find out who's responsible," Luke said.

Martha's face relaxed. "I'm relieved to know where you were last Thursday. If my daed suggests you had anything to do with last Thursday's vandalism, I can tell him you were here working for John all day."

Luke grimaced. "Is that why you came here today? To check up on me and see where I was during the wedding? Did you think I'd stayed away from the wedding so I could sneak over to your place and vandalize it? Is that what you thought?"

Martha dropped her gaze to the floor. "I didn't really think that, but I needed to be sure."

He sighed. "I guess everyone's a suspect until proven otherwise, huh?"

"Jah." She reached into the black handbag draped over her shoulder and pulled out a writing tablet. "If you really want to help, how about reading my list of suspects and telling me what you think?"

Luke nodded. "I'd be happy to take a look, but if my name's on the list, I'll have to scratch it off right away!"

As Ruth moved about Abe's kitchen, trying to get breakfast on the table for his family, a feeling of weariness washed over her like a drenching rain. Although she tried to act as if nothing was bothering her when she arrived at Abe's house each morning to help get his children ready for school, she'd felt drained ever since she and her family had gotten home from Sadie and Toby's wedding last Thursday and discovered the vandalism. Each attack reminded her of the tragic event that had taken Martin's life nearly a year ago. Despite her love for Abe and his children, she wasn't sure she would ever completely get over Martin's death.

Ruth shook her head, trying to clear her thoughts. Thanksgiving was only a few days away, and despite the things that had been going on at her folks' place, she really did have a lot to be thankful for.

"Are you feeling all right, Ruth?" Abe asked as he joined her in front of the stove.

"I. . .I'm fine. Just feeling kind of drained this morning."

"Didn't you get enough sleep last night?"

"I slept okay." Ruth sighed as she stirred the eggs around in the pan.

A shadow of worry crossed his face. "Are you still fretting over what happened at your folks' place?"

Ruth nodded as her throat constricted.

Abe touched Ruth's arm, and she shivered when his warm breath tickled her neck. "I'll be glad when we're married. Then you won't have to worry about being vandalized or threatened anymore."

"That's what Martin said before I married him, and look what happened."

Abe's fingers closed gently around her arm. "There are no certainties in this life, Ruth, but we must trust the Lord."

"Jah, I know, and I'm trying to do that, but whenever another attack occurs, my faith begins to waver." Ruth glanced over her shoulder and spotted Esta and Owen staring at her. Abe's family had been through a lot in the last few years, too—first losing Alma when she was struck by lightning and then losing young Willis when he drowned in the pond. "Maybe we should talk about this later," she said, keeping her voice low.

Abe nodded. "You're right. We'll continue this discussion after the kinner have gone to school."

Ruth was tempted to remind Abe that he needed to go to work as soon as he'd finished breakfast, but she figured Ivan would probably open the harness shop if Abe wasn't there right away.

"Papa, I can't wait 'til you marry Ruth," Esta spoke up from her place at the table.

"I'm looking forward to our wedding day, too." Abe gave Ruth's arm a gentle squeeze; then he returned to his seat at the table.

"After you're married, we can all start calling Ruth *Mama*," Esta said with an enthusiastic nod.

Josh, Owen, and even Abe's youngest child, two-and-a-half-year-old Molly, nodded, but Gideon, who'd just turned thirteen, sat staring at his empty plate. Was he unhappy about Ruth marrying his dad, or did the boy have something else on his mind? Ruth was on the verge of asking but changed her mind. If something was bothering Gideon, Abe would deal with it. She wasn't in any frame of mind to deal with anything right now. It had taken all her energy just to show up for work today.

How am I going to handle things once Abe and I are married? Ruth wondered. *Am I really ready to become Abe's wife and mother to his five children?* She drew in a deep breath and tried to focus on the job at hand. She wished she felt free to tell Abe how she felt, but she didn't want him to know the conflicting emotions swirling in her mind. He might not understand her doubts and take them to mean she didn't want to marry him. *I wish Aunt Rosemary were here. She's so easy to talk to and seems to understand me better than anyone.*

No one in Ruth's family had heard anything from Rosemary for the last few weeks, and Ruth had begun to worry that her aunt might not arrive in time for the wedding in January. She gripped the spatula as a feeling of trepidation crept up her spine. *If I don't get some problems resolved in my mind, I'm not sure I can go through with the wedding.*

Chapter 6

"Are you getting tired, Ken? I'd be happy to drive for a while if you are," Rosemary said as she leaned over the backseat in her son's minivan and touched his shoulder.

Ken shook his wavy blond head. "I'm fine, Mom." He nodded at his wife sleeping in the seat beside him. "Sharon's the one who's tired."

Rosemary smiled. Her daughter-in-law had fallen asleep soon after they'd left their hotel this morning. Five days of traveling had taken its toll on all of them. She was glad Ken and Sharon had been able to take vacation time from their jobs at the bank in Boise. It would have been a long, lonely trip to Ohio if Rosemary had made it on her own. It had been much more pleasant riding in Ken's minivan and having her own car towed behind the moving van she'd hired to move her things. She looked forward to introducing her son and his wife to her Amish family, and she was glad they would be able to share Thanksgiving dinner together.

"We should be in Holmes County by late afternoon," Ken announced. "Do you want to go straight to the house you've bought, or do you want to see your brother and his family first?"

"Let's drop by my house to see if the moving van's arrived with my furniture and car, and then we can drive over to Roman's place."

"Sounds like a plan."

Rosemary leaned back in her seat and tried to relax as memories from the past crowded her mind. She'd only been eighteen when she'd left home to try out the English way of life. Then she'd met fun-loving, charismatic Bob, and it had been love at first sight. They'd gotten married soon after and moved to Boise, Idaho. Rosemary had written a letter to her folks, letting them know where she was, but had never gotten a response. She'd written several more letters, but there was no reply. Finally, deciding that her family wanted nothing to do with her, Rosemary had quit writing. It wasn't until shortly before Bob's death that he'd confessed to intercepting those letters and throwing them away so she would have no contact with her Amish family.

Rosemary had always known Bob was the controlling type, but she'd never dreamed he would do anything that would sever the ties with her family in Ohio. It had taken Rosemary several months after Bob's death to come to grips with what he'd done. Once she'd been able to forgive him, she'd made a trip to Ohio in the hope of being reconciled to her family.

Rosemary was anxious to see Roman and his family again and hoped nothing had changed between them while she'd been in Boise getting ready to move to Holmes County permanently. She only wished she'd been able to talk Ken and Sharon into moving there, too. But they both had good jobs at the bank in Boise and didn't want to relocate. Since children were not in their immediate plans, they'd become committed to their careers.

Rosemary leaned closer to Ken. "Are you sure you're okay with the idea of me moving to Ohio? I still feel bad about leaving you and Sharon."

"It's okay, Mom. I want you to be happy. If moving back to your birthplace does that, then you have my blessing."

Rosemary touched his shoulder. "Thank you, Ken. It means a lot to know I have your support."

"Of course," he added with a chuckle, "that doesn't mean I understand your desire to leave the modern world behind and live among the Plain people."

She rapped the back of his head lightly with her knuckles. "I'm not leaving the modern world. I just feel the need to be near my Amish family. They've gone through some rough times lately, and I can't offer my complete support if I'm living in Idaho."

"I understand, Mom." Ken remained silent for a time; then he glanced in the rearview mirror and said, "Are you thinking about becoming Amish again?"

Rosemary pursed her lips. She'd thought about it, but she'd been English too long and didn't think she would feel comfortable wearing plain clothes and driving a horse and buggy again.

"Mom? Does your silence mean you're considering joining the Amish faith?"

"Oh, I don't think so. But I do plan to live a simpler life and keep my focus on God, family, and friends, not all the fancy, modern things the world has to offer."

He shrugged. "You will come to visit us, I hope."

"Of course, and I'd like you and Sharon to come visit me whenever you can, too."

"We'll make a trip to Ohio at least once a year," he said.

Rosemary smiled. She was thankful for her son and glad he hadn't turned out like his father.

Martha had just stepped out of the barn when she saw a minivan pulling into the yard. She didn't recognize the driver, but when the back door of the van opened and Aunt Rosemary stepped out, she knew the driver must be Aunt Rosemary's son.

Martha sprinted across the yard and raced up to the car. "Aunt Rosemary! It's so good to see you!"

Aunt Rosemary held her arms out and gave Martha a hug. "It's good to see you, too, sweet girl."

"We hadn't heard from you in a while and didn't know for sure when you'd be coming."

Aunt Rosemary smiled. "We wanted to surprise you, and I thought it would be nice if we could celebrate Thanksgiving together."

"I'm glad you're here, and I know Mom and Dad will be, too." Martha gave Aunt Rosemary another hug. "Did you have a good trip?"

"Yes, and we saw lots of interesting sights along the way, which was one of the reasons I suggested we drive rather than fly." Aunt Rosemary motioned to the young man with wavy blond hair, and the woman whose dark brown hair was pulled into a ponytail. "Martha, I'd like you to meet my son, Ken, and his wife, Sharon." Smiling at the couple, she added, "This is my niece Martha. She's Roman's youngest daughter."

Ken was the first to extend his hand. "It's nice to meet you, Martha."

"Same here." Martha shook Ken's hand then turned to his wife. "It's nice to meet you, too."

Sharon smiled, although it appeared to be forced. Her gaze traveled slowly around the yard as though she was scrutinizing everything.

Aunt Rosemary gave Martha's shoulder a gentle squeeze. "How's your kennel business doing?"

"Heidi had another batch of puppies a few weeks ago, and Polly just had a litter of seven pups."

"I always wanted a dog when I was a boy, but my dad never let me." Ken chuckled. "I'm making up for it now, though. Sharon and I own two dogs—a beautiful black Labrador retriever and a frisky cairn terrier."

Martha glanced at the minivan. "Did you bring your dogs along?"

Ken shook his head. "We thought it would be an inconvenience, so we boarded them near our home."

"I'd like to be able to board dogs someday," Martha said wistfully, "but I'm not set up for that yet."

"Are you still working for Irene Schrock, or are the dogs taking up all your time these days?" Aunt Rosemary asked.

"I work for Irene a few days a week. If I ever make enough money with the dogs, I'll probably quit that job." Martha pursed her lips. "Of course Irene would have to find someone to replace me. She's so busy with the dinners she serves tourists these days that there's too much work for her and Carolyn to do by themselves."

"I'm sure she appreciates your help." Aunt Rosemary motioned to the house. "Is the rest of the family at home? We stopped by Roman's shop on the way up the driveway and discovered it was closed."

"It's getting close to supper, so Dad's probably up at the house by now. Mom and Ruth were in the kitchen when I went out to the barn a short time ago." Martha grimaced. "I'll probably get a lecture for taking so long with the dogs and shirking my kitchen duties."

Aunt Rosemary looked at her watch. "I hadn't realized it was almost time for supper. Since we're two hours behind you in Boise, I guess my time's still off."

"No problem. I'm sure the folks will insist on you eating supper with us."

"That would be an imposition. I think we should drive back to Berlin and eat at one of the restaurants there." Sharon's dark eyes darted from Martha, to Ken, and back to Martha again. The young woman was clearly uncomfortable.

"There's no need for that," Martha said with a shake of her head. "Mom always fixes way more than the four of us can eat. Besides, we can visit while we share our meal."

"Judith is a wonderful cook," Aunt Rosemary said. "I think you and Ken will enjoy eating one of her delicious meals—not to mention getting the opportunity to know my brother and his family."

Ken reached for his wife's hand. "Let's go inside and meet everyone, shall we?"

Martha slipped her hand in the crook of Aunt Rosemary's arm. "I'll make the introductions first, and then I'll run up to Grace and Cleon's place and see if they'd like to join us for supper."

"Would you pass me the basket of biscuits, please?" Luke's stomach rumbled as the savory aroma of freshly made stew and biscuits wafted up to his nose. He'd worked hard and felt hungrier than usual.

"I noticed that you didn't get after that wood I asked you to chop this morning," Mom said as she handed him the biscuits.

"I was running late and didn't have time to do it before I left for work."

Mom's eyebrows pressed together. "Is that the truth, or are you giving me another one of your excuses for not getting things done around here?"

Luke shook his head. "It's not an excuse."

"From what I hear, you work hard enough for John Peterson, but around here you tend to slough off," Mom said.

Luke grunted. "Are you saying I'm lazy?"

She slathered a biscuit with butter. "You're not exactly lazy, but you sure don't do what I ask these days. It seems you've always got something else on your mind other than what you're supposed to be doing. You've been kind of moody lately, too. Don't you agree, Elam?"

Luke glanced across the table to gauge his dad's reaction, but Pop just sat there, dipping a biscuit up and down in his bowl of stew as though he hadn't heard a word that had been said.

Mom leaned closer to Luke and looked him right in the eye. "I think you need to quit fooling around and make a decision about getting baptized and joining the church."

Luke grunted and reached for another biscuit. "I will when I'm ready. In the meantime, I've got a lot on my mind."

Mom squinted at him. "A lot on your mind?"

"Jah."

"What kind of things could be on your mind that would keep you from joining the church?"

"Just things, that's all."

"Maybe he's got some woman on his mind," Pop spoke up.

"A woman?" Mom nudged Pop with her elbow. "If he had a woman on his mind, he'd be more than ready to join the church." She gave a little gasp as she covered her mouth with her hand. "Ach, Luke! Please don't tell me you've found an English girlfriend and she's the reason you haven't joined the church."

Luke's mouth dropped open. " 'Course not. I don't have any girlfriend, much less one who's English." He hoped his mother didn't press him on this, or he might end up admitting that he had more than a passing interest in Martha Hostettler.

"Whether you've got your eye on any particular woman or not, I think it's past time for you to get baptized and join the church."

Luke opened his mouth to argue the point, but Pop interceded with a raised hand. "And I think it's time we drop this subject, don't you, Betty?"

Mom gave Pop a quick nod, but Luke could see by the look on her face that she was none too happy about it. Fact was, if Pop hadn't put a halt to the conversation, Mom probably would have pestered Luke all the way through supper.

Luke reached for his glass of milk. *If the folks knew I had a truck hidden in the woods and had been hanging around with some rowdy English fellows, I'd probably be in for another lecture.*

"Are we still going to Henry and Luann's house for Thanksgiving?" Luke asked, deciding it was time for a change of subject.

Mom nodded. "Your big brother's looking forward to having us, as well as your four other brothers and their families, over that day."

"Henry's not that much older than me," Luke said with a frown. "How come you referred to him as my 'big brother'?"

"It's just a figure of speech," Pop said before Mom could reply. "Why do you have to be so nitpicky all the time?"

"I wasn't. I was just making a point."

Mom laid a gentle hand on Luke's arm. "Let's not have any more fussing tonight, okay?"

Luke nodded. Tempers had flared and harsh words had been spoken at their supper table more in the last few months than in all of Luke's twenty-two years. If only Mom and Pop would quit pestering him about joining the church. If they'd just let him live his life the way he thought best.

"Have you asked your boss about joining us for our Thanksgiving meal?" Mom asked.

Luke nodded. "I mentioned it to John this morning, but he said he'd made other plans. He'll be out of town until Saturday, so his shop won't be open again until then."

Pop's eyebrows arched upward. "He's single, with no family in the area. What other plans could he have made?"

"I don't know and didn't ask."

Pop grunted. "No wonder you don't have an *aldi*. You never think of anyone but yourself."

Luke gritted his teeth. Was Pop trying to start another argument by bringing up the fact that he didn't have a girlfriend? "I didn't press John for details because I didn't think it was any of my business."

"Even if John doesn't have other plans for Thanksgiving, he might not feel comfortable with the idea of having dinner with people he doesn't know," Mom said.

Pop reached for his glass of water. "He knows Luke."

"That's true, but he doesn't know us that well."

Luke pushed his chair away from the table and stood. He'd had enough supper conversation.

"Where are you going?" Mom motioned to Luke's half-eaten bowl of stew. "You haven't finished your meal."

"I'm full right up to here." Luke touched his chin. "And I've got somewhere I need to go."

Pop's forehead creased. "And where might that be?"

"I'm going outside to take care of that wood Mom's been after me to chop," Luke said as he grabbed his stocking cap off the wall peg near the back door.

"That can wait until tomorrow," Mom called.

Luke rushed out the door. Even though he was in no hurry to chop wood, it would be better than sitting at the table being nagged at throughout the whole meal.

As the Hostettlers sat around the kitchen table with Aunt Rosemary, her son, and his wife, Ruth couldn't help but notice how uncomfortable Sharon appeared to be. Was she shy, or did she feel out of place sharing a table with a group of people she didn't know?

Everyone else seemed relaxed and happy, as Aunt Rosemary and Dad caught up on each other's lives, and Ken alternated between talking to Martha about her dogs and to Cleon about his bees and honey. Grace juggled the baby on her lap while keeping Anna entertained, and Mom kept trying to engage Sharon in conversation. It felt good to have the whole family together–almost as if everything in their life was normal.

But it's not normal, Ruth thought regretfully. *My family is still under attack by someone who wrote a note reminding us that it's not over yet. To make matters worse, I'm having doubts about whether I should marry Abe or not.*

"If our Thanksgiving meal is anything like this meal, then I sure have something to look forward to," Ken said as he took another helping of chicken potpie.

"We'll be eating at Grace and Cleon's place on Thanksgiving, and Grace is a fine cook," Mom said. "I'm sure you'll enjoy every bite."

Grace smiled as her cheeks turned pink. "I won't be the only one cooking that day, Mom. You'll be furnishing the pies."

Mom nodded. "Ruth's planning to make a fruit salad, and Martha will bring some of those sweet potato biscuits Irene taught her to make."

Ken patted his stomach. "Sounds good to me." He looked over at Ruth and smiled. "I understand you'll be getting married in January."

"That's right–the second Thursday," Ruth replied.

"I'll bet you're getting excited already," Sharon spoke up.

Ruth nodded and forced a smile.

Aunt Rosemary reached over and touched Ruth's arm. "If you're like most brides, you're probably feeling a few prewedding jitters."

"She's got nothing to be nervous about," Dad put in from his place at the head of the table. "Ruth's marrying the finest man in these parts. I'm sure they'll have a real good marriage."

"Yes," Aunt Rosemary said before Ruth could respond, "but that doesn't mean she's not feeling a bit nervous." She leaned close to Ruth and whispered, "As soon as we've finished supper and the dishes are done, how about the two of us having a little heart-to-heart chat?"

Ruth nodded as a sense of relief flooded her soul. If anyone could help her deal with the unsettled feelings swirling around in her head, it was Aunt Rosemary.

As Rosemary stood at the kitchen sink, doing the dishes after supper, she thought about how quiet Sharon had been during the meal and wondered how she was getting along in the living room with Grace and Judith. The men and Martha had gone out to the barn, and at Ruth's suggestion, she and Rosemary had become the designated dishwashers.

"Are you ready for that talk now?" Rosemary asked Ruth. "Or would you rather wait until we're done with the dishes?"

Ruth reached for a clean plate to dry. "We can talk while we work, if you like."

"I could tell by the way you responded when Sharon asked about your upcoming wedding that things aren't quite as they should be."

"No. No, they're not."

Rosemary sloshed the dishrag along the edge of the glass and waited to see if Ruth would continue. After a few minutes, Ruth spoke again.

"I love Abe, and I want to be his wife, but I'm not sure I'm ready to get married again."

"Is it because you still love your first husband?"

Tears pooled in Ruth's eyes. "There will always be a place in my heart for Martin, but there's more to what I'm feeling than that."

"Is there a problem with Abe's children? They've all accepted you, right?"

"All but Gideon. He's been so moody and unpredictable lately. I can't be sure what he's thinking."

"He's probably struggling with the idea of someone moving into their home and taking over the role of his mother."

"But I've been working as Abe's *maad* for some time."

"Even so, a maid's not the same as a new wife for Gideon's father."

"True." Ruth's gaze dropped to the floor.

"Is there something else troubling you?"

"Jah. I'm afraid for my family. We're still being attacked, Aunt Rosemary. The last act of vandalism included a threatening note." Ruth drew in a shuddering breath. "Abe thinks I'll be safe living at his place, but even if I am, I'll still be worried about my family. What if the attacks get worse? What if—"

Rosemary lifted her hand from the soapy water. "You mustn't borrow trouble."

More tears filled Ruth's eyes. "But you know what happened to Martin and me. The attacker rammed us off the road, and—"

Rosemary shook her head. "You don't know that the person who rammed your buggy is the same one responsible for the attacks against your family."

"I—I don't know it for a fact, but I feel it in my heart."

"Worrying about your family won't solve a thing." Rosemary dried her hands on a clean towel and touched Ruth's shoulder. "Your folks wouldn't want you to set your happiness aside and continue living here just because you're worried about their safety. If something's going to happen, it will happen whether you're living here or not."

"I suppose you're right."

"Was the sheriff notified after the last attack?"

"No."

"Why not?"

"Dad didn't think it was necessary. He thinks if the sheriff really wanted to put a stop to the attacks, he would see that the area is patrolled more often."

"After I get settled into my new home, I might pay a call on Sheriff Osborn. In the meantime, I want you to commit everything to God and start counting the days until your wedding."

Ruth gave Rosemary a hug. "It's real good to have you back, Aunt Rosemary."

"Thanks. It's good to be here."

Chapter 7

As Luke crawled out of bed on Thanksgiving morning, a wave of nausea hit him with the force of a speeding horse. He groaned and clutched his stomach. They were supposed to have dinner at his brother Henry's home, but the thought of eating all that Thanksgiving food made him feel even worse.

Another wave of nausea came, and Luke dashed into the bathroom just in time to empty his stomach. When he stepped out several minutes later, his stomach lurched again at the smoky odor of bacon coming from the kitchen. He felt light-headed, and his legs trembled so badly he could barely stand. He inched his way down the hall to the kitchen. "Have you got a bucket I can use?" he asked his mother, who was at the stove.

"What do you need a bucket for?" she asked over her shoulder.

"I'm grank, and I don't think my shaky legs will keep taking me to the bathroom."

Mom whirled around. "Ach, Luke, you must be sick. Why, your face is paler than a bucket of goat's milk!" She quickly pulled out a chair at the table. "You'd better sit down."

He grasped the back of the chair and shook his head. "I–I just need a bucket so I can go back to my room."

"I'll get one right away." Mom opened the door to the utility closet and handed Luke the bucket she used for mopping floors. "Do you think you've got the flu?"

Luke grimaced. "Sure looks like it. Either that or I've got a bad case of food poisoning. Even the thought of food makes my stomach churn."

"I don't think it could be food poisoning," Mom said. "You ate the same thing your daed and I ate for supper last night, and neither of us feels sick."

"John and I had lunch in town yesterday," Luke said. "It could have been something I ate there."

Mom slowly shook her head. "I'm sorry you're not feeling well. Guess you won't be up to going with us to Henry's this afternoon."

"No, I just want to go back to bed." Another wave of dizziness hit Luke, and he closed his eyes.

"Your daed's out in the barn right now." Mom slipped her arm around Luke's waist. "I'd better help you back to your room."

Luke didn't argue. He felt too weak to resist. Clinging to the bucket with one hand and holding onto Mom's arm with the other, he made his way upstairs. There would be no turkey and pumpkin pie for him today. All he wanted to do was crawl back in bed and sleep until he felt better.

"If everything looks as good as it smells, I think we're in for a real treat," Ken said as everyone gathered around Grace and Cleon's table.

"I'm glad you and Sharon could join us," Grace said with a smile. "It's always nice when family can be together for a special holiday." She glanced over at Cleon. "I wish your folks could have joined us today, too, but by the time I invited them, your mamm had already planned a big Thanksgiving dinner and invited your brothers and sisters to join them."

Cleon nodded. "I think she would have liked it if we could have been there, too, but we'd already made plans to have your family here."

Grace knew Cleon wasn't trying to make her feel guilty. He was just stating facts. She looked down the long table to where Abe sat with his children and smiled. Having them here would make the day go easier for Ruth. Last Thanksgiving, Martin had still been alive. Despite the fact that Ruth would soon be marrying Abe, Grace figured her widowed sister was probably feeling some sorrow and regret today.

"Now that everyone's seated, let us bow for silent prayer," Dad said.

All heads bowed, and Grace offered her private prayer. *Heavenly Father, bless our family this day, bless the food we're about to eat, and help us to remember to trust You as we face each new day. Amen.*

Dear Lord, Martha silently prayed, *bless this food, bless my family, and help me find out who's responsible for the attacks that have been made against my family.*

When she ended her prayer and looked at the faces around the table, a lump formed in her throat. *If only things could be as peaceful and joyous every day as they are today. If only we no longer had to worry about being under attack.*

"Martha, would you please get the potatoes going?" Mom asked when everyone had opened their eyes.

"Jah, sure." Martha reached for the bowl of mashed potatoes and passed it to Sharon, who sat to her right.

"Danki."

Martha's mouth dropped open. "I'm impressed. You've only been here a couple of days, and already you know how we say thank you."

"Rosemary taught us a few simple words on the drive here from Idaho," Sharon explained.

"I'm surprised she remembered any German-Dutch," Dad spoke up from his seat at the head of the table. "It's been so long since she spoke our language."

Aunt Rosemary's cheeks turned pink. "I may not be able to speak it as fluently as I did when I was a girl, but the language of my youth has never left me."

Martha shifted uneasily in her chair. Was Dad trying to embarrass Aunt Rosemary? If so, it made no sense; the two of them had made their peace several months ago.

As if sensing her discomfort, Dad leaned closer to Rosemary and said, "I wasn't trying to embarrass you, sister. I was just surprised, that's all."

She smiled and patted his arm. "Pleasantly, I hope."

He nodded. "You never cease to surprise me."

Martha breathed a sigh of relief. She was glad things were still okay between Dad and Aunt Rosemary.

"Gemaeschde grummbiere." Ruth said when Sharon handed the bowl of potatoes to her.

Sharon tipped her head. "What was that?"

Ruth pointed to the potatoes. "Gemaeschde grummbiere—mashed potatoes."

Abe's youngest daughter, Molly, who sat beside Ruth in a high chair, bobbed her head up and down. *"Es bescht."*

Ruth nodded. "Jah, mashed potatoes are the best."

Abe, sitting on the other side of Molly, spoke up. "If there's one thing my little girl likes, it's potatoes."

"I like 'em, too, Papa," nine-year-old Esta said. "So does Owen and Josh." She looked over at her older brother, Gideon, and frowned. "I ain't so sure 'bout him, though. Gideon don't like much of anything these days."

"It's 'I'm not' not 'I ain't,' Esta," Abe said. "And let's not get anything started between you and your *bruder* right now."

"Argumentative kids—that's one of the reasons my wife and I have decided not to have any children," Ken said with a shake of his head. "I don't think either of us has the patience for it."

"Raising children isn't just about dealing with arguments," Mom said. "It's a joy to watch your children grow up." She patted Martha's hand. "I wouldn't trade being a mother for anything."

A lump formed in Ruth's throat. She had wanted to be a mother for such a long time, but the tragic accident that had claimed Martin's life and left her unable to have any children of her own had ended those hopes. She glanced at Abe out of the corner of her eye and realized he was smiling at her. *Thank You, Lord, for bringing this kind man into my life. Thank You for giving me the chance to be a mudder to Abe's special kinner.*

As the family continued to eat their Thanksgiving meal, they talked about the beautiful fall weather they'd been having, Martha's dog venture, Cleon's bee business, Dad's woodworking shop, and Ruth's upcoming wedding.

Finally, pushing his empty plate away from him, Dad announced, "Now that we've eaten such a good meal, I think we should take turns saying what we're thankful for. I'll get things started by going first." He leaned back in his chair. "I'm thankful we're all in good health and able to be together today. God has walked by our side this past year, and I think our faith has been strengthened, despite the attacks against us." He nodded at Mom. "Judith, why don't you go next?"

Mom smiled and had just opened her mouth to speak, when—*ka-boom!*—an earth-shattering noise from outside rattled the windows.

Everyone jumped up and rushed out the door.

As they started down the driveway, Ruth saw smoke and flames shooting into the air.

"It's my shop!" Dad hollered. "It's been blown to bits!"

Chapter 8

Martha ran down the driveway after the men. Her heart leaped into her throat when she saw what was left of Dad's shop. Pieces of wood and burning debris lay everywhere.

"Someone, run to the phone shed and call 911!" Dad shouted as he, Cleon, Abe, and Ken raced for the two hoses connected to the water faucet near his shop.

"I'll call on my cell phone," Ken hollered.

Martha glanced around the yard, hoping to spot the person who had done this horrible deed. Except for her family and their Thanksgiving guests, who were now all gathered on Mom and Dad's front porch wearing stunned expressions, she saw no one in sight. Whoever had blown up Dad's shop had taken a chance doing it in broad daylight.

Martha's heart nearly stopped beating. No. The person responsible for this attack must have known they were having their meal at Cleon and Grace's place.

"Oh, dear Lord," Martha said, "how can this be happening to us?"

Grace and Ruth joined her on the lawn, but Mom remained on the porch with Sharon and the children.

"I. . .I can't believe this." Ruth's voice quavered, and her eyes widened with obvious fear. "Must we let these attacks keep going on until someone else is hurt?"

Martha put her arm around Ruth's waist. "Ken's called 911. I'm sure the sheriff will be here soon. Once he finds out what's happened, he'll hopefully try to find out who's responsible for blowing up Dad's shop."

Ray and Donna Larson dashed into the yard just then. "We heard an explosion and saw smoke and flames coming from your place!" Ray shouted. "I phoned the fire department right away!"

"My cousin phoned them, too, for all the good it will do," Martha said with a shake of her head. "Dad's shop is gone."

Ray turned to Donna. "You stay here with the women. I'd better go see if I can lend Roman a hand."

"I don't know what Dad's going to do without his shop," Ruth said to no one in particular. "How's he going to earn a living with no place to do his woodworking?"

"Maybe he'll decide to move," Donna spoke up. "I'd certainly encourage Ray to move if something like this happened to us."

"Dad will never move," Grace was quick to say.

Martha couldn't stand there and listen to the women's conversation any longer. She needed to see how things were going with the men. With a quick, "I'll be back," she sprinted down the driveway. Halfway to the shop, she heard sirens blaring in the distance. A few minutes later, two fire trucks pulled in, with Sheriff Osborn's car and John Peterson's rig right behind them.

The next few days went by in a blur. As upset as Roman was over losing his shop, he took comfort in knowing no one had been hurt. He'd been overwhelmed when his friends and family had rallied around, offering supplies and money so he could start up his business again. With winter around the corner, he'd decided to temporarily use one section of the barn as his shop and to rebuild in the spring. The sheriff had promised to do a thorough investigation and said he would keep a closer watch on the Hostettlers' place.

"I hope he means it this time," Roman mumbled as he headed for the barn on Saturday morning. The sheriff had made that promise before, but had he? *No!* He'd used the excuse that he was either too busy or couldn't spare the men to patrol the area regularly. Roman had begun to think the sheriff didn't care. But when he'd shown up on Thanksgiving Day, he'd acted genuinely concerned—even said he was thankful no one had gotten hurt.

When the attacks had first begun, Roman hadn't wanted to involve the sheriff. He'd figured they'd been random acts by rowdy kids looking for a good time. But as the attacks continued, he'd become more concerned. Of course he hadn't told Judith or his daughters the way he really felt. He was trying to set an example—show them how strong his faith was and that he was trusting God to protect them. Despite Roman's resolve to remain strong, his nerves were beginning to wear, and Judith's were, as well. Since Thanksgiving, she'd had trouble sleeping. She'd also been acting jittery as a June bug. He wondered how much more she could take.

Roman glanced at the field behind their place. The cows and horses grazed peacefully, basking in the early morning sun. A few dried-up wildflowers lined the fence, and birds chirped from the trees.

If only life could be calm and undisturbed like the scene set before me, he thought regretfully. *If we could just put the past behind and forget about all the frightening things that have been done to us.* He grunted. *Guess that won't happen until this horrible nightmare ends—if it ever does.*

As Roman stepped into the barn, two pigeons that had been roosting in the hayloft swooped down and landed on the floor. His heart leaped into his throat, and he jumped back. *Get a grip,* he told himself. *You can't let every little noise set you off.*

He moved to the nearest shelf, grabbed a book of matches, and lit a lantern. *I just need to continue to pray and seek God's direction.*

As Rosemary stood in her driveway, saying good-bye to Ken and Sharon, a lump formed in her throat. Moving away from her only son was harder than she'd thought it would be. Even so, her place was here in Holmes County right now. Her Amish family needed her more than ever.

"I wish you'd forget about staying here and come home with us,"

Ken said with a worried expression. "I'm concerned for your safety, Mom."

"I'll be fine," she assured him. "The attacks have only been made on the Hostettlers, not me. Besides, I'm trusting God to protect me."

Sharon slowly shook her head. "Look where trusting God's gotten the Hostettlers."

Rosemary clasped her daughter-in-law's hand. "There are times when it seems as if God has abandoned us, but that's when we need to draw closer to Him."

Ken nodded as he put his arm around Rosemary. "You're right, Mom. It won't be easy not to worry about you, but if you're determined to stay here, then Sharon and I will remember to pray every day—for you and for your Amish family."

Rosemary smiled as tears clouded her vision. "I'll be praying for you and Sharon, too."

Ken looked over at Sharon. "If you're ready, I guess we'd better hit the road."

She nodded. "I'm ready."

Rosemary gave them both another hug, and as their vehicle pulled out of her driveway, she heard a cow's mournful *moo* in the distance. A sense of unease tightened her stomach. Did she really have the faith to believe everything would be all right?

Proverbs 29:25 popped into her mind: *"The fear of man bringeth a snare: but whoso putteth his trust in the Lord shall be safe."*

She drew in a deep breath and closed her eyes. "Help us all to trust You completely, Lord."

Luke stepped into John's woodworking shop on Saturday morning and found John on his knees, sanding the underside of an old chair. "Hard at work already, huh?"

John looked up and smiled. "Since we didn't work on Thursday or Friday, I thought I'd better get an early start today."

"Which is why I'm here fifteen minutes sooner than you told me to be. I figured you'd want to make the most of our day." Luke removed his jacket and stocking cap and hung them on the coat tree. "What would you like me to do first?"

"Why don't you get those stained?" John motioned to a set of cabinets on the other side of the room. "There's a new bed-and-breakfast opening in Sugarcreek in a few weeks, and they'd like the cabinets done by the first of next week."

"I'll get right on it," Luke said as he got out a can of walnut stain.

They worked in silence for a time; then Luke looked over at John and said, "You're doing a nice job on that chair."

"Guess it comes from years of practice."

"You're not that old. I doubt you could have been doing woodworking all that long," Luke said as he dipped his brush in the can of stain.

"I started working part-time for a carpenter out in Oregon when I was sixteen. By the time I'd turned eighteen, I was working full-time." He grunted. "Of course I didn't really have much choice, since my stepdad had died, leaving Mom and me to fend for ourselves."

"Does your mother live in Oregon?"

"She did, but she died a few years after Harold, my stepdad, did."

"What about your real dad? Is he still living?"

John shook his head. "He died when I was two. I don't even remember him." He grabbed another piece of the sandpaper and started working on the chair legs.

"Do you have any brothers or sisters?"

"Nope."

"What about grandparents, aunts, uncles, or cousins?"

John stood and arched his back. "Can we talk about something else? Family—or the lack of it—is not my favorite topic of conversation."

"Sure, no problem." Luke was surprised John had told him as much as he had. In all the time he'd been working here, John hadn't told him much more than the fact that he was single and had no family living in the area. Hearing John's story made Luke realize those in his Amish community weren't the only ones who suffered hurts and disappointments. It also made him appreciate the family he had.

"Did you hear what happened at the Hostettlers' place on Thanksgiving?" John asked.

"I spent Thursday and Friday in bed with the flu, so I haven't heard much of anything. What happened at the Hostettlers'?"

"Roman's shop was blown up."

Luke's mouth dropped open. "Are you sure about that?"

John nodded. "I saw the fire trucks speeding down the road on my way home Thanksgiving night. When they turned in at the Hostettlers', I followed to see what had happened."

"I thought you were going out of town and weren't planning to be back until Friday night."

"My plans changed, so I had Thanksgiving dinner at a restaurant in New Philadelphia and headed for home soon after that."

"And you say Roman's shop was blown up?"

"Yep. From what I heard, they'd just finished eating their Thanksgiving meal when the big bang occurred." John's forehead wrinkled. "You should have seen the mess it made. There was nothing left of Roman's shop, and he lost all his woodworking tools and everything else in that explosion."

"That's terrible. Was it an accident, or do they think it was another attack?"

"The sheriff and the fire marshal said they would conduct an investigation. From what I heard, it sounded like they think there was foul play involved."

Luke slowly shook his head. "What's Roman going to do? I mean, without his woodworking business, how's he going to support his family?"

"I asked him about that, and he said he planned to work out of his barn until he can build another shop. I'm planning to go over there later today and give Roman a few tools. I'm sure he'll get some help from some of the families in his community, too."

Luke nodded. Whenever anyone in their community had a need, everyone always rallied. He just wished he felt free to offer his help, as well. Unfortunately, any help he might offer Roman would be flatly refused.

"I can't believe the kind of luck the Hostettlers have had," John said. "It sure seems like someone's out to get them, doesn't it?"

Luke nodded. *I may not be able to help Roman, but I can help Martha try to figure out who's responsible for blowing up her daed's shop.*

Chapter 9

Clutching a flashlight, Martha tiptoed out of her room. She took the steps slowly, being careful not to wake Mom, Dad, or Ruth. The last thing she needed was for one of them to see her sneaking outside to search for clues. She'd been planning to do this on Friday evening but had been so tired she'd fallen asleep and hadn't woken up until morning. This was the first chance she'd had to really look things over, and she hoped she might find one or two clues—anything to learn who had blown up Dad's shop.

When Martha reached the bottom of the steps, she grabbed her jacket from the wall peg and slipped out the back door. As she stepped into the yard, the cold night air jabbed at her skin. Winter would be here soon.

As she passed the barn, the sour, pungent aroma of horse manure wafted up to her nose. Dad would probably clean the horse stalls sometime tomorrow. Otherwise, he'd never be able to work in the barn.

The gravel under Martha's feet crunched as she headed down the driveway, using her flashlight to illuminate the way. A quiver of expectation crept up her spine. Would she find anything in the rubble left from Dad's shop that might give her some clue as to who had done this horrible thing? Maybe the sheriff and fire marshal had missed something.

As Martha approached the spot, she lifted the flashlight and rotated it from side to side, letting the light shine all around. She kicked at a charred piece of wood with the toe of her sneaker and groaned. "I'll never find anything in this mess."

"Probably not, and you shouldn't be out here alone in the dark."

Martha whirled around, her heart pounding against her rib cage. "Luke! You scared me half to death! What are you doing here, anyway?"

"Same as you. I came to look for some clues." He lifted the flashlight he had in his hands.

"I guess you heard what happened here on Thanksgiving then."

"When I got to work this morning, John told me about your daed's shop being blown up."

She nodded. "John stopped here soon after the fire trucks arrived. He said he'd seen them racing down the street and followed them when he realized where they were headed."

"John's going to give your daed some of his extra tools. Said he couldn't believe the kind of luck your folks have been having."

"I wouldn't call it luck." Martha frowned. "I'd say it's more of a curse than anything."

"So have you found anything in this mess?" Luke asked, shining his light on the rubble.

She shook her head. "But then, I haven't been here very long."

"Was the sheriff called this time?"

"Jah. Both he and the fire marshal came over on Friday morning and checked around. They concluded that Dad's air compressor must have blown up."

"What'd your daed say about that?"

"Dad said he's sure he didn't leave the compressor running when he closed his shop the night before. He couldn't figure how the power could have been turned on. He's sure someone broke into his shop and tampered with the compressor so it would blow up."

"If the sheriff and the fire marshal didn't find anything helpful, what makes you think you will?" Luke asked.

Martha resisted the urge to scream. Didn't Luke think she was smart enough to figure anything out? "Do I look stupid?" she asked a bit too sharply.

"Sorry. I was out of line for making it sound as if I thought you were *dumm*." He stepped closer to her. "I don't think that, Martha. I think you're one of the smartest, bravest women I know. I'm just worried about you, that's all. It's not safe for you to be out here in the middle of the night, searching for clues." He made a sweeping gesture of the debris with his flashlight. "What if whoever did this came back tonight and found you out here alone?"

Martha smiled. Luke obviously cared for her, if only as a friend, or he wouldn't seem so upset about finding her here. "I told you before that I was going to do some investigating," she said. "This was the first chance I've had to come out here and look around."

"I can't believe anyone would do this to your daed's shop." Luke slowly shook his head. "These attacks have gone on so long it's almost unreal. Seems by now someone would have caught the culprit in the act of doing at least one of these things, doesn't it?"

She nodded. "Dad thinks our faith is being tested. He said the other night that being afraid of what people might do to us is unnecessary if we trust in God."

"I don't think that means we should sit back and let these kinds of things happen without trying to put a stop to them."

"That's why I want to find out who's responsible for doing this."

"Have you looked for footprints?" Luke asked.

"No, but the sheriff did. He said since our driveway and the parking lot by Dad's shop are graveled, no prints showed."

"How does he know the attacker came up the driveway?" Luke turned toward the field closest to them—the one separating their property from the Larsons'. "Maybe we should search for clues farther away from your daed's shop. Whoever did this might have come onto your property that way and left some clues."

Martha shined her flashlight in that direction. "Do you really think so?"

"It's worth looking, don't you think?"

"I suppose it is."

"Then let's head over there and see what we can see."

Luke led the way as they trudged through the field, shining their flashlights in every direction.

"This would be a whole lot easier in the light of day," he mumbled. "If there *was* any evidence, we could step right over it and not even know."

"I know, but I feel led to keep looking for a while."

Luke moved on, continuing to shine his light. Suddenly, he came to a halt.

"What is it, Luke? Why'd you stop?"

"Look here." He bent down and picked up a wrench. "I'm guessing the person who blew up your daed's shop might have used this to damage the valve on the air compressor so it wouldn't release the pressure, which would cause it to blow sky high."

"We'd better take the wrench to the sheriff so he can check for fingerprints."

A cold sweat trickled down Luke's back as he shook his head. "That's not a good idea, Martha."

"Why not?"

He shined the light on the wrench. "Now that I foolishly picked this up, my fingerprints are on it. If anyone else's prints were on the wrench, now they're all messed up."

In the soft glow of the moonlight, Luke saw Martha tremble. He took a step back, resisting the desire to pull her into his arms. "Any idea what we should do with the wrench?"

"I suppose I could hide it somewhere—at least until we've had time to do more investigating."

A sense of relief flooded his soul. "I think that's a good idea—unless you'd rather I take the wrench home with me."

She shook her head. "I'll find a place to hide it."

Luke handed the wrench over to her. "Guess I'd better get on home. My daed gets up early to milk the cows, and if he goes to my room looking for help and discovers I'm not there, he'll have a conniption."

"I need to get back up to my room, too." Martha turned toward her house but whirled back around. "You wouldn't have blown up my daed's shop, would you, Luke?"

"Of course not! I can't believe you would even ask me that question." A sense of irritation tinged his voice. "I thought by now you had figured out that I was innocent and wanted to help you find out who's behind the attacks so we can keep your family safe and clear my name."

"I'm sorry, Luke. I'm just feeling confused and a little bit scared right now."

Throwing caution to the wind, Luke stepped forward and pulled Martha into his arms. "You don't have to be scared when you're with me," he murmured against the top of her head.

Martha leaned heavily against Luke's chest, and the nearness of her was almost his undoing. He wanted to tell Martha how much he'd come to care for her. He wanted to ask if he could court her. But it was too soon for that. He needed to clear his name before he could declare his intentions.

Slowly, Martha pulled away. "I'd better go now. Good night." She hurried off before Luke could find his voice.

Boom! Boom!

Roman bolted upright in bed. *That sounds like gunfire. Is someone hunting nearby?* He had posted No Hunting signs on his property several weeks ago, so surely whoever was hunting couldn't be too close.

Boom! Boom! Boom! More gunfire in rapid succession.

"Roman, that sounded like gunfire!" Judith exclaimed.

"I know, and I think it's real close." Roman scrambled out of bed and slipped into his trousers.

"Where are you going?"

"Outside, to see what's up."

Judith scrambled out of bed and raced to the window. "It's not even fully light."

"It's light enough for me to see, and I'm going to check things out. If someone's hunting on our property, I'll run 'em off."

Judith clutched his arm. "But they've got a gun. What if they're not hunters at all? What if—"

He held up his hand to silence her. "I'll be okay, Judith."

She grimaced, a look of desperation on her face. "How can you be so sure?"

"There are no certainties in life, but as Christians, we're supposed to trust God to take care of us."

"That doesn't mean we should put ourselves in danger foolishly."

"There's nothing foolish about a man going out to see if someone's hunting on his property." Roman slipped into his boots then turned to face her. "I'll be back in a few minutes. While I'm gone, why don't you get breakfast started?"

"I won't be able to fix breakfast until you're back in the house and I know everything's all right."

He patted her shoulder. "I'll be fine; you'll see."

When Roman stepped outside a few minutes later, he was greeted by the chattering of squirrels eating from one of the bird feeders. He listened for more gunfire but heard none. Apparently, the shooter had either bagged a deer or moved on.

Just to be sure everything was okay, he decided to walk the fence line. He started with the fence closest to the house and moved on back. When he came to the pasture where he kept his beef cows, he halted. Five of them lay dead! That gunfire hadn't been from a hunter at all. Someone had deliberately shot his cows!

Martha groaned and rolled over in bed. She'd been dreaming about someone shooting a gun and chasing after Luke. She rubbed her forehead, trying to clear her mind. It hadn't been a dream. She'd heard a gun go off; she was sure of it.

Martha scrambled out of bed and raced over to the window. Someone stood in the pasture where Dad's beef cows were kept. She squinted against the early morning light. It looked like Dad, and he seemed to be bent over something. Alarm rose in her chest. Had someone been shot?

She slipped into her sneakers, threw on her robe, and dashed from the room. She met Mom in the hallway at the bottom of the stairs. "What's going on? I thought I heard a gun go off, and when I looked out the window, I saw Dad in the pasture."

"It was gunfire," Mom said. "Your daed thought someone might be hunting on our property. Against my wishes, he went outside to check on things."

Martha raced out the back door, tore across the yard, and headed straight for the pasture. She found Dad kneeling in front of a cow. He looked up and slowly shook his head. "It's been shot dead, along with four others."

Martha gasped then covered her mouth with her hand, horrified. It was bad enough that five of Dad's prized cows were dead. What if whoever had shot the cows had been lurking in the field last night when she and Luke had been looking for clues? If the shooter had discovered them, their lives could have been in danger.

Chapter 10

Martha touched her father's trembling shoulders. "Why would someone want to shoot your cows?"

"Why would they have done any of these terrible things to us?" He slowly shook his head. "Someone's got a grudge against me. The question is who?"

A shiver shot through Martha's body. She rubbed her hands briskly over her arms and drew in a deep breath. Luke had a grudge against Dad—or at least, Dad thought he did. If she told Dad about Luke being here last night and that the two of them had been looking for clues, would he believe her? Or would Dad think Luke had been skulking around, waiting to attack?

"Will you let the sheriff know about this?" Martha asked.

He grunted. "Wouldn't have to if he'd been doing his job better. After what happened to my shop on Thanksgiving, I figured he'd be keeping a close watch on our place like he said he would."

"The sheriff can't be everywhere at once."

"Maybe not, but he's got deputies working for him. You'd think with my shop being blown to bits just a couple of days ago, someone would at least have been keeping an eye on our place. Every morning when I get out of bed, I ask myself, 'What will this day bring?' And each time there's another attack, I try to keep the faith, but it's getting harder to believe the attacks will ever come to an end."

Martha cringed when she heard the anger and pain in her father's voice. Despite his resolve to remain hopeful that the attacks would stop, he was obviously feeling discouraged. If only she could say something to make him feel better. If she could just do something to solve the mystery of who was behind these horrible attacks.

"*Was is letz do?*" Mom asked breathlessly as she stepped up to Martha.

"I'll tell you what's wrong here–someone's shot five of my beef cows!" Deep lines etched Dad's forehead, and his clenched jaw revealed the extent of his despair.

Mom gasped as she stared at the cows lying in the pasture. "Ach! Roman, why would anyone do such a terrible thing?"

He rose to his feet. "You know why, Judith. Someone's got an axe to grind against me."

"You don't know that," she said with a shake of her head. "This might have been done by that reporter fellow. Grace still thinks he came to Holmes County in order to make her pay for breaking up with him when she was going through rumschpringe."

"I don't think so. If it was Gary Walker, and he was only after Grace, then only she would have been attacked." Dad touched Mom's arm. "Think about it. Most of the attacks have been done to our property, not hers."

"But some were done to Grace," Martha spoke up. "Don't forget about her and Cleon's house being burned."

"That's true, but most of the attacks have been done here." He motioned to the dead cows. "Guess I'd better notify the sheriff about this mess, and then I'm going to see if some of our friends and neighbors will help me cut and process these critters so I can share with others. No point in all this good meat going to waste."

Mom turned toward the house, her shoulders slumped. "I'll be in the kitchen fixing breakfast."

Martha looked at Dad. "Do you need my help, or should I go up to the house with Mom?"

"There's not much you can do here," he replied. "You may as well help your mamm."

Martha nodded and hurried off. She stopped by the barn to

check on her dogs. Finding them to be okay, she went straight to the house.

When she stepped into the kitchen, the savory aroma of sizzling bacon filled the room. Ruth was busy setting the table, and Mom stood in front of the stove.

"What can I do to help?" Martha asked.

Mom turned, and her hand trembled as she pushed a wayward strand of hair away from her face. "If you'd like to get out some eggs and scramble them in a bowl, it would be much appreciated."

Martha nodded. "Jah, sure, I can do that."

Steam rose from the whistling teakettle, and the heat of the kitchen brought a film of perspiration to Mom's flushed cheeks. She turned back to the stove and turned the bacon.

As Martha headed to the refrigerator, Ruth stepped up to her and whispered, "Mom told me what happened to Dad's cows. She's really upset about this."

"There's no need to whisper," Mom said, "and you needn't talk about me behind my back. I'm not going to fall apart, if that's what you're worried about."

Ruth looked at Martha and shrugged her shoulders. Martha gave a slow nod. She knew her sister was probably thinking the same thing she was: that despite Mom's denial, she was definitely not herself.

"You look like you could have used a few more hours sleep last night," John said when Luke entered the shop, yawning. "What'd you do–stay up all night counting sheep?"

Luke couldn't tell John he'd been over at Roman's place in the middle of the night searching for clues, so he merely shrugged and said, "Yeah, something like that."

John stretched his arms over his head and yawned. "Just looking at your bloodshot eyes and dark circles makes me feel tired."

Luke snorted as he plucked off his stocking cap. "I don't think I look all that bad."

"Well, as long as you can give me a fair day's work, I don't care what you look like." John motioned to the rocking chair he'd been working on. "Speaking of work, I'd like you to go in the back room and get some coffee going while I get back to work on this old gem."

Luke nodded and headed for the back room. He was happy working here and didn't mind when John asked him to do the grunt work. At least John didn't yell at him the way Roman used to.

Luke got the coffeemaker going and thought about the night's activities while he waited for the coffee to brew. *I wonder what Martha did with that wrench we found. It was sure stupid of me to pick it up. I wonder if Martha will keep her promise and not tell anyone about the wrench.*

As Martha entered the barn to get her horse ready to go to Irene's that afternoon, she looked up at the hayloft and thought about the wrench she'd hidden there. Had she been right to agree not to tell anyone about it? The wrench did have Luke's fingerprints on it.

Could Luke have tampered with Dad's compressor and dropped the wrench in the field as he was fleeing? Was that why he'd picked it up and made such an issue of his fingerprints being on it?

Martha remembered the expression on Luke's face when she'd asked if he would have blown up Dad's shop. He'd looked at her as if she'd asked if he would consider lighting his own house on fire.

She grimaced. What was there about Luke that made her emotions so unstable? Trust one minute, confusion and mistrust the next. She had to make up her mind whether she trusted him or not. She couldn't keep changing her mind like this.

"I trust Luke," she murmured as she led Gid out of the barn. "I *have* to trust him."

Martha had just finished hitching her horse to the buggy when Aunt Rosemary's car pulled into the yard. "Where's your dad?" Aunt Rosemary called to Martha as she stepped out of her vehicle. "I have something for him."

"He's in the barn with Cleon. They're taking the hide off a couple of his cows."

Aunt Rosemary quirked an eyebrow. "He's butchering cows? I figured he'd be busy trying to set up his shop in the barn. That is where he plans to do his woodworking until he can build a new shop, right?"

Martha nodded. "Five of Dad's beef cows were shot and killed early this morning." She motioned to the pasture out back. "Abe Wengerd and Cleon's brother, Ivan, are out there loading the rest of the cows on one of our wagons."

"What?" Aunt Rosemary's jaw dropped.

"It's true. We heard shots while we were still in bed, and then Dad discovered the cows lying dead in the pasture."

"I can't believe this." Aunt Rosemary shook her head. "First your dad's shop, and now his cows? How much more can your family take?"

"I don't know. I just don't know."

Aunt Rosemary opened her purse and removed her cell phone.

"What are you doing?"

"I'm calling the sheriff; that's what I'm doing."

Martha shook her head. "You don't need to do that. Dad called Sheriff Osborn from our phone shed earlier this morning, and the sheriff came out right away."

"I'm glad to hear that. It's about time my brother decided to notify the sheriff right after one of these attacks has occurred."

"Dad had the sheriff called when the shop blew up. Finding some of his cows dead this morning only magnified his feelings of frustration."

"He has good reason to be frustrated." Aunt Rosemary started for the barn. "Maybe when he sees what I brought him, he'll feel a little better about things."

When Rosemary entered the barn, she spotted Roman and Cleon removing the hide from one of the cows hanging from the rafters.

"I just talked to Martha," she said, stepping close to Roman. "I'm sorry about your cows."

He shrugged. "At least the meat won't go to waste."

"Martha says the sheriff came out this morning."

"Jah."

"What'd he have to say?"

"Said he'd double his patrol time around our place."

"He's said that before," Cleon put in, "but the attacks haven't stopped, have they?"

"Maybe the sheriff will catch the guilty party this time." Rosemary hoped her voice sounded more optimistic than she felt. After speaking to the sheriff herself a couple of times, she didn't feel he cared that much about the things that had happened at her brother's place. She wondered if he might be prejudiced against Roman because he was Amish. She'd even wondered if—

"What brings you over today?" Roman asked, breaking into Rosemary's disconcerting thoughts.

She reached into her purse and pulled out a check. "I came to give you this. It's to help rebuild your woodworking business."

Roman took the check, and as he studied it, an awkward silence filled the space between them. Finally, he spoke. "I can't take this."

"Why not?"

"It's for five thousand dollars. That's way too much."

"No, it's not. I love you and your family, Roman. I want to help out." Rosemary touched his arm. "Christmas is just a few weeks away, you know."

"So?"

"I'm sure you can use some money to buy your family a few presents, not to mention all the supplies you'll need to purchase to replace what was lost when your shop was destroyed."

A muscle on the side of his face quivered. "I'm touched by your generosity, sister," he said in a near whisper. "Especially after the way I acted when you first came back home."

She smiled as tears clouded her vision. "That's in the past. It's over and forgiven. It's the *now* that counts."

"Your sister's right," Cleon said. "It does no good to dwell on the past."

Roman nodded as he offered Rosemary a smile. "Danki, sister." He held up the check. "Danki for this and for moving back to Holmes County."

Chapter 11

As Grace entered the schoolhouse, where Anna and the other schoolchildren would be putting on their Christmas program, weariness settled over her like a heavy fog. The past few weeks had been stressful for everyone. Not only had Dad's shop been blown up and his cows killed, but also two days ago, Dad and Mom had come down with a bad case of stomach flu, which meant they wouldn't be able to attend Anna's program tonight. Grace hoped no one else in the family came down with the flu.

At least there have been no attacks in the last two weeks, she thought as she took a seat behind Anna's desk. Anna had scurried behind the curtain at the front of the room, and Cleon stood near the back, holding Daniel.

She glanced around the room and spotted Abe standing at the back near Cleon. Cleon's brother Ivan was there, too, along with his girlfriend, Amanda. Grace figured it was just a matter of time before Ivan and Amanda became engaged. Soon Cleon's folks would only have Carolyn living at home.

Children grow up too quickly, she thought as she spotted Abe's daughter Esta slip behind the curtain, along with her brothers Josh, who'd recently turned eleven, and Gideon, the oldest. Ruth sat at a desk with Abe's youngest boy, five-year-old Owen, beside her, while she held little Molly in her lap.

Grace smiled when Ruth nuzzled the top of Molly's blond head. *My sister will make a good mudder to Abe's kinner. I'm glad she's found love again.*

"How are your folks feeling?" Aunt Rosemary asked as she took a seat across the aisle from Grace. "I hear they've both got the flu."

Grace nodded. "They're still pretty sick. Martha stayed home to see to their needs so Ruth could be here to watch the program."

Aunt Rosemary's eyebrows puckered. "Does that mean they're going to miss Christmas?"

"It looks that way. You're still invited to our house on Christmas Eve, and we're planning to come to your place on Christmas Day. If no one else gets sick, that is," Grace quickly added.

"We'll have to pray they don't."

"Jah."

Grace turned toward the front of the room as the children's teacher stepped in front of the curtain. "Welcome to our Christmas program," she said. "We'll begin with some recitations and poems by our first and second graders."

The first graders gave their recitations first, and then it was Anna's turn. She glanced at Grace and smiled. "A long time ago, a sweet baby was born. God's Son, Jesus, came to earth that special morn."

Grace smiled and gave Anna a nod to let her know she'd done a good job reciting the poem.

As the program continued, Grace thought about what Christmas meant to her. It was a joyful, peaceful time of the year, when family and friends gathered to celebrate the birth of Jesus and thank God for His many blessings. She thought about the sacrifice God had made to send His Son to earth to die for the sins of the world and how Jesus had suffered so those who believed in Him might have eternal life.

Nothing we've had to go through can compare with the suffering Jesus endured, Grace thought. *Even what Mary and Joseph went through as they searched for a place where Mary could give birth had to have been stressful.*

She watched Esta, dressed as Mary, enter carrying a baby doll in her arms. Grace thought about how God had told Joseph to take Mary and Jesus and flee to Egypt because Jesus' life was in danger. Trials and suffering would always be part of life, she realized, but it was how people chose to get through those trials that made the difference. They could either cry about their troubles and live in fear, or they could trust God and rely on Him to see them through. Tragedies either drove people away from God or drew them closer to Him. Grace hoped everyone in her family would draw closer to God during this Christmas season and keep their focus on Him, not the unpleasant circumstances that had been brought into their lives.

Martha pulled the heavy quilt on her bed aside and sank onto the crisp, white sheets. She'd spent all day waiting on Mom and Dad and was exhausted. She rolled onto her back, watching the evening shadows dance across the ceiling and trying to relax. As tired as she felt, sleep refused to come.

Ping! Ping! Ping!

Martha bolted upright in bed and turned on the battery-operated lamp by her bed. It sounded like someone was throwing something against her window. She jumped up and raced over to the window, pulling the curtain aside. A man wearing Amish clothes, bathed in the light of the full, bright moon, appeared to be staring up at her room.

She opened the window and stuck her head out, hoping to see who it was.

"*Psst.* Martha! Can you come down?"

The man looking up at her was Luke. Martha willed her heart to stop throbbing.

"I'll be right there!" She closed the window and slipped out of her nightgown and into a dress and sneakers. She quickly did up her hair, set her kapp in place, and tiptoed out of the room. When she reached the bottom of the stairs, she stopped and listened, hoping Mom and Dad weren't awake. Except for the soft snores coming from their room, all was quiet. She grabbed her jacket from the wall peg and slipped out the back door.

The smile Martha gave Luke when she stepped up to him took his breath away. "Luke, what are you doing here?" she asked.

"Came to see you."

She glanced around. "I don't see your horse and buggy. I hope you didn't walk all the way over here in the cold."

He shook his head. "I drove over in my truck, parked it down the road a piece, and came the rest of the way on foot. Didn't want to take the chance of anyone hearing me come in." He leaned casually against the trunk of a tree and reached into his jacket pocket, hoping she wouldn't know how nervous he felt. "I wanted to give you this," he said as he pulled out a paper sack.

"What is it?"

"Just a little something for Christmas."

"Ach, Luke, I wish you hadn't done that."

"Why not?"

She dropped her gaze to the ground. "Because I have nothing for you."

"That's okay. I didn't expect anything." Luke pushed the paper sack at her, and she lifted her gaze. "It's not much, but I thought you might like it."

With another smile that warmed Luke's heart, Martha took the sack and peered inside.

"It's a book on grooming and boarding dogs. I figured since you've had some trouble breeding dogs, you might like to try something different for a change."

Martha removed the book from the sack and stood staring at it.

"If you don't like it, I can take it back. I bought it at a bookstore in New Philly, so it won't be hard for me to return."

Martha shook her head. "No, no. I like the book. Danki, Luke."

"You're welcome."

"I've actually thought about boarding dogs, but the notion of grooming dogs has never occurred to me. It's something to consider for the future."

"If you got into boarding and grooming dogs, would you continue to breed them, too?"

"Probably so."

"At least the dogs you raise are well cared for, and you always make sure they get good homes."

"Jah. John Peterson is taking good care of Flo, and the same holds true for the Larsons and Esta Wengerd." Martha's forehead wrinkled. "Unfortunately, I won't be able to keep in close contact with everyone who buys my dogs."

"Most folks who spend the money to buy a purebred dog will see that it's cared for, don't you think?"

"I hope that's always the case."

Luke glanced up at the house. "I didn't wake your folks when I threw pebbles at your window, I hope."

She shook her head. "Mom and Dad have been down with the flu. I'm sure they're asleep."

"What about Ruth?"

"She went to the Christmas program at the schoolhouse with the Wengerds, and she's not back yet."

Luke blew out his breath, wishing he could say all that was on his mind.

Martha pulled her jacket tighter around her neck and shivered. "It's sure cold out here. I wish I could invite you in for some hot chocolate, but–"

He held up his hand. "It's okay; I understand. If your daed knew you were out here talking to me, that would be bad enough. If he found me sitting in your kitchen sipping hot chocolate and eating cookies, he'd probably have a heart attack."

She playfully poked his arm. "Who said anything about cookies?"

He snickered. "Guess my stomach was doing some wishful thinking."

"I don't know when or how it's going to happen, Luke, but I feel confident that one day Dad will finally realize you're a good man."

"And that I'm not the one responsible for the attacks against your family," he added.

"That, too." Martha groaned. "I'm sure you heard about some of my daed's cows being shot a few weeks ago."

He nodded and was about to express his concerns, when he heard the distinctive *clippety-clop* of a horse's hooves on the road out front.

"That might be Abe bringing Ruth home," Martha said.

"I'd better go in case it is." Luke started to walk away but turned back. "Would it be all right if I come over to see you at Irene's place sometime? I'd like to talk some more about the attacks and who I think might be responsible."

"I'd like that, too, but I don't think it's a good idea for us to talk in front of Irene or Carolyn. Maybe we can meet somewhere in town."

"Okay. When and where do you want to meet?"

She shrugged. "The next few weeks will be busy with Ruth and Abe's wedding coming up, so I probably won't have much chance to meet with you until that's behind us."

"I understand. If we have a minute to talk after the wedding, maybe we can decide on a time and place then."

The sound of the horse drew closer. Luke turned and saw the silhouette of a horse and buggy starting up the driveway. He had to go. "Have a Merry Christmas, Martha," he called before racing around the side of the house and into the field.

Chapter 12

As Ruth stood in front of the stove, stirring a pot of chicken soup, she thought about last Christmas Eve and how her whole world had been turned upside down. When they'd climbed into Martin's buggy that night, Ruth had never imagined it would be the first and last Christmas Eve she would spend with her husband.

"Are you sure you don't want me to stay here with Mom and Dad so you can join Grace and her family this evening?" Martha asked, halting Ruth's thoughts.

Ruth turned and forced a smile. "You stayed home last night so I could go to the Christmas program at the schoolhouse. It's your turn for an evening out."

"I wouldn't mind staying home again."

"I'll be fine here with Mom and Dad," Ruth said. "Besides, if they're feeling up to it, we'll all be going to Aunt Rosemary's for dinner tomorrow afternoon."

Martha nodded. "I checked on them a few minutes ago, and they said they felt well enough to eat some of this delicious soup they've smelled."

"If they're getting their appetites back, it's a good indication that they're feeling better."

Martha slipped into her coat and picked up the pan of frosted brownies she'd made. "I still feel guilty about leaving you here."

Ruth waved a hand. "Well, don't. You can't always be the one making sacrifices. You deserve to have some fun."

"Jah, okay. I'll see you later then." Martha slipped out the back door.

A few minutes later, Mom and Dad entered the room. Dad ambled over to the stove and peered at the soup. "Ah, there's nothing better than a pot of homemade chicken soup," he said.

"Especially after a body's been without food for a couple of days." Mom moved over to the stove. "What can I do to help?"

Ruth shook her head. "Not a single thing. You and Dad have a seat at the table, and I'll bring you some soup and crackers."

Mom looked like she might argue the point, but Dad nudged her and said, "Just do as your daughter says, Judith. You're still weak and shaky; you ought to rest."

"You're right. I am a bit unsteady on my feet." Mom pulled out a chair and sat down. Dad took his chair at the head of the table.

Ruth ladled soup into three bowls and brought them over to the table, along with a basket of saltine crackers. "Would either of you like anything else?" she asked as she took her seat.

"Soup and crackers will be plenty for me," Mom said.

Dad nodded in agreement. "Shall we offer our thanks now?"

All heads bowed, and when the silent prayer was over, Ruth handed the crackers to her mother. "When I went out to the chicken coop awhile ago, the air felt like it could snow. I wonder if we'll have a white Christmas."

"It would be nice to have snow for Christmas," Mom said. "As long as it doesn't snow heavy and cause the roads to be icy, the way it did last year." She covered her mouth and gave a muffled gasp. "Ach, Ruth, I'm sorry for bringing that up."

"It happened, Mom. Not talking about it won't change a thing." Ruth blew on her soup and took a tentative taste.

"Even so, it's Christmas Eve, and I think we should focus on positive things," Mom said. "It always amazes me the way God can take a bad situation and turn it into something good."

"Are you referring to anything specific?" Dad asked.

"Jah. I was thinking that even though both Ruth and Abe lost their mates, God brought them together. Why, in just a few weeks,

Abe will have a new fraa and a mudder for his kinner." Mom looked over at Ruth and smiled. "And you have been given the opportunity to raise Abe's kinner."

Ruth swallowed around the lump that had formed in her throat. "I'm not marrying Abe just so I can be a mother, you know."

Mom reached over and patted Ruth's arm. "No, of course not. I know you love Abe, as well."

Thump! Thump! Thump!

Ruth jumped at what sounded like boots clomping up the back stairs. A loud knock sounded on the door.

"I wonder who that could be," Mom said.

"Well, there's only one way to find out." Dad started to push away from the table.

Ruth jumped to her feet. "I'll get it, Dad. Why don't you stay here with Mom and finish your soup?"

He nodded.

Ruth hurried out of the room and opened the back door. Sheriff Osborn stood on the porch, holding a small box in his hand.

"Good evening, Ruth," he said. "I just dropped by to see how you folks are doing and also to bring you this." He handed the box to Ruth. "It's a fruitcake from the bakeshop in Berlin."

"That's very nice. Thank you." Ruth smiled. "Mom and Dad are in the kitchen, eating some soup. They're just getting over a bout with the flu; otherwise, I'd invite you in."

"That's okay," the sheriff said. "I need to be on my way home. Don't like to keep the wife and kids waiting on Christmas Eve." He started to walk away but turned back. "Oh, would you give your dad a message?"

"Of course."

"Tell him I still have no leads on who shot his cows or blew up his shop, but I have requested that one of my deputies patrol your area throughout the holidays. Hopefully, that will keep the one responsible from doing anything else." He popped a piece of gum in his mouth. "Have a Merry Christmas."

"You, too, Sheriff Osborn."

Ruth returned to the kitchen with an uneasy feeling in the pit of her stomach. Even if one of the sheriff's men patrolled the area, that didn't guarantee the attacks would end.

Martha watched Grace and Cleon, as they interacted with their children at the supper table. A pang of jealousy stabbed her heart. *Unless someone takes an interest in me, I may never marry and have children.* She toyed with the napkin beside her plate. *Luke's the only man I want, but that seems impossible.*

She thought about Luke throwing pebbles at her window. She'd been so surprised when he'd given her a Christmas present. *I wish I'd have had something to give him. He probably thinks I don't appreciate him helping me find out who's been attacking our family.*

"How are Mom and Dad feeling tonight?" Grace asked.

"Better. When I left the house, they were getting ready to join Ruth for a bowl of soup."

"Do you think they'll be up to eating supper at my house tomorrow?" Aunt Rosemary asked.

"I hope so." Martha smiled. "If Dad doesn't come, I'll eat his share of pie."

"I'll be sure to send some pie home with you in case they don't come." Aunt Rosemary sighed. "I wish Ken and Sharon could have come to Ohio for Christmas, but they used the last of their vacation time helping me move."

"Had you considered going back to Idaho for Christmas?" Cleon asked.

She nodded. "With everything that's gone on with Roman lately, I didn't feel good about leaving. I'm needed here more than ever."

"We appreciate having you here, too," Grace said with a smile. "It means a lot to Dad to have you living in Holmes County again."

Anna looked over at Martha. "I wish you could have been at the Christmas program last night. It was lots of fun, and Esta got to be Mary."

"I'm sorry I missed it," Martha said, "but I needed to be at home taking care of your grandpa and grandma."

"Anna said a real nice poem." Grace gave her daughter's arm a little squeeze. "Why don't you recite your poem so Aunt Martha can hear it?"

Anna looked over at Martha.

Martha nodded. "I'd like to hear the poem, Anna."

"Okay." Anna sat up straight, and in a clear, sweet voice, she said, "A long time ago, a sweet baby was born. God's Son, Jesus, came to earth that special morn."

"That was very nice, Anna," Martha said with a nod. "You said your lines perfectly."

Anna beamed. "Maybe next year, when I'm older, I'll get to be an angel in the Christmas program."

"Maybe you will."

"Or maybe you'll get to play the part of Mary," Aunt Rosemary put in.

Anna's eyes widened. "You think so?"

Aunt Rosemary nodded. "As well as you said that poem, I'm sure your teacher will consider you for a really good part."

Anna's smile stretched ear to ear as she reached for a biscuit and slathered it with butter.

Martha smiled, too. Aunt Rosemary had a special way with everyone in the family. It was a good thing she'd come back to Holmes County.

"Grace, why don't you let Martha and me do the dishes?" Rosemary suggested when dinner was over and the women had begun to clear the table. "You worked hard preparing the meal, so I think you should go in the living room and enjoy being with your family before it's time to put the children to bed."

Grace hesitated but finally nodded. "If you're sure you don't mind, that does sound nice."

"I don't mind, do you?" Rosemary asked looking at Martha.

Martha shook her head. "Don't mind at all."

"Okay, danki." Grace cleared the rest of the glasses from the table and headed for the living room.

Martha followed Rosemary over to the sink. "Can I ask your opinion on something?"

"Of course."

"I've been wondering if I should give up on the idea of raising dogs and do something else."

Rosemary smiled. "Are you thinking about getting married and raising a family instead of dogs?"

Martha's face turned bright pink. "I'd need to find a man who was interested in marrying me first."

"I wouldn't think that would be a problem for someone as smart and pretty as you."

Martha dropped the sponge into the pan of soapy water, and tiny bubbles rose to the ceiling. "I've never thought of myself as smart or pretty."

"Then you're not taking a close enough look." Rosemary gave Martha's shoulder a gentle squeeze. "Is there something you'd rather do than raise dogs?"

Martha shrugged. "I've thought about boarding dogs, but Dad hasn't given his approval on that idea yet." The color in her face deepened. "I've also considered grooming dogs, and the book Luke gave me says—" She clamped her hand over her mouth. "I mean—"

"Luke gave you a book on dog grooming?"

"Jah."

"When was this?"

"Last night." Martha's voice lowered to a whisper. "He came over to our place after the folks were in bed and said he had something he wanted to give me for Christmas."

"The book on dog grooming?"

Martha nodded as she sucked in her bottom lip. "Dad doesn't want Luke to come around our place anymore, so he came over when he thought Mom and Dad would be asleep.

"I see." Feeling the need to put Martha's mind at ease, Rosemary said, "Your folks won't hear about Luke's visit from me."

"Danki."

"You know," Rosemary said, "dog grooming might actually be something for you to consider."

"Jah, I'm going to give it some serious thought, but I probably won't do anything like that for some time. It would take awhile to learn everything, and it might take even longer to line up some customers."

Rosemary picked up a dish towel and reached for the first plate, when a wave of nausea hit her. "Oh no," she groaned.

"What's wrong?"

"I think I might be coming down with the flu." She raced out of the kitchen and headed straight for the bathroom.

Christmas Day dawned with snow lightly sprinkled on the ground and clinging to the trees like a dusting of powdered sugar.

Martha had just returned from Grace and Cleon's place, where she'd gone to pick up her aunt. Since Aunt Rosemary had been so ill last night, Grace had insisted she sleep in their guest room. Thankfully, Aunt Rosemary was feeling a bit better, although she was still weak and shaky. Since Cleon's parents were expecting Grace, Cleon, and the children for Christmas dinner, Martha had suggested she bring Aunt Rosemary home with her. Now she was upstairs resting in Grace's old room. It wasn't the Christmas they had planned, with dinner at Rosemary's house, but at least none of them would have to be alone on Christmas Day.

As Martha scurried around the kitchen getting breakfast, she thought about Luke and the gift he'd given her. Since she didn't want Mom and Dad to know he'd been here or that he'd given her a gift, she'd hidden the book in the bottom drawer of her dresser.

I hate sneaking around like this, she thought ruefully. *I wish I felt free to tell Mom, Dad, and the rest of the family how much I care for Luke and that the two of us are working together to figure out who's been attacking us.*

"Do you need any help in here?" Ruth asked.

Martha whirled around. "Ach, Ruth, you scared me."

"Didn't you hear my slippers scuffling down the hall?"

"No, I was deep in thought."

"What were you thinking about?"

"Nothing much—just Christmas and such."

Ruth sighed and took a seat at the table. "With Dad and Mom just getting over the flu, and now Aunt Rosemary coming down with it, this isn't much of a Christmas, is it?"

"It's not the worst Christmas we've ever had."

Ruth slowly shook her head. "No, it's not. Last Christmas was the worst."

When Martha saw the sorrowful look on her sister's face, she wished she could take back what she'd said. She hurried across the room and took a seat beside Ruth. "I'm sorry, Ruth. My words were not the best choice, and—"

Ruth held up her hand. "No need to apologize. I can't expect everyone to walk on eggshells because of me. I'm just a bit oversensitive right now."

Martha gave Ruth's shoulder a gentle squeeze. "I understand. It's not easy to lose someone you love, and when their death occurs on a holiday, every time that holiday comes around, it's a painful reminder of what you lost."

Ruth leaned over and gave Martha a hug. "When did my little *schweschder* get to be so *schmaert*?"

Martha patted Ruth's back and said, "I think maybe being around my two big sisters so much is what's made me smart."

When Ruth pulled back, tears clung to her eyelashes. "I think maybe being around Aunt Rosemary has made us all a little smarter, don't you?"

"She does have some pretty good advice." Martha glanced at the door leading to the hallway. "Not that Mom's not schmaert; she's taught us plenty of things. It's just that Mom tends to be kind of emotional about certain things. I think maybe it clouds her judgment sometimes."

Ruth tipped her head. "Are you thinking of anything in particular?"

"Not really. It's just that whenever I try to talk to her about anything, she never sees things my way and starts getting all emotional."

"You mean the way she gets when she thinks you spend too much time with your dogs?"

Martha nodded. "I don't think either Mom or Dad understands why I keep trying to get my kennel business going, in spite of the setbacks I've had."

"I would think Dad should understand. Look at the setbacks he's had with his woodworking business, yet he keeps on going."

"Speaking of going. . ." Martha rose from her chair. "We need to get breakfast going so you can get ready to spend Christmas Day at Abe's."

Ruth smiled. "I am looking forward to that. Thanks to Aunt Rosemary's good counsel, I'm also looking forward to my wedding day in a few weeks."

Chapter 13

As Martha sat on a wooden bench inside Grace and Cleon's house, watching Ruth and Abe say their vows, she was filled with mixed feelings. The look of contentment she saw on Ruth's and Abe's faces made her happy, but she couldn't keep her jealousy at bay. *Will I ever know the kind of love my sisters share with their husbands?*

Martha glanced across the room to where the men and boys sat. She spotted Luke sitting beside his cousin Raymond. At least he hadn't missed Ruth's wedding because of work. Although if Luke was going to miss any wedding, Ruth's would be the one, since he and Ruth had dated for a while.

Martha watched Luke's expression for any sign of jealousy over Ruth marrying Abe but couldn't detect anything. Luke stared straight ahead with a placid look on his face.

At one time, Ruth had thought Luke might be the one attacking their family. She'd even believed it was Luke's truck that had rammed their buggy last Christmas Eve. After Ruth had learned that, except for a quick trip to borrow something from a neighbor earlier in the day, Luke had been home that evening, she'd seemed to accept that he couldn't have been responsible for Martin's death. Ruth's close relationship with Aunt Rosemary and falling in love with Abe had helped heal her broken heart and given her a sense of peace and purpose in life.

Martha glanced over her shoulder. Aunt Rosemary sat beside Cleon's mother, Irene. Martha was glad Aunt Rosemary felt well enough to be here today. She'd come down with a bad cold after her bout with the flu.

Aunt Rosemary gave her a smile and a nod. Martha smiled in return. Having Aunt Rosemary living nearby had not only been good for Ruth but also for everyone in the family. Dad seemed mellower when Aunt Rosemary was in the same room. Mom and Grace related well to her, too. Martha had discovered that she and her aunt had one important thing in common—they both wanted to find out who was behind the attacks that had been done to her family.

Rosemary was about to head for Roman's place, where the wedding meal would be served, when someone tapped her on the shoulder. She turned.

A tall Amish man with faded blond hair and piercing blue eyes gave her a slanted grin. "Well, if it isn't my little sister who 'yanked over.' Roman said you'd come home."

Rosemary had heard that the Amish who lived in Geauga County referred to Englishers as *Yankees* and that when an Amish person left the faith, it was said that he or she had *yanked over*. Her mouth went dry. The man who stood before her was none other than her brother who lived in Geauga County. "Walt? Is. . .is it really you?"

He nodded. "Came down for Ruth's wedding."

Rosemary wanted so badly to give her brother a hug, but she thought it might not be appreciated. So she smiled and said, "It's good to see you again, Walt."

He gave a quick nod. Wasn't he glad to see her? Did he harbor ill feelings toward her because she'd left the Amish faith?

As if sensing Rosemary's discomfort, Walt reached out and touched her arm. "Roman says you've decided to move here permanently."

She nodded. "That's right. My son and his wife helped me move. I wish you could have met them."

He glanced around. "They're not here now?"

She shook her head. "They used their vacation time to help me move. They both work at a bank in Boise, Idaho."

"It's too bad they couldn't be here today. It would've been nice to meet them," Walt said with a genuine smile. Maybe he wasn't angry with her, after all.

"Where's your family?" she asked. "Are they all here today?"

He shook his head. "Just me and Mary came down. Our two sons live in Wisconsin, and our four daughters have settled in Pennsylvania."

Rosemary smiled. "I'd like to meet Mary. Where is she?"

"She's still in the house talking to Judith and Grace. Let's head in there now, and I'll introduce you."

Rosemary smiled. It really was good to be home again.

As Luke headed down the driveway toward the Hostettlers', he thought about Martha and how pensive she'd looked throughout most of her sister's wedding. Had she been thinking about Ruth and wondering if things would go better for her being married to Abe than they had when she'd been married to Martin?

Luke was almost to the house, when someone tapped him on the shoulder. Toby was walking beside Sadie. The two of them had only been married a few months, but already Toby had a good beard.

"I'm surprised to see you here," Toby said with a scowl. "Since you had to work the day Sadie and I got married, I figured you'd be working again today."

Luke shook his head. "We're getting caught up at work, so John said I could have the day off."

"I see." Toby nudged Sadie's arm. "Why don't you go on into the house?"

"Aren't you coming?"

"I want to talk to Luke for a few minutes, but I'll be in soon."

Sadie shrugged and headed for the back porch.

"What'd you want to talk to me about, Toby?" Luke hoped they weren't going to have another one of their disagreements.

Toby folded his arms and stared hard at Luke. "There was an article in the paper yesterday morning about some windows that were broken at the schoolhouse in Charm."

"That's too bad."

"The article said someone who lives near the school saw a black truck cruising around the area the night before."

"What's that got to do with me?"

"Duh! You own a black truck."

Luke stiffened. "I hope you're not suggesting that I had anything to do with those broken windows."

Toby shrugged. "I'm not accusing; just wondering is all."

"Wondering if I broke the windows?"

"Jah."

Luke gave a small rock a hefty kick. "I had nothing to do with those windows being broken, and I wasn't out driving my truck in the middle of the night."

"Can you prove it?"

Luke leaned closer to Toby. "I don't need to prove it. Especially not to you."

Toby scowled at Luke. "You think you can do whatever you want and get away with it, don't you? It's just like when we were kinner, and the two of us got caught doing something we weren't supposed to do. You always got off easy, while I was punished."

Luke sucked in his breath. So that was the problem. How immature to be carrying a grudge around all these years. Truth be told, Toby probably wished he had owned a truck during his running-around years. But since Toby's dad was the bishop, he probably hadn't dared make waves. Luke was tempted to defend himself and try to make Toby see reason. But what was the use? He'd never been able to make Toby see things as they were in the past, so why try now? Luke turned on his heel and stalked off toward the Hostettlers' barn.

When Martha saw Toby enter the house with a red face, she knew something was up. She glanced around but didn't see any sign of Luke.

"I'll be back in a few minutes," she whispered to Ruth, who sat beside her new groom.

"Where are you going? We'll be eating soon."

"I need to go outside and check on something."

Ruth released an exasperated sigh. "You're not going to check on those puppies again, I hope."

"Well, I–"

"You checked on them before the wedding, and they were fine."

"I know, but–"

"It's all right," Abe put in. "If Martha checks on her hundlin, then she'll come back to the house and enjoy the rest of the day." He looked up at Martha and smiled. "Isn't that so?"

"Jah." Martha gave her sister's shoulder a gentle squeeze then scooted out of the room.

When she entered the barn, she spotted Luke inside one of the stalls, petting a beautiful black gelding. "When I didn't see you inside, I wondered if you might have come out here," she said, stepping up to him.

He nodded.

"Are you okay? Are you upset about something?"

"I'm upset all right. Upset and irritated with my so-called friend, Toby."

"What did Toby do?"

Luke grunted. "He as much as accused me of breaking out some windows in the Charm schoolhouse."

"What?" Martha's mouth dropped open. "When did that happen?"

"Toby said he read about it in yesterday's paper. I guess it happened the night before."

"What makes him think you had anything to do with it?"

"Someone saw a black truck cruising around the area."

Martha's throat constricted. What if Luke had been driving his truck near the schoolhouse that night? What if–

Luke grabbed her arm. "I didn't have anything to do with those broken windows, Martha. You believe me, don't you?"

She swallowed around the lump in her throat. She wanted to believe him; she really did. But if a black truck had been seen–

"It wasn't my truck," Luke said.

His grip tightened on her arm, and she winced. "You're hurting me."

Luke let go of her arm and stepped back. "I'm sorry. I sure didn't mean to hurt you, Martha."

Tears pricked the backs of her eyes. "I'm okay."

"My truck's still parked in the woods, and I haven't driven it in over a week. Not since the last time I went to the mall in New Philadelphia with Tim and Rod."

"Are they some of the English fellows you've been hanging around?"

He nodded.

"If I ask you a question, will you be honest with me?"

"Jah, sure."

"How come you've become friends with those English fellows who everyone knows are rowdy?"

Luke shifted his weight from one foot to the other and stared at the straw-covered floor. "I. . .uh. . .can't really say."

"Can't or won't?"

He lifted his gaze to meet hers. "If I tell you what I've been up to, do I have your word that you won't repeat it to anyone?"

Martha nodded. She hoped Luke wasn't about to tell her that he'd decided to jump the fence and go English.

Luke cleared his throat. "When I first started hanging around Tim and Rod and some of their friends, it was to have a good time. But then when I got wind that they'd pulled some pranks in the area, I decided to stick around them and try and find out if they might be the ones responsible for the attacks on your family."

"Really?"

He nodded. "At first, it was only because I wanted to clear my name with your daed. But then, when things got really bad, I realized you—all of you—could be in danger. So I've been trying to figure out who's been doing the attacks, and I figured if I gained Tim's and Rod's trust, sooner or later, one of them would spill the beans."

"Have they?"

He shook his head. "Not yet."

"Maybe they aren't the ones responsible."

"That could be, but they have pulled some pranks around the area."

"Like what?"

"They admitted that they'd toilet-papered a few places, turned over some schoolhouse outhouses, and tipped some cows." Luke grunted. "I wouldn't be surprised if they aren't the ones who broke the windows at the school in Charm—which is why I need to keep hanging around them so I can find out."

"Does either of them own a black truck?"

He shrugged. "Not that I know of, but just because a truck was seen cruising the area the night before the windows were broken doesn't mean the driver of the truck's the one who broke 'em."

Martha nodded. "Good point." Hearing Luke's reasons for hanging around the English fellows gave her hope that Luke really was innocent.

"In case you haven't figured it out, one of the reasons I haven't joined the church yet is so I'd be free to investigate the attacks."

Martha nodded slowly. She knew if her father found out she was trying to investigate the attacks, she'd be in for a lecture.

"So when I said I'd be willing to help you find out who's been trying to hurt your family, I really meant it," Luke added.

"I appreciate that, because I need all the help I can get. You know that wrench you found in my daed's field?"

He nodded.

Martha motioned to the hayloft. "Well, I hid it up there, and when I was looking for the right spot to put it, I discovered some initials engraved on the handle."

Luke's eyebrows lifted. "What were the initials?"

"H. C." Martha pursed her lips. "I don't know anyone with those initials, do you?"

"I sure don't." His forehead creased. "Let's get together to talk about this some more, okay?"

Martha opened her mouth to reply when Grace stepped into the barn. "I figured I'd find you out here. Were you checking on your dogs?"

"Uh. . .jah, I was planning to."

"Well, Ruth's looking for you, so I hope you'll check on the dogs and get back to the house soon." Grace glanced over at Luke.

He shuffled his feet nervously, gave Martha a nod, and said, "Guess I'd better get back inside, too. If I don't show up soon, my mamm will probably come looking for me."

Ruth smiled at Aunt Rosemary and said, "I'm glad you could be here for our wedding."

Aunt Rosemary looked over at Abe and smiled. "You take good care of my niece, you hear?"

He nodded. "Of course I will."

"I'll leave you two to enjoy your meal, but before I go, I was wondering if I could ask a favor."

"What's that?" Abe asked.

"Would it be all right if I take a few pictures of your children so I can send them to Ken and Sharon? Since they couldn't be here for the wedding, I'm sure they'd enjoy seeing how cute the little ones looked today."

Abe glanced at Ruth, as though seeking her approval.

"They're your children," she said.

He touched her arm. "Now that you're my wife, the kinner belong to both of us."

"If you have no objections to Aunt Rosemary taking the kinner's pictures, then I'm in agreement with it," she said, smiling at Abe.

"All right then." Abe rose from his chair. "I'd better gather up our brood, because they're scattered all around the room."

As Abe and Aunt Rosemary left, Martha took a seat next to Ruth. She smiled and placed a small package on the table.

"Is this a wedding present?"

Martha nodded. "I know it's not customary for the bride and groom to receive gifts if they've both been married before, but I wanted to give you something anyway."

Ruth tore the wrapping off the package and withdrew a lovely sampler. Her and Abe's names had been embroidered on it, as well as the names of his five surviving children—her children now.

She thought about the sampler Martha had given her when she'd married Martin. After his death, she'd packed the sampler away because it had hurt too much to look at it and be reminded of her loss. But now that Abe and his children were in Ruth's life, she felt as if she was being offered a second chance, and for that she was grateful.

"The sampler is beautiful," she said, tears clogging her throat. "Danki, Martha."

"You're welcome."

Just then, Abe's daughter Esta stepped up to the table and handed Ruth a small box wrapped in white tissue paper. "This is for you. Papa helped me pick it out, and I paid for it with some money I earned cleanin' the floor in Papa's harness shop."

Ruth smiled and took the gift from the child. "It was sweet of you to think of me."

Esta's eyes twinkled as she wiggled around. "Aren't you gonna open it?"

"Jah, of course." Ruth tore the paper off the box and lifted the lid. Inside lay a delicate hanky with white lace around the edges. She gave Esta a hug. "Danki, it's beautiful."

"I'm glad you like it—" The child hesitated then leaned close to Ruth's ear. "Is it all right if I call you Mama now?"

Ruth nodded and swallowed around the lump in her throat. "I'd like that very much. I hope your *brieder* and little schweschder will call me Mama, too."

"I'm sure my sister will. After all, Molly's been callin' you *mammi* ever since you came to work for Papa." Esta frowned. "I'm not sure about the brothers, though—at least not Gideon. He's such an old sourpuss these days. He might refuse to call you Mama just 'cause he's so stubborn."

Ruth glanced around. "Where are Molly and your brothers?" she asked, making no comment about Gideon's recent behavior. Today was a special day, and she didn't want to think about anything negative. "Did your daed gather all of you together so my aunt Rosemary could take your picture?" she asked, patting Esta's arm.

Esta's head bobbed up and down. "After the picture takin' was done, Molly started to fuss, so–"

"Grace took our little girl over to her house," Abe said, stepping up beside Esta.

"See you later, Mama." Esta gave Ruth a quick hug and darted away.

Abe reclaimed his seat and leaned close to Ruth. His warm breath against her neck caused her to shiver. "Grace and Cleon volunteered to keep our brood until tomorrow morning, so it'll just be you and me staying here with your folks tonight."

Ruth's cheeks warmed at the thought of spending the night with Abe sleeping next to her. Would he find her desirable even though she could never give him a baby? Would he be tender and loving, the way Martin had been?

As if sensing Ruth's reservations, Abe reached under the table and gave her fingers a gentle squeeze. "Tomorrow, after we've helped clean things up here, we'll take our kinner home to our place and begin a new life together."

Ruth smiled and squeezed Abe's fingers in response. "I'm looking forward to that."

Chapter 14

Ruth was getting ready to put a pot roast in the oven for supper, when Gideon stepped into the kitchen. "Are you just getting home from school?" she asked, glancing at the battery-operated clock above the refrigerator. "The others have been here for nearly an hour already."

Gideon scrunched up his nose. "Teacher kept me after school. Didn't Esta tell you I was gonna be late?"

Ruth's forehead wrinkled. "No, she just said you hadn't walked with them. I figured you'd walked by yourself through the woods or had decided to walk with some of your friends."

"I ain't got no friends," he said, shaking snow off his stocking cap.

"*Don't have any*," she corrected. "And what makes you think you don't have any friends?"

Gideon hung his coat and hat on a wall peg and flopped into a chair at the kitchen table. " 'Cause nobody wants to be around me, that's what!"

Ruth put the roast into the oven and took a seat in the chair opposite him. "Does this have something to do with you having to stay after school?"

He shrugged.

"Gideon, I need to know what's going on. I can't help if you don't talk about it."

"I don't wanna talk about it, and you ain't my mamm, so I don't need your help, Ruth!" Gideon pushed his chair away from the table and rushed out the door as the chair toppled over with a crash.

Ruth sighed. All of Abe's children except Gideon had begun calling her *Mama*. She had a hunch he hadn't because he resented her marriage to his dad. Could that resentment be the cause of Gideon's problems at school?

As Martha directed her buggy horse toward Irene's house, a feeling of despair settled over her like a drenching rain. She was thankful for this job but wished she could become self-supporting through her kennel business.

Without telling her folks about the book Luke had given her, she'd mentioned the possibility of dog grooming to them the other night. Dad had said he thought it would be too much work because Martha had enough to do right now with her job at Irene's and raising puppies. Mom's only comment was that she thought Martha should give up working with dogs altogether and find a husband.

Thinking about marriage made Martha's thoughts turn to Luke. She'd only seen him once since Ruth and Abe's wedding—at their biweekly preaching service, which had been held at his folks' house. After the service, Luke had disappeared, so she hadn't been able to say hello, much less ask if he'd had any success finding out who was behind the attacks.

Of course I haven't learned anything yet, either, she thought ruefully. Preparations for Ruth's wedding had kept Martha busy for weeks. She'd also had her dogs and her job at Irene's. During the holidays, they'd been busier than ever, serving dinners to the employees of several local businesses that had decided to host their Christmas parties at an Amish sit-down dinner.

Tonight, they would be cooking for people who worked at the newspaper in Millersburg. Since they'd been too busy to accommodate the group before Christmas, it would be an after-the-holidays gathering.

Having taken care of her horse and buggy, Martha stepped into the kitchen and found Irene and Carolyn scurrying around, faces glistening with perspiration. Even on a chilly winter day, the kitchen was hot. Martha figured by the time their guests arrived they would all be sweating.

Irene turned from cutting up chicken and smiled. "Ready for another big dinner?"

"Ready as I'll ever be," Martha replied. "What do you need me to do?"

Irene motioned to another chicken lying on the cutting board. "You can begin by cutting that, and then there are ingredients for a tossed green salad in the refrigerator."

Martha slipped into her work apron and set right to work. She kept so busy that she barely took notice when the group of Englishers arrived and took their seats at the table. It wasn't until a deep male voice said something to Irene that Martha glanced that way. Gary Walker, the reporter who'd dated Grace during her rumschpringe days, stood near the door that separated the kitchen from the dining room.

She leaned casually against the counter and listened to his conversation with Irene.

"I'm hoping to write another article about your business here," Gary said. "The last one I did generated a lot of reader response, which made my boss happy."

Irene smiled. "Soon after the article was printed, several more people made reservations for a meal."

"That's good to hear, Mrs. Schrock," Gary said in his usual, charming voice. He glanced over at Martha and winked. "Maybe after this article comes out, you'll have to hire a few more lovely women to help with your dinners."

Martha averted her gaze and busied herself filling water glasses that had been set by each plate.

For the remainder of the evening, she stayed busy in the kitchen, returning to the dining room only when necessary. The sight of Gary flirting with the dark-haired woman beside him was enough to make Martha's stomach churn. She couldn't figure out what Grace had ever seen in that arrogant man.

When the meal was over and the guests began to file out of the house, Martha breathed a sigh of relief. Maybe now she could focus on something other than the irritating man in the other room.

She'd just gone outside to deposit a bag of trash in the garbage can, when Gary stepped onto the porch and leaned against the railing. "Nice night, isn't it?"

She shivered and knew it wasn't from the chilly night air. "I thought everyone had gone home."

"Everyone but me." He moved to stand beside her. "I decided to stick around awhile so I could talk to you."

"What about?"

"I have a few questions I'd like to ask about your dog business."

"My dog business?"

"Yeah. I'd like to know if I can come by your place tomorrow and take a look at your kennels."

"Are you interested in buying a dog?"

He grunted. "Hardly! I hate dogs. Have ever since one bit me on the nose when I was a kid."

Martha dropped the sack into the trash can and started walking back to the house.

Gary followed. "I'm interested in writing a story about your kennel business for the newspaper."

"Why would you want to write a story about me? I only have a few dogs. I don't think there's much about my struggling business that would be worthy of a write-up in the newspaper."

He eyed her curiously. "It's struggling, huh?"

"I've been trying to get it going for some time, but either my dogs aren't able to get pregnant, or something happens to one of the pups." Martha felt like biting her tongue. She had no idea why she'd answered any of Gary's questions, and she certainly wasn't going to allow him to come to her house and nose around. Grace would be upset if Gary came anywhere near their place. Besides, Martha didn't trust the man as far as she could toss one of Dad's buggy horses.

Her thoughts went to the article that had been in the paper several weeks ago, accusing some Amish of running puppy mills and abusing their dogs. If Martha gave Gary an interview, he might write something that would make her look bad.

"I'm not interested in having an article written about me or my dogs," she mumbled.

"Why not? If your business is struggling, a newspaper article might be just the thing that would bring in more customers."

She shook her head.

Gary followed her onto the porch. "What are you afraid of?"

"I'm not afraid of anything."

He shrugged. "You must have something to hide if you won't let me do a story about your dogs."

A brigade of shivers ran up Martha's spine. What was Gary trying to prove? Was he hoping to find something at her kennels to make her look bad? "I have nothing to hide," she said.

"That's good to hear. For a minute there, I thought you might be running one of those puppy mills and didn't want me to know about it."

Martha's anger outweighed her fear. "I am not running a puppy mill! I take good care of my dogs, and I have a kennel license!"

Gary tipped back his head and roared.

Her defenses rose. "What's so funny?"

His laughter slowed to a few chuckles and then stopped. "You remind me of Grace in many ways, only you're prettier."

"I have nothing more to say, so if you'll excuse me, I have work to do." Martha tromped across the porch, jerked open the door, and stepped into the house. She wished Gary Walker would leave Holmes County for good!

Chapter 15

As Martha sat around the breakfast table with her folks a week later, she was shocked to discover an article in the newspaper written by Gary Walker. It was about Amish puppy mills again, only this time he mentioned her as a breeder who had refused an interview. *"Could Ms. Hostettler be running a puppy mill?"* the article read. *"Is that why she wouldn't allow this reporter to see her kennels or ask any pertinent questions?"*

Martha slammed the paper down so hard it jiggled her mother's cup, spilling some of the coffee.

"Ach! Martha, watch what you're doing!" Mom grabbed a napkin and mopped up the spill.

"What's wrong with you this morning?" Dad asked crossly. "You shouldn't be reading the paper while we're trying to eat."

"This is what's wrong!" Martha pointed to the newspaper. "There's an article by Gary Walker. He insinuates that I might be running a puppy mill!"

Mom's mouth dropped open. "Where would he get such a notion?"

Dad snatched up the paper. He studied it a few seconds then slapped it down hard, jostling his own cup of coffee. "That man has some nerve saying those things!"

"What'd he say, Roman?" Mom asked. "Did he accuse Martha of running a puppy mill?"

"Not in so many words, but he said Martha's a dog breeder and that she refused an interview with him. It also says he suspects she might be running a puppy mill." Dad looked over at Martha and frowned. "Any idea where he got such a notion?"

Martha reached for her glass of orange juice and took a drink, hoping to buy some time. Dad was upset enough; she didn't want to say anything that might rile him even more.

Dad leaned closer to Martha and tapped his finger against the newspaper. "Have you talked to that nosy reporter recently?"

Martha nodded. "He came to Irene's last week with some others who work at the newspaper. After everyone else had left, Gary cornered me and started asking a bunch of questions."

"What'd you tell him?" Mom asked.

"I just said my business was struggling, and when he asked if he could come by our place to take a look at my dogs and interview me, I turned him down."

"Ah, I see how it is." Dad frowned deeply. "You got Mr. Walker riled when you refused to let him interview you, so he's trying to get even by writing things that aren't true."

"Well, I–"

"If an Englisher raises more than one breed of dog and doesn't have a license, it's considered 'enterprising.' If an Amish person raises more than one breed and has a license, it's called 'running a puppy mill.' "

"Some Amish and Englishers probably don't take good care of their dogs," Martha said. "But I'm not one of them."

"Of course you're not," Mom said. Her hand shook a bit as she patted Martha's arm.

Dad gave the newspaper another good rap and grunted. "If that man comes around here asking a bunch of nosy questions, I'll give him a piece of my mind. Fact is, I've got half a notion to go over to that newspaper office and have a little talk with Gary's boss. He ought to know one of his reporters is writing things that aren't true."

Martha figured if her father hadn't gone to the sheriff when most of the attacks had occurred, he wasn't likely to go to the newspaper office and file a complaint.

"Calm down, Roman. You're getting too upset about this," Mom said. "I'm sure anyone reading that article will know it's not true." She added more coffee to her cup. "Would. . .would you like more coffee, Roman, or another piece of toast?"

Dad shook his head and pushed away from the table. "I've lost my appetite, so I think I'll head out to the barn and get busy on that new set of cabinets the bishop ordered the other day. Nothing gets me calmed down better than work."

Dad grabbed his stocking cap from the wall peg and slipped into his jacket. He turned and looked right at Martha. "If you ever see that reporter again, don't say a word to him. Is that clear?"

"Jah, Dad," she mumbled. She hoped she hadn't made a promise she might not be able to keep, because if she ran into Gary again, she'd probably give him a piece of her mind.

As Luke headed home from work that afternoon, he spotted Toby's rig pulling out of his folks' driveway. *I wonder what he was doing at our place.* Luke lifted his hand in a wave, but Toby looked the other way and kept on going.

When Luke entered the house, he found his mother sitting at the kitchen table massaging her forehead. His dad sat across from her wearing a frown. Something must be wrong.

"What's going on?" Luke asked. "Why was Toby here?"

Pop glared at him. "You don't know?"

"I have no idea."

"He came about that stupid truck of yours."

"My. . .my what?"

"Don't play dumm with me, Luke." Pop's voice raised an octave, and a muscle on the side of his neck quivered. "Toby told us you have a truck you keep hidden in the woods so we won't know about it. Is it true?" He leveled Luke with a piercing stare. "Well, is it?"

Luke dropped his gaze to the floor. "Jah, it's true."

Pop slammed his fist on the table, sending the napkin holder sailing across the room. "I might have known you'd go behind my back and do something like that!"

"Now, Elam, please calm down." Mom's voice was pleading, and Luke figured she was close to tears. She had never approved of yelling in the house.

Apparently, Mom's cocker spaniel, Cindy, didn't care for Pop's yelling, either, for the shaggy little dog left her place by the woodstove and ducked under the table.

"I won't calm down!" Pop shouted. "Not until our son gets rid of that truck!"

"I've not joined the church yet, so I have every right to own a motorized vehicle." Luke's defenses rose. "What all did Toby say that's got you so riled and demanding that I sell my truck?" he asked.

"He said a black truck matching the description of yours was seen cruising around the schoolhouse near Farmerstown last night."

"I wasn't riding around in my truck last night."

"Jah, well, Toby says the fellow driving the truck was wearing a baseball cap like you sometimes wear." Dad grunted. "You oughta be wearin' an Amish man's hat, not what the Englishers wear."

"So someone was driving a truck that looks like mine, and he was wearing a baseball cap," Luke said, making no reference to what he should or shouldn't be wearing. "What does that prove?"

"It proves that whoever egged the schoolhouse during the night could have been the same one driving the truck."

Luke's eyebrows lifted high on his forehead. "The schoolhouse was egged?"

Pop nodded. "The public school in Charm had some windows broken out awhile back, and now the Amish schoolhouse in Farmerstown's been singled out."

"I hope you don't think I egged the schoolhouse or broke those windows in Charm."

"I'm not saying you did either of those things," Pop replied, "but Toby believes you did because he saw your truck in the area."

"So it was Toby who supposedly saw me, huh? A minute ago you said Toby told you someone else had seen my truck." Luke clenched his fists. "That *someone* was Toby, wasn't it?"

Pop nodded slowly.

"Well, he's lying! I wasn't driving my truck last night, and I didn't egg the schoolhouse."

"We believe you, Luke," Mom said. "But we don't want folks making accusations."

"If the bishop's son is the one making those accusations, then people are likely to listen," Pop added.

Luke folded his arms. "I don't care what other people think. I didn't vandalize either of those schools, and I'm not the one responsible for any of the attacks against the Hostettlers."

Mom shot out of her chair. "Now where'd you come up with that? Your daed never accused you of–"

"He didn't have to," Luke interrupted. "I already know Roman thinks I'm the one responsible for the things that have been done at their place." He rocked back and forth on his heels. "I don't know why, but it seems as if Toby's trying to make me look bad, even to my own parents."

"You don't look bad," Mom said with a shake of her head. "It's just that we want you to–"

"Get rid of that truck!" Dad said. "That way if anybody sees someone driving a black truck and wearing a baseball cap, they won't accuse you."

Luke shook his head. "I'm not selling my truck because Toby's likes to *blabbermaul.*"

"He may like to blabber, but if he can convince others that you're responsible–"

"I don't want to sell my truck. At least not now."

"If you don't, then you'll likely be blamed for everything that happens in this area." A vein on the side of Pop's neck bulged, and Luke knew he was walking on thin ice.

"I'll have a talk with Toby if you like," Luke said. "Maybe I can talk some sense into him–make him realize it wasn't me who did all those things."

Pop shook his head. "Forget talking to Toby. I want you to sell that truck!"

"And if I don't?"

"Then you'll have to move out."

Luke turned sharply toward the door. "Fine then, I'll move out!"

"Please, don't do that!" Mom grabbed the sleeve of Luke's jacket. "Where would you go?"

"Guess I'll head for the woods and sleep in my truck."

"It's too cold to be sleeping in your truck." Mom turned pleading eyes on Pop. "Please say something to convince Luke he shouldn't move out."

Pop shrugged his shoulders. "Betty, there's not much I can say if the boy wants to live in his precious truck."

Luke moved toward the door, but Mom positioned herself in front of it. "I won't sleep a wink tonight if I have to lie in bed thinking about you freezing to death. Please, don't go, Luke. Stay here and we'll work things out."

"There's not much to work out unless he agrees to sell his truck," Pop said, shooting a piercing glance at Luke.

Luke drew in a deep breath and released it with a huff. He didn't like seeing his mother so upset. Truth was, he really didn't want to sleep in his truck—especially in the dead of winter. "I'll tell you what," he said, reaching into his pocket and withdrawing his truck keys. "How about I leave these with you for two weeks? During that time, if any attacks occur where a black truck is seen, then you'll know I wasn't driving the truck or doing the dirty deed."

Pop held out his hand and accepted the offered keys. "All right then. It's agreed."

When Martha went out to the barn to feed her dogs the following morning, she discovered Fritz, her male sheltie, lying in the corncrib on a pile of dried corn. Her heart gave a lurch. Had someone come into the barn and let the dog out? No, that was impossible; the barn door had been locked. She was just being paranoid.

"How did you get out of your kennel, boy?" Martha murmured, reaching out to pat Fritz's head. "And what are you doing here in the corncrib?"

The dog lifted his head and responded with a lethargic grunt. He was obviously quite comfortable.

Martha was sure she had latched all the cage doors securely last night. She glanced around, wondering if any of the other dogs had gotten out. To her relief, there was no sign of them.

"Come on, Fritz. You can't stay here all day." Grasping the dog's collar, Martha led him back to his kennel. The door to his cage was hanging open, although the latch didn't appear to be broken. Could Fritz have figured out some way to open the gate? If that were the case, she would have to rig something up so he couldn't get out. Martha put Fritz back in his cage and inspected the rest of the cages. Everything was just as it should be.

Smiling, she leaned against the wire fence that enclosed the dog run and watched Heidi's growing puppies scamper around, yipping and nipping at one another in play. She glanced at her beagle Polly and was pleased to see that her pups were nursing. The little scamps were sure growing. Maybe she would run an ad in the *Bargain Hunter* and sell some of the puppies for Valentine's Day.

I hope that article by Gary Walker won't hurt my sales.

Pushing her disconcerting thoughts aside, Martha hurried to get the dogs fed and watered. She didn't have to work for Irene today, so after breakfast, she planned to head to Berlin to do some shopping for Mom.

Should I lock the door? Martha wondered as she left the barn a few minutes later. *No, everything will be fine. I'm just feeling anxious for nothing.* Martha closed the barn door and headed for the house to help Mom with breakfast.

"I can't get over that article Gary Walker wrote in yesterday's newspaper," Grace said.

Cleon nodded as he scooped his lunch pail off the counter. "The man ought to get his facts straight before he writes a story like that."

"I think he wrote those things about Martha on purpose, just to make our family look bad."

Cleon grunted. "You don't still think he's trying to get even with you for breaking up with him when you were a teenager, do you?"

"I don't know. He's denied it several times, but I don't trust him." Grace sighed. "After the way he treated me when we were dating and the upsetting things he's said to me since he came to Holmes County, I wouldn't put anything past him."

Cleon glanced at the kitchen table where eight-year-old Anna sat eating her oatmeal. Daniel was seated in his high chair next to her. "We shouldn't be talking about things like this in front of the kinner," he said, lowering his voice. "I don't want them to live in fear that something bad's going to happen."

"Daniel's not old enough to know what's going on," Grace said. "Anna's another story. She's already been through a lot, so I'll try to be more careful what I say in front of her."

Cleon gave Grace a hug. "There haven't been any more attacks for a while, so try not to worry."

As Grace stood in the doorway, watching Cleon walk down the driveway toward her father's barn, she whispered a prayer. "Dear Lord, please put an end to these attacks."

As Martha left the hardware store, where she'd purchased some new feeding dishes for her dogs, she spotted Luke coming out of the market with a disposable camera in his hands.

Luke waved.

She waved back, wondering if he would make his way across the parking lot to say hello. To her delight, he did.

"What are you doing in town in the middle of the day?" she asked as he stepped up to her. "I figured you'd be working."

He nodded. "I am. John sent me to town to pick up a few things he needed, so I decided to make a stop of my own."

"For that?" she asked motioning to the camera in his hand.

"Jah."

"Why do you need a camera?"

"To take pictures, of course."

"Of what?"

Luke's voice lowered to a whisper. "Since I'm trying to help you figure out who's behind the attacks, I figured I might get some pictures."

She tipped her head in question.

"If another attack occurs, I'll come out with my camera and take pictures of the damage and any evidence that might be there."

Martha lifted her gaze to the sky. "Like my daed's going to let you do that."

"He doesn't have to know. I'll do it when he's not around."

Martha shook her head. "I don't think that's a good idea, Luke."

"Why not?"

"Even if you did get some pictures without my daed seeing you, what good would the pictures do?"

"If the pictures show anything helpful, I guess I could take 'em to the sheriff." Luke shrugged. " 'Course, I'm not sure how much good that would do, since he hasn't done much to stop the attacks. Makes me wonder. . ."

"Did you see that article in yesterday's paper written by Gary Walker?" Martha asked.

"Nope. I haven't even read yesterday's paper. What was it about?"

"It had to do with the rumors that some Amish in the area are running puppy mills." Martha shook her head. "Gary insinuated that I might be running a puppy mill."

Luke's mouth dropped open. "You're kidding."

She shook her head. "He attended dinner at Irene's a few weeks ago, and before he left, he cornered me, asking if he could come to our place and interview me about my dogs."

"What'd you tell him?"

"I said I wasn't interested in being interviewed for the newspaper." Martha rubbed a sore spot on the side of her head, knowing she was on the verge of a full-blown headache. "I figure he probably wrote that article to get back at me for refusing to let him do a story about my kennel business."

Luke grunted. "Gary Walker is not a nice man. In fact, he's near the top of my list of suspects."

Martha nodded. "Mine, too."

"You know what I think we should do?"

"What's that?"

"I think we should plan to meet somewhere again and go over our lists. I have a few ideas I'd like to talk to you about."

"When did you want to meet, and where?"

"What are you doing this Saturday?"

"I'm not working that day, and I have no special plans."

"How about we meet at Keim Lumber? It's always crowded there on Saturdays, and we'll probably go unnoticed."

"You want to sit in the parking lot in our buggies and talk about the attacks?"

Luke shook his head. "I figured we could meet there and then drive somewhere out of the area in my pickup where we're not likely to be seen by anyone we know."

Martha's heart began to race. She'd only seen Luke's truck when it was parked in the woods, and she certainly never expected to take a ride in it. What if someone she knew saw her getting into his truck? Would they tell Dad? Would they think she and Luke were courting?

Before she could formulate a response, Luke snapped his fingers and said, "Rats! I almost forgot."

"What?"

"I can't go anywhere in my truck because my daed has the keys."

"You gave him the keys to your truck?"

He nodded.

"I didn't think your folks knew you had a truck."

"Thanks to that blabbermouth Toby, my folks found out." Luke grimaced. "Toby told Pop he saw a truck like mine cruising around the schoolhouse in Farmerstown the night it was egged. Pop thinks once the word gets out that I've got a truck and someone spotted a truck like mine near the schoolhouse, I'll be blamed for the vandalism. He was so upset about all this that he demanded I get rid of the truck."

"What'd you say?"

"I refused. Then he said I'd have to move out." Luke tugged his earlobe. "When I said I would leave, Mom got real upset. The next thing I knew, I'd opened my mouth and suggested that I leave my truck keys with my daed for the next couple of weeks. Then I said if a truck was seen anywhere near a place that had been vandalized, Pop would know I hadn't done the dirty deed."

Martha stood, too dumfounded to speak. If Toby had been so brazen as to tell Luke's folks about his truck and that he thought Luke might be involved in the schoolhouse vandalism, what else was Toby saying about Luke, and to whom was he saying it?

Luke touched Martha's arm, and the strange tingle she felt made her wish even more that they were a courting couple.

"The uncertain expression on your face makes me wonder if you believe I'm responsible for those acts of vandalism."

"No, I—"

"I didn't do it, Martha. You've got to believe me."

"I do believe you."

"Then you'll still meet me on Saturday?"

She nodded. "If the roads aren't too bad, maybe we could take separate buggies and meet somewhere other than Keim Lumber. That way, if someone should see us, it won't look like we're together."

Luke groaned. "I hate sneaking around all the time. I ought to have the right to see you without having to hide it."

"Well, if you'd just–"

Luke snapped his fingers. "Why don't we meet in Mt. Hope at Mrs. Yoder's restaurant? It's not likely we'll see anyone we know up there."

"That's true, but even if we do see someone we know, they'll probably think we came there separately and are sharing a table."

"I'll see you at Mrs. Yoder's on Saturday then. In the meantime, I'd better get back to work before John comes looking for me."

Martha smiled. "It was good seeing you, Luke."

"Same here."

As Luke sprinted toward his buggy, Martha smiled. She could hardly wait until Saturday.

Chapter 17

As Martha took a seat at a table near the window in Mrs. Yoder's restaurant, her heart started to pound. She could hardly wait to see Luke. The more time she spent with him, the more she realized that she'd foolishly allowed herself to fall in love with him.

She stared out the window, watching a slow-moving truck follow a horse and buggy up the road, but her thoughts remained on Luke. Was he telling the truth about giving his truck keys to his father? Was she absolutely sure Luke could be trusted? Did he really want to help her learn the identity of the person who'd done the attacks?

If Dad knew I'd fallen in love with Luke and that I've been seeing him on the sly, he'd be furious. Martha gripped the edge of the table until her knuckles turned white. *If Luke knew how much I cared, what would he think?*

"A nickel for your thoughts."

Martha jerked at the sound of Luke's voice. "Oh, I didn't know you were here."

"I just arrived and saw you sitting here by yourself so figured I might join you."

"Jah, please do." Martha smiled and glanced around. If anyone they knew saw them together, Luke was doing a good job of making it look like they'd accidentally met and had decided to share a table. She hated to be sneaking like this, but she didn't know any other way they could meet and talk about the attacks.

"How are things with you?" Luke asked as he took a seat across from her.

"Okay. And you?"

He shrugged. "Things are kind of tense at home, but at work, things are fine and dandy."

"You enjoy working with wood, don't you?"

He nodded, and a sparkle of light danced in his dark eyes. "I'd like to have my own shop someday, but I guess that's not likely to happen."

"What makes you say that?"

He leaned both elbows on the table. "Think about it. Your daed owns one woodworking shop in our area, and John owns the other. I don't think there's a need for three, do you?"

"Probably not." Martha felt sorry for Luke. It seemed like nothing was going right for him these days. Of course things weren't going all that well for her, either. She'd spent the last couple of years putting most of her time and money into raising dogs, and she wasn't much further along now than when she'd first started.

"Maybe John would consider making you his partner," she suggested.

Luke shook his head. "I rather doubt that. He seems to like being the boss. Besides, I don't have enough money saved up to buy half his business."

"I can relate to that. I'd like to buy several more breeds of dogs to raise, but that takes money, and until I sell enough dogs—"

"Have you two decided on what you'd like to order?" their young Mennonite waitress asked, stepping up to the table.

"I'll have the salad bar," Martha replied.

Luke nodded. "I'll have that, too."

Martha tipped her head. "Is that really all you're having?"

"Jah." He patted his stomach. "I had a very big breakfast this morning."

"Would you like anything to drink other than water?"

Luke shook his head, and Martha did the same.

"Help yourself to the salad bar then."

Martha pushed away from the table and smiled at Luke as he walked beside her. This almost felt like a real date.

As Luke sat at the table eating his salad and watching Martha eat hers, a deep sense of longing filled his soul. If things weren't so mixed up right now, and if he knew he could gain Roman's approval, he would probably ask to court Martha.

"You look kind of *verwart*," Martha said, breaking into Luke's thoughts. "Is something wrong?"

Luke took a drink of water before he spoke. "I. . .uh. . . This whole thing with the attacks is enough to make anyone feel perplexed."

She nodded. "If only we could find out who's been attacking us and make him stop, things would be back to normal."

"Have you come up with any new ideas on how we're going to do that?"

"Not really. I thought I'd make a trip to see the sheriff."

"What for?"

"To tell him that I plan to do some investigating on my own and say that I'd like his help."

Luke shook his head vigorously. "I don't think that's a good idea, Martha."

"Why not?"

He leaned forward and lowered his voice. "I've been mulling things over the last few days, and I've put the sheriff on my list of suspects."

"What?" Martha's mouth dropped open. "Why would you think Sheriff Osborn had anything to do with the attacks?"

"Think about it. The attacks have been going on since before Grace married Cleon. Wouldn't you think by now the sheriff would at least have some leads?"

"Maybe he'd have some leads if my daed had told him about the attacks sooner."

"But he knows now, and nothing's been done."

"He's been keeping an eye on our place ever since Dad's shop was blown up."

"How long do you think he'll keep doing that?"

She shrugged. "I don't know."

"Doesn't it seem strange that a man who's sworn to uphold the law and do all he can to keep people safe hasn't done much more than drop by your place and make your daed a few promises to keep an eye on things?"

"That could be Dad's fault. By the time Sheriff Osborn has found out about most of the attacks, the perpetrator's trail's grown cold."

Luke nearly choked on the water he'd just put in his mouth. "Perpetrator? What have you been reading lately—Nancy Drew mystery novels?"

Martha's face flamed, and she blinked a couple of times. "Are you making fun of me?"

"Sorry," he mumbled.

"I'll admit I have read a few mystery stories. I know for a fact that if too much time passes after a crime is committed, it's that much harder to determine who did the crime." Martha folded her arms. "I've also thought about questioning some of the suspects on my list during my free time."

Luke shook his head. "That's not a good idea, either."

"Why not?"

"If the person you're questioning turns out to be the one responsible for the attacks, you could be in danger."

"I'm not afraid."

"Well, you should be. Look what happened to Ruth and Martin. If the person who rammed their buggy is the same one who did all the other things to your family, then he—or she—won't think twice about harming you."

Martha's face paled. "You really think I could be in danger?"

"It's possible." Luke reached across the table and touched her arm. "Promise you won't do anything foolish?"

"I promise."

Chapter 18

When Martha returned home from her meeting with Luke, she was filled with a sense of hope. Not only did he want to help her find the person responsible for the attacks, but also he was concerned for her safety. She saw it as a sign that he might care for her—hopefully as more than a friend. She wondered if Luke might decide he wanted to court her once they found out who was behind the attacks.

"That's probably wishful thinking," Martha murmured as she stepped into the barn to put her horse away.

"What's wishful thinking?"

Martha whirled around. "Dad, I didn't know you were in here."

He stepped out of the shadows near the back of the barn. "Came in to get a roll of wire. One of our fences in the back pasture has been cut. If I don't get it fixed right away, the horses will all be out."

"Not another attack," she said with a moan. "I was hoping now that the sheriff has been watching our place more, the attacks would end."

Dad reached out to stroke her horse's ear. "Someone's obviously trying to get even with me for something."

"Or maybe they want our land."

He huffed. "I won't be run off this place, and I won't spend my days living in fear."

"Would you mind if I go with you to fix the fence?" Martha asked. Maybe she would discover some clue as to who had cut the wire.

He shrugged. "If you've got nothing better to do, you're welcome to come along."

"I'm free for the rest of the day." Martha glanced toward the barn door. "Should I run up to the house first and tell Mom where we'll be so she won't worry in case she comes looking for you?"

He shook his head. "Your mamm's not home. She went over to Abe and Ruth's place to see how things are going with them. I doubt she'll be back until it's time to start supper."

"Okay. I'll put my horse away, and then I'll be ready to head out."

When Luke stepped onto the back porch of his home, he heard voices coming from the kitchen. One he recognized as his mother's; the other he was sure belonged to Judith Hostettler.

As Luke opened the door, he heard Judith say, "This afternoon, Roman discovered someone had cut the fence in our back pasture." She groaned. "I'm getting so tired of these attacks."

"I hope Roman doesn't think Luke had anything to do with it. I know he's accused him of doing some of the other things."

Luke's spine went rigid as he halted. He could see the back of his mother's head through the doorway to the kitchen on the other side of the utility room.

"I think my husband was wrong when he accused your son," Judith replied. "I know Luke's going through rumschpringe and all, but I can't imagine he would do any of the horrible things that have been done to us."

Mom nodded. "Luke tends to be impulsive and stubborn at times, but he's a good boy. We've raised him to respect other people's property."

"Our Martha's the same way—stubborn and impulsive but always polite and respectful."

Luke edged closer to the back door. Should he make himself known, keep on listening, or turn around and head back outside?

"What's Roman going to do about the fence?" Mom asked Judith.

"He was planning to fix it right away."

"I meant, what's he planning to do about the vandalism that keeps happening at your place?"

"There's not much he can do."

"He could notify the sheriff."

Judith sighed. "The sheriff's supposedly been watching our place, but obviously it hasn't kept the attacker from thinking up more things to do."

"How do you feel about all this?"

Judith gave another long sigh. "Each attack makes me feel more nervous, but I'm asking God to calm my fears, and I'm praying that eventually the one who's been doing these things will either be caught or will decide to quit tormenting us on their own."

Luke pressed his weight against the wall. *I wonder what Mom and Judith would say if they knew Martha and I were trying to find out who's responsible?*

Judith's chair squeaked as she pushed away from the table. "Well, I'd best be on my way. I told Roman I was going over to see Ruth, and if I don't get there soon, it'll be time to turn around and head home again so I can start supper."

Luke knew if he didn't do something soon, his presence would be known. He quietly opened the back door and slipped outside. Maybe he would head over to the Hostettlers' place and check on the fence that had been cut. By the time he got there, Roman should be finished with his repairs. This would be a good chance to take a few pictures and look for some evidence.

Ruth settled into the rocking chair with Molly in her lap, leaned her head back, and closed her eyes. She'd had another disagreement with Gideon this morning, and it had left her feeling drained and more discouraged than ever. If only there was something she could say or do to make the boy happy and compliant. If she could just think of a way to get through to him—make him understand that she cared about him and needed his acceptance. Ruth felt that Gideon needed her, too; he just didn't realize it.

She thought about Abe—the steady, gentle man she'd married. She felt blessed to be his wife and hoped she could make him happy.

As Ruth rocked the bundle of sweetness in her lap, she sang an old song her mother used to sing when she and her sisters were young. *"Well, I don't care if the birds don't sing; I don't care if the bells don't chime; just as long as you love me. I don't care if the world don't turn; I don't care if the fire don't burn; just as long as you love me."*

Ruth was close to drifting off when the back door creaked open. She turned her head. Thinking it might be Abe, she was surprised to see Mom enter the room.

Ruth nodded at the sleeping child in her lap. "Let me put her on the sofa, and then we can go to the kitchen for a cup of tea."

Mom smiled. "She's awfully *schee*, isn't she?"

"Jah, she's a very pretty child." Ruth stood and placed Molly on the sofa; then she quietly followed her mother into the next room.

It wasn't until they were seated at the table and had cups of tea in their hands that she noticed her mother's furrowed brows and grim expression.

"Is something wrong, Mom? You look upset."

Mom sighed deeply. "I am upset. Someone cut your daed's fence near the back pasture."

"Did any of his cows or horses get out?"

Mom shook her head. "Luckily, your daed found the cut before that happened."

Ruth reached over and took her mother's hand. "Oh, Mom, are these attacks ever going to end?"

Mom stared into her cup and slowly shook her head. "I don't know. I just don't know." She lifted the cup with a shaky hand and took a sip of tea. "Your daed seemed pretty calm about the whole thing. He told me earlier that he's still trusting God to put an end to all this. In the meantime, he plans to keep a closer eye on things."

Ruth released a heavy sigh as she leaned heavily against her chair. "Why does everything have to be so unsettled? Why can't things be safe and peaceful?"

"I'm afraid we'll never know complete peace until we're face-to-face with our heavenly Father."

"I realize that. I just wish—"

"You look troubled, too, Ruth," Mom said. "Are things okay between you and Abe?"

"Everything's fine. It's my relationship with Gideon I'm worried about."

"What seems to be the problem?"

"Gideon's so defensive whenever I say anything to him. He won't join any family games or contribute much to our conversations. He just wants to be off by himself. Abe has an awful time getting the boy to even do his chores."

"Do you think Gideon's still mourning his mudder's death?"

"Jah, I do. I also think he resents me being his daed's new fraa."

"Give him more time, Ruth. I'm sure the boy will come around eventually."

"I hope so, because it's getting harder to deal with, especially when Abe's other four kinner are sweet and compliant."

Mom took another sip of tea. "God has blessed you by bringing Abe and his kinner into your life. I think you should keep your focus on that right now."

Ruth nodded and reached for her cup. "You're right, Mom. We all need to focus on the positive things."

"Danki for helping me fix the fence," Dad said, smiling at Martha. "Since I have no sons, it's nice to have a daughter who's not afraid to get her hands dirty."

"Jah, that's me—Martha the tomboy."

"So, how was your morning, and where all did you go?" Dad asked, as they moved away from the fence.

"My morning was fine. Since most of the snow has melted, the roads were good. I did a little shopping, and then I went out to lunch." Martha was careful not to mention who she'd had lunch with.

"I'm glad you were able to get away for a while. You spend too much time around here with those hundlin of yours."

"I like spending time with my dogs."

"I know, but you're a young woman and need to be thinking of finding a suitable mate so you can marry and raise a family. Don't you agree?"

Martha shrugged. There was no way she could tell her father that she'd already found someone she'd like to marry. Dad would ask who, and if she told him it was Luke, she was certain he would become angry and forbid her to see Luke again. Of course she wasn't really seeing Luke in a boyfriend-girlfriend sort of way. They were just friends trying to solve a mystery together.

"Guess I'd better get going," Dad said, pulling Martha out of her musings. "Ray Larson's driving me to Millersburg right after lunch so I can get some supplies I need. I'd better get back to the barn and lay some things out for Cleon to do while I'm gone." He turned and started walking away. "Are you coming?"

"It's not as cold today as it has been. I think I'll go for a walk, but I'll head for the house soon."

"Jah, okay," he said with a wave.

Martha was glad Dad had given no objection to her taking a walk. She wanted to snoop around a bit and see if she could find anything that might give some clue as to who had cut the fence.

She walked along slowly, checking the stubble of grass sticking through the clumps of melting snow. Several feet from the fence, in a cluster of bushes, she spotted a worn-looking glove.

"Hmm, what have we here?" She bent to pick up the glove.

"What's that you're holding?"

Startled by the deep voice behind her, Martha jumped up and whirled around. There stood Luke, holding his camera. "You. . .you scared me."

"Sorry about that." Luke glanced around with an anxious expression. "Your daed's not anywhere nearby, I hope."

She shook her head. "He was here a few minutes ago—fixing our fence that someone cut."

"I heard about it."

"Who told you?"

Luke's face colored. "I'd just gotten home from having lunch with you, and when I stepped into the house, I heard your mamm and my mamm talking in the kitchen. When your mamm said your fence had been cut, I decided to hightail it over here and do a little investigating." He gazed at the fence. "Which part was cut?"

"Right here." Martha moved over to stand by the fence and pointed to the spot her father had fixed.

Luke lifted his camera and took a picture; then he turned to Martha and said, "Did you find that glove somewhere nearby?"

She nodded. "Found it in the bushes right before you showed up."

"Mind if I have a look-see?"

She handed him the glove.

"Looks like a work glove to me. I'm guessing whoever cut the fence must have dropped the glove when they were running away."

"That's what I figured, too," Martha said with a nod. "Do you think we should keep the glove or tell the sheriff about it?"

He shook his head. "Like I said at lunch, I'm not sure he can be trusted. Besides, we have no definite evidence as to who the attacker might be, so I think it's best that we keep all the evidence we find to ourselves. Don't you?"

"I suppose. If we get more evidence and decide the sheriff doesn't have anything to do with the attacks, we can turn everything we've found over to him."

Luke nodded, handed the glove back to her, and snapped another picture.

"Do you really think that's going to do any good?"

Luke shrugged. "You never know. The other glove might show up somewhere. If it does, I'll know who it belongs to."

"But if we keep the glove, we won't need a picture of it."

"Good point." He grinned. "Guess I'm not real good at this detective thing yet. Maybe the camera was a dumb idea."

"It was a good thought," Martha was quick to say, "but I really don't think taking pictures will help that much." She tucked the glove under the band of her apron. "Guess I'd better keep this in a safe place for now."

"Did you check for footprints?"

She shook her head. "I haven't gotten that far yet."

"Then let's do it now."

Martha and Luke spent the next several minutes scrutinizing the area around the part of the fence that had been cut. "There's the print of my sneaker," Martha said, pointing to the footprints her shoes had made. "And there are some boot prints, but I can't be sure whether they were made by the person who cut the fence or by my daed." She grunted and slapped the side of her head. "Guess I should have thought to look for footprints before Dad and I started working on the fence."

"Where are you gonna put the glove?" Luke asked.

"Probably in the hayloft where I hid the wrench."

"Are you sure no one will find it there?"

She nodded. "It's in a box under a mound of hay where the cats like to sleep. Dad keeps all the hay he needs for feeding the horses in one side of the barn, so he really has no reason to go into the hayloft for anything right now."

"Okay. I'd better go. Can we meet somewhere soon to discuss things more?" Luke asked.

Martha's heartbeat picked up speed, the way it always did whenever she thought about spending time with Luke. "I have next Saturday off."

"Where do you want to meet?"

"How about Heini's Cheese? That's a public place, and if someone sees us, they'll figure we just met there accidentally and are talking. Would two o'clock work for you?"

Luke smiled and nodded. "I'll see you at Heini's then."

As Roman and Ray drove through Millersburg in Ray's station wagon that afternoon, they passed the newspaper office. It made Roman think about Gary Walker and the article he'd written. He had threatened to have a talk with Gary about the things he'd written that weren't true. Maybe this was the time to make good on his threat.

He turned to Ray and said, "Would you mind dropping me off at the newspaper office?"

Ray blinked. "I thought you wanted to go to the Wal-Mart store."

"I do, but if you don't mind, I'd like to run into the newspaper office first. I have something I need to take care of there."

"Sure, no problem." Ray pulled over to the curb. "This a no-parking zone, so I'll drive around the block a few times, and when I see you standing out front, I'll pick you up. How's that sound?"

"Sounds good to me." Roman stepped out of the car and closed the door. Then he hurried up the steps and entered the building. He spotted a young woman sitting at a desk just inside the front door. "Excuse me, but is Gary Walker in his office today?"

The woman shook her curly blond head. "Gary Walker doesn't work here anymore."

"He–he doesn't?"

"No. Gary took a job at a newspaper in Redding, California. He's been gone for over a week."

Roman heaved a sigh of relief. If Gary had been attacking them, the attacks would finally be over. If he wasn't responsible, then it had to be some-one else on his list of suspects.

Chapter 19

As Martha headed for the barn, a biting wind stung her cheeks, and huge flakes of snow landed on her woolen jacket.

When she stepped into the barn, she brushed the snow off her jacket and started for the kennels.

Woof! Woof! Fritz bounded up to Martha, planting both paws on her knees.

"Fritz! What are you doing out of your cage again?" Martha gently pushed the dog to the floor.

The sheltie responded with another loud bark and a couple of wags of his tail.

"Come on, boy. Let's get you back to your cage." Martha headed in the direction of the kennels with Fritz at her side. When she arrived at his cage, she halted. The door hung wide open.

"I can't believe this," she groaned. "How are you managing to get that latch undone?"

Fritz stared up at her with sorrowful brown eyes and released a pathetic whimper. Was it possible that he'd figured out a way to open the door to his cage, or could someone have let the dog out on purpose? But if that were so, then why only Fritz and not the rest of her dogs?

Martha put Fritz back in his cage, closed the door, and waited to see what he would do. Fritz gave a friendly wag of his tail and scurried off to his doghouse.

"Of course you're not going to do anything while I'm standing here." Anxious to finish her chores in the barn so she could speak to her father, Martha hurried through the feeding process. When that was done, she returned to the house.

"You're right on time," Mom said as Martha stepped into the kitchen. "I just started putting breakfast on the table. Since it's so cold and snowy this morning, I fixed a big pot of oatmeal."

Martha removed her coat and hung it on a wall peg near the back door. "That's good to hear. I'm hungry and more than ready to eat." She hurried across the room and washed her hands at the sink.

Dad looked up from where he sat, reading the morning newspaper. "How'd it go in the barn? Did you get the dogs all fed and watered?"

"The feeding went okay, but I found Fritz out of his cage again." Martha flopped into the chair opposite him. "It makes no sense how he keeps getting out."

"Did you close and latch the cage doors last night?" Mom asked.

"Jah, of course. I even checked them twice to be sure."

"Maybe Fritz has figured out a way to unlatch his door." Dad folded his paper and set it aside. "Some animals, even the smaller breeds, can be real clever when it comes to things like that."

"Fritz may be clever, but he's never gotten out of his cage until recently."

"Here's the oatmeal," Mom announced.

As soon as Mom was seated at the table and their silent prayer was done, Martha said, "I'm thinking of sleeping in the barn for a couple of nights."

"Why would you want to do that?" Mom asked.

"So I can keep an eye on things—see how Fritz is getting out of his cage."

"That's just plain *narrisch*. It's too cold to be sleeping in the barn," Dad said with furrowed brows.

"Your daed's right; sleeping in the barn in the dead of winter would be a foolish thing to do," Mom agreed.

"But I've got to find out if Fritz is escaping on his own or if someone is sneaking into our barn during the night and letting him out."

Mom blinked a couple of times. "You think someone's doing it on purpose?"

"Don't be *lecherich,*" Dad said. "I've been locking the barn at night, so there's no way someone could be sneaking in. Besides, I've got a hunch we don't have to worry about being under attack anymore."

"What makes you think that?" Martha asked.

"When Ray and I were in Millersburg yesterday, I had him drop me off at the newspaper so I could talk to Gary Walker about that article he wrote about you and your kennel business."

"You spoke with that reporter fellow?" Mom's eyes were huge.

He shook his head. "Never got the chance. The young woman at the front desk gave me some very good news."

"What?" Martha asked.

"Said Gary had taken a job at some newspaper in Redding, California." Dad took a drink from his coffee mug. "Guess he's been gone a week already."

"I'm glad to hear Gary's left Holmes County again, and I'm sure Grace will be, too," Martha said. "But isn't it possible that someone else is responsible and that they've been getting into the barn through the hayloft?"

Mom's mouth dropped open, and Dad's forehead wrinkled. "You think someone's climbing a ladder and coming in the small window leading from the outside to the barn?"

Martha nodded. "I think it's a possibility."

He shook his head and grunted. "No way! It would take a tall ladder to reach that window, and I keep all my ladders inside the barn."

"Maybe whoever's doing it brings his own ladder."

"Now that is lecherich," Dad said with a snicker. "What reason would anyone have for sneaking into our barn through the hayloft in the middle of a cold, snowy night and releasing one of your dogs?"

"I don't know, but Fritz getting out of his cage has me worried, and I won't rest until I know how he's been getting out."

"Well, you're not sleeping in the barn," Dad asserted. "So if you're done talking about this, I need to get out to my temporary shop and get some work done."

"Speaking of your shop," Mom said. "I was wondering when you think you'll build a new one."

"In the spring, after the snow's all gone." He grunted. "I'll be glad to get out of that smelly barn. I get tired of hearing Martha's dogs yapping from their kennels."

"I can understand that, and—"

Martha tuned out her parents' conversation as she continued to mull over her problem with Fritz. If she couldn't sleep in the barn, she'd have to come up with some other way to find out how he'd been getting out of his kennel.

Luke had just stepped away from the checkout stand inside the hardware store in Berlin when he spotted Toby entering the store.

"What are you doing here?" Toby asked as Luke approached. "Shouldn't you be at John's place by now?"

Before Luke could reply, Toby added, "Or did you get fired from that job, too?"

Luke clenched his fingers. Why did Toby find it necessary to say cutting things every time they saw each other? "For your information, I'm still working for John." He lifted the paper sack in his hands. "And I came here to get a few things he needed before I head to work. What are *you* doing here so early? Shouldn't you be at Keim Lumber by now?"

"I don't have to be to work until ten today," Toby said. "I came to town to buy a new pair of work gloves."

"Did your old ones wear out from lifting all that heavy lumber at work?"

"Nope. I lost 'em, that's what."

Luke stared at his used-to-be friend. "You lost your work gloves and came all the way to Berlin to get a new pair?"

"Uh-huh."

"Don't they provide you with gloves at the lumber store?"

"Jah, sure, but this is the second pair I've lost in the last month, and my boss said if I lost another, I'd have to buy my own."

"I see."

"First I lost both gloves when I left 'em lying on a stack of lumber." Toby squinted. "Then the other day, one of my new gloves came up missing."

"It did, huh?"

"That's right." Toby snickered. "Sadie says she never realized how forgetful I was until we got married. Maybe it's 'cause I've got a lot more on my mind now that I have a wife to provide for."

Luke nodded. Was it possible that Toby had cut Roman's fence? Could that have been *his* glove Martha found near the fence? He was tempted to say something but changed his mind. No point in alerting his used-to-be friend that he was on to him. Not until he had some clear-cut evidence.

Roman had just lit the gas lamps in his shop, when the door opened and clicked shut. Figuring it was probably Cleon, he called over his shoulder, "*Guder mariye.* You can begin sanding that chair my sister ordered if you want."

"I don't know anything about a chair your sister ordered, but I'd like to have a word with you," a deep male voice said.

Roman whirled around. Just inside the door stood the pushy land developer who'd come around a few years back, asking to buy Roman's property.

"Remember me?" the man asked. "My name's Bill Collins, and I—"

"I know who you are. I thought you'd left Holmes County for good."

"I was gone for a time, but now I'm back, looking to purchase more land in this area."

Roman grimaced. In the area. . .out of the area. What was up with this man, anyway? For that matter, Gary Walker had been in and out of Holmes County a few times in the last couple of years, too. Didn't anyone stay put anymore?

"What do you want with me, Mr. Collins?" he asked.

"I was hoping you had changed your mind about selling and were ready to reconsider my offer to buy your property."

Roman folded his arms as he shook his head. "I wasn't interested when you came around before, and I'm not interested now."

Bill raked his fingers through the sides of his salt-and-pepper hair and plastered a smile on his face. "I heard while I was gone that there was some trouble around here."

A muscle on the side of Roman's face began to pulsate; but he made no comment.

"Heard you were the victim of some vandalism and other attacks." Bill took a step forward. "Guess some of them were pretty bad, too."

Roman grunted. Was this pushy man trying to intimidate him? Did Bill Collins think he could just show up out of the blue and talk him into selling his land?

"Here's the set of figures I offered you before," Bill said, reaching into his pocket and pulling out a slip of paper. "I'm prepared to offer you even more now."

"Forget it!" Roman took a seat behind his desk. "I told you then, and I'm telling you now: I'm not interested in selling."

Bill tapped the toe of his boot. "You strike me as a man who loves his family and wants to protect them. Am I right about that?"

"Of course."

"It seems to me if someone's out to get you, the best thing you could do for the sake of your family is to sell out and move far away from here. Go someplace where you won't be bothered."

Roman's face heated up. "Are you threatening me, Mr. Collins?"

"Not at all. I just thought I'd bring it to your attention that if you sold your land you'd be protecting your family from further harm." Bill placed both hands on the desk and leaned so close to Roman that he could smell the spicy aroma of the man's aftershave. "I think you'd do well to give my offer some serious consideration, Mr. Hostettler."

"I won't run from the problem. My family and I are trusting God to take care of this in His time, and I'm not selling out: plain and simple."

Bill snickered. "That's the dumbest thing I've ever heard. If God was going to protect you, then why didn't He stop all those terrible things from happening to you?"

"How'd you know about the attacks anyway?" Roman asked, ignoring the man's ridiculous question.

Bill leveled him with a piercing gaze. "I have friends in the area. I also subscribe to the local newspaper, so I keep well-informed."

Roman cringed. *Could this man be responsible for the things that have been done to us? Did Bill Collins hire someone to do them so I'd knuckle under and agree to sell him my land? I can't let him know I'm scared, and I'm not going to be bullied into moving from here.*

He stood. "I'd appreciate it if you'd leave right now, Mr. Collins. And please, don't come back again."

Bill looked at Roman as if he didn't quite believe him. Then, with a lift of his shoulders and a muffled grunt, he sauntered out of the shop, slamming the door behind him.

Roman moved back to his chair and sank into it with a moan. "Oh, Lord, what am I going to do?"

Chapter 20

On Friday night as Martha prepared for bed, she made a decision. She'd found Fritz out of his cage two more times this week and wanted some answers. Since Dad wouldn't allow her to sleep in the barn, she'd decided to sit in a chair by her upstairs window and watch the barn with the binoculars she'd gotten for Christmas. From her upstairs room, she had the perfect view of the small outside window that led to the hayloft.

After only a short time of sitting in front of the window, staring through the binoculars, Martha's eyes became heavy and her arms started to ache. She flopped onto her bed with a groan. This wasn't working as well as she'd hoped. Besides, it had started snowing again, obscuring her vision.

Sometime later, she awoke with a start. She glanced at the clock on the table by her bed. It was almost four o'clock.

She dressed quickly. Grabbing the flashlight she kept by her bed, she slipped quietly out of the room and tiptoed down the stairs. When she reached the bottom step, she halted, listening for any sounds coming from her parents' bedroom. All she could hear was the steady *tick, tick, tick* of the living room clock mingling with Dad's muffled snores.

Martha hurried to the utility porch, slipped into her jacket and boots, and tied a woolen scarf around her head. Then she removed the key to the barn from the nail where it hung and stepped outside into the chilly night air. The snow swirled around her in clustered flakes, and she pulled her jacket tighter around her neck as she trudged through the snow toward the barn.

A few minutes later, with fingers stiff from the cold, she undid the padlock and entered the barn. It was dark, and her teeth began to chatter. Even so, she knew it wasn't a good idea to light a lantern. If Dad woke up and looked out the window, he'd probably notice the light in the barn and come to investigate.

With trembling fingers, Martha lifted the flashlight and shined a quick beam of light around the barn. Everything seemed fine–just as it should be. Drawing in a deep breath, she made her way toward the kennels in the back of the barn. She was relieved to see that all the cage doors were shut and the dogs were sleeping in their beds.

"Now I need to find a comfortable place to sit." She spotted a bale of hay inside one of the empty horse stalls and decided that would have to do. It was close enough to watch the kennels, but far enough away that she could stay out of sight should someone come into the barn.

Martha shivered as she plunked down on the hay. *I should have brought an old quilt from the house.* She shined the light around the stall and spotted a well-used horse blanket. It smelled like horse sweat but would help dispel the cold, and she couldn't afford to be choosy.

She clicked off the flashlight so she wouldn't run the battery down and leaned against the wall behind her, wrapping the smelly blanket around her shoulders. If someone opened one of the cage doors, she was bound to hear them.

What will I do if someone does come into the barn? I can't very well knock them to the floor and make them tell me why they've been letting my dog out of his cage or ask if they've been vandalizing our place.

A feeling of guilt coursed through Martha. She had not only disobeyed Dad by coming to the barn in the wee hours of the morning, but she'd been sneaking around seeing Luke without Dad's knowledge. *Maybe I shouldn't meet Luke at Heini's tomorrow. Maybe I should. . .*

Click. . .click. . .clang!

Martha bolted upright.

Squeeeak.

Someone must have opened one of the cage doors.

She held her breath and listened.

Woof! Woof! She recognized Fritz's deep bark. *Woof! Woof! Woof!* The other dogs chimed in.

Martha clicked on the flashlight and shined the light on the kennels. Sure enough, Fritz was out, and his cage door hung wide open. She sent a beam of light around the area. No one was in sight. If someone had come into the barn and opened Fritz's door, she would have heard them moving about. Besides, why would they open only Fritz's cage door?

Martha stepped out of the stall, and Fritz bounded up to her, wagging his tail. "You little stinker," she said, bending to pat his head. "I don't know how you're doing it, but you've figured out some way to get your cage door open, haven't you?"

Fritz gave a couple of barks, and Heidi, the female sheltie, followed suit. Soon Polly and Bo and both sets of puppies woke up and started barking, yapping, and running around their kennels.

"*Shh.* . .you'll wake up Mom and Dad." Martha grabbed Fritz's collar and led him back to his kennel. Fritz looked up at her and gave a pathetic whimper.

"You're not getting out so you can run all over the barn," she said with a shake of her head.

Using the flashlight to guide her steps, Martha hurried to the other side of the barn where some tools and supplies were kept. She returned to the kennels a few minutes later with a piece of sturdy wire, which she tied around the latch on Fritz's cage door. "That ought to hold you."

She shined the flashlight around the kennels one last time then hurried out of the barn. Mom would probably be up soon, and they'd need to start breakfast.

Luke's heart kept time to the rhythm of the horse's hooves as he headed to Berlin in his buggy. Since it had snowed again and the roads were a bit slippery, he wasn't sure if Martha would meet him at

Heini's or not. He'd been tempted to stop at her place and ask, but that wasn't a good idea.

Luke grimaced as he gripped the reins tighter. *If Roman knew Martha and I had plans to go anywhere together, he'd probably pitch a fit.*

A black truck whizzed by, honking its horn and splattering wet slush across the buggy window. The horse reared up then took off on a run.

"Whoa! Steady, boy," Luke said as he fought to keep his gelding under control.

The buggy wheels slipped on the snowy pavement, causing the buggy to slide first to one side and then the other. Just when Luke was sure his rig was going to tip over, the horse calmed down and started moving at a slower pace.

Luke wished he could have driven his truck today. It would have been safer than being out on the snowy road in a buggy with a skittish horse. He only had a few days left until his dad gave the truck keys back. He was glad there'd been no more episodes at the Hostettlers' place since the fence had been cut. To Luke's knowledge, his dad didn't know about that event, but even if he did find out, Luke had an alibi—he'd been home in bed. Since his dad had the truck keys, he couldn't accuse Luke of driving his truck or being anywhere near the Hostettlers' place.

"I need to get to the bottom of these attacks," Luke muttered under his breath. Maybe when he told Martha about Toby's missing glove and said he thought Toby might be responsible for the attacks, they'd be able to come up with a way to catch Toby in the act.

As Rosemary placed her breakfast dishes in the sink, she decided it might be a good time to pay a call on Sheriff Osborn. She'd gone there a few weeks ago, but he hadn't been in his office. Since then, her brother's fence had been cut, and she was determined to see the sheriff.

She glanced out the window and noticed that it had finally quit snowing. Hopefully, the roads had been cleared enough so she could make the trip to town without any problems. *Maybe I'll stop by and see Ruth on my way,* she decided. It had been awhile since they'd had a good visit, and she wanted to see how Ruth was getting along with her new family.

Half an hour later, Rosemary pulled her car into the Wengerds' driveway and headed for the back door. Ruth answered her knock, red-faced and teary-eyed.

"Ruth, what's wrong? Have you been crying?"

Ruth nodded and hiccupped on a sob. "I'm afraid I'll never be a good stepmother."

Rosemary stepped into the house and shut the door. Then she put her arm around Ruth's waist and led her to the kitchen. "What's troubling you?" she asked, guiding Ruth into a chair.

Ruth took a napkin and wiped her nose. "I. . .I had another run-in with Gideon this morning."

"What happened?"

"I asked him to take out the garbage, and when he didn't do it right away, I asked him again." Ruth dabbed at the tears running down her cheeks. "Then he reminded me that I'm not his mudder and said I shouldn't be telling him what to do."

Rosemary's forehead wrinkled. "What did Abe have to say about his son speaking to you that way?"

"He'd already gone out to his harness shop, so he didn't hear Gideon's belligerent tone." Ruth drew in a shaky breath. "I'm trying so hard to get through to Gideon, but he just won't respond to me."

Rosemary gave Ruth's shoulder a gentle squeeze. "I know this is a difficult situation, but don't give up. Keep reaching out to the boy."

"I've been trying to, but he's not making it easy."

"Mammi." Little Molly toddled into the room.

"Come here, sweet girl," Ruth said, holding her arms out to the child.

"Mammi," the little girl said again as Ruth lifted her onto her lap. She smiled at Rosemary. "Would you like a cup of coffee or some tea?"

Rosemary nodded. "I could use something hot to drink before I head out again. It's pretty nippy this morning."

Martha's nose twitched when she stepped into Heini's Cheese Store and smelled the tangy aroma of smoked sausage and Swiss cheese. She glanced around the room, and her breath caught in her throat when she spotted Luke standing in front of one of the cheese counters.

Luke looked up as she approached and offered her a wide smile. "I'm glad to see you made it. With the weather turning snowy, I wasn't sure you'd be able to come."

"I used one of our easygoing horses and took my time coming in, so everything was fine."

"Wish I could say the same for my trip to town."

"What do you mean?"

"Some goofy driver in a pickup splashed slush all over my front window, and then my horse spooked and nearly ran away with my buggy." Luke poked another piece of cheese with a toothpick and popped it into his mouth. "My buggy swayed so much I thought it was gonna topple over." He reached for another toothpick. "Would you like a hunk of cheddar cheese?"

"No thanks." She tipped her head and studied him. "You look pretty calm. I take it you got things under control with your horse and buggy?"

He gave her a smug little grin. "Sure did."

She smiled. "There's a bench out in the entryway. Should we sit there and talk?"

"Sure." Luke headed that way, and Martha followed.

Once they were seated, she told him what had happened with Fritz and how she'd discovered that the dog had been opening his own cage door.

Luke chuckled. "That dog must have wanted freedom really bad to have figured out a way to escape."

She nodded. "Jah, but I solved the problem by wiring the door shut."

"That's good thinking."

"Another problem's been solved this week, too."

"What's that?"

"Gary Walker isn't working for the Millersburg newspaper anymore. Dad found out that Gary took a job at a newspaper in California." Martha smiled. "So that's one name we can delete from our list of suspects."

"That's good to hear." Luke's voice lowered as he leaned closer to Martha. "I've got some information I think you should know about, too."

"What is it?"

"You know that work glove you found near the fence?"

She nodded.

"I think I know who it belongs to."

"Who?"

"Toby King."

Martha's eyebrows shot up. "What makes you think the glove belongs to Toby?"

"I ran into him the other day at the hardware store, and he mentioned that he'd lost a pair of gloves." Luke sucked in his lower lip. "He was buying a new pair."

"That doesn't prove he was anywhere near our place when he lost his glove."

"Doesn't prove he wasn't, either."

"What reason would Toby have for cutting our fence?"

Luke shrugged. "Maybe to get even with me."

"How would cutting our fence get even with you?"

"I told you before. . .Toby's got a grudge against me. I think he might be trying to make it look like I'm responsible for the attacks."

Martha drew in a quick breath. "I can't believe our bishop's son would be involved in anything so mean or destructive." She shook her head. "*Nee*, I can't conceive of it at all."

"Well, someone's been doing those things."

"Seems like our list of suspects keeps growing," she said.

He nodded. "Now all we have to do is figure out who it is."

Chapter 21

As Rosemary entered Sheriff Osborn's office, a whiff of smoke filled her nostrils. She was allergic to cigarette smoke; it gave her a headache. She would state her business and get out of the sheriff's stuffy office as quickly as possible.

The sheriff plunked his elbows on his desk and leaned slightly forward. "I heard you'd come back to the area. What can I do for you, Mrs. Cole?"

Rosemary took a seat. "I'm here about the attacks that are still being made against my brother and his family."

Sheriff Osborn's eyebrows shot up. "There has been another attack?"

She nodded slowly. "It was over a week ago."

"What happened this time, and why wasn't I informed?"

"The fence on Roman's back pasture was cut, and the reason you weren't informed is probably because Roman felt it wasn't serious." Rosemary grimaced. "At least not compared to some of the other things that have happened."

The sheriff grabbed a tablet and pen. "You'd better give me the details."

Rosemary spent the next few minutes telling the sheriff what had happened and that something needed to be done to protect her family before another attack occurred.

"I can hardly prevent things from happening when I'm usually the last one to know." He grunted. "I'm doing the best I can, but I don't have enough manpower to patrol the Hostettlers' place every minute of the day."

"I realize that, but–"

"If you want my opinion, the best thing Roman could do to protect his family is to move somewhere else."

Rosemary's skin prickled. When she'd first come to Holmes County to see Roman and his family, Judith had mentioned something about a land developer wanting to buy their land. She'd also heard one of Roman's neighbors had offered to buy his property.

"I don't think my brother has any plans to move," she said. "And I don't believe anyone should be allowed to get away with attacking him and his family in order to make him knuckle under and sell out."

The sheriff leveled her with a piercing gaze. "What makes you think the person doing the attacks is after Roman's land?"

"Isn't that what you were insinuating when you suggested he move?"

The sheriff shrugged.

"So there's nothing more you can do to stop these attacks?"

He shook his head. "I'm doing the best I can with whatever information I've been given."

Rosemary stood. She'd obviously made a mistake in coming here. It didn't appear as if Sheriff Osborn cared that much about the things that had been done to her brother and his family.

"Thank you for taking time out of your busy day to speak with me, Sheriff." She turned and marched out of the room, her snow boots clomping against the wooden floor.

Once outside, Rosemary drew a couple of deep breaths, relieved to be breathing fresh air again. *I think I'll stop over at Heini's Cheese Store for a little snack, and then I'm going over to Roman's place and have a talk with him.*

As Luke continued to talk with Martha about Toby, her thoughts swirled like a windmill going at full speed. "I know Toby has something

against you," she said. "That's obvious by the way he acts whenever the two of you are together."

Luke nodded.

She pursed her lips. "I don't see how he could have done all the attacks, though—especially when he was someplace else when most of them happened."

"Huh?"

"Take that day when our house was egged and we found a headless scarecrow in our yard. We'd been at Toby and Sadie's wedding, and the attack had to have occurred while we were there."

"So?"

"So, if Toby was at the wedding, which he obviously was, then he couldn't have been at our house throwing eggs or cutting off that old scarecrow's head."

Luke tapped his finger against his clean-shaven chin. "Maybe he had someone else do it for him."

"Who?"

"Beats me. All I know is Toby's no longer my friend, and I don't trust him as far as I can throw a mule."

"Some of the attacks might have been done by pranksters—maybe those English fellows you've been hanging around with."

He gave a quick nod. "Which is why—"

"Well, hello there, Martha. I didn't expect to see you here today."

Martha's head snapped around. "Aunt Rosemary! I didn't think I'd be seeing you here, either."

Aunt Rosemary smiled, first at Martha and then at Luke. "Hello, Luke. I'm surprised to see you here, as well."

His face colored, and he reached up to swipe at the sweat on his forehead. "I was just. . .uh. . .tasting some cheese, and Martha showed up, so—"

"So we came out here to talk awhile," Martha said, finishing Luke's sentence.

"I see." Aunt Rosemary took a seat beside Martha and patted her arm. "It's always good to see you."

"Same here."

Luke cleared his throat a couple of times. Martha could tell he was uncomfortable about having been seen with her. Truth was she felt a little apprehensive about it, too. At least it was Aunt Rosemary and not Dad who'd seen her sitting beside Luke.

"I'd better go," Luke said, rising to his feet. "I've got some errands to run, and then my daed needs my help this afternoon." He glanced over at Martha and gave her a half smile. "I'll be seeing you around."

She smiled and nodded in return.

Luke cast a quick smile in Aunt Rosemary's direction then hurried away.

"Luke seems like a nice enough fellow," Aunt Rosemary said, "but he acted kind of nervous, don't you think?"

Martha shrugged then leaned closer to her aunt and whispered, "I hope you won't say anything to my folks about seeing me and Luke together. Dad wouldn't like it."

"Why not?"

"He thinks Luke might be responsible for the attacks against us."

"Is that what you think, Martha?"

"I don't believe he is. In fact–" Martha halted her words. Should she tell Aunt Rosemary that she and Luke were trying to find out who was responsible for the attacks, or should she just say she'd been trying to find out on her own?

"Is there something troubling you, Martha? Something more than me seeing you with Luke?"

Martha nodded. "I'm concerned about the terrible things that have been done to my family, and I've decided to try and find out who's behind the attacks."

"You, too?"

Alarm rose in Martha's chest. Did Aunt Rosemary already know Luke was doing some investigating of his own? "What do you mean?"

Aunt Rosemary glanced around as though she was worried someone might hear their conversation, but no one was within earshot, as far as Martha could tell.

"I've just come from Sheriff Osborn's office," Aunt Rosemary whispered. "I went there to see if he's come up with any leads and to let him know about your dad's fence being cut."

"Did the sheriff have anything helpful to say?"

"I'm afraid not. He thinks he could help more if he was told right away whenever something happens." Aunt Rosemary released a lingering sigh. "To tell you the truth, I don't think the sheriff cares all that much what happens to your family, and I. . ." Her voice trailed off.

"You what?" Martha prompted.

Aunt Rosemary glanced around once more. "I'd rather not discuss this with you here. Is there a time you can come by my house so we can visit privately?"

"I work for Irene all next week, but I'm free on Monday of the following week."

"Why don't you come over around eleven thirty? We can talk while we have lunch together." Aunt Rosemary gave Martha's arm a gentle pat. "You'll be the first lunch guest in my new house."

"You've had others over to eat in that house."

"That's true, but I was only renting the place then. Now that the home is mine, I'm starting fresh with my entertainment list."

Martha chuckled. She always felt relaxed when she was with Aunt Rosemary.

Aunt Rosemary stood. "I think I'll buy a couple packages of cheese and some trail bologna, and then I'll be on my way."

Martha smiled. "I'll see you next Monday for lunch."

"I'm done with those cabinets you wanted me to stain," Cleon said. "Did you want me to make those deliveries for you now?"

"Jah, sure," Roman answered with a nod.

"While I'm in Berlin, I'd like to stop by a couple of the shops that sell my honey and see if their supply's running low."

"No problem. Take your time."

Cleon smiled. "I appreciate you letting me continue with my honey business while working for you. I enjoy working with my bees, and it would be hard to give it up."

"Everyone in the family enjoys the honey your bees provide."

Cleon nodded. "I'd best get those chairs loaded up and head out. I should be back shortly after noon."

"No problem. Take your time."

The barn door clicked shut behind Cleon, and Roman resumed his work on some rusty hinges.

Some time later, the door opened, and Rosemary stepped into the barn.

"This is a surprise," Roman said, moving over to the door to greet his sister. "What brings you out on this cold winter day?"

"I came to see you, of course." Rosemary gave him a hug.

"I'm glad you did. How are things going? Are you all settled in?"

She nodded. "Now that all the unpacking is done, I need something else to keep me busy."

He chuckled. "I'm sure you'll find something to do. Even when you were a *maedel*, you always had to be busy."

"That's true," she admitted. "Most of the girls I knew were happy playing with their dolls, but not me. I felt I should be doing something more constructive."

"Are you thinking of finding a job?" he asked.

She shook her head. "Between the money from my husband's insurance policy and the sale of our home, I should be fine."

"But if you need to keep busy, a part-time job might be what you need."

"Maybe later. Right now, I've got something else I want to do."

He nodded toward the metal desk he'd set up in his temporary shop. "Why don't you have a seat and tell me about it?"

"Are you sure you have the time?"

"Jah, sure. I can take a little break."

Rosemary sat down, and he pulled a wooden stool over and joined her.

"So what's this 'something else' you're wanting to do?" he asked.

"I'd like to investigate the attacks that have been made against you."

His eyebrows shot up. "It's not your place to do any investigating; that's the sheriff's job."

"It should be," she said with a nod. "However, I don't think he's doing a very good job, or else we would know who's behind the attacks by now, and the culprit would be behind bars."

Roman grunted. "The sheriff blames me for that. He thinks I should call him right away whenever we've had an attack."

"Why haven't you called him every time, Roman?"

"I feel that it shows a lack of faith on my part if I go running to the law every time someone pulls a prank on us."

"I'll admit, some of the things that have been done to you have seemed like simple pranks, but other things, like Martin's death, were obviously not."

Roman massaged the back of his neck. "We don't know for sure that the person who's done vandalism here is the one who rammed Ruth and Martin's buggy off the road. That could have been a hit-and-run driver who'd had too much to drink on Christmas Eve or was speeding and lost control of his vehicle in the snow."

Rosemary slowly shook her head. "You don't really believe that, do you?"

Roman shrugged. "I don't know what to believe anymore. These attacks have gone on longer than I thought they would. Now that irritating land developer's back in the area, asking to buy my land." He grimaced. "When the attacks first began, I was convinced Luke was doing them."

"And now?"

"Now I'm not so sure. It's possible that the land developer hired someone to do the attacks so he could scare me into selling my land."

"I've been thinking that, too."

"I haven't ruled out the possibility that Luke's somehow involved," Roman said. "That fellow seems sneaky, and I know he hasn't liked me since I fired him for being late to work too many times."

"Do you have any other suspects?"

"At first I thought it might be Steven Bates, who got mad at me after the set of cabinets Luke delivered fell off the wagon. But then after Luke started acting so weird about things, I figured it was probably him." Roman crossed his arms. "At least we know it's not that reporter fellow, since he's moved out of the area again."

"We can speculate until the sheep are all sheared, but we won't know anything for sure until this mystery is solved."

He clutched her arm and shook his head. "I don't want you playing detective; you could get hurt."

She laughed. "I'm not a little girl anymore. I don't need my big brother watching out for me."

"You may not be a little girl, but you're a woman whose curiosity could get her in trouble if this person gets wind that you're trying to catch him."

She patted his hand in a motherly fashion. "I appreciate your concern, but I'll be fine, Roman. Just keep the faith and put your trust in God."

He drew in a deep breath and offered up a silent prayer. *I do trust You, God. I just don't trust my nosy sister to keep out of trouble.*

Chapter 22

As Martha headed for the barn on Monday morning, a week later, she spotted Ray Larson standing near the fence that divided their property. He held a pair of binoculars and seemed to be looking at something in their yard.

I wonder what he could be looking at, and what's he doing up so early on such a cold winter day?

This wasn't the first time Martha had seen Ray with his binoculars trained on their place. *Maybe I should ask what he's doing.*

She shook her head. *I'm being paranoid again. I need to feed my dogs and get back in the house so I can help Mom with breakfast. Then I've got to clean my room and do a few other chores before I leave for Aunt Rosemary's.*

Martha unlocked the barn door. The familiar odor of sweet-smelling hay and horseflesh greeted her. She lit a gas lamp and carried it to the back of the barn where her kennels were located. All the cage doors were shut, including Fritz's, which she'd been securing with a piece of wire every night. Since Fritz wasn't getting out anymore, she knew for certain it hadn't been foul play.

She smiled when Heidi's pups bounded up to the door of their cage. They were old enough to sell now, so she would run an ad in the paper later this week. Polly's pups would be ready soon after that. With any luck, Martha would soon have some money in her bank account.

As she got out the sack of dog food and began the feeding process, she thought about the article Gary Walker had written about her kennel business several weeks ago. Gary might be gone now, but the article he'd written could still influence someone's decision about whether to buy one of her puppies or not.

I'm glad that irritating reporter took a job in California, Martha thought as she put the bag of dog food away. *At least we know now that he wasn't responsible for the attacks.*

Rosemary had just set a kettle of soup on the stove to heat when she heard a horse and buggy pull into the yard. She looked out the kitchen window and saw Martha climb down from her buggy.

A few minutes later, Martha entered the house through the back door. "Something sure smells good," she said as she stepped into the kitchen.

"It's cheddar chowder." Rosemary motioned to the stove. "I took the recipe from one of my favorite Amish cookbooks, and I got the cheddar cheese at Heini's the other day."

"I'm sure it'll taste as good as it smells." Martha hung her coat over the back of a chair. "Is there anything I can do to help?"

Rosemary shook her head. "The table's set, and I've got some rolls warming in the oven. So if you'd like to have a seat, we can visit while we wait for the soup to finish heating."

"Okay." Martha plunked down in the chair where she'd draped her coat.

"How were the roads? Has the snow melted any?"

Martha nodded. "There was just a bit piled along the side of the road from the snowplows."

"Winter will be over soon. Hopefully we won't see much more snow before spring comes."

"Uh-huh."

Rosemary knew she was sharing idle chatter, but she wasn't quite ready to talk about what was really on her mind. Should she tell Martha what had been said when she'd visited with Roman last week, or would it be better to begin by asking Martha some questions—find out how much she knew about the attacks?

"Last week at Heini's," Martha said, "you started to tell me something, and then you stopped and said you'd tell me later, when we were alone. I've been wondering what you wanted to say."

Rosemary turned down the burner on the stove and took a seat across from Martha. "Since the sheriff hasn't done anything about the attacks, and since your dad isn't making any effort on his own to find out who's behind them, I've decided to do some investigating of my own." She paused. "And since you said the other day that you were trying to find out who's responsible for the attacks, I was wondering if you had made a list of suspects."

Martha nodded.

"Me, too, and I plan to question everyone on the list."

"Do you think that's a good idea, Aunt Rosemary? It could be dangerous for you to go poking around."

"That's what your dad said, too."

"You've spoken to Dad about this?"

Rosemary nodded. "I stopped by his temporary shop after I left Berlin last Saturday. I asked who he thought might be responsible for the attacks."

Martha's cheeks turned pink. "He still thinks it's Luke, doesn't he?"

"Maybe. But he's beginning to suspect that land developer Bill Collins—I think that's his name."

"If Dad thinks it could be the land developer, then maybe he won't care if—" Martha stopped speaking and stared at the table.

"Won't care if what?" Rosemary prompted. "Does this have anything to do with Luke?"

"Yes."

"Are you in love with Luke?"

Martha's head moved slowly up and down, and the color in her face deepened. "For all the good it'll do me."

"You mean because Luke's not one of your dad's favorite people?"

"That, and I'm also afraid I'm going to say or do something stupid when I'm with Luke."

"Like what?"

"Like blurt out to Luke the way I feel about him."

"Maybe he already knows. Maybe he feels the same way about you as you do him."

"What makes you say that?"

"I saw the way he looked at you when we were at Heini's." Rosemary chuckled. "I've seen that look on a man's face before, and it's called love, dear heart."

Martha's face lit up like a full moon. "You really think so?"

"I do." Rosemary sniffed the air. "I also think my soup's done, so we'd better eat." She stood and moved back to the stove. "We can talk more while we have our lunch."

For the next hour, Rosemary and Martha ate their meal and talked about the attacks. They worked on a timeline and wrote down the sequence of the attacks, as well as any clues, motives, and possible suspects. They talked about Luke and why Martha was convinced he was innocent. Then Martha told Rosemary that Luke was watching for clues, too.

Rosemary's mouth dropped open. "He is?"

Martha nodded. "According to Luke, he's been investigating for some time, but now we're working together on this."

"Has he gathered any evidence that would point to anyone in particular?"

Martha opened her mouth but then closed it again.

"What were you going to say?"

"Well, I–I promised Luke I wouldn't tell anyone who he thinks did it. Since he's not really sure at this point, it wouldn't be fair to speculate."

"I guess you're right. What we need is some cold, hard evidence."

"Will you promise not to tell anyone that Luke and I are working together on this?" Martha asked.

Rosemary nodded. "Unless I see some reason to tell, it will be our little secret."

As Martha headed down the road toward home, she thought about stopping to see Ruth but realized there wasn't time. She needed to be at work for Irene by three o'clock, and she'd stayed at Aunt Rosemary's longer than planned.

But the discussion we had was good, she thought as she gave her horse the freedom to trot. *Knowing Aunt Rosemary's also investigating gives me more hope of finding out who's behind the attacks.*

A horn tooted from behind, and a truck came alongside Martha's rig. Her heart skipped a beat when she realized Luke was in the driver's seat.

He motioned her to pull over, and then he pulled up ahead and stopped his vehicle along the shoulder of the road.

Martha guided her horse to the right and pulled her buggy in behind him. Luke hopped out of the truck, skirted around to the side of Martha's buggy, and opened her door.

"I'm surprised to see you driving your truck," she said.

"My daed returned my keys." Luke smiled. "I'm heading to New Philadelphia right now to meet a couple of my English friends."

Martha's heart took a nosedive. Wouldn't Luke ever give up his running-around days and settle down?

"There's no reason to look so upset," he said, shaking his head. "It's not what you think."

"How is it then?"

"My daed read in the newspaper this morning that a couple of outhouses at Amish schoolhouses were tipped over last night. I aim to find out if any of the English fellows I know did it."

"What makes you think that they might have tipped over the outhouses?"

"They've done it before—told me so, plain and simple."

"It seems that every time there's another prank pulled somewhere, our place gets hit next." Martha swallowed a couple of times. "I really have to wonder if those English fellows might be the ones making the attacks."

"At first I thought they were, too, since I know for a fact that they've pulled some ugly pranks around the area." He lifted the edge of his stocking cap and rubbed the side of his head. "But that was before I started suspecting Toby."

"You don't really think Toby's been out late at night tipping over outhouses, do you?"

"I didn't mean the outhouses. I'm sure those were done by the Englishers I know. What I'm worried about are the attacks that have been made against your family." Luke reached for Martha's hand. Even through her woolen glove, she could feel the warmth of his touch. "I wouldn't want anything to happen to you, Martha." He rubbed his thumb over her knuckles. "I care for you, and I—I wish I could court you."

Martha bit her lip to keep from breaking into tears. It seemed like she'd waited a lifetime to hear those words. If only she and Luke were free to court.

"Your silence makes me wonder if I've spoken out of turn. I was hoping you might have feelings for me, too, but I guess I was wrong."

"You're not wrong." Martha lowered her gaze. "I realized some time ago that I had feelings for you, but I never thought you'd return those feelings."

Luke lifted her chin with his thumb, and the look of tenderness Martha saw on his face let her know he really did care for her.

They gazed into each other's eyes, until a passing car broke the spell. With an embarrassed giggle, Martha said, "I wish I could stay and visit longer, but I'll be late getting to work if I don't leave now."

"I understand." Luke smiled, and there was a twinkle in his eye. "I'll see you soon, Martha."

As Martha guided her horse onto the road again, she said a prayer for Luke—that he would quit hanging around his English buddies and join the church.

Chapter 23

"Where's my backpack?" Gideon fussed as he rummaged around the living room on a Friday morning in late February. Ruth sat holding Molly, who had run into a chair after being chased by Owen.

"Where did you put it last night?" Ruth shouted above Molly's screams. "You had it out when you did your homework."

Gideon pointed to the sofa. "Had it right here, but somebody must've took it." He glared at Josh. "I'll bet you hid it, didn't you?"

"Did not." Josh grabbed his own backpack that sat near the front door and wrinkled his nose. "We're gonna be late for school if you keep foolin' around."

"I ain't foolin' around," Gideon shot back. "If you'd help me find my backpack instead of standin' there lookin' so smug, we might be on our way to school already." He stomped across the room, bumping into the rocking chair where Ruth sat with Molly.

The little girl let out another piercing scream, and Ruth gritted her teeth to keep from screaming herself. With Molly hollering in her ear, she could barely think, much less try to resolve Gideon's problem.

Esta's sheltie darted into the room, with Esta right behind him. "Come back here, Winkie," she yelled. "Your paws are muddy and you're not supposed to be in the living room with dirty feet!"

Ruth opened her mouth to scold Esta for letting the dog in the house, when Owen, who'd been cowering in one corner of the room since he'd bumped into Molly, jumped up and started chasing the dog.

"I'll get him for you, sister!" he shouted.

Esta and Owen darted for Winkie, and their heads collided.

"Ouch!" Esta rubbed her forehead and glared at Owen. "You oughta watch where you're going."

"I was only tryin' to help." His chin trembled, and tears welled in his eyes.

"Aw, don't start bawlin' now," Gideon grumbled. "It's bad enough we have to listen to Molly screaming all the time."

Esta shook her finger at Gideon. "Don't be talkin' about our little sister that way. She's got every right to cry if she wants to."

"All right, that's enough!" Ruth lifted Molly from her lap and was about to stand, when Winkie leaped over her foot. She bent down and grabbed the dog's collar. "Get your dog, Esta." Then she turned to Owen and said, "I want you to take Molly out to the kitchen and find something to keep her entertained." She looked back at Esta. "After you've put Winkie away in the dog run, you and Josh had better head out to school."

"What about Gideon?" Esta questioned.

"He can catch up to you after he finds his backpack."

Owen grabbed Molly's hand and led her to the kitchen, while Josh and Esta rushed out the back door. Gideon stood facing Ruth with his arms folded. "Don't see why I have to look for my backpack. Can't I go to school without it?"

She shook her head. "Your homework is in the backpack, and so are your schoolbooks. You need to think about where you put it last night before you went upstairs to bed."

"Put it right there." Gideon pointed to the floor near the door.

"Well, it's not there now, so I suggest you think of some other places to look."

He stared at Ruth as though daring her to make him move.

She tapped her foot impatiently. "Do I need to go out to the harness shop and get your daed?"

Gideon's face turned red, and he shuffled his feet a few times. Finally, with a disgruntled grunt, he turned and stomped up the stairs.

Ruth debated about going up to his room to help search for the backpack but decided he might not appreciate it. Instead, she went to the kitchen to see what the younger children were up to. She found Molly sitting on the floor playing with two empty kettles and a wooden spoon. Owen sat at the table coloring a picture.

When Owen spotted Ruth, he hopped off his chair. "Is it okay if I go upstairs and color in my room?"

"Don't you want to sit here in the kitchen where it's warm and cozy?" she asked.

He shook his head. "Molly keeps makin' noise with those pots she's bangin'."

"Okay."

Owen had no more than left the room, when Gideon showed up carrying his backpack. "Found it," he announced.

"Where was it?"

"Under my bed." He sauntered out the back door before Ruth could comment.

Ruth poured herself a cup of tea and headed back to the living room. She needed a few minutes of solitude.

She set her cup on the coffee table, took a seat in the rocking chair, and closed her eyes. *I don't know how much more of this I can take. Maybe I made a mistake marrying a man with five children. Maybe I'm not cut out to be a mother.*

Ruth's eyes snapped open when she heard a pathetic whimper coming from the kitchen.

Thinking something must be wrong with Molly, she sprang from her chair and rushed to the kitchen. She found the child sitting on the floor, this time with a kettle on her head.

With tears streaming down her cheeks, Molly pointed at the kettle. *"Fascht."*

"I know you're stuck." Ruth lifted the kettle off Molly's head and sank to the floor beside her. As she held the little girl in her lap, she started to laugh. With all the serious stuff that had gone on in this house lately, she'd almost forgotten how to look for humor.

"Hungerich," Molly said, tugging on Ruth's sleeve.

"Well, then, if you're hungry, I think the two of us should have a little snack." Ruth clambered to her feet, grabbed a box of crackers from the cupboard, and placed them on the table. Then she set Molly in a chair and spread several crackers on the table in front of her.

As Ruth joined Molly at the table, she realized she'd been taking things too seriously lately. What she should be doing was asking God to help her with Gideon, not arguing with the boy or trying to solve things on her own.

She glanced over at Molly and smiled. *And I definitely need to laugh and smile a lot more.*

Thump-thump-thump! Martha jumped when she heard someone knocking at the front door. None of their friends or relatives ever used that door.

"I'll get it," Mom said as she placed her kitchen towel on the counter. She hurried from the room and returned shortly with a smile on her face. "There's someone here to look at the hundlin you have for sale."

Martha dried her hands on the towel and hurried from the kitchen. Apparently, someone had read the ad she'd put in the newspaper. Either that, or they'd seen the sign posted out front by the driveway advertising sheltie and beagle puppies.

When Martha went to the door, she discovered a middle-aged English couple on the porch. "My mother says you're interested in seeing some of my dogs?"

"Oh yes," the dark-haired woman said with a nod. "We read your ad in the *Bargain Hunter*, and we're interested in seeing the sheltie puppies." She smiled at the balding man who stood beside her. "I've wanted a sheltie for some time. Isn't that right, Philip?"

He nodded. "Can we take a look at the pups now?"

"Yes, of course. I'll just get my jacket, and then I'll take you out to the kennels." Martha hurried to the utility room where her jacket hung and then rushed back out to the porch where the couple waited. "Follow me," she said, leading the way across the yard toward the barn.

She found the barn door unlocked but figured Dad had already been out there this morning before he and Cleon had left for Sugarcreek to deliver some cabinets. What she hadn't figured on was the sight that greeted her when she stepped inside the barn and lit the nearest gas lantern. Heidi and Polly were both running free, and so were their puppies. Had the dogs figured out how to get their cage doors open now, too?

"Oh, my! What's that awful smell?" the woman asked, sniffing the air. "It smells like fresh—"

"Horse manure," the man said, finishing her sentence. "And there's the reason we smell it." He pointed to one of the beagle pups. "That dog's hair is covered with manure."

"Eww!" The woman wrinkled her nose. "That's really disgusting!"

Yip! Yip! Yip!

Martha gasped when she spotted a puppy tail sticking through a thin opening in a nearby wooden crate. Its mother, Polly, let out an ear-piercing howl and jumped up, planting both paws on the woman's jean-clad knees.

"Get down!" the woman shrieked, pushing the dog away. She looked over at Martha and frowned. "What kind of business are you running here anyway?"

"I assure you—"

"She's running a puppy mill, that's what." The man made a sweeping gesture with one hand. "No one running a respectable kennel would allow their dogs to run all over the place, rolling in horse manure, getting stuck in wooden crates, and who knows what else!"

The woman turned toward the door. "Let's go, Philip. I would never buy a puppy from anyone who neglects their dogs in such a way!"

"I don't neglect my dogs," Martha mumbled as the couple left the barn. She glanced down at Heidi, who was looking up at her with sorrowful brown eyes. "I would never mistreat any of my dogs."

A sudden realization came to Martha. Someone must have sneaked into the barn and let the dogs out. Someone wanted to make it look like she wasn't taking good care of her dogs.

"Where do you think you're going?"

Luke halted at the bottom of the stairs and turned to face his father. "I'm heading to work."

"Without breakfast?" his mother asked, as she stepped out of the kitchen and into the hall.

"I slept later than I should have. If I don't leave now, I'm going to be late."

Pop grimaced and shook his head. "You got in late last night, didn't you?"

Luke nodded.

"I heard your truck rumble in, and when I looked at the clock, it was after midnight." Pop grunted. "Where'd you park that truck, anyway? Not on our property, I hope."

Luke shook his head. "I parked it behind some bushes along the side of the road, not far from our driveway."

Pop grunted again.

"Where were you at such a late hour, Luke?" Mom asked.

"I was in New Philly most of the evening, and then I drove around for a while."

"Drove around, huh? Don't you know we were worried?" Pop's voice rose, and a vein on the side of his neck bulged.

Luke massaged the back of his head. He'd woken with a headache—no doubt from lack of sleep. "I'm sorry if I made you worry, but as you can see, I'm fine and dandy."

Pop planted both hands on his hips. "You're fine and dandy all right—out all hours on a weeknight, driving around in that fancy truck of yours, doing who knows what." He stared at Luke. "I want to know exactly where you were and what you were doing."

Luke's jaw dropped. "I'm not a little buwe, Pop. I don't think I should have to account for every minute I'm away from the house."

Pop clapped his hands, and Mom jumped.

"Really, Elam, do you have to shout at our son like that?"

Pop scowled at her. "I do when he's being disrespectful, not to mention rebellious and defiant." He shook his finger at Luke. "I don't think you'd have been out so late last night if you'd been driving a horse and buggy, now would you?"

"Probably not, but–"

"It's that fancy truck that's causing you problems. I demand that you put it up for sale, and you'd better do it today!"

Luke shook his head. "I need my truck, Pop."

"What do you need it for?" Mom spoke softly, and Luke could see by the strained look on her face that she was struggling not to cry.

"I can't say why I need it."

"Can't or won't?" Dad hollered.

Luke shifted from one foot to the other, wondering how much he dared say to his folks without telling them the real reason he felt he needed to own a truck right now. "I'm still going through my rumschpringe, you know."

"Like we needed that reminder." Pop slowly shook his head. "You've been going through your running-around years long enough. It's time to settle down and make a commitment to God and to our church."

"I'm not ready."

Pop moved closer to Luke, until they were nose to nose. "I'm tired of all this, boy. If you won't sell that truck, then you'll have to move out of my house."

Mom gasped. "Ach, not this again! You can't mean it, Elam!"

He nodded soberly. "I do mean it."

Mom stepped forward and placed her hand on Luke's arm. "I'm begging you. Please do as your daed asks."

Luke swallowed hard. He didn't want to disappoint his mother, but he wasn't ready to make a decision about joining the church yet.

Pop nudged Luke's back with his elbow. "What's it gonna be, son?"

Luke turned and grabbed his jacket off the wall peg by the door. "I'm not willing to sell my truck at this time, and I'm not ready to join the church yet. If you're opposed to me living here under those conditions, then I guess it is time for me to move out." Before either of his folks could respond, Luke jerked open the back door. "I'll be back after work to get my things!"

Chapter 24

As Luke sped out of his parents' driveway, his emotions dipped like a roller coaster. Why wouldn't Pop believe him? Why hadn't he been able to find out who was responsible for the attacks against the Hostettlers? Should he give up looking for clues? Should he sell his truck and join the church? Would it be better for all if he forgot about being Amish and became English?

He gripped the steering wheel until his fingers started to throb. *If I jump the fence and go English, I'll have no chance with Martha.*

By the time Luke arrived at John's shop, he'd made a decision. He needed to continue trying to find out who was behind the Hostettler attacks, which would clear his name with Roman. Then, and only then, would he make the commitment to join the church.

When Luke entered the shop, John looked up from the paperwork he was doing and pointed to the clock sitting on his desk. "You're half an hour late, Luke. Did another buggy wheel fall off?"

"Not this time. I drove my truck this morning."

"Did it break down on the way here or what?"

"No. I had a disagreement with my folks." Luke yanked the stocking cap off his head and tossed it on the closest workbench. "It was mostly with my dad, I guess."

"That made you late to work?"

Luke nodded. "My dad wants me to sell my truck and join the Amish church. He said if I didn't, I'd have to move out. So I left."

John's eyebrows lifted high on his forehead. "You mean you moved out of your folks' house?"

"That's right." Luke released a gusty sigh. "Guess I'll have to sleep in my truck until I can find some place to live."

John scrubbed a hand over his clean-shaven chin. "I suppose I could set up a cot for you in the back room. The sink and toilet would give you the basic necessities. I've also got a small microwave and a hot plate I could let you use."

"You'd really do that for me?"

"You need somewhere to stay. I can't have my best employee living out of his truck, now can I?"

"What do you mean, John? I'm your *only* employee."

John chuckled. "That's right, and since we've got a lot of work to do today, I think we'd better quit chewin' the fat and get busy, don't you?"

Luke nodded and grabbed a leather work apron from the nail near his workbench. "Thanks, John. Thanks for everything."

As Martha headed for the barn, she spotted Ray Larson looking over at their place with his binoculars again. She had plenty of time this morning, so maybe she should find out what their neighbor found so interesting.

She hurried across the pasture separating their place from the Larsons', and when she reached the other side, Ray trained his binoculars on her. " 'Morning, Martha. What brings you over to our place?" he asked with a smile.

"I was heading to the barn to feed my dogs when I noticed you leaning over the fence with your binoculars. I wondered what you were looking at."

He lowered the binoculars. "I was studying an unusual bird that flew toward your place. Haven't seen one like it around here before, and I wanted to get a better look."

"What did the bird look like?"

"It had an orange head and a black body." Ray scratched the side of his head. "No, I think its head was more of a yellow color."

Martha opened her mouth to comment, but Ray rushed on.

"I checked my bird identification book, and the closest I've been able to come to what I saw is the yellow-headed blackbird. But those birds are usually found in marshy areas, and I've never seen one around here." He looked right at Martha. "You didn't happen to see it, did you?"

She shook her head. "I wasn't looking for birds this morning. I was focused on getting my dogs fed."

"Speaking of your dogs, how's the kennel business doing these days?"

"Not so well. I placed an ad in the paper, and there's a sign out by the road, but so far, I haven't sold any of Heidi's or Polly's puppies." Martha thought about telling Ray about the incident with the English couple who'd come to look at puppies but decided it was best left unsaid. No point in giving Ray, who had a tendency toward gossip, something to spread around the neighborhood.

"That's too bad," Ray said with a shake of his head. "We've been real happy with the dog we bought from you. I would think anyone buying one of your pups would be satisfied, too."

Martha sighed. "Guess I'll have to keep trying."

He smiled. "That's right. I never did like a quitter."

Martha turned toward home. "I'd better get to the barn and feed those dogs, or they'll be yapping up a storm."

"Tell your folks I said hello," Ray called.

"I will," Martha said with a farewell wave.

Sometime later, with the dogs fed and watered, Martha stepped out of the barn, relieved that she'd found no messes this morning and that all the dogs had been in their cages. She was about to head for the house, when a dark blue car came up the driveway. She didn't recognize the vehicle or the middle-aged man with thinning brown hair who got out of the car. She walked up to him and was about to ask if he was looking for her father's woodworking shop, when he spoke first.

"I'm here to see my granddaughter. Is she at home?"

Martha squinted. *Granddaughter?* She figured the man must be lost.

"What's your granddaughter's name? If she lives around here, I probably know her and can give you directions to her house."

"Her name's Anna, and she lives with her mother, Grace."

Martha's mouth fell open. "Are. . .are you Carl Davis?"

He nodded.

Martha knew Carl Davis was the father of Grace's deceased English husband. He was the one who'd brought Anna to live with Grace almost two years ago. Martha hadn't been home at the time, so she'd never met the man in person; Grace had told her and the rest of the family how Carl's wife had died and that he'd been having health problems and had decided Anna would be better off with her mother.

"Is Anna here or not?"

Martha shook her head. "She's in school today."

"What time will she be home?"

"Later this afternoon."

"What about Grace? Is she at home?"

Martha's heart began to pound. Except for a few letters and some gifts Carl had sent to Anna, he'd never made any other contact or come to visit the child. Martha knew from what Grace had said that she was glad he hadn't come around. It would have probably confused Anna, or maybe made her want to go back to live with the man she called "Poppy." Grace had lost Anna once, after her husband's death when his parents had taken Anna to live with them. Martha knew it would break her sister's heart if she lost Anna a second time.

She shifted uneasily, not knowing how to respond to Carl's question. It wouldn't be right to lie, but if she told Carl where Grace lived and he went over there demanding to take Anna away, Grace would be devastated.

"Did you hear what I said? I'd like to see Grace," Carl persisted.

Martha pointed to the driveway leading to Grace and Cleon's house. "Grace and her husband live up there now."

A look of relief spread over Carl's face. "Thanks. I'll leave my car parked here and walk up."

Martha wished there was some way she could warn Grace that Carl was coming. Maybe she should walk with him to Grace's house.

At least that way, she'd be there to offer Grace some support.

"I think I'll walk along," she said as Carl started up the driveway.

He shrugged. "Suit yourself."

Grace had just diapered Daniel and put him down for a nap when she heard the back door open and close. She knew it couldn't be Anna, because she was at school. It wasn't likely to be Cleon, either, since he and Dad had a backlog of orders right now and were hard at work in Dad's shop in the barn. *It must be Mom or Martha.*

"It's me, Grace," Martha called up the stairs. "Are you up there?"

"Jah, just putting Daniel down for his morning nap."

A few minutes later, Martha entered the baby's bedroom. A worried-looking frown creased her forehead.

"What's the matter? You look upset." Grace rushed to Martha's side. "Please don't tell me there's been another attack."

"No, but there's someone downstairs, and I don't think you'll be too happy to see him."

Grace's mouth went dry and her palms grew sweaty. "Is it Gary Walker? Has he come back to Holmes County?"

Martha shook her head. "It's Anna's grandfather."

Grace squinted. "Dad?"

"The other grandfather."

"Carl Davis?"

"Jah. He pulled into our driveway as I was coming out of the barn, and he asked to see Anna."

Grace's legs wobbled, and she sank to the edge of her bed. "What did you tell him?"

"I said Anna wasn't here, that she was in school." Martha took a seat beside Grace. "Then he asked to see you, so I brought him up here." She reached for Grace's hand and gave it a gentle squeeze. "He's in the living room, waiting to speak with you."

Fear gripped Grace like a vise, and she clutched her sister's hand. "What does he want, Martha? Why, after all these months, has Carl come to Holmes County?"

"I don't know. He only said he wanted to speak with you."

Grace took a couple of deep breaths and tried to think. "What if he wants Anna back? What if he's come to make trouble?" Tears welled in her eyes, blurring her vision. "I couldn't bear to lose my little girl again."

Martha shook her head. "You're not going to lose her. You need to go down there, listen to what the man has to say, and if it's what you fear, then tell him in no uncertain terms that your daughter is staying with you."

"When Carl first brought Anna back to me, I told him I would never give her up again."

"Of course you won't. You love Anna, and she's happy here with you and Cleon." Martha patted Grace's arm. "Anna loves you. I'm sure she wouldn't want to leave, even if Carl wanted her to."

Grace drew in one more deep breath and rose to her feet. "I'd better see what he wants."

"Do you want me to go with you or wait here with Daniel?" Martha asked.

"Daniel will be okay in his crib." Grace managed a weak smile. "I'd like to have you with me for moral support."

Martha nodded. "You've got it."

When they entered the living room, Grace spotted Carl sitting on the sofa. He jumped up as soon he saw Grace and moved quickly across the room. "It's nice to see you again," he said, extending his hand.

Grace didn't want to be rude, but it was all she could do to shake Carl's hand. She motioned to the sofa. "Please, have a seat."

He sat down, and Grace and Martha took seats in the chairs across from him.

"I'm surprised to see you." Grace moistened her lips with the tip of her tongue. "I–I had no idea you were coming."

"I wrote you a letter saying I was planning to come."

Grace shook her head. "I've received no such letter."

He shrugged. "It must have gotten lost in the mail."

"How's your health?" she asked, for want of anything better to say.

"Are you feeling better than the last time you were here?"

He nodded. "My doctor discovered that I had a yeast overgrowth throughout much of my body."

"What was that caused from?" Martha asked, leaning slightly forward.

"I've had trouble with sinus infections most of my life," Carl said. "Consequently, I've taken numerous courses of antibiotics, which not only killed the bad bacteria in my body but the good ones, as well. That's how the yeast overgrowth began. But with proper diet and the right supplements, it's under control. I'm feeling much better now."

Grace was glad Carl's health had improved, but she felt concern over why he'd come. "What are you doing in Holmes County?" she asked.

"I came to see Anna. I've missed my little girl something awful."

"I missed her, too, when she was living with you and your wife and I had no idea how to find her." Grace couldn't keep the bitterness out of her voice, and she blinked several times against stinging tears.

"As I told you before, I'm sorry about that. It wasn't right for us to keep Anna from you, but all that's in the past, and it can't be undone."

"I'm sure you've missed Anna," Grace said, keeping her voice steady and low, "but I don't want my daughter seeing you and getting confused about things."

"Why would she be confused?"

"She might think you've come to take her away, and if you did—"

Carl held up his hand. "I did not come here to take Anna away."

Grace hoped Carl was telling the truth, but she couldn't be sure. "I'm sorry you came all this way, because as my sister's already told you, Anna's at school."

Carl stood. "I've checked into a hotel just outside of Sugarcreek, so I'll head there now, but I'll be back this evening to see Anna."

"This evening won't work."

"Why not?"

"I. . .uh. . .need time to prepare Anna for seeing you." Grace paused and swiped her tongue over her bottom lip. "It took her some time to adjust to living here, and—"

"Are you afraid if she sees me again, she won't want me to go or might want to go with me?"

Grace nodded, as tears stung the back of her eyes.

He took a step forward. "As I said, I haven't come to take Anna away. But I did come to see her, and I'm not leaving until I know how she's doing. So if I can't see Anna this evening, then how about tomorrow evening or Saturday?"

"You can come by on Saturday morning," Grace finally agreed.

Chapter 25

I'm going home to get some of my clothes and a few other things," Luke told John after they'd finished work for the day.

"No problem," John said. "You've got a key to the shop, so when you get back, let yourself in and you can settle into the back room."

Luke smiled. "I sure appreciate this, John."

John thumped Luke on the back. "Not a problem. I'm heading over to my place now to get a few more things you might need. If I don't see you when you get back with your clothes, I'll see you in the morning."

"Thanks." Luke headed for his truck. He hoped Pop wasn't home from work yet. The last thing he needed was another confrontation, which would probably lead to a full-blown argument. He wasn't as concerned about seeing Mom, except that she might get emotional and beg him to come home and make restitution. Why couldn't his folks allow him to go through rumschpringe the way other fellows his age did, without laying down so many rules and stipulations? Others he knew had trucks and cars. Why couldn't he?

Luke loosened his grip on the steering wheel. He needed to be calm when he arrived home.

As Grace stood at the kitchen sink, peeling potatoes for supper, she struggled to stay focused on the job at hand. For a long time after Carl had left this morning, she'd paced the floor, asking God to give her the wisdom to know how to tell Anna that her English grandfather had come for a visit. At least Grace hoped it was just for a visit. What if Carl had been lying when he'd said he hadn't come to take Anna away?

The back door opened and slammed shut. "Guess what, Mama?" Anna asked, as she burst into the kitchen. "Karen Miller's got twin baby sisters!"

"That's exciting news." Grace motioned to the umbrella stand near the door. "Put your umbrella and coat away, and then you can have some hot chocolate and cookies while you tell me about it."

"That sounds *appeditlich.*"

Grace smiled. "I think hot chocolate and cookies are always delicious."

A short time later, they sat at the table, each holding a cup of hot chocolate with a plate of cookies between them.

Between bites of cookie and slurps of hot chocolate, Anna told Grace about Karen's news and that her parents had named the babies Lorine and Corine. When Anna finished her story, she turned to Grace and said, "I wish I had somethin' exciting to share with the kinner at school."

"Are you hoping another *boppli* will be added to our family?" Grace asked.

Anna shook her head. "Not unless it can be a baby sister this time."

Grace chuckled and patted Anna's hand. "If and when I have another boppli, it will be up to God to decide whether it'll be a buwe or a maedel."

Anna nodded and reached for another cookie. "Where's Daniel? How come he's not eatin' cookies with us?"

"Your little bruder was fussy most of the afternoon, so I put him down for a nap about an hour ago. He's still sleeping."

Anna's eyebrows drew together. "I'm glad I don't have to take naps anymore. When I was livin' with Poppy and Grandma Davis, I had to take a nap every day."

Grace flinched. Should she tell Anna about Carl having been here earlier today? She'd wanted to discuss things with Cleon first and had hoped he would help her decide the best way to tell Anna. She'd gone out to the barn to speak with him earlier, but Dad had said Cleon was out making some deliveries.

Maybe I should tell Anna now. Grace opened her mouth, but a shrill cry coming from upstairs halted her words.

"Daniel's awake," Anna announced.

"You finish your cookies, and I'll go get him," Grace said with a nod. Maybe it was better that she hadn't said anything yet. It might be best to wait and talk to Cleon first.

Martha had just started down the road after leaving her job at the Schrocks' house, when a truck passed, going in the opposite direction. She thought she recognized the driver, and when he rolled down the window and motioned her to pull over, she knew it was Luke.

Martha guided her horse and buggy to the side of the road and waited for Luke to turn his truck around and park behind her. When he stepped up to the driver's side of her buggy, she opened the door.

"I'm glad to see you," he said breathlessly. "Something happened today, and I wanted to let you know."

"It's starting to rain," she said. "Why don't you get in and tell me about it?"

Luke climbed into the buggy as soon as Martha slid to the passenger's side. "I moved out of my folks' house this morning," he said.

Martha's mouth dropped open. "Why?"

"I had a disagreement with my daed because I got home late last night." Luke grunted. "He said if I didn't sell my truck and join the church, I'd have to move out."

"But that's lecherich. A lot of Amish fellows going through rumschpringe have cars or trucks."

Luke nodded. "It might seem ridiculous to you and me, but not to Pop. He's got old-fashioned ideas, and he's been after me to sell my truck ever since he found out I had one and kept it hidden in the woods." He grunted again. "I wish Toby hadn't told them I had it."

Martha's heart went out to Luke. She could see by the droop of his shoulders and the pinched look on his face that he was grieving over this conflict with his folks. "What are you going to do now? Have you found another place to stay?"

"Jah. John said I could sleep in the back room of his shop until I find something more permanent." He motioned to his truck. "I just came from my house, where I picked up my clothes and few personal items. Thankfully, my folks weren't at home, or I'm sure we'd have ended up in another disagreement."

She touched his arm. "I'm sorry, Luke."

"Maybe it's for the best," he said with a shrug. "Living away from home without Pop watching my every move will give me a better chance to play detective."

"I suppose. Even so–"

"What's new with you?" he asked, changing the subject. "Have you found any more clues or done more investigating?"

She shook her head. "Not really, although I did see our neighbor, Ray Larson, looking over at our place this morning with his binoculars."

Luke's eyes narrowed. "Any idea why?"

"I went over there and asked. He said he was looking for some unusual bird he'd seen earlier."

"Did you believe him?"

"I guess so." Martha shivered, as a gust of wind blew in through the cracks around the opening of the buggy flap. "I know it's ridiculous, but I'm starting to think everyone I know is a suspect."

"Does that include me?"

She shook her head. "No, Luke. Not anymore."

Luke reached for Martha's hand. "It's nice to know at least one member of the Hostettler family believes I'm innocent. I just wish I could prove it to everyone else."

Chapter 26

Grace had just cleared their breakfast dishes from the table and was about to run some water into the sink, when a knock sounded on the back door. Her heart gave a lurch. Could that be Carl? He'd said he would return on Saturday, but she hadn't expected it would be this early or that she would feel so unprepared.

Thursday night, after Anna had gone to bed, Grace had told Cleon about Carl's visit. Cleon hadn't seemed too upset by the news. He'd even said he thought it might be good for Anna to spend some time with her English grandpa, since they had once been so close. Grace wasn't sure about that. She was still worried that even if Carl hadn't come to take Anna way, the child might want to go with him.

Grace had waited until last night to tell Anna about her grandfather's visit, when the child was preparing for bed. Anna had been so excited about the prospect of seeing her poppy that it had been hard for her to fall asleep. Grace half expected to find Anna up at the crack of dawn this morning, but Anna had slept longer than usual and had come down to breakfast still wearing her nightgown. Now the child was upstairs in her room getting dressed.

Another knock sounded at the door, a little louder this time. With a sigh, Grace went to answer it, wishing Cleon was here, but he'd gone to check on his bee boxes as soon as he'd finished breakfast.

When Grace opened the door a few seconds later, she found Carl standing on the porch holding a vinyl doll with bright red hair in his hands. "This is for Anna," he said. "She is here, I hope."

"She's upstairs getting dressed. We. . .uh. . .didn't expect you so soon." Grace opened the door wider. "If you'd like to wait for Anna in the kitchen, I'm sure she'll be down soon."

Carl seated himself at the table, and a few minutes later, Anna bounded into the room. "Poppy! You're really here!" She threw herself into his arms.

"Oh, I've missed you, Anna girl." He nuzzled her head with his chin. "But I hardly recognized you in those plain clothes."

"I dress Amish now." Anna kissed his cheek. "You look the same, only better."

"Why don't we go into the living room and sit down?" Grace suggested. "I think it will be easier for us to visit there."

Holding her grandfather's hand, Anna led the way. Grace followed. When they entered the living room, Grace took a seat in the rocking chair, and Carl sat on the sofa with Anna in his lap.

"Can you stay and visit all day, Poppy?" Anna gazed up at Carl with a look of adoration.

"I'd like to, Anna, but I have an appointment this afternoon."

Anna's lower lip protruded. "You're goin' home?"

He shook his head. "I'm going to see about renting a house in Berlin."

"Why would you need to rent a house if you're only here for a visit?" Grace asked.

"I'm thinking about moving here so I can be closer to Anna."

Grace's hands turned cold and clammy. Things were complicated enough in her life; she didn't need Carl moving to Holmes County and complicating them further.

"If you move to Berlin, I can see you all the time," Anna said excitedly. "Berlin's not far from here. Right, Mama?"

Grace opened her mouth to respond, but Daniel's shrill cry halted her words. "I need to tend to the baby," she said, looking at Carl.

"I didn't realize you had a baby."

"His name's Daniel, and he's my little brother," Anna answered for Grace. "Daniel still cries and wets his *windle* a lot."

Carl quirked an eyebrow as he looked back at Grace.

"Windle means diapers," she explained.

"Oh, I see."

Grace stood and held out her hand to Anna. "Why don't you come upstairs with me while I see about Daniel?"

Anna shook her head. "I wanna stay here with Poppy."

Grace struggled with the need to tend Daniel or remain in the living room. *What if Carl takes Anna while I'm upstairs? He has a car. He could get away quickly, and there wouldn't be a thing I could do about it.*

As if Carl could read her mind, he smiled and said, "Anna will be fine; I promise."

Daniel let out another ear-piercing scream, and Grace bolted for the stairs. She'd only gotten halfway up when someone knocked on the front door. Turning back around, she went to see who it was.

Rosemary lifted her hand to knock on Grace's door for the third time, when the door suddenly swung open. Grace stood there with a panicked expression on her face.

"Is everything all right?" Rosemary asked, feeling immediate concern.

Grace touched her flushed cheeks. "Daniel's crying, and I need to go to him. But I've got company in the living room."

"Would you like me to entertain your company while you take care of Daniel?"

"I'd appreciate that." Grace led Rosemary into the living room, where a middle-aged man sat on the sofa with Anna in his lap. "Carl, this is my aunt Rosemary." She looked at Rosemary then nodded at Carl. "This is Anna's grandfather, Carl Davis."

"It's nice to meet you," Rosemary and Carl said in unison.

Daniel's howling increased, and Grace excused herself, leaving Rosemary alone with Carl and Anna. She took a seat in the chair opposite them.

"Do you live around here?" Carl asked.

"I'm Roman Hostettler's sister. I grew up in Holmes County but moved away when I was a young woman. I married an English man, and we moved to Idaho." She paused a moment to see if he would comment, but when he said nothing, she continued. "My husband died several months ago, so I came home to see my family."

"So you're just here for a visit?"

"No, I've recently purchased a house nearby. Where are you from?"

"I've been living in Nevada for the last several years, and I'm also widowed."

"Poppy came here to see me," Anna put in.

Rosemary smiled at the exuberance she saw on the child's face. Anna was obviously happy to see her English grandfather.

"Anna's mother was married to my son, Wade, at one time," Carl said. "Wade was killed in a car accident when Anna was a baby."

"Yes, I know about that."

Carl looked like he was about to say something more when Grace returned to the room, carrying Daniel.

"Can I hold him?" Rosemary asked.

Grace nodded and handed the little boy to Rosemary.

Rosemary rubbed her chin along the top of Daniel's downy head as she breathed in the sweet smell of him. Oh, how she wished she could have had more than one child, but she was grateful God had given her Ken.

"I hate to cut this visit short," Carl said looking at his watch, "but I'm supposed to meet a Realtor in Berlin in half an hour, and I don't want to be late." He placed Anna on the sofa and stood.

With a panicked expression, Anna grabbed his hand. "Please, Poppy, don't go away again!"

He bent down and gave her a hug. "I'm going to look at a house, but I'll be back to see you soon."

"You promise?"

"Yes, I promise."

Anna clung to Carl's hand as she walked him to the door. Grace followed.

When Grace and Anna returned to the living room, Grace nodded at Anna and said, "Why don't you take Daniel to the kitchen and see if you can find some cookies for the two of you?"

"I don't want any cookies. I want Poppy," Anna said tearfully.

"He said he'd come back soon."

Anna sniffed and swiped at her tearstained cheeks. "What if he doesn't? What if he goes away like he did before?"

Feeling the need to offer Grace some support, Rosemary jumped in. "Anna, your grandfather said he was going to look at a house to rent in Berlin. If he wasn't going to stay awhile, do you think he would do that?"

"I. . .I guess not."

Rosemary set Daniel on the floor and pulled Anna into her arms. "Your grandpa will be back soon, just like he promised." She gave the child's back a little pat. "Now take your brother into the kitchen like your mama said and find some cookies to eat."

"Okay." Anna grabbed Daniel's hand and scooted out of the room.

Grace released an audible sigh and collapsed onto the sofa.

Rosemary took a seat beside her. "You're not happy about Anna's grandpa coming to Holmes County, are you?"

Grace's eyes filled with tears. "I'm afraid he might try to take her again."

"Would he be renting a house in Berlin if kidnapping was on his mind?"

"I. . .I guess not."

"I think Carl Davis has plans to stay in Holmes County so he can be closer to Anna." Rosemary took Grace's hand and gave it a gentle squeeze. "The best thing you can do is try to relax and leave this in God's hands."

"It won't be easy," Grace said with a slow nod, "but I'll try."

Martha left Spector's store in Berlin, where she had gone to buy material for a new dress, and headed across the parking lot to the hitching rail. She'd only taken a few steps, when she halted. Her horse and buggy were missing!

"What in all the world?" She gritted her teeth and tried to think. She was sure she'd tied her horse near the end of the hitching rail.

She looked around helplessly, but the horse and buggy were nowhere in sight. Could this be another attack or just a prank some kids had decided to play? Were other buggies missing, or had only hers been targeted?

With heart pounding and palms sweaty, Martha ran around to the front of the building, calling her horse's name. No sign of Gid or the buggy, either. She looked up and down the main street but saw nothing out of the ordinary.

Should I call the sheriff or maybe Aunt Rosemary? Yes, I'll use the phone at Spector's; Aunt Rosemary will know what to do.

Martha dashed back to Spector's and had just reached the parking lot when she spotted Luke and John getting out of John's SUV. Luke waved at her, and as the two men started across the parking lot, Martha rushed up to them. "My horse and buggy are missing!"

Luke looked at her as if she'd lost her mind. "How could they be missing?"

"I don't know, but they are." Martha pointed across the parking lot. "I tied Gid to the hitching rail before I went into Spector's. When I came out again, Gid and my buggy were gone."

"Maybe you didn't tie the horse securely enough," John said.

"Yes, I did; I'm sure of it."

"Then he probably got restless and broke loose," John said.

"Or else someone untied the horse and let him go free," Luke put in. "That has been known to happen on occasion."

"What am I going to do?" Martha transferred her package from one hand to the other. "My horse could be most anywhere by now."

"If he broke free and no one's driving him, then he's probably headed for home," Luke said.

Hope welled in Martha's chest. "Do you think so?"

"Makes sense to me."

"I agree with Luke," John said with a nod. "Let's get in my rig and look for your horse and buggy."

Chapter 27

There they are, Luke! There's my horse and buggy!" Martha shouted as they headed out of Berlin in John's SUV.

"Can you tell if there's a driver in the buggy?" John asked, craning his neck.

"Doesn't look like it," Luke hollered.

Martha's heart pounded like a blacksmith's anvil. Gid ran wild, and the buggy swayed precariously. What if her horse veered into oncoming traffic and caused an accident? What if—

"Oh no, the buggy's going over!" Luke shouted.

Martha gasped as she watched her buggy topple onto its side. Gid continued to trot, dragging the buggy along.

John pulled his rig to the side of the road. They all jumped out and ran down the road after the runaway horse and buggy. About fifty feet beyond where the buggy had fallen over, Luke grabbed the horse's reins and got him stopped.

"Is Gid hurt?" Martha panted as she caught up to them.

"Doesn't seem to be," John said. "But I don't know about your buggy."

"Let's get it up and assess the damage." Luke handed the reins to Martha, and he and John set the buggy upright.

Martha breathed a sigh of relief when she saw that the only real damage was to the mirrors and blinkers on the right side, which had both been smashed.

"The rig should be okay to drive if you think you're up to driving it,"

John said to Martha.

She nodded slowly, although her hands shook so badly she wasn't sure she could hold the reins.

"I'll ride with Martha and drive the horse." Luke turned to John and said, "If you don't mind following so you can give me a ride back to your shop, that is."

John nodded. "Sure. No problem."

Martha smiled. "I appreciate you both helping me get home."

Roman was heading up to the house to see if Judith had supper started, when he spotted Martha's horse and buggy pulling into the yard. To his surprise, Luke was in the driver's seat, and Martha sat beside him. The horse was lathered up, and he noticed that the mirror and right blinker on the buggy had been smashed.

Roman rushed toward the buggy just as John Peterson's SUV came up the driveway. "What's going on?" he called as Luke stepped down from the buggy. "What happened to my daughter's rig, and why are you driving it instead of her?"

Martha scrambled out of the buggy, holding a package. She spoke before Luke could respond. "Gid broke free when I was at Spector's, and Luke and John helped me track him down." She motioned to the sweaty horse. "When we spotted him on the road a short ways out of town, he was running wild, and the buggy was being whipped from side to side."

"When the buggy flipped over," Luke added, "the horse dragged it a ways before we got him stopped."

Roman looked over at John, wondering if he would agree with what Luke had said.

John nodded. "It's true. It happened just the way Luke said."

"If I hadn't run into Luke and John in Spector's parking lot and if they hadn't offered to help me look for the horse, I don't know what would have happened." Martha looked over at Luke with a strange expression. Was it merely gratitude, or was there something else? Could Martha have a romantic interest in Luke?

Roman massaged his temples, hoping to clear his thinking. No, she was just reacting to the frightening situation; that had to be it. He looked first at John and then at Luke. "I. . .uh. . .appreciate you coming to the aid of my daughter."

"No problem," John said. "We were happy to do it."

"I'm just glad Martha and her horse and buggy are okay," Luke added, as he shuffled his feet a few times.

Martha took a step closer to Luke. There was that look again. Was it more than gratitude Roman saw on his daughter's face?

"You'd better get in the house and see about helping your mamm with supper," he said, nudging Martha's arm. "I'll put Gid in the barn and rub him down." He smiled at John and gave Luke a quick nod. "Again, I appreciate what you did."

"See you, John. See you, Luke." Martha gave Luke another smile and scurried into the house.

As Luke and John climbed into John's rig and drove away, Roman headed to the barn with the horse. *I sure hope Luke has no designs on my daughter. If he does, he's got a big surprise coming.*

Grace yawned and leaned her head against the back of the sofa. She was glad to have both children tucked into bed. Now maybe she and Cleon could have some time alone. They needed to talk. Ever since Carl's visit earlier today, she'd been a ball of nerves. What if Carl rented a house in Berlin and decided to stay in the area permanently? Would he want to see Anna all the time? What kind of influence would he have on the child? Grace feared that Anna might become dissatisfied with the Amish way of life if she spent too much time with Carl. What if, despite Carl's promise, he tried to take Anna away?

"Are you feeling okay tonight?" Cleon asked as he took a seat beside Grace. "You look all done in."

"I am awfully tired," she admitted. "It's been a very long day."

"Was Daniel fussy?"

"Jah. He's cutting another tooth." She released a sigh. "And then there's the problem with Anna."

"What problem is that?"

"When I tucked her in bed, all she could talk about was her poppy and how she couldn't wait to see him again." She drew in a shuddering breath. "Oh, Cleon, what if he tries to influence her against the Amish ways?"

"Did he say anything that might make you think he would do that?"

Grace shook her head. "No, but I don't trust him. He and his wife took Anna from me once. I won't give him the opportunity to do it again."

"From what you've told me, taking Anna and not leaving an address or phone number where you could reach them was mostly his wife's doing."

"That's true. Even so—"

Cleon reached for her hand. "Anna is the man's only grandchild. Do you think it's fair to deprive her of spending time with him?"

Grace clenched her teeth so hard her jaw ached. "Do you want Anna to go away?"

Cleon's furrowed brow and the squint of his eyes let Grace know she'd said too much. "How can you even say such a thing? Of course I don't want Anna to go away."

"Are you sure? I mean, it wasn't too long ago that you and she didn't get along so well."

"Things are fine with me and Anna now; you know that. I love that little girl as if she were my own."

Tears clouded Grace's vision. "Maybe I'm being overly sensitive. I'm probably overreacting to Carl's visit earlier today."

"Maybe you're trying too hard to protect Anna."

Heat flooded Grace's cheeks, and she sat up straight. "If caring about my daughter and seeing that she's safe is being overly protective, then so be it."

Cleon grunted. "This isn't getting us anywhere, Grace, and I don't want to argue."

"Neither do I."

"Then let's make a compromise."

"What kind of compromise?"

"Anna can spend time with Carl, but only when you, me, or someone from your family is with them. He can take her shopping or out to lunch, but someone from the family will accompany them." Cleon gently stroked her shoulder. "He's also welcome to come here to visit Anna. Agreed?"

She nodded slowly. "Jah, okay."

Chapter 28

Rosemary groaned as she bent to pull a clump of weeds from a flower bed near her house. This was the second week of March, and spring was on its way. So was a backache if she didn't take it a bit easier. She smiled, despite the knot that was beginning to form in her lower back. It felt good to be back in her home state, living close to Roman and his family. Ken and Sharon were getting along fine on their own, and in Ken's last letter, he'd said they were planning to build a new house in a few months.

A cool breeze rustled through the trees, and Rosemary turned her thoughts back to the weather. Now that the snow was gone, she planned to take a day sometime soon and drive up to Geauga County to see where Walt and his family lived.

Rosemary straightened when she heard a car pull into the driveway and was surprised when a middle-aged man with thinning hair got out and came up the sidewalk. She realized it was Carl Davis.

"Remember me?" he asked, stepping up to her.

"I remember, Carl. We met at Grace's."

He smiled and nodded. "I was driving down the road and spotted you standing in your yard, so I decided to stop and say hello, since we're almost neighbors."

Rosemary tipped her head. "Oh?"

"I'm renting a house about a mile from here."

"You're planning to stay in Holmes County then?"

He nodded. "Anna's my only granddaughter. I want to be close to her."

Rosemary's jaw clenched. She knew how Grace felt about Carl showing up out of the blue. She also knew Grace was afraid he might try to take Anna away from her again. But if Carl planned to stay in the area, then it wasn't likely he had kidnapping on his mind.

He shifted from one foot to the other. "I don't know how much Grace has told you about my wife and me taking Anna away from her, but–"

"You owe me no explanations," Rosemary said with a raised hand.

"I know I don't, but I was hoping once you heard my story you might be willing to talk to Grace for me–smooth the way, if you will."

Irritation welled in Rosemary's soul. "Look, Mr. Davis, I barely know you, and I really don't think–"

"Won't you please hear me out?"

She motioned to the porch. "Shall we have a seat?"

Carl stepped onto the porch and lowered himself into one of the wicker chairs near the front door. Rosemary took the seat beside him.

"I never meant to hurt Grace by taking Anna," he said. "My wife convinced me that it was the best thing for the child." He clasped his hands around his knees and grimaced. "She said we'd be doing Grace a favor by removing the burden of raising a child without a father."

"Did you think to offer your son's widow a home, too?"

Carl dropped his gaze to the porch as he slowly shook his head.

"Why not?"

"Bonnie convinced me that Grace was an unfit mother and our son had told her that if something happened to him, he wanted us to raise Anna." He lifted his gaze to meet hers. "My wife was a very controlling woman. In order to keep the peace, I went along with most everything she wanted."

Rosemary swallowed hard. She could relate to Carl's last statement. She'd done many things during the time she'd been married to Bob in order to keep the peace. She knew well what it was like to be married to a control freak.

"Shortly after my wife died, I decided that Anna would be better off with her mother. I was having some health problems and didn't think I could care for the child on my own." Carl sucked in his bottom lip and released it again. "After my meeting with Grace the other day, I realized she felt threatened by my showing up and wanting to see Anna."

"That's understandable, don't you think?"

He nodded. "She has no reason to feel threatened. I'm not here to take Anna away. I just want to be close to my granddaughter. My health has improved, and I want to be able to do all the things for Anna that a grandparent should do."

"I understand."

"Do you really?"

"I believe so."

"Will you speak to Grace on my behalf? Will you assure her that I'm not here to make trouble for her or take Anna away?"

"I'll act as a go-between if necessary, but I think you should talk to Grace yourself and tell her what you've told me."

"Yes, yes, I'll do that."

"Grace and her family have been through enough with the attacks against them. Grace doesn't need anything else to stress about."

Carl's eyebrows pulled together. "Attacks? What kind of attacks are you talking about?"

"I figured Grace had probably written and told you."

Carl shook his head. "She only responded to a couple of my letters after I brought Anna to her, and she never mentioned any attacks having been made on her family." He leaned slightly forward, as deep creases formed in his forehead. "Can you tell me what happened?"

Rosemary cleared her throat a couple of times as she tried to formulate a proper response. How much should she share with this man she barely knew? If she told him the details of the attacks and he became concerned for Anna's safety, he might change his mind and try to take Anna away after all.

"For the last two years, my brother and his family have been the victims of some acts of vandalism," she began. "They don't know who did the attacks or why."

"What kinds of things have been done?"

"Break-ins, tools stolen, clothes cut in two, a fire started at Grace and Cleon's place, and–"

"Their house was set on fire?"

Rosemary nodded and drew in a deep breath. "Grace's sister Ruth and her first husband, Martin, also had their buggy rammed off the road, and Martin was killed in the accident. Of course we aren't sure the accident was related to the other attacks."

Carl's face blanched as he rose to his feet. "Grace should have told me about this! Anna's life could be in danger. It's my duty as her grandfather to see that she's protected from potential danger." Without another word, he rushed off the porch, climbed into his car, and sped down the driveway.

Rosemary gripped the armrests on her chair. "Oh, Lord, what have I done?"

"Cleon, what are you doing?" Grace asked when she entered the kitchen and spotted him sitting at the table with a pen and piece of paper. "I figured you had left for work by now."

"I'll be heading out soon. I wanted to make a list of some supplies I need for my beekeeping business first. I've thought about building a small shop near the front of our property, where I can sell honey and beeswax candles, but as long as your daed needs my help in his woodworking shop, I probably won't follow through with the idea."

Grace pulled out a chair and took a seat beside him. "If you really want to quit working for Dad and go out on your own, I'm sure he could find someone else to take your place in his shop."

Cleon shook his head. "I don't want to leave him in the lurch right now. He's been through enough with having to deal with all the attacks."

Grace shuddered. "That land developer is back in the area, you know, and he's after Dad to sell."

"That's about as likely to happen as one of Martha's hundlin giving birth to a baby bee." Cleon pushed away from the table and bent to give Grace a hug. "If there are any problems today, come out to the barn and get me, okay?"

"I will."

Cleon started for the door but turned back around. "I mean it, Grace. If you need me, I'll come."

Grace forced a smile. "I'm sure everything will be fine."

When Cleon headed out the door, Grace went upstairs. She found Anna sitting on the floor in her room, playing with the doll Carl had given her. "Why aren't you dressed yet?" she asked. "Have you forgotten that you have school today?"

Anna dropped the doll and scrambled to her feet just as a shrill scream came from across the hall.

"I'd better tend to your bruder," Grace said, hurrying from the room.

A short time later, Grace had Daniel in his high chair, and Anna was seated at the table eating breakfast.

"When's Poppy coming to see me again?" Anna asked.

Grace shrugged and reached for a piece of toast.

"I hope he comes soon."

Grace made no comment, thinking Anna might change the subject if she didn't answer her question.

"I can't wait 'til school lets out for the summer," Anna continued. "Then I'll be able to see Poppy a lot. He's gonna move here, isn't he, Mama?"

"Maybe." Grace pointed to Anna's plate. "Finish eating and then clear your dishes. You don't want to be late for school."

Much to Grace's relief, Anna ate the rest of her breakfast in silence. When she finished, she put her dishes in the sink and grabbed her lunch pail off the counter. With a cheery smile, she said, "See you after school, Mama," and skipped out the door.

Grace had just started cleaning scrambled eggs off Daniel's face when she heard a car pull into the driveway. She finished up with Daniel, scooped him out of his chair, and headed for the door. When she opened it, she found Carl sitting in one of the wicker chairs, with Anna in his lap.

"What are you doing here, Carl?" Grace asked as she stepped onto the porch and took a seat in the chair beside him, placing Daniel in her lap.

"Poppy wants me to see his new house," Anna said, her blue eyes twinkling like fireflies, and her lips curving upwards. "Can I go there now?"

Grace shook her head.

"How come?"

"Because you have to go to school, and if you don't leave now, you're going to be late. Aunt Martha's planning to give you a ride, and I'm sure she's waiting down by the barn with her horse and buggy by now."

"Can I go with Poppy after school?"

"No."

Anna opened her mouth as if to say more, but Carl spoke first. "Anna, why don't you run on now? I'll come again soon, and then we can talk some more."

Anna hesitated a moment but finally gave Carl a hug and headed down the driveway toward the barn.

Carl turned to face Grace. "We need to talk."

"About what?"

"About the attacks that have been made against your family and about the safety of my granddaughter."

"Who told you about the attacks?"

"It doesn't matter who told. What matters is that Anna might not be safe living here."

Grace's face heated up. "Are you saying my husband and I aren't capable of protecting our daughter?"

Carl squinted. "*Your* daughter, Grace. Anna's your daughter and *my* granddaughter, and I won't stand by and watch her be victimized by some lunatic who's determined to hurt your family. Therefore, I'd like Anna to move in with me for a while."

Her mouth dropped open. "What?"

"I'd like Anna to move in with me. Just until the attacker has been caught and I know it's safe for her to come back here."

"Absolutely not! Anna is not moving in with you!"

"I'll be back to see Anna sometime soon." Carl reached into his pocket and pulled out a slip of paper. "Here's my new address and also my cell phone number, so if you change your mind about Anna moving in with me, bring her over or give me a call."

As Martha headed for town, a strange feeling came over her, as though something was wrong. Was it the way Gid pulled against the reins when she tried to make him run, or was it the absence of cars on the road that made her feel so odd? Usually at this time of the morning, several cars would be heading toward Berlin. Today, however, her horse and buggy seemed to be the only things moving on this stretch of road.

"Giddyap there, boy." Martha flicked the reins. "I thought you liked to trot."

The gelding whinnied and flipped his head from side to side.

"What's wrong with you, Gid? Are you getting old and lazy?" She snapped the reins again and was shocked when they broke in two. Gid bolted down the road as the buggy, now out of Martha's control, bounced and swayed behind him.

"Whoa! Hold up there!" she hollered.

The horse kept running, and all Martha could do was grip the edge of her seat and hope he would decide to stop before they ran off the road or were hit by some other vehicle.

She spotted a truck coming down the hill and said a prayer out loud. "Dear God, don't let Gid drag this buggy to the other side of the road."

"I've got to stop that horse!" Luke whipped his truck into the other lane and pulled ahead of Martha's horse. When he slowed his truck, the horse halted. A sense of relief shot through him as he shut off the engine and hopped out of the truck. He sprinted around and grabbed the horse's broken reins. "Are you okay?" he called to Martha.

"I'm fine. Shaken up a bit, but not hurt." She jumped down from the buggy and started toward him. "The horse's reins broke, and–"

"They didn't break, Martha. From what I can tell, they were cut."

Martha's eyes widened, and she gasped. "No wonder Gid was acting so skittish when I smacked the reins and tried to make him trot."

"Have you got any rope?"

"I think there's some in the buggy." Martha scurried around to the back of the buggy and returned a few minutes later with a piece of paper in her hands.

"Where's the rope?" Luke asked as she approached him.

"There wasn't any. I found this lying on the floor where the rope should have been."

Holding on to the horse, Luke took a step toward her. "What is it?"

"It's a note. I. . .I think it was written by the person who's been attacking my family."

"What's it say?"

"Someone needs to pay." Martha's voice quivered. "Oh, Luke, just when we think this nightmare might finally be over–just when my hopes begin to rise–something else happens to let us know that the attacker isn't done with us yet, and the hope I felt sinks like a rock thrown into the pond." She drew in a deep breath. "Someone cut Gid's reins, and if you hadn't happened along when you did and gotten the horse stopped. . ." Her voice faltered.

Luke let go of the broken reins and pulled Martha into his arms. His insides twisted with the thought of what could have happened to Martha. "I'm concerned for your safety," he said, gently patting her back.

Martha opened her mouth as if to say something, but Luke spoke again. "Are you going to tell your daed about this?"

"About the note or the cut reins?"

"Both."

She shrugged. "I suppose he needs to know about the reins, but I'm afraid to mention the note–at least not in front of my mamm."

"How come?"

"It'll upset her too much. She tries to hide it, but she's been a ball of nerves since the last few attacks."

"Then do whatever you think's best. Maybe you can talk to your daed about this when your mamm's not around." Luke motioned to Gid. "If you don't mind leaving your horse and buggy here, I'll drive you over to Abe's harness shop and we'll see about getting some new reins."

"Danki. I appreciate your help with this."

Luke struggled with the desire to kiss Martha, but a van came by just then, so he pulled away. The last thing he needed was for someone they knew to see them hugging or kissing. That kind of news would probably get back to Roman, and then both he and Martha would be in trouble. He gave her arm a gentle squeeze. "Let's go, shall we?"

Chapter 29

As Martha sat at the supper table, she thought about the events of the day: discovering her horse's reins had been cut, the note she'd found in the back of the buggy, the concern Luke had shown her today. She didn't see how anyone could think he had anything to do with the attacks. Luke was trying to help her find out who was behind them, and the handwriting on the note had obviously not been his. Besides, what opportunity would he have had to cut the reins, and for what reason? She knew she needed to tell Dad about this but wasn't sure what to do about Mom.

"You're looking very thoughtful there," Mom said, nudging Martha's arm. "You've hardly touched your chicken potpie."

"I'm not so hungry tonight. I've got a lot on my mind."

Dad grunted. "More than likely you're thinking about Luke Friesen. Probably wishing he'd give you another hug."

Martha's mouth dropped open, and Mom let out a gasp. "Roman, what are you saying?"

Dad picked up his spoon and gave his coffee a couple of stirs. "Toby King came by to see me today, and he had some story to tell."

"What story is that?" Mom asked.

"Said he'd been riding with Howard Kemper in his van and saw Luke and Martha standing beside her buggy. They were locked in each other's arms."

Martha nearly jumped out of her chair. "Dad, it wasn't like that. I can explain–"

"I should hope so!" Dad's face turned as red as an apple. "I'd like you to tell me and your mamm what you were doing with Luke today, and why you had your arms around each other."

"My horse's reins broke, and Luke offered to drive me over to Abe's place and get a new set of reins." She would explain that the reins were cut later, when she could talk to Dad alone.

"Did you ride in Luke's truck?"

Martha's heart started to pound. "You know about his truck?"

Dad's fist came down hard on the table, jostling the silverware and nearly knocking over his glass of water. "I know all about Luke's truck! Toby filled me in on that bit of information, too."

Martha reached for her glass of water and took a drink. Her mouth felt so dry she could barely swallow. If Toby had told Dad about Luke's truck and said he'd seen the two of them hugging, then that must have been him riding in the vehicle that had passed when she and Luke had been talking beside her buggy. And if Toby had felt the need to blab that to Dad, then he really must have something against Luke.

"Have you and Luke been courting behind our backs?" Mom's question drove Martha's thoughts aside.

Martha wasn't sure how to respond. Even though she and Luke weren't officially courting, they had gone a few places together. He'd also said he wished they could court. She gulped down some more water. "No, we're. . .uh. . .not courting."

"Then why was he hugging you?" Dad asked.

"We weren't really hugging. Luke was trying to comfort me."

"Comfort you?" Mom's eyebrows furrowed. "Why did you need comforting, Martha?"

"Because I was upset about my horse's reins having been cut," Martha blurted out.

"What?" Mom and Dad said in unison.

"I thought at first they were just broken, but Luke's the one who discovered they'd actually been cut, and then—" Martha saw Mom's hands begin to shake, and she caught herself in time before blurting out the part about the note she'd found in the back of her buggy.

"Ach, Martha," Mom said shakily. "You could have been hurt."

"We'll talk about the reins being cut later," Dad said, staring hard at Martha. "Right now I'd like to deal with the issue of Luke having his hands all over you."

Martha shook her head vigorously. "He didn't, Dad. Luke was just—"

Dad slammed his fist on the table again. "I will not allow it to happen a second time! I forbid you to see Luke again!"

Martha's eyes filled with tears as she pushed back her chair and rushed from the room.

Judith released a shuddering sigh. "Ach, Roman. Why'd you say such a thing to our daughter? Can't you see how much it hurt her?"

"I don't care if it did. She shouldn't be sneaking around and meeting up with Luke behind our backs." Roman grunted. "Hugging him right there on the side of the road where everyone could see. What was that girl thinking?"

"Maybe it's the way she said. Luke might have just given her a hug to comfort her."

"Over some broken reins?"

"They weren't broken. You heard what Martha said." Judith paused and drew in a quick breath. "Those reins were deliberately cut, Roman. It was another attack."

He grabbed his glass of water and took a drink. "I doubt Martha was upset enough to need the kind of comforting Luke was offering. I think Luke just used it as an opportunity to put our daughter in a compromising position and make her look bad."

"Why would he do that?"

"For the same reason he's been doing all those horrible things to us. He's trying to get even with me for firing him."

"Please don't start with that again, Roman." She touched his arm. "I thought you'd decided the land developer was probably behind the attacks."

"I said it *could* be the land developer, but I have no proof."

"We never will know for sure who's responsible until the sheriff catches him."

"Jah, right! Like Sheriff Osborn's going to camp out on our property and wait for someone to pull another prank."

"They aren't pranks, Roman. Whoever's behind the attacks is out for more than a good time."

"You're right about that." He scratched the side of his head. "Fact is, I've been thinking and praying about this a lot lately."

"Will you speak to the sheriff again and see if he has any leads?"

He shook his head. "I'm thinking I might do a little investigating on my own."

Her eyebrows lifted high on her forehead. "What kind of investigating?"

"I haven't come up with a plan yet, but when I do, you'll be the first to know. In the meantime, I've got other things that need to be done. I talked with Cleon this morning, and we've decided to get started on my new shop, hopefully in the next week or so."

"Will you have a work frolic then?"

He nodded. "Probably so. It'll be good to be in my own shop again. I've had about as much of working in that smelly barn with Martha's yappy dogs as I can take."

"I hope Poppy comes over to see me soon," Anna said as she swirled her noodles around on her plate with a fork. "I wanna show him Papa's bees."

"You know you're not to go near my bee boxes," Cleon said with a shake of his head. "I've told you before that you might get stung."

Anna's lower lip protruded. "I never get to have any fun."

"There's nothing fun about seeing my bee boxes."

"Then how come you go out there all the time, Papa?"

"Because I have things that need to be done."

"What kind of things?"

"I have to check on the honeycombs, and when the time is right, I extract the honey."

Anna smacked her lips. "I love peanut butter and honey sandwiches. Sure wish we could've had that for supper tonight."

"You had a peanut butter and honey sandwich for lunch," Grace reminded the child.

"I could eat another one now. It might help me not miss Poppy so much."

Cleon reached over and patted Anna's hand. "He's going to be renting a place near Berlin, and that's not far away, Anna. I'm sure you'll be able to see him a lot this summer when you're out of school. Maybe your mamm will take you to see his new house sometime later this week."

Anna's face lit up. "How about tomorrow after school?"

"We can talk about that later," Grace said.

Cleon turned to face Anna. "In the meantime, you need to finish eating your supper."

Anna's forehead wrinkled. "Daniel don't have to eat his supper."

Grace glanced over at her son, sitting in the high chair next to the table. "That's because he's already eaten. I fed him earlier, remember?"

"Then how comes he's sittin' in his chair with a cracker and a cup of milk?"

"So he can feel like part of the family and be near us," Cleon answered.

They ate in silence for the rest of the meal. Grace hoped Anna would be willing to take Daniel into the living room to play after supper, because she needed to talk to Cleon and tell him what had happened when Carl had shown up this morning saying Anna wasn't safe living with them.

"It's later now," Anna said. "Will you take me to see Poppy tomorrow after school?"

"I don't think so." Grace gritted her teeth. *I wish Wade's dad hadn't come back to Holmes County. I wish he would stay out of Anna's life.*

"How come?" Anna persisted.

"I've got too much to do tomorrow."

Anna gave Cleon an imploring look. "Will you drive me to Berlin so I can see Poppy?"

"Your daed will be working tomorrow afternoon," Grace said.

Anna bumped the tray on Daniel's high chair, and Daniel let out an ear-piercing wail. Grace grabbed a couple of napkins to wipe up the milk that had spilled out of his cup.

"Stop that *gegrisch*!" Anna said, covering her ears with the palms of her hands.

"He's only hollering because you bumped his tray and spilled his milk."

"He's hurtin' my ears." Anna pinched Daniel's arm, and he screamed even louder.

Grace's hands shook as she lifted Daniel from his chair and placed him in her lap. "Anna, tell your bruder you're sorry for pinching him."

Anna shook her head. "He's too young to know what I'm sayin'. Besides, he shouldn't have yelled in my ear like that."

"Either apologize or go to your room," Grace said through tight lips.

With tears in her eyes, Anna glanced over at Cleon.

"You'd better do as your mamm says," he said.

"But I haven't had my dessert."

Grace's face heated up. "Then apologize to Daniel!"

Anna shook her head and dashed from the room.

Cleon's forehead wrinkled as he looked over at Grace. "Did you have to yell at her like that?"

Grace's defenses rose. "She acted like a pill throughout the meal, and when she pinched Daniel, I'd had enough."

"She's upset about not being able to see her grandpa tomorrow."

Grace wrapped her arms around Daniel and held him tightly, hoping the gesture might offer her some comfort. "I'm not sure Anna should ever see Carl."

"Why not? I thought we agreed that she could see him if someone in the family was with them."

"He found out about the attacks against my family, and he doesn't think Anna's safe living here." Grace gulped on the sob rising in her throat. "He said he wants Anna to move in with him."

A muscle on the side of Cleon's neck quivered, and he blinked rapidly. "I won't let that happen, Grace. I promise you'll never lose your daughter again."

Chapter 30

The following morning as Grace stood at the stove, stirring a pot of oatmeal, she thought about Carl's suggestion that Anna come to live with him, and it upset her all over again. She did want Anna to be safe, but not at the risk of letting Carl take control of her again. No, Anna's place was here, with them.

Forcing her thoughts aside, Grace turned from the stove, cupped her hands around her mouth, and called, "Anna, breakfast is ready!"

No response.

"Maybe she's in the bathroom," Cleon said as he stepped into the kitchen.

Grace shook her head. "I'm sure I would have heard her come down the stairs."

"Maybe she took them softly for a change." Cleon moved toward the high chair and ruffled Daniel's curly hair. "Or Anna might have come downstairs during one of this little guy's yelling matches. No one can hear much of anything when he gets to hollering."

Grace bit back a chuckle. Daniel had become pretty verbal lately. "Would you mind checking the bathroom to see if Anna's there while I finish making the pancakes?"

"Don't mind at all." Cleon left the room and returned a few seconds later. "No sign of Anna in the bathroom. Want me to check upstairs and see if she's still in her room?"

Grace nodded.

Cleon left again, and when he returned, he was frowning.

"What's wrong?"

"Anna's gone."

"Gone?"

"She's not in her room, and when I looked in her closet to see if she might be there, I discovered that her suitcase was missing."

Grace gasped. Had Anna been kidnapped, or had she run away?

As Luke bounced along in the passenger's seat of John's SUV, he was surprised when he spotted Grace's daughter, Anna, walking along the edge of the road in the opposite direction of the schoolhouse, lugging a small suitcase. "Hold up there, would you, John? I know that little girl, and I'd like to find out where she's going with that suitcase."

When John slowed his rig and pulled to the shoulder of the road, Luke hopped out. "Where are you going, Anna?" he called.

Anna merely shrugged and kept on walking.

"The direction you're heading is not the way to the schoolhouse," Luke said, walking beside her.

"I know that."

"Would you like us to give you a ride to school?"

She shook her head.

"Then get in the car, and we'll take you home."

"I don't wanna go home. I'm goin' to see Poppy."

"Poppy?"

Anna nodded. "Poppy's my *grossdaadi*, and I wanna be with him."

Luke had never heard Anna refer to Grace's dad as "Poppy" before. Could Anna be talking about her other grandfather—the one she'd been with before she'd come to live with Grace?

"Where's your grossdaadi live?" Luke asked.

"In a house in Berlin. He's livin' there now."

"Do you know which house, Anna?"

She shook her head. "No, but I'll find him!"

Luke touched Anna's shoulder. "If you want to visit him, then you'd better ask your mamm, don't you think?"

Anna's blue eyes flashed angrily, and her chin jutted out. "Mama said no, but she can't stop me from bein' with Poppy. Nobody can keep us apart."

"I'm sure no one wants to keep you apart, Anna."

"Uh-huh. Poppy asked if I could go to his house to see him, and Mama said no, not today."

Luke was sure if Grace knew Anna was out on the road by herself, heading toward Berlin in search of her grandfather, she would be worried sick.

"Look, Anna, if you get in the car we can talk about this better."

Anna hesitated but finally climbed into John's rig. Luke grabbed her suitcase and climbed in, too. "Head for Cleon's place," he mouthed to John after he'd taken his seat and shut the door. John nodded and pulled onto the road.

Martha had just stepped out of the barn when she heard a vehicle pull into the yard. Her breath caught in her throat when she saw Luke getting out of John Peterson's SUV. Didn't he know better than to come here uninvited? What if Dad came out of his shop and saw Luke and Martha together? After the scene Dad had made the other night when he'd confronted her about seeing Luke, Martha knew he would be hopping mad if Luke showed his face around here again. She still hadn't had the chance to speak to Dad alone and tell him about the note she'd found in the back of her buggy. She wasn't even sure she wanted to bring up the subject, for fear of riling Dad again.

Martha took a step toward Luke but halted when he turned and lifted Anna out of the SUV. "What in the world?" She rushed over to them. "What's Anna doing in John's rig? I figured she'd be home having breakfast or in Cleon's buggy on her way to school."

"That's what I thought, too, when I saw her walking along the edge of the road in the opposite direction of the schoolhouse." Luke nodded toward Grace and Cleon's place. "You want to come along while I walk Anna up to her house?"

Martha was about to reply, when Anna hollered, "I don't wanna go home! I wanna see Poppy!"

The child pivoted toward the road, but Martha reached out and grabbed her arm. "You can't go running off by yourself," she said firmly. "We'll go up to your house, let your mamm know you're okay, and then you can talk about seeing your grandpa."

Anna dug in her heels. "I need to see Poppy!"

Martha gritted her teeth. "You don't even know where he lives. You're coming with me!"

"Let me talk to her." Luke squatted beside Anna. "We know you want to see your grossdaadi, but let's go up to your house and talk to your mamm and daed a few minutes. I'm sure we can work things out."

Anna finally nodded and reached for Luke's hand.

Luke picked up Anna's suitcase, and as he and Anna started up the driveway, Martha turned to John, who still sat in his vehicle. "Thanks for bringing her home, John."

"Sure, no problem. We couldn't let the little tyke skip school and try to find her grandfather's house all alone."

"I appreciate that." Martha smiled. "Would you like to come up to the house with us?"

John shook his head. "I think I'll head to the barn and see your dad. I heard he's planning to rebuild his shop soon."

Martha nodded. "Would you do me a favor, John?"

"What's that?"

"Would you please not mention anything to Dad about Luke being here?"

"How come?"

"Dad doesn't care much for Luke, and—"

"Sure, no problem. I won't say a word."

"Thank you." Martha turned and hurried up the driveway behind Luke and Anna.

When Grace heard footsteps on the back porch, she jerked open the door. There stood Anna holding Luke Friesen's hand. "Anna! Oh, Anna!" she cried.

"Where have you been?" Cleon asked, as he joined Grace on the porch, holding Daniel in his arms. "You sneaked out of the house without telling your mamm or me where you were going, and I was just getting ready to go out looking for you."

Anna gave no reply as Luke herded her up the stairs.

"John and I were heading to Berlin, and we saw her walking along the side of the road in the opposite direction of the schoolhouse," Luke said as they stepped onto the porch.

"She was going to see her grandpa Davis," Martha added as she followed behind Luke.

"What!" Grace and Cleon said in unison.

"I. . .I wanted to see Poppy." Anna's voice quivered, and her blue eyes filled with tears. "Poppy loves me."

Grace dropped to her knees and wrapped her arms around the child. "Oh, Anna, we love you, too."

"But we can't have you skipping school," Cleon said. "You don't even know where your grandpa Davis lives. You would have gotten lost on your own, and it's dangerous for you to be out by yourself like that."

Anna sniffed. "C-can I see Poppy after school today?"

"Not today." Grace patted Anna's back. "We'll see about going there some Saturday when you have no school."

When Grace and Cleon took Anna inside, Martha remained on the porch with Luke.

"Danki for bringing Anna home," she said, leaning on the railing as she faced Luke, who stood with his back to the door.

"It scared me when I saw her lugging a suitcase and heading in the direction of Berlin by herself," he replied. "When I found out what she was up to, I figured her folks were probably worried and that we needed to get Anna home as quick as we could."

"You really do care about my family, don't you?"

"Of course I care." Luke glanced down the driveway, where John's rig was parked near the barn. "I even care about your daed. Although I'm sure he'd never believe that."

Martha grimaced. "Dad can be pretty stubborn at times. It's not easy to make him see that he's wrong about something."

"Well, he's wrong about me, and I aim to prove it. I just wish there were more clues that would help us find out who's behind the attacks." Luke grunted. "I don't think we've done such a good job of investigating things, Martha. To tell you the truth, I'm beginning to wonder if we'll ever find out who's behind the attacks."

"I have some information I think is worth thinking about," she said.

His eyebrows shot up. "You do?"

She nodded.

"What is it?"

Martha motioned for Luke to come closer. "I recently discovered that Ray Larson has set up a bird feeder close to our fence line that borders his property."

Luke's mouth fell open. "You don't really think your nice neighbor has anything to do with the attacks."

"I hope not, but when I asked Ray about the feeder, he said he'd put it there so he could watch certain birds." She frowned. "I think he might be watching us and not the birds. I'm hoping to find out what he's up to."

"How are you planning to do that? Since you're working for Irene more now than ever, you're not always home to keep an eye on things."

"That's true, but I'll watch when I am here, and—"

Luke held up one hand as Cleon stepped out the door.

"I didn't realize you were still here, Luke," Cleon said. "Figured you and John would be headed for work by now."

"He closed his shop for a few hours this morning," Luke replied. "The two of us were headed to town when we spotted Anna." He nodded toward the barn. "John's visiting Roman right now, so I figured I may as well hang around here 'til he's done."

"I'm heading to work at the barn myself," Cleon said. "Should I tell John you're waiting up here at the house, Luke?"

Luke nodded. "But I'd appreciate it if you didn't mention that

I'm talking to Martha. Roman wouldn't like it."

Cleon gnawed on his lower lip but finally nodded.

"Maybe I should wait in John's rig," Luke said when Cleon stepped off the porch. "No point in borrowing trouble."

"Cleon said he wouldn't tell Dad you're with me."

"Even so, I think I'd better go." Luke turned and sprinted down the driveway.

Martha turned and started up the steps leading to her sister's house, figuring Grace probably needed a listening ear.

"How are things with you these days?" John asked Roman as he stood near one of the workbenches that had been set up in the barn.

Roman shrugged his shoulders. "Fair to middlin'."

"There haven't been any more attacks, I hope."

"Not for a while." Roman saw no need to mention that the reins of Martha's horse had been cut.

"That's good to hear. It's kind of worrisome to think there might be a deranged person running around our community, ready to terrorize some other unsuspecting family at any moment."

"So far, we're the only ones who have been attacked." Roman blew out his breath. "If the person behind the attacks was planning to hit other folks' homes, I'm sure they'd have done it by now."

"What about the vandalism done at some of the schools?"

"I'm sure those were done by pranksters. Same holds true for the other mischief that's been pulled."

"You're probably right about that," John said with a nod.

"So, what brings you by here this morning?"

"Luke and I were headed to Berlin and spotted your granddaughter Anna heading in that direction. After Luke talked with her awhile, we brought her back home."

Roman's forehead wrinkled. "Anna was heading to Berlin by herself?"

"That's right. She said she was going to see her grandpa."

"Carl Davis?"

John shrugged.

A car door slammed, and Roman glanced out the window. He spotted Luke getting into John's SUV.

John glanced out the window then, too. "Guess I'd better get going."

"All right then. Thanks for bringing my granddaughter home."

"No problem. We were glad to do it." John headed for the door but turned back around. "Oh, I heard you were going to start building a new shop soon."

"That's right. Hope to get started on it in the next week or so."

"Let me know if you need any help."

"Thanks, John, I will."

Roman watched as John got into his truck. Despite the fact that he didn't care much for Luke, he was grateful he'd brought Anna home; he just couldn't muster up the words to say so.

Chapter 31

Crash! Bam! Thump, thump, thump!

Roman sat straight up in bed and snapped on the battery-operated light. His heart pounded as he looked at his and Judith's bedroom window. It had been shattered, and a brick lay on the floor near their dresser.

Judith bolted upright and let out an ear-piercing scream.

With no thought for the broken glass covering the floor, Roman rushed over to the window and pulled the curtain aside. The moon was hidden by clouds tonight, and the yard was shrouded in darkness.

"What is it, Roman? Do you see anyone out there?" Judith's voice quavered, and when Roman turned to look at her, he saw tears on her cheeks.

"It's too dark for me to see," he said, moving back to the bed. "I'm sure whoever threw that brick isn't hanging around so he can get caught. No doubt, the culprit's long gone."

"Oh, Roman," she sobbed, "I. . .I don't think I can take much more of this. I wish you c–could make it stop."

He lowered himself to the bed and took hold of her hand. "If there was something I could do about these horrible attacks, don't you think I would?"

Judith started rocking back and forth, holding her hands against her temples.

He touched her shoulder. "Judith, are you okay?"

No response.

"Judith, are you listening to me?"

She continued to rock, staring vacantly across the room.

Suddenly, Martha burst into the room. "Did you hear that big boom? It sounded like—" Her gaze went to the window, and then to the floor. "Did. . .did you see who threw that brick, Dad? Were either you or Mom hurt?"

Roman shook his head, but Judith continued to sit and rock as though in a daze.

Martha rushed over to the bed and took a seat beside her. "Mom, are you okay?"

"She's fine; just a little shook up is all."

Martha turned to face Roman. "Are—are you sure she's all right? She looks like she's in shock."

"She was talking to me a few seconds ago. She seemed kind of shaky, but I don't think she's in shock."

"Maybe Mom should lie down in bed."

"That might be a good idea." Roman helped Judith lie down, and he made sure her head was resting on a pillow. "Martha, why don't you run to the kitchen and get your mamm a cup of herbal tea?"

Martha hesitated a moment, took a quick glance at her mother, and bolted from the room.

Martha entered the kitchen, lit the gas lamp hanging above the table, and put a kettle of water on the stove to heat. Then she hurried across the room, grabbed a flashlight from the top drawer, and opened the back door. Clicking on the flashlight, she shone the beam of light around the yard. No sign of anyone. Of course that didn't mean no one was lurking in the shadows. If she hadn't been so concerned about Mom, she would have ventured into the yard and searched for the culprit who'd thrown that brick.

I'll never find out who's been doing these things to us if I don't find some clues, she fumed. *But I'd better not go outside and look for them now.*

Martha stepped back into the house and closed the door. She would look for some clues first thing in the morning. In the meantime, she needed to check on Mom and give her some tea.

"Where's your mamm? I figured she'd be here making breakfast," Dad said when he stepped into the kitchen after finishing his chores the following morning.

Martha turned from the stove, where she'd been frying bacon. "Mom's still in bed."

Dad's eyebrows shot up. "It's not like her to sleep so late."

"I'm not sure she's sleeping, Dad. I think she may still be upset over what happened last night with the brick."

"I can understand her being upset last night," Dad said as he washed his hands at the sink. "But I boarded up the window, cleaned up the glass, and promised to notify the sheriff, so there's no reason for her to be lying in bed feeling *naerfich*."

Martha pursed her lips.. "I think Mom has every right to feel nervous. These attacks have been going on too long, and it's enough to put anyone's nerves on edge."

"Which is why I agreed to notify the sheriff."

"When do you plan to call him?"

"Sometime today, but not until I've had some breakfast and have checked on your mamm."

Martha set a plate of toast on the table just as Dad took a seat. "Don't you think you ought to call the doctor and see about getting Mom in as soon as possible?"

He shrugged his shoulders. "I think she just needs a good rest. She's been working awfully hard around here lately, you know."

Martha released an exasperated sigh. "Mom's not in bed because she's tired and needs a good rest. She's—"

He held up one hand to silence her. "If she's not feeling better by noon, I'll take her to the clinic in town. In the meantime, I'm going up to Grace and Cleon's place to tell them what happened last night."

"Dad, what's wrong? You look like you didn't sleep a wink last night," Grace said when her father entered the kitchen as she was getting breakfast on the table.

He moaned and sank into a chair. "There was another attack during the night."

"Ach, no!" Grace gasped, and Cleon reached out to grab her hand.

"What happened?" Cleon asked.

"Someone threw a brick through our bedroom window."

"Were either of you hurt?"

Dad looked up at Grace and shook his head. "Not physically, anyway."

"What do you mean, Dad?"

He tugged his ear. "It's your mamm. She's not acting like herself at all."

"What's wrong with Mom? How's she acting?"

"Like she's in some kind of daze. Won't say a word to anyone and doesn't seem to know where she is."

Grace covered her mouth with the palm of her hand. "I knew it. I knew this was coming."

Dad looked up at her and tipped his head. "What's that supposed to mean?"

"Mom's been on edge ever since the attacks first began, but with each one that's happened, she's gotten worse." Grace slowly shook her head. "I'm afraid the brick being thrown through your window might have pushed her over the edge."

"I don't think so." Dad's eyelids blinked in rapid succession. "I'm sure she'll snap out of it soon and be back to her old self."

"Mom hasn't been her old self for a long time, Dad." Grace moved over to the row of wall pegs by the back door and grabbed a sweater.

"Where are you going?" Cleon asked.

"To see Mom, of course. Can you take care of things here while I'm gone?"

Cleon looked over at Dad. "What about work? Are you planning to open the shop today?"

Dad shook his head. "No, no. I think I'd better spend the day with Judith." He rose from his chair. "I'll walk back to the house with Grace now, and we'll let you know later how things are going."

Anna spoke up for the first time. "What about Poppy? Don't I get to see him today?"

"Not today, Anna," Cleon said. "Your grandma Hostettler is sick, and your mamm has to look after her."

Grace didn't wait to hear Anna's response. She rushed out the door with Dad behind her. *Oh, dear Lord,* she silently prayed, *please help my mamm.*

As Martha headed outside after the breakfast dishes were done, all she could think about was her mother lying in her room, refusing to get out of bed. Mom hadn't eaten anything from the breakfast tray Martha had prepared for her, nor had she spoken a word to either Martha or Dad. Martha worried that Mom might be on the verge of a nervous breakdown.

"I hope Dad decides to take Mom to the doctor," Martha muttered as she zigzagged across the yard, searching for clues that might give some indication as to who had thrown the brick into her parents' room the night before. It wasn't fair, this nightmare they'd been living since the first act of vandalism that had taken place over two years ago. Martha was sure if it had been some kids playing pranks it would have ended long before now. No, someone was definitely trying to get even with someone in her family. The questions remained: who and why?

As Martha made her way along the edge of the flower bed near the house, she spotted an empty beer bottle lying in the grass. *Whoever threw that brick must have been drinking and dropped the beer bottle.*

She was about to head into the house when something shiny sticking out of the dirt caught her eye. She bent to investigate and discovered a ballpoint pen. She didn't recognize it as belonging to anyone in her family, but she thought she might have seen it, or at least one like it, somewhere before.

Clutching the pen tightly in her hand, she hurried back to the house to check on Mom. She'd just entered the kitchen and had slipped the pen in a drawer, when Dad showed up with Grace.

"Where's Mom?" Grace asked with a panicked expression.

"She's in her room, resting," Martha replied.

Grace moved in that direction, but Martha stepped between her and the hallway door. "Why don't we let Dad check on Mom first? That will give the two of us a chance to talk."

Grace looked like she might argue, but she finally nodded and took a seat at the table.

Dad hurried down the hall toward his bedroom.

Martha took a seat beside Grace. "I think Mom needs to see the doctor. She's not doing well at all."

Grace's head moved slowly up and down. "Dad said she won't speak to anyone and acts like she doesn't know where she is."

"That's right. She's been like that since the brick was thrown through the window during the night."

"Is Dad going to phone the doctor?"

Martha shrugged. "He said that if Mom wasn't feeling better by noon, he would."

"If she's as bad as you say, then I don't think we should wait that long, do you?"

"Probably not."

Grace pushed her chair away from the table and stood.

"Where are you going?"

"Into Mom's room to see for myself how she's doing." Deep wrinkles formed in Grace's forehead. "If I think she needs to see the doctor, I'm going to insist that Dad make the phone call right now."

Luke glanced at the clock on the far wall of John's shop. It was after eight and still no John. Luke didn't remember John saying the night before that he planned to run any errands this morning, but maybe something had come up at the last minute and John had decided to run into town.

"He should have called to let me know he was going to be late," Luke mumbled as he glanced at the phone sitting on John's desk. It had only rung once this morning, and that call had been a wrong number. "Guess I'd better get busy and find something to do, because when the boss does get here, I'm sure he won't be too happy if he sees me standing around."

For the next hour, Luke stayed busy staining a set of cabinets that were supposed to be finished by the end of the week. When those were done, he put the can of stain away and started sanding an antique rocking chair that had been brought into the shop the day before for restoration.

At nine thirty, the shop door opened, and John stepped into the room. "I overslept. Why didn't you call me?"

"Figured you might call me," Luke replied.

John's forehead wrinkled. "How could I call if I was sleeping?" He tromped across the room and dropped into the chair at his desk with a groan. "The battery in my stupid alarm clock must have gone dead, because it never rang this morning."

"I would have called if I'd known you'd just overslept, but I thought maybe you had run some errands in town."

"No errands today." John glanced across the room, where the coffeepot sat on a table. "Is there any coffee made?"

Luke nodded. "Made some first thing this morning."

"Good. A steaming cup of hot coffee is just what I need." John left his desk and ambled across the room, stretching his hands over his head and releasing a yawn. "I never feel right when I oversleep. It'll probably take my brain the rest of the day to thaw out so I can get some work done."

Luke gestured to the cabinets he'd just stained. "As you can see, I've got those ready to go." He pointed to the rocking chair. "I also started on that."

"Glad to hear it," John said as he poured himself a cup of coffee and added three teaspoons of sugar. Luke had never figured out why John liked his coffee so sweet. He preferred his black.

"Have you heard anything from your folks lately?" John asked when he returned to his desk.

"I saw Mom from a distance in town the other day but didn't get a chance to speak to her."

"Do you think your folks are still mad at you?"

"I'm not sure." Luke scrubbed his hand across his chin. "I think they're more disappointed than anything."

"Because you haven't joined the Amish church?"

Luke nodded. "By the time Dad was my age, he was already married, and Mom was expecting her first baby."

John took a swig of coffee. "How much longer do you plan to sleep in my back room?"

"Do you need me to find another place to stay? Because if you do–"

John lifted his hand. "I didn't say that. I just don't think it's an ideal living arrangement."

"I hope to have some answers soon. Then maybe I can make a decision that will give my parents some peace."

"What kind of answers are you talking about?"

"I'll explain things when I can." Luke motioned to the rocking chair. "In the meantime, I'd better get back to work on that."

John set his coffee cup down. "I'd better try to get something done myself."

Chapter 32

Martha paced the kitchen floor and kept glancing at the clock on the far wall as she waited for Dad and Grace to come out of Mom's room. By noon, Mom still hadn't responded to anything Dad or Grace had said to her, and at Grace's insistence, Dad had phoned the doctor and gotten Mom an appointment for this afternoon. Then he'd called Rosemary and asked if she would give them a ride to the doctor in Millersburg. Grace and Dad had gone into Mom's room forty-five minutes ago to help Mom get dressed.

What could be taking so long? she fretted. *Surely it couldn't take Mom this long to get dressed.*

Martha had known for some time that her mother was upset over the attacks that had been done to them. After the last several acts of vandalism, Mom had acted jittery for days. But she'd never freaked out like she had last night or gone into her own world, refusing to talk to anyone.

Martha sank into a chair at the table and let her head fall forward into her open palms. She feared the worst where her mother was concerned. Mom rarely got sick, and whenever she did, she usually bounced right back. What if Mom didn't bounce back this time? What if. . .

Martha jumped when she heard her parents' bedroom door open. She raced into the hallway and was pleased to see Mom standing there, fully dressed. Grace and Dad stood on either side of her with their arms around Mom's waist.

"How are you feeling?" Martha asked, rushing to her mother's side.

Mom blinked a couple of times and gave Martha a blank stare.

"She'll be better once she sees the doctor," Dad said with a nod.

"Would you like some lunch before you go?"

"I've already eaten," he replied.

"No, I meant Mom."

"She might feel better if she had something to eat," Grace said. "Would you like some tea and a boiled egg before you go, Mom?"

"I. . .don't care for any."

Hope welled in Martha's soul when Mom replied to Grace's question. If Mom was speaking again, maybe she would be all right and wouldn't need to see the doctor after all. She was about to voice that thought when a horn honked from outside.

"That must be Rosemary," Dad said. "We're supposed to be at the doctor's in half an hour, and if we don't go now, we'll be late. We can get something to eat on the way home." He ushered Mom quickly out the door, calling over his shoulder, "If you're coming with us, Martha, you'd better get a move on."

"She's going to be all right," Grace whispered as Martha headed out the door. "She *has* to be all right."

As Ruth washed the breakfast dishes while Esta dried, she glanced over her shoulder and smiled at Molly sitting on the floor, playing with one of her dolls.

"Can I go over to Anna's when we're done with the dishes?" Esta asked. "I want to take Winkie along and show her the new tricks I've been teaching him."

Ruth nodded. "I suppose it would be all right. But only if Gideon goes with you."

Esta wrinkled her nose. "How come he has to go along?"

"Because you'll need someone to drive the pony cart."

"I can drive it. Cinnamon's a tame pony and does just what I say."

"That may be, but I won't have you out on the road by yourself in the pony cart." Ruth added a few more squirts of detergent to her sink full of dishes. "Either Gideon goes along, or you'll have to stay home."

Esta's lower lip jutted out. "Gideon's always so cranky. Can't Josh go instead?"

The back door flew open, and Josh tore into the room. His face was red and his breathing labored. "You'd better come quick, Mama. Gideon fell on a broken beer bottle out by the barn, and he's bleedin' real bad!"

A broken beer bottle? Ruth had no idea how a beer bottle would have gotten there; no one in their family drank anything with alcohol in it. She supposed it could have belonged to one of the men who came to Abe's harness shop, but what would they have been doing up by the barn?

Shaking her head to clear her thoughts, Ruth opened a drawer and grabbed a clean dish towel. "Esta, stay with Molly while I check on Gideon," she instructed as she rushed out the back door.

Ruth found Gideon lying on the ground not far from the barn, moaning and clutching his leg. Nearby lay the shattered remains of a beer bottle.

"Gideon, let me have a look at your leg," she instructed.

The boy groaned and pulled his bloody fingers away from the spot he'd been holding. Ruth bent for a closer look, and her stomach clenched when she saw how deep the cut was.

"You need to go to the hospital for stitches," she said, wrapping the towel securely around Gideon's leg.

"Can't you just slap a bandage on it?"

She shook her head. "The cut's too deep and wide for that. Besides, we can't take the risk of infection setting in."

"But Papa's gone shopping in Berlin today," Gideon said. "So how am I gonna get to the hospital?"

"I'll call for a ride and take you there myself."

Gideon looked like he might protest, but to Ruth's surprise, he nodded and said, "Jah, okay."

After Rosemary dropped Judith, Roman, and Martha off at the

doctor's, she decided it was time to pay the sheriff another visit. He needed to know about this latest attack, and he needed to find a way to make the attacks stop. She hoped he was in his office today and not out patrolling.

When Rosemary entered the sheriff's office a short time later, she was relieved to find the sheriff there.

"What can I help you with?" he asked, as she took a seat on the other side of his desk.

"There's been another attack at my brother's house."

He lifted both arms and laced his fingers together as he placed his hands behind his head. "What's happened now?"

"Someone threw a brick through Roman and Judith's bedroom window last night."

"I see."

Irritation welled in Rosemary's chest. Didn't the man even care? Wasn't he concerned that someone may have gotten hurt?

"My brother and his wife are over at the doctor's right now," she said through tight lips.

"Was one of them hit by the brick?"

She shook her head. "But they could have been."

He dropped his arms and placed both hands on his desk. "If they weren't hurt, then why the trip to the doctor's?"

"Judith's been a nervous wreck since the last several attacks, and this one. . .well, it sort of put her over the edge."

He leaned slightly forward. "Did she suffer a nervous breakdown? Is that what you're saying?"

"We're not sure, but she wouldn't talk to anyone for a while, and—"

"I'm sorry to hear about the broken window and Mrs. Hostettler's shattered nerves, but unless I'm given some evidence to go on, there's really not much I can do."

Rosemary released an exasperated sigh. "It's my impression that you promised my brother you'd keep a closer eye on his place."

He gave a curt nod. "I did say that, but I'm a busy man. You can't expect me to spend all my on-duty hours camped across the road from the Hostettlers', waiting for the next attack to occur."

Rosemary's face heated up, and she gripped the strap on her purse. "You don't have to be so harsh."

"I'm just stating facts as I know them." Sheriff Osborn gave her a half smile. "As I'm sure you know, that brother of yours is a stubborn man. He's given me little or nothing to go on and rarely notifies me when there's been an attack."

"He planned to tell you about this one," she was quick to say. "He got detained when we had to take Judith to the doctor's."

The sheriff picked up his pen and jotted something on a piece of paper. "I'll stop by Roman's place later today and see what information I can get out of him."

"Will you check around the place for evidence?"

"Of course."

She rose from her chair. "Thank you, Sheriff."

As Rosemary left the sheriff's office, she felt a small sense of relief. At least he'd been notified about the brick and the broken window, and he was planning to speak to Roman about it. She knew Roman might not appreciate her having gone to the sheriff without his permission, but that didn't matter. They had to find out who was behind the attacks and, in the meantime, protect Roman's family.

As Rosemary headed to her car a few minutes later, she was surprised to see Carl Davis walking up the sidewalk across the street. She hadn't seen him since the day he'd stopped by her house, but she knew after talking with Grace the following day that Carl had suggested Anna come live with him so she would be safe. Of course Grace had vetoed that idea because she feared Carl might try to take Anna away again, and Rosemary couldn't blame her for that. She'd had the same thought when Carl had visited with her.

She hurried to her car, hoping Carl wouldn't see her. The last thing she needed was for him to find out about the latest attack. He'd probably be even more determined to take Anna from Grace.

Rosemary opened the door, slid quickly behind the wheel, and started the engine. A short time later, she pulled up to the doctor's office. She found Martha and Judith sitting in the waiting room, while Roman paced the floor.

"Where have you been?" he growled. "We've been waiting for thirty minutes!"

"I had an errand to run." She glanced at Judith then back at Roman. "What'd the doctor have to say?"

Roman shook his head and motioned to Judith. "I'll tell you later."

As Ruth sat in the backseat of Donna Larson's car, with Gideon at her side, her mind replayed the events that had happened since she'd found Gideon on the ground with a cut leg. After she'd taken him into the house, she'd gone to Abe's shop and phoned Aunt Rosemary, hoping she'd be free to give them a ride to Millersburg. Aunt Rosemary obviously wasn't at home, for all Ruth had gotten was the answering machine. Then she'd called Donna Larson and was relieved when Donna answered and said she'd be glad to give them a ride to the hospital. Since Ivan was alone in the harness shop, she didn't feel free to ask him to go up to the house to watch the children while she was gone, so she'd left a message on her folks' answering machine, asking if either Mom or Martha might be free to watch the children. In the meantime, she'd put Esta and Josh in charge of the younger ones, which she hoped hadn't been a mistake.

The trees lining the road blurred as they sped along in Donna's car, and Ruth offered a silent prayer. *Dear Lord, please protect the kinner while I'm gone.*

A short time later, Donna pulled up to the hospital emergency entrance. "I'll let you and Gideon out here and then find a place to park."

"We could be awhile," Ruth replied. "If you have some errands to run while you're in town, you'll probably have time to do them."

"I might run over to the post office, but I shouldn't be long. I'll come inside and check on you as soon as I get back."

"Thanks." Ruth opened the car door and stepped out; then she turned to help Gideon. Hobbling on one foot, he gave no resistance as she led him into the emergency room. Once he was seated, she went to the front desk.

"If you'd like to have a seat, someone will be with you soon," the woman behind the desk said after Ruth had filled out some paperwork.

Ruth took a seat next to Gideon. "It's going to be okay," she whispered.

"I–I'm scared of gettin' stitches." His chin quivered slightly. "It's gonna make my leg hurt worse; I just know it."

Ruth reached over and touched his arm. "When I was a little girl, I fell and broke my arm. I was scared then, too."

"You were?"

She nodded. "But my mamm was with me when I went to the hospital, and I knew God was with me, too."

Gideon looked over at her with tears clinging to his lashes and smiled. "Danki for comin' with me today, Mama."

Ruth swallowed against the lump lodged in her throat as she gently squeezed his fingers. At least one good thing had come from Gideon's accident.

Chapter 33

That evening after supper, Martha decided to ride her bike over to Abe and Ruth's so she could tell them what had been going on with their mother. Since Ruth had been depressed for several months after Martin's death, Martha hoped Ruth might have some suggestions as to what they could do to help Mom.

As she peddled her bike along the shoulder of the road, her thoughts wandered. The attacks that had begun over two years ago with the break-in of their house and then Dad's shop had gone on far too long. They needed to find out who was responsible for the attacks and make them stop. If they didn't, someone else might get hurt or end up dead, like Martin. Martha had been trying for several months to figure out who the attacker was, but she was no further along in finding him now than she had been when she'd first decided to do some detective work. The only thing she was sure of was that Luke was not the attacker. He wouldn't be helping her if he were. Martha was certain that Luke wanted to find out who the attacker was as much as she did, if for no other reason than to clear his name with Dad.

A horn honked from behind, and Martha jumped. Her bike swerved to the right, but she righted it before running into the ditch. She glanced over her shoulder and was surprised to see John Peterson's SUV pull alongside of her.

He leaned over and rolled down the window on the passenger's side. "Need a ride?"

She pointed to her bike. "Thanks anyway, but I've got a ride."

He smiled. "I can see that. I just thought if you had a ways to go, I'd put your bike in the back of my rig and I could give you ride to wherever you're going."

"I'm heading over to Abe and Ruth's place, so I don't have much farther to go."

John's smile widened. "No, I guess you don't. How are things with the Wengerds these days? I haven't talked to Abe in a while."

"Last I heard, things were fine and dandy with my sister and her husband." Martha grimaced. "My family's still having problems, though."

"What kind of problems? Have there been more attacks?"

She nodded. "Someone threw a brick through my folks' bedroom window last night, and Mom's been pretty upset ever since." No point in giving John all the details. Martha was sure her dad wouldn't like it if everyone in the area knew Mom was on the verge of a nervous breakdown.

"That's too bad. No one was hurt, I hope."

"No, but they could have been."

"Did your dad report it to the sheriff?"

"Aunt Rosemary did while Dad and Mom were at the doctor's."

"What were they doing at the doctor's?"

"As I said before, Mom was pretty upset, and Dad wanted her to get something from the doctor to help settle her nerves."

"That makes good sense. I'll drop by your dad's shop soon to see if there's anything I can do to help."

"I'm sure he'd appreciate that."

"I'll let you get to your sister's, and I'd better get home myself. It's been a long day, and I'm bushed."

"Okay. Thanks for stopping, John."

"Sure thing." John rolled up the window and pulled back onto the road.

Martha smiled. Even in the face of adversity, it was nice to know they had caring neighbors like Donna and Ray Larson and John Peterson.

Ruth had just stepped onto the porch to check on the children playing in the yard when she spotted Martha peddling up the driveway on her bike. "It's good to see you," she called as Martha climbed off the bike and leaned it against the barn. "I left a message on the folks' answering machine earlier, but you must not have gotten it until now."

"What message was that?" Martha asked as she stepped onto the porch.

"The one about me needing you or Mom to come over here and watch the kinner while I took Gideon to the hospital for stitches."

Martha's forehead wrinkled. "What happened to Gideon? Is he all right?"

Ruth nodded. "He cut his leg on a broken beer bottle someone threw in our yard, but he'll be fine." She took a seat in one of the porch chairs and motioned Martha to do the same. "I called Donna Larson for a ride to the hospital, and then we took Gideon in for stitches."

"Who watched the kinner?" Martha asked, glancing at the children playing in the yard.

"I figured you or Mom would be coming over, so I left Esta and Josh in charge of the two younger ones. But when I got home, I found out that Ivan had closed the shop and come up to the house to watch them himself."

"What about Abe? Where was he when all this happened?"

"He'd gone to Berlin to get some things he needed in his shop."

Martha moaned. "What a *verhuddelt* day this has been for all of us."

"How has the day been mixed-up for you?"

"Someone threw a brick through Mom and Dad's window last night."

"Ach, that's *baremlich*! Were either of them hurt?"

"Not physically. The worst part was how Mom reacted to it. She was so upset that she didn't want to get out of bed this morning. Except for a couple of words, she wouldn't say much to Dad, Grace, or me, either."

Ruth covered her mouth with her hand as she struggled to control her emotions. "How's Mom doing now?" she asked.

"Well, Dad called Aunt Rosemary this afternoon, and we took Mom to see the doctor."

"What'd the doctor have to say?"

"He thinks Mom's on the verge of a nervous breakdown."

"Ach, no!"

Martha nodded. "The doctor wanted to put Mom in the hospital, but Dad said no to that idea. So the doctor gave Mom a prescription for something to help her relax and said she needed to rest."

Ruth jumped up from her chair. "I'd better go over there now and see how she's doing. Maybe she needs my help. Maybe—"

Martha put a restraining hand on Ruth's arm. "She's already in bed. There's nothing you can do right now except pray."

Ruth swallowed around the lump in her throat. "Has the sheriff been notified?"

"Jah. Aunt Rosemary went to see him while Dad, Mom, and I were at the doctor's."

"Is the sheriff going to come out and check for evidence?"

Martha shrugged. "I don't know about that, but I did find a couple of things on my own when I was looking around outside this morning."

"What'd you find?"

"There was a ballpoint pen lying in the flower bed, and not far from it was a beer bottle."

"A beer bottle?"

Martha nodded.

"Gideon fell on a beer bottle this morning. That's how he cut his leg." Ruth rocked back and forth in her chair as she mulled things over. "You don't suppose—"

"That the beer bottle Gideon fell on was left by the same person who dropped a beer bottle at our place?" Martha said, finishing Ruth's sentence.

"That's exactly what I was thinking." Ruth bit down on her lip so hard she tasted blood. "I wonder if the person who threw the brick into Mom and Dad's window came over here last night with the intent of doing the same thing but got scared off by Winkie. I did hear the dog barking once during the night."

Martha shrugged. "I suppose that's possible, but I'm wondering why none of my dogs barked last night. If they'd heard an intruder, I'm sure they would have been howling like crazy."

"I think Abe needs to know about this," Ruth said as she moved toward the door. "He's in the living room, rocking Molly to sleep."

"It'll be dark soon, so I'd best be getting home," Martha said. "I'll say hello to the kinner and be on my way."

"Tell Dad I'll be over to see Mom in the morning," Ruth called over her shoulder.

On an impulse after John had closed his shop for the day, Luke decided to go for a ride in his truck. It had been a long, busy day, and he needed to relax—needed to get out of the small room in the back of John's shop where he'd been staying at night since he'd moved out of his folks' house.

Maybe I'll drive over to Walnut Creek and see what's doin', Luke told himself as he started down the road in that direction.

He'd only gone a little ways when he spotted Martha riding her bike along the shoulder of the road. He pulled over behind her and tooted his horn.

Martha stopped the bike and got off.

Luke turned off the engine and hopped out of the truck. He swallowed hard when he saw how flushed Martha's cheeks were. Several strands of dark hair had escaped her kapp, no doubt from the wind. It was all he could do to keep from pulling her into his arms and kissing those rosy cheeks.

"Where're you headed?" he asked.

"I just came from Ruth and Abe's place, and now I'm headed home. I'm really glad to see you, Luke. We need to—"

"You're losin' daylight," Luke interrupted. He looked up at the darkening sky. "It's not good for you to be out on the road alone." He motioned to the back of his truck. "Why don't you let me put your bike in there and give you a lift home?"

Martha hesitated as she glanced around kind of nervouslike. Was she worried someone they knew might drive by and see her talking to him? Probably so, he decided, since she didn't want her dad to know they'd been seeing each other. Luke was on the verge of telling her to forget the offer of a ride and suggesting he follow behind her bike in his truck, when she said, "I'd be happy for a ride home. It'll give us a chance to talk."

Luke lifted the bike with ease and set it in the back of his pickup. "Aren't you worried what your daed will think when I bring you home?" he asked as Martha opened the door and climbed into the passenger's seat.

"I figured you could drop me and my bike off at the end of our driveway. That way, Dad will be none the wiser."

"Guess that makes good sense." Luke skirted around to the driver's seat and started up the truck. Before he pulled onto the road, he turned to Martha and said, "I've got to tell you, though, I'm getting tired of sneaking around in order to see you. Every time we want to see each other, we have to meet some place in secret." He thumped the steering wheel with his knuckles. "It's not right that a fellow in love has to sneak around to see his *aldi*."

Martha's mouth dropped open, and her eyes widened. "Did you mean what you just said?"

"What? That I'm sick of sneaking around in order to see you?"

She shook her head. "The part about being in love and me being your girlfriend."

Luke reached across the seat and took hold of her hand. "It's true, Martha. I'm in love with you."

She sat there several seconds, staring at his fingers, intertwined with hers. "I. . .I love you, too, Luke, but I don't know if I can ever truly be your aldi."

"Because of your daed?"

She nodded. "If we could just find out who's behind the attacks—"

Luke stopped her words with a kiss. Her favorable response made him wish all the more that he had the right to court her.

"Oh, Luke," she murmured, pulling slowly away, "I'm afraid things will never be the way we want them to be. You see, what I wanted you to know is that there's been another attack, and even though I found some evidence, I still don't know who threw the brick."

Luke squinted as he studied her face. "What are you talking about? What evidence? What brick?"

"Last night, someone threw a brick through my folks' bedroom window. No one was hurt, but it left Mom really shaken." Martha paused to take in a quick breath. "This morning, I was looking around the place for evidence, and I found a ballpoint pen and a beer bottle that I believe the attacker must have dropped. The pen came from the Farmstead Restaurant, so whoever dropped it probably has eaten there."

"What'd you do with the evidence?"

"I threw the beer bottle out and put the pen in a kitchen drawer."

"Did your daed call the sheriff?"

"My aunt Rosemary spoke to the sheriff while Dad and I sat with Mom at the doctor's."

Luke's brows furrowed. "What was she doing at the doctor's?"

"This morning, Mom wouldn't respond to Dad or me, so we knew she needed to see the doctor."

Luke sat silently, trying to digest all that Martha had said. "What did the doctor say about your mamm?"

"He thinks she might be having a nervous breakdown, so he prescribed some medicine to calm her down and said she needed to rest." Martha squeezed Luke's fingers. "I'm afraid if the attacks don't stop soon, Mom might get worse and never fully recover."

Luke groaned as he leaned against his seat. "Your mamm's mental condition is one more reason why we need to find out who's behind the attacks. I don't know about you, but I plan to step up my investigation."

"What are you planning to do?"

"I don't know, but when I come up with a sensible plan, I'll let you know."

Martha drew in her bottom lip. "What if we never find out who's doing these horrible things to my family? What if–"

Luke put one finger against her lips. " 'With God, all things are possible.' Isn't that what the Bible says?"

She nodded slowly. "It's hard to hope and have the faith to believe when things keep going from bad to worse."

"Don't give up," he said as he pulled onto the road. "Maybe by the time we meet again, I'll have come up with a better plan."

Chapter 34

The following morning, Roman looked out the kitchen window and spotted Sheriff Osborn's car pulling in. As the sheriff stepped onto the porch, Roman went to open the door.

"Your sister came by my office yesterday and said someone had thrown a brick through your bedroom window," the sheriff said.

"Took you long enough to get here," Roman mumbled.

The sheriff stiffened. "I'm doing the best I can."

"Jah, well, I don't see how you're ever going to find out who's responsible for the attacks that have been done here if you don't keep a closer watch on our place." Roman grunted. "Doesn't make much sense for us to notify you when something happens if you don't care enough to check things out right away."

"It's not that I don't care. If you'll recall, you haven't always notified me right away."

"That may be true, but you were notified this time, and you don't show up until today."

The sheriff cleared his throat a few times and raised himself to his full height. "I'm a busy man, and I don't have time to stand around here all day debating the issue with you. I came to see if I could find any evidence, and that's what I plan to do." He moved toward the porch steps. "You want to show me exactly which window the brick came through?"

"Jah, sure." Roman followed the sheriff down the steps, and they walked across the grass. "That's the one." Roman pointed to the first floor window he'd patched with a piece of plywood.

"I'll take a look around out here in the yard," the sheriff said. "There might be some footprints showing or some other evidence that could help me find out who threw that brick."

Roman stood off to one side as Sheriff Osborn studied the lawn and the ground beneath the bedroom window. After several minutes of looking, the sheriff shook his head and said, "No footprints in the flower beds, and it would be hard to spot any in the grass unless there was snow on the ground. Don't see anything lying around that might give me any clues, either." He glanced at the house. "Mind if I have a word with your wife?"

Roman shook his head. "That's not possible."

"Why not?"

"Judith's asleep in our room right now."

"I can come by later this afternoon."

"No, I. . .I don't think Judith will be up to talking to you at all." Roman rubbed the back of his head. "You see, Judith kind of went into shock after the brick flew through the window, and I had to take her to the doctor's yesterday."

The sheriff nodded. "Yes, your sister mentioned that."

"The doctor gave Judith some medicine to take–something to calm her nerves and allow her to sleep." Roman continued to rub the spot on the back of his head. "Even if she was feeling up to talking to you today, she wouldn't have anything more to say than I've already told you."

"How about your daughter, Martha? Was she at home when this happened?"

Roman nodded.

"Is she here now?"

He nodded again.

"Mind if I speak with her?"

Roman moved toward the house. "I'll get her now."

Martha had just slipped a batch of sticky buns into the oven when the back door opened and Dad stepped into the kitchen. "Sheriff Osborn's here," he said. "He wants to speak with you."

Martha's forehead wrinkled. "What does he want?"

"Said he wants to question you about the brick being thrown through our bedroom window. Guess he wants to know if you heard or saw anything suspicious."

Martha nibbled on her bottom lip as she contemplated how much she should tell the sheriff. Not that she knew that much, really. She'd been asleep when the incident happened and hadn't seen anyone in the yard. But she had found that beer bottle and the ballpoint pen when she'd looked around the yard yesterday morning.

Dad rubbed the back of his head and squinted like he might be in pain.

"Have you got a headache?" she asked.

"Jah. Feels like a bunch of horses have been stamping on the back of my head. When things calm down around here, I may have to see the chiropractor."

"That's probably a good idea."

He inched toward the door. "Are you comin' or not?"

Martha nodded. "I'll be right there. Just let me set the timer so these buns don't burn."

"I'll see you outside then."

Moments later, Martha went outside. "My dad says you want to speak to me," she said to the sheriff, who stood on the porch, leaning against the railing.

He nodded. "Just wondered if you saw or heard anything the other night when the brick was thrown through your folks' bedroom window."

"The only thing I heard was the loud noise from the window being broken."

"Did you find any evidence?"

Martha wasn't sure how she should answer the sheriff's question. She didn't want to lie, but she didn't feel she should tell him about the pen she'd put in the kitchen drawer, either. Not with him being on their list of suspects. "I. . .uh. . .found a broken beer bottle in the yard."

"Where is it now?"

"I threw it away so no one would step on it."

"That's just great." The sheriff moaned. "I thought I told you before not to touch any evidence you found after one of these attacks. How are we supposed to check for fingerprints if you toss the evidence?"

Martha's face heated up. "I'm sorry."

"Please remember, the next time you find any evidence, leave it there, and call me right away."

Ruth's heartbeat matched the rhythm of the horse's hooves as she traveled down the road toward her folks' place in one of Abe's buggies. She'd left Molly and Owen with Aunt Rosemary for a few hours so she could see how Mom was doing. She feared if the attacks didn't stop, Mom might never be the same.

As Ruth approached her parents' driveway, she spotted Sheriff Osborn's car pulling out. He glanced her way, lifted one hand in a quick wave, and tore off down the road.

I wonder if the sheriff came to talk to Dad about the brick being thrown through their window. Hopefully he'll be able to find out who's behind these attacks and put a stop to them, once and for all.

Just as Ruth pulled her horse and buggy up to the hitching rail, Cleon stepped out of the barn. "If you're going to be here awhile, I'll put your horse in the corral," he offered.

"Danki," she said with a smile. "I came to check on Mom, so I'll probably be here a few hours."

Cleon's forehead creased. "She's not been the same since that brick was thrown through your folks' bedroom window. I think it really put her over the edge."

Ruth nodded. "She's been getting more nervous after each attack."

"The sheriff came to see your daed this morning, so maybe he'll have some answers soon," Cleon said as he helped Ruth out of the buggy.

"I hope that's the case." She slowly shook her head. "These horrible attacks have gone on long enough. We all need some answers."

"You're right about that." Cleon started to unhitch the horse.

"When I get your horse put away, I'll be in the barn working with your daed. When you're ready to go home, come get me, and I'll take care of hitching your horse to the buggy again."

"I will. Danki." Ruth hurried toward the house. When she entered the kitchen a few minutes later, she was surprised to see Mom fully dressed and sitting at the table, drinking a cup of tea. "It's good to see you up," Ruth said, bending to give her mother a hug. "I thought I might find you in bed."

Mom stared at Ruth as though she was looking right through her and said in a placid tone of voice, "I'm having a cup of tea."

Ruth nodded and looked over at Martha, who sat in a chair on the other side of the table.

"We need to talk," Martha whispered.

"Talk. . .talk. . ." Mom shook her head. "No, I'm too tired to talk."

Martha slid her chair back and stood in front of Mom. "Why don't I walk you down to your room so you can rest awhile?" she said, placing one hand on Mom's shoulder.

Mom stood silently and walked slowly out of the room. Martha followed.

Ruth sighed and reached for the teapot sitting in the middle of the table. Mom might be up and dressed, but she was definitely not herself.

Martha returned to the kitchen a few minutes later and took a seat. "I'm glad you came by. As I said, we need to talk."

"About Mom, you mean?"

Martha nodded.

"If Grace is at home, maybe we should see if she'd like to be in on this discussion. Dad, too, for that matter," Ruth quickly added.

"I've already talked to Grace, but I need your input before we can talk to Dad."

Ruth leaned forward with her elbows on the table. "Mom's not doing well at all, is she?"

Martha shook her head. "If not for the medication the doctor put her on, she wouldn't even be out of bed or saying much of anything to us."

"But the little she said to me didn't make much sense. It was as though she hasn't a care in the world—like she's in a daze or something."

"Exactly." Martha poured herself a cup of tea and took a sip. "The medication is helping Mom get out of bed, but it's keeping her so doped up that she can barely respond to things going on around her. She can't spend the rest of her life taking medication for her nerves, and we can't continue to live our lives in fear that there will be another attack."

Ruth fingered her untouched cup of tea. "Is there anything we can do about this?"

"I think the first thing we need to do is figure out some way to help Mom—something that doesn't involve her taking a lot of medication to keep her calmed down."

"Do you have any ideas?"

Martha nodded. "When I spoke with Grace last night, she suggested we send Mom up to Geauga County to stay with Dad's brother, Walt, and his wife, Mary, for a while."

Ruth rubbed her chin as she contemplated the idea. "How's that going to help?"

"Mom will be safe at Walt's place, and if any more attacks take place here, she won't know about them or have to deal with the fear of what might happen." Martha picked up the jar of honey sitting on the table, added a bit to her cup of tea, and stirred it around with her spoon. "I think if Mom has some time away from all this, her nerves might heal."

"What's Dad think about the idea?"

"Neither Grace nor I have said anything to him yet. We wanted to get your opinion first."

Ruth nodded. "I'm all for it. Even if Mom's nervous condition doesn't improve up at Walt's, at least we'll know she's in a safe place."

Martha pushed away from the table. "While Mom's taking her nap, maybe I'll go up to Grace's house and get her; then the three of us can have a little talk with Dad."

Chapter 35

Roman looked up when the barn door opened, and his eyebrows furrowed when all three of his daughters stepped up to his desk.

"What are you three doing out here, and who's keeping an eye on your mamm?" he asked.

"Mom's taking a nap, and we decided this was a good time for us to talk to you about something," Grace said as she shifted a sleeping Daniel in her arms.

He stood and motioned to his chair. "I'm sure that boy's getting heavy. Maybe you'd better sit here."

"Better yet, let me take him," Cleon said stepping up to Grace. "I'll sit with him over at my workbench, so you're free to talk with your daed and sisters."

"Danki." Grace handed their son to him.

"What's this all about?" Roman asked, lowering himself into the chair again.

"It's about Mom," Martha spoke up. "We think she needs to go away for a while."

His forehead wrinkled. "Go away?"

All three sisters nodded.

"We were thinking it might be good if you took Mom up to Geauga County to stay with Uncle Walt and Aunt Mary," Ruth said.

He leaned forward, placing his elbows on his desk. "How's that gonna help anything?"

"Mom will be safe from the attacks there," Martha said. "Being in a safe place with people she knows might help her nerves to settle."

Grace nodded. "Maybe she'll be able to get off the medication that's making her act so spacey and out of touch with what's going on around her."

Roman sat massaging his forehead as he contemplated the idea. Maybe taking Judith to Geauga County would be a good thing. He could let people know that he planned to take Judith to visit his brother, Walt, for a few days and that he would be staying there with her until she got settled in and used to the idea of being away from home. Hopefully, the culprit would hear that Roman was leaving and plan another attack, believing that no one was at the Hostettler home. Roman would return home sooner than planned without telling anyone. Then he'd hide out in the house. With any luck, he could catch the person in the act. Of course this plan would mean that he'd have to get Martha out of the house, too.

Roman looked up and smiled at his daughters. "I think you've got a good idea. I'll get in touch with Walt right away and see if it's agreeable with them. If it is, I'll see if Rosemary's free to drive us up there. She's been wanting to go up to Geauga County to see where Walt lives, anyway. We can spend a few days having a little family reunion," he added.

"I'm glad you're in agreement with this," Ruth said with a look of relief.

"Of course this means I'll have to put my plans to begin building the new shop on hold awhile longer, but that's not as important as getting your mamm away from here right now." He looked over at Martha. "I think it would be a good idea if you went with us to Walt's."

Her mouth dropped open. "How come?"

"I wouldn't feel comfortable leaving you home alone. It might not be safe."

"But I can't go," she argued. "I'm needed here to care for my dogs. Not to mention my job at Irene's."

"Martha can stay with us," Grace was quick to say. "That way, you won't have to worry about her being alone in the house, and she'll be able to fulfill her responsibilities to Irene and still care for her dogs."

Roman nodded. "That sounds fine to me." He looked back at

Martha. "You can go to the barn to do what you need to do with the dogs whenever Cleon's around, but I don't want you going there alone. And no going into the house while I'm gone, either. Is that clear?"

"Jah," Martha said with a slow nod. He could tell by her frown that she wasn't happy about it.

"When do you think you'll be able to leave for Geauga County?" Grace asked.

He shrugged. "I'd like to head out tomorrow morning, but that will depend on whether Rosemary's available to take us or not."

"If she's not, maybe you can hire Ray Larson to drive you and Mom up there," Ruth suggested. "He's driven you plenty of other places."

"That's true," Roman said with a nod. "But Rosemary's been wanting to see Walt and his family, so I think it would be best to wait until she's free to drive us."

"I have several errands I need to run in Millersburg, and I'll probably be gone the rest of the day," John said as he slung his jacket over his shoulder and headed for the door. "See if you can get those cabinets finished up while I'm gone, okay?"

Luke nodded. "Unless we get a bunch of customers, I should have them finished by closing time."

"Great. See you tomorrow then."

A short time later, the shop door opened, and in walked Rod and Tim, two of the English fellows Luke had been hanging out with for some time.

"What are you up to?" Tim asked, coming to stand near Luke.

"I'm trying to finish up a set of cabinets for my boss," Luke replied.

Rod glanced around. "Where is your boss, anyway?"

"He had an appointment in Millersburg today." Luke dipped his paintbrush into the can of stain. "So what are you two doing here?"

"Came by to see if you'd like to go to New Philly with us. There's a new sports bar that just opened there, and we thought—"

Luke shook his head and pointed to the cabinets. "You'd better count me out. I've got work to do."

Rod stuck his head close to Luke. "Since your boss ain't here, then you oughta be able to take off a little early, don't ya think?"

"Not if I want to keep my job."

"Puh!" Tim grunted. "You're such an old stick-in-the-mud these days. Haven't wanted to do anything fun since you started hanging around that little gal who raises dogs."

Luke grimaced. He'd never told Tim or Rod that he'd been seeing Martha.

"Don't look so stunned." Rod leaned over and rapped Luke on the head. "There isn't much that goes on around here that me and Tim don't know about."

"Do you know that Martha's folks had a brick thrown through their bedroom window the other night?" Luke asked pointedly.

Rod looked at Tim then back at Luke. "Nope. Never heard a thing."

Luke spread some stain over one of the cabinet doors as he contemplated what to say next. If Rod and Tim were responsible for the attacks, they'd probably never admit it, but he felt that he needed to ask.

"I know you two have pulled a couple of pranks around here over the last few years," he began. "I thought you might have had something to do with the brick that was thrown."

Rod shook his head. "Nope. The only pranks we've been involved in were some outhouse tipping and vandalism at a few of the local schools. We've had nothing to do with what's been done at the Hostettlers.' " He looked over at Tim. "Ain't that right, Tim?"

Tim nodded. "We might like to have a little fun now and then, but we're not stupid enough to single anyone out or do anything that might get the law on us."

"The law could get on you for vandalism at the schools if they knew you were the ones who'd done it," Luke reminded.

Rod squinted his dark eyes at Luke. "Who's gonna tell–you?"

Luke shook his head.

Tim grunted and poked Rod's arm. "Lay off Luke, would ya? He's never given us any reason not to trust him, so don't be accusing him now."

Rod scowled at Tim. "I never said I didn't trust him. Just wanted to know if he was planning to rat on us or not."

"Doesn't sound like he is to me." Tim looked back at Luke. "Do you want to go to New Philly with us or not?"

"I appreciate the offer, but I'd better not. Don't want to risk getting my boss mad at me for sloughing off."

Rod nudged Tim's arm. "Let's go then. We're burning daylight."

Tim nodded and headed across the room. "See you soon, Luke," he called as they went out the door.

Luke grimaced. If Rod and Tim knew he'd been hanging around with them all this time just so he could find out if they were the ones responsible for the attacks, who knew what they might do?

I just don't think either Rod or Tim has anything to do with those attacks, Luke thought as he continued his work. *It's got to be someone who has a grudge against someone in Martha's family.*

Luke sucked in his breath. An image of Toby flashed into his mind. *He may not have any specific grudge against the Hostettlers, but he does have a grudge against me. I think I'll go over to Toby's house after I close the shop for the day and have a little talk with him. It's time we get a few things straightened out between us. If Toby's responsible for the attacks, maybe I can get him to admit what he's done.*

Chapter 36

That evening after work, Luke headed straight over to Toby's. As he climbed the back porch stairs, he prayed that God would give him the right words.

He lifted his hand to knock on the screen door, but the door swung open before his knuckles connected with the wood. Sadie stood on the other side of the door, her apron covered with a dusting of flour. "Luke! I'm surprised to see you," she said. "I heard a buggy rumble into the yard and figured it must be Toby."

"Toby's not here?"

Sadie shook her head. "He hasn't come home from work yet." She motioned to one of the wooden chairs sitting near the door. "If you'd like to wait for him, I'm sure he'll be here soon."

Luke shifted from one foot to the other as he contemplated what to do. Sadie seemed uncomfortable, so maybe it would be best if he came back some other time. Or he could try to catch Toby over at Keim Lumber. Maybe he hadn't left yet. He smiled at Sadie and said, "I think I'll head over to Charm and see if I can catch Toby before he gets off work."

"He might have already left," she said. "Are you sure you wouldn't rather wait for him here?"

Luke rubbed his chin thoughtfully and shook his head. "I'd better not." He turned and was about to step off the porch, when Sadie said, "I saw Martha earlier today when I stopped by their place to look at one of her pups as a possible birthday present for my mamm."

"How are things with her?" Luke asked.

"Okay with the kennel business but not so good with her mamm."

"She told you about the brick and Judith's reaction to it?"

Sadie nodded, her dark eyes looking ever so serious. "I guess Judith has been getting more nervous after each of the attacks. This one must have put her over the edge."

"That's what I understand. From what I heard, the doctor had to put her on medication in order to calm her down."

"Jah, and now Roman's decided to take Judith away for a while. Martha said they're hoping a change of scenery and being in a safe place might help heal her shattered nerves."

"Where are they going, do you know?"

"To Geauga County, where Roman's brother, Walt, lives."

"Is Martha going with them?"

Sadie shook her head. "She said she has to be nearby to care for her dogs, and she's got that part-time job with Irene to worry about."

Alarm flooded Luke's soul. If Martha wasn't going with her folks, did that mean she would be home alone? He was about to ask when Sadie said, "Martha plans to stay at Grace and Cleon's place while her folks are gone."

Luke blew out his breath. "That's good to hear."

Sadie tipped her head and smiled at him. "You love her, don't you?"

"Who?"

"Martha, of course. That's who we've been talking about, right?"

He nodded as a flush of heat covered his face. "I do care for her," he admitted. "For all the good it's doing me."

"You mean because of her daed?"

"Jah." He stared at the floorboards beneath his feet. "Unless I can prove to Roman that I've had nothing to do with the attacks, I'm afraid there's no chance of Martha and me ever being together as a couple."

Sadie touched his arm. "Where there's a will, there's a way. Where love's involved, there's always hope." She giggled, kind of embarrassed-like. "Look at Toby and me. For a long while, I thought we'd never get married, but look at us now. We're an old married couple."

"Come on, Sadie, you and Toby haven't even been married a year yet."

She smiled. "That's true, but there are days when it feels like we have."

Luke wasn't sure what Sadie meant by that, but he didn't feel he had the right to ask. Besides, he needed to get back in his buggy and head for Charm if he was going to catch Toby before he left work.

"I'd best be on my way," he said, turning to go. "If I should miss Toby, would you let him know I was here and that I'd like the chance to speak with him soon?"

"Jah, sure." Sadie gave Luke another smile and stepped into the house.

As Luke headed for the buggy, an idea popped into his head. If no one would be at Roman's house for several days, it would be the perfect time to go over there and look around. He might camp out in the barn for a few days. If the culprit showed up at the Hostettlers' again, Luke hoped he might catch him in the act.

Luke unhooked his horse from the hitching rail and was about to climb into his buggy, when Toby showed up. *Good. That'll save me a trip to Charm.*

Toby scowled as he climbed down from his buggy. "What are you doin' here, Luke?"

"I came to speak with you, but when Sadie said you weren't home from work yet, I decided to head over to Keim Lumber and see if I could catch you there."

"What did you want to talk to me about?" Toby asked as he unhitched his horse.

"It's about the attacks that have been going on at the Hostettlers'."

Toby grunted. "You'd know more about that than me."

Luke balled his fingers into the palms of his hands. "What makes you so sure I'm the one behind the attacks, and how come you've been trying to make it look as if I'm the guilty one?"

"You've been irritated with Roman ever since he fired you." Toby led his horse to the barn, and Luke followed.

"I'll admit, I was irritated at first, but I've got a better job now working for John. I'm not carrying a grudge against Roman. I'm not the one responsible for any of the attacks against them." Luke ground his teeth together. "You, on the other hand, have been carrying a grudge against me for some time, and it makes me wonder if–"

"If what?" Toby put the horse inside its stall and leveled Luke with a piercing look. "What are you accusing me of?"

"For some time now, you've been bad-mouthing me to my folks, to Roman, and to anyone who'll listen." Luke's voice shook as he struggled to keep control of his emotions. He should have had this discussion with Toby a long time ago.

Toby grabbed a brush from the shelf overhead and started grooming his horse.

"You know, Toby," Luke went on to say, "instead of pointing fingers at me, you ought to be more concerned about making yourself look innocent."

"Innocent of what? I've done nothin' wrong."

Luke grunted. "You think running off at the mouth and telling tales about me isn't wrong?"

Toby's face turned bright red. "Well, I–"

"I have to wonder if it's not you who's been terrorizing the Hostettler family."

"Me? What reason would I have to hurt the Hostettlers?"

Luke shrugged. "The only thing I can think of is that you did it to get even with me."

"Huh?"

"You thought that if you could make it look like I was the one doing the attacks, then I'd be in trouble with the Hostettlers–not to mention the law."

Toby shook his head. "No way! You don't know what you're talking about, and you sure have no proof of such a crazy notion."

Luke nodded. "I think I do have some proof."

"Wh-what kind of proof?" Toby sputtered.

"Martha and I have found some evidence, and a couple of the items point to you."

The color in Toby's cheeks deepened. "I don't know what you're talking about. What kind of evidence did you find that points to me?"

"A work glove and a ballpoint pen."

"What?"

"I said–"

Toby held up one hand. "I know what you said. I just can't figure out what a pen and a glove would have to do with me."

"A work glove," Luke said through clenched teeth. "Just like the ones you wear at Keim Lumber."

Toby's eyebrows furrowed. "I told you that I'd lost my glove, so what does that prove? And I don't know anything about a pen."

"The pen Martha found came from the Farmstead Restaurant in Berlin. I know you eat there a lot, so you could have picked up the pen during one of your meals."

Toby shook his head. "I had nothing to do with any of those attacks, and unless you can prove otherwise, I'd appreciate it if you'd stay away from me!"

"Fine then!" Luke started to walk away but turned back. "Just remember one thing. I'll be watching you, Toby!"

Martha was about to leave Irene's for the day, when she spotted Luke's buggy coming up the driveway. She stepped up to his buggy when he pulled up at the hitching rail. "This is a surprise," she said. "I didn't expect to see you today."

"I wasn't sure if you were working for Irene today or not, but I thought I'd stop by, just in case." Luke's face was bright red, and he swiped his hand across his forehead, glistening with sweat.

Alarm rose in Martha's chest. "What's wrong? You look really upset."

He nodded. "I just came from Toby and Sadie's place, and I wanted you to know what all was said before you heard Toby's version of things."

Martha's forehead wrinkled. "What are you talking about?"

Luke motioned to his buggy. "Let's have a seat, and I'll tell you what happened."

"Okay." Martha stepped into the passenger's side of Luke's buggy, and he slipped in beside her.

Luke cleared his throat a few times and reached for her hand. "Do you still believe I'm innocent of the attacks against your family?"

"Of course I do. I trust you, Luke. Really, I do."

"Good." He drew in a quick breath and released a puff of air that lifted the hair off his forehead. "I've told you before that I think Toby might be the one doing the attacks and that he's been doing them in order to get even with me. In the process, he's trying to make me look guilty."

"I thought you were thinking those rowdy English fellows you've been hanging around with might be responsible for the attacks."

"I did think that at first, but not anymore. As time's gone on, I've become more and more convinced that the attacks have been done by Toby." Luke chewed on his bottom lip and grimaced. "Remember that work glove we found that looked like one of Toby's?"

She nodded.

"And then there was that ballpoint pen you found. It had the name of the Farmstead Restaurant on it. Toby eats there a lot. I wouldn't be surprised if that pen was his."

Martha groaned. "I hate to think our own bishop's son could have done anything so terrible. He's a baptized member in our church, not to mention that he's married to Ruth's best friend."

"I know, I know." Luke sat staring at the floor. Finally, he lifted his gaze and turned to face her. "I had it out with Toby. . .told him what I suspect."

"What'd he say?"

"He denied it, of course. Said if I thought he was the one doing the attacks, I'd have to prove it." Luke's eyes narrowed. "Which is exactly what I plan to do, and I think it might be soon."

"Why?"

"Before Toby got home from work, I spoke with Sadie. She mentioned that she'd talked to you earlier today when she came over to your place to look at a puppy."

"That's right," Martha said with a nod.

"Sadie told me your daed's planning to take your mamm and go up to Geauga County with the hope that it will settle her nerves."

"Jah. I'd planned to tell you all this as soon as I saw you again. I guess Sadie beat me to it, though."

"It doesn't matter how or when I found out," Luke said. "The important thing is that I know."

"Why's it important for you to know?"

"Because having your house sit empty for several days is exactly what I need."

"Huh?"

"I'm planning to hide out in the barn during the nights your folks are gone, and if the attacker comes around again, I'll hopefully catch him in the act."

Martha's mouth fell open. "Are—are you sure that's a good idea? I mean, what if someone sees you there, or what if—"

"You worry too much. I'll be just fine." Luke leaned over and gave her a kiss.

Rosemary glanced in the rearview mirror at Judith asleep in the backseat of her car; then she looked over at Roman, sitting up front in the passenger seat, chewing on his fingernails. "You're not nervous about taking Judith to Walt and Mary's place are you?" she asked.

"Huh?" He dropped his hands to his lap. "Uh. . .no, I'm just. . . well, I've come up with a plan, and—" He turned and looked over his shoulder. "Good, Judith's asleep. I'm glad we decided to head out this evening rather than wait until tomorrow morning."

"I suppose it is a good idea to get Judith away from home as soon as we can."

Roman glanced in the back again. "I wouldn't want her to hear what I'm about to say." He turned toward the front and rubbed the bridge of his nose. "Not that she'd probably give much response. That medication the doctor prescribed keeps her so calm and relaxed she barely notices what's going on around her."

Rosemary nodded. "Maybe after some time at Walt and Mary's, she'll relax and her medication can be cut in half."

"I'm hoping that's the case."

"How long are you planning to stay in Geauga County?"

"Uh. . .that's what I wanted to talk to you about. I'm only planning to spend the night, and then I'll ride home with you after supper tomorrow evening."

"Roman, I hardly think one night at Walt's place is going to put Judith at ease enough to return home."

He shook his head. "Judith will stay with Walt as long as necessary. I'll be going home tomorrow with you."

"You're leaving Judith alone?"

"She won't be alone; she'll be in good hands with our brother and his wife. When I talked with Walt on the phone last night, he said Judith could stay with them for as long as necessary."

"Is this about you not wanting to be gone from your business?"

"No." Roman's voice lowered, and he cast another quick glance over his shoulder.

Rosemary looked in her rearview mirror again. Judith was still asleep. "What is it you're not telling me, brother?"

"I'm planning to return home and hide out in the house, hoping there will be another attack."

"What?" Her mouth dropped open. "Why on earth would you want another attack to occur?"

"So I can catch the one doing it." Roman pursed his lips. "I told as many people as I could think of that I'm taking Judith to my brother's place and that we'll be gone for several days. I did it in hopes that the word would get back to the one doing the attacks and he'll think with no one at home that he'll have the perfect opportunity to attack again."

She slowly shook her head and groaned. "That's the most foolhardy thing I've ever heard you say. It could be downright dangerous."

He folded his arms in a stubborn pose. "I don't care if it is. I'm tired of these attacks, and I've decided it's time to take matters into my own hands."

"What about trusting God to take care of your family?"

"I am trusting God. I'm trusting Him to help me learn who the attacker is and bring these harassments to an end."

Chapter 37

Grace had just said good-bye to Anna, who was being driven to school in Martha's buggy, when she spotted Sheriff Osborn's car coming up their driveway. "I wonder what he wants," she murmured.

"Who?" Cleon called from the kitchen doorway.

"Sheriff Osborn. He's heading this way."

Grace stepped outside, and Cleon joined her on the porch. A few minutes later, the sheriff parked his car and got out. "I was down at Roman's house looking for him, but no one was there," he called. "Thought maybe he might be up here."

Cleon shook his head. "Roman's out of town."

Sheriff Osborn stepped onto the porch. "For how long?"

"Several days, I believe," Grace said. "He took Mom up to Geauga County to his brother's place for a while."

"Hmm. . .I see. Well, I just wanted your dad to know that I've been doing more investigating lately, and I've ruled out several of his original suspects." The sheriff leaned on the porch railing. "I think I might know who's responsible for the attacks, but I won't know for sure until I follow up on a couple more leads."

"What kind of leads?" Cleon asked.

"I'd rather not say anything more until I know something definite and the criminal's been caught." The sheriff raked his fingers through the back of his hair. "With your folks being gone for several days, it might be an open invitation for another attack, so I'm planning to keep a close watch on their place–hopefully catch the attacker in the act."

Grace drew in a deep breath and released it slowly as a sense of hope filled her soul. Was it possible? Did the sheriff really know who had done the attacks? It would be such a relief for all of them if the person was caught. Maybe it would happen while Mom and Dad were gone. Maybe soon the family would find some peace.

As Martha guided her horse and buggy down the road toward Anna's school, she thought about her folks being gone and how this would be the perfect chance to do some investigating without anyone knowing what she was doing or asking a bunch of questions. She planned to keep a close watch on things. If the attacker struck again, she would hopefully see who it was.

"Mama said she would take me over to Poppy's new house soon, but probably not 'til Grandpa and Grandma Hostettler get back from Geauga County."

Martha reached across the seat and touched Anna's hand. "I know you want to see your poppy again."

"Jah." Anna fiddled with the strap on her backpack. "Is Grandma Hostettler gonna die?"

Anna's unexpected question took Martha by surprise. "Ach, no, Anna. What makes you ask such a thing?"

Tiny wrinkles marred Anna's forehead. "Mama says Grandma's sick, and when my other *grossmudder* got sick, she died."

Feeling the need to reassure the child, Martha reached across the seat and took Anna's hand. "Grandma Hostettler's not going to die. She just needs to rest and calm her nerves. That's why Grandpa and Aunt Rosemary took her up to Geauga County to see my uncle Walt and aunt Mary."

A look of relief flooded Anna's face, and she smiled. "When they get back home, will Grandma be better?"

"I hope so, Anna. I surely do."

Anna remained silent for the rest of the ride, and Martha hoped it was because the child's mind was at ease.

Now if someone could only put my mind at ease.

As Luke headed down the road in his truck toward John's shop, he glanced at the clock on the dash and grimaced. It was getting close to the time when he should be opening the shop, and if John showed up and Luke wasn't there, he'd have some explaining to do. Since he was supposed to be sleeping in the back of the shop, John would expect him to be there and to open the place on time.

Maybe I should tell John where I spent last night. Luke shook his head. *No, John's a gabber. He might say something to one of his customers.*

Luke had told John last night that Roman was planning to take Judith up to Geauga County and would be gone several days, but he didn't want anyone but Martha knowing he'd spent last night in Roman's barn and planned to continue doing so until Roman returned home. If the attacker heard that Roman and Judith were out of town, that could be a good thing, because he'd probably think he had free run of the place. But if the attacker thought anyone was hiding out with the intent of discovering who was responsible for the attacks, it could prove to be disastrous.

Luke had just passed the Amish schoolhouse when he noticed Martha's buggy pulling out of the parking lot. Figuring she must have driven Anna to school, he waited until her buggy was ahead of him; then he pulled up beside her and waved her off the road.

"Wie geht's?" Martha asked when he stepped up to her buggy.

"I'm kind of sore and stiff after sleeping in your daed's barn all night." Luke reached around to rub a sore spot in his lower back.

Her mouth fell open. "You stayed there last night?"

He nodded. "Said I was going to, didn't I?"

"Well, jah, but I figured you wouldn't start sleeping there until I could get you a key to open the padlock so you'd be able to get into the barn." Her forehead wrinkled. "How did you get into the barn, anyhow?"

"I brought my ladder along and went in through the small window that opens into the hayloft."

She slowly shook her head. "I might have known you'd pull something like that."

He offered her a sheepish grin. "I'm surprised you didn't know I had slept there."

"How would I know? I stayed up at Grace and Cleon's place last night, and there isn't a good view of my daed's barn from there. Just the rooftop can be seen from the second floor."

"I knew you were staying at Grace's, but I figured you'd show up at the barn to feed your dogs this morning and that you'd find me sleeping in the hayloft."

She shook her head. "Grace asked me to take Anna to school this morning. She was running late, so I decided the dogs could wait to be fed until I got back from the schoolhouse."

"Ah, I see."

"Did you see or hear anything unusual during the night?" she asked.

"Nope, and it wasn't because I was in a deep sleep, either." He grunted and rubbed his back again. "What little sleep I did get was not restful. I think I'll take the mattress off the cot I've been using in John's back room and take that with me when I sleep in the barn tonight."

Martha reached into her handbag and handed him a key. "You'd better take this with you then, because it would be kind of hard to carry the mattress up the ladder and squeeze it through the window."

"Good thinking." Luke took the key and shoved it in his pants pocket, but as he thought things through, his eyebrows drew together. "If I take your key, then how are you gonna get into the barn when you need to?"

"Cleon has a key. I'll ask to use his."

"Won't he think it's a bit strange that you'd need his key when you have one of your own?"

"I'll tell him it was in my purse but it's not there now."

"You'd tell your brother-in-law a lie?"

"I wouldn't really be lying, because the key won't be in my purse—it'll be in your pocket."

Luke chuckled. "Good point. No wonder I fell in love with you—you're a real schmaert woman."

Martha's cheeks turned pink, and if a car hadn't been passing just then, he would have kissed her.

"I'd best be on my way," Luke finally said. "I need to get to work before John gets there, or he'll want to know why I didn't sleep in his back room last night."

"John doesn't know what you're planning to do?"

He shook his head. "Figured the fewer people who knew about my plan, the better. No point getting the word spread around that someone's hiding out in your daed's barn hoping to catch the attacker."

"You think John would blab if you asked him not to?"

"Probably not intentionally, but he's quite the gabber. Who knows what he might let slip to one of his customers?"

Martha nodded. "Maybe it's best that you don't say anything then."

He smiled. "On that note, I'd better be off. Maybe I'll see you in the morning."

"If I get out to the barn to feed my dogs before you leave." She reached out and touched his arm. "Please be careful, Luke. I couldn't stand it if anything happened to you."

Luke clasped her hand. "You be careful, too."

Chapter 38

"Are you sure it's going to work out for you to stay here?" Rosemary asked as she pulled along the shoulder of the road several feet from Roman's driveway.

Roman nodded. "I'll be fine."

"Does Cleon know what you're planning to do?" she asked.

He nodded. "He's agreed to keep quiet about it."

"What if something happens while you're asleep?"

"I'll stay awake at night and try to sleep during the day. Cleon will be at the shop in the barn most of the day. I doubt anyone would be dumb enough to come around then, anyway."

"I suppose you're right." Rosemary leaned across the seat and gave him a hug. "Please be careful, and if you need anything, I'm only a phone call away."

"I'll remember that. Thanks for driving me and Judith up to Walt's place. I feel a lot better knowing I've left her in good hands."

"You're welcome."

Roman opened the car door and stepped into the night. As Rosemary drove away, he sent up a silent prayer. *Lord, please help Judith get better soon, and help me to find out who's behind the attacks.*

Luke pulled his truck off the road and parked it behind a clump of bushes about a quarter of a mile from the Hostettlers' place. He didn't dare drive it onto their property and give away the fact that he was there.

He reached under the seat and grabbed a flashlight. "Oh no," he groaned. "I forgot to bring that mattress with me."

Luke hesitated, wondering if he should go back to John's shop and get the mattress. He decided it would take too much time. It was dark, and he needed to get to the barn and keep watch as soon as possible.

"I guess one more night on a bed of straw won't kill me," he muttered as he started in the direction of the Hostettlers', being careful to stay hidden behind the trees. Some time later, he came to their driveway, but rather than walking up it, he stayed off to one side where a hedge of bushes grew.

He continued his walk up the driveway until he came to the barn; then he slipped his hand into his pants pocket and withdrew the key Martha had given him that morning. He'd just unlocked the padlock on the door, when he heard a noise. It sounded like a door had slammed up at Roman's house. But how could that be? No one was supposed to be at home there.

Swish! Luke jumped when an owl flew past his head, and he dropped the key.

Thump. . .thump. . .thump. . . Another noise came from the house, and he whirled in that direction.

I'd better check things out before I get settled in the barn.

Using only the light of the moon, Luke crept along the edge of the lawn. He was almost to the house when he felt someone's hand touch his shoulder.

"What do you think you're doing?"

Luke's mouth went dry as he whirled around. Holding the flashlight in front of him, he directed the beam of light at the man who'd startled him. "Roman! What are you doing here? I thought you'd taken Judith to Geauga County."

"I did take her, but I came back so I could keep an eye on my place." Roman's eyes narrowed as he glared at Luke. "What I'd like to know is what *you're* doing on my property in the middle of the night." A muscle on the side of Roman's neck quivered as he held his hand in front of his face. "For heaven's sake, put that flashlight down! You're gonna blind me with it!"

"Sorry," Luke mumbled as he lowered the flashlight.

"You came here to do another act of vandalism, didn't you?"

"No, I–"

"I'll just bet you didn't. What other reason would you have for sneaking around my place in the dark?"

"I was heading for the barn so I could–"

"What? Do something to one of the animals there?"

Luke opened his mouth to reply, but Roman rushed on. "I've spent the last couple of years trying to deal with these attacks by choosing to look the other way, but I've come to the conclusion that there are times when God expects people to put feet to their prayers."

"What's that supposed to mean?"

"It means, I left Judith in Geauga County and came back home so I could keep an eye on our place and hopefully catch whoever's been doing the attacks to us." Roman leaned so close that Luke could feel his hot breath blowing on his neck. "It looks like the Lord's finally answered my prayers and has helped me learn who the culprit is." He grabbed Luke's arm before Luke could offer a word in his own defense. "You're comin' with me."

"To where?"

"To the phone shed. I'm calling the sheriff to let him know I caught you trespassing on my property in the middle of the night. I'm going to tell him that I think you were about to commit another act of vandalism."

Luke shook his head. "No, that's not why I'm here. I–" He glanced around nervously, hoping no one had seen the two of them out here. If the attacker had decided to strike again and had found them standing out here on the lawn, he'd be long gone.

"Look," Luke said in the calmest voice he could muster, "why don't the two of us go into your house and talk things through? If you'd just give me a chance to explain things to you–"

"You can explain it to the sheriff!"

"I'll tell you what. If you promise to hear me out, and then if you decide I'm still the guilty party, I'll phone the sheriff myself."

"Fine then." Holding onto Luke's arm, Roman led the way to his house. Once they were in kitchen, he turned to Luke and said, "All right now, let's hear your story."

Luke took a seat at the kitchen table and proceeded to tell Roman how for the last several months he and Martha had been trying to find out who was responsible for the attacks. He ended by saying that he'd spent last night in Roman's barn and had planned to sleep there again tonight, hoping the attacker would show up so he could catch him in the act of committing another crime.

"That's some story you told."

The room was dark so Luke couldn't see Roman's face clearly, but he knew from the tone of Roman's voice that he didn't believe him.

"It's the truth; just ask Martha if you don't believe me."

"I'm not asking my daughter anything that has to do with you." Roman grunted. "Besides, I told her to stay away from you some time ago, and I don't think she'd go against my wishes."

"She didn't deliberately go against your wishes, but she wants these attacks to come to an end as much as I do."

"As much as you do? What reason would you have for wanting the attacks to end?"

"Because I'm in love with Martha, and she loves me. I'd like your permission to court her."

"That will never happen!"

Luke swallowed around the lump in his throat. This wasn't going well, and if he couldn't convince Roman that he and Martha had been working together and that he wasn't the one responsible for the attacks, he'd probably be heading for jail before the night was over.

"If Martha and I aren't working together, then why'd she give me this?" Luke reached into his pocket to retrieve the key Martha had given him but found it empty. That's when he remembered that he'd dropped the key by the barn.

"What's in your pocket?"

"Nothing. I mean, I did have a key to your barn, but I dropped it."

"How'd you get a key to unlock my barn?"

"Martha gave it to me so I could get inside to spend the night."

"I don't think my daughter would be dumb enough to give anyone outside of our family a key to my barn."

"She did give me the key. Let's go to the barn now, and I'll look for it."

"I think you're trying to pull a fast one; that's what I think."

"No, I'm not. Please, let's go to the barn."

"Give me a few minutes to think about this some more."

Martha woke up in a cold sweat. She'd been dreaming that someone had broken into the barn, taken the wrench and glove she'd hidden in the hayloft, and had set the barn on fire. What if it was true? What if–

She threw the covers aside, jumped out of bed, and raced to the window. From the second floor guest room at Grace's house, she could only see the top of Dad's barn. No smoke or flames shot out from it.

Martha leaned against the window ledge. That dream had been so real. She drew in a deep breath and tried to relax. What she needed most was some assurance that she was doing the right thing in trying to solve the mystery of the attacks.

Last night, before Martha had gone to bed, Grace had told her that the sheriff had stopped by that day and said he thought he might know who was responsible for the attacks and that he'd let them know more when he could.

Martha shuddered as a new realization hit her. If the sheriff thought he was getting close to catching the one responsible, then he couldn't be the culprit.

She turned on the battery-operated lamp by her bed and picked up the Bible lying on the nightstand. How long had it been since she'd read God's Word and sought guidance from Him?

She opened the Bible to Proverbs, one of her favorite books. Her gaze went to the third chapter, verses 5 and 6. She read the passage out loud. " 'Trust in the Lord with all thine heart; and lean not unto thine own understanding. In all thy ways acknowledge him, and he shall direct thy paths.' "

"I haven't been doing that, Lord," she murmured. "I've been trying to take matters into my own hands and haven't trusted You to direct my paths. Maybe what I need to do is go out to the barn, get the evidence I have hidden in the hayloft, and take it to the sheriff in the morning."

Martha removed her nightgown, put on a dress, slipped into her sneakers, and tied a black scarf over her head. If Luke was in the barn, as he said he would be, she wanted to explain to him her decision to turn over the evidence to the sheriff.

With that settled in her mind, she grabbed the flashlight from her nightstand and tiptoed out of the room so she wouldn't wake Cleon, Grace, or the children.

Downstairs, she slipped quietly out the back door and hurried into the night air.

She found the barn unlocked and figured Luke must be inside, but when she stepped through the doorway, a sudden chill shot up her spine. She thought about that morning several months ago when she'd been doused with white paint because someone had rigged a bucket of paint above the door. Instinctively, she looked up. There was nothing.

I'm just being paranoid, she told herself. *Everything's fine. 'Be of good courage, and he shall strengthen your heart, all ye that hope in the Lord,'* she quoted from Psalm 31:24. It was a verse she'd learned as a child.

"Luke, are you awake?" she called, shining her flashlight toward the hayloft.

Woof! Woof!

"Quiet, Heidi; it's only me." Martha recognized her female sheltie's bark and figured she must have taken the dog by surprise when she'd entered the barn.

Holding the flashlight in front of her, she moved toward the back of the barn where the kennels were located. Heidi wagged her tail when she saw Martha, and Martha was glad to see that everything was okay. She just needed to talk to Luke and get the evidence she'd hidden under the mound of hay in the loft.

She reached through the wire fence and patted the top of the dog's head. "Go back to sleep, girl. I'll see you in the morning."

Martha made her way to the ladder leading to the hayloft and climbed up. "Luke, are you up here?"

No response.

She shinned the light around but saw no sign of him. *I wonder where he could be? Maybe he's in one of the empty stalls.*

She dug through the mound of hay, opened the box, and picked up the wrench and glove.

Thump! Thump!

"Luke, is that you?"

No response.

There was a muffled grunt, and then an arm reached out and grabbed her around the waist.

"Luke, I–"

Slap!

Martha gasped as a hand connected to her face. She dropped the glove, but her fingers tightened around the wrench.

"You're gonna pay for every year I suffered. You and your family are gonna pay!"

Martha swallowed against the bitter taste of bile rising in her throat. Even without seeing the man's face, she knew who it was.

Chapter 39

Rosemary punched her pillow and tried to find a comfortable position. She'd been tossing and turning in bed for nearly two hours. She couldn't seem to relax, couldn't keep the negative thoughts out of her head. What if Judith never got better? What if the attacks continued and they never found out who was doing them? What if Roman had put himself in danger by hiding out at his house?

The words of Romans 12:12 popped into her head: *"Rejoicing in hope; patient in tribulation; continuing instant in prayer."*

Rosemary slipped from her bed and went down on her knees. "Heavenly Father, the attacks against my brother and his family have affected each one in a different way. I pray that You will give everyone a sense of peace and the faith to put their hope in You. Help them learn patience in waiting for answers and remind us all that our strength comes from You. Amen."

As Rosemary got to her feet, she made a decision. She would get dressed and drive over to Roman's house. Since she couldn't sleep anyhow, the least she could do was keep him company during his nighttime vigil.

"Did ya hear what I said? You're gonna pay—each and every one of you has gotta pay!"

"What are you talking about?" Martha pointed the flashlight at John. "Why are you dressed in Amish clothes?"

He yanked on her arm, pulling her over to a bale of hay, and shoved her down. She smelled alcohol on his breath, and his clothes reeked of smoke. How odd. She'd never known him to drink or smoke. But then, she didn't really know him that well. None of them did. John had moved to the area a few years ago and opened a woodworking shop nearby. He'd been helpful and kind–like any good neighbor should–but they didn't really know him.

John sank down beside Martha and clutched at his head. "He. . . he made me do it."

"Who made you do what, John?" Martha hoped her voice sounded calmer than she felt.

"It. . .it's Roman's fault–Harold said so."

"Who's Harold?"

John groaned. "Said it was 'cause I liked wood. Said I reminded him of Roman."

Martha had no idea what John was talking about or why he was dressed in Amish clothes, but she knew by the tone of John's voice that he was deeply troubled.

"Say, where'd you get that?" John pointed to the object Martha held in her hand.

She glanced at the wrench and wondered if she dared–

"I said, where'd you get that?" He leaned closer and snatched the wrench out of her hand.

"I. . .uh. . .Luke found it in the field after my dad's shop was blown up." *Luke. Oh, Luke, where are you?* Martha shined the flashlight around the hayloft. She couldn't see a mattress. If Luke was here, there should be a mattress. But if Luke wasn't here, why had she found the barn door unlocked? The padlock wasn't broken. Could John have crawled up a ladder and entered the barn through the small window in the hayloft like Luke had last night? Or could he. . .

"Gimme that!" John snatched the flashlight out of Martha's hands, clicked it off, and tossed it on the floor. "What was Luke doin' in the field with Harold's wrench?"

"Who is Harold?"

"Harold Crawford–my stepdad." John sounded more coherent.

Maybe the effects of the alcohol were beginning to wear off.

"Did the wrench belong to your stepdad?"

"Harold's dead. Mom gave me his tools. Guess she figured I needed somethin' to remember him by." John's tone was bitter, and a groan escaped his lips. "I've got a lot more'n a few tools to remember Harold by."

A shaft of light from the moon shone in through the hayloft window, and Martha's mouth went dry as she saw John run his fingers over the bridge of his crooked nose. A nose that had obviously been broken at some point.

She looked at the wrench in his hands and thought about the initials she'd seen engraved there. *H. C. Those must stand for Harold Crawford.*

Martha didn't understand why John had brought up his stepdad, or how the man's wrench had ended up in their field. She was about to ask, when John leaned forward and began to sob. "No! No! Don't hit me no more, Harold. Ple-ease it's not my fault. I didn't do nothin' wrong."

Martha wasn't sure what to do. John was clearly upset, but he'd also been drinking. Should she try to run away from him or stay here and try to offer comfort?

She reached out and touched John's shoulder. "Did your stepdad abuse you, John?"

John's head jerked up, and he leaned so close to Martha that she could feel and smell his hot, putrid breath on her face. "Harold—worked for Roman—till he got fired." His words were short and choppy, and he spoke to Martha as if she were a stranger.

"Who got fired?" Martha asked.

"Harold."

"My dad fired your stepdad?"

"Roman fired Harold."

"How come?"

John rubbed his forehead with one hand and clung to the wrench with the other hand. "Harold came to work late—after he'd been drinkin'." He paused, drew in a quick breath, and released it with a shudder. "Got fired—went out drinkin' some more—came home—beat the stuffing outta me and Mom."

Martha gasped as a light began to dawn, but John spoke again before she could comment. "Harold begged Roman—'Gimme my job back'—Roman said no—Harold drank even more."

"Did Harold try to find another job?"

"Said he couldn't find one. Moved us to Oregon 'cause that's where his brother lived. Said he might have a job for Harold." John clutched Martha's arm, and his nails dug into her flesh. "Harold hated Roman for firin' him. I hate Roman, too! It's *his* fault Harold drank. It's *his* fault Harold beat me and Mom when he got drunk." John touched the side of his nose again. "I never shed a tear at his funeral, neither."

"I'm sorry you and your mother were mistreated, but—"

"Roman's gotta pay! It's Roman's fault Harold couldn't find a job. It's Roman's fault Harold hated me! Roman's gotta pay for every year we suffered!"

Martha's heart pounded so hard she heard it echo in her head. "Are. . .are you the one who's done all those horrible things to us?" she asked, already knowing the answer but not wanting to believe it. Ever since John had moved to Holmes County and opened his own woodworking business, he'd been nice to them, loaning Dad tools, buying Martha's dog, and offering his assistance in any way it was needed. It was unthinkable that he could have done such hateful things. It was as if he were two different people—one kind and helpful, the other hateful and full of revenge. John Peterson was a sick man who obviously needed help.

"I did most of those things." John emitted a high-pitched laugh. "Made it look like it was Luke."

It was all coming together. John had befriended Luke and then tried to make it look like Luke had been the culprit so no one would suspect it was John.

"Why did you come here tonight?" Martha dared to ask.

"Came to burn this barn down; that's why I came."

Martha's palms grew sweaty as she thought about the dream

she'd had where the barn was on fire. Had it been a warning of things to come?

"You can't do this, John." Martha struggled not to cry. She had to remain calm. She couldn't let him know how frightened she felt.

Dear God, she silently prayed, *show me what to do.*

"Who's gonna stop me from burnin' the barn?" Before Martha could respond, John grabbed her around the neck and jerked her to his side. "If you tell Harold, you're gonna burn, too."

"I wish you'd believe me, Roman," Luke said as he paced in front of the kitchen table. Even though it was dark in the kitchen and Roman couldn't see Luke's face, he could tell by the tone of his voice that he was agitated.

Well, I'm agitated, too. I can't believe that one of our own could stoop so low as to attack a fellow Amish man. Roman gritted his teeth and clasped his fingers tightly together. *And I can't believe one of my own daughters would betray me by falling for the one who's been attacking us.*

"I'd really like to go look for that key," Luke said.

Roman was about to reply when the back door opened and clicked shut.

"Roman, are you here?"

"I'm in the kitchen," Roman replied, recognizing his sister's voice.

"It's dark in here. How come you don't have a gas lamp lit?"

"Didn't think it'd be a good idea to light up the place and let anyone know I was here."

"Oh, right." Rosemary's voice grew closer as she moved across the room.

"Hello, Rosemary."

"Luke? Is that you?"

"Jah."

"What's going on here?"

Roman could see Rosemary's silhouette as she came closer. "Luke and I are havin' a little discussion," he mumbled. "I caught him sneaking around in the yard."

"I wasn't sneaking," Luke defended himself. "I was just checking things out by the house; then I was going to the barn to spend the night so I could keep an eye on things, when Roman came up and startled me."

"You were planning to sleep in the barn?" Rosemary's tone was one of disbelief.

"That's right. I knew Roman and Judith were gone, so I figured I'd take advantage of the fact that nobody was around and hide out in the barn a few nights."

"Whatever for?"

"He made up some wild story about him and Martha working together to find out who's been attacking us," Roman said before Luke could respond. "Did you ever hear such a tale?"

Rosemary cleared her throat a couple of times. "Actually, Martha did tell me she and Luke—"

"I know, I know. She and Luke are *in love.*"

"It's true we are," Luke spoke again. "That's one of the reasons I need to clear my name and find out who's responsible."

Rosemary moved over to the table and placed her hand on Roman's shoulder. "Before you interrupted me, I was going to say that Martha told me she and Luke were doing some investigating because they wanted to find out who was behind the attacks. I believe Luke when he says he was planning to sleep in the barn so he could keep a watch on things. Maybe we should go up to Grace and Cleon's place and ask Martha to confirm what Luke's said," she suggested.

Roman shook his head. "No way! It's the middle of the night, and I'm not waking my daughter out of a sound sleep so she can tell me how much she loves Luke." He grunted. "She'd probably say most anything to keep him out of trouble."

"Then at least let's go out to the barn so I can look for the key I dropped," Luke said.

"What key?" Rosemary asked.

"The key to the padlock that locks the barn. Martha gave it to me so I could get inside at night."

Rosemary touched Roman's shoulder again and gave it a gentle squeeze. "I think we should see if the key is there, don't you?"

Roman ground his teeth as he mulled things over. Should he go look for the key to please Rosemary, or should he phone the sheriff?

Chapter 40

John slipped the wrench into his pants pocket and stood. "There's been enough talk!" He reached into his shirt pocket and withdrew a cigarette lighter; then he bent down and grabbed a handful of hay. "If ya don't wanna burn with the barn, then you'd better get outa here now."

Martha squeezed her eyes shut and started to pray. *Please, God, don't let John do this. Give me the right words to say.* She opened her eyes and drew in a deep breath. "I. . .I don't know all the details of how things were between my dad and your stepdad, but I'm sorry your stepdad took his anger out on you and your mother."

The stubble of hay crackled under John's feet as he shifted his position. "Roman's gonna be sorry." His voice cracked. "He ruined my life. He's gotta pay."

"Your life's not ruined, John. You have a good business, a well-trained dog that's devoted to you, and you've got your whole life ahead of you. If you'd just–"

"Shut up!" John flicked the lighter, and a glow of light illuminated his face. Deep lines etched his forehead. His eyes looked red and swollen. He pointed to the hayloft ladder. "Go down!"

Martha did as he requested, praying with each step she took. There had to be a way to get through to John. She couldn't let him burn Dad's barn. Her throat felt clogged as she thought about her dogs in their kennels near the back of the barn. She had to save them–Dad's horses, too. Maybe if she made a run for the door, she could dash up the hill to Cleon and Grace's place and get help before it was too late. Or should she stay and keep talking to John—try to make him see the error of his ways? After all, John needed saving, too.

When John stepped off the bottom rung of the ladder behind her, she turned to him and said, "Luke really likes you, John. He's said many times what a good boss you are. He enjoys working for you."

"Luke's a good guy, not like Roman."

Martha cringed. If John liked Luke so much, then why had he tried to make Luke look like the one who'd done the attacks?

"My dad's not a bad person, John," she said. "It's not his fault your stepdad drank or beat you."

"Uh-huh. Harold said it was. Someone's gotta pay."

"Harold said that because he couldn't face up to his own problems," Martha said. "It was Harold's drinking that got him fired, and he beat you and your mother because he needed help for his drinking problem and uncontrollable temper, not because my dad fired him." She paused to gauge John's reaction, but he said nothing.

"Do you believe in God, John?"

He rocked back and forth on his heels. "Mom did. She read her Bible. She prayed when Harold got drunk." He snorted. "For all the good it did her! God never answered Mom's prayers. God didn't care about us. If He had, He would've done somethin' to make Harold stop. Roman needs to pay."

"God doesn't *make* us do anything," Martha said, carefully choosing her words. "He gave us a free will to choose between right and wrong. You can't blame my dad for the actions of your stepdad, either. Harold chose to drink and abuse his family; nobody made him do it."

John gave no reply, but he made no move to light the barn on fire, either. He snapped the cigarette lighter closed and shoved it in his pocket. Martha took that as a good sign and continued with what she felt God had laid on her heart.

"Instead of hating your stepdad and my dad, you need to forgive them."

John shook his head. "I can't."

"In your strength, you can't, but with God's help, you can. In Matthew 6:14, God's Word says: 'For if ye forgive men their trespasses, your heavenly Father will also forgive you.' " Martha touched John's arm. "The things you've done to my family are wrong. The only way you'll ever find peace in your heart is to seek God's forgiveness."

John drew in a ragged breath and blew it out with another snort. "There's only one way to find peace. I've gotta end it all."

End it all? Was John saying he planned to commit suicide? Was he going to burn the barn with him in it? Or was he planning to do worse things to them?

As Roman, Luke, and Rosemary approached the barn, Roman noticed that the door was slightly open. He turned to Luke. "Did you unlock the lock before you dropped the key?"

Luke nodded. "Said I did, didn't I?"

"Did you open the door?"

"No, I never got that far."

Roman frowned. "But it's open now, so that means someone must be in the barn." He turned to Rosemary. "You'd better stay out here. Luke and I will go in and see what's up."

She touched his arm. "Listen, I hear voices. Do you hear them, Roman?"

He tipped his head and listened. "You're right. Someone must be inside."

"Maybe it's Cleon and Martha. Could be they came to feed her dogs," Rosemary said.

"At this hour?" Roman blew out an exasperated breath.

"I'm going in," Luke said, pushing past them.

As soon as Roman stepped inside, he realized that one of the voices was Martha's.

"She's talking to someone," Luke whispered as they crept along in the dark.

"Maybe it's Cleon." Roman followed the sounds of Martha's voice. As they drew closer, he saw the back of her head. He shined his flashlight in that direction, and she turned to face him.

A man dressed in Amish clothes stepped out from behind Martha.

Luke rushed forward. "John! What are you doing in Roman's barn in the middle of the night, wearing Amish clothes?"

"That's what I'm wondering, too," Roman said.

John kicked a hunk of straw with the toe of his boot and mumbled, "Came to burn down the barn."

Rosemary gasped, and Roman gripped the flashlight so hard his fingers ached. "You were going to do what?"

John's finger shook as he pointed it at Roman. "Came to make you pay for what you did to me and Mom!"

Roman's forehead wrinkled as he slowly shook his head. "I don't understand. I've never done anything to you. I don't even know your mother."

"John's stepdad used to work for you," Martha spoke up. "I guess he had a drinking problem and you fired him because of it." Her voice was thick with emotion. "John said his stepdad used to beat him and his mother, and–"

Roman's jaw dropped. "Harold Crawford? Was he your stepdad, John?"

John nodded. "I vowed to make you pay for turnin' the only man I'd ever known as a father into an evil monster."

"So you're the one who did these things against the Hostettlers?" Luke stepped between John and Martha. "And you tried to make it look as if it was me?"

"That's right. Roman's gotta pay for every year Harold smacked me and Mom around."

Roman trembled as he struggled to keep his emotions under control. Violence went against the Amish ways, but at this moment, he wanted to do something that would make John pay for all the horrible things he had done to Roman's family.

"I was just telling John that he doesn't have to hate you or his stepdad," Martha said. "I told him he could ask God to forgive his sins and choose to forgive those who have hurt him."

"Martha's right," Luke added. "You can release your pain to God and forgive Roman, your stepdad, and yourself."

John's gaze went to Martha, back to Luke, and finally to Roman. With a shuddering sob, he dropped to his knees.

Martha and Luke went down beside him, each with their hands on John's trembling shoulders.

Rosemary touched Roman's arm. "Let's move over there." She motioned to the other side of the barn. "Let's give Martha and Luke a chance to talk to John."

Roman hesitated but finally nodded. He lit one of the gas lamps hanging from the rafters and followed Rosemary across the barn.

She stopped near one of the stalls and turned to face him. "Are you finally convinced that Luke's not holding a grudge against you?"

He nodded and swallowed hard, unable to speak around the thick lump in his throat.

"What are you going to do about John?" she asked.

"What do you mean?"

"John needs help for his emotional problems. And he'll have to pay for his deeds. Do you want me to phone the sheriff?"

Roman was about to reply when he heard a car pull into the yard. He opened the barn door and stepped out just as Sheriff Osborn got out of his car.

"Roman, what are you doing here?" the sheriff asked. "I heard that you took your wife up to Geauga County."

"I did, but I left her with my brother and came back so I could keep an eye on my place." Roman moved over to stand by the sheriff. "Did someone call and ask you to come over here?"

The sheriff shook his head. "I was out patrolling tonight, and since I was in the area and knew you were gone, I decided to swing by your place and check on things. Then I spotted two black trucks parked out by the road—one about a quarter of a mile from here and one on the other side of your driveway. It made me suspicious. When I came up the driveway, I spotted a car parked near your house."

"That's my sister's car," Roman said.

"Where is she?"

Roman pointed to the barn. "In there, with Martha, Luke Friesen, and John Peterson."

The sheriff's bushy eyebrows pulled together. "What's going on?"

Roman drew in a quick breath and told the sheriff everything that had transpired since he'd caught Luke in the yard. He ended by saying, "John confessed to the attacks against us."

The sheriff grunted. "I figured as much. I've been watching John for some time and waiting for him to make his next move so I could catch him in the act. He'll pay for his crimes; I can assure you of that."

"I won't press charges against him—it's not the Amish way," Roman was quick to say.

"I realize that, but if John's the one who killed Martin, then the state will press charges. He can't be allowed to get away with the other things he's done to your family, either."

"I'm not saying he should get away with it," Roman said. "I'm just saying I won't press charges."

The sheriff nodded. "Let me worry about the details." He walked swiftly toward the barn, and Roman followed. They found John still on his knees with Martha, Luke, and Rosemary standing around him in a circle.

"John says he knows he'll have to pay for what he's done," Martha said when she spotted the sheriff walking toward them with Dad at his side.

"You got that right," the sheriff said with a nod. He read John his rights and handcuffed him. "I'll drop by some time tomorrow to ask a few more questions," he said to Dad as he led a very quiet and remorseful-looking John out of the barn.

"Flo. I've gotta get Flo," John mumbled as he approached the sheriff's car. "I can't leave my dog alone."

"Don't worry about Flo," Luke called to John. "I'll take care of her for you."

As the sheriff's car headed down the driveway, Dad swiped a hand across his face. "Whew! After all this time of living in fear and wondering when and where the next attack might occur, I can't believe it's finally over."

"Maybe now things will get back to normal and we'll know some peace," Martha said.

"Speaking of peace," Luke said, "I'll need to make my peace with Toby, since I now know he had nothing to do with the attacks."

"And speaking of peace—" Rosemary nudged Dad's arm. "Isn't there something you'd like to say to Luke?"

The rhythm of Martha's heartbeat picked up as she waited to see how Dad would respond. He needed to apologize to Luke, but because Dad was a stubborn man, it was hard for him to admit when he was wrong.

Dad cleared his throat and took a step toward Luke. "My sister's right: I do have something to say to you."

Luke stared at the floor.

"I need to ask your forgiveness, Luke." Dad's voice quavered, and Martha wondered if he might break down in tears. This whole ordeal had to have been terribly stressful on him.

"No need to apologize," Luke said in a voice barely above a whisper. "What's done is done. It's in the past now."

Dad shook his head. "I do need to apologize. I was wrong about you, Luke, and I. . .I ask your forgiveness."

Luke lifted his gaze and stared at Dad. He, too, seemed to be struggling with his emotions. "I accept your apology."

"There's something else I'd like to say," Dad said.

"What's that?"

"Now that John will be going to jail, his shop will be closing down. So, I. . .I was wondering if you'd like to come back to work for me."

"Well, I—"

"Don't worry. I've learned my lesson. I promise not to be so harsh and demanding. If you've got an idea you want to share about woodworking, I'll listen."

"Jah, I would like to come back to work for you, Roman." Luke looked over at Martha and said, "But there's something I'd like even more."

"What's that?" Dad asked.

"I'd like permission to court Martha."

Martha held her breath as she waited for Dad's reply.

Dad stood, mulling things over. Finally, he nodded and said, "You've got my permission, but on one condition."

Luke tipped his head to one side. "What's that?"

"That you sell your truck, get baptized, and join the church."

Luke smiled. "No problem there. That's exactly what I'd planned to do once my name was cleared."

Martha threw herself into Dad's arms and gave him a hug. "Now we just need to get Mom well so she can come home where she belongs."

"That's right," Aunt Rosemary spoke up. "And if I'm not mistaken, you'll probably need your mother's help making a wedding dress soon."

Martha's cheeks burned hot as she looked over at Luke. She was relieved when he stepped forward and whispered in her ear, "You're definitely going to need a wedding dress."

Epilogue

Six months later

As Martha sat at the corner table with her groom and their attendants, her heart swelled with joy. She'd just become Luke's wife, and now that the attacks were behind them, her family had finally found a sense of peace. Sheriff Osborn had come by the other day and given Dad a letter from John, who was still in jail. John admitted that he'd been drinking the night Martin was killed but said he hadn't rammed the buggy with the intent of killing anyone. He also said he'd been reading his Bible every day and that his faith was growing. He'd also been getting some counseling, which was helping him deal with his past and the abuse he'd suffered from his stepdad. John ended the letter by saying that he planned to move back to Oregon when his jail time had been served, and he apologized for all the horrible things he had done.

Martha was glad John was doing well, and she knew that, despite what John had done, God wanted her to forgive him. She also knew that in order to heal, she must forgive.

She glanced across the room to where Mom and Dad sat talking with Luke's parents. Although quiet and reserved, Mom was feeling much better these days. She no longer needed medication for her nerves, and the smile on her face as she leaned close to Dad told Martha that Mom was happy and at peace.

Martha shivered when Luke's warm breath tickled her ear as he leaned close and whispered, "Have you noticed how happy Cleon looks today? I think he was relieved when your daed said he was free to quit working at the shop with us and go out on his own with his honey and candle-making business."

"I'm happy for Cleon and also for his brother Ivan. He and Amanda make a wonderful couple."

Martha motioned to Grace, sitting beside Cleon with Daniel in her lap. "I'm also happy to see Grace looking so peaceful. Now that the attacks have ended and things are better between her and Carl Davis, she always seems to be wearing a smile."

Martha glanced at the table where Aunt Rosemary sat beside her son and his wife. She was glad Ken and Sharon had been able to take vacation time and come to Holmes County for her wedding. Aunt Rosemary was all smiles as she visited with them.

"Did I tell you my cousin Ken and his wife are expecting a baby?" Martha asked.

"You have mentioned that a time or two," Luke said with a chuckle. "I'm glad for them and will be even happier when our time comes."

"Jah, me, too." Martha's gaze went to her aunt again. "Aunt Rosemary's real good with kinner. I think she'll make a fine grossmudder, don't you?"

"I'm sure she will. She's also a good cook, so she'll probably do real well taking over your place at Irene's with all the dinners she serves." Luke motioned to Carl Davis, who sat on the other side of Rosemary with Anna by his side. "From what I hear, your aunt's been seeing a lot of Carl lately, which may be another reason she's wearing such a big smile today."

"Maybe there'll be another wedding in our family sometime soon."

"You mean Rosemary and Carl?"

Martha nodded. "They seem to have a lot in common."

Luke reached for her hand. "Like us, you mean? We both enjoy being outdoors, we like to go fishing, and we take pleasure in working together with the dogs in your kennel business."

Martha smiled. "I appreciate the time you took to make me those new dog runs. Now, not only can I raise my dogs, but I can board and groom other dogs, as well."

He gently squeezed her fingers. "A man will do most anything for the woman he loves."

Her cheeks warmed. No matter how long she and Luke were married, she didn't think she would ever get tired of hearing him say he loved her.

"You two look happier than a couple of kids with a box of candy," Toby said as he and Sadie stepped up to the corner table. "I'm glad everything's worked out so well for you."

"Jah, and for you and me, too," Luke said with a nod. "For quite a while there, I thought our friendship might be over."

Toby clasped Luke's arm. "I feel bad for the trouble I caused. I don't know how I could have ever thought you were behind the attacks on the Hostettlers."

Luke grimaced. "I can't believe I thought it was you, either."

"That's in the past, and we've made our peace, so let's look to the future," Toby said.

"Jah, I agree."

As the men continued to visit, Martha turned to Sadie and said, "How are you feeling these days?"

Sadie's smile seemed to light up the room. "Other than some bouts of heartburn and a bit of morning sickness, I'm feeling right as rain."

"Are you getting anxious for your boppli to be born?"

"Oh, jah." Sadie placed one hand on her bulging stomach. "February can't come soon enough for me." She leaned closer to Martha and whispered, "I'm glad things have worked out for you and Luke. You both deserve to be happy."

"Danki." Martha glanced across the room to where Ruth and Abe sat with their family. God had blessed Ruth when she'd married Abe.

Sadie nudged Toby's arm. "Should we go back to our table now and let the bride and groom visit with their other guests?"

"Jah, sure." Toby smiled at Luke. "I'll talk to you later."

Toby and Sadie had no sooner gone back to their table when Ray and Donna Larson stopped by. "We wanted to offer our congratulations on your marriage," Ray said.

"And say how much we're going to miss you, Martha, now that you won't be our neighbor anymore," Donna put in.

Martha smiled. "I won't be living that far away–just a few miles down the road in the house Dad, Luke, and Cleon built for us on the backside of Luke's folks' property."

Donna patted Martha's arm. "Do come by and see us whenever you can."

"We will," Martha and Luke said in unison.

"We left your wedding present on the back porch," Ray said. "It's a birdhouse that will attract the martins that come into our area every spring."

"Thank you. That's very nice." As Martha watched the Larsons walk away, she thanked God that her suspicions concerning Ray had been wrong. Ray and Donna had been good neighbors for many years.

"There's sure a lot of food here today," Luke said, pushing Martha's thoughts aside. "I'll be so full by the end of the day that I probably won't have to eat for a week."

She snickered and poked him in the ribs. "If I know you, come tomorrow morning, you'll be the first one at the breakfast table."

He laughed and motioned to the table where his folks sat with Martha's parents. "From the looks of my daed's plate, I'd say he's eating more than his share today."

"I guess you take after him then, huh?"

Luke shrugged as his face sobered. "I hope not too much."

"What do you mean?"

"When we have kinner of our own, I hope I never distrust them the way my daed did me when I was going through rumschpringe."

She touched his arm. "Things are better between you and your folks now, so it might be best to keep your focus on that."

Luke smiled and took her hand. "How'd I find myself such a schmaert wife?"

"The same way I found such a smart man. I'm thankful God brought us together," she said.

He nodded. "And I'm thankful you never quit believing in me or lost hope that God would answer your prayers."

Martha released a contented sigh as she leaned her head on Luke's shoulder. Whatever they might have to face in the future, she could be at peace, knowing their love for God and for each other would see them through.

About the Author

Wanda E. Brunstetter enjoys writing about the Amish because they live a peaceful, simple life. Wanda's interest in the Amish and other Plain communities began when she married her husband, Richard, who grew up in a Mennonite church in Pennsylvania. Wanda has made numerous trips to Lancaster County and has several friends and family members living near that area. She and her husband have also traveled to other parts of the country, meeting various Amish families and getting to know them personally. She hopes her readers will learn to love the wonderful Amish people as much as she does.

Wanda and her husband have been married over forty years. They have two grown children and six grandchildren. In her spare time, Wanda enjoys photography, ventriloquism, gardening, reading, stamping, and having fun with her family.

In addition to her novels, Wanda has written three Amish cookbooks, an Amish devotional, several Amish children's books, as well as many novellas, stories, articles, poems, and puppet scripts.

Visit Wanda's website at www.wandabrunstetter.com and feel free to e-mail her at wanda@wandabrunstetter.com.

A *Sister's Secret* Discussion Questions

1. When Grace Hostettler's secret was revealed, how did each of her family members respond to it? Who was the most supportive? Who was the most judgmental?

2. Grace knew her father was upset about his sister leaving the Amish faith when she was a young woman. Was Grace justified in using that as an excuse not to tell her family the truth about her past?

3. Was Roman's unforgiving attitude really directed at Grace for the secret she'd kept, or did it have more to do with the disappointment from his past?

4. Was Cleon's reaction to Grace's secret reasonable? Did he have a right to feel betrayed?

5. Do you know of a person who tried to hide a secret of their youth from their spouse? Does it ever pay to keep silent about the past?

6. What rights does a spouse have to know everything about the past?

7. Are there any secrets that would be considered grounds for a biblical divorce, if they happened before marriage?

8. When Grace's family became the victims of random attacks, Roman chose not to report it to the sheriff. How would you react if someone broke into your house?

9. Have you ever witnessed acts of random violence? How do you respond to violence when you don't know who is to blame?

10. Even though the Hostettlers chose to "turn the other check" when they were under attack, each family member had trouble dealing with what had been done. How would you feel if something like that happened to you or a member of your family?

11. With each subsequent attack, Grace became more convinced that Gary Walker was responsible, and eventually she confronted him about it. Do you think that was the best choice of action? What would you do if faced with a similar situation?

12. After Roman fired Luke for being late to work, Roman began to have suspicions that Luke might be the one doing the attacks, in order to get even. Was Roman justified in firing Luke? Was there enough evidence to make Luke appear guilty?

13. Have you ever been accused of something and had no way to prove your innocence?

14. What life lessons did you learn from reading this book?

15. How did reading *A Sister's Secret* help you have a better understanding of the Amish way of life?

A *Sister's Test* Discussion Questions

1. What do you think was the hardest test Ruth had to face? How did she deal with each of her tests?

2. What do you think caused Ruth to be so despondent? Was it what actually happened to her during the accident she was in, or did her thoughts and attitudes about what happened make her feel depressed?

3. Ruth's aunt, Rosemary, helped Ruth through the roughest times. Can you think of anyone who's helped you during a difficult time? Did your relationship become stronger because of the help they gave you? What are some ways you can help others going through depression?

4. What was it about Rosemary that made her able to reach Ruth when others in the family could not?

5. Do you think Ruth didn't want to love again because she had lost so much and was afraid if she found another man it would be dishonoring Martin's memory? What does the Bible have to say about remarriage when one's spouse dies?

6. What were a couple of tests that Ruth and Abe had in common? What test did Abe have that Ruth did not? How did Abe cope with the tests he was faced with?

7. Abe's oldest son, Gideon, felt guilty for the loss of his younger brother. Was the accident really Gideon's fault? Have you ever felt responsible for something that wasn't your fault? How did you come to grips with it?

8. Why do you think Ruth's father, Roman, wouldn't notify the sheriff whenever they suffered an attack?

9. Why was Roman so unforgiving toward his sister? Do you think he was being unreasonable? Have you ever carried a grudge against someone who did something that hurt your entire family? Was the situation between you and that person resolved?

10. Why do you think Rosemary's husband destroyed the letters she'd written to her family? If you'd been Rosemary, would you have kept writing anyway? Do you think she gave up because she felt that her family no longer loved her? Have you seen a real-life situation similar to the one Rosemary experienced?

11. Do you think Cleon realized he was favoring his new baby over Grace's daughter, Anna? Were any children in your family favored by your parents? Were you the favored or neglected one?

12. How does it affect a child when one of their siblings is favored? Do stepchildren often feel less loved and accepted than biological children? Is there anything a child can do when they feel as if a sibling is favored?

13. Everyone in Ruth's family had a different idea about who might be responsible for the attacks being made on them, yet no one had any real evidence. Is it human nature to try to figure things out on our own and jump to conclusions before we know the facts? What might be a better approach to such a problem as the Hostettlers faced?

14. What was the most important thing you learned from reading *A Sister's Test*? Was there one thing in particular that helped strengthen your faith?

A *Sister's Hope* Discussion Questions

1. The Hostettler family was under attack for many months and didn't know who was responsible. How would you feel if something similar happened to your family? Would you have handled it differently than the Hostettlers did?

2. Why was Roman so convinced it was Luke doing the attacks? Have you ever accused someone of something without knowing the facts?

3. Have you ever been accused of doing something you didn't do? How did it make you feel, and how did you respond to the accusation?

4. Why wouldn't Luke's parents believe or support him? Have you ever been let down by those you love most? If so, how did you handle it?

5. Why was it so important to Luke's parents that he get baptized and join the Amish church? Do you think they encouraged him in the right way? If they had been more supportive, do you think he might have joined the church sooner?

6. Was Roman right in forbidding Martha to see Luke? Could prohibiting her have made Martha want to see Luke even more?

7. One of the reasons Martha wanted to find out who was doing the attacks was so she could clear Luke's name. Have you ever wanted to accomplish something so much that you took chances or risked your life in order to do so? Was Martha right in trying to solve the mystery on her own?

8. Do you think Grace was unreasonable in her reactions to Carl's request to see Anna? Was she being over-protective or just cautious?

9. Was Carl right in asking Grace to let Anna move in with him? If your child was in danger would you allow them to move in with someone you didn't trust?

10. Roman's sister, Rosemary, was a positive influence on all three of Roman's daughters. Do you think Rosemary had any regrets about having left the Amish faith? Why do you think she chose to remain English?

11. Why did it take so long to learn who the attacker was? Would you have felt abandoned by God because it took so long to get results? Do you ever feel abandoned by God when you don't see answers to your prayers as quickly as you would like?

12. What life lessons did you learn from reading *A Sister's Hope*? In what way did it help strengthen your faith?

Other books by Wanda E. Brunstetter

Adult Fiction

Kentucky Brothers Series
The Journey
The Healing

Brides Of Lehigh Canal Series
Kelly's Chance
Betsy's Return
Sarah's Choice

Indiana Cousins Series
A Cousin's Promise
A Cousin's Prayer
A Cousin's Challenge

Brides Of Webster County Series
Going Home
Dear to Me
On Her Own
Allison's Journey

Daughters Of Lancaster County Series
The Storekeeper's Daughter
The Quilter's Daughter
The Bishop's Daughter

Brides Of Lancaster County Series
A Merry Heart
Looking for a Miracle
Plain and Fancy
The Hope Chest

White Christmas Pie
Lydia's Charm

Children's Fiction

Rachel Yoder—Always Trouble Somewhere Series

The Wisdom of Solomon Lapp

Nonfiction

Wanda E. Brunstetter's Amish Friends Cookbook
Wanda E. Brunstetter's Amish Friends Cookbook Volume 2
Wanda E. Brunstetter's Amish Friends Cookbook: Desserts
The Simple Life
A Celebration of the Simple Life